STORIES
FROM THE MARSHALL ISLANDS

BWEBWENATO
JĀN AELŌÑ KEIN

PALI Language Texts
Department of Linguistics
University of Hawai'i

Byron W. Bender
General Editor

STORIES FROM THE MARSHALL ISLANDS

BWEBWENATO JĀN AELŌN̄ KEIN

JACK A. TOBIN

University of Hawai'i Press
Honolulu

Printed in the United States of America

07 06 05 04 03 02 5 4 3 2 1

Library of Congress Cataloging-in-Publication Data

Tobin, Jack A., 1920–
Stories from the Marshall Islands : Bwebwenato Jan Aelon Kein / Jack A. Tobin.
p. cm. — (PALI language texts)
Includes bibliographical references and index.
ISBN 0–8248–2545–4 (cloth : alk. paper)—ISBN 0–8248–2019–3 (pbk. : alk. paper)
1. Tales—Marshall Islands. 2. Marshallese language—Texts. I. Title. II. Series.
GR385.M37 T63 2001
398.2'099683—dc21

2001046283

University of Hawai'i Press books are printed on acid-free paper and meet the guidelines for permanence and durability of the Council on Library Resources.

Printed by Maple-Vail Book Manufacturing Group

Cover art: A Marshallese stick chart, used by traditional navigators as a mnemonic device, showing island locations and resultant wave patterns.

N̄an Ri-M̧ajeļ

For the Marshallese People

CONTENTS

PREFACE

The stories and other cultural material presented here were collected by me over the years 1950–57 and 1967–74, and part of 1975, in the Marshall Islands. My duties as District Anthropologist in the first period and Community Development Advisor in the second gave me the opportunity to learn the language and the culture of the Marshallese people. Indeed, this was necessary in order to do my job properly. I returned to the Marshalls in early 1975, after the termination of my employment there, to collect additional folk tales and related material.

When I first came to the Marshall Islands, I met with traditional leaders individually, explained my official role, and told them of my interest in learning Marshallese culture. Without exception, I was able to obtain their assistance. They gave me valuable information, and also identified and referred me to other knowledgeable people and specialists in different activities. Other Marshallese helped me in this manner as well. I was able to gather folk tales and ethnographic, historical, and other data in many locations and situations during the course of my daily routine, and on field trips to the outer islands of the archipelago, while at sea and ashore, and at appointed times and places at the informants' convenience, usually in their homes or nearby. Information was also collected during casual conversations with friends and acquaintances.

In many instances, an informant would volunteer information or tell a story or a proverb *(jabōnkennaan)* in order to make a point that he or she wanted to get across, or to educate me in some aspect of Marshallese culture. Often I just asked informants to tell me some stories of the past *(bwebwenato in etto),* and a free flow of narrative followed. My requests for specific information, no matter of what kind, were never refused by anyone. Of course, I avoided asking anything that I thought might cause the particular person or persons with whom I was speaking any discomfort for personal, cultural, or political reasons. All of my informants seemed to like giving me information, and all of them agreed that it would be beneficial to record the stories for future generations of Marshallese as well. Indeed, this was my main purpose in collecting this material, as well as to add it to the body of Marshallese folklore that has already been recorded—for the benefit of scholars and others who are interested in Marshallese culture.

All translation was done by me, except where indicated. I have identified the interpreters in these cases. Words and expressions in the ancient language *(kajin etto)* and those of a specialized nature with which I was unfamiliar, as for example, canoe language *(kajin wa),* fishing language (*kajin eọn̄wōd*), navigation language *(kajin meto),* and the like, were explained to me by my informants in the course of the narration.

Each story is preceded by the name of the person who told it to me, or other identification, followed by the place where and year when the story or information was obtained. I use the term "informant" to refer to this person. It is a term that has had long and widespread usage among anthropologists and other social scientists to refer to an individual who provides information to the researcher from his or her stock of knowledge. The Marshallese equivalent is *ri-bwebwenato* 'storyteller'. *Bwebwenato* means 'talk' (both verb and noun) or 'story'. The *ri-bwebwenato* is one who is knowledgeable in the oral tradition of the Marshall

Islands—more so than others. Such individuals are well known and respected, and are, in effect, living repositories and transmitters of traditional Marshallese culture. They can be described as the native historians. Their role in preliterate Marshallese society and on up to the present time will be discussed in more detail later. The term *ri-bwebwenato* is also used for one who has given information, a speaker who may or may not be a specialist, so to speak, endowed with a great store of traditional knowledge.

As I have indicated, there are stylistic differences among informants in the telling of tales, and there are some dialectical differences as well. This will be apparent in the Marshallese texts to those who know the language. I have tried to translate as literally as possible and yet avoid stilted or clumsy language, and not sacrifice clarity.

Those conversant with the Marshallese language will recognize the use of the present tense to describe past actions in some instances. As linguists Carr and Elbert (1945:xxii) point out: "In vivid narrative style the present is used for the past except for direct quotations." They describe this as "the narrative present." In the stories told to me, the present tense was sometimes used as Carr and Elbert have described. However, I have used the past tense in the English translation when it was more meaningful and was clearly the intent of the narrator to be past action. I did not change tenses in the Marshallese text, however. The Marshallese equivalent of the English conjunction "and" is frequently used in the Marshallese narrative style. I have translated it in every case, although it may appear superfluous to those not conversant with the Marshallese language.

I have identified and listed the motifs in the stories, using Bacil Kirtley's (1955) motif-index as a model. This work analyzes and classifies Oceanic narratives according to the system developed by Thompson (1932–36).

Marshallese folklore, indeed the folklore of any people, cannot be more than superficially understood or appreciated without some knowledge of the particular culture. The more one knows, of course, the better one can understand and appreciate the references and nuances in these stories. For this reason, some basic information is presented for the benefit of those who may be unfamiliar with the Marshall Islands and the Marshallese people. I have also included explanatory notes for most of the stories. Many of them are from my unpublished field notes.

I have included more than one version of several of the stories to show the variation in content and style that exists in Marshallese folk tales.

The orthography used by me was in common use when I recorded the stories. It is based on the Protestant Bible translation orthography. However, my Marshallese text has been transcribed into the more recent official/standard orthography so that it can be used in the government schools in the Marshalls.

Acknowledgements

My thanks go to Mr. Alfred Capelle, President of the College of the Marshall Islands, and formerly CEO of the Alele Museum. His early and continuing interest and encouragement are greatly appreciated. I thank Mrs. Carmen Bigler, Secretary of Internal Affairs, who funded the initial computerization of the manuscript at Mājro. My thanks go also to Professor Robert C. Kiste, Director, Pacific Islands Studies Program, and to Professor Byron W. Bender, Department of Linguistics, University of Hawai'i at Mānoa, for their interest and support in facilitating the publication of this book. I greatly appreciate Professor Bender's contribution as editor, which included the transcription of the Marshallese text into the official standard orthography with the assistance of Alfred Capelle, Takaji Abo, and others at Mājro. I am also indebted to Mark Nakamura of the University of Hawai'i Center for Instructional Support for assistance with the maps.

In conclusion, I want to thank the Marshallese, *ri-bwebwenato* and others, who helped me so much in the collection of these stories and other information that I was able to gather in my over fifteen years in their homeland. I deeply appreciate their confidence, patience, hospitality, courtesy, and kindness. I will never forget this. To those who are living and to the memory of those who are no longer with us, thank you very much!

N̄an Ri-M̧ajeļ remour im ilo ememej eo eņ ro remej: Koņ kanooj in eņņool kōn ami jipan̄ im jouj eļap.

J. A. T.
Honolulu 1996

"... like all other elements of human culture, folktales are not mere creatures of chance. They exist in time and space, and they are affected by the nature of the land where they are current, by the linguistic and social contacts of its people, and by the lapse of the years and their accompanying historic changes."

Stith Thompson (1951:13)

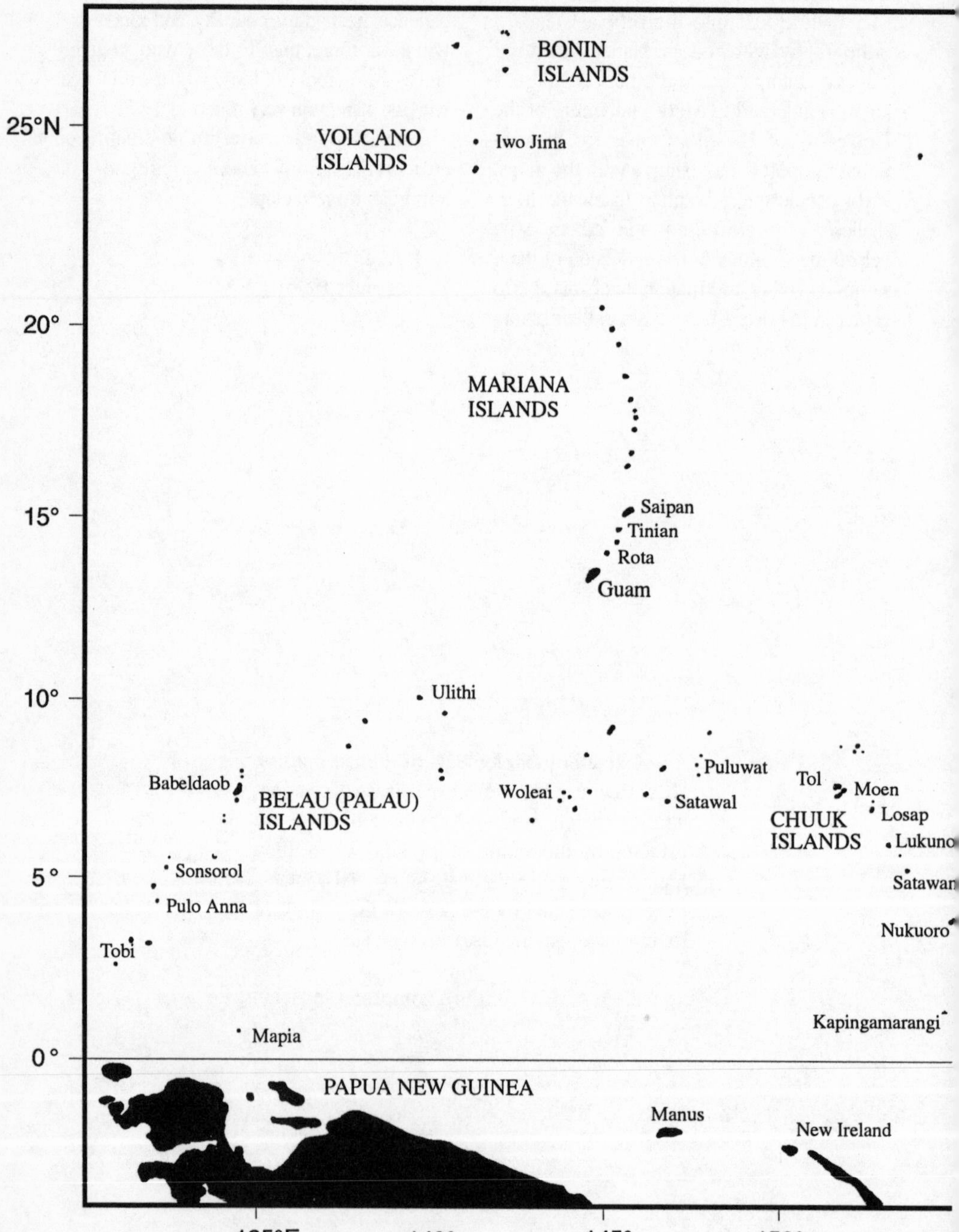

BONIN ISLANDS
VOLCANO ISLANDS
Iwo Jima
25°N
20°
MARIANA ISLANDS
15°
Saipan
Tinian
Rota
Guam
10°
Ulithi
Puluwat
Tol
Moen
Babeldaob
BELAU (PALAU) ISLANDS
Woleai
Satawal
Losap
CHUUK ISLANDS
Lukunor
5°
Sonsorol
Pulo Anna
Satawan
Nukuoro
Tobi
Kapingamarangi
Mapia
0°
PAPUA NEW GUINEA
Manus
New Ireland
135°E
140°
145°
150°

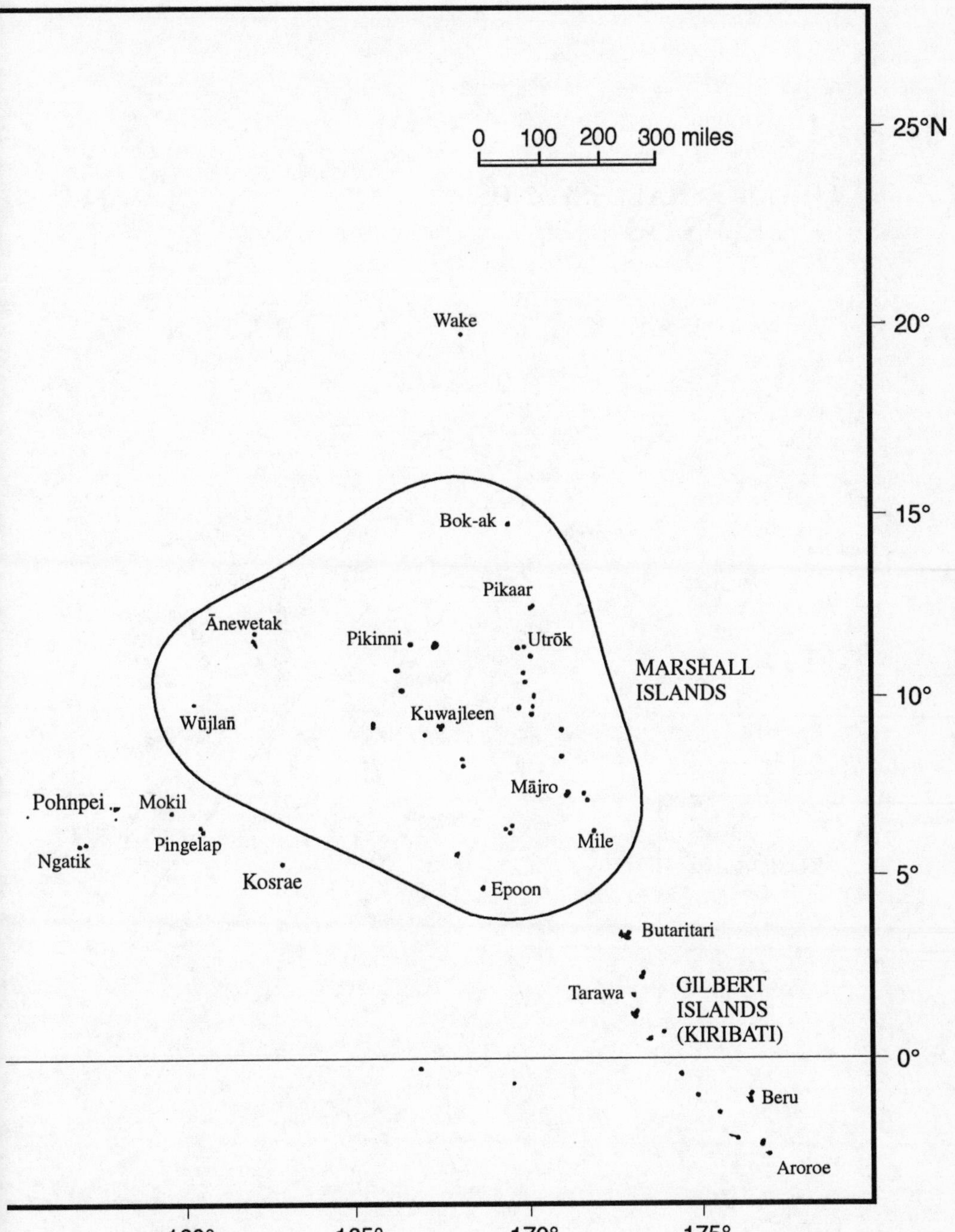

0 100 200 300 miles
25°N
20°
15°
10°
5°
0°
160°
165°
170°
175°
Wake
Bok-ak
Pikaar
Ānewetak
Pikinni
Utrōk
MARSHALL
ISLANDS
Wūjlañ
Kuwajleen
Mājro
Pohnpei
Mokil
Pingelap
Ngatik
Kosrae
Mile
Epoon
Butaritari
Tarawa
GILBERT
ISLANDS
(KIRIBATI)
Beru
Aroroe

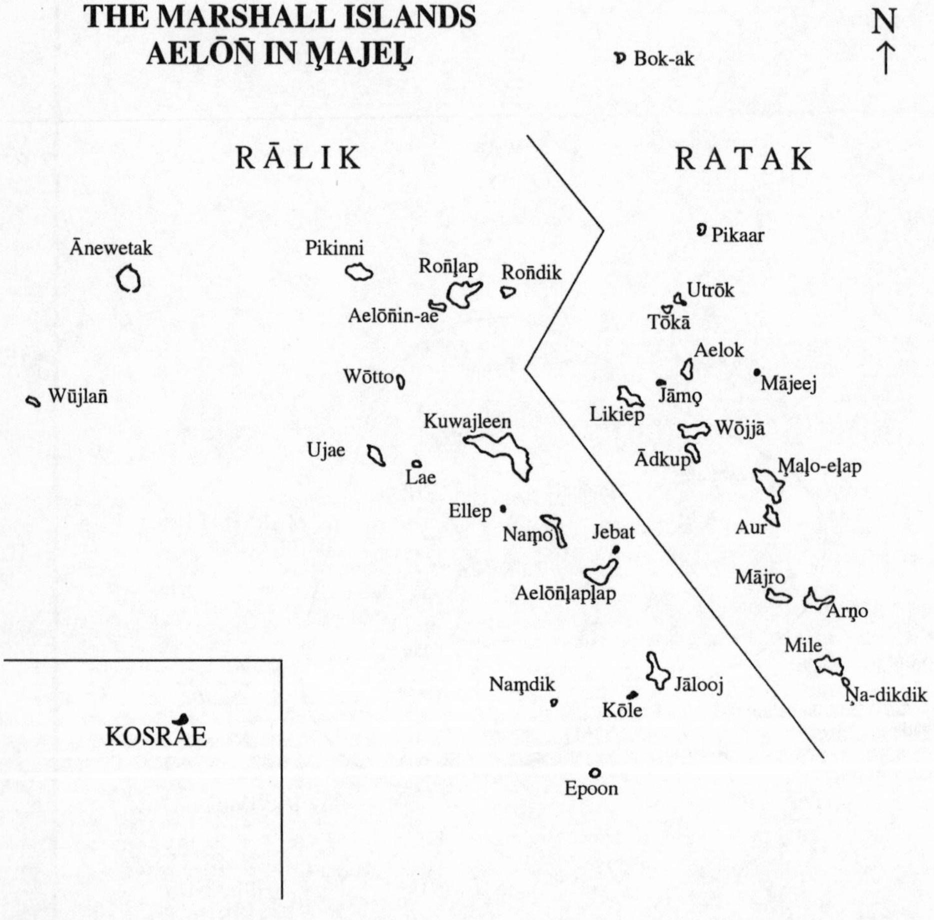
THE MARSHALL ISLANDS
AELŌÑ IN M̧AJEĻ
N
Bok-ak
RĀLIK
RATAK
Pikaar
Ānewetak
Pikinni
Roñļap
Roñdik
Aelōñin-ae
Utrōk
Tōkā
Aelok
Wōtto
Mājeej
Wūjlañ
Jāmo̧
Likiep
Kuwajleen
Wōjjā
Ujae
Ādkup
Ļae
M̧aļo-eļap
Ellep
Aur
Nam̧o
Jebat
Mājro
Aelōñļapļap
Arņo
Mile
Nam̧dik
Jālooj
Ņa-dikdik
Kōle
KOSRAE
Epoon

INTRODUCTION

The Setting

The archipelago known as the Marshall Islands (*Aelōn̄ in M̧ajeļ* or *Aelōn̄ Kein*) is located in the North Central Pacific Ocean, about 2,000 miles west-southwest of Honolulu. It consists of two chains of atolls and single islands, the eastern named Ratak and the western Rālik. They lie nearly parallel to each other in a northwesterly and southeasterly direction, and are part of the vast geographic/cultural area of Micronesia. They are the easternmost of the former districts of the United States Trust Territory of the Pacific Islands, and are just to the north of the Gilbert Islands (Kiribati), another Micronesian group.

The total land area of the Marshalls is quite small. It consists of only about seventy-four square miles of dry land area. This is distributed over twenty-nine low-lying coral atolls and five low coral islands, which are widely scattered over 375,000 square miles of ocean. The atolls (and single islands) are seldom more than six feet above sea level; the highest point being only thirty-three feet or so above the ocean. Some of the islands are as much as ten miles long, but seldom exceed 400 yards or so in extent. Lagoons are from less than a mile to thirty miles across and up to seventy-five miles or more in length. The largest lagoon, the largest atoll in the world, is Kuwajleen (Kwajalein) in the northern Marshalls, with a lagoon area of 839.30 square miles. The extensive reef areas protect the islands and provide a habitat for the rich and important marine life.

The Marshall Islands have a tropical oceanic climate that is tempered by the winds from the sea and by frequent rains. The temperature is usually around eighty degrees Fahrenheit most of the year, with practically no variation from season to season. However, the trade winds that blow steadily from the northeast from December through March moderate the heat considerably. Both the days and evenings are pleasant. In summer and autumn, the winds shift and decrease in intensity. Then the rains increase. The northern Marshalls get about eighty inches of rain a year, compared to the southern Marshalls, which receive about 160 inches. The figures are deceptive, however, as the downpour is quickly absorbed by the porous sandy and light soils. The better soils and more luxuriant vegetation of the southern Marshalls reflect this rainfall differential.

Although climatic conditions are generally favorable in the Marshalls, the soils are relatively poor as compared, for example, to the high islands of Pohnpei (Ponape), Kosrae (Kusaie), Chuuk (Truk), and other volcanic islands to the west in Micronesia. The variety of plants in the Marshalls is, therefore, somewhat limited. Coconut palms and pandanus are the most plentiful, and are well suited to an atoll environment. They furnish food for the people, as well as building materials and materials for fine handicraft: mats, fans, hats, handbags, and the like, which the women are experts in making. In the past, canoe sails, weapons, agricultural implements, and wearing apparel were made from these invaluable trees.

The only cash crop is copra, the dried meat of the coconut, and Marshallese copra is considered to be among the best in the world. Over fifty percent of the copra produced in the Trust Territory, as of 1984, came from the Marshall Islands. Breadfruit trees are also important for the food that they produce. The huge breadfruit trees furnished the sailing canoe hulls and other parts in the past, and other items as well. Other important food plants have been arrowroot and taro, but the cultivation of taro is minimal today. Banana and papaya trees also provide food to a lesser extent.

The animals on these tiny and remote islands are few; however, the lagoon, reefs, and surrounding ocean are rich in marine life. They teem with fish and shellfish of many kinds. Porpoises are caught occasionally, and turtles come ashore to lay their eggs, as do seabirds, providing another source of food for the islanders. Pigs and chickens furnish the main source of protein from the land. However, canned meat and canned fish are used to a large extent nowadays, especially by the people at the urban centers on Kuwajleen and Mājro atolls.

Food and other consumer goods have been imported for many years, as the Marshallese have moved from a subsistence to a mixed economy. This has accelerated with increased cash income, greater availability of consumer goods, and government feeding programs. Today imported food forms a large part of the Marshallese diet.

While the economy has long been based on copra production, income is also derived by the Marshallese from lease payments for the use of their land on Kuwajleen Atoll by the military, thus enhancing the value of the land. Compensation for land use and damages to land and to people caused by the past nuclear weapons testing programs provides an income for others. Cash income is also obtained by many Marshallese from employment with their government and at the missile base on Kuwajleen. Employment with businesses or as independent businessmen and businesswomen is another important source of income for a considerable number of Marshallese, primarily at the urban centers. It should be noted, however, that the unemployment rate is high.

History in Brief

The consensus of most authorities is that the Marshallese came from Southeast Asia many generations ago, as did the ancestors of other Pacific Island groups. They were, it is believed, pushed down by stronger groups through the areas of South China and the Malay Peninsula (a natural corridor and migration route), and on out to the archipelagoes and larger islands to the east. They then voyaged on to the scattered islands and atolls where their descendants now live.

The Marshallese have no knowledge as to the exact place of their origin. Only vague clues exist in their folklore. Those who have taken trips in small vessels, especially sailing canoes, even for relatively short distances, can appreciate the hardships of the hazardous and extended voyages that were necessary to reach the Marshall Islands. Undoubtedly many canoes and lives were lost on the voyages that resulted in the settlement of these islands.

The oral tradition tells us that there was a great deal of warfare between the chiefly *(irooj)* clans for political control of various atolls. (Early European accounts also report such activities.) Civil wars also occurred, and political control fluctuated, as in other cultures in Oceania and elsewhere.

As far as can be ascertained, the two chains, Ratak and Rālik, were never united under one paramount chief *(irooj ļapļap/*

irooj eļap), although the Rālik chain once was. Both Ratak and Rālik are divided into several chiefdoms today. The westernmost atolls of Wūjlañ and Ānewetak were long isolated and were independent political entities, and Mājeej Island in northern Ratak was allegedly never conquered by outsiders.

The Marshall Islands were first sighted by the Spanish captain Garcia de Loyasa, who sailed through and past the northern Marshalls in 1526. A few other sightings were made by other Spanish captains during the sixteenth century. These were all incidental to the voyages of the Manila Galleons from Acapulco, Mexico, to Manila in the Philippines.

The British captain Wallis was at Roñdik in 1767, and in 1788 his compatriots, captains Marshall and Gilbert, explored the archipelagoes that were later named after them. Sporadic visits were subsequently made throughout the Marshall Islands by other European vessels.[1] Northern Ratak was explored by Lieutenant Otto von Kotzebue of the Imperial Russian Navy in the brig *Rurik* in 1816, 1817, and 1824. Considerable information was obtained by the officers and scientists on these expeditions, and invaluable drawings were made by the artist Louis Choris of the people, their activities, and items of their material culture. The Spanish never exercised control over the Marshalls as they did in the Marianas, and in the Carolines to a much lesser extent and later in time. Nor did they engage in missionization in the Marshalls as they did in other parts of Micronesia.

European and American whaling ships were common in the area beginning in the middle of the nineteenth century. The needs of these vessels for fresh water and food supplies were better satisfied by the high islands of Kosrae and Pohnpei, however, so they were more frequented by the outsiders than were the Marshalls with their scantier resources.

The copra trade developed during this period, and traders from different countries established stations on several of the atolls. German traders, with the assistance of the Jaluit [Jālooj] Gesellschaft, a quasi-governmental commercial concern, became the most influential in the archipelago. The German Empire annexed the Marshalls in 1885 and established a rather small administrative center on Jebwad Island, Jālooj Atoll, in the southern Marshalls. During the latter part of the German regime, German ethnographers collected and subsequently published considerable data, including some folk tales. Items of material culture were also collected and sent back to museums in the homeland. The German administration continued until the outbreak of World War I, when Japanese naval forces seized the Marshalls.

The Japanese ruled the Marshalls (and the Carolines and the Marianas, less Guam) until 1944. They had, in violation of the League of Nations Mandate, heavily fortified many islands in the Marshalls and elsewhere in Micronesia, including the construction of air bases in preparation for the war in the Pacific. The Japanese were defeated by the American armed forces after bitter and bloody fighting on the atolls of Kuwajleen and Ānewetak. Other military installations were also destroyed.

The United States assumed control and administered the area as a strategic trust territory for over forty years, while using part of it for the testing of nuclear weapons, and for the ongoing missile testing program.

Constitutional self-government became effective in the Marshalls on May 1, 1979.

1. See Krämer and Nevermann (1938:1–10) for a listing of ship sightings of islands and atolls, and visits in the Marshall Islands.

On March 12, 1982, President Amata Kabua issued an official proclamation designating the Marshall Islands a republic. The Compact of Free Association with the United States resulted from U.S. Public Law 99239, which was approved by the U.S. Congress and the President of the United States in January of 1986. This was implemented and funded on October 1, 1986. The United States will continue to finance governmental functions in the Marshalls, and to be responsible for defense matters. The missile testing program will also continue.

The People

The Marshallese have been described as follows: "In physical type the Marshallese are closely related to the Polynesians to the east. To the observer however, the Marshallese appear distinctly as a non-homogenous people. Their physical characteristics indicate a mixture primarily of Mongoloid and Caucasoid elements, though in the absence of a thorough study of physical anthropology of Micronesia only the most general statements can be made. The Marshallese are of medium stature, with light brown skin that becomes heavily tanned through exposure to the sun. The hair is black and ranges from straight to wavy, epicanthic fold is rare. Nose form is variable. Perhaps the most common characteristic is a marked lateral prominence of the zygomatic arches" (Spoehr 1946:25–26). There has been a certain amount of admixture as a result of over a century of contact with people from Europe, North America, and the Orient. There has also been some mixture with other Micronesians, especially Gilbertese castaways from earlier times.

The Marshallese population has increased markedly after a decline due to imported diseases. It was only 10,131 in 1939 (U.S. Navy 1943:19). The increase has probably been due to improved medical care in the post–World War II period. However, much more needs to be done in the area of public health, which has reportedly worsened in recent years, with a marked increase in serious health problems. The present population is about 46,000. The birth rate greatly exceeds the death rate. This is a young population and it continues to increase. This trend will probably continue, resulting in overpopulation and its concomitant problems. Population distribution is imbalanced now.

The Urban Trend

Many Marshallese, attracted by employment opportunities, a different life-style, or for other reasons, have left their home atolls to live on tiny Epjā (Ebeye) Island on Kuwajleen Atoll, adjacent to the missile base, and around the capital on Mājro Atoll. Over one-half of the population of the Marshalls now live at these two sites. This heavy concentration of people on very limited land areas has created serious social, economic, and public health problems. It has also been an important factor in social change.

Marshallese have moved to Hawai'i and the mainland United States in recent years for purposes of education and employment. Whether a significant number of them will become permanent residents remains to be seen.

Social Organization

The traditional social organization is based on control of land, and land-use rights. The Marshallese belong to matriclans *(jowi/jou)* and to matrilineages *(bwij)*, through which they inherit their primary land-use rights and status. Patrilineal affiliation is important but secondary. However, primary rights in land and chieftainships have been inherited patrilineally when matrilineages have become extinct *(bwij eļot)*. The Ānewetak Atoll chiefs traditionally inherit their rank patrilineally, as did the original Wūjlañ Atoll chiefs. Everyone inherits land-use rights at birth. Land has always been considered to be their most valuable asset by the Marshallese. The traditional land tenure system is operative today, albeit modified in some respects.

Familial ties are strong and widely extended. Mutual aid and support are important and expected among kinfolk. See Erdland (1914:101), Krämer and Nevermann (1938:190–193), Mason (1947:53–54), Spoehr (1949:74–79), and Tobin (1958:16–21; 1967:71–102) for details of the Marshallese sociopolitical system. Marshallese folklore is replete with stories of chiefs *(irooj)* and chiefesses *(lerooj)*. This is not surprising, considering the structure of traditional Marshallese society.

Marshallese culture has become quite westernized due to the long period of sustained contact with outsiders, which has intensified since World War II. It is a rapidly changing culture, with accompanying problems, including those brought about by the intrusion of the nuclear weapons testing programs (displacement of atoll communities from their ancestral lands and radioactive contamination of people and land). Change has also brought economic and career opportunities for the Marshallese. Despite the changes that have taken place, many of the old customs and beliefs have survived.

The Language

Marshallese belongs to the large language family known as Austronesian or Malayo-Polynesian. Languages of this family are widely distributed throughout the Pacific Ocean area and in parts of mainland Southeast Asia. A language of this family is spoken on Madagascar in the Indian Ocean, off the coast of Southeast Africa. Marshallese is closely related to the other languages of "nuclear" Micronesia, which include Ponapean, Kosraean, Trukese, and Woleaian, to the west of the Marshall Islands, and Gilbertese to the south. These languages are more distantly related to Yapese, Chamorro, and Palauan, which are spoken in the westernmost part of Micronesia, and to Nukuoro and Kapingamarangi, Polynesian Outlier languages spoken in Pohnpei of the Federated States of Micronesia. See Alkire (1977:11–12) for a succinct discussion of the classification of the languages of Micronesia and their possible origins.

As noted previously, there are slight dialectal variations in Marshallese as spoken in Ratak and Rālik, and on the more isolated atolls such as Wūjlañ and Ānewetak. The use of the Rālik dialect in the translation of the Bible many years ago, and the acceleration of interatoll travel and interpersonal contact and communication have had a leveling effect on the language. Modified foreign words have been incorporated into the language as well.

Religion

One of the most significant agents of change in Marshallese culture has been the introduced religion, and accompanying western education and literacy. The government schools that were established later have also been important agents of change.

The Marshallese are Christians of long standing. The majority of them are Protestants. The Congregational Church was established on Epoon Atoll in 1857 by American missionaries, and subsequently spread throughout the Marshalls with the aid of native Hawaiian missionaries. Wūjlañ and Ānewetak were converted by Micronesians. The Congregational mission church has been taken over completely by the Marshallese. It is a Marshallese church with American church connections. The Roman Catholic faith was brought in by German missionaries in the early part of the German period. Other sects have been introduced since the immediate post-World War II period. The church is an important part of the lives of the Marshallese.

The Aboriginal Religion

Marshallese folklore is replete with references to supernatural beings of various kinds. Indeed, they are central figures, primarily as forces of evil, in many stories. They are very much alive in the Marshallese consciousness today, despite over a century of acceptance of Christianity. It is easy to find parallels in other cultures, of course. In his description of the aboriginal/traditional religion, Spoehr (1949:228–229) states, "In addition to the culture heroes, the old religion recognized a large number of spiritual beings of different sorts. German accounts do not entirely agree on the kinds and varieties of these spiritual beings, no doubt because there were some inter-atoll differences and because the old religion was perhaps not highly systematized and hence resulted in considerable variation in interpretation among individual Marshallese. A German writer as long ago as 1886 commented on the decline of the old religion (Hager 1886:101). As for spiritual beings, Erdland mentions the *ekjöb [ekjab],* a hierarchical order of beings in human form that reside in and around an atoll—in the sky or in stones, trees, and other natural objects—and the *anij,* spirits that have names and for the most part are dangerous and harmful to man, except for a few such as *anjinmar,* good-natured little people who live in the bush (Erdland, 1914:312–314)."

I found the belief in the animistic beings still extant in varying degrees among individuals with whom I came in contact: spirits or *ekjab* that were associated with natural phenomena such as reef formations, rocks, birds, waves, certain trees, portions of ground, and marine creatures as described by the early German ethnographers. Although a hierarchy of priesthood as found, for example, in aboriginal Polynesia, did not exist in the Marshall Islands culture area, offerings of food, mats, and other objects were made to the *ekjab*. Human or other living sacrifices were apparently never made, contrary again to the general aboriginal Polynesian practices.

The various *ekjab* are still known, and allegedly respected, as indicated. Many Marshallese believe that supernatural malevolent beings known as *tiṃoṇ* 'demons' (an obvious loanword from English) cause sickness and sometimes death. There are, according to the believers, many kinds of demons, categorized by their habitat: demons of the beach, demons of the sea, demons of the bush, and the like.

The references to demons and the devil in the Bible, in the teachings of the introduced religion, may very well have reinforced the traditional beliefs in supernatural beings that harm people, and perhaps facilitated acceptance of the new belief system. (The absence of an organized religion and a priestly hierarchy in the Marshalls were also factors that perhaps made it easy for the Marshallese to accept Christianity.) The belief in ancestral spirits persists today throughout the Marshalls and functions as a form of social control and explanation of events.

The guardian spirits of the chiefs *(irooj)* are considered to be much more powerful than those of the commoners *(kajoor)*, some in particular more than others. This is an obvious reflection of the stratified social system, and has undoubtedly enhanced the prestige and authority of the chiefly class.

Here again, there were (and are) parallels in the introduced religion. The Holy Ghost/Spirit is an integral part of the triune god, the Holy Trinity, and the concept of souls and an afterlife is, of course, integral to Christianity. This is comparable to traditional Marshallese beliefs. There are a number of references and stories about spiritual beings and their activities, often of a miraculous nature, in both the Old and the New Testament. This might very well have made their traditional folktales more believable to the Marshallese, and certainly more defensible.

Marshallese Chants *(Roro)*

The Marshallese chants or *roro* were, and in some cases still are, used for various purposes: to obtain supernatural assistance in warfare, fishing, hunting turtles, hunting bird and turtle eggs, and to obtain strength for carrying out group activities such as launching and beaching canoes, and the like (work chants). They were used while making magic, either benevolent or malevolent, to bring about the death or illness of an enemy, to drive away evil spirits (demons), to gain the favor of a desired member of the opposite sex, or to obtain influence with a chief or others in a position to help one. Chants are also used to commemorate a famous person or legendary person or event.

One of the more important uses of the *roro* was as an aid to navigation *(meto)*. The navigation signs or sea marks (*kōkļaļ* or *kakōļļe*) that are associated with a particular island, atoll, or ocean area were recited in the *roro* to help the navigator (*ri-meto*) reach his destination. Other chants are used for amusement purposes. Some of the *roro* are of an erotic nature and must not be overheard by those with whom one has a respect or taboo relationship. The psychological value of the *roro* was and is an important one to the Marshallese in their attempts to obtain a desired result. The *roro* content varies from one section of the Marshalls to another. Most atolls possess their own particular *roro,* especially of the type used in time of war to taunt the enemy and inspire and stimulate self-confidence. Most of the latter type were composed at the time of a particular incident or war.

The *roro* used by the navigators were secret, as were the *roro* used by the experts at divination *(ri-bubu),* the practitioners of magic *(ri-anijnij),* the specialists in weather forecasting *(ri-lale-lañ),* and the practitioners of traditional medicine *(ri-wūno).* The *roro,* sometimes referred to as *al* 'songs', and the special knowledge associated with them, are retained by these experts who may specialize in several areas. They pass the information on to their special students. Other *roro* are common knowledge, as, for example, the work chants. However, few of the younger generation today know the less commonly used *roro,* nor do they seem to be interested in them. Some of the *roro* will, of course, disappear along with the activities with which they have been associated, as, for example, the sailing-canoe *roro. Roro* are integral elements in many Marshallese folktales. They add a dramatic quality to the narration, and they entertain as well as explain, as do the stories themselves.

The typical *roro* consists of four to six lines that are chanted in a low rhythmic monotone; initially slowly, but usually ending hurriedly with a rising inflection. The few *ikid* 'song-story' are much longer. Some of the work chants, for example, the *roro* used in launching or beaching canoes, are done in statement-response or point-counterpoint style, with one half of the work group chanting a line and the other half chanting another.

Some of the words in the chants are in the archaic language *(kajin etto).* Hence the meanings of some of the words and phrases are unknown to most Marshallese. Some of the *roro* contain words that have hidden or double meanings, or are metaphorical. This is called *m̧wilaļ* (deep), and is similar to the Hawaiian *kaona:* "hidden meaning in Hawaiian poetry; concealed reference as to a person, thing or place . . ." (Pukui and Elbert 1971:121). These same archaic words and phrases are found in a number of Marshallese folktales.

The Role of the *Ri-bwebwenato* (Storyteller) and the Function of the Stories

Although stories were and are known and told by different individuals in the Marshallese culture, there are some individuals who know more than others and who have a greater repertoire of stories and associated lore. They are known as *ri-bwebwenato* or storytellers, and are the older members of the society, as might be expected. They usually received this knowledge from their kinsmen.

The folktales are not only entertaining but are valuable as teaching devices as well—as part of the socialization process. The young Marshallese, sitting at the feet of the *ri-bwebwenato,* or in other situations, learned important information about their culture and had other information augmented. The stories, which have been transmitted orally over the years, commemorate historical events and individuals, as well as legendary figures and events. They explain natural phenomena and the origins of geological forms, plants, and animals, they explain aspects of animal and human behavior, and they describe social organization and the supernatural. The auditors (of whatever age) could learn many essential things necessary for survival, including the techniques for living with and exploiting the environment. They could learn, through the successes or failures of the characters in the stories about their social environment and the values of their society. In this way, the proper respect relationships, social obligations, avoidance patterns, and other appropriate interpersonal and group behavior and relationships would be explained, validated, and reinforced (for the ultimate benefit of all members of the culture). Folklore supplemented the other informal education of observation, advice, and teaching by relatives, peers, and others—and actual experience.

Accounts of actual events, transmitted orally over the generations, become part of the body of folklore of a people. Changes in details may, and often do, occur in the retelling of the stories over the years. But such stories help in the historical reconstruction of a society, and the old folktales provide information about traditional customs and material culture that may no longer exist, or may exist in an attenuated form. The young people of the rapidly changing Marshallese culture of today apparently have little if any interest in Marshallese folklore or other traditional lore, as older Marshallese men and women have told me. The introduced educational system has taken over the role of educator, although in a Western mode, and has supplanted the *ri-bwebwenato* in this area, and the church also continues to provide information to the Marshallese.

The traditional storyteller cannot compete in terms of entertainment either. The Marshallese find this in the ubiquitous transistor radios, and in radio and motion pictures at the urban centers of Mājro and Epjā. Television has become available and very popular there in recent years, and will probably spread to the outer islands when electricity becomes available there. All of these have more audience appeal than the traditional entertainment afforded by the storytellers. The lack of interest, motivation to learn, and consequent lack of recruitment of replacements will undoubtedly result in the eventual disappearance of the *ri-bwebwenato,* living repositories of traditional Marshallese culture.

On a more optimistic note, the Marshall Islands Museum (Alele) has reportedly begun collecting and taping folktales for the benefit of those Marshallese who may be interested in them now or in the future, and, it is assumed, for study by folklorists and other researchers. Folktales have reportedly been aired on local television. This is certainly a worthwhile effort that should be encouraged and supported by the government of the Marshall Islands. Folklore is obviously a very important part of the heritage of the Marshallese people, and should be preserved.

1: THE BEGINNING OF THIS WORLD

As told by Jelibōr Jam̄, Kuwajleen 1975

(This is the longest and most important story in the Marshall Islands. Old people know it. But the young people do not know it. They are not interested. They only want to learn the knowledge of the white men.)

In the beginning, there were four posts. They remained there. And the post in the east fell down and made the sky in the east. And it was given the name Ļōkōm̧raan.[1] It remained a short while, and the post in the south fell down to make the sky in the south. Its name was Ļōrōk. A short while later, the post in the north fell down to make the sky in the north. Its name was Ļajibwinām̧ōņ. It remained a short while, and the post in the west fell down to make the sky in the west. Its name was Iroojrilik.

The sky was very foggy. It remained there, and two men appeared from the sky. The names of these men, Ļowa and Ļōm̧tal. And Ļowa made the islands with his voice. He said, "Ļowa and reefs." And there were reefs. And he spoke again, "Ļowa and rocks." And there were rocks. And he spoke again, "Ļowa and islands." And there were islands. And he spoke again, "Ļowa and human beings." And there were human beings.

The sky remained foggy. One could not see afar.

Now Ļōm̧tal. He made the sea. He said with his voice, "Kick out in the depths of the sea and make it flow to the east. It flows to the east." And he again said with his voice, "Kick out in the depths of the sea and make it flow to the south. It flows to the south."

And he spoke again, "Kick out in the depths of the sea and make it flow to the north. It flows to the north." And he spoke again, "Kick out in the depths of the sea and make it flow west. It flows west."

Now there was much water. And now he made fish. And he said, "Kick out in the lagoon of Ep and flow." Fish flowed in. (Ep is the name of an island. We have not seen it.)[2]

He spoke again, "Kick out in the lagoon of Ep and flow."

The birds of the sky came. Now there were many islands, many seas. And all of the things belonging to them.[3]

After a while, two more young men came. These men came to tattoo. (In the ancient

---

1. The informant explained that Ļōkōm̧raan means *bwe in kōm̧m̧an rear* 'in order to make the day or east'. In response to my question as to who or what gave it the name, he said, "I do not know who, but the story is thus."

2. Ep/Eip/Uab is the name of a legendary island to the west of the Marshall Islands, and figures in a number of folktales. One is tempted to link it with the island of Yap in the Western Carolines (see the story of Liwātuonmour and Lidepdepju on page 54.) Compare this with the Hawaiian story of "the four chief gods, dwelling high in the heavens, but at times appearing on earth" (Johnson 1981:iii).

3. Compare the formation of the world and the calling up and naming of all living things by Ļōm̧tal and Ļowa, and by Ļewōj and Ļaneej, with the analogous Hawaiian creation myth, the description of the emergence, and the identification of living things in the Kumulipo, the Hawaiian Hymn of Creation (Johnson 1981:1–17; Ka Wa Akaha—Chant One), and Beckwith (1951:55–83): The Birth of Sea and Land Life. The creation of the world and all living things and the naming of the animals by the first man as described in the Bible (Genesis 1:1–19) has been known to the Marshallese for over a century. The similarities to the Marshallese creation myth may have facilitated acceptance of the new religion by the islanders.

language, *kabuñ eǫǫn* means 'to make tattoos'.) These people saw these men come down from the sky there at the northern end of Buoj [Island, Aelōñļapļap Atoll]. The name of the land parcel there was Jiṃwinne, as it is to this day.

Now the two came to begin their tattooing. And they came to make their tattooing paint (dye). (*Ṃaṃwij* in the ancient language means 'to make paint [dye] for tattooing from earth': black, green, white, yellow, blue; many kinds.) And they came to paint all of the living things.

And one of the men, Ļewōj, called all of the fish. And said, "One come here." And one came, and the other man, Ļaneej, colored it. And said, "Your name is *kupañ* [*Hepatus triostegus* Linn., convict tang; *Acanthurus triostegus* triostegus Linn., surgeon fish, tang]. And released it into the sea.

And the one man, Ļewōj, again called a fish, and the other man Ļaneej, painted it and said, "Your name is *bwebwe*" [yellowfin or bluefin tuna]. And released it into the sea. Ļewōj again called one, and Ļaneej again colored it and released it into the sea and said, "Your name is *mao*" [*Chelinus chlorourus*, wrasse; *Scarus jonesi,* parrot fish]. And thus the two of them did to all of the fish in the sea. And Ļewōj called all of the birds in the air, and Ļaneej again colored them a different way and gave each one of them a separate name. And Ļewōj again called everything that crawled on the island. And he colored them with individual kinds of paint.

And he named each one of them. And he called the human beings. And he improved the appearance of their faces from one another, so that they would not all be the same, but should be separate from each other. And it is thus to this day.[4]

But the sky was not light yet. It was still dark.

A woman became pregnant through the power of love. And after nine or eight months, this woman gave birth to her child, a ripe coconut. (Because it was not yet light. And food had not yet appeared. But people and animals and all kinds of living things were ready.)

And the woman named the coconut Ļakaṃ. (Ļakaṃ is the name for this ripe coconut in the ancient language. Only one.) And she treasured it highly.

And the woman pondered a lot about her

---

4. The theme of supernatural beings originating the art of tattooing by painting fishes is also found in the folklore of ancient Tahiti (Henry 1928). She explains, "In the genealogy of the gods, Tohu was named as the god of tattooing" (377, 380). He was supposed to have painted the fishes in beautiful colors and patterns, which human beings imitated upon themselves and so men who made tattooing their profession invoked Tohu to aid them in their work. They were called ta-tau (tattoo adepts)" (234). "Birth of the Gods: . . . The sea rolled and night passed until the night of 'Ohua (Becoming Circular) came, and there was born Vave'a (Towering Wave): he caused the waves to become breakers out at sea and on the reefs. There followed Vero-huti-i-te-ra'i (Storm-producer-in-the-sky). Then there came Tohu (Pointer) who painted patterns upon the fishes; he dwelt in the caves of the ocean" (377). ". . . Other sharks [other than the great blue shark] were messengers for Tino-rua (Body-of-two-natures). Lord of the ocean, and their young were messengers for Tohu (Pointer), who painted the fishes in different hues and stripes and patterns" (389).

In the Ratak version of the creation myth, Wūllep and Lejṃaan, male and female worms and the first living things, live in a shell. They raise the upper part of the shell. This becomes the sky. And the lower part becomes the earth. See Knappe (1888:65–66) and Erdland (1914:309). Variants of the sky-raising motif have been found in southern and central Polynesia and in Polynesian outlier cultures in Melanesia and Micronesia, as well as in other Micronesian cultures, including the Gilbert Islands (Kiribati). See Luomala 1950b:719–721.

child, the coconut. After three days, she took the coconut and went out and planted it. And looked to see what was the result. And she checked on it. (*Ajimonone* in the ancient language is 'to check on something'.) And after one or two weeks, the sprout appeared. And the woman said to herself, "Will it be good to eat?"

And she went and took hold of the sprout and tried to eat it. And it was not good. And she returned. After three days she went again and looked. And said to herself, "Is it good?" It was *mejeneor.* (One or two inches of sprout had appeared in the eyes of the coconut.) And now it was *epeijojo* (a coconut sprouted to one foot, spread out in the shape of the fins of a flying fish: *pe-i-jojo*).

And she went and cut, and cut the front of the sprouted coconut *(iu)* and tried to eat it. And it was bad.

And she returned. After three days, she returned and looked at her child the coconut. She went and, where it had been *peijojo,* it was now *denkiaie.* (*Denkiaie* is a sprout about six feet long.) And she was surprised about its length and she said to herself, "What is this thing, my son, going to do, woman?" And she again returned and looked again. When she looked, there were small fronds. And she again spoke to herself, "What will these things be finally?"

The sky was not yet light and it was still dark. And she came to the coconut and thought a lot about what would be good.

And she took hold of the coconut frond and spoke to herself, "It will be good for what?" Now she pulled out a part of the frond and tried to eat it. It was bad. And she began to think about many kinds of ideas. And she again returned and just reflected upon it.

A few nights later, she went out and again looked. She looked and the *utak* [sheathed efflorescence] had grown out. And she did not want to move it or take hold of it. And she again returned.

After a few nights she again went and looked. Then the *utak* had broken open, and she saw many *kwaļini* [small nuts or seeds of the coconuts, that is, the beginning]. And thought a lot about these things. She saw inside the coconut as it grew older and revealed all of these things.

And she said to herself, "I will not move these things that appear now until when everything will be clear later."

And she spent almost one month and did not go and look at the coconut. When the time she waited there was ended, she again went out.

Then many ripe coconuts were under the coconut tree. And there were many coconuts on the branches.

Now she thought about the fronds. "What could they be used for?"

Now she saw the *inpel* [cloth-like spathe around the base of coconut fronds: coconut cloth]. And she said, "What can these *inpel* be used for?"

Later she took hold of the ripe coconut and said, "And this ripe coconut, why is it like the boy, my son, Ļakaṃ?"

And she picked one young coconut and again reflected upon it. And she husked the coconut. And Ļakaṃ [the nut] appeared. And she took it, and went to open it up. And she tried to eat it. And it was very good to eat.

Now she again returned to the young coconut that she had picked before, and husked it and drank. She drank. It was very good. And she reflected upon all the things that appeared from the coconut.

But the sky was still dark. And she again took and husked it and opened it up and grated it—as she had thought about it within. And when she grated it, she said, "I make the coconut fall while grating it, Ļakaṃ." (In the ancient language, the meaning of *iṃukṃuk* is 'to make it fall while grating it'.)

The reason she said, "Iṃukṃuk Ļakaṃ" was because she hoped that it would be food and it would be for all of the people. And when she ate, she began to think that she could make houses from the coconut tree trunks. And make large baskets *(kilōk),* small baskets *(iiep* and *banonoor),* and many other different things.

The coconut cloth, the woman said, can be used to make fires and some other things. The husk, the woman said, can be used for firewood. And the coconut shell can also be used to make fires and other things.

And she thought about the coconut husks. And she tried to put them in the salt water [lagoon] for a month to see if they would be as she had thought.

When one month was passed, she went and looked. When she looked, the husk was soft. And she took it and beat it a little and washed it and took it and sun-dried it.

The sky had not yet cleared.

And she did as she had thought, and pulled out part of the coconut husk. And when there was a lot of it, she did as she had thought, and made coconut sennit [plaited cordage]. When she saw that it was good, she continued and made sennit.

After a week, the sennit was very long.[5] One day she was just starting to make sennit when she saw a bird. The name of this bird is *keār* [*terna fuscata serrata,* sooty tern]. Now she brought the sennit line and cast a sling shot. She put a rock in the front part of the line and threw it at the bird. (This activity was called *luewor* in the ancient language. And *likito ion* in the language of today. People today do not know much about this.)

The sennit line went out and wrapped around the bird's legs. And she pulled it down.

When the bird fell down, the sky cleared. (In the ancient language, *jeļļo̧k lan̄* means 'the sky cleared, opened up, became visible'.) And it was very light. And all of the people also began to think (previously they were like rocks). And some people thought about making canoes. And some thought about making houses. And some thought about making medicine. Thus enlightenment came to each person at the time of thought.

At this time, they took care of each other very well. And as brothers and sisters take care of each other.

And there was an idea that they should make a canoe. And they made the keel. When it was completed, they made the end pieces [for bow and stern]. And when they were completed, they made the top-strakes. And it was not ready.

And the men who were constructing the canoe previously stopped their work. And other men took over from them (changed shifts), and again chopped a tree—again chopped a breadfruit tree. And again brought and cut it and put it together [repeated their previous effort]. And it was not good. And they discarded it.

And again some men came. And they chopped a breadfruit tree and brought it and again put it together. And it was not good. Now a man came and brought the parts of the things that they had made before, and tried to put them together. When he began putting them together, the men who had worked on the canoe previously said, "It cannot be completed, for we have discarded those things. But if you construct new ones, it should be good. And the man who made the top-strake said, "I will just try, but I do not know whether it can be completed."

The next day he went out alone to the canoe. And thought a bit. And called two

---

5. Note the use of the introduced concept of a unit of time, one week, and the loanword *wiik.* Also hour, *awa,* month (for which *allōn̄* 'moon' is used), and year, *iiō.* These have all been incorporated into the traditional folktales. This shows how folktales change in details over the years. (See the Marshallese text of this and other folktales.)

young men to help him. And he did it, and it was very good. When it was evening, they [the other men] came to the canoe and were surprised because it was very good. At that time, they were angry with one another, because they had not been able to complete the canoe. And they said, "You alone by yourself, and I alone by myself." (They separated from one another.)

Now they said, "I am Irooj and you are Ļajjidik and you are Errōbra, you are Ri-Kuwajleen." (Because the man who made the canoe [had made it so] that [it] was good, they said, "Ri-Kuwajeleen.") (I have forgotten some of the clan names in this story.) "And you are Ṃōkauleej; You are Tilañ (six real clans); You are Ri-Lobareņ."

Now they were clans and they separated from each other. And made many different clans in these atolls [the Marshalls].[6]

Now the woman said, "It is bad to separate from each other, for it was just like this from the beginning." Some knew how to make the islands. And some how to make oceans. And some knew how to color all the living things, and separate them from each other.

"Well, it is just like this with us now. Some knew the work and thus it is that this canoe is completed. And I say to you that it is bad to separate from each other. For beginning the work before, thus this is your canoe. And I say to you: 'your canoe'" (in the ancient language, the canoe of everyone). "Canoe together, canoe to make us fortunate, canoe to destroy us" (because one time it would be wrecked and destroy them). "Canoe of *jokier.*" (In the ancient language, *jokier* means that [you should] never mind if your life is not good; if you see the canoe, it will be good there. Well, you will be prosperous.)

Now she saw the light was better. The woman brought two supports and placed one at the east and bent it and extended it to the west. Now she again brought the other stick and placed it at the south and bent it and extended it to the north.

And the name of the support at the north: Kationi. And the name of the support at the south: Katirōk. And the name of the support at the east: Kōṃlañ. And the name of the support at the west: Kōṃlaļ. And it is like this to this day.[7]

Now the sky could not fall down (because there were supports). And thus the light increased and everything could be seen.

Now they thought about making houses. And they made [one] as they thought about it. And it was completed. When it was completed, the woman said, "Dig it in, and pound in the posts of the house and the contents." (*El* in the ancient language means 'house'—any kind of house; people, goods, all kinds can stay in it.)

And now the woman spoke to the people and said, "It is not good to separate from each other in doing big tasks. And do not harbor trouble with one another." (Now that woman taught them that they should work together and love each other and not be separated from each other.)[8]

Therefore they obeyed the teachings of the woman very well.

And the light of the sun was extremely great coming from the east. And they named it "*raan.*" When it went and set in the west it became dark.

---

6. Here is an explanation of the origin of the matriclans: clan fission.

7. Note the explanation of the separation of earth and sky, and of light and darkness, as well as the origin of the points of the compass (the major directions). The separation motif is found throughout Polynesia.

8. This tells of the establishment of a code of behavior, ideal interpersonal relations. (These specific teachings are part of the Marshallese value system today.)

And the people were worried again. And the woman said, "Do not be worried about something we do not know about." When it was dark, stars appeared and lighted it up a little. And the people were less worried.

And they called it "Night, Iroojrilik!" And the sun again rose, and when it became afternoon, it shined on Ļakam̧ [coconut tree], and he became ill.

And they asked Ļōkōm̧raan about this (why he became ill from the sunshine and heat).

And Ļōkōm̧raan did not speak, but he would do what they sought the next day. When it was sunrise and noon, a haze appeared for three days.

And at night, the stars did not appear. And it was very dark. After three days it was again sunrise. And the haze was gone, and Ļakam̧ was flourishing. And many different kinds of vegetation appeared: breadfruit, pandanus, *ut, kiden, kōjbar, arm̧we, wūjooj, marļap, markinenjojo, marjej, atat.* All kinds of vegetation. And they were very healthy.

And Ļewōj and Ļaneej colored them and gave them separate names.

And when the light increased, and when the situation was very good for the animals and human beings, they began to think about food. And they tried to eat all kinds of things, but they were not good.

And the woman again brought out the breadfruit and they ate. And pandanus and arrowroot.[9] And the woman separated the breadfruit and put it in the words of the testament to Ļōkōm̧raan and Ļōrōk that they should take the responsibility to make the time for planting. And she gave it the name *rak* (summer). This woman again gave the responsibility for pandanus and arrowroot to Iroojrilik and Ļajibwinām̧ōņ. And she gave it the name *añōneañ* 'winter'.

And the woman gave the responsibility for the sea to Ļewōj and Ļaneej (because there were many edible things there, and they would be able to feed the people with fish and clams and all the things in the sea: sharks, and whales and fluted clams, and everything).

And the woman said, "Let there be high tide and low tide and very low tide and very high tide."

And she made moonlight in the dark. In order to make very low tide and very high tide.

Now the woman revealed the ways of the sun to these people, and said, "If it is in the east: morning. If it is in the middle, noon. If it is in the west, evening." And she again explained the ways of the moon. "If it is in the west, the name is *takatakinae.* If it is in the west, in the middle: *limeto.* If it is in the middle: *lipepe.* If it is in the east in the middle: *limetak.* If it is in the east: *tutuinae."*

(These were the directions named after the sky had been supported, and divided. These are used for sailing when conditions are good.)

Now she again made it so that there would be many fruits on all of the vegetation. And she said, "I am taking the responsibility [for all the winds]. And make it so that there will be many fruits of all of the vegetation, and every kind of edible fruit."

And she said, "Let the wind fall down from the east." And it came from the east. And she gave it the name *jonin itok i rear* 'comes from the east' (in the ancient language, *jonin* is 'comes').

And she again said, "Let the wind come in the west." And she named it *jonin ketak* 'comes from the west'.

And she again said, "Let it come in the south." And she named it *jonin kitak* 'comes from the south'.

9. Note the explanation of the beginning of the diet of human beings, established by the female culture hero, who advised them and taught them useful knowledge for their survival.

And the woman again said, "Let it come from the north." And she named it *jokļā* 'comes from the north'. (These terms are used today; connected with sailing at the right time for certain destinations.)

Now the wind blew and moved through the branches of all the trees. And many different kinds of flowers appeared.

And she also made currents that went to and fro, westward and eastward. And also the northward moving current. And also the southward moving current.

(Thus the old people believed the appearance of all fruit: breadfruit, pandanus, and flowers occurred. But not coconuts. Coconuts came before. The rest came through the agency of the wind, as this story tells.)

After a few days, the woman separated the winds from each other. And for three months the wind came from the east. And for three months it came from the west. And for three months it came from the south. And for three months it came from the north.

And this is the way the wind worked in making the westward current and the eastward current. And the southward current and the northward current. And she again made it so that the wind would fall from the middle of the sky. And she again named it *jinobōdelañ* of the wind. And she also wanted it to be calm, and with no wind, so that it would make a good current.

And the following day when it was afternoon, the flowers, grass, and things shriveled up. (All kinds, they were in bad condition.)

And the woman first sent *wōtm̧welañ* (a light shower). And the grass, breadfruit, *kōjbar, ut, kūtaak, arm̧we,* and all of the vegetation did not grow very well.

And she again sent *wōtatkoņ* (another kind of rain, rains a lot but only falls briefly).

And she saw that it was not good. She sent *wōtwǫ* (a little longer in duration than *wōtatkoņ*—the sound "W-O-O-O" comes, and it stops).

And when it was not very good, she sent *wōtmijeljel* (a lot of rain that decreases slowly, an extended rain).

And she saw that this was good for the life of all the growing things. And it is like this to this day. (Now there was rain. There was none before.)

When everything was prepared, she laid down words of testament to all the young men and the women at that time that they should not separate from each other. Never mind if they have different clans. But it will be bad to separate. And she gave another word. She said, *"Del lik | Del ar ilo wāto in kein | Ajri jiddik ipinnidrik."* (Wherever you go from ocean to lagoon | No matter what lies you hear | Do not obey them.) That is, do not talk against people and obey lies. Do not be like small children who tell lies. (*Ipinnidik* in the ancient language in this chant means not to obey lies.) The woman taught this to the people.

And she said, "If you do great work, it will be bad if you do not help each other (cooperate). It will be best if you help each other. For you will be in the word that says *'Ko make iwaļapļap eo iwaļapļap eo jañi jeram̧ōl ke iio jipakwe | Kwe eo.'*"

(The meaning, the deep meaning in this word, a word in the ancient language, is like if you alone try to build a large canoe it cannot be completed because there are no people with you. *Jeram̧ōl* in the ancient language is 'no people with [some]one'. Like if Irooj Ļōjjeiļañ had no people with him: *jeram̧ōl*.)[10]

And she strongly made the testament to them that they should not separate from each other. "And when you eat breadfruit (during the breadfruit season), see that you do not waste the food." (In the ancient language *wūdin* is 'waste food'.) "But conserve it for a time when there will be no food. Also pandanus, conserve it. Also arrowroot, again conserve it. And do not waste food, for [there will come] a time [when] there will be none."

And she again made a testament that when it would be the breadfruit season they should make their means of hastening it (perform the ritual for ripening of the fruit).[11]

"In this manner, you will do it: *Boktok joṃa eo.*" (In the ancient language, it is like the breadfruit is to ripen quickly.) "And place it in a pile. And choose six men from the top people of the lineages (the number one clan). And they should walk just before dawn (before the cock crows). And cry out and say, *'Ni mi to O-O-O | Ni mi to O-O-O'.*"

(The meaning of this in the ancient language is 'Coconut, come here! | Coconut, come here!' Because the coconut, Ļakaṃ, appeared before everything. Because the coconut tree produces coconuts all the time. Not just one time. They wanted the breadfruit tree to produce its fruit like coconut trees. This is the reason they cried out like this.)

And they came to the side of the pile of breadfruit, and two men stood, one to the east, and one to the south. And the two of them called to four men, their companions. And they began from the east. And said, "One man come here and take a breadfruit and turn to the east. And say, *'Mā in Kijmelañ jabuweo i rear eo Ļōkōṃraan | ibōk taļǫk | ibōk taļǫk | Likūti i nabwij jān iṃōn Ļōkōṃraan'.*" (Breadfruit of Kijmelañ over there—in the east Ļōkōṃraan | I take it to the east | I take it to the east | I place it outside of the house of Ļōkōṃraan.) (These are the words of their worship, the words of prayer to Ļōkōṃraan.)

Now he took it to the east about six feet. And put the breadfruit down and stood.

(To this day the Marshallese put breadfruit inside the church. And they sing. And they put it within the church. And they pray in thanksgiving to God to this day. At the beginning of the breadfruit season and the beginning of the pandanus season. Sometimes they put coconuts inside.)[12]

And the two young men again called a young man to come from the south. And he stood south of the pile. And went forward six feet and took hold of a breadfruit, and returned and said, *"Mā in Kijmelañ jabuweo irōk eo—Ļōrōk | Ibōk rōñaļǫk | Ibōk rōñaļǫk | Likūti i nabwij jān iṃōn Ļōrōk."* (Breadfruit of Kijmelañ over there—in the south—Ļōrōk | I take it to the south | I take it to the south | I put it outside of the house of Ļōrōk.)

And he took it away about six feet, and stood. And two stood next to the pile of breadfruit.

And the two young men again called and said, "Come here, man from the north." And the man from the north came forward six feet and took hold of the breadfruit and returned and said, *"Mā in Kijmelañ jabuweo eañ eo—Ļajibwināṃōņ | Ibōk niñaļǫk | Ibōk niñaļǫk | Likūti i nabwij jān iṃōn Ļajibwināṃōņ."* (Breadfruit of Kijmelañ over there—in the north—Ļajibwināṃōņ | I take it to the north | I take it to the north | I put it outside of the house of Ļajibwināṃōņ.)

He went another six feet and put the breadfruit down and stood.

And the two young men and their companions again said that man should come

10. The informant was making the point that everyone needs other people for support. In the case of the *irooj* (chief), he needed his *kajoor* (commoners) to support him as warriors and workers in the olden days, and as workers today. A strong mutual support system was obviously vital for survival in these small island communities where the natural resources were (and are) rather limited.

11. This is an increase ceremony, an important ritual for obvious economic reasons in many parts of the world, from antiquity to the present.

12. Here is an interesting example of syncretism/adaptation of the traditional beliefs to the introduced religious system.

from the west. And he came forward six feet and took hold of a breadfruit and turned westward and said, *"Mā in Kijmelañ jabuweo irilik eo—Iroojrilik | Ibōk toļok | Ibōk toļok | Likūti i nabwij jān iṃōn Iroojrilik."* (Breadfruit of Kijmelañ over there to the west—Iroojrilik | I take it to the west | I take it to the west | I put it outside of the house of Iroojrilik.)

He went about six feet and put the breadfruit down and stood.

Now these men cried out with a great sound and said, *"Emelim O | Emelim!"* (It is permitted O | It is permitted!)

And when all of the people heard [this], they ran up to the men and the pile of breadfruit. And their food, breadfruit.

Now it was permissible for anyone to be free to harvest breadfruit at any time. (They ate breadfruit for the first time now. They did not [eat it] previously.)

Thus they were free every day. And when there was a great amount of breadfruit, they rotted. Because there were so many that they could not eat them all. And they remembered the word of the woman when she said, "Do not waste food."

And they were careful of their harvesting, but the breadfruit just fell down. (They fell down because they were ripe.) And they began their processing [to preserve the breadfruit]. And they processed for four months. (In the ancient language, *allōñiju* is 'month'.)

And the breadfruit was finished and there was none now. They ate from *bwiro* [breadfruit preserved in a pit] and *jāānkun* [cooked and sundried breadfruit] and *ṃōņakjān* [dried *bwiro*] for eight months. And it was the right time for the coming of pandanus.[13] At this time, when the pandanus fruit began to appear, they revealed a law to all of the people. And the woman said, "It is forbidden to chew the pandanus and discard the segments when the pandanus are ripe." (In the ancient language *pittōr* means 'to chew the pandanus and discard the segments'.)

And she again called six men, the top men of the clans, so that they would be ready to awaken just before dawn on the following day. On that day, they made a pile of pandanus fruit, and prepared it for the following day. And when it was just before dawn of the following day, the men rose and walked in the area on the island and cried out with a loud voice and said, *"Ni Mi To-O-O-O | Ni Mi To-O-O-O."* (Coconut come here | Coconut come here.) And they again called out the second time, *"Ni Mi To-O-O-O."* (Coconut come here.)

Thus was their cry. And all the people heard their cry and said, "O-O. Those are demons!" But some said, "Those are gods! It will be permissible to chew pandanus and discard the segments now!"

And the men came to the pile of pandanus. And one stood at the north, one at the south, one at the east, and one at the west.

And two stood next to the pile of pandanus. And the two called the man from the north. And he came forward to the pile, six feet, and took a pandanus fruit and picked it up and turned to the north and said, *"Bōb in Kijmelañ jabuweo iōñ eo—Ļajibwināṃōņ | Ibōk niñaļok | Ibōk niñaļok | Likūti i nabwij in iṃōn Ļajibwināṃōņ."* (Pandanus of Kijmelañ over there to the north—Ļajibwināṃōņ | I take it to the north | I take it to the north | I put it outside of the house of Ļajibwināṃōņ.) And he put it down and stood.

And the two young men again said, "The man from the west should come here." And

13. Note the explanation of the origin of preservation of the seasonal breadfruit, and the teaching of the need for this conservation in the subsistence economy. The story treats the very important pandanus in the same manner.

the man from the west came forward six feet and took hold of the pandanus fruit and picked it up. And said, *"Bōb in Kijmelañ jabuweo i rilik eo—Iroojrilik | Ibōk toļọk | Ibōk toļọk | Likūti i nabwij in iṃōn Iroojrilik."* (Pandanus of Kijmelañ over there to the west—Iroojrilik | I take it to the west | I take it to the west | I put it outside of the house of Iroojrilik.) And he put it down and stood.

The two young men again called the man from the east. And the man from the east came forward six feet and took hold of the pandanus fruit. And picked it up and said, *"Bōb in Kijmelañ jabuweo i rear eo—Ļōkōṃraan | I bōk taļọk | I bōk taļọk | Likūti i nabwij in imōn Ļōkōṃraan."* (Pandanus of Kijmelañ over there to the east—Ļōkōṃraan | I take it to the east | I take it to the east | I put it outside of the house of Ļōkōṃraan.) And he put it down and stood.

The two young men said for the man to come from the south. And the man from the south came forward six feet and took hold of the pandanus and picked it up and said, *"Bōb in Kijmelañ jabuweo rōk eo—Ļōrōk | I bōk rōñaļọk | I bōk rōñaļọk | Likūti i nabwij in imōn Ļōrōk."* (Pandanus of Kijmelañ over there to the south—Ļōrōk | I take it to the south | I take it to the south | I put it outside of the house of Ļōrōk.) And he stood, and when he was finished, he cried out with a loud voice and said, "*Emelim O-O | Emelim | Emelim bittōr O-O!*" (It is permitted O-O | It is permitted | It is permitted to chew pandanus and discard the segments O-O!)

Now all of the people ran up on the following day (at sunrise) to the pile of pandanus, to the man and took their food, pandanus.

(This time was the beginning of people eating pandanus in this world. They did not eat pandanus previously.) And they were free to chew pandanus segments, and throw away the pandanus segments (after chewing them) in the area.

And they chewed the pandanus segments and many pandanus fruits fell down (because they were very ripe). And they again remembered the word of the woman when she said, "It is bad to waste food." And they began their processing (to preserve) and made *jankwōn* [cooked and sundried pandanus fruit]. And *tipijek* (sundried pandanus fruit—not made today).

They ate these things for eight months. And thus the woman again told them that if they did any big work, they should take time to pray. And remember their suffering and their happiness because it came to pass.

And she said that she would go on a road, and she left her footprints. And they quickly disappeared. And the people who were there with the woman at that time died and changed into different things after death (like rocks, birds, fish, and so forth). They are signs (navigation markers) to this day.[14]

(All of the people who died at that time are located in all of the areas of the Marshalls.)

And the woman's footprints are still to be seen at Orjej. So that people should not forget.

And Iroojrilik was the chief over everything at this time when the woman, their mother, went away. And they named the woman Jineer ilo Kōbo. (I do not know what this means.)

After some time, a boy was born and his mother named him Bōrraan. He was the maternal nephew of Iroojrilik. When older, he was very haughty in his way of living.

14. The *kōkļaļ/kakōļļe* (navigation signs or sea marks) were very important in navigating the sailing canoes between the islands and atolls of the Marshallese archipelago. A specific sign was (and is) associated with specific islands or atolls or locations in the sea between landfalls (see story 30, "The Ikid of Ļainjin," page 131, and references in many other Marshallese folktales).

And he broke all of the rules of the woman, his mother. And Iroojrilik oversaw all of the people in those times.

And because Bōrraan was haughty, he told Iroojrilik, his *aļap* [maternal uncle, lineage head] that he should take all of the food from the ocean, and Bōrraan should take all of the food from the land.

And Bōrraan told Iroojrilik that he should come and see the large amount of food on the land. And Iroojrilik came and saw that there was a great deal. And he told the maggot that he should go and eat the breadfruit. And the *menkōk* [an insect] and the *kauļaļo* [a spider]. And they destroyed all of the food-producing plants and their fruit.

And Iroojrilik told all of the fish that they should beach themselves, and all of the birds of the air. And the fish beached themselves. And waves of fish flowed over the island. And they named the island Tutu. As it is to this day.

Bōrraan saw the strength of his uncle and was very frightened.[15] But he continued in his bad actions. And he went away and is gone to this day.

And they again built the second canoe, Ļowa and Ļōm̧tal [did]. They built the canoe on Pikinni Atoll. On an island named Nam̧. The name of the land parcel was Jinbwi.

They used a *kañal* [*Pisonia grandis,* a tree] as a measurement for the canoe.

Ļewōj and Ļaneej made tattoos the second time on Ujae Atoll. The name of the land parcel there was Bati-Ļaneej, on the main island.

The place where they stirred up, in a well, is there to this day. And the water there is very good. But at the time they dug it up, many, many coconut husks appeared.

And some people again made houses the second time on Aelōñļapļap [Atoll] on the land parcel named Ekweren, on Wōja Island.

And all of the people at that time opened their minds to all aspects of work.

At this time, all of the people from the beginning were gone. And Ļajibwinām̧ōņ took the responsibility for the children of sustenance (real people). And at this time, many kinds of people were born. Some human beings and some *ņooniep,* and some *riikijet* and some *rimmenanuwe,* and some *ripitwōdwōd.*

(*Ņooniep* are like human beings. Sometimes they appear and talk with human beings. And they can see people but sometimes people cannot see them. *Riikijet* are like human beings. *Riikijet* live in the water. *Ņooniep* live on land. And *rimmenanuwe* are short but are like people. They can talk with people.)

The *jebwa* [stick dance] was revealed by a *riikijet* on Ujae.

The *ripitwōdwōd* are tall [and] large. They walk on the sea. They do not speak to people. They harm people.

At this time, a young man was born. And they named him Ļe-Etao. [Informant chuck-

15. Note admonition of the disrespectful nephew by his uncle because of the nephew's violation of the respect due him. A special respect relationship exists between a maternal uncle and his nephew, who belong to the same lineage and clan.

Although the informant did not know where Tutu Island in the story was located, there is a Tutu Island on the northeastern side of Arņo Atoll, near a pass. (The name Tutu, appropriately enough, means 'wet' or 'bathe'.) Stories of floods are widespread. The catastrophe told in Genesis is part of the Judeo-Christian heritage, of course. For stories of floods in Polynesian folklore, see Beckwith (1970:314–320). She also points out that "although tidal waves on high islands are not so disastrous as the myth would represent, a small inhabited coral island is subject at irregular intervals to a complete inundation from which a small remnant may escape. . . . And there are records throughout the South Seas of occasions in which whole islands have disappeared utterly." Such tidal waves may very well have been the historical basis of the Marshallese flood stories.

led after he mentioned the name of this famous trickster.]

And one time some of the people, the children of sustenance (the real people), were sick. (They were real human beings. They ate, and they had blood. The people previously did not eat. They tasted the food and threw it away—many thousands of years ago.)

And Ļajibwinām̧ōņ said, "When they die, you bury them. Do it with the top of their heads pointing toward Ļajibwinām̧ōņ."

(The meaning of this in the ancient language and custom is to bury people with their heads to the north, to Ļajibwinām̧ōņ. As Marshallese did from long ago. But not all of the time these days.)

"The reason for this is if they die in sin and are resurrected, I will eat them. But if they keep (follow) the words of teaching of the woman Jineer Ilo Kōbo when they die, Ļajibwinām̧ōņ will give freedom to them."

Although it was thus, the young man Ļe-Etao's will was very strong. And he tricked many people with lies. The first lie of Ļe-Etao was a canoe that he built and put on a reef.

This canoe was very good. However, the wood of the canoe was only of *kōne* [*Pemphis acidula,* ironwood], a very heavy wood.

And he went and said to the chief at that time that he should take his canoe to sail it.

And the chief said "But why don't you sail the canoe that you made?" And Ļe-Etao answered the chief and said, "Because that canoe is very good and appropriate for you."

And the chief went to look at the canoe. And he liked it very much and was very happy with it.

And the chief released his canoe and gave it to Ļe-Etao. And Ļe-Etao sailed away quickly. Later the chief went to sail on the canoe that had been Ļe-Etao's. [Informant laughed again, in anticipation of the denouement of the trick.]

And when the chief launched the canoe into the sea from the reef to sail, it (the canoe) sank and remained in the sea.

And the chief was very angry at this time, but Ļe-Etao had gone, for he would be killed (if he had remained there). [Informant laughed and said, "Ļe-Etao was bad!"]

And they searched for Ļe-Etao but they have not seen him to this day. But his bad deeds persist to now.

At this time, people were sick. Some of them died, and some of them lived. (The beginning of sickness and death. There was none previously. Because now people were "children of sustenance.")

And they buried those who died as they knew they should, pointing them toward Ļajibwinām̧ōņ.

The place where they began burying them was on Jalwōj Atoll, on Piñlep [island] and M̧ōn-bōd land parcel.

At this time, the people were having a wake. And Ļe-Etao appeared at the time of the wake and came to the people who were dead. And moved their eyes and it was as if they were alive. And no human beings knew about this [what Ļe-Etao was doing] but only the *ņooniep.* And the *ņooniep* was sorry for the people who were alive and revealed to them the way Ļe-Etao had done [how he had tricked them].

At this time, when the people spoke, Ļe-Etao again spoke just like them. And they said, "Echo." And they said, "Voice of Ļe-Etao."

From that time to this day, people do not believe in the deeds of Ļe-Etao. (But many believe and they are harmed.)

The way they buried those people who died at that time, they made *wura.* (In the ancient language the meaning of this is to put a person inside the grave.) And later on they put a rock inside in place of a person. Chiefs and commoners before. And later enlightenment came—before the missionaries arrived.

And at the time of eating, they put their food on the grave for six nights. And after six nights, they placed pebbles on the grave and cleaned around it. For, at that time, the deceased separated from the people [and] changed into a demon.

The chief said, "*Emelim ākūt em ma kamaañōñōñ ioon Anij | Kiki O-O | Kiki in etoñ.*" (It is permitted to delouse and pound on the demon | Sleep O-O | Sleep deeply.) (The meaning of *ma* in the ancient language is 'pound'.)

And their giving of food was concluded [placing food on the grave].

(According to the ancient custom of the olden days, when a chief died, no one could pick coconuts, harvest pandanus fruit, delouse, [or] pound pandanus leaves for six days. If a commoner died, only his relatives had to do like this.

And after six days, it was forbidden to go to the grave. But it was permitted to delouse, and to harvest pandanus fruit, and to pick coconuts.

You could go and clear away trash and weeds and clean up the area good. And it was bad if you did not do your work.

All of the people do not do like this today. Only a few old men and old women obey it. I obey this custom. And I tell my children that they should not go to the graveyard if they do not have any work to do there.[16]

And now if the person who died had led a good life, he would be free. But if he had been bad, Ļajibwinām̧ōņ would eat him.

[Informant laughed and said, "But Ļajibwinām̧ōņ did not put people in jail. There were no jails in the Marshalls before."])

At this time, there was trouble between brothers and sisters. And when they remembered the words of teaching from long ago, some of them did not obey them. And some of them did obey. And at that time when the islands separated from each other by flood (*ikijik* is the ancient word for 'flood'), they began their spreading about in canoes (many canoes). And they were able to go from atoll to atoll. However, only one island did not appear, but it remained within the sea. At that time, one man and two of his relatives sailed. They searched for where it was (the island).

For there were many people and living things and *ņooniep* and *riikijet* on all of the islands. And they (the three men) did not want to stay on these islands.

And they sailed and made magic to find out where they were.

And then the fold on the pandanus leaf strip called *ņokemen* appeared. (In the ancient language the meaning of *eļǫk wōttok* is 'then came', or 'appeared'.)

And the man said, "The canoe should stop here. And give me one thing." (In the ancient language, *kewaretok* is 'give'.)

And one of the men in the canoe gave him a ripe coconut. And he seized it and threw it away. And he said again, "Give me one thing."

The young men gave him a piece of wood. And the man seized it and again threw it away.

And he again said, "Give me one thing." And they again gave him a coconut husk. And he seized it and again threw it away. And he again said, "Give me one thing."

Now his young daughter who was sailing came out of the cabin. And gave him a core of a pandanus fruit (without segments).

And the man seized the core and wrapped coconut sennit around it. And lowered it down into the water.

And said, "*Ņokemen eo lio deo | Kewaretok Kāājinpit i ņa Likļǫkwe | Āne im ke āne?*

16. Note the history of changes in burial customs explained.

| *Rakijbadke jen ro kijbadke em kijbadbad.*" (Give the hook in the pandanus and fish up the island | What island? | It appears | We two go to it | And we remain there.)

(*Kijbadke* and *kijbadbad* are words in the old language. And the name of the girl now is N̦okemen.)

The man pulled on the line. It was very heavy. And they all came to pull it up. When it appeared, they said, "The atoll rises up. Here it is."

And they came to the atoll and remained there. The name of the atoll: Mile.

(This is its name because N̦okemen revealed Mile.)

Now there were many people on all of the atolls in the Marshalls. And all kinds of living things.

(The navigation signs *[kōkļaļ]* of Mile are four *kowak* [*Numeius tahitiensis,* bristle-thighed curlew] that stay to the south and east of Mile, to the south of N̦adikdik [Atoll]. And six *kōtkōt* [*Arenaria interpres,* turnstone] that stay south of Mile [and N̦adikdik] to the west.

And when you see the navigation signs of Mile, you know that you are beside Mile.

The [pandanus leaf magic] fold of the *kowak* is named N̦okemen—the name of the young girl.

And the fold of the *kōtkōt* is named Irinbwe—the thing to make the fold: magic to foretell.

If you see these things, you know that you are near Mile. If the birds fly out from the island to the sea, you know you are near the island. And if you see birds flying out from the sea to the island, you know you are far away from the island.)

However, the *n̦ooniep* lived and were just like human beings.

They also completed their separation from each other again and lived like human beings. And they stayed in all the world. But human beings could not see them.

But the *n̦ooniep* could appear to humans at any time. [That was] because the *n̦ooniep* did not obey Etao all of the time. But the *n̦ooniep* obeyed the words of teaching from long ago. And they lived like people, but people could not see them.

One time, the Chief of the N̦ooniep sailed. And the name of the captain: Lo̧meto. The name of the chief: Kabua.

And the *riikijet* were living also like *n̦ooniep*. However, they stayed under the island.

Etao was not able to deceive the *riikijet.* But the *riikijet* dislike Etao to this day.

In this manner, Etao went back and forth throughout the world and deceived many people. And some obeyed the things (tricks) that Etao did.

There were two examples for people in those times. One obeyed Etao. And he disappeared to this day. One obeyed the law and words of teaching from long ago. And she remains free [up until] now.

The name of the person who obeyed the word of law and the word of teaching: Lim̧kade.

The name of the person who did not obey the word of law and the word of teaching: Bōrraan.

There are fingernails of Lim̧kade to this day on the atoll of Wōtto. They are like *kūkōr* [mollusks] [their shells].

Some of the people of Mile long ago were good because they worked with spirits and revealed the atoll of Mile. However, those who obeyed Ļe-Etao were bad.

(Of all of the people in the world, those who obeyed Ļe-Etao were bad. And those who did not obey him are good to this day. And those who obey Ļe-Etao and lie and hurt people are bad.)

This story is ended.

There are also other stories that come out of this story, such as Tōboļāār and other stories about Ļe-Etao, and so forth.

Ŋooniep love people. And if there is a mistake made, it is bad with the *ŋooniep*. If *ŋooniep* mate with a woman, a human being, a half-caste will be born: half *ŋooniep* and half human being.

But the *riikijet* sometimes do bad things to humans. They like to mate with female humans. If a *riikijet* mates with a female human, children cannot be born. Or if they can, I have not heard of it.

Comments

As one can see, this long story is more than an origin story. It contains a wealth of information and explanation, and must have been a useful device for the education of Marshallese children and a valuable oral history of the culture as well. It incorporates several motifs and stories that are also narrated separately—for example, the Ļe-Etao/Etao adventures, the story of Iroojrilik, the story of Bōrraan, and description of other supernatural beings such as the *ŋooniep, ripitwōdwōd, riikijet,* and the *rimmenanuwe.* One wonders if these elements were indeed part of the original story of "The Beginning of This World" and became separate stories, as the informant said, or if they were added to the original creation story. Whatever the case, informant Jelibōr Jam impressed me with the importance of the story (as he stated at the outset). Indeed, one can see why he felt that way.

Fishing for an island by a culture hero is a widespread theme in Polynesian folklore, and is found in Micronesia as well. In Polynesia, this marvelous feat is associated with the culture hero/trickster Maui/Mauitikitik, and in Micronesia it is associated with other characters. In another Marshallese story, Mile Atoll is fished up with a special hook by a character named Lañinperan. See the comments on story 71, "The Chant of Mile—Fishing Up from the Bottom of the Sea," page 315, for references to the literature of island fishing. In the chant referred to, Bukonmar is the principal character, and Lañinperan plays a secondary role. For Polynesian cosmogonic myths and trickster stories ("The Maui Cycle"), see Dixon (1964:4–56). Luomala (1950b:720) states that "the Marshalls and Gilberts have cosmogonies which leave no doubt of historical connections with Polynesia."

Another explanation of clan origins was given to me by Ekpap Silk on Mājro in 1972. "The *Ri-Kuwajleen* (People of Kuwajleen), *Ri-Meik* (People of Meik), and the *Ri-kapin-aelōn̄-in* (People of the western end of the atoll) originated many years ago as follows: They (all of the people on Kuwajleen) were all *Ri-Kuwajleen.* They split up. Those at the northwest of the atoll, Epatōn Island and that area *(kapinmeto),* became *Ri-kapin-aelōn̄-in.* Those to the east became Ri-Meik, after Meik Island. And those to the south became *Ri-Kuwajleen,* after the main island (*eoonene*) of the atoll."

This story is an indigenous explanation of clan fission, which functioned to increase the availability of mates in an exogamous clan system, which the Marshallese have. As stated earlier, clan *(jowi/jou)* membership, lineage *(bwij)* membership, and primary land-use rights are matrilineal. However, Marshallese also consider themselves to be part of their patrilineal clans and lineages, thus extending kinship ties even further. This has obvious social, political, economic, and psychological value.

A legend from Pohnpei (Ponape) Island, to the west of the Marshall Islands, also describes the origin of the coconut tree. "It is said that one man of the Masters of the South became sick and died, and they buried him in the earth and eventually a coconut sprouted from his grave and made a coconut palm. This was the beginning of the first coconut tree in the world. And it multiplied in the land, and a ripe coconut floated hither from that land, floating here and there in the sea until it reached Ponape and washed ashore at Metolanim" (Bernart 1977:128). For two other versions of this Pohnpeian legend, see Bernart 1977:152, 156). The first beneficiary of the coconut tree in the story from Pohnpei (156) is named Lakam. And in the Marshallese story ("The Beginning of This World" in this chapter), the one who became the first coconut tree is named Ḷakaṃ. This is apparently a case of diffusion of a story and role reversal of a principal character.

In other Marshallese stories of the origin of the coconut tree, the principal character is named Tōboḷāār (also spelled Tebolar or Debolar). Erdland (1914:299–302) recorded a story of Tōboḷāār where the coconut tree originated on Epoon Atoll. Similar legends of the coconut tree's origin are found in other cultures in Oceania. See Beckwith (1970:102–104) for coconut origin legends from Polynesia and Melanesia.

1: JINOIN LAḶ IN

Ri-bwebwenato: Jelibōr Jam, Kuwajleen 1975

(Bwebwenato in eḷap an aetok im eḷap tokjān jān aolep bwebwenato ilo Aelōñ in Ṃajeḷ. Rūtto ro rejeḷā bwebwenato in. Ak ro reddik rejaje. Rejjab bōk itoklimo kake. Rōkōŋaan katak jeḷāḷọkjeŋ an ripālle wōt.)

Ilo jino in eaar or emān joor. Pād innām eoḷọk joor eo irear im kōṃṃan mejatoto irear. Im ŋa etan Ḷōkōṃraan. Pād jidik innām eoḷọk joor eo i rōk bwe en kōṃṃan mejatoto in rōk. Etan: Ḷōrōk. Jidik iien emootḷọk eoḷọk joor eo eañ bwe en kōṃṃan mejatoto in eañ. Etan: Ḷajibwināṃōŋ. Pād jidik iien eo eoḷọk joor eo i rilik. Bwe en kōṃṃan mejatoto in rilik. Etan: Iroojrilik.

Mejatoto ekanooj tab. Pād innām ewaḷọk ruo eṃṃaan jān mejatoto. Etan ḷōṃarein Ḷowa im Ḷōṃtal. Innām Ḷowa ej kōṃṃan āne kōn ainikien. Eaar ba, "Ḷowa im pedped." Innām eor pedped. Innām eaar bar ba, "Ḷowa im dekā." Innām eor dekā. Innām eaar bar ba, "Ḷowa im āne." Innām eor āne. Innām eaar bar ba, "Ḷowa im armej." Innām eor armej.

Mejatoto ej tab wōt. Jejjab lo ijoko rōttoḷọk.

Kiiō Ḷōṃtal. Ej kōṃṃan lọjet. Eaar ba kōn ainikien, "Bwijlọkwe ikijet im katọọr taḷọk. Etọọr taḷọk." Innām eaar bar ba kōn ainikien, "Bwijlọkwe ikijet im katọọr rōñaḷọk. Etọọr rōñaḷọk."

Innām eaar bar ba, "Bwijlọkwe ikijet im katọọr niñaḷọk. Etọọr niñaḷọk." Innām eaar bar ba, "Bwijlọkwe ikijet im katọọr toḷọk. Etọọr toḷọk."

Kiiō elōñ dān. Innām kiiō ej kōṃṃan ek. Im eaar ba, "Bwijlọkwe ar in Ep. Em kōtọọre." Etọọr ek. (Ep etan āne. Jejjab loe.)

Eaar bar ba, "Bwijiḷọke ar in Ep im katọọre." Itok bao in mejatoto. Kiiō elōñ āne, elōñ lọjet. Im men otemjej ilowaer.

Pād innām itok ruo likao. Ḷōṃarein rej iten kabuñ eọọn. (Ilo kajin etto meḷeḷein "kabuñ eọọn" ej kōṃṃan eọ.) Etan ḷōṃarein Ḷewej im Ḷaneej. Ijo armej ro raar lo an ḷōṃaro to jān eañ ie i jabōn Buoj tu-iōñ. Etan wāto eo ijeŋ Jiṃwinne, ñan rainin.

Kiiō rejro iten jino aer kabuñ eǫǫn. Innām rejro iten m̧am̧wij. ("M̧am̧wij" ilo kajin etto ej kōm̧m̧an uno in eǫ jān bwidej: kilmeej, maroro, mouj, iaļo,būļu: elōñ kain.) Im rej iten uno aolep mennin mour otemjej. Innām ļeo juon, Ļewej, ej kūrtok aolep ek. Im ba, "Itok juon." Innām ej itok juon im ļeo juon, Ļaneej, ej unoke. Im ba, "Etam̧ kupañ." Im kōtļǫke n̄a i lǫjet.

Im ļeo juon, Ļewej, ej bar kūrtok juon ek im ļeo juon, Ļaneej, ej unoke im ba, "Etam̧ bwebwe." Im kōtļǫke n̄a i lǫjet.

Ļewej ej bar kūrtok juon im Ļaneej ej bar unoke im kōtļǫke n̄a i lǫjet im ba, "Etam mao." Im āindein aer kōm̧m̧an ñan aolep ek ko otemjej ilo lǫjet. Im Ļewej ej kūrtok bao ko in mejatoto im Ļaneej ej bar leļǫk uno ñan er kajjo wāween im kōjpel etāer jān doon. Im Ļewej ej bar kūrtok aolep men otemjej, ko rej tōbalbal ioon āne. Im unook er kōn kajjo kain uno.

Im ej kōjpel etāer jān doon. Bwe ren jab āinwōt juon. Ak ren jepel jān doon. Innām āindein ñan rainin.

Ak lañ ejjañin meram. Ej marok wōt.

Kōn kajoor in iǫkwe ej bōrǫro juon kōrā. Im ļǫkun ruwatimjuon ak ruwalitōk an allōñ kōrā in ej keotak juon nājin waini. (Kōnke ejjañin meram. Im m̧ōñā ejjañin waļǫk. Ak repojak armej im kidu im aolep kain men-ninmour.)

Innām kōrā in ej likūt etan waini eo Ļakam̧. (Ļakam̧ ej etan waini ilo kajin etto. Juon wōt.) Im kanooj in kaorōke.

Innām kōrā eo eļap an kōļmānļǫkjen̄ kōn waini eo nājin. Ļǫkun jilu raan ej bōk waini eo im iļǫk im kalbwini. Im lale ej alikkar ta? Innām ej ajimonene. ("Ajimonene" ilo kajin etto ej etalitok.) Innām ļǫkun juon ak ruo wiik ej eddōk mejān. Innām kōrā eo ej ba ippān make, "Enaaj em̧m̧an ke m̧ōñā?"

Innām ej etal im jibwe māj eo im kajjeoñ in m̧ōñā. Innām ejjab em̧m̧an. Innām ej bar rǫǫl. Im ļǫkan jilu raan ej bar etal im lale. Im ej ba ñan e make, "Ejako ke?" Eaar meje-

neor. (Juon ak ruo inij an mejān ni e waļǫk.) Ak kiiō epeijojo. (Mejen ni ñan juon ne im jekjek āinwōt pein jojo.)

Innām ej etal im bukwe pein rājet im kajjeoñ m̧ōñā. Im enana.

Im ej bar jepļaak. Ļǫkun jilu raan ej bar iļǫk im lale waini eo nājin. Eļak iļǫk ejako ke eaar peijojo ak ej dānikiaie. (Dānikiaie ej mejān ni eo ñan jiljino ne aetokan.) Innām ebwilōñ, kōn an aetok im ej ba ñan e make, "Enaaj kōm̧m̧an ta menin nejū, lim̧a?" Im ej bar jepļaak im kaļǫk jiljino boñ. Āindein ej iļǫk im bar lale. Ke ej lale emetete kimej en̄. Im ej bar konono ippān make, "Enaaj ta jem̧ļǫkin menkein?"

Lañ ejjañin meram ak ej marok wōt. Innām ej itok ñan ni eo im kanooj in ļōmn̄ak enaaj em̧m̧an ta?

Im ej jibwe kimej eo im konono ippān make, "Enaaj em̧m̧an ñan ta?" Kiiō ej tūm̧wi juon kimej im kajjeoñ kañe. Enana. Innām elōñ kain ļōmn̄ak ej ijjino an ļōmn̄ak kaki. Innām ej bar jepļaak im kōļmānļǫkjen̄ bajjek.

Ļǫkun jet boñ ej iļǫk im bar lale. Ļak lale eddek utak. Innām ejjab kōn̄aan kōm̧akūti ak jibwe. Innām ej bar jepļaak.

Ālikin jet boñ ej bar etal im lale. Ļak iļǫk em̧ōj an rup utak eo. Im ej lo elōñ kwaļinni. Im ej bar jepļaak im kanooj ļōmn̄ak kōn men kein ej loe ilo an ni eo rūttoļǫk im kwaļǫk men kein wōt otemjej.

Innām ej ba ñan e make, "Ijāmin kōm̧akūti men ko rej waļǫk kiiō ñan ñe enaaj alikkar jabdewōt tokālik."

Innām ej joļǫk enañin juon allōñ im jab etal im lale ni eo. Ke ej jem̧ļǫk iien ko eaar kōttar ie ej bar etal.

Ļak iļǫk elōñ waini rej pād ium̧win ni eo. Ak elōñ ni iraan. Kiiō ej ļōmn̄ak kōn kimej ko. "Enaaj ta ekkar ñan kōjerbali?"

Kiiō ej lo inpel eo. Im ba, "Enaaj ta ekkar ñan inpel kein?"

Tokālik ej jibwe waini ko im ba, "Ak waini in, etke āinwōt ļadik eo nājū Ļakam̧?"

Innām ej ļote juon ni im bar kōļmānļọkjeŋ kake. Innām ej joļọk bweọ eo in waini eo. Innām ewaļọk Ļakaṃ. Innām ej bōke im etal im rupe. Im kajjeoñ ṃōñā. Innām ennọ an ṃōñā. Ekanooj in ennọ.

Kiiō ej bar jepļaak ñan ni eo ar ļote ṃokta im joļọk bweọ eo im idaak. Eļak idaak. Ekanooj ennọ. Innām ej kōļmānļọkjeŋ kōn aolep men ko rej waļọk jān ni eo.

Ak lañ ej marok wōt. Im ej bar bōk juon waini im dibōje im rupe im raankeiki. Āinwōt ilo an kar ļōmŋak kake. Innām ke ej raanke ej ba, "Imukmuk waini Ļakaṃ." (Ilo kajin etto meļeļe in "iṃukṃuk" ej kọwōtlọk waini ke ej raankeiki.)

Unin an ba "Iṃukṃuk Ļakaṃ" kōnke ej kōjatdikdik ke enaaj ṃōñā im enaaj ñan armej otemjej. Kab mennin mour otemjej. Innām ke ej ṃōñā epeļļọk an ļōmŋak bwe emaroñ kōṃṃan eṃ kōn kāān ni eo im kōṃṃan kilōk, iiep, banennor, im bar elōñ jabdewōt men ko.

Inpel eo lio ej ba emaroñ kōṃṃan kijek im bar men ko jet. Bweọ ko lio ej ba emaroñ kōṃṃan kane im barāinwōt ļat in ni eo emaroñ kōṃṃan kijeek im jabdewōt men ko.

Innām ej ļōmŋak kōn bweọ in ni eo. Innām eaar kajjeoñ in door ŋa i lọjet iuṃwin juon allōñ ej etal im lale. Ļak lale ekōt bweọ eo. Innām ej bōktok im dōñļọkwe jidik im kwale im bōkļọk im kōjeeke.

Lañ ejjañin peļļọk.

Innām ej kōṃṃan āinwōt ej ļōmŋak. Im kōṃṃan idaap jān bweọ eo. Innām ke ej lōñ ej kōṃṃan āinwōt an ļōmŋak. Im eokkwaļ. Ke ej lo ej eṃṃan ej wōnṃaanļọk wōt kake im eokkwaļ.

Ke ej ļọk juon wiik ekanooj aetok eokkwaļ eo. Ilo juon raan ejja eokkwaļ wōt ak ej alikkar ilo mejān juon bao. Etan bao in "keār." Kiiō ej bōktok eokkwaļ eo im luewor. (E likūt juon dekā ŋae iṃaan eokkwaļ im joļọk ñan bao eo.) (Etan jerbal in "luewor" ilo kajin etto im lo kajin ran kein ej likito. "Armej rainin rejjab kanooj jeļā.")

Etal eokkwaļ eo im pọputi pein bao eo. Innām ej kanōk laļ tak.

Ke ej wōtlọk bao in im jeļļọk lañ. (Ilo kajin etto meļeļe in "jeļļọk lañ" ej peļļọk lañ.) Im ekanooj in ļap an meram. Innām aolep armej rej barāinwōt peļļọk aer ļōmŋak. (Ṃokta rej āinwōt dekā.) Im jet armej ļōmŋak in kōṃṃan wa. Ak jet rej ļōmŋak in kōṃṃan eṃ. Ak jet rej ļōmŋak in kōṃṃan uno. Innām āindein an kar meram in kar kepeļļọk an kajjojo armej ro kar ilo iien eo ļōmŋak.

Iien in ekanooj eṃṃan an armej lale doon. Im āinwōt an jemjānjemjātin lale doon.

Innām eor juon ļōmŋak bwe ren kōṃṃane juon wa. Innām raar jek jooj eo. Ke ej ṃōj rej jek jiṃ ko. Innām ke ej ṃōj rej jek jenil. Innām ke ej ṃōj rej jek dilep. Innām ej jab tōprak.

Innām ļōṃaro raar jekjek ṃokta rej bwijrak jān aer jekjek ak ebaj etal jet eṃṃaan. Em bar jek juon wōjke. Bar jek juon mā. Im bar bōktok im karōke. Im ejjab eṃṃan. Innām rej joļọk.

Innām bar itok jet eṃṃaan. Im jek juon mā im bar bōktok im bar karōke. Ak ejjab eṃṃan. Kiiō eitok juon im bōktok ṃōttan men ko raar jeki ṃokta im kajjeoñ karōke. Ke ej karōke ļōṃaro ṃokta rej ba, "Eban tōprak bwe men ŋe kōm ar joļọke. Ak ñe kwōnaaj kar jektok juon ekāāl enaaj kar eṃṃan." Innām ļeo ej kōṃṃane dilep eo ej ba, "Ij baj kajjeoñ wōt ak ijaje en tōprak ke."

Raan eo juon ej make ļọk iaan im etal ñan wa eo. Im ļōmŋak bajjek. Im ej kūrtok ruo likao bwe ren jipañe. Innām ej kōṃṃane im ekanooj eṃṃan. Ke ej jota ļọk rej itok ñan wa eo im bwilōñ kōn an kanooj eṃṃan. Iien in rejwōj illu jān doon. Kōnke eaar jab tōprak wa eo ippāer im eļap aer illu. Innām rej ba kwe wōt kwe ak ña wōt ña. (Ejepel wōt kōtaerro.)

Kiiō rej ba, "N̄a Irooj ak kwe Ļajjidik ak kwe Errōbra, kwe Rū-Kuwajleen." Kōnke ļeo eaar kōm̧m̧ane wa eo im ej em̧m̧an rej ba, "Rū-Kuwajleen." (Imeļǫkļǫk jet iaan etan jowi ilo bwebwenato in.) "Ak kwe M̧akauliej, kwe Tilan̄." (Jiljino lukkuun jowi.) "Kwe Ri-Lobaren."

Kiiō errein jowi ko im raar jepel ļǫk jān doon. Im kōm̧m̧an elōn̄ wāween jowi ilo aelōn̄ kein.

Kiiō kōrā eo ej ba, "Enana jepel ļǫk jān doon bwe ej ja kar āindein wōt jān jinoin. Jet raar jeļā kōm̧m̧an āne. Im jet raar jeļā kōm̧m̧an lǫjet. Im jet raar jeļā kōm̧m̧an uno kan̄ meninmour otemjej. Im kōjepeli jān doon.

"Ekwe ejja āindein n̄an kōj kiiō. Jet rejeļā jerbal im en̄iin ej tōprak wa in. Innām ij ba n̄an kom̧ ke enana jepel jān doon. Bwe jinoin jerbal eo m̧okta en̄iin ej wa n̦e waami. Innām ij ba n̄an kom̧ ke wa-kuk." (Ilo kajin etto "wa e wami" an aolep.) "Wa-jim̧or, waan kōjban kōj." (Waan kejeraam̧m̧an kōj.) "Waan kǫkkure kōj." (Kōnke juon iien enaaj jorrāān im kǫkkure er.) "Waan jokkwier." (Kajin etto: jekdǫǫn enana am̧ mour n̄e kwōj loe wa eo ej em̧m̧an an pād. Ekwe ijo en pād ie, im em̧m̧an.)

Kiiō ej loe ej em̧m̧anļǫk wōt an meram. Kōrā eo ej bōktok ruo aun̄wōļā im kate juon n̦ae i rear im kiele im katļǫke n̦ae irilik. Kiiō ej bar bōktok aļaļ eo juon im kate m̧aan n̦ae i rōk im kiele im katļǫke n̦ae ean̄.

Innām etan aun̄wōļā i ean̄: Katiōn̄. Im etan aun̄wōļā eo i rōk: Katirōk. Im etan aun̄wōļā eo i rear: Kōm̧lan̄. Im etan aun̄wōļā eo irilik: Kōm̧laļ. Im ej ainwōt n̄an rainin.

Kiiō eban wōtlǫk lan̄. (Kōnke elōn̄ aun̄wōļā.) Innām āindein an ļap ļǫk an meram im alikkar men otemjej.

Kiiō rej jino ļōmn̦ak in kōm̧m̧an em̧. Innām rej kōm̧m̧an āinwōt aer ļōmn̦ak kake. Innām ej tōprak. Ke ej tōprak, kōrā eo ej ba, "Katkat em̧ kate n̦a joor in el in, el in kobban eo in."

("El" ilo kajin etto ej em̧. Jabdewōt kain armej, m̧weiuk, aolep kain maron̄ pād ilowaan.)

Innām lio ej bar kōnnaan n̄an armej ro im ba, "Enana jepel jān doon ilo jerbal ko rōļļap. Innām kom̧in jab likūt inepata ilo buruomi n̄an doon." (Kiiō lien ej kōm̧m̧an katak n̄an er bwe ren jerbal jim̧or im jokwe jim̧or im jab jepel jān doon.)

Āindein aer kanooj in eǫron̄ naan in kauwe ko an kōrā in.

Innām ke ej kanooj ļap an meram aļ ej tak je rear im rej n̦a etan "raan." Ke ej ilǫk in tulǫk irilik ej marokļǫk.

Innām armej rej bar inepata. Innām eo ej ba, "Jab inepata kōn men ko jejjab jeļā kake." Ke ej marok ej waļǫk iju ko im kōmeram jidik. Innām edik an armej ro inepata.

Innām rej n̦a etan, "Bon̄, Iroojrilik!" Innām ebar tak aļ, im ke ej raelep ļǫk ekōjeje Ļakam̧ im nana an mour.

Innām rej likūt ilo aer kajjitōk ippān Ļōkōm̧raan. (Āinwōt ta wūnin an kōjeje im enana an mour, an mān̦āān̦.)

Innām Ļōkōm̧raan ejjab konono, ak enaaj kōm̧m̧an āinwōt aer kōn̦aan n̄an raan eo juon. Ke ej tak aļ im raelep ej waļǫk juon tab (Āinwōt enaaj kōm̧m̧ane ta eo rej kōn̦aan.) Eļap ium̧win jilu raan.

Im ilo bon̄ ejjab waļǫk iju. Ak eļap an marok. Ļǫkun jilu raan ej bar tak aļ. Im ejako tab eo ak ekanooj in wāmurur Ļakam̧ im elōn̄ jabdewōt men in eddek ko rej waļǫk: mā, bōb, ut, kiden, kōjbar, arm̧we, wūjooj, marļap, markinenjojo, marjej, atat. Aolep kain mennin eddek. Im ekanooj em̧m̧an aer mour.

Innām Ļewej im Ļaneej rej unoki im kōjpel etāer jān doon.

Im ke ej ļapļǫk an meram im kanooj em̧m̧an an meninmour kab armej pād, rej jino ļōmn̦ak in m̧ōn̄ā. Innām raar kajjeon̄ in m̧ōn̄ā aolep kain, ak enana.

Innām kōrā eo eaar bar kwaļǫk mā im rej m̧ōn̄ā. Kab bōb im m̧akm̧ōk. Innām kōrā in eaar kōjpel mā im likūt ilo an naan in kallim̧ur ñan L̗ōkōm̧raan im L̗ōrōk bwe ren bōk eddo in kōm̧m̧an iien aer kallib. Innām eaar ŋa etan "rak." Kōrā in eaar bar lelo̧k eddo in bōb kab m̧akm̧ōk ñan Iroojrilik kab L̗ajibwinām̧ōŋ. Im eaar ŋae etan "añōneañ."

Im kōrā eo ar lel̗o̧k eddo in lo̧jet ñan L̗ewej im L̗aneej. (Kōnke elōñ mennin m̧ōñā ie. Im remaroñ naajdik armej kōn ek im kapwor im aolep mennin lo̧jet: pako im raj im mejānwōd im aolep men otemjej.)

Innām kōrā eo eaar ba, "Bwe enaaj wor ibwijtok im pāātl̗o̧k kab idik kab iōl̗ap."

Innām eo ej kōm̧m̧ane meram in allōñ ilo marok. Bwe en kōm̧m̧an idik kab iōl̗ap.

Kiiō kōrā in ej kwal̗o̧k wāween al̗ ñan armej rein, im ba, "N̄e ej pād i rear: jibboñ. N̄e ej pād iol̗ap: raelep. N̄e ej pād irilik: jota." Im ej bar kōmel̗el̗e wāween allōñ. "N̄e ej pād rilik etan: Takatakinae. N̄e ej pād rilik im iol̗ap: Limeto. N̄e ej pād iol̗ap: Lipepe. N̄e ej pād i wetan iol̗ap: Limetak. N̄e ej pād i rear: Tutuinae."

(Erkein rej iial̗ ko raar ŋa etāer ālikin em̧ōj an kōm̧m̧an aunwolā in lañ im em̧ōj an ajej lañ. Rej kōjerbali in jerakrōk ñe em̧m̧an.)

Kiiō ej bar kōm̧m̧an bwe en lōñ leen aolep mennin eddek otemjej. "N̄a ij bōk eddo in. Im kōm̧m̧an bwe en lōñ leen aolep mennin eddek kab leen kein ikkan otemjej."

Innām ej ba, "En wōtlo̧k kōto jān rear." Innām ej itok jān rear. Im ŋa etan "Jonin itok rear." (Ilo kajjin etto "Jonin" ej itok.)

Innām ej bar ba, "En itok i rilik." Im ŋa etan "Jonin ketak." (Itok jān rilik.)

Im lien ej bar ba, "En itok i rōk." Im ŋa etan "Jonin kitak." (Itok jān rōk.)

Im lien ej bar ba, "En itok jān eañ." Im ŋa etan Jokl̗ā. (Itok jān eañ.)

(Rej kōjerbal āt kein ñan rainin ilo jerakrōk ilo iien ekkar ñan jet jikin.)

Kiiō kōto ej uki raan wōjke otemjej im ej jabar elōñ kain kajjo ut.

Innām ej barāinwōt kōm̧m̧an bwe en aeto im aetak. Im barāinwōt aelukeañ im barāinwōt aelukrōk.

(Āinwōt rūtto ro raar tōmak raar wal̗o̧k aolep leen wōjke: mā, bōb, ut, āindein. Ak ejjab ni. Ni eo ar wal̗o̧k m̧okta. Ak ko jet men kein raar wal̗o̧k jān kōto āinwōt bwebwenato in ej ba.)

Ālikin jet raan lio ej kōjpel kōto jān doon. Innām jilu allōñ kōto ej itok i rear. Im jilu allōñ ej itok rālik. Im jilu allōñ ej itok i rōk. Im jilu allōñ ej itok eañ.

Innām ej wāween dein an jerbal kōto im kōm̧m̧an aeto im aetak. Im aelukrōk im aelukeañ.

Innām eaar bar kōm̧m̧an bwe kōto en wōtlo̧k jān lukkuun lañ. Im eaar ŋa etan Jinnobōdelañ in kōto. Im eaar barāinwōt kōŋaan bwe in lur im ejjel̗o̧k kōto. Bwe en kōm̧m̧an ae em̧m̧an.

Innām raan eo juon ke ej raelepl̗o̧k, eaemerl̗o̧k ut, wūjooj, im men ko āerl̗o̧k wōt. (Aolep kain, enana aer mour.) Innām kōrā eo eaar jilkinl̗o̧k m̧okta wōtm̧welañ eo.

(Wōt dikjidik.) Innām ejjañin kanooj in em̧m̧an an eddek wūjooj, mā, kōjbar, ut, kūtaak, arm̧we im aolep men in eddek.

Innām ej bar jilkinl̗o̧k wūtatkoŋ eo. (Bar juon kain wōt. El̗ap ak jidik wōt an wōtlo̧k.)

Im eaar lo bwe ejjab em̧m̧an. Eaar jilkinl̗o̧k wōtwo̧. (Aetokl̗o̧k jidik jān wūtatokoŋ. Ej itok ainikien "W-O-O-O." Im ejem̧l̗o̧k.)

Im ke ejjab kanooj in em̧m̧an eaar jilkinl̗o̧k wōtmijeljel eo. (El̗ap an wōt im ej dikl̗o̧k an jem̧l̗o̧kin.)

Innām eaar loe bwe em̧m̧an an mennin eddek otemjej mour. Im ej āinwōt in ñan rainin. (Ej kab wōt kiiō. Ejjel̗o̧k m̧okta.)

Ke ej dedel̗o̧k men otemjej eaar likūt an naan in kallim̧ur ñan aolep likao ro im kōrā ro ilo iien in. Bwe ren jab jepel jān doon. Jekdo̧o̧n ñe renaaj kajjo jowi im pād. Ak enana ñe eor jepel. Innām eaar lel̗o̧k juon bar ennaan. Ej ba, "Del lik | Del ar | ilo wāto kein | Ajri jiddik | ipinnidik."

Roro ej ba: Ilo jabdewōt jikin kwōj etal jān lik ñan ar jekdǫǫn ta riab ko kwōj roñ. Kwon jab pokaki. Āinwōt kwōn jab ruruwe. Enjab āinwōt ajri jiddik im riab bajjek āinwōt ajri jiddik rej riab.

(Meļeļe in naan in ipinnidik, naan in kajin etto ilo roro in, ej juon naan jiddik ñe riab, kwōn jab pokake. Lien ej katak ñan armej.)

Innām eaar ba, "Eļañňe koṃ naaj kōṃṃan jerbal eļap enana ñe koṃij jab jipañ doon. Eṃṃantata eļañňe koṃij jipañ doon. Bwe koṃ naaj pād ilo naan eo ej ba, "Ko make iwaļapļap eo iwaļapļap eo jañi jeraṃōl ke iio jipǫkwe | Kwe eo."

(Meļeļe ak ṃwilaļ eo ilo naan in naan ilo kajin etto, ej āinwōt eļañňe kwōnaaj make iaaṃ im kōṃṃane juon wa eļap eban tōprak kōnke kojeraṃōl. Jeraṃōl ilo kajin etto ej ñe ejjeļǫk armej ippān, āinwōt Irooj Ļōjjeiļañ ñe ejjeļǫk armej ippān, ejeraṃōl.)

Innām ej kanooj kalliṃure er bwe ren jab jepel jān doon. "Im ñe enaaj itok in ṃōñā mā (ilo iien mā) lale bwe koṃin jab wūdin ekkan."(Ilo kajin etto "wūdin" ej kǫkkure ekkan.) "Ak koṃin kōjparoke, bwe juon iien enaaj ejjeļǫk ṃōñā.

"Barāinwōt bōb. Koṃin kōjparoke. Barāinwōt ṃakṃōk. Koṃin bar kōjparoke. Im jab wūdin ekkan, bwe juon iien enaaj ejjeļǫk."

Innām eaar bar kalliṃur bwe eļañňe enaaj iien mā, ren kōṃṃan aer mennin ṃōkajkaj kake. (Kōṃṃan kabuñ in kōkalo.)

"Wāween dein, ami naaj kōṃṃane: Bōktok joṃōkaj eo." (Ilo kajin etto āinwōt mā eo ṃōkaj in kalo.) "Im likūt ilo juon ejouj. Im kālet jiljino eṃṃaan jān jeban bwij ko (jowi nōṃba juon). Im ren etetal ilo joraanļǫk. (Ṃokta jān [an] ikkūr kako.) Im laṃōj im ba, 'Ni mi to O-O-O!'"

(Meļeļe in menin ilo kajin etto ej, "Ni itok ñan ijin! Ni itok ñan ijin!" Kōnke ni ej waļǫk ṃokta jān aolep men otemjej, Ļakaṃ. Kōnke ni ej kwaļǫk ni aolep iien. Ejjab juon wōt iien. Rōkōŋaan [bwe] mā en kōṃṃan leen āinwōt ni. Wūnin rej laṃōj āinwōt [in].)

Innām rej itok ñan turin ejouj in mā im ruo eṃṃaan rej jutak; juon i rear im juon i rōk. Im rejro ikkūr ñan ļōṃaro emān, ṃōttāer. Im rej jino jān i rear. Im ba, "En itok juon im bōk juon mā im rǫǫl taļǫk. Im ba, 'Mā in Kijmalañ jabuweo i rear eo Ļakaṃran | ibōk taļǫk| ibōk taļǫk| Likūti i nabwij jān iṃōn Ļakaṃran'." (Naan in kōṃṃan aer kabuñ, naan in jar ñan Ļakaṃran.)

Kiiō ebōk taļǫk tarrin jiljino ne. Im door mā eo im jutak.

(Ñan rainin rū-Ṃajeļ rej door mā iloan ṃōn jar. Ak rej joļǫk al eo. Ak rej doore iloan ṃōn jar. Im rej jar im kaṃṃoolol ñan Anij ñan rainin. Ilo jinoin mā im jinoin bōb. Jet iien rej door ni iloan.)

Innām ebar ikkūr likao ro ruo itok ļeo jān rōk. Innām ļeo eaar jutak irōk in ejouj ej wōnṃaantak jiljino ne im jibwe juon mā im rǫǫl rōñaļǫk im ba, "Mā in Kijmalañ jabuweo irōk eo| Ļōrōk| ibōk rōñaļǫk | ibōk rōñaļǫk | Likit i nabwij jān iṃōn Ļōrōk."

Im ej bōktok tarrin jiljino ne, im jutak. Im ruo ej jutak iturin ejouj in mā eo.

Innām likao ro ruo rej ikkūr im ba, "Itok ļeo jān eañ." Im ļeo jān eañ ej wōnṃaantak jiljino ne im jibwe mā eo im rǫǫl im ba, "Mā in Kijmalañ jabuweo eañ eo Lajibwineṃṃan | ibōk niñaļǫk | ibōk niñaļǫk | Likit i nabwij jān iṃōn Ļajibwināṃōŋ."

Ke ej etal bar jiljino ne im doore mā eo im jutak.

Innām likao ro ruo ṃōttāer rej bar ba en itok ļeo jān rālik. Innām ej wōnṃaantak jiljino ne im jibwe juon mā im rǫǫltoļǫk. Im ba, "Mā in Kijmalañ jabuweo eo. Iroojrilik | ibōk toļǫk | ibōk toļǫk | Likit i nabwij jān iṃōn Iroojrilik."

Ke ej etal tarrin jiljino ne im door mā eo im jutak.

Kiiō ļōṃaraŋ rej laṃōj kōn ainikien eļap im ba, "Emelim O | Emelim!"

Innām ke armej otemjej ro rej roñ rej

ettōrtok ñan ippān ļōṃaro kab ejouj in mā eo. Im ebbōk kijeer mā.

Kiiō emālim an jabdewōt armej anemkwōj im kōṃkōṃ mā ilo jabdewōt iien. (Rej kab ṃōñā mā kiiō. Raar jab ṃokta.)

Āindein aer anemkwōj ilo raan otemjej im ke ej bwijleplep in an lōñ mā eiten jorrāānļǫk mā. Kōnke eļap an lōñ reban kañi. Innām rej kememej naan eo an lio eaar ba, "Koṃ in jab wūdin ekkan."

Innām rej kōjparok aer kōṃkōṃ ak ej bōlōk wōt mā ko. (Mā ko rej wōtlǫk kōnke re kalo.) Innām rej jino aer ṃadṃōd. Innām raar ṃadṃōd iuṃwin emān allōñiju. (Ilo kajin etto "allōñiju" ej allōñ.)

Innām emaat mā im ejjeļǫk kiiō. Rej ṃōñā jān bwiro kab jāānkun kab ṃōņakjān ko, iuṃwin ruwalitōk allōñiju. Innām ejejjet iien an itok bōb. Ilo iien in ke ej jino waļǫk leen bōb ko rej kwaļǫk juon kien ñan aolep armej. Im kiiō kōrā eo ej ba, "Emo bittōr eļañne enaaj kalo [owat] bōb ko." (Ilo kajin etto meļeļein "bittōr" ej wōdwōd bōb im joļǫk pej ko.)

Innām ej bar kūr ñan jiljino eṃṃaan, ļōṃaro jeban bwij ko. Bwe ren pojak ñan joraanlǫk in raan eo ilju. Ilo wōt raan eo rej kōṃṃane juon ejouj in bōb. Im kepoji ñan raan eo juon. Innām ke ej joraanlǫk raan eo juon, ļōṃaro rej ruj im etetal peļaak in āne eo im laṃōj kōn ainikien eļap im ba, "Ni-mi- to- O I O-O." Innām rej bar laṃōj kein ka ruo, "Ni- mi- to- O- O I O- O."

Āindein aer laṃōj. Im armej otemjej rej roñjake laṃōj im ba, "O-O. Tiṃoņ ro rein!" Ak jet rej ba, "Anij ro rein! Enaaj melim bittōr kiiō."

Innām ļōṃaro rej itok ñan ejouj in bōb eo. Im jutak juon eañ, juon i rōk, juon i rear, im juon i rilik.

Im ruo ej jutak iturin ejouj in bōb eo. Im rejro kūrtok ļeo jān eañ im ej wōnṃaanļǫk ñan ejouj eo, jiljino ne, im bōk juon bōb im kotake im ṛǫǫl niñaļǫk. Im ba, "Bōb in Kijmalañ jabuweo iōñ eo—Ļajibwināṃōņ I I bōk niñalik I I bōk niñaļǫk I Likūti i nabwij in iṃōn Ļajibwināṃōņ." Innām ej jutak.

Innām likao ro ruo rej bar ba, "En itok ļeo jān rilik." Innām ļeo jān rilik ej wōnṃaanļǫk jiljino ne im jibwe bōb eo im kotake. Im ba, "Bōb in Kijmalañ jabuweo i rilik eo Iroojrilik I ibōk toļǫk I ibōk toļǫk I Likūti i nabwij in iṃōn Iroojrilik." Innām ej bar doore im jutak.

Likao ro ruo rej ba itok ļeo jān rōk. Innām ļeo jān rōk ej wōnṃaanļǫk jiljino ne im jibwe bōb eo im kotake im ba, "Bōb in Kijmalañ jabuweo i rear eo. Ļakaṃran I ibōk taļǫk I ibōk taļǫk I Likūti i nabwij in iṃōn Ļakaṃran." Innām ej doore im jutak.

Likao ro ruo rej ba itok ļeo jān rōk. Innām ļeo jān rōk ej wōnṃaanļǫk jiljino ne im jibwe bōb eo im kotake im ba, "Bōb in Kijmalañ jabuweo i rōk eo Ļōrōk I I bōk rōñaļǫk I I bōk rōñaļǫk I Likūti i nabwij in iṃōn Ļōrōk." Innām ej jutak im ke ej ṃōj rej ļaṃōj kōn ainikien eļap im ba, "Emelim O-O. Emelim I Emelim bittōr O-O."

Kiiō aolep armej [rej] ettōrtok ilo rujļǫkin raan eo ñan ejouj in bōb eo im ippān ļōṃaro. Im ebbōk daer bōb.

(Iien in ej jinoin [an] armej ṃōñā bōb i laļ in. Raar jab ṃōñā bōb ṃokta.) Innām rej anemkwōj aer iien wōdwōd bōb. Im joto jotak pej ņa i meļaaj.

Innām raar wōdwōd bōb ak elapļǫk an poļǫk bōb ko. (Kōnke ekalo [eowat].) Innām rej bar kememej naan eo an kōrā eo ke eaar ba, "Enana wūdin ekkan." Innām rej jino aer ṃadṃōd im kōṃṃan jāānkun, kab tipijek. (Rej kab kōṃṃan tipijek rainin. Kar ṃokta ej leen bōb. Ej āinwōt juka; āinwōt ṃakṃōk.)

Men kein rej ṃōñā iuṃwin ruwalitōk allōñ. Im āindein kōrā eo [eaar] bar ba bwe eļañne jabdewōt jerbal eļap rej kōṃṃane ren joṃōkaj in jortak eo.

Innām eaar ba bwe enaaj etal ilo juon iiaļ innām ej likūt jāānkun im jidimkij an jako. Im armej ro raar pād ippān lio iien eo raar mej im erom jabdewōt kain meninmour. (Āinwōt dekā, bao, ek, im āinwōt.) Rej kōkļaļ ñan rainin.

(Aolep armej raar mej ilo iien eo repād ilo aolep peļaak in M̧ajeļ.)

Im jenokwōn an kōrā rej barmej in Wōdmeej. Bwe armej ren jab meļo̧kļo̧k.

Innām Iroojrilik ej irooj ioon men otemjej ilo iien in ke ejako kōrā eo im n̄a etan Jineer ilo Kōbo. (Ijaje meļeļe in men in.)

Ālikin jet iien eļotak juon ļaddik im jinen likūti etan Bōrraan. Ej maan̄den Iroojrilik. Ke ej rūttoļo̧k eaar utiej būruon ilo mour eo an. Im ko̧kkure aolep kien ko an kōrā eo jineer. Im Iroojrilik ej lale ñan aolep armej ro ilo iien ko.

Innām kōn an Bōrraan utiej būruon eaar ba ñan Iroojrilik, aļap eo an, bwe en babar (bōkedoon lo̧jet) to meto eo. Ak Bōrraan ej babar to āne eo. (Bwe en bōktok aolep m̧ōñā jān lo̧jet im Bōrraan enaaj bōktok aolep m̧ōñā jān āne.)

Innām Bōrraan eaar ba Iroojrilik en itok in lo joñan an lōñ m̧ōñā ioon āne. Innām Iroojrilik eaar itok im lo ekanooj ļap an lōñ. Innām eaar ba ñan likaakrak eo bwe en etal in kañe m̧ōñā ko. Kab menkōk eo kab kauļaļo eo. Innām aolep keinikkan kab men ko leer raar jorrāān.

Innām Iroojrilik eaar ba ñan aolep ek bwe ren jidaak ioon āne, kab aolep bao in mejatoto. Innām eaar jidaak ek ko. Im n̄o in ek ko raar to̧re āne eo. Im rej n̄a etan Tutu ñan rainin.

Bōrraan eaar lo kajoor eo an aļap eo an im kanooj mijak. Ak eaar jerbal nana wōt. Im ejako ñan rainin.

Innām rej bar jek wa eo kein ka ruo. Ļowa im Ļōm̧tal. Ijo rejro jekjek wa ie ilo Aelōñ in Pikinni. Ilo juon āne etan Nam̧. Etan wāto eo Jinbwi.

Joñak ko raar kōjerbali ñan wa eo raar doori n̄a ilo juon kañal. Ļewej im Ļaneej raar kabuñ eo̧n̄ kein karuo ilo Aelōñ in Ujae. Etan wāto ie Bati-Ļaneej, ioon eoonene eo.

Ijo raar itemomij ie ilo juon aebōj ej pād ñan rainin.

Im dān eo enno̧. Ak ilo iien eo raar kūbwiji ej waļo̧k bwijin bweo̧.

Innām jet armej raar bar kōm̧m̧ane m̧weo kein karuo ilo Aelōñļapļap ilo wāto Ekweren ioon āne in Wōja.

Innām aolep armej ilo iien in epeļļo̧k aer ļōmn̄ak ñan aolep menin jerbal.

Iien in aolep armej ro jān jinoin rejako. Innām Ļajibwinām̧ōn̄ eaar bōk eddo in armej ro nājin ekkan. Innām iien in eaar ļotak elōñ kain armej. Jet armej ak jet n̄oon-iep, im jet riikijet, ak jet rimmenanuwe, jet ripitwōdwōd.

(N̄ooniep rej āinwōt armej. Jet iien rej waļo̧k im bwebwenato ippān armej. Ak remaroñ lo armej ak jet iien armej rejjab maroñ lo er. Rūkijet rej āinwōt armej. Rūkijet rej jokwe ilo dān. N̄ooniep rej jokwe ioon āne. Im rimmenanuwe rej kadu, ak āinwōt armej. Remaroñ bwebwenato ippān armej.)

Jebwa eaar waļo̧k jān juon riikijet i Ujae.

(Ripitwōdwōd rej aetok im kilep. Rej etetal ioon lo̧meto. Rej jab konono ippān armej. Rej ko̧kkure armej.)

Iien in ej ļotak juon likao. Im rej likūti etan Ļe-Etao. Innām juon iien enañinmej jet iaan armej ro nājin ekkan. (Lukkuun armej; rej m̧ōñā im eor bōtōktōk. Armej m̧okta rej jab m̧ōñā. Kar edjoñ m̧ōñā im jo̧ļo̧k; elōñ taujin iiō remootļo̧k.)

Innām Ļajibwinām̧ōn̄ ej ba, "Eļañne renaaj mej kom̧in kab kalbwini im jitinek ļo̧k Ļajibwinām̧ōn̄. (Meļeļe in men in ilo kajin etto im m̧anit eo ej kallib armej kōn bōrāer ñan eañ, ñan Ļajibwinām̧ōn̄. Āinwōt rū-M̧ajeļ rej kōm̧m̧ane jān etto. Ak ejjab aolep iien raan kein.)

"Unin ñe renaaj mej ilo nana im jerkakpeje, enaaj kañ er. Ak eļañne renaaj kōjparoke naan in katak ko an kōrā eo Jineer Ilo

Kōbo im ñe renaaj mej, Ļajibwinām̧ōņ enaaj leļǫk anemkwōj ñan er."

Meñe kar āindein ak likao eo Ļe-Etao in kajoor an kilan im ukot elōñ armej ñan riab ko. Kein kajuon riab an Ļe-Etao ej juon wa eaar jeke im door ioon juon wōd.

Wa in ekanooj in em̧m̧an. Ijoke wōjke in wa eo wōt kōñe. (Juon aļaļ kanooj in eddo.) Innām ej ilǫk im ba ñan irooj eo ilo iien eo bwe en leļǫk wa eo waan bwe en jerak kake.

Innām irooj eo ej ba, "Ak wa eo kwar kōm̧m̧ane, etke kwōj jab jerak kake?" Innām Ļe-Etao ej uwaak irooj eo im ba, "Kōnke wa eņ ekanooj in em̧m̧an im ekkar ñan kwe." Im irooj eo ej ilān lale wa eo. Im eļap an kōņaan im em̧m̧ōņōņō kake.

Im irooj eo katarļǫk wa eo waan im leļǫk ñan Ļe-Etao. Im Ļe-Etao ej m̧ōkaj in jerak. Tokālik irooj eo ej etal in jerak kōn wa eo kar waan Ļe-Etao.

Innām ke irooj eo ej bwiļǫke meto ļǫk wa eo jān wōd eo in jerak, wa eo eruñļǫk im pād ibuļōn lǫjet.

Im eļap an irooj eo illu iien in ak ejako Ļe-Etao bwe en kar m̧ane. (Jinoin nana ej mejaļ armej kake.)

Innām raar pukot Ļe-Etao ñan rainin ak rejjab loe. Ak kōm̧m̧an ko an rej nana ļǫk ñan kiiō.

Ilo iien in armej ro raar nañinmej. Eaar mej jet iaer ak eaar mour jet iaer. (Jinoin nañinmej im mej. Kar m̧okta ejjeļǫk. Kōnke kiiō armej rej "nājin ekkan.")

Im armej ro raar mej raar kalbwini er āinwōt aer jeļā jitinekļǫk Ļajibwinām̧ōņ.

Ijo raar jino kallib ie ilo aelōñ in Jālooj ilo Piñlep, wāto M̧ōn-bōd.

Ilo iien in aolep raar ilomej. Ak Ļe-Etao eaar waļǫk ilo iien ilomej eo im itok ippān armej ro remej. Im kōm̧akūtkūt mejāer im āinwōt ñe ren mour. Innām ejjeļǫk armej eaar jeļā kake ak ņooniep wōt. Im ņooniep eaar būrom̧ōj kōn armej ro remour im kwaļǫk wāween an Ļe-Etao kōm̧m̧an.

Ilo iien in ke armej rej konono Ļe-Etao ej bar konono āinwōt er. Innām rej ba, "Wōn in." Innām rej ba, "Ainikien Ļe-Etao." Jān iien in armej rejjab tōmak jerbal ko an Ļe-Etao ñan rainin. (Ak elōñ rej tōmak im rej jorrāān.)

Wāween aer kalbwin armej rein raar mej, ilo iien in raar kōm̧m̧an ura. Kajin etto, raar likūt juon armej lowaan lōb eo. Im tokālik rej leļǫk dekā ejjab armej. Irooj im armej m̧okta. Ak tokālik meram ej jerbal. M̧okta jān [an] mijinede [ro]itok.

Im ilo iien m̧ōñā re kōm̧m̧an kijeer ñan ñe eļǫk jiljino boñ. Innām ālkin jiljino boñ rej eor bwe ilo iien in ejepel jān armej. Eoktak ñan kamanij.

Irooj eo ej ba, "Emelim ākūt im ma kamaañōñōñ ioon anij | Kiki | O-O | Kiki in etoñ."

(Meļeļe in men in "ma" ilo kajin etto ej noe.)

Innām ejem̧ļǫk aer leļǫk m̧ōñā.

(Ilo m̧antin etto ilo raan ko m̧okta, eļaññe juon irooj ar mej, ejjeļǫk armej emaroñ entak ni, okok bōb, ākūt, innin maañ ium̧win jiljino raan. Eļaññe kajoor, nukwin wōt aikuj āinwōt.)

Innām ļǫkun jiljino raan emǫ itok ñan wūliej. Ak emelim ākūt, im okok bōb, im entak ni. Komaroñ etal in rarō im karreoiki; em̧m̧an. Ak enana ñe ejjeļǫk am̧ jerbal.

(Aolep armej rej jab kōm̧m̧an āinwōt kiiō. Jet wōt ļōļļap im leļļap rej pokake. Ña ij pokake m̧anit in. Im ij ba ñan ro nājū bwe ren jab etal ñan wūliej eņ ñe ejjeļǫk aer jerbal ie.)

Ak kiiō eļaññe armej in eaar mej eaar jerbal em̧m̧an enaaj anemkwōj an. Ak eļaññe enana Ļajibwinām̧ōņ enaaj kañe.

[Ri-bwebwenato eo eaar ettōñ im ba, "Ak ej jab kalbuuj armej. Ak ejjeļǫk kalbuuj ilo aelōñ in M̧ajeļ m̧okta [jān an] ripālle [kar] itok."]

Iien eaar wor inepata ikōtaan jemjānjemjātin. Innām ke rej kemejej ennaan ko naan in katak jān etto rejjab pokake jet iaer. Ak jet iaer rej pokaki. Innām iien in ke eṃōj an jepel āne jān doon jān ikijik ("ikijik" ilo kajin etto ej ṇo eḷap rej kọkkure āne). Rej jino aer jeplōklōk ilo wa. (Elōñ wa.) Im remaroñ etal jān aelōñ ñan aelōñ. Ijoke juon wōt āne eaar jab waḷọk ak ej pād wōt ibuḷon lọjet. Ilo iien eo juon eṃṃaan kab ruo nukwin rej jerak. Rej pukot ijo ej pād ie. (Āne eo.)

Bwe aolep āne elōñ armej im menin-mour, ṇooniep im riikijet. Innām (ḷōṃaro jilu) rejjab kōṇaan pād ioon āne kein.

Innām rej jerak im bubu ia eo epād ie. Innām eḷak wōttok (ilo kajin etto meḷeḷe in men in ej eḷak itok) etan bwe Ṇokemen. (Kakōlle in bubu ioon maañ eo.) Innām ḷeo ej ba, "Wa [eo] en bwijrak ijin. Ak keware-tok men juon." (Ilo kajin etto "kewaretok" ej leḷọk men juon.) Ilo juon iaan ḷōṃaro i wa eo ej leḷọk ñane juon waini. Innām ej jibwe im joḷọke. Ak ej bar ba, "Kewaretok men juon." Likao ro rej leḷọk juon aḷaḷ. Im ḷeo ej jibwe im bar joḷọke.

Ak ej bar ba, "Kewaretok men juon." Im rej bar leḷọk juon bweọ. Im ej jibwe im bar joḷọke. Ak ej bar ba, "Kewaretok men juon."

Kiiō ledik eo nājin ej jerkak im diwōj jān pelpel eo. Im leḷọk juon ed in bōb.

Innām ḷeo ej jibwe tok ed in bōb eo im okleiki kōn juon eokkwaḷ. Im door laḷ ḷọk ilọjet. Im ba, "Nokemen eo lio deo | Keware-tok kajin Piti ne em liklọkwe | Āne im ke āne? | Rakijbadke jān ro kijbadke em kijbadbad."

(Meḷeḷe in naan ko an ḷeo: "Leḷọk kāāj ioon bōb eo im tōbwe āne | Ta āne? | E waḷọk | Kōjro etal ñan e | Im pād ie.")

("Kijbadke" im "kijbadbad" rej kajin etto. Im etan lien kiiō: Nokemen.)

Ḷeo eḷak kanōke eokkwaḷ eo. Ekanooj in eddo. Innām rejwōj aolep tok iten tōbwe. Ke ej waḷọk rej ba, "Āne eo eron ne eowa."

Innām rej itok ñan āne eo im pād ie. Etan āne eo: Mile. (Etan bwe ej kwaḷọk Mile: Nokemen.)

Kiiō aolep aelōñ in Ṃajeḷ elōñ armej ie. Im mennin mour kajjojo wāweer.

(Kōkḷaḷ in Mile: rej emān kowak rej pād i rōk im i rear in Mile, irōk jān Ṇadikdik. Im jiljino kōtkōt rej pād irōk in Mile [im Ṇadikdik] tu rilik. Innām ñe kwōj loe kōkōḷaḷ in Mile kwōjeḷā kwōj pād iturin Mile.

Bwe in kowak etan Nokemen, etan ledik eo. Im bwe in kōtkōt etan Irinbwe. [Kein kōṃṃan bwe, bubu.] Ñe kwōj loe men kein kwōjeḷā kwōj pād epaak ñan Mile. Ñe bao rej kāmetotak kwōjeḷā ettoḷọk āne eo.)

Ijoke ṇooniep ej mour im āinwōt armej. Eṃōj aer bar jepel jān doon im barāinwōt armej. Im pād ilo aolepān laḷ. Ak armej rej-jab maroñ in lo er. Ak ṇooniep ej maroñ in waḷọk ñan armej jabdewōt iien. Kōnke ṇooniep eaar jab po ippān Etao ilo iien otemjej. Ak ṇooniep eaar pokake naan in katak ko jān etto. Im ej mour āinwōt armej ak armej rejjab maroñ loe.

Juon iien irooj in ṇooniep eaar jerak im etan kapen eo: Ḷemeto. Etan irooj eo: Kabua. Ak riikijet ej mour āinwōt bar ṇoon-iep. Ijoke ej pād iuṃwin āne.

Etao eo eaar jab ṃane riikijet. Ak riikijet rej dike Etao ñan rainin.

Wāween dein an Etao itoitak ilo peḷaakin laḷ im ṃan elōñ armej. Im jet rej po ilo Etao ko an.

Eor ruo jemenāe ñan armej ro ilo iien ko.

Juon eaar pokake Etao. Im ejako ñan rai-nin.

Juon eaar kōjparok kien kab naan in katak ko jān etto. Im ej pād ilo anemkwōj ñan kiiō.

Etan armej eo eaar pokake naan in kien kab naan in katak: Liṃkade. Etan armej eo eaar jab pokake naan in kien im naan in katak: Bōrraan.

Eor akki in Liṃkade ñan rainin ilo aelōñ in Wōtto. Rej āinwōt kūkōr.

Jet iaan armej in Mile etto rej eṃṃaan kōnke raar jerbal in jetōb im kwaḷọk aelōñ in Mile. Ijoke ke ro raar po ippān Ḷe-Etao im nana.

(Aolep armej in laļ, ro rej po ippān Ļe-Etao rej nana. Im ro rejjab po ippān, rej eṃṃan ñan rainin. Im ro rej po ippān Ļe-Etao im riab im kọkkure armej rej nana.)

Ejeṃļọk bwebwenato in.

Bar eor bwebwenato rej waļọk jān bwebwenato in. Āinwōt Tōboļāār im bar bwebwenato in Ļe-Etao, im āinwōt.

N̄ooniep rej iọkwe armej. Im eļañe bwōd, enana ippān n̄ooniep. Eļañe n̄ooniep rej bōk kōrā, armej, naaj waļọk apkaaj: jimettan n̄ooniep, jimettan armej.

Ak riikijet jet iien rej kōṃṃan nana ñan armej. Rōkōn̄aan bōk kōrā (armej.) Eļañe riikijet ej bōk juon kōrā eban waļọk nājin. Ak ñe eor nājin iaar jab roñ kake.

2: STORY ABOUT BŌRRAAN

As told by Jelibōr Jam, Kuwajleen 1975

Bōrraan, a boy, did not stay with his mother and grandmother at the times when he was older.

When he was a young man, he went away to his *aļap* [maternal uncle; lineage head].[1] The age of the *aļap* at this time was one hundred and thirty winter seasons past.[2] When he went away to his *aļap*, his uncle sent him away and told him that he should go look for the girl, his sister. And Bōrraan replied, "Yes, I will go away." But he did not go at all. This was the first wrong against his *aļap*.

He stayed there and the *aļap* also [told him of the] need, when he would go fishing, to see that he should not take even one of the fish of his catch, but he should bring all of them [to the *aļap*].

Bōrraan did not obey. This was the second wrong against his *aļap*.

The third: Iroojrilik ['chief of the west'] (the name of his *aļap*), said to him, "Go take away that fish trap over there and place it in the water." And he said, "Yes, I will take it away."

When he took it away, Iroojrilik said, "See that you do not move the rock of entering."[3] (The meaning of *ikūr* in the ancient language is 'move'.)

Bōrraan replied, "Yes, I will never move the rock of entering."

But Bōrraan deceived his *aļap* and took the fish trap away and placed it in the water and moved the rock of entering. (It was prohibited [taboo] to move it. This was the beginning of the wrong of Bōrraan.)

When three nights had passed, Iroojrilik said to Bōrraan, "Go and check the fish trap" [for fish]. (We say, reveal or show the fish trap.)[4]

When Bōrraan went, no fish had entered, because he did not obey his *aļap*.[5] When Bōrraan had not done as his *aļap* had commanded him three times, the *aļap* was angry

---

1. The *aļap* 'lineage head' is "manager" of the lineage *(bwij)* land. A special respect relationship exists between the maternal uncle, whether lineage head or not, and his sisters' sons. They belong to the same matriclan and lineage, and are associated with the same land rights, whether chiefly *(irooj)* or commoner *(kajoor)*. The senior nephew owes special respect to his maternal uncle.

2. Informant explained: "There were no 'years' before the white men came. But *añōneañ* 'winter season' is like a year. One *añōneañ*, one year. I am not really sure how old the *aļap* was." Compare this to the old age attributed to biblical characters such as Noah ("The whole lifetime of Noah was nine-hundred and fifty years; then he died" [Genesis 9.29]) and Shem's descendants (Genesis 11.10–12 and passim). Marshallese appear to have a tendency to describe an old person as being much older than he or she actually is.

3. Informant explained the Dekā in Jelāmej 'Rock of Entering'. "It is a rock that they place in front of the fish trap *(u)* and tie bait (crabs and coconut meat, and such as that) onto, so that the fish should come inside the fish trap. The people of today do not do this. One time I did it, and there were very many fish caught because I did not remove the rock of entering."

4. The word used by Iroojrilik was *ibwaik,* and the informant explained that this meant *kwaļọk* 'reveal or show' in ordinary Marshallese.

5. Note the supernatural punishment for disobedience of a junior (the maternal nephew [*mañden*]) to a senior (his maternal uncle [*rukoreān* in Rālik, *wūllepān* in Ratak] and *aļap*). This is obviously an exemplary and didactic element of this story. Indeed, it is the leitmotif of the tale.

and said, "You do as you wish. Because you do not obey me."

Because Bōrraan knew that very many breadfruit, coconuts, pandanus, and any kind of food were with his *aļap,* he said, "Iroojrilik, you bring food from the sea, for I will bring food from the island. And after one or two moon stars,[6] you just come and look at much food. Because any kind of food will be full on the branches, because of their hanging down."

(In the ancient language, the meaning of *jurri* is 'to see who has much food with him', *bōbaar tometo* is 'bring food from the sea', *bōbaar toānin* is 'bring food from the island', and *ebbib* is 'full'.)

And Iroojrilik said to his *ṃaanladdik* 'senior maternal nephew' [Bōrraan], "Why do you do thus, making ready anything that I have planted, [which] you come to give me? Well, I will come and see if there is much food on that island, your island."

Bōrraan said, "You just come, right now."

And Iroojrilik said, "Well, I will come." And they separated.

The next day Iroojrilik spoke to the living things that can destroy all the things that can produce food [trees and plants] and all the food there. [He spoke to the insects.]

Iroojrilik said, "Go forth, Ļajeia, Ļajañaro,[7] and see the things [items] of food there, and those [other] things, Leia."

And Ļajañaro went and climbed up on all the things that produce food and destroyed them, as much as he could.

And Iroojrilik again summoned an insect that was very destructive to things that produce food. The name of this insect: *kūļōļō.*

And said to the *kūļōļō* (he gave the names of men to these insects), "Go away, Ļakūļōļō, and look at the leaves, the leaves of the breadfruit trees, and the fronds of the coconut trees, and the leaves of the pandanus trees, and their fruits!"

And Ļakūļōļō went as Iroojrilik said.

And Iroojrilik again called Ļakwe and said to him: "Go on, sir, Ļakwe, and look at those things, the fruit of the breadfruit [and the] pandanus, and destroy them!"

And Ļakwe went and destroyed the foods.

And Iroojrilik again called Ļamenkuk and said to him, "Go away, Ļamenkuk, and destroy all the fruit of the breadfruit trees!"

And Ļamenkuk went and destroyed all the fruit of the breadfruit trees.

And Iroojrilik again called to Ļalikaakrak ["Mr. Maggot"], and said that he should go and destroy all of the coconuts, sprouted coconuts, pandanus, [and] breadfruit. All foods.

And Ļalikaakrak went.

Iroojrilik again called to Ļōmōñ that he should come and destroy all the foods.

Iroojrilik again called to Ļōkōrōr that he should come and go to destroy all the foods.

(Perhaps there were more insects. I do not know, but I forget.)

When it was just dusk,[8] Bōrraan came to his *aļap* and said, "When will you come? As there is much food ready for you. And hurry

6. *Allōñ iju* 'moon in the west, second phase of the moon [lit. "moon star"]'. The Marshallese use the word *allōñ* 'moon' for one month.

7. *Le-* and *Li-* are the female prefixes for personal names, and *Ļa-* and *Ļō-* are the male prefixes. In this and other stories, these prefixes are also used with the names of animals to anthropomorphize them. Making animals humanlike is common in the folktales of other areas, including Europe, Africa, and the Americas. The stories of Aesop, La Fontaine, and the Grimm brothers include examples of this phenomenon, as do the Jātaka and Panchatantra stories. Many of the European animal tales were derived from the Jātaka tales, which came from the Buddhist tradition, and many of the Indian Panchatantra stories also derive from the Jātaka tales (see Leach 1949(2):543).

8. *Jota-dikdikļọk* 'dusk, about six p.m., when it is beginning to get dark *(jinoin marok)*'.

and bring food from the sea. As it is the time of many flies, the summer season [of] your food" [that is, breadfruit]. (*Itōknonu* 'the time of many flies', it is a word seldom used today.)[9]

Iroojrilik replied: "Tomorrow, when the sun is in the middle of the sky, I will go with you."

They slept that night, and then the following day, Bōrraan again went and looked at the breadfruit and the pandanus, coconuts, taro, [and] bananas. When he went away and saw all the fruits of the breadfruit trees, they were dried out, brown.

The leaves of the breadfruit trees, many *kūļōļō* there, and Ļakūļōļō had destroyed all the things that produce food. (It is one kind of white insect. We see it today. These things are very destructive.)

At the time of the story, Iroojrilik remained [lived] a long time, but Ļajibwinām̧ōņ [Man-of-the-north] and Ļōkōm̧raan [Man-of-the-east] and Ļōrōk [Man-of-the-south] died before.[10]

Iroojrilik had only a *mañden,* maternal nephew. But because he, the nephew, did not stay with his mother and his grandmother, he did not obey; he did not know how to obey. Because he thought he was tough and did not need to obey his *aļap.*[11]

Because Ļakūļōļō is on all of the things that produce food. When it was afternoon Bōrraan went away to pick breadfruit and take it away so that they should finish all the fruit of the breadfruit trees. And half of them there were dried-up [and] brown, because Ļakwe had finished entering inside the fruit of all the breadfruit trees and destroyed them.

Also, Ļalikaakrak had finished entering inside some breadfruit and ripe coconuts, and destroyed them, and people could not eat [them.]

At the time when it was noon, Iroojrilik looked for Bōrraan, as Bōrraan had said he should go out and see his share of food [that is, his food]. When Iroojrilik went, Bōrraan was ashamed because of all of the things he had been proud of, all of them people could not eat [that is, people could not eat any of the things of which he was proud].

Now Iroojrilik said, "Where are the things you said I should come and see? For I'm ready to eat now."

Bōrraan replied, "All of the things are destroyed, for I don't know why they are dried up and brown, and you cannot eat [them] now.

Iroojrilik said, "Bōrraan, do you remember when you said I am to bring food from the sea?"

"Well, you will see now." And Iroojrilik said, *"Bwijilǫke, ikijet em katǫǫre, ettǫǫrtok ļōjabwil!"* (In the ancient language *ikijet* is 'sea'.) ("Kick out, press out [with one's leg] into the sea and make it flow, flow in the fish to here: *ļōjabwil!* [*Katesuwonis pelamis,* Oceanic bonito].")

And again he said, *"Bwijilǫke, ikijet em katǫǫre, ettǫǫrtok: bwebwe!"* ("Kick out, press out into the sea and make it flow, flow in the fish to here: *bwebwe!* [yellowfin or bluefin tuna].")

He again said, *"Bwijlǫke, ikijet em katǫǫre, ettǫǫrtok: ļōjkaan!"* ("Kick out, press out into the sea and make it flow, flow in the fish to here: *ļōjkaan!* [*Xiphias gladius,* swordfish].")

---

9. "All insects in this story exist today," said the informant (storyteller).

10. These supernatural beings, who mark the four directions, figure in other Marshallese tales (for example, "The Story of Irooj" told to me by Leroojj [chiefess] Litarjikūt Kabua in 1951). They obviously had an important function in the supernatural world of the Marshallese, and high status as well.

11. Ideal behavior described, flouted by Bōrraan, who was punished for misbehaving toward his *aļap.*

He again said, "*Bwijlǫke, ikijet em katǫǫre, ettǫǫrtok: wūjinleep!*" ("Kick out, press out into the sea and make it flow, flow in the fish to here: *wūjinleep!* [*Istiepherus greyi,* Pacific marlin].")

And again he said, "*Bwijlǫke, ikijet em katǫǫre, ettǫǫrtok: m̧ōlm̧ōl!*" ("Kick out, into the sea and make it flow, flow in the fish in here: *m̧ōlm̧ōl!* [*Scomber japonicus,* mackerel].")

Again he said, "*Bwijlǫke, ikijet em katǫǫre, ettǫǫrtok: pāti!*" ("Kick out, into the sea and make it flow, flow in the fish in here: *pāti!* [*Trachurops crumenophthalmus,* horse mackerel].")

Again he said, "*Bwijlǫke, ikijet em katǫǫre, ettǫǫrtok: ettōū!*" ("Kick out, press out into the sea and make it flow, flow in the fish in here: *ettōū!* [*Trachurops crumenopthalmus,* mackerel].")

And again he said "*Bwijlǫke, ikijet em katǫǫre, ettǫǫrtok baļōj!*" ("Kick out, press out into the sea and make it flow, flow in the fish in here: *baļōj!* [unidentified; possibly a variant of *bakōj,* Pomacentrid: *Abudefduf saxatilis*].")

He again said "*Bwijlǫke, ikijet em katǫǫre, ettǫǫrtok: ļooj!*" "Kick out, press out into the sea and make it flow, flow in the fish in here: *ļooj!* [*Sarda sarda,* bonito].")

He again said "*Bwijlǫke, ikijet em katǫǫre, ettǫǫrtok: raj!*" ("Kick out, press out into the sea and make it flow, flow in the fish to here: *raj!* [*Cetacea,* whale, porpoise].")[12]

When he finished [naming and bringing up] these fish,[13] all the fish came in and beached up on the island (*jirak* [*kajin wa em ek* 'canoe and fish language']).

When the waves of the fish wet the island, they flooded it greatly with water, and swept away all the food there, the food Bōrraan had been proud of [had bragged about] to his *aļap.*

And all the island was full of fish and Bōrraan looked and was very much surprised. And his *aļap* said, "Why are you surprised when you said I should bring food from the sea; and you would bring food from the island. And all of the things you have prepared are gone?"

At that time Bōrraan said nothing, but he thought that he should go away from his *aļap.* And he said, "Well, it is clear I will go away from you any which way I want to go."

(The name of the island to this day is Tutu, on Arņo [Atoll.] The reason they named it Tutu is because of the very high wave of fish that flooded all of the island.)[14]

And Bōrraan stayed there, and after one day, he sailed and came to Mājro and broke all the laws on the atoll of Mājro.

When Iroojrilik heard about this, he said, "You [plural] say to Bōrraan that he should not break the laws of long standing."

Bōrraan did not obey his *aļap* but did as he wanted to.

After he stayed on the atoll of Mājro, he made a round [trip][15] in the atolls of the Marshalls and came to Aelōñļapļap. The reason

12. The word *raj* 'whale' is also used for porpoise in Rālik; they are called *ke* in Ratak. The dichotomy is not as distinct on the local and archipelago-wide levels. In any event, this would seem to indicate that the Marshallese recognize that whales and porpoises do belong to the same order *(Cetacea).*

13. Note the motif of bringing up animals and naming them by a supernatural being.

14. Note the explanation for a place name. Tutu Island is on the windward side of Arņo (Mejāniañ) Atoll near a large pass, and is thus vulnerable to waves and flooding. And *tutu* means 'wet, bathe' as in *jikin tutu* 'bath place', *(i)m̧ōn tutu* 'bath house'.

15. *Rawūn* is from English *round,* meaning 'a circuit, or round trip'. The field trip ships are known as *waan rawūn.*

he came to Aelōn̄ļapļap was because the keel of his canoe was damaged, and the part at the top of the mast through which the rigging passes was broken. And he came to Buoj [island] and stayed there.

Sometimes he went away and broke all of the laws, and because he was so immoral, he was almost destroyed at times. But he was not destroyed.

He left his canoe on Wōja, Aelōn̄ļapļap, and came to Naṃo, Ellep, Kuwajleen, Lae, Wōtto, Ron̄dik, Ron̄ļap, Pikinni, Aelōn̄inae, Ujae, and again returned to Aelōn̄ļapļap. And made the top part of the canoe mast and the keel on his canoe.

And Bōrraan went and constructed/chopped the keel and the top part of the canoe mast from the *kōn̄e* [*Pemphis acidula,* ironwood tree] that his *aļap* had told him he should not move.

When Bōrraan finished making the top part of the canoe mast and the keel, he sailed. And because Bōrraan did not obey, a big wind came and damaged his canoe, and it drifted.

When it drifted, Bōrraan said, "Maybe [this is] because I did not obey my *aļap*."

Bōrraan drifted on the sea for a great many days. And he drifted in to an island.

The name of the atoll is the Atoll of Ep. (I do not know where it is. It is not in the Marshalls.)[16]

When he drifted in to the island, all of the people who were with him (in the canoe, I do not know how many) were weak. And some were dead. But some were alive. At the time, a young man came and met the canoe, and said to Bōrraan, "You see, all of the laws that you broke, those things turned back to you now.

"This atoll is the atoll/island[17] of Ep. You cannot leave it. Look to the east. See the smoke of that island, Tawoj? Do you see that this island is long?"

Bōrraan replied, "Yes, I see it."

The young man said, "Well, they were warming our mother there [*tabuki:* heat treatment using hot stones wrapped in leaves]. Because you chopped our mother and made the keel and the top part of the mast of that canoe. And half of her is gone."

(The real mother of Bōrraan was a *kōn̄e* [tree]. But Bōrraan did not know it was his mother that he [had] chopped. But Iroojrilik knew.)

"Bōrraan, the reason for your misfortune is because of your bad behavior."

(In the ancient language *kotarkōlkōl* is bad behavior: *"enana ṃwilūṃ."*

And he continued speaking. "You will see all the things that are bad. From now on out."[18]

"Are you going fishing now?" Bōrraan replied and said, "Well, I want to go fishing as you say."

And the young man said, "Well, take the bait here. And put it on the hook and throw it [the hook and line] to the west into that pool!" (*Kōṃọọre kāāj* in fishing language means 'put the bait on the hook'.)

And Bōrraan threw out the hook and a tuna came: *ajbōk juon* (in the ancient lan-

---

16. The legendary land to the west of the Marshalls (also called Waab), from whence came the supernatural clan founders Liwātuonmour and Lidepdepju. Ep figures in other Marshallese stories as well. Could it also be Yap (called Iaab or Waab) by the Marshallese? Yap Island is also far to the west of the Marshalls, and recorded drift voyages have been made from there to the Marshalls (see Riesenberg 1965:162). So the possibility obviously exists that ancestors of Marshallese did come from there.

17. The word *aelōn̄* 'atoll' is sometimes also used for a single island without a lagoon (as, for example, Aelōn̄ in Kōle) instead of the word *āne* 'island, islet'.

18. Note the motif of harming mother by an ignorant mistake, with punishment following to the culprit. Note also the motif of the mother being a tree or plant.

guage, the size and method of measuring the size that one man can carry).[19] And it ate [took] the hook. When it ate the hook, the young man said, "Try hard! Pull it in!" And Bōrraan pulled in the tuna and threw it beside himself and the other young man.

And the other young man said to Bōrraan, "Bring our knife to cut that tuna. For I'm only standing here watching your cutting that tuna."

Bōrraan said, "How shall I cut it, sir, my older brother?"

The other young man said, "I will show you how to cut it."

And Bōrraan said, "Well, show me so that I can learn."

And the other young man said, "Cut the stomach and put it next to the fish. When you have finished cutting the stomach, you just look over at me." (In the ancient language, *jowōj* means 'put'. And the stomach is the best part to eat of fish like tuna and some other fish. It is the food of the chiefs.)[20] [Informant sketched the area reserved for the chiefs *(irooj ro)* in my notebook. It covered most of the ventral part of the fish.]

When Bōrraan finished cutting the stomach, he put the stomach beside the fish and looked over to the other young man.

He looked over and saw that the other young man had finished cutting his [own] stomach like Bōrraan had cut the stomach from the fish.

When Bōrraan saw the open stomach of the young man, he was surprised. And said to himself, "Why, sir, is the stomach of that young man open?"

The other young man again said, "Well, cut those fins, the fins of that fish [lateral fins] and put them beside it."[21]

And Bōrraan cut the fins and put them next to the fish. And the other young man now said, "Look over here at me."

Bōrraan then looked over. The hands were gone. The hands of the other young man. At that time, he was very much surprised about the nature of what he had just seen. Now the young man said, "The way that you cut our mother. And thus they healed, the wounds—the wounds that you cut.

"Now you can never again return, but thus the people of this island will do to you. For you filled up all your life with evil, and did not listen to your *aļap*. That [is to be your] misfortune."

It is ended.

(The meaning of this thing: The words to Bōrraan from Iroojrilik said, "*Ekkwǫǫl aļap.*" That is 'obey our older (senior) people': our mother and father, grandmother, grandfather and our *aļap;* all of our older [senior] people.)

There are many stories of Bōrraan in all of the atolls of the Marshalls. But Bōrraan did not remain in the Marshalls, because he went to the atoll/island of Ep, as the story tells.

Bōrraan damaged many places in the

---

19. *Ajbōk ruo* is the size that two men can carry, and *ajbōk jilu* the size that three men can carry. Informant explained that this is the way of measuring fish that the Marshallese used before the white men taught their way of measuring to the people of these atolls. The Marshallese do not use these words very much today, just a little bit. The fish are carried at one's side with arm extended down, full length. This is obviously used only for larger fish, such as tuna; smaller ones can be carried in baskets, threaded on cord, or hand-carried.

20. Food of the chiefs *(kijen irooj),* special cuts of fish and turtles, were reserved for the chiefs, as seen in this story. This was a custom throughout Micronesia and Polynesia. The heads and stomachs of the large fish were special delicacies. The *ṃǫle* (Ratak, *ellōk* Rālik) '*Siganus rostratus,* rabbit fish' was also prized by the chiefs (Tobin 1958:67–68, 1967:82).

21. The word for lateral fin is *pā (pei-)*, the same word used for the hands and arms of humans and the wings of birds.

Marshalls: reefs and coral heads, and islands and fish.

There is a fish named *dāp* [family *Muraenidae* sp., moray eel] that Bōrraan stretched to its full length. This is the reason eels are long now.[22]

There are reefs on Lae and Ujae and on some of those atolls that Bōrraan damaged.

The *kōn̄e* [ironwood] on the lagoon beach on Aelōn̄ļapļap in the story remains to this day. On the island of Wōja, it is on Wōja to the east—the mother of Bōrraan.

2: BWEBWENATO IN BŌRRAAN

Ri-bwebwenato: Jelibōr Jam, Kuwajleen 1975

Bōrraan, juon ļadik eo eaar jab pād ippān jinen im jibwin ilo iien an rūttoļǫk.

Ke ej likao ej ilǫk n̄an ippān aļap eo an dettan aļap eo ilo iien in eo jibuki jilin̄oul an̄ōnean̄ emootļǫk.[23] Ke ej ilǫk [n̄an] ippān aļap eo an, aļap eo an ej jilkinļǫk im ba en etal in pukot ledik eo jātin. Innām Bōrraan ej uwaak, "Aet, inaaj ilǫk." Ak eaar jab etal n̄an jidik. Kein ka juon in an bwōd ņae aļap eo an.

Pād innām aļap eo ej bar aikuji. Bwe n̄e enaaj eǫn̄wōd [en] lale bwe en jab baj bōk juon iaan ek ko koņan ak en bōktok aolep.

Bōrraan eaar jab pokake. Ej kein ka ruo in an bōd ņae aļap eo an.

Kein ka jilu Iroojrilik (etan aļap eo an) ej ba, "Kwōn bōkļǫk u ņe in joone." Innām ar ba, "Aet, inaaj bōkļǫk."

Ke ej bōkļǫk Iroojrilik ej ba, "Lale kwaar jab ikūr dekā in jelāmej" (kajin etto ikūr ej kōm̧m̧akūt).[24]

Bōrraan ej uwaak, "Aet, ijāmin ikūr dekā in jelāmej."

Ak Bōrraan eaar m̧oņe aļap eo an im bōkļǫk u eo im joone im ikūr dekā in jelāmej. (Emǫ an kōm̧akūti. Ej jinoin an jorrāān Bōrraan.)

Ke ej ļǫk jilu bon̄, Iroojrilik ej ba n̄an Bōrraan, "Kwōn etal in ebbwāik u eo" (āinwōt kwaļǫk u eo).

Ke Bōrraan ej etal ejjeļǫk ek eaar deļǫn̄. Kōnke eaar jab pokake aļap eo an. Ke ej jilu alen an Bōrraan jab kōm̧m̧an āinwōt an aļap eo ijjilōk n̄ane, aļap eo ej illu im ba, "Kwōn kōm̧m̧an āinwōt am̧ kōņaan. Bwe kwōj jab pokake eō."

Kōn an Bōrraan jelā ke ekanooj lōn̄ mā, ni, bōb, im jabdewōt kain m̧ōn̄ā eaar juri aļap eo an, im ba, "Iroojrilik. Kwoņam̧

---

22. Note explanation of natural phenomena (for example, the shape of eels) by the act of a supernatural being. This is a motif found in Marshallese folklore, and elsewhere in the world. Also note the trickster motif, similar to that of Etao and Maui, and others worldwide (see Leach 1950, 2: 1123–1125). See Erdland (1914:204–206) and Krämer and Nevermann (1938:262–263) for other versions of the adventures of Bōrraan. Also compare the calling up and naming of the marine creatures in this story with the same action in story 1, "The Beginning of This World," and with the Hawaiian Kumulipo (Beckwith 1951 and Johnson 1981).

23. Ri-bwebwenato eo ej komelele: ejjeļǫk iiō m̧okta ripālle ar itok. Ak an̄ōnean̄ ej āinwōt juon iiō. Juon an̄ōnean̄ ej juon iiō.

24. Dekā in jelāmej (dekā in deļǫn̄ tok) ej juon dekā raar likūti m̧aan u im lukoj m̧ǫǫr (baru ak waini im āinwōt) ioon. Bwe ren itok ek iloan u eo. Armej in rainin ejjab kōm̧m̧ane. Juon iien iaar kōm̧m̧ane. Im kanooj lōn̄ ek, kōnke iaar jab kōm̧m̧akūt dekā in jelāmej.

bōbaar tomento ņe bwe ij bōbaar toāniin. Innām ļọkun juon ak ruo allōñ iju, kwōn kab itok in aluje an loñ ṃōñā. Bwe aolep keinikkan otemjej eipeep loraer kōn aer kouwa."

(Ilo kajin etto meļeļein *jurri* ej 'lale wōn eo elōñ mōña ippān'. "Bōbaar tomento" ej 'bōktok ṃōñā jān lọmeto'. "Bōbaar toāniin" ej 'bōktok ṃōñā jān āne'. Im "eipeep" ej 'ebooļ'.)

Innām Iroojrilik eaar ba ñan ṃaan ļadiķ eo an [Bōrraan], "Etke kwōj kōṃṃan āindein ta eļakke ededeļọk jabdewōt ke iaar kalbwini kwōj iten jurri eō? Ekwe inaaj iwōj in lale elōñ ke ṃōñā ioon āņņe āneeṃ."

Bōrraan eaar ba, "Kwōnaaj baj itok. Kiiō wōt."

Innām Iroojrilik ej ba, "Ekwe, inaaj iwōj." Innām rejro jepel jān doon.

Raan eo juon Iroojrilik eaar konono ñan mennin mour ko remaroñ in kọkkuri aolep keinikkan kab ṃōñā ko ie.

Iroojrilik e ba, "Teļọk ṃōk Ļajeia, Ļajañaro em lale keinikkan kaņ kab men kaņ Leia."

Im Ļajañaro eaar etal im'tallōñ ilo aolep keinikkan ko im kọkkuri joñan wōt an maroñ.

Ak Iroojrilik ebar kūrtok juon kij, ekanooj kọkkuri keinikkan. Etan kij in, kūļōļō. (Ej ņae etan kij kaņe ṃōṃaan.) "Iļọk ṃōk ļe, Ļakūļōļō, im lale ṃōk bwilkōn, bwilkōn mā kaņ, kab kimej in ni kaņ, kab ṃaañ in bōb kaņ, kab men kaņ leer!"

Innām Ļakūļōļō ej etal āinwōt Iroojrilik ej ba.

Innām Iroojrilik ej bar kūrtok Ļakwe im ba ñane, "Etal ṃōk ļe, Ļakwe, im lale men kaņ leen mā, bōb, im kọkkuri!"

Innām Ļakwe ej etal im kọkkuri ṃōñā ko.

Innām Iroojrilik ej bar kūrtok Ļemenkuk im ba ñane, "Iļọk ṃōk, Ļemenkuk, im kọkkuri aolepān leen mā kaņ."

Innām Ļemenkuk ej etal im kọkkuri leen mā ko.

Innām Iroojrilik ej bar kūr ñan Ļalikaakrak in ba en etal im kọkkuri aolepān waini, iu, bōb, mā. Aolep ṃōñā.

Im Ļalikaakrak ej etal.

Iroojrilik ej bar ikkūr ñan Ļōmōñ. Bwe Ļōmōñ en itok im kọkkuri aolep ṃōñā ko.

(Bōlen eor bar kij ijaje ak imeļọkļọk.)

Ke ej jota dikdik Bōrraan ej itok ñan ippān aļap eo an im ba, "Kwōnaaj itok wōt ñāāt? Ke ekanooj in lōñ ṃōñā ko repojak ñan eok. Innām kwōn ṃōkaj in bōbaar tomento ņe. Ke ejja itoknonu rak e kijōṃ." ("Itoknonu" ej juon naan jejab kanooj in kōjerbal rainin. Meļeļe eo ej iien eo eļap an ļọñ.)

Iroojrilik ej uwaak, "Ilju, pād in aļ ioļap inaaj iwōj."

Rōkiki boñon eo im ļak rujiļọkōn eo Bōrraan ej bar etal im lale mā ko kab bōb ko, ni ko, pinana ko. Ke ej iļọk ej lo mā ko rōṃōņakņak. Bōlōk in mā ko elōñ kūļōļō ie. Im aolep ekkan ko eṃōj an Ļakūļōļō kọkkuri. (Ej juon kij emouj. Jej loe rainin. Eļap an kọkkuri men kein.)

Ilo iien bwebwenato Iroojrilik etto an pād, ak Ļajibwināṃōņ, Ļōkōṃraan, im Ļōrōk rej mej ṃokta.

Eor wōt mañden ippān Iroojrilik. Ak kōnke eaar jab pād ippān jinen im jibwin, ejjab pokake, ejaje pokake. Kōnke ej ļemņak in kakijoñjoñ im ejjab pokake aļap eo an.

Kōnke Ļakūļōļō ej pād ilo aolep keinikkan.

Ke ej raelepļọk Bōrraan eļak iten kōṃkōṃ mā in bōkļọk bwe ren kōmat aolep leen mā im ṃōņakņak jimettan ier. Kōnke eṃōj an Ļakwe deļọñ iloan mā im kọkkuri.

Barāinwōt jet mā ak waini eṃōj an Ļalikaakrak deļọñ ilowaer im kọkkuri. Innām armej rejjab aikuj in ṃōñā.

Ilo iien eo ke ej raelepļọk, Iroojrilik ej pukotļọk Bōrraan. Āinwōt an kar Bōrraan ba in iļọk in lale ṃōñā ko kijen. Ke Iroojrilik ej etal, Bōrraan ejook bwe aolep men ko eaar utiej būruon kaki, aolep im armej reban ṃōñā.

Kiiō Iroojrilik ej ba, "Erri men ko kwaar ba in itok in lali im ṃōñā? Ke ña ipojak in ṃōñā kiiō."

Bōrraan ej uwaak im ba, "Aolep men ko im jorrāān, kōnke ijaje ta wūnin aer ṃōṇakṇak. Innām kwōj jab maroñ in ṃōñā kiiō."

Iroojrilik ej ba, "Bōrraan kwōj emeemej ke kwaar ba ña ij bōbaar tomento e?

"Ekwe, kwōnaaj lale kiiō!" Innām Iroojrilik ej ba, "Bwijlọkwe ikijet em katọọre, etọọrtok: ḷōjabwil!" (Ilo kajin etto "ikijet" ej lọjet.)

Innām eaar bar ba, "Bwijlọkwe, ikijet em katọọre, ettọọrtok: bwebwe!"

Ej bar ba, "Bwijlọkwe, ikijet em katọọre, ettọọrtok: ḷōjkaan!"

Eaar bar ba, "Bwijlọkwe ikijet em katọọre, ettọọrtok: wūjinleep!"

Innām eaar bar ba, "Bwijiḷọke, ikijet em katọọre, ettọọrtok: ṃōlṃōl!"

Ej bar ba, "Bwijlọkwe, ikijet em katọọre, ettōrtok: pāti!"

Eaar bar ba, "Bwijlọkwe, ikijet em katọọre, ettōrtok: ettōū!"

Innām eaar bar ba, "Bwijlọkwe, ikijet em katọọre, ettōrtok: baḷōj!"

Ej bar ba, "Bwijlọkwe, ikijet em katọọre, ettōrtok: ḷooj!"

Eaar bar ba, "Bwijlọkwe, ikijet em katọọre, ettōrtok: raj!"

Ke ej maat ek kein aolep ek rejwōj ettōrtok im jerak (kajin wa im ek). Ke rej jerak ṇo in ek ko rōkatutu āne eo im ekanooj in ḷap an eppej kōn dān. Im tọre [eo] aolep ṃōñā ko Bōrraan eaar kautiej būruon kaki ñan aḷap eo an. Ak eobrak aolepān āne eo kōn ek im Bōrraan eaar lale ḷọk im kanooj in bwilōñ. Im aḷap eo an ej ba, "Etke kwōj bwilōñ ke kwaar ba in bōbaar tomento e; ak kwe toene ṇe. Innām aolep pojak ko aṃ rejako?"

Ilo iien eo ejjeḷọk an Bōrraan konono ak ḷōmṇak eo an bwe en etal jān ippān aḷap eo an. Innām eaar ba, "Ekwe, alikkar ke ña inaaj etal jān kwe jabdewōt ijo ikōṇaan etal ieḷọk."

(Etan āne eo ñan rainin Tutu, i Arṇo. Wūnin rej ṇa etan Tutu kōnke ṇo in ek lōñlōñ eo eaar jerak im eppej aolepān āne eṇ.)

Innām Bōrraan eaar pād im ḷak juon raan ej jerak im itok ñan Mājro. Im kọkkuri aolep kien ko ilo aelōñ in Mājro.

Ke Iroojrilik ej roñ ej ba, "Koṃin ba ñan Bōrraan bwe en jab kọkkuri kien ko jān etto."

Bōrraan eaar jab pokake aḷap eo an ak eaar kōṃṃan āinwōt an kōṇaan.

Ṃwijin an pād ilo aelōñ in Mājro ej rawūn ilo aelōñ in Ṃajeḷ in im itok ñan Aelōñḷapḷap. Wūnin an itok ñan Aelōñḷapḷap kōnke ejjorrāān erer eo i wa eo waan. Kab bwilọk ḷot eo.

Innām ej itok ñan Buoj im pād ie.

Jet iien ej ilọk im kọkkuri aolepān kien ko ak kōn an kijoñ enañin jorrāān jet iien. Ak ejjab jorrāān.

Eaar door wa eo waan ṇa ilo Wōja, Aelōñḷapḷap. Im itok ñan Naṃo, Ellep, Kuwajleen, Lae, Wōtto, Roñdik, Roñḷap, Pikinni, Aelōñinae, Ujae, im bar jepḷaak ñan Aelōñḷapḷap. Im kōṃṃane ḷot eo kab erer eo i wa eo waan.

Innām Bōrraan ej etal im jektok erer eo kab ḷot eo jān ijo aḷap eo an eaar ba lale bwe enjab kōṃakūt kōñe eo ilo Aelōñḷapḷap.

Bōrraan ejjab pokake ak eaar etal wōt im jekjek an erer kab ḷot ilo kōñe eo aḷap eo an eaar ba enjab kōṃakūti.

Ke ej ṃōj an Bōrraan kōṃṃane ḷot eo im erer eo ej jerak. Im kōn an Bōrraan jab pokake, eitok juon kōto eḷap im kọkkure wa eo waan im epeḷọk. Ke ej peḷọk Bōrraan ej ba, "Bōlen kōnke iaar jab pokake aḷap eo aō."

Ekanooj lōñ raan in an Bōrraan peḷọk i lọmeto. Im eaar eọtōkḷọk ilo juon āne etan aelōñ eo, aelōñ in Ep. (Ijaje epād ia. Ejjab pād ilo Ṃajeḷ.)[25]

Ke ej eọtōkḷọk aolep armej ro kar ippān (ilo wa eo, ijaje jete), rōṃōjṇọ. Im jet raar mej. Ak jet raar mour. Ilo iien eo eaar itok juon likao in wōnṃaeki wa eo. Im ba ñan Bōrraan, "Lale ṃōk aolepān kien ko kwaar kǫkkuri erkein rej oktak ñan eok kiiō. Aelōñ in, aelōñ in Ep. Kwōj jab maroñ in diwōjļǫk jāne. Kwōn erre tawōj ṃōk. Lale baat irōk ņe iaar in āne, Tawōj? Kwōj lo ke an aetok ānin?"

Bōrraan ej uwaak, "Aet, ij lo wōt."

Likao eo ej ba, "Ekwe jinerro ņe rej tabuki. Kōnke jinerro eo kwaar jeke im kōṃṃan erer in wa ņe kab ļot. Innām ejako jimettanin."

(Lukkuun jinen Bōrraan ej kōñe. Ak Bōrraan ejaje ej jinen im eaar jeke. Ak Iroojrilik eaar jeļā.)

"Bōrraan, wūnin aṃ jerata ņe kōnke kotarkelel" (kajin etto: 'enana ṃwiliṃ').

Innām ej konono wōt, "Kwonaaj lo men otemjej ko renana. Jen kiiō im ilǫk."

"Kwoeañwōd ke kiiō?" Bōrraan ej uwaak, im ba, "Eokwe, ikoņaan eañwōd āinwōt aṃ ba."

Innām likao eo ej ba, "Ekwe, lewōj mǫǫr eo ieo. Im komǫǫre kāāj ņe im jotowōj ņa ilo ļwe ņe."

Innām Bōrraan ej jotoļǫk kāāj eo im itok juon bwebwe. Ajbok juon (kajin etto: 'dettan wōt juon eṃṃaan maroñ bōke').[26] Em kan kāāj eo. Ke ej kan kāāj eo, likao eo ej ba, "Kate eok! Tōbwe!" Innām Bōrraan ej tōbwe bwebwe eo im jotok ņe iturierro likao eo juon.

Innām likao eo juon ej ba ñan Bōrraan, "Bōktok di eo nejirro im bukwe bwebwe ņe. Bwe ña ij jutak wōt ije im lale aṃ bukwe bwebwe ņe."

Bōrraan ej ba, "Ewi wāween aō naaj bukwe ļe jeiū?"

Likao eo juon ej ba, "Inaaj kwaļǫk wāween aṃ bukwe."

Innām Bōrraan ej ba, "Ekwe, kwaļǫk tok ṃōk bwe in ekkatak."

Innām likao eo juon ej ba, "Kwōn bukwe je ņe im jowoj ņa iturin wōt ek ņe. N̄e eṃōj am bukwe je ņe, kwōn kab erretok ṃōk lale eō." (Kajin etto: *jowōj* ej 'door'. Im *je* ej 'lǫjien ek', ennǫtata ṃōttan ek āinwōt bwebwe im ko jet ek. Ej kijen irooj.)

Ke ej ṃōj an Bōrraan bukwe je eo ej door je eo ņa iturin ek eo im erreļǫk ñan likao eo juon.

Eļǫk erreļǫk im lale likao eo juon eṃōj bukwe lǫjien im āinwōt an kar Bōrraan bukwe je eo jein ek eo.

Ke Bōrraan ej lo an peļļǫk lǫjien likao eo, ebwilōñ. Im konono ippān make, im ba, "Ta wūnin an peļļǫk lǫjien likao eņ, ļōṃa?"

Likao eo juon ej bar ba, "Ekwe kwōn bukwe pā kaņe pein ek ņe im doori ņa iturin." Innām Bōrraan ej bukwe pā ko im doori ņa iturin ek eo. Im likao eo juon ej ba kiiō, "Erretok ṃōk lale eō."

Bōrraan eļak erreļǫk ejako pā ko pein likao eo. Iien eo eļapļǫk an bwilōñ kōn wāween eo ej kab loi. Kiiō likao eo ej ba, "Wāween de ņe aṃ kar jeke jinerro. Innām eñeņ rej tabuki kinej ko. Kōnjān aṃ kar jeki.

"Kiiō bar jepļaak ak enaaj āindein an armej in āniin kōṃṃan ñan eok. Bwe kwaar booļe aolep mour eo aṃ kōn nana. Im jab eǫroñ aļap eo aṃ. Jerata ņe ijōņe."

Ejeṃļǫk.

(Meļeļe in menin: Naan eo ñan Bōrraan jān Iroojrilik ej ba, "Ekkwǫǫl aļap." Āinwōt pokake rūttoro ad, jined im jemād, jiṃṃaō, būbū, im aļap: aolep rūtto ro ad.)

---

25. [Bōlen Iaab (Yap) ilo aelōñ in Kapilōñ ke? Āne in Ep epād ilo ko jet bwebwenato in Ṃajeļ.—J. A. T.]

26. Im ajbok ruo, drettan wōt ruo eṃṃaan maroñ bōke kōn peir, kōn peir wōnlaļļǫk. Ajbok jilu, drettan wōt jilu eman maroñ bōke. Ej wāween joñan an dri Ṃajeļ ṃokta ripālle raar katak wāween joñan eo aer ñan ri-Aelōñ Kein. Rejjab kanooj in kōjerbal naan kein rainin. Jidik wōt.

Elōñ bwebwenato an Bōrraan ilo aolep aelōñ in M̧ajeļ. Kōnke eaar rawūni aolep aelōñ in M̧ajeļ. Ak Bōrraan ejjab pād ilo M̧ajeļ. Kōnke ej etal ñan aelōñ in Ep. Āinwōt bwebwenato ej ba.

Elōñ jikin ilo M̧ajeļ Bōrraan ar kǫkkure: pedped, ak wōd, ak āne, ak ek.

Juon ek etan dāp Bōrraan eaar kankan. Wūnin [an] dāp rej aetok kiiō.

Eor pedped i Lae im Ujae em ilo aelōñ kaŋ jet eo Bōrraan ar kǫkkure.

Kōñe in ar i Aelōñļapļap, ilo bwebwenato ej pād ñan rainin. I aelōñ i Wōja epād i Wōja i tu rear—jinen Bōrraan.

3: STORY OF THE HEAVEN POST MEN

As told by Litarjikūt Kabua and interpreted by Jetñil Felix, Mājro 1951

There were four men: Ļajibwinām̧ōņ, Ļōkōm̧raan, Ļōrōk, and Irooj Rālik. They made heaven posts by standing up and holding heaven.[1] They stood up all the time to keep heaven from falling. Ļajibwinām̧ōņ is the north post, Ļōkōm̧raan is the east post, Ļōrōk is the south post, and Irooj Rālik is the west post.

The north post man eats people. The east post man makes light. Ļōrōk supplies food for the world. And Irooj Rālik made the *irooj bwij* [chiefly lineage/clan]. The north man fell down and went to sleep to the north. The man to the east got tired and went to sleep and fell to the east. Ļōrōk fell to the south. Irooj Rālik fell to the west.

These men had power before but did not use it. They were too busy holding up heaven (the sky). When they fell down they used their power.

The north man used his power to make people die. (There had been no death before this.) *"Kol e":* he used his power to kill (by his voice). He swallowed by the power. People's bodies came into his mouth when he made a sound: "I want a man to eat!" A man would come and he would eat him. (Marshallese would not move a sick person to the north. To the south it was all right. Also to the east and west it was all right. This is still done.)

Ļōkōm̧raan: his work was to make light, the day. He wanted to help Ļōrōk, to make light so that Ļōrōk would make food for the people. If Ļōkōm̧raan had not made light, Ļōrōk would not have time to make food.

Ļōrōk had to make food twice a year: *iien rak* (summer): *rak mā* [breadfruit time]; *añōneañ* [winter]: *bōb* [pandanus] and *m̧akm̧ōk* [arrowroot].

Irooj Rālik was the first *irooj.* He made the *bwij* of *irooj.* Ļōrōk and Ļōkōm̧raan made *ekkan* [tribute of food and other goods] to him. They gave him everything: days and food.

Irooj Rālik stayed at Ep, an underworld place. (Some people say that Ep is in the Palau Islands. I say that it is not.)

There are still north, east, south, and west. Light and food. People die. And there are *irooj* now.

These four men: three agreed to work together, but Ļajibwinām̧ōņ was against the others. He killed people, caused sin, and so forth (like Satan). The three agreed to help people to live well and happily—to learn and so forth.

It is not clear to me how Irooj Rālik started the *irooj bwij.*

---

1. This creation myth and others tell us how the Marshallese saw their universe. It indicates their conceptualization of how the world was bound, as well as how it was structured. The motif of posts or pillars erected to hold up the sky is found elsewhere in Oceania. For example, the creation myth of the southernmost Polynesians, the New Zealand Maori, explains that the god Tane provided four poles or *toko* on which Rangi (the sky-parent) was supported (Reed 1963:24–25). In the neighboring Chatham Islands, the raising of the heavens was upon the pillars, set one above the other (Dixon 1964:34–35).

Etymological note: The word *irooj* 'chief' comes from the words *er wōj* meaning 'you are all of them'. That is, powerful. Hence *irooj* as the designation for the leader of the people (M̧ak Juda, Mājro 1968). The word *kajoor* itself means strength or power ('strong' or 'powerful') and is the word used to describe the commoner class, the bulk of the population and base of the social structure of Marshallese culture. The more *kajoor* an *irooj* had in his domain, the greater the work force and number of warriors he had at his disposal, and obviously the stronger he was, as older Marshallese have told me.

4: THE ORIGIN OF TATTOOING

As told by Litarjikūt Kabua and interpreted by Jetñil Felix, Mājro 1951

The story came from the northwestern islands. The *ri-bwebwenato* [storyteller] [was] Ļatōb. He came from a *bwij in bwebwenato* [lineage of storytellers.] The stories are passed on from father to son.

Two men came from heaven. They were named Ļewej and Ļaneej. Both were irooj [chiefs] of the Ļajjidik *bwij (jowi)* [lineage, clan.] They came to Buoj [island], Aelōñļapļap [atoll.]

They brought tattoo ink *(m̧am̧ōj)* to *eo̧o̧n* (tattoo). They also brought a tattoo house *(im̧ōn eo̧o̧n).* After they brought that house, they called all the people to come and have a tattoo.

The *irooj* were tattooed on the face. After they finished tattooing the *irooj* and the people and the fish; all the animals, they put colors on everything. There were no colors before that.

Some people came in late. They became demons—*daak ad* 'drank blood'—from people's tattoo wounds, and became demons by this act. (Prayers were said before tattooing in the Marshalls. People gathered together.)

When you go to Aelōñļapļap, you may see at Buoj pass, between Buoj and Pikaajļā islands, that there is a line of coral heads. These are the demons who drank the *ad.*

The *atlo* [are] the people who have power in their mouth by words. [An *atlo*] may speak to a rock and the rock may let out fire or go to

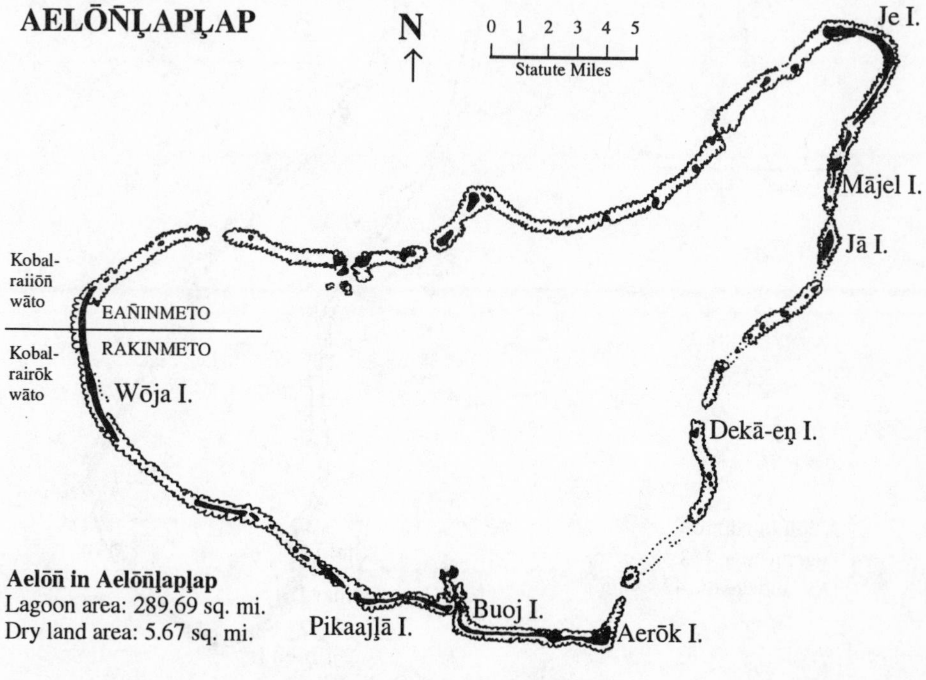

pieces. One *jowi* (clan) had this power: Rikipin-aeliñ-in 'people of the west of the atoll'.

Some have a little power now. But not all in this *jowi* had this power. There were sexual taboos connected with this during the time it was desired to use the power. Usually males used this.

Irooj Ļewej turned the demons into reef rocks because they did not come to be tattooed on time. Now Ļewej and Ļaneej returned to Ep. Irooj Rālik was before them. Note: Only chiefs were allowed facial tattoos.

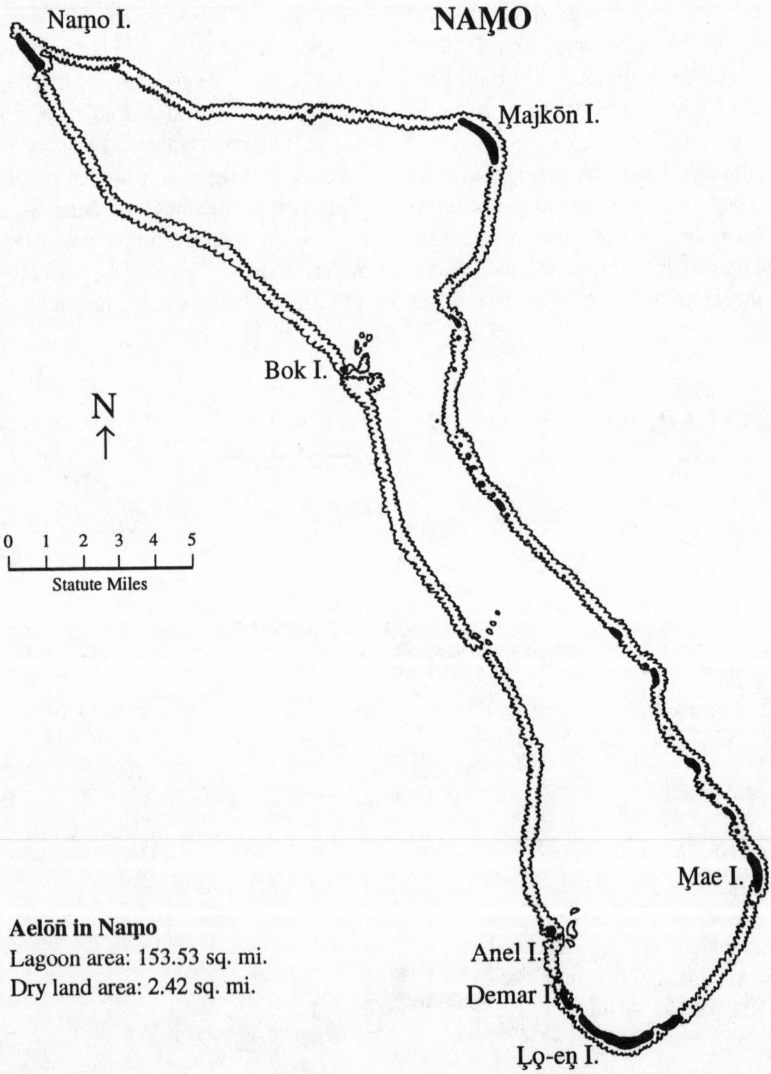

Aelōñ in Nam̧o
Lagoon area: 153.53 sq. mi.
Dry land area: 2.42 sq. mi.

5: THE ORIGIN OF THE *IROOJ* (CHIEFS) OF THE MARSHALL ISLANDS

As told by Raymond DeBrum, Mājro 1952

Many years ago, two sisters named Liwātuonmour and Lidepdepju came to the Marshall Islands in a canoe from the distant land of Ep.[1] They were pillars of hard stone (of the kind not found in the Marshalls.) The canoe landed at Naṃo Island on Naṃo Atoll.[2]

Liwātuonmour remained on Naṃo, but Lidepdepju sailed on to Aur Atoll.[3]

The two became the mothers of the *irooj* (chiefs) of the Marshall Islands. Liwātuonmour, the stone pillar, remained at Naṃo on a piece of land near the lagoon beach. The people worshipped her and made offerings of food, flowers, and mats to her. (The piece of land on which she dwelled was one of only two places in the Marshalls where people did not have to *badikdik* (bow down low in a stylized position, when they passed in front of the chiefs).

This worship continued until an American Protestant missionary, Dr. Rife, came to Naṃo.

In order to stamp out "pagan" practices, he cast Liwātuonmour into the deep waters of the lagoon, despite the warnings of the Marshallese of divine retribution (from Liwātuonmour).

It is ended.

[Thus, a possible valuable clue to Marshallese prehistory was lost forever.]

Comments

Information concerning Lidepdepju was given to me by Jọwej on Mājro in 1951. He was talking about various landmarks in the Ratak chain of the Marshalls. And he stated, "There is another rock *(dekā)* at Tōbaaḷ Island on Aur Atoll. It is buried in the sand now. It was placed on another rock. And it was washed away by the last typhoon. People are going to look for it.

"This rock is Lidepdepju, the younger sister of Liwātuonmour who is at Naṃo Atoll. This (Lidepdepju) is a large rock. Everyone knows where it is. People sharpened their knives and spears on it before.

"People say that it returned after being dropped in the ocean. And people think that it will return this time. It is a person.

"In the old days, people worshipped this rock.

"*Jurōk* was done here. Only at this place. *Jurōk* is a special method of fishing. It consists of blocking the exit to a bay with people holding palm branches in the water, and catching the fish as the water goes out with the tide.

---

1. Ep figures in other Marshallese stories. Could it perhaps be Yap, also a distant land, far to the west of the Marshall Islands?

2. Naṃo is in Rālik, the western chain of the Marshalls.

3. Aur is in Ratak, the eastern chain of the Marshalls.

"This special fishing was done once or twice a year. And all of the people of the atoll helped. Ordinary fishing was allowed the rest of the year.

"There were many fish at this place.

"There was an old taboo *(mǫ)* rule in the Marshall Islands that no woman could look at an *irooj eṃṃaan* (a commoner *[kajoor]* married to a chiefess *[lerooj]*). But at this place (where the rock was) any woman could look at him or flirt with him, or take his fish from the waistband of his loincloth, where he had tucked them.

"Men could look at or flirt with the *lerooj* as well at this time.

"The ṛules against sexual intercourse did not change at this place, however."

This licensed familiarity is similar to the relaxation of the rules of conduct at the site of Liwātuonmour on Naṃo.

There the custom of *badikdik* (bowing down) was waived, as noted.

I heard the story of Liwātuonmour and Lidepdepju from several other Marshallese. It is obviously a very important part of the oral history of the Marshallese people.

The meddlesome, iconoclastic, and officious Dr. Rife was outwitted and squelched by Iroojļapļap Kabua in another matter, Jǫwej said. (We were talking about the chiefs of the Marshall Islands.)

"Kabua and Litōkwa were involved in a dispute over land. And Dr. Rife came to Jālooj (uninvited) to settle this trouble.

"While the two chiefs were discussing the matter, Kabua called Dr. Rife to come closer to them. (Dr. Rife had said 'I will settle your trouble. Divide your land between yourself and Litōkwa'.)

"Kabua replied: 'Where is your money?' Dr. Rife asked: 'Why?' Kabua answered: 'I think it would be best for you to divide your money with me'."

"Dr. Rife departed in haste."

Jǫwej concluded that Kabua was a very shrewd man—much more so than the American missionary. (Obviously so, judging from this incident, one could say.)

6: LIWĀTUONMOUR

As told by Litarjikūt Kabua and interpreted by Jetñil Felix, Mājro 1951

She was a goddess. She helped the people. She was on Naṃo Atoll, on Naṃo Island. She lived there all the time.

All the *irooj* (chiefs) got sick or died. They were taken to Naṃo and brought to her. Everyone got together around the dead or sick *irooj* and sang a song to the spirit. After the people sang the song, the *irooj* recovered. (*Pinek* is the name of that song.) There was no medicine. They sang and laughed.

She [Liwātuonmour] was *ṇakṇōk in irooj*.[1] Some say that people say that she was the mother of the *irooj*. But they do not know. Most of the *irooj* do not know this (in Ratak). This is a Northern Rālik story.

She was a guardian of the people [and] brought *irooj* back to life. She is not here now.

The stone pillar, (Liwātuonmour) the stone, was on Naṃo. A missionary came to Rọñrọñ [island on Mājro Atoll]. Some old men went to Rọñrọñ and told him the story (of Liwātuonmour). And he went to Naṃo and threw the stone into the ocean. The people of Naṃo were angry and surprised at his act.

The stone had helped them very much in getting food and so forth.

The missionary, Rife, sailed to Kosrae. A storm arose in between. An old Marshallese man told Rife, "There is an old custom. If you take a stone or something from an island, something will happen to us. If you throw the stone into the ocean, we will all be all right."

Rife threw the stone away and the weather calmed down.

The place of Liwātuonmour remains the same even if sand is still placed on it, it drifts away.

There was only one stone, not two.

The story was told to me years ago by Ļowa, an old *irooj*.

---

1. The most powerful, highest chief. The chief of chiefs.

7: THE STORY OF LIWĀTUONMOUR AND LIDEPDEPJU

As told by Ļamān and Jekkein, Mājro 1955

The *out* of Rālik is Naṃo. It is the place of the *irooj eļap* (paramount chiefs). The *out* of Ratak is Mājro and is likewise the place of the paramount chiefs.[1]

There are only two *out* in the Marshall Islands.

Bōke-eņ *wāto* (land parcel) is the *out wāto* on Mājro Island, Mājro Atoll. And Libuojar *wāto* is the *out wāto* on Naṃo Island, Naṃo Atoll.

Libuojar *wāto* is important because the high power Liwātuonmour once lived there.

Liwātuonmour and her sister Lidepdepju came to the Marshall Islands long, long ago from the land of Uap in the west in a canoe.

They landed on Ero Island in Kuwajleen Atoll. All of the *jowi* (clans) in the Marshall Islands came from those two women on Ero Island. After a while, they left Ero. Liwātuonmour went to Naṃo Atoll, and Lidepdepju went to Aur Atoll.[2]

Liwātuonmour was the *dekā* (stone) located on Libuojar *wāto* on Naṃo Island. When walking on Libuojar *wāto,* one does not have to *badikdik* (bow down when passing in front of people), even to the *irooj.* Because the higher power, Liwātuonmour, once lived there.

In the olden days and even today, this exception to the rule of homage and respect to the *irooj* is observed.

The people worshipped Liwātuonmour and made offerings of food and mats to her.

Then the missionaries came to the Marshall Islands. Dr. Rife came to Naṃo and threw the stone (Liwātuonmour) into the ocean. The people had told him, "If you move the stone, your ship (Morning Star) will be destroyed."

---

1. Interesting and valuable information was frequently uncovered when unfamiliar words contained in *roro* 'chants' were explained to me. For example, the explanation for the word *out* used in one of the *roro in lañ* 'weather forecasting chants' led to "The Roro of Lijiruk" by informant Ļamān, which revealed the story of the *out* of Rālik and the *out* of Ratak. *"The Roro of Lijiruk Tokkanwut: N̄un̄ur Lijiruk kolañin | Ekni ioon āne wut im lañin Joon | Ej ejarakrak ekni ioon out!"* (The sound [thunder] of Lijiruk [goes along the sky] | Joon is sailing| Look along the *out* [important place of the *irooj* (chief)].) (*N̄e jourur ejañ* 'if it thunders' is *ekni* in Kajin Lañ 'the language of weather', and *kolañin* is 'it goes in the sky.' Joon was an *irooj* of long ago.)

2. I had previously heard the legend of the two sisters who came from the land of Ep or Uap from other informants, and similar versions are to be found in Erdland (1914:35), Mason (1947:32), and Spoehr (1949:78). One is tempted to find a parallel or to identify the land of Ep/Uap with Yap in the western Carolines, and the two stone pillars are apparently symbolic of the ancestral founders of Marshallese matriclans, but this is just speculation, of course.

Although the rock *(dekā)* was thrown into the sea many years ago, the story is still known on Naṃo or was when I visited there in 1951. I was shown the place on Libuojar *wāto* (land parcel) where Liwātuonmour formerly lived. The *deka* was described to me by Dwight Heine, who was with me at the time, as about one foot in height and dark colored (basalt? Yap is of volcanic origin and is partially basaltic). I was also told about the exception to the custom of *badikdik* 'deeply bowing down before the chiefs' in honor of Liwātuonmour, the spirit who once dwelled on this spot. This is still respected, I was told, only at this place. It is indeed unfortunate, to say the least, that a possible clue to the origin of the Marshallese people has been lost because of the misguided action of an overly zealous missionary. He was obviously trying to eliminate the competition.

Dr. Rife wanted to prove this warning false, so he went ahead with his original plans and removed the stone and threw it into the deep water off Naṃo Atoll. However, nothing happened to his ship.

(I studied the Bible under Dr. Rife.)

People used to worship Lidepdepju also. (*Ruprup* means to destroy and throw away. And *Li-* is the feminine prefix.) She is still on Aur Island in Aur Atoll.

[Ḷamān then chanted the following *roro:*]

"Luerkolik ej ño diun ña duireañ | Lidepdepju erbet inij eo." (Luerkolik [a reef in Arṃo Atoll lagoon, close to Tutu Island] is destroying me [in the canoe] because of my sin to Lidepdepju. Is destroying all of us. Lidepdepju is destroying the fleet [of canoes].)

There is a reason for the spirits to destroy people, but I do not know why myself.

Luerkolik is like a person, a woman: same size and appearance and physically is the reef, a large coral head. But she can appear to people in the shape of a woman.

There are many *ekjab* (indwelling spirits throughout the Marshalls, for example:

Ḷalukluk: a male *ekjab* (spirit) near Ujae. West of the main island *(eonene)* in the lagoon.

Ḷatarbwin: a male *ekjab* in the lagoon near Bok Island.

Likōttarbok: A female *ekjab* in the lagoon near Bok Island.

Liñijiḷọk: A female *ekjab* in the lagoon near Bok Island.

Laranbok: A female *ekjab,* a *bar* (hillock) on Bok Island.

Ekjab are like people in appearance at the times of their appearance to humans.

Roro of Likōttarbok: *"Tartar iere | kominro kōttarbok."* (Sail to the east, sit on the center platform. | All of you wait for the sand [beach] of the island.) [*Kōttar* means 'wait', and *bok* means sand or beach.]

Roro of Liñijiḷọk: *"Merik Liñijiḷọk | jenme kotto eo."* (Pay homage to Liñijiḷọk | so that she will bring forth [create] good winds.)

Laranbok (also on Roñdik) is a *barulep* [*Birgus latro,* coconut crab.] But it is all red, not partly brown, and so forth, like ordinary crabs. (It looks like a cooked crab.)

If it appears on Roñdik, perhaps an *irooj* (chief) will die.[3] People have seen this *ekjab.*

Roro of Laranbok: *"Lakaketok maañ eo an Laranbok. | Likit ṇa i kubaak akake wa in."* (Hurry up and bring the *maañ* 'prepared pandanus leaves' of Laranbok so that this canoe will swim.) (That is, make a sail for the canoe from pandanus. Bring it to the canoe and hoist it. Sails were made of pandanus in the olden days.)

---

3. This belief is an obvious indication of the importance attached to the chiefs by the Marshallese. An analogous belief but without a specific spirit involved was prevalent in Hawai'i: "When abnormally large schools of certain fish especially the alalauwa and moi and uiui were seen, they were regarded as omens of some unusual event, sometimes a change of power among the high chiefs, but usually death" (Titcomb 1952:45). A legend from Hawai'i, over two thousand miles northeast of the Marshalls, also tells of two women who voyaged from the west, from Kuaihelani, a land far distant in the west. "In the dirge of Kahahana it is the land of the deified dead. . . . It lies to the west, for two chiefesses who travel thence voyage eastward to Hawai'i; after a voyage of forty days the sweet smell of kiele flowers hails their approach to its shores" Beckwith (1970:79). There are obvious similarities with the Marshallese tale of Liwātuonmour and Lidepdepju. And this may be a clue to the migration route of the ancient voyagers of the Pacific.

8: ABOUT A WOMAN NAMED LŌKTAÑŪR

As told by Jelibōr Jam, Kuwajleen 1975

This woman had eleven or twelve children, boys. These boys grew older and looked out for each other very well and obeyed their mother Lōktañūr.[1]

When they became young men, they began to think that they should each build a canoe.

When the canoes were finished, they decided together that they should arrive at the east [race to the east] and that the one who arrived there first would be the chief.

These canoes did not have sails but were only paddling canoes. One day they took the canoes seaward to the ocean so that they should paddle and arrive at the east.

And their mother came with a big bundle wrapped up in mats. (The reason it was a big bundle was because the booms and the sail and the mast and the lines—the lines of the sail—and the cleats for the lines and the rest of the sail, and the posts for the lines and the halyards were in it.)

And her sons were afraid to take their mother aboard. And their mother came to where their canoes were and carried the big bundle on her shoulder, and said, "Take me aboard, Tūm̧ur."[2] (Tūm̧ur was the oldest.) Now Tūm̧ur said to his mother, "Ride in Mājlep's canoe." Lōktañūr said to Mājlep, "Take me aboard, Mājlep." Now Mājlep said, "Ride in L̦ōbōl's canoe."

Now the old woman said, "Take me aboard, L̦ōbōl." L̦ōbōl said, "Ride in Jāpe's canoe." The old woman said, "Take me aboard, Jāpe." Jāpe said, "Ride in L̦ōmejdikdik's canoe." The old woman said, "Take me aboard, L̦ōmejdikdik." L̦ōmejdikdik said, "Ride in Jitata's canoe." The old woman said, "Take me aboard, Jitata." Jitata said, "Ride in L̦ak's canoe."

The old woman said, "Take me aboard, L̦ak." L̦ak said, "Ride in Jeljelimkouj's canoe." The old woman said, "Take me aboard, Jeljelimkouj." Now Jeljelimkouj said, "Ride in L̦ōkañebar's canoe." The old woman said, "Take me aboard, L̦ōkañebar." L̦ōkañebar said, "Ride in L̦āātbwiinbar's canoe." The old woman said, "Take me aboard, L̦āātbwiinbar." L̦āātbwiinbar said, "Ride in Jebro̧'s canoe."[3] The old woman said, "Take me aboard, Jebro̧." Jebro̧ said, "Come, my mother, and ride!"

His mother said, "My child, Jebro̧, nevermind if you cannot be chief, for you are just the youngest." Jebro̧ said, "Yes."

Now Tūm̧ur, the oldest man, said, "Paddle now." Now everyone paddled. Only Jebro̧ remained and did not paddle. But the old woman took her bundle seaward and said to Jebro̧—the word that the old woman said, "Well, bring the sail and load the mast aboard and erect it.

"Take a line ahead to the forward part of the canoe there. The name of that line is 'Jo̧m̧ur'. Take a line to the after part of the canoe. The name of all of these lines is 'Jo̧m̧ur'. Take a line to the outrigger float. The name of that line is 'To-kubaak'. Now 'Jerak' is the name of the line forward (the line to raise the sail).

"Well, put on the cleats. One aft and one

---

1. Alpha Aurigae (Capella)
2. Alpha Scorpio (Antares)
3. See comments on page 58 for identity of Jebro̧ and his canoe.

forward. And put on the posts. One forward and one aft.

"My son, are those things completed?" Jebrǫ replied, "Everything is completed." His mother said, "Well, launch that canoe. Now ride." And Jebrǫ boarded the canoe and rode it. And his mother said, "Pull in the line of the sail to tack." They tacked. And the canoe sped ahead and passed Tūm̧ur's canoe.

Tūm̧ur said, "Give me your canoe, Jebrǫ." Jebrǫ said, "Mother, why does my older brother say [that I should] give him this canoe?" His mother said, "It is good to give him this canoe. But take the forward cleat and the after post."

And they (Lōktañūr and Jebrǫ) came close to Tūm̧ur's canoe and boarded it and rode on in it (after they exchanged canoes). And Tūm̧ur went to the canoe that had been Jebrǫ's. And Tūm̧ur pulled the line taut to tack, and the canoe went very fast running to the south.

But Jebrǫ and his mother were not paddling yet, and his mother brought out a fish from within her purse and said to Jebrǫ, "Place that fish in front of the canoe so that it will run to the east."

Jebrǫ placed the fish there and the canoe ran to the east, to the island to which they were racing. Tūm̧ur's canoe was fast, but tacked off course from side to side for a long time and was slow, because Jebrǫ had taken the other cleat and the other post (because there was only one of each now on the canoe). And Tūm̧ur was slow in reaching the island. But Jebrǫ went on and reached the east before all of his older brothers arrived. A huge wave came and took Jebrǫ's canoe and carried it to the middle of the coconut trees.

And Jebrǫ and his mother disembarked from the canoe and went inland and stayed in a house. And his mother made a very good skirt for Jebrǫ. It was made from *atat* [*Triumfetta procumbens* forst.].

And Jebrǫ did not move around or walk about, but remained in the house.

A few days later, Tūm̧ur's canoe arrived. When he came, there were no footprints in the sand of the island. And Tūm̧ur said, "Oh, men"—he was speaking to the two men in his canoe—"I alone am chief, for no one has reached the island. For there are no footprints of people, just white sand crabs."

Tūm̧ur now stood in front and Jebrǫ came to the lagoon. The skirt that Jebrǫ was wearing was very good. And he brought the bottom part of a pandanus fruit in his hands and gave it to Tūm̧ur, because he honored him. (According to the custom of honoring, you do not give the top part to a chief, only the bottom part.)

Tūm̧ur was angry with Jebrǫ and said to Jebrǫ, "The back of my head to you, younger brother." (This means, "I do not want to see your face.")

Now Tūm̧ur said, *"Reje Tūm̧ur im leto, n̄ōn̄ati. Mājlep ej bun̄."* ("Load up. Tūm̧ur takes it to the west, a big wind. *Mājlep* has come down.") (In the ancient language *reje* is 'load aboard', *leto* is 'take to the west', and *n̄ōn̄ati* is 'big wind'.)

After Tūm̧ur had spoken these words, there was a very big wind and waves! Like [a] typhoon. And the people in the canoes, Tūm̧ur's younger brothers, suffered greatly, because Tūm̧ur said there would be big wind and waves.

And Jebrǫ was sorry about this and said, *"Jebrǫ ededle rear. Ekōm̧anm̧an aejet. Eeǫkwe armej."* ("Jebrǫ has come to the east. He calms the ocean. He loves the people.") (In the ancient language, *ededle* is 'came' and *aejet* is 'on the ocean'.)

Now there were no waves and no wind, and the older brothers were very happy with Jebrǫ and went with him to see what Tūm̧ur's thoughts were. When they got there, Tūm̧ur was very angry and said, "Whoever loves me, well, he should come here with me. But if you love Jebrǫ, well, go with him." And only Jeljelimkouj and Ļōkañebar and Ļāātbwiinbar loved Jebrǫ. But Mājlep and Ļōbōl and Jāpe loved Tūṃur.

Ļōmejdikdik and Jitata and Ļak did not know where to go, because they were sorry for Tūṃur, but they were sorry for Jebrǫ, and they stayed in the middle.

At this time, when it was clear to all the people and all the fish and the birds in the sky that Jebrǫ was chief, they were very happy about what Jebrǫ had said, "Jebrǫ has arrived at the east. He calms the sea. He loves people."

And all the living things came to honor him. (In the ancient language, *jorek* means to honor, to pay homage to a chief, and to give happiness.) And only two living things did not go to honor Jebrǫ. In the ocean, a fish called *aol,* and a bird named *le.* And Jebrǫ rejected them and they suffered misfortune. (*Kaliaiki* means 'reject' in the ancient language.)

The *le,* if it flies and sees the leaves on the island, dies. The *aol,* if he swims downward a little, will be eaten by fish. If he swims upward, he will be eaten by the birds.

And all of the people were very happy at the time when Jebrǫ was in the east, because everything was good.

And Tūṃur and some men were angry and went away from Jebrǫ in the wintertime. And Ļōmejdikdik and two young men went away from Jebrǫ between winter and summer. (In the ancient language *kōtōboņboņ in rōk* [means] 'between winter and summer, in the middle'.)

And Jebrǫ and some young men went in the summer, and all of the people and every living thing.

And when Jebrǫ comes in the east, the thoughts of the people and everything are good.

(The reason this story appeared was because it is an example concerning humility, just as Jebrǫ was humble.)

The stars are in the sky now. And all of the brothers are in the sky. And Lōktañūr.

Thus Lōktañūr said.

(The reason the men—Tūṃur, Mājlep, and all of the younger brothers of Tūṃur—did not load her on their canoes was because their mother had a big bundle, and they did not have one. And they did not want to take it on their canoes, and perhaps lose.)

Comments

Jebrǫ is the Pleiades (The Seven Sisters of Greek mythology), a constellation called Jeleilōñ in the Ratak chain. The ancient Greeks believed that "the Pleiades were daughters of Atlas, and nymphs of Diana's train. One day Orion saw them and became enamoured and pursued them. In their distress, they prayed to the Gods to change their form, and Jupiter in pity turned them into pigeons, and then made them a constellation in the sky. Though their number was seven, only six stars are visible . . ." (Bulfinch 1978:206).

"The Polynesian year, as stated by Ellis, Fornander, Morenhout, and others, was regulated by the rising of the Pleiades, as the month of Makali'i began when the constellation rose at sunset, i.e., about November 20" (Malo 1976:36 nn.). Beckwith (1970:367–368) discusses the legends associated with the Pleiades in Hawaiian and other Polynesian cultures. Canoe racing, sibling rivalry, and rejection of a mother do not figure in the legends, which vary from one Polynesian culture to another. In old Hawai'i, Beckwith explains, "not only is

Aldebaran, traditional steering star from Hawaii-Loa, named Makali'i (Na-hui-hui-a-Makali'i) or nets of Makali'i (Na-koko-a-Makali'i). 'Makali'i's rainbow-colored gourd-net hangs above' (Huihui-koko-a-makali'i-kau-iluna) is the saying." Makali'i (eyes of the chief) was the chief navigator of Hawaii-Loa, the discoverer and the settler of the Hawaiian islands, according to Hawaiian legend (363).

The Pleiades (and other heavenly bodies) were used by Polynesian and Micronesian navigators to reach their often-distant destinations.

8: KŌN JUON KŌRĀ ETAN LŌKTAÑŪR

Ri-bwebwenato: Jelibōr Jam, Kuwajleen 1975

Kōrā in eor joñoul-juon ke ak joñoul-ruo nājin ļaddik. Ļadik rein raar rūttoļǫk im kanooj eṃṃan aer lale doon kab pokake ainikien jineer Lōktañūr.[4]

Ke rej likao ej jino juon ļōmņak ippāer bwe ren kajjo wa in jekjek. Ke ej ṃōj wa ko rej pepe ippān doon bwe ren kōttōpar rear bwe eo ej tōpare enaaj irooj.

Wa kein ejjeļǫk wōjļā[ier] ak waan aōņōōņ wōt. Juon raan rej bōk metoļǫk wa ko ñan lǫjet bwe ren aōņōōņ im kōttōpar rear.

Innām jineer ej itok kōn juon jepjep ļapļap. (Wūnin an ļap jepjep in kōnke rojak kab wōjļā kab kiju kab to ko—toon wōjļā eo—kab dipākāāk kab jidukli kab iep in wōjļā ak li.)

Innām likao ro nājin remijak in ektake jineer. Innām jineer ej itok ñan ānein wa ko im ineek jepjep eo an im ba, "Ektake eō, Tūṃur."[5] (Erūttotata Tūṃur.) Kiiō Tūṃur ej ba ñan jinen, "Kwōn pād in uwe i waan Mājlep." Lōktañūr eba ñan Mājlep, "Ektake eō, Mājlep." Kiiō Mājlep ej ba, "Kwōn pād in uwe i waan Ļōbōl."

Kiiō leļļap [eo] ej ba, "Ektake eō, Ļōbōl." Ļōbōl eba, "Kwōn pād in uwe i waan Jāpe." Leļļap eo eba, "Ektake eō, Jāpe." Jāpe eba, "Kwōn pād in uwe i waan Ļōmejdikdik." Leļļap eo eba, "Ektake eō, Ļōmejdikdik." Ļōmejdikdik eba, "Kwōn pād in uwe i waan Jitata."

Leļļap eo eba, "Ektake eō, Jitata." Jitata ar ba, "Kwōn pād in uwe i waan Ļak." Leļļap eo ar ba, "Ektake eō, Ļak." Ļak eba, "Kwōn pād in uwe i waan Jeljel-im-kouj."

Kiiō Jeljel-im-kouj eba, "Kwōn pād in uwe i waan Ļōkañebar." Leļļap eo eba, "Ektake eō, Ļōkañebar." Ļōkañebar eba, "Kwōn pād in uwe i waan Ļāātbwiinbar." Leļļap eo eba, "Ektake eō, Ļāātbwiinbar."

Ļāātbwiinbar eba, "Kwōn pād in uwe i waan Jebrǫ."[6]

Leļļap eo eba, "Ektake eō, Jebrǫ." Jebrǫ eba, "Itok jinō im uwe!"

Jinen eba, "Nājū Jebrǫ, jekdǫǫn ñe kwōjjab irooj bwe diktata bajjek." Jebrǫ eba, "Iññā."

Kiiō Tūṃur, ļeo erūttotata, ej ba, "Aōņōōņ kiiō." Kiiō aolep aōņōōņ. Jebrǫ wōt ej pād im jab aōņōōņ. Ak leļļap eo ej

4. Alpha Aurigae (Capella)

5. Alpha Scorpio (Antares)

6. The Pleiades ("Jiljilimjuon Jemjān Jemjatin Kōrā Ro") ilo bwebwenato an Ri-Kriik (Ri-Greek) ro etto-im-etto). Ilo Ratak rej ņaetan Jeleilōñ. Ej juon bukun iju.

bōk metoļǫk jepjep eo im ba ñan Jebrǫ. Naan eo leļļap eo ej ba, "Ekwe bōkwōj wōjļā em ektakewōj kiju e im kajutake. Bōkwōj juon to ŋa iṃaan wa ŋe tujabdik. Etan to ŋe, 'Jǫṃur'. Bōkļǫk juon to ŋa i tujabļap. Etan to kein aolep, 'Jǫṃur'. Bokļǫk juon to ŋa i kubaak. Etan to ŋe 'Tokubaak'. Kiiō 'jerak' etan to ŋe iṃaan (to in kanōk wōjļā).

"Ekwe kōṃṃane dipāākāk ko. Juon iwajebļap im juon i wajabdik. Kōṃṃane jirukli ko. Juon wajebdik, juon wajebļap.

"Nājū, eṃōj ke men kaŋe?" Jebrǫ eba, "Eṃōj aolep." Jinen eba, "Ekwe bwillǫke wa ŋe. Kiiō uwe." Innām Jebrǫ euwe. Innām jinen eba, "Ŋatoon kiiō." Eļak ŋatoon eļōñjak wa eo em ettōr em joļǫk ŋe wa im ioon wa eo waan Tūṃur.

Tūṃur eba, "Letok ŋe waō, Jebrǫ." Innām Jebrǫ eba, "Jinō, etke jeiū ej ba leļǫk in waan?" Jinen eba, "Eṃṃan leļǫk in waan. Ak kwōn bōk dipāākāk ŋe i tujabdik kab jidukli ŋe i tujabļap."

Innām rejro (Lōktañūr im Jebrǫ) kepaaktok wa eo waan Tūṃur em uwe ie. (Eṃōj aer jānij wa ko.) Ak Tūṃur etal ñan wa eo kar waan Jebrǫ. Innām Tūṃur eŋatoon em wa eo ekanooj in ṃōkaj an tōbtōb rōñaļǫk. Ak Jebrǫ im jinen rejro ejjañin aōŋōōŋ innām jinen ej kwaļǫktok juon ek jān lowaan iep eo an em ba ñan Jebrǫ, "Kwōn likūt ek ŋe ŋa i ṃaan wa in. Bwe in ettōr kake ñan rear."

Jebrǫ ej ṃōj wōt an likūti ek eo [ak] ettōr wa eo ñan rear, āneo rej kōttōpare. Ak wa eo waan Tūṃur eṃōkaj ak eto an jeje. Eruṃwij kōnke [eṃōj] an Jebrǫ bōk dipāākāk eo juon kab jidukli eo juon. (Kōnke juon wōt.)

Innām eruṃwij an Tūṃur tōprak āne. Ak Jebrǫ etal im tōpar rear ṃokta jān aolep ļōṃaro jein ke rej tōprakļǫk.

Eitok juon ŋo kileplep em bōk wa eo waan Jebrǫ em bōkļǫk ŋa iuṃwin ni ko.

Innām Jebrǫ im jinen rōto jān wa [eo] em wōnǫǫjļǫk em pād iṃōko. Innām jinen ej kōṃṃane juon an Jebrǫ in, ekanooj in eṃṃan. Kōṃṃan jān atat. Innām Jebrǫ ejjab ṃakūtkūt im etetal ak pād wōt iṃweo. Ļǫkun juon raan epotok waan Tūṃur. Eļak itok ejjeļǫk jenkwan ne ioon bok in āneo.

Innām Tūṃur ej ba, "Io ļōṃa" (ej konono ñan ļōṃaro ruo ioon wa eo waan), "Ña wōt irooj bwe ejjeļǫk juon enañin tōpartok āniin. Bwe ejjeļǫk jenkwan neen armej kab karuk."

Tūṃur ejja jutak wōt iṃaan wa eo waan ak ej wōnartak Jebrǫ. Ekanooj in eṃṃan in eo Jebrǫ ej kōŋaktok. Ak ioon pein Jebrǫ ej bōktok juon ajbok in bōb im leļǫk ñan Tūṃur. Kōnke ej kautiej e. (Ilo ṃantin kautiej kwōjjab leļǫk ṃak ñan irooj ak ajbok wōt.)

Tūṃur ellu ippān Jebrǫ im ba ñan Jebrǫ, "Meja wōt kapin bōra ñan kwe jatū." (Meļeļein: Ijjab kōŋaan loe mejaṃ.)

Kiiō Tūṃur eba, "Reje Tūṃur im leto, ñōñati Mājlep ej buñ." (Ilo kajin etto *reje* ej 'ektake' im *leto* ej 'bōkļǫk turilikin'. Im *ñōñati* ej 'eļap kōto'.)

Ej ṃōj wōt an Tūṃur ba naan in ak ekanooj in ļap kōto im ŋo! (Āinwōt taibuun.) Innām armej ro ioon wa ko, ļōṃaro jatin Tūṃur, rōkanooj eñtaan kōn an kar Tūṃur ba en ļap kōto im ŋo.

Innām Jebrǫ ej būroṃōj kake er im ba, "Jebrǫ ededle rear. Ekōṃanṃan aejet. Eeǫkwe armej." (Ilo kajin etto *ededle* ej 'eaar itok' im *aejet* ej 'ioon lǫjet'.)

Kiiō ejjeļǫk ŋo. Ejjeļǫk kōto. Im ļōṃaro jein rekanooj in ṃōŋōŋō ippān Jebrǫ em etal wōt ippān im lale ta an Tūṃur ļōmŋak. Ke rej ilǫk ekanooj in ļap an Tūṃur illu, em ba, "Jabdewōt ej iǫkwe eō, ekwe en itok ippa tok. Ak ñe koṃ iǫkwe Jebrǫ, ekwe koṃin etal ippān ļǫk." Innām Jeljelimkouj kab Ļōkañebar kab Lāātbwiinbar wōt rej iǫkwe Jebrǫ. Ak Mājlep kab Ļōbōl kab Jāpe reeǫkwe Tūṃur.

Ļōmejdikdik kab Jitata kab Ļak rejaje rej etal iaļǫk. Kōnke rōburoṃōj kōn Tūṃur ak rōburoṃōj kōn Jebrǫ. Innām rej pād ioļap.

Iien in ke alikkar an Jebrọ irooj ippān armej otemjej kab ek otemjej kab bao in mejatoto rōkanooj in ļap aer m̧ōņōņō kōn an kar Jebrọ ba, "Jebrọ ededle rear. Ekōm̧anm̧an aejet. Eeọkwe armej."

Innām aolep men kein otemjej raar jorek. (Ilo kajin etto *jorek* ej 'kautiej', 'kairooj', 'leļọk m̧ōņōņō'.) Innām ruo wōt iaan menninmour raar jab ilān jorek Jebrọ. Ilo lọjet juon ek etan aol. Kab juon bao etan le. Innām Jebrọ eaar kaliaiki, innām rejerata bajjek. (Ilo kajin etto *kaliaki* ej āinwōt 'joļọk jān ļōmņak' ak 'kajekdọọn'.) Le eņ ñe ej kātok im lo bwilikōn āne, emej.

Aol eņ eļaññe ej wanlaļļọk jidik, ek enaaj kañe. Eļak wanlōñļọk, bao eloe im kañe.

Im aolep armej rekanooj in m̧ōņōņō ilo iien in Jebrọ ej pād i rear kōnke em̧m̧an men otemjej. Ak Tūm̧ur im ļōm̧aro jet rellu im rej etal jān Jebrọ ilo añōneañ. Ak Ļōmejdikdik im likao ro ruo rej etal jān Jebrọ ilo kōtōboņboņ im rak. (Ilo kajin etto meļeļe in *kōtōboņboņ* ej 'kōtaan añōneañ im rak; ioļap'.)

Ak Jebrọ im likao ro jet rej etal ilo rōk kab aolep armej im mennin mour otemjej.

Innām ñe ej tak Jebrọ i rear, em̧m̧an an armej ļōmņak kab mennin mour otemjej.

(Wūnin an waļọk bwebwenato in kōnke ej menin jemān-āe ñan jabdewōt kōn ettā būro. Āinwōt Jebrọ ar ettā bōro.)

Iju [kein] repād i lañ kiiō. Im aolep ro jein im jātin repād i lañ. Kab Lōktañūr.

Āinwōt Ļainjin ar ba.

(Wūnin [an] ļōm̧aro Tūm̧ur, Mājlep, im aolep ļōm̧aro jātin Tūm̧ur jab ektake jineer ioon wa ko waer kōnke eļap jepjep eo ippān. Im ejjeļọk ippāer. Im rej jab kōņaan bōk men eo ioon wa ko waer. Im maroñ luuj.)

9: THE STORY OF LŌKTAÑŪR

As told by Rev. Pijja Matauto, Kuwajleen 1975

Lōktañūr was the mother and is a constellation *(bukun iju)*—a specific constellation. Tūm̧ur was the eldest brother, also a constellation (The Big Dipper or *Waan Tūm̧ur* 'Tūm̧ur's Canoe').

Jebrǫ was the younger brother and was also a constellation (The Pleiades). This is called Jeļeilōñ in both Rālik and Ratak.

The brothers were competitive in life. They became star constellations. One cannot rise without the other. This started with a canoe race. Lōktañūr asked a number of her sons to take her from Jebat Island to Je, Aelōñļapļap. All refused except the youngest son, Jebrǫ.

The others refused because the canoes were full and they thought they would lose.

Jebrǫ took her anyway and she showed him how to handle sails. She deceived Tūm̧ur so the sail was let go by Jebrǫ and Tūm̧ur's back was broken.

All of them, canoes and all, went into the sky and you can see them today. Jebrǫ in the east is a sign of good luck; good crops, breadfruit, et cetera. And calm seas. All good things.

Comments

Reverend Matauto is the pastor of the Protestant Church on Ebeye (Epjā) Island on Kuwajleen Atoll. He is in his early thirties and is fluent in English, in which he told me this folktale.

In another explanation of the origin of the Pleaides, from Mangaia in Polynesia, to the southeast of the Marshalls, the story says: "The Pleiades were originally one star, and so brilliant that Tane was angry. He got Sirius and Aldebaran to help him and pursued Matariki, who fled behind a stream. Sirius drained the waters dry and Tane flung Aldebaran and broke Matariki into six small pieces" (Beckwith 1970: 368).

As Leach (1950, 2:874–875) points out, "The Pleiades has been an important constellation to the peoples of both hemispheres from earliest times. It was well known to the early Hebrews; both Egyptian and Greek temples were dedicated to its rising . . . .

"Almost everywhere in the world the rising of these stars is significant as marking the beginning of a new year and is celebrated with feasts, rejoicing, and special rites."

10: STORY ABOUT JEBWA

As told by Jelibōr Jam, Kuwajleen 1975

The meaning of the word *jebwa* is not clear. The *ņooniep*[1] revealed the *jebwa* to a human being on Ujae in the *ņooniep* language.

Ņooniep only knew their own language. We are not able to translate it.

The *jebwa* began in Kapinmeto, the western Marshalls area, but now all Marshallese know it, and they learned it before the white man came.

Formerly the missionaries said it was bad, because they did not know the meaning of this thing. But now perhaps they know.[2] Today *kǫṃōt* (church committee members) and *eklejia* (church members) do it.[3]

Rijek appeared at the time *ņooniep* revealed the *jebwa*. They came in from inside a pool on Epāju, Ujae [Atoll]. They were big like human beings, and had long beards. And one appeared. He was very handsome, and he did the *jebwa* and his *jebwa* was much better than that of the *ņooniep*. (When he appeared and danced, all of the women watched because his dancing was good.)

When that man finished his dancing, he dived down inside the pool and did not [re]appear.

There were many *rijek* before. They did not steal and they did not harm human beings. They helped human beings. Only one appeared.

[A group of] many *ņooniep* killed the *rijek*. He appeared [for] three days. On the third day,[4] the *ņooniep* killed him (with spears) and threw his body in the sea. And the *ņooniep* returned and [did the] *jebwa* [for] many nights.[5]

There were many [*ņooniep*] before, on all the atolls of the Marshalls. They stole many women, and returned them months later. And later they went and did not return. They lived on the island and hid from people. Their size is similar to human beings.

If human beings wrong the *ņooniep*, they [the *ņooniep*] harm them. If they are good to the *ņooniep*, they help them—like when people get fishhooks and fine mats from them.[6]

---

1. The *ņooniep* are humanoid creatures who are usually benevolent and who figure in many Marshallese folktales.

2. Note the tolerant evaluation by the informant of the intolerant Protestant missionary attitudes toward the dance.

3. Attitudes and rules have obviously changed in regard to the traditional dances. This is comparable to the history of the *hula* in Hawai'i. The New England Protestant missionaries, who later came to the Marshalls, tried to eliminate dancing, which was a very important part of Hawaiian culture. Their efforts were partially successful, but they never succeeded in eliminating the *hula*. And there has been a renaissance of this ancient art form in recent years. *Kǫṃōt* is another English loanword, from *committee*, as in *rūkoṃat* 'committee person' or 'committee man'.

4. Here again we see the ritual number three used—three times.

5. The motif is that of battles between supernatural beings, *rijek* and *ņooniep*. Perhaps this is a hazy rememberance of an actual event that occurred in the distant past, a battle between human invaders and human defenders of the island. Or a strong individual may have challenged the authorities, the chief and his supporters, only to be defeated and killed as the *ņooniep* killed the *rijek*.

6. This is analogous to the relationship between humans and little people of European folklore: the leprechauns, elves, fairies, brownies, and the like—a relationship marked by reciprocity.

Rimmenanuwe are very small people. They were in the atolls of the Marshall Islands long ago. But we do not know exactly when.[7] People do not believe in them or in *ņooniep* today. I do not believe [in them].

Comments

Stick dances, which is what the *jebwa* is, are found in many parts of the world. As Leach (1949:1082) explains: ". . . [they are] folk and ritual dances distinguished by the manipulation of sticks and staves. They are found in many parts of the world in various forms, almost always as a male prerogative."

And in Micronesia, "the Mortlock stick dances . . . have persisted to the present. In these, men take large staves and leap about, striking the sticks sharply together in fixed patterns. When performed at top speed it is considerable gymnastic exercise. A similar dance is also performed by Pingelap men. Similar dances are known in Western Micronesia" (Fischer and Fischer 1957:207).

This description is that of the *jebwa* as I have seen it done. The Marshallese performers also chant, and in one instance that I witnessed on Arņo in 1950, an old woman led the chanting and set the pace of the dancing of the male performers.

The Marshallese men dress in coconut leaf skirts and wear flower garlands *(ṃarṃar)*. And they are bare above the waist, and barefoot.

It is quite a vigorous and stirring performance that requires agility and coordination. And, using spears, it would have been an excellent exercise and stimulating device for the warriors, which may very well have been one of its functions, as well as for entertainment.

There has been a revival of the *jebwa* in recent years. The late *iroojļapļap* (paramount chief) Ļōjjeiļañ Kabua had a group. And there have been others in the post–World War II period in the Marshalls.

There was a *jebwa* contest (with other dances) sponsored by the Marshall Islands Museum (The Alele) at Mājro in 1984. This event reportedly attracted a great deal of interest by the Marshallese and bodes well for the continuance of this traditional art form.

7. The *rimmenanuwe* are analogous to the *menehune (menahune)* of Hawaiian folktales. They are obviously cognatic, and perhaps there is a historical relationship between the concept and stories of the little people of the Marshalls and those of Hawai'i and other parts of Polynesia. See Luomala (1955:123–136) for a discussion of these "little people." She points out that "other Polynesian islands have comparable bands of spirits with similar attributes but different names" (135). Stories of little people may have a common ancestoral source, or they may have been brought into the Marshalls by Hawaiian sailors on early European or American ships, or—and this seems doubtful—by native Hawaiian missionaries. The *rimmenanuwe* are obviously analogous to the little people who are known to practically every people in the world (see Leach [1949:365–366] for a discussion of this belief, and Keightley [1978] for a "World Guide" to these beings).

10: BWEBWENATO IN JEBWA

Ri-bwebwenato: Jelibōr Jam, Kuwajleen 1975

Meļeļein naan in jebwa ejjab alikkar. Ņooniep eaar kwaļọk ñan juon armej ioon Ujae ilo kajin ņooniep. Eor kajin ņooniep im kajin etto im kajin raan kein.

Ņooniep ejeļā wōt kajin eo aer. Jejjab maroñ ukote.

Jebwa ej jino i kapinmeto ak kiiō aolep ri-Ṃajeļ rejeļā. Im raar katak ṃokta jān an ripālle kar itok.

Kar ṃokta mijinede [ro] raar ba enana. Kōnke rejaje meļeļein menin. Ak kiiō bōlen rejeļā. Rainin kọṃōt im eklejia rejeļā rej kōṃṃane.

Rijek rej waļọk [aolep] iien ņooniep rej kwaļọk jebwa. Rej deļọñ jān ilowaan juon ļwe ilo Epāju, Ujae.

Rōkilep āinwōt armej. Im aetok aer kodeak. Im juon [ej] waļọk. Ekanooj wūlio. Im ej jebwa im ekanooj eṃṃan an jebwa jān ņooniep. (Ke ej waļọk im ikkure, aolep kōrā rej lale bwe eṃṃan an ikkure.)

Ke eṃōj an ikkure, ļeo ej tulọk ilowaan ļwe eo im jab [bar] waļọk.

Elōñ rijek ṃokta. Rej jab kọọt im rejjab kọkkure armej. Rej jipañ armej. Juon wōt ar waļọk.

Elōñ ņooniep raar ṃane rijek eo. Eaar waļọk jilu raan. Ilo raan eo kein kajilu, ņooniep ro raar ṃane (kōn ṃade) im joļọk ānbwin eo an ñan lọjet. Im ņooniep raar bar rọọl im jebwa elōñ boñ.

E[kar] lōñ ņooniep ṃokta ilo aolep aelōñ in Ṃajeļ. Elōñ kōrā raar kọọt, im kōrọọle ālikin allōñ. Im tokālik raar etal im jab [bar] rọọl. Raar jokwe ioon āne im ņojak jān armej. Āinwōt dettan armej. Ñe armej rej kōṃṃan bōd ñan ņooniep, rej kọkkure er. Ñe rej eṃṃan ñan ņooniep, rej jipañ er. Āinwōt ñe armej [rej] bōk kāāj im nieded jān er.

Rimmenanuwe rej armej jidikdik. Raar pād aelōñ in Ṃajeļ ṃoktaļọk. Ak lukkuun ñāāt ijaje. Armej rej jab tōmak er ak ņooniep rainin. Bar ña. Ijjab tōmak.

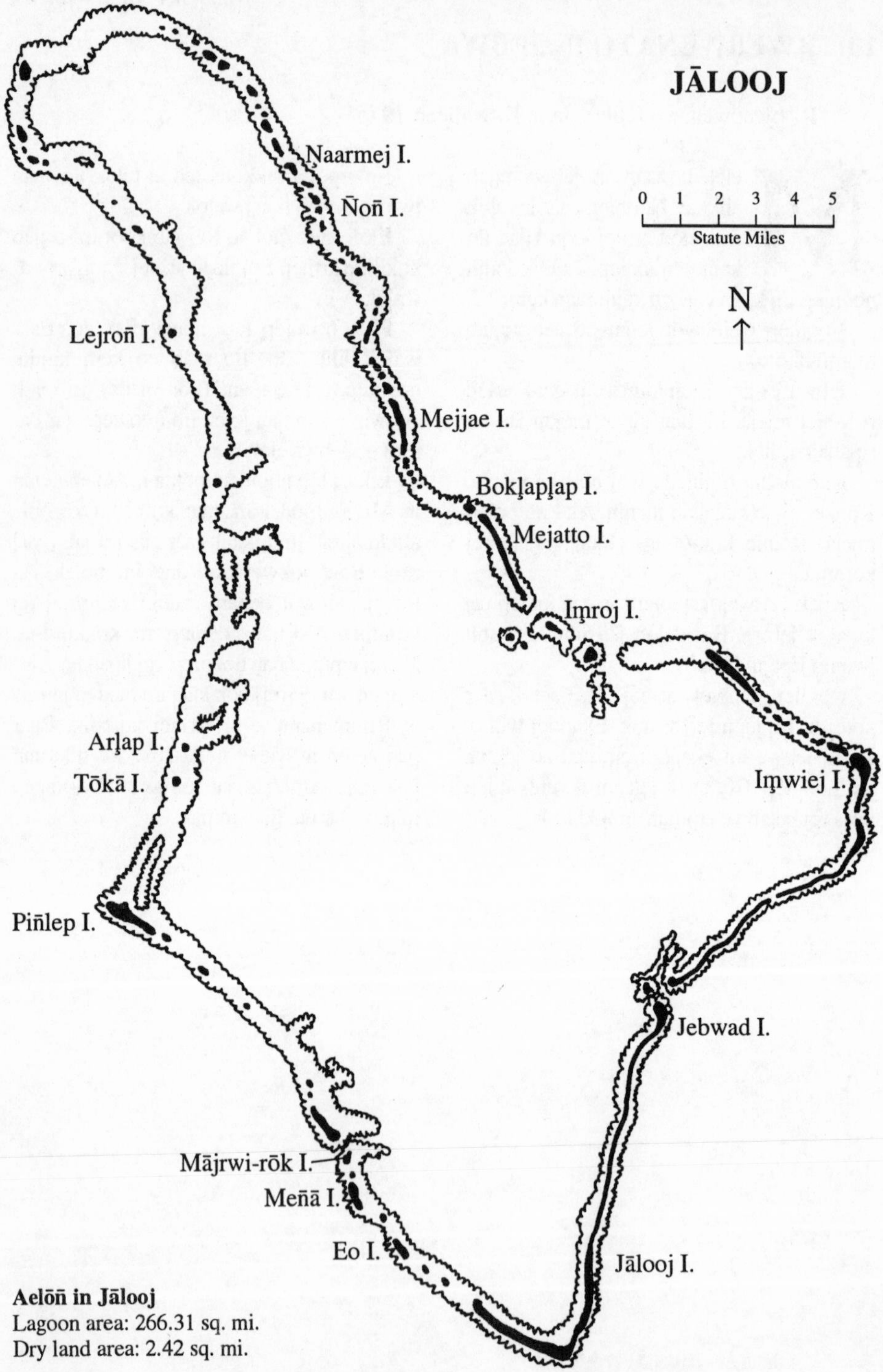

Aelōñ in Jālooj
Lagoon area: 266.31 sq. mi.
Dry land area: 2.42 sq. mi.

11: ABOUT A YOUNG MAN OF JĀLOOJ: STORY ABOUT ANIDEP

As told by Jelibōr Jam, Kuwajleen: 1975

The name of the young man was Ļōm̧aanjidep. He made an *anidep* [a small stuffed cube of plaited pandanus leaves].[1] And he took it to women of Jālooj and taught them. In the beginning, they threw [it] back and forth with their hands. Over a lot of time they learned [to play *anidep*] with their hands.

And when they became accustomed to it, the *anidep* did not land on the ground, [and] they were very good at playing with it. And they also discovered a procedure whereby if the *anidep* should fall down and fall on the ground, a person would come and seize the *anidep* and run with it.

And all the women would go with him and take the *anidep* from the person and run with it.

And Ļōm̧aanjidep also saw that men should also play with the *anidep*. (He said that men should learn now.) And the men did not play with their hands, but they played with their feet.

However, it was not like the women played, and when their playing was better, they again made people seize the *anidep* at the time it would fall. And run away with it.

When the women and men were better with their playing with the *anidep,* now the people began to go watch their playing with their *anidep.*

After some time when watching their *anidep* was more renowned and good, the daughter of the *irooj* [chief] began to go and play with the women.

And the men and women joined together and played the *anidep* with their hands.

There were many, many people in these times.

The chief's daughter would go to these games. And they made food. (All of the people on the main island of Jālooj.) And they brought it to the place of *anidep.*

After a time, they all threw the *anidep* back and forth and there were some women who beat a drum to the playing[2] (because playing was a new thing).

And the woman sang and said, *"Ļōm̧aanjidep, | item dāpļo̧ke anidep eo nājū. | Joļo̧k ñan lije uweo. | Lije uweo dāpļo̧ke. | Joļo̧k ñan ļōje uweo. | Ļōje uweo dāpļo̧ke. | Joļo̧k ñan juko eņ. | Juko, dāpiji."* ("Ļōm̧aanjidep, | come and kick up with feet or hands the *anidep* my child [my *anidep*] | Throw it to those girls over there | Those girls over there kick it | Throw it to those men over there | Those men over there kick it | Throw it to that *juko* | Juko, grab it.")

(The *juko* is the person outside [the group of players] who has been chosen by the *lerooj* [chiefess] to take the ball.)

And the *juko* took the *anidep* and ran with it. And all the people chased him. And when they caught the man, they would return to the place of *anidep.* But if they did not catch him, well, the *anidep* playing was

1. It is used in a special "ball" game which is widely spread throughout the Pacific and Southeast Asian culture areas, under different names.

2. The traditional drums (*aje*) were hourglass shaped, and carved out of breadfruit wood, with drumheads made of the skin of shark stomach. They were used for dancing, in warfare (signaling and encouraging the warriors), and apparently, as in this story, to celebrate an important event, the advent of a new game—an important occasion.

over for one day. And they [would] wait until the following day.

And they again played *anidep*. After they had played *anidep* a long while, a demon who was like a human being came to the *anidep* [game].

And the girl, the chief's daughter, when she saw the demon, she thought it was another human being. And the girl, the daughter of the chief, said to the demon, "You, you will be *juko* today."

And the demon walked outside of the people and looked [for] where the *anidep* would fall, so he could seize it and run with it.

When the *anidep* fell down, the demon came close to the *anidep*, and seized it and picked it up, and said, "Throw it to that *juko*. Juko, grab it."

And he turned and ran. When he ran, the girl, the child of the chief, ran with the demon and seized the *anidep* and brought it, and *anidep* [was] played again.

And people said to the girl, "Because you are so fast, only you can catch the young man." And they again threw the ball up.

And the women again drummed their play about the *anidep* and said, "*Ļōm̧aanjidep, | item depļǫke anidep eo nājū | Joļǫk ñan lije uweo. | Lije uweo depļǫke. | Joļǫk ñan ļōje uweo. | Ļōje uweo depļǫke. | Joļǫk ñan juko eņ. | Juko, dāpiji.*" "Ļōm̧aanjidep, | come and kick with feet or hands the *anidep,* my child. | Throw it to those girls over there. | Those girls over there kick it. | Throw it to those men over there. | Those men over there kick it. | Throw it to that *juko*. | Juko, grab it."

And the *juko* seized the *anidep* and ran; the girl, the child of the chief, ran with him. And seized the *anidep*, but because the thing was a demon, he knew very well what he should do at the time.

He did not run far. But only for a little while, in order to seize the girl.

And when the two of them were far away from the people, the demon turned around and seized the girl and ran with her to his house. And the demon was putting the girl inside his house. And when he came to put her in, it was closed. And the demon said, "*N̄iln̄il melan̄lan̄ im̧ōn anij eiō. | n̄iln̄il peļļǫke.*" (It really was closed and he could not open it. In *kajin etto,* the ancient language, *melan̄lan̄* means 'open'.) [Literal translation of the chant: "Fit tightly, open the house of the spirit there. | Fit tightly, open it."][3]

And it opened. When it opened, he put the girl inside. And he closed it again. When the house was closed, he said, "*N̄iln̄il melan̄lan̄ im̧ōn anij eiō. | N̄iln̄il kilōk.*" (Fit tightly, open the house of the spirit there. Fit tightly closed.)[4]

Now the house was closed and nothing could open it!

And now he went and told his mother that she should make a fire. "For I your child am going to pick breadfruit, our food."

And he took an implement for picking breadfruit and went and climbed up [a breadfruit tree.] When he was climbing, he greatly hoped that when he finished picking breadfruit he would descend and go pick

---

3. Note the magic password (formula) to open and to close doors. It is analogous to the motif in the story of Ali Baba and the Forty Thieves in the Arabian Nights Entertainment: "Open, O Simsim!" (or Sesame). And "Close, O Simsim!" This is a widespread folktale motif (see Leach 1949:36). Lessa (1961:334–346) discusses the "open sesame" motif and its distribution in detail. He cites its distribution in Malaysia, Melanesia, Micronesia (although he does not include a reference to it in the Marshalls), and in Polynesia. See Alpers 1970:118–129 for a story with this motif from Tahiti, in which a cave is opened by magical formula.

4. The actual meaning of many words in chants or elsewhere in the ancient language *(kajin etto)* has been lost, or is not known by the informants, so that translations may be obscure in some cases.

coconuts that would be for his mother's food.[5] When he was picking, he sang on the branch of the breadfruit tree. This is the song he sang; he said, *"N̄e ekar jab ba lieņ nājin irooj eņ eaar ba jen kōm̧ji ak mā kein kōm̧ij iuweo | Kab iuweo | Ak uweo | Ejja pād in kaļo̧ļo̧k."* "If the child of that chief had not said that we should pick these breadfruit, we would pick over there. | And over there. | Or way over there. | Just a while for them to ripen" [we have to wait for the word from the girl to pick the breadfruit].

When he finished picking, he climbed down and took the breadfruit and brought them to his mother. And his mother cooked them. When the first breadfruit were cooked, the demon went and took them and went to the side of his house and ate the sweet smell (of the girl) to the west in the house (with the breadfruit).

During the time he was eating, he smiled very much and was just happy. And when his mother saw his happiness, his mother talked to herself and said, "What is this he is happy about? I will go away and see what it is. When the demon is gone."

When the demon finished eating, he went to bring coconuts. And when the demon was gone, his mother went to the demon's house and looked at it; it was locked.

And she opened it again. When she opened it again, she said: *"N̄iln̄il im̧ōn anij eiō. | N̄iln̄il peļļo̧k!"* "Fit tightly, open the house of the spirit there. | Fit tightly, open!"

After the door was opened, the woman saw the girl, the child inside. And she was sad about it, for when the demon would return, he would come eat the girl.

And the demon's mother took the girl out of the house. And gave three *kor in ni* (old coconut shells without husks)[6] to the girl, the child of the chief. The eyes of these coconut shells were plugged up and the eyes were not open.

And when the girl took the coconut shells [containers], she said to the woman, "What are these things?" And the woman said, "You take them and run with them! And when the demon comes, I know he will search for you. For he wants very much to eat you. And when he will run toward you [next to you] to grab you, you throw one coconut shell down first.

"You will try very hard to throw it down so that the coconut shell will break."

When the demon returned and went to

---

5. The *kein kōm̧kōm̧* (thing or tool to pick breadfruit)is a long wooden pole with a smaller piece lashed to the upper end at an angle. The stems of the breadfruit are twisted by the user who stands on the ground or on lower branches of the tree. And the large, delicious, and nutritious breadfruit drop to the ground, where they are collected. Breadfruit were and to lesser extent still are an important source of food. Part of the harvest was processed and stored in pits for future use, when the breadfruit season was over. This is called *bwiro*. Breadfruit were also sun-dried and preserved as were the fruit of the pandanus, called *jāānkun* and *mokwaņ*, respectively. The tubers of the arrowroot plant (*Tacca leontepetaloides, m̧akm̧ōk*) were also processed and preserved.

These foods were vital in periods of shortages and famine caused by drought. They are less important today, as the Marshallese have become increasingly involved in a cash economy and as many have left their home atolls for the urban centers of Mājro and Epjā (Ebeye). Famine is no longer a threat because of a central government with access to food supplies from abroad, if necessary, and an improved transportation/communication system. Imported foods have become part of the regular diet of all of the Marshallese. Rice and flour are staples, and have been for many years. This change in the economic and dietary pattern has obviously brought about important changes in the social system, and has attenuated the function of the chiefs and lesser authorities in their roles as organizers, conservators, and distributors of resources.

6. These were used as containers for water, coconut oil, and the like, and also for making magic (as I have seen).

open his house, he did not look inside the house. But he put out his hand and groped for the girl, for when he seized the girl he would be very happy.[7]

But he became tired from groping, but he did not seize her.

When he did not seize her, he looked inside the house. And he searched for her. But did not see her. When he did not see her, he took his net and ran perhaps one hundred some *ñeñe* [one *ñeñe* is one fathom, or six feet]. And he met the girl. When he went to seize the girl, the girl threw down one of coconut shells.

And it broke. And *kallep* [large black ants] were scattered there. The ants were highly valued by the demon. And he cried. And again looked for coconut shells.

When he saw another coconut shell, he took it and cried. And gathered the insects and placed them inside the coconut shell. And said, *"Men jidik, men jidik ko. | Nājimro jinō kein. | Men jidik, men jidik ko ia kein?"* "Little things, little things./ These children[8] of mother and me. | Little things, little things where did they come from?"

When he finished gathering up the ants, he went to search for the girl. She had gone.

And the demon again ran. And when he met the girl, he went to grab her, but the girl again threw down another coconut shell. And the coconut shell broke and scattered ants from inside of it. And the demon again cried, and was sad about the ants, his children.

And he gathered them and said, *"Men jidik, men jidik ko. | Nājimro jinō kein. | Men jidik, men jidik ko ia kein?"* "Little things, little things. | These children of my mother and me. | Little things, little things where did they come from?"

And he gathered them inside another coconut shell, and again went to search for the girl. She had gone.

Because he wanted to eat the girl so much, he ignored his fatigue and ran to seize the girl. When he got close to the girl, he said, "I will eat you now!" [Informant laughed after he said this.] And the girl was very frightened.

Because of her fright and exhaustion, the girl stood [stopped] and cried. And the demon said, "Do not cry, friend! For I cannot do anything [to you]. For you are my child!" (He was just lying.)

When the demon came to seize the girl, the girl threw the third coconut shell. And the coconut shell broke. And ants were scattered. And the demon looked for the coconut shell to gather up the ants. But he could not find the coconut shell [lit., it was not clear that he should find the coconut shell]. And he circled there (the area) and looked for the coconut shell.

At that time, the girl's exhaustion was gone, and she tried to run.

A little while later, the demon saw a coconut shell. And he gathered up the ants, and hastened to run.

At that time, he was very close to the house of the girl and the people. And the chief, her father.

Taking no heed, the demon ran to seize the girl, for he said that he would eat her.

When he came near to the girl to seize her, the girl had no more coconut shells.

And the girl ran to the *kōņņat* [*Scaevola frutescens*, a tree], and broke off a branch and covered her chest with it.[9]

But the demon only ran and stood next to the girl and cast his net and pulled in the girl

7. Note the analogy to the Hansel and Gretel story. The motif of the cannibalistic ogre or ogress and the child/children it attempts to devour is a widespread story/motif.

8. The word *nājin* 'his/her child(ren), child(ren) of' in the Marshallese text is also used with certain classes of property to indicate ownership, which is probably the meaning in this story.

[in the net], and returned and carried her over his shoulder (in the net).

But at that time, when the demon pulled in the girl in the net, because there were many *kōņņat* branches with the girl, the branches were caught in the net and fouled it (*ļorak,* this is *kajin añkō* 'anchoring language [or terminology]' and *kajin eǫñōd* 'fishing language [or terminology]') within the net. And the girl fell out, for the demon's mother cut open the bottom of the net. For she knew that the demon would continue to carry the net. (There was a piece of wood at the top of the net that the demon was carrying over his shoulder and going [along]. But the bottom of the net was gone.)

The girl ran to her house [to be] with her father, and the demon returned and went to his house. He did not examine the net, because it was very heavy, and he thought the girl remained inside. But the branches of the *kōņņat* were the only things that were heavy within the net [weighed down the net].

When the demon reached his house, his mother came and questioned him, and said, "Where do you come from, my child?"

The demon said, "I brought these, our things from the girl, she who came and brought them, but you did not see her" (he was lying to his mother). "And [you] go and make that fire, to cook our food, for I am going to lie down a while, for I am exhausted because of that bad girl. It was not the girl, but the girl who has gone" (he lied to his mother).

And his mother said, "Where is the girl that you say, 'Because of that bad girl?' What, did you bring her here?"

The demon answered, "I did not." But he hastened to open his house and enter and close it. And he brought the net. He then examined the net. The girl was gone. And there were only *kōņņat* branches [in it]. The demon was very angry at the time and thought to go and eat his mother. But because his mother was also a demon, she knew all of his thoughts [she could read his mind].

And his mother quickly went away to Lōļlaļ [a big *wāto* (land parcel) on Jebwad Island, Jālooj Atoll, southern Marshalls]. And the demon remained in his house on Deñōjeņ [an island of Jālooj]. And the girl remained with her father on the main island of Jālooj.[10]

The story is ended.

(This is how *anidep* and *juko* began. Today there is not *juko,* only *anidep.*)[11] Because *juko* causes trouble, as the story tells. As the mother (demon) was separated from her son (demon).

The way we have played the game in these days [modern times] is like this: The players form a circle. The women use their hands, and the men use their feet. When both men and women play together, we do it the same way. The one who misses the ball (*anidep*) goes outside of the circle. [It is a process of elimination.] The one left is the winner. And the *irooj* (chief) might give him or her a *wāto* (land parcel) or food. Nowadays nothing is given or gambled.

[*Anidep* is still played in the Marshalls, although baseball and volleyball have become more popular with the young people.]

---

9. Here is the motif of the flight of the hero/heroine from the pursuing monster, and the attempts (usually successful) of the intended victim to evade/slow down the pursuer by throwing objects down in the path of the monster. This is also a widespread folktale motif: Obstacle flight or magic flight (see Leach 1950, 2:811).

10. The triumph of the intended victim of a cannibalistic ogre or ogress is widespread in folklore (see Leach 1950, 2:478).

11. Here we have another explanation through a folktale.

Comments

I sketched the actions of the characters in this story: the movements and positions of the players of the new game, of the women beating the drum, and of the girl and the demon, in my notebook. I did this under the gaze and for the approval of the storyteller so that I would be sure I understood the story.

Marshallese folktales such as this one give one a feel for the traditional subsistence economy, and for the social structure.

11: KŌN JUON LIKAO IN JĀLOOJ: BWEBWENATO IN ANIDEP

Ri-bwebwenato: Jelibōr Jam, Kuwajleen 1975

Etan likao eo Ļōm̧aanjidep. Eaar kōm̧m̧ane juon anidep. Innām eaar bōktok kōrā in Jālooj ro im katakin er. M̧okta rej joto jotak kōn peier. Iom̧win elōñ iien in aer katak kōn pā.

Innām ke rej imminene ejjab jok laļ anidep eo ekanooj em̧m̧an aer ikkure kake. Innām raar bar lo juon kōl bwe [ñe] enaaj wōtlǫk anidep eo im buñit laļ enaaj itok juon armej im jibwe anidep eo im ettōr kake.

Innām aolep kōrā renaaj lukwarkware in bōk anidep eo jān armej eo eaar jibwe im ettōr kake.

Innām Ļōm̧aanjidep eaar bar lo bwe em̧m̧aan ro ren bar ikkure kōn anidep. Innām em̧m̧aan rej jab ikkure kōn pā ak rej ikkure kōn ne.

Ijoke ejjab barāinwōt an kōrā ro ikkure im ke ej em̧m̧anļǫk aer ikkure kake raar bar kōm̧m̧an armej bwe ren jibwe anidep eo ilo iien eo ñe ej wōtlǫk im ko kake.

Ke kōrā im em̧m̧aan rej em̧m̧anļǫk aer ikkure kōn anidep. Kiiō ej jino an armej etal in aluje aer ikkure kōn anidep.

Ālikin jet iien ke ej buñbuñļǫk im em̧m̧an aer aluje aer anidep ledik eo nājin irooj eo ej jino an etal im ikkure ippān kōrā ro.

Innām em̧m̧aan im kōrā rej koba ippān doon im anidep kōn pā.

Ekanooj ļap an lōñ armej ilo iien kein.

Leddik in irooj eo ej etal ñan ikkure kein. Innām rej kōm̧m̧an m̧ōñā (aolep armej in eonene in Jālooj). Im bōktok ñan jikin anidep eo.

Ļak juon iien rej wōj joto jotak anidep eo ak eor jet kōrā rej pinniktake aer ikkure (kōnke ikkure ej juon men kāāl).

Innām kōrā ro rej al im ba, "Ļōm̧aanjidep, | item depļǫke anidep eo nājū | Joļǫk lije uweo. | Lije uweo depļǫke. | Joļǫk ñan ļōje uweo. | Ļōje uweo depļǫke. | Joļǫk ñan juko eņ. | Juko dāpiji."

Innām juko eņ ej bōk anidep eņ im ettōr kake. Innām aolep armej rej lukwarkware. Innām ñe rej jibwe ļeo renaaj bar rǫǫl ñan jikin anidep eo im bar anidep. Ak eļañña rej-jab jibwe ekwe em̧ōj m̧okta anidep ilo juon raan. Innām rej kōttar ñan raan eo ilju.

Innām rej bar anidep. Kōn an baj to aer ikkure kōn anidep juon tim̧oņ ej āinwōt armej im itok ñan anidep eo. Innām ke ledik eo nājin irooj ej lo tim̧oņ eo ej ļōm̧ņak bar armej.

Innām ledik eo nājin irooj eo ej ba ñan tim̧oņ eo, "Kwe kwōnaaj juko rainin?"

Innām tim̧oņ eo ej etetal ilikin armej ro im lale ijo enaaj wōtlǫk anidep ie. Bwe en jibwe im ettōr kake.

Ke ej wōtlǫk anidep eo, tim̧oņ eo ej

keṃaantak [im bōk] anidep eo. Im jibwe anidep eo im kotake anidep eo im ba, "Joļǫk ñan Juko eņ. Juko dāpiji."

Innām ej rǫǫl im ettōr. Ke ej ettōr ledik eo nājin irooj eo ej ettōr ippān tiṃoņ eo im jibwe anidep eo im bōktok im bar anidep.

Innām armej ro rej ba ñan ledik eo, "Kōn aṃ ṃōkaj, kwe wōt komaroñ in jibwe likao eo." Innām rej bar jolōñļǫk anidep eo.

Innām kōrā ro rej bar pinniktake aer ikkure kōn anidep eo im ba, "Ļōṃaanjidep, item dāpļǫke anidep eo nājū. | Joļǫk ñan lije uweo. | Lije uweo dāpļǫke. | Joļǫk ñan ļōje uweo. | Ļōje uweo dāpļǫke. | Joļǫk ñan juko eņ. | Juko dāpiji."

Innām juko eo ej jibwe anidep eo im ettōr. Im ledik eo, nājin irooj eo, ej ettōr ippān. Im jibwe anidep eo, ak kōnke tiṃoņ men eo, ekanooj in jeļā ta eo en kōṃṃane ilo iien eo.

Ejjab ettōr ettoļǫk. Ak ṃōttan wōt jidik. Bwe en jibwe ledik eo.

Innām ke rejro ettolok jān armej ro, tiṃoņ eo ej rǫǫl liktak im jibwe ledik eo im ettōr kake ñan ṃweo iṃōn.

Im tiṃoņ eo ej kadeļǫñ ledik eo ņa ilowaan ṃweo. Im eļak iten kadeļǫñe, ekilōk. Innām tiṃoņ eo ej ba, "Ñilñil melañlañ iṃōn anij eiō. | Ñilñil peļļǫke."

Innām epeļļǫk. Ke ej peļļǫk, ej kadeļǫñ ledik eo. Innām bar kili. Ke ej kili ej ba, "Ñilñil melañlañ iṃōn anij eiō. | ñilñil kiļǫk."

(Meļeļe in al eo ej lukkuun kilōk. Im eban peļļǫk. *Melañlañ* ilo kajin etto ej 'peļļǫk'.)

Kiiō ekilōk ṃweo im ejjeļǫk emaroñ kōpeļļǫkwe! Ak kiiō ej etal im ba ñan jinen ke en kōjǫ juon kijeek. "Bwe ña nājiṃ ij etal in kōṃkōṃ kijerro."

Innām ej bōk kein koṃ eo im etal im tallōñ. Ke ej tallōñ eļap an kōjatdikdik bwe ñe enaaj ṃōj an kōṃkōṃ enaaj to im etal im entak tok ni bwe en kab ṃōñā jinen. Ke ej kōṃkōṃ ej al iraan mā eo; eñin al eo ej al kake: ej ba, "Ñe ekar jab ba lieņ nājin irooj eņ eaar ba jen kōṃji ak mā kein kōṃij iuweo | Kab iuweo | Ak uweo | Ejja pād in kalo ļǫk."

Ke eṃōj an kōṃkōṃ, ej tolaļļǫk im būki mā ko im bōkļǫk ñan jinen. Im jinen ej kōmatti. Ke ej mat mā eo ṃoktata tiṃoņ eo ej etal im bōke im etal ñan turin ṃweo iṃōn im jelleik ñaj eo i turilik in ṃweo.

Ilo iien eo ej ṃōñā ekanooj in ļap an ettōñ im eṃṃōņōņō bajjek. Innām ke jinen ej lo an eṃṃōņōņō jinen ej konono ippān make. Im ba, "Ta eņ meneņ ej eṃṃōņōņō kake? Inaaj ilǫk ṃōk, lale ta. Ñe enaaj jako tiṃoņ eo."

Ke ej ṃōj tiṃoņ eo ṃōñā ej etal im ebbōktok ni. Innām ke ejako tiṃoņ eo, jinen ej etal ñan ṃweo iṃōn tiṃoņ eo im ļak lale. Ekilōk.

Innām ej bar kōpeļļǫke. Ke ej kōpeļļǫke, ej ba, "Ñilñil melañlañ iṃōn anij eiō | ñilñil peļļǫk!"

Eļak peļļǫk ṃweo kōrā eo ej lo ledik eo nājin irooj eo ilowaan. Im ej būroṃōj kake bwe ñe enaaj rǫǫltok tiṃoņ eo enaaj iten kañ ledik eo. Innām jinen tiṃoņ eo ej kadiwōj ledik eo jān ṃweo. Im leļǫk jilu kor in ni ñan ledik nājin irooj eo.

Kor kein eṃōj pinej mejāer em ejjab peļļǫk mejāer.

Im ke ledik eo ej bōk kor ko, ej ba ñan kōrā eo, "En ta kein?" Innām kōrā eo ej ba, "Kwōn būki wōt im ettōr kaki! Innām ñe ej itok tiṃoņ eo ijeļā enaaj pukot eok. Bwe ekanooj kōņaan kañ eok. Innām ñe enaaj ettōr wōj im jibwe eok kwōn kadelaļ kōņ juon kor ṃokta. Kwonaaj kanooj kate eok kadelaļ bwe en rup kor eo."

Ke tiṃoņ eo ej jepļaak tok im ilām kapeļļǫk ṃweo iṃōn ejjab reilǫk ñan ilowaan ṃweo. Ak ej leļǫk pein im jatoļe ledik eo bwe ñe ej jibwe ledik eo enaaj kanooj in eṃṃōņōņō. Ak eṃōk in jatoļ ak ejjab jibwe.

Ke ejjab jibwe ej erreilǫk ñan ilowaan ṃweo. Im pukote. Ak ejjab loe. Ke ejjab loe ej bōk ok eo im ettōr bōlen jibuki jiṃa ñeñe. Im ej iioon ledik eo. Ke ej ilān jibwe ledik eo, ledik eo ej kadelaļ kōn juon iaan kor ko.

Im ej rup. Im ej jeplōklōk kallep ko ie. Kallep ko rōaorōk ippān tiṃoŋ eo. Innām ej jañ im bar kappoktok kor.

Ke ej lo juon bar kor ej bōktok im jañ. Im āti kallep ko ŋa ilowaan kor eo. Im ba, "Men jidik, men jidik ko. | Nājimro jinō kein. | Men jidik, men jidik ko ia kein?"

Ke ej ṃōj an āti kallep ko, eļak pukot ledik eo; emootļǫk.

Innām tiṃoŋ eo ej bar ettōr. Im ke ej iioone ledik eo, ej iten jibwe wōt, ak ledik eo ej bar kadelaļ kōn kor eo juon. Innām erup kor eo in jeplōklōk kallep ko jān ilowaan. Innām tiṃoŋ ej bar jañ, im būroṃōj kōn kallep ko nājin. Im āti im ba, "Men jidik, men jidik ko. | Nājimro jinō kein. | Men jidik, men jidik ko ia kein?"

Im ej āti ŋa ilowaan bar juon kor. Im bar ļak pukot ledik eo; emootļǫk.

Kōn an kanooj ijoļe [kañ] ledik eo. Ej kōjekdǫǫn an ṃōk im ettōr in jibwe ledik eo. Ke ej epaaktok ledik eo, ej ba, "Inaaj kañ eok kiiō!" Innām eļap an ledik eo mijak.

Kōn an ledik eo mijak im ikkijeļǫk ledik eo ej jutak im jañ. Im tiṃoŋ eo ej ba, "Kwōn jab jañ jera! Bwe iban kōṃṃan jabdewōt. Bwe nājū kwe!" (Ej riab bajjek.)

Ke tiṃoŋ ej ilān jibwe ledik eo, ledik eo ej kadelaļ kōn kor eo kein kajilu. Im erup kor eo. Im ej jeplōklōk kallep ko. Innām tiṃoŋ eo eaar kappok kor in āti kallep ko. Ak ejjab alikkar an elolo kor. Innām ej kūtpooļe ijo im kappok kor.

Ilo iien eo ejako an ikkijeļǫk ledik eo. Innām ej kate ettōr. Ṃaanļǫk jidik, tiṃoŋ eo ej lo juon kor. Im āti kallep ko. Im kairi im ettōr.

Iien e ekanooj epaaktok ṃōko iṃōn ledik eo kab armej ro.

Im irooj eo jemān. Jekdǫǫn ak tiṃoŋ eo ej ettōr im jibwe ledik eo. Bwe ej ba enaaj kañe.

Ke ej kepaakļǫk ledik eo in jibwe, emaat kor ko ippān ledik eo. Innām ledik eo ej ettōr ñan kōŋŋat eo im ruje jān raan im jiburlepi ŋa ioon ubōn.

Ak tiṃoŋ eo ej ettōr wōt im jutak iturin ledik eo im leļǫk ok eo an im bǫuri ledik eo. Im rǫǫl im ineke im ettōr.

Ak ilo iien eo, ke tiṃoŋ ej bǫuri ledik eo, kōn an lōñ raan kōŋŋat ippān ledik eo, ra ko rōļorak ŋa ilowaan ok eo. Ak ledik eo ewōtlǫk bwe jinin tiṃoŋ eo eaar bukwe kapin ok eo. Bwe eaar jeļā wōt ke tiṃoŋ eo enaaj kar bōk ok eo. (Eor juon aļaļ ilōñ in ok eo im tiṃoŋ eo ej ineke im etal. Ak kapin ok eo ejako.)

Ledik eo ej ettōr ñan ṃōko ippān jemān. Ak tiṃoŋ eo ej jepļaak im etal ñan ṃweo iṃōn. Ejjab lale ok eo bwe eļap an eddo. Im ej ļōmņak ledik eo ej pād wōt ilowaan. Ak ejjab wōt ke raan kōŋŋat men ko rej eddo ilowaan ok eo.

Ke tiṃoŋ eo etōparļǫk ṃweo iṃōn, jinen ej itok im kajjitōk ippān, im ba, "Kwōj itok jān ia, nājū?"

Tiṃoŋ eo ej ba, "Iaar bōktok men kā nājirro jān ippān ledik eo eaar itok im bōki ak kwojab loe." (Ej riab ñan jinen.) "Innām kwōn ilān kōjǫ kijek eŋ. In kōmat kijerro bwe ij itok in babu jidik bwe ikkijeļǫk kōn ledik nana e. Ejjab ledik eo ak ledik eo emootļǫk."(Ej riab ñan jinen.)

Innām jinen ej ba, "Ewi ledik in ke kwōj ba, 'Kōn ledik nana e.' Ta, kwaar bōktok ke?"

Tiṃōŋ eo ej uwaak, "Iaar jab." A ej kaiuri im kapeļļǫk ṃweo iṃōn im deļǫñ im kili. Im bōktok ok eo. Ļak lale ok eo ejako ledik eo ak raan kōŋŋat wōt. Eļap an tiṃoŋ eo illu ilo iien eo im ļōmņak in ilān kañ jinen. Ak ke jinen bar tiṃoŋ, ejeļā aolep ļōmņak ko an.

Innām jinen ej ṃōkaj im ilǫk ñan Lōļlaļ [juon wāto eļap ioon Jebwad]. Ak tiṃoŋ eo ej pād wōt ilo ṃweo iṃōn ilo Deñōj-eŋ [juon āne ilo aelōñ in Jālooj]. Ak ledik eo epād ippān jemān ionene in Jālooj.

Ejeṃļǫk bwebwenato.

(Men eo wōt jinoin anidep im juko. Rainin ejjeļọk juko, anidep wōt. Kōnke juko ej kōm̧m̧an inepata āinwōt bwebwenato ej ba. Āinwōt ej jepel jinen (tim̧oŋ) jān nājin (tim̧oŋ).

Eindein kilen ikkure in raan kein: Rūkkure ro rej kōm̧m̧ane juon douluul.

Kōrā ro rej kōjerbal peier, im ļōm̧a ro rej kōjerbal neer. N̄e em̧m̧aan im kōra rej ikkure ippān doon, eindein ikkure. Eo erōļọk bọọļ (anidep) eŋ ippān ediwōj n̄an likin douluul eŋ. (Wāween dein an ietetļọk rūkkure.) Eo epād wōt ilo douluul eŋ āliktata ewiin. Im irooj eŋ emaron̄ leļọk juon an wāto ak leļọk kijen m̧ōn̄ā. Raan kein ejjeļọk men eŋ jej bōk ak kauwiinin kake.

[Ej wōr wōt jet ri-M̧ajeļ rej anidep, ijoke ekkā wōt an jọdikdik in raan kein iakiu im baļebọọļ.]

12: A YOUNG MAN WHO SAW JEBRỌ

As told by Jelibōr Jam, Kuwajleen 1975

(Jebrọ is a star that has seven stars in it. They are very small. It is like a sail of a canoe of these atolls. It is in the east in June and July, August, September, October, November, December, January, February, and March. In April and May it is in the west. Only two months. It comes from the east a long time. The name of this is Jebrọ.)[1]

A man had a child, a boy. This person was a fisherman. He went fishing every day. And he took the boy, his son when he was two years old. And he went fishing. Never mind if it was raining, he took his son. Never mind if it was very windy.

When the boy was older, perhaps seventeen years old, his father built a canoe.

When the canoe was almost finished, the old man died. Now the boy completed the canoe and again went fishing as his father had done. And one day he told his mother that he would go get bait, in order to go and fish for flying fish. (In the ancient language the meaning of *enen* is 'to go'.)

Now he took his canoe seaward and paddled it. He looked out and saw a canoe. It came from north to south.

The canoe came up alongside his canoe.

The boy said, "Greetings to you all." The young men (seven) in the canoe said, "Greetings to you!" Now the men in the canoe said, "Do you know who we are?" The boy said, "I do not know you."

Now the men in the canoe said, "Have you heard about Jebrọ?" The boy said, "I have heard in stories."

Now the men in the canoe said, "Well, this canoe is Jebrọ's canoe." The boy looked at the canoe and saw that the men all looked alike in every way.

The boy said, "Why do the men in your canoe all look alike?"

Now the men said, "Well, we are all Jebrọ. Bring your canoe close to us." And the boy paddled and brought his canoe close and against the side of their canoe.

And the men gave him a stalk of bananas and said to the boy, "This *kōḷowan* is your food. Go and dig a hole and throw in a pandanus segment. And put that stalk of bananas inside the hole and plant it. And after six days you will go again and dig it up. And take it and feed all of the people. And see that you do not say that you saw Jebrọ."

Now the boy returned to the island and gave his catch of fish to his mother.

Now his mother said, "Why have you been gone so long, son?" The boy deceived his mother and said, "Because I caught a shark with a hook and line, and this is the reason why I have been gone so long."

The mother said, "Well, you go into the house and lie down, for I will go bring your food."

The boy said, "Mama, I am not hungry." His mother said, "Why not?"

"Because there is one thing I am thinking about." (In the ancient language *ḷemake* means to think.)

His mother said, "What is that?"

The boy said to his mother, "After six days, I will say."

Six days later, the boy went and took the stalk of bananas he had planted, and called his mother to him and said, "This is the thing I was thinking about. Come here and see it."

---

1. The Pleiades. Also known by the Marshallese as Jeḷeilōn̄. A group of stars in the Constellation Taurus known to the ancient Greeks as The Seven Sisters.

When his mother came to see it, she was surprised and said, "What is that?" The boy replied, "This thing is called '*kōḷowan*'. Feed all the people."

Now his mother called all of the people to her and fed them. All of the people were very surprised.

"Where did this thing come from?" they asked.

The boy did not reveal to them from whence the thing came.

Every day the people asked, "Where did it come from?"

The boy did not tell them, because Jebrǫ had so willed it, and told him not to reveal it to anyone. For if he never told, he would live forever. He would never die. And the boy did not tell anyone.

After some time, his mother died, and his wife died. Now the boy took another wife, and the woman asked (as had the first wife), "Where did this come from?"

The boy did not answer at all. The woman grew old and died (as had the first wife). But the boy remained the same as before. He did not become older. Now the woman heard the story about the *kōḷowan* and again asked. The boy did not speak. A little while later, the woman again asked. And said, "Why do you not reveal it?"

The boy did not speak. Now all the people were surprised about how long the boy had lived and had not aged, but was still a young man. But his many, many wives and children aged and became old women and old men and died. But he just remained the same as ever.

Because his wife asked him so many times, he said to her, "Well, tomorrow I will reveal it."

When it was the right time, the boy said, "Bring food here and tell all of the people who are now alive to come here. If they come here, I will come and reveal the thing that you have heard about in the story."

Now he began to speak, "I will now reveal to you the thing that you wanted to know about. The name of the thing is *kōḷowan.* This food is very famous for its deliciousness."

Now the hair on his head (and face) turned white. The people turned to look, the young man was gone. He had been a young man and now he was an old man.

The young man spoke again, "I saw Jebrǫ's canoe." Now his right arm fell off. "When they gave me *kōḷowan* they said I should not reveal it to any person."

Now his left arm fell off. The boy spoke again now, "If I reveal it, I will die quickly. But the reason I have lived a long time here is because I did not reveal the testament of Jebrǫ to me. Now today I tell you never to bury me for I will become dust.

"Well, I say farewell to all of you." The people looked for him, but he was gone.

Now they were very surprised and sad, and said, "See, if he had not broken the testament, he would have lived into the future." Thus Ḷainjin said.[2]

---

2. This refers to Ḷainjin, the famed navigator and culture hero. Here we see the motif of one who brings a new kind of food to the people. And that of prolonged youth, and outliving contemporaries and their descendants. These are widespread motifs. They are found in the folklore of many cultures.

12: JUON LIKAO AR LO JEBRỌ

Ri-bwebwenato: Jelibōr Jam, Kuwajleen 1975

(Jebrọ ej juon iju eaar jiljilimjuon iju ilowaan, kanooj dik. Ej āinwōt juon wōjḷā in wa in Aelōn̄ Kein. Ej pād ilo rear Juun, Juḷae, Ọkwōj, Jeptōm̧ba, Oktoba, Nobōm̧ba, Tijem̧ba, Janwōde, Pāpode, im M̧aaj. Eprōḷ im Māe epād rālik. Ruo wōt allōn̄. Etto an itok jān rear. Etan iju eo, Jebrọ.)[3]

Juon em̧m̧aan eor juon nājin ḷaddik. Kijak eo rieọn̄wōd. Aolep raan ej eọn̄wōd. Innām ej bōk ḷadik eo nājin ke ej ruo an iiō. Im ilām eọn̄wōd kake. Jekdọọn ewōt. Ebōk ḷadik eo nājin. Jekdọọn eḷap kōto. Ke ej rūttoḷọk ḷadik eo, bōlen joñouljiljilimjuon iiō, jemān ej jekjek wa.

Ke eiten m̧ōj wa eo, emej ḷōḷḷap eo. Kiiō ḷadik eo ekam̧ōjḷọk wa eo im bar jerbal eọn̄wōd āinwōt jemān. Ḷak juon raan eba n̄an jinen bwe en etal in bōktok mọọr in. Bwe enen eọn̄wōd jojo.

(Ilo kajin etto meḷeḷe in *enen* ej 'ilān'.)

Kiiō etal im bōk metoḷọk wa eo waan em aōn̄ōōn̄. Eḷak reilọk elo juon wa. Ej tar-rōkean̄. Itok wa eo im ippān. Ḷadik eo eba, "Iokwe kom̧!" Likao ro (jiljilimjuon) i wa eo rōba, "Iọkwe eok!" Kiiō ḷōm̧aro i wa rōba, "Kwōjeḷā ke kōm?" Ḷadik eo eba, "Ijaje kajjiemi."

Kiiō em̧m̧aan in wa eo rōba, "Kwaar ron̄ ke kōn Jebrọ?" Ḷadik eo eba, "Iaar ron̄ ilo bwebwenato." Kiiō em̧m̧aan in wa eo rōba, "Ekwe, wa e waan Jebrọ." Ḷadik eo eḷak erreilọk n̄an wa eo im lale em̧m̧aan ro ie āin-wōt juon.

Ḷadik eo eba, "Etke āinwōt juon em̧m̧aan in wa n̄e?"

Kiiō ḷōm̧aro i wa eo rōba, "Ekwe kōm Jebrọ aolep. Kwōn kepaaktok wa n̄e waam̧."

Im ḷadik eo eaōn̄ōōn̄ im kepaakḷọk wa eo waan im katartare.

Im ḷōm̧aro releḷọk juon uroor in pinana im ba n̄an ḷadik eo, "Eo kōḷowan eo kijōm̧ eo. Kwōn etal im kubwij juon ron̄ em ejjolọk wūdin bōb. Innām leḷọk pinana n̄e ilowaan ron̄ eo em kalbwini. Innām ḷọkun jiljino raan kwōnaaj etal bar kubwiji. Innām būki im etal im naajdik aolep armej. Innām lale kwaar kennaan ke em̧ōj am̧ lo Jebrọ."

Kiiō ḷadik eo erọọl n̄an āne em leḷọk ek ko kon̄an n̄an jinen.

Kiiō jinen ej ba, "Etke enan̄in to am̧ jako nājū?" Ḷadik eo em̧on̄e jinen im ba, "Kōnke iaar kōkọjeki juon pako em wūnin an to aō jako in."

Jinen ej ba, "Ekwe, iwōj im babu bajjek im̧ōn̄e. Bwe ij ilān bōktok men kaŋ kijōm̧."

Ḷadik eo eba, "M̧am̧a, ejjab itok aō kōn̄aan m̧ōn̄ā." Jinen eba, "Ta wūnin?"

"Kōnke juon e men ij ḷemake." (Meḷeḷe in *ḷemake* ilo kajin etto ej 'ḷōmn̄ak'.)

Jinen eba, "Ta n̄e?" Ladik [eo] eba n̄an jinen, "Ḷọkun jiljino raan, inaaj ba."

Ej ḷọk jiljino raan ak ḷadik eo ej etal in bōktok uroor in pinana eo eaar kalbwini. Im kūr tok jinen em ba, "En̄iin men eo iaar ḷōmn̄ak kake. Innām lale m̧ōk."

Ke jinen ej iten lale, ebwilōn̄ im ba, "Kar ta in?" Ḷadik eo ej uwaak, "Men in etan 'kōḷowan'. Kwōn naajdik aolep armej."

Kiiō jinen ej kūr tok aolep armej em naaj-dik er. Innām aolep rej kanooj in bwilōn̄. "Jān ia men eo?" rej kajjitōk.

Ḷadik eo ej jab kwaḷọk men eo ej itok jān ia.

Aolep raan armej rej kajjitōk, "Ej itok jān

---

3. Pleiades eo ilo kajin pālle.

ia?" Ļadik eo ejjab kwaļǫk. Kōnke Jebrǫ eaar kallimur, em ba en jab kwaļǫk ñan jidik. Bwe ñe ejāmin kwaļǫk enaaj mour iumin iien otemjej, ejāmin mej. Innām ļadik eo ejjab kwaļǫk jabdewōt.

Ālikin jet iien, emej lio jinen kab lio koņaan pāleen. Kiiō ļadik eo ebar bōk juon pāleen innām kōrā eo ej bar kajjitōk, "Jān ia men in?"

Ļadik eo ejjab uwaak ñan jidik. Erūttoļǫk lio im bar mej. Ak ļadik eo ejja dettan deo wōt. Ejjab ļōļļapļǫk. Kiiō kōrā eo eaar roñ bwebwenato kōn kōļowan eo em bar kajjitōk. Ļadik eo ejjab kōnono. Ļǫkun bar jidik iien kōrā eo ebar kajjitōk. Em ba, "Ta wūnin aṃ jab kwaļǫke?"

Ļadik eo ejjab kōnono. Kiiō aolep armej rej bwilōñ kōn an etto an ļadik eo mour im jab ļōļļapļǫk ak likao wōt. Ak ekanooj lōñ pāleen im nājin rej rūttoļǫk im leļļap im ļōļļap im remej. Ak ejja dettan deo wōt.

Kōn an lōñ alen an lio kajjitōk, ar ba ñane, "Ekwe, ilju inaaj kwaļǫk ñane."

Ke ej jejjet raan eo ļadik eo eba, "Kōṃṃan tok ṃōñā kab ba aolep armej ren itok ro remour ñan rainin. Ñe remoottok ņa ijōņe inaaj itok im kwaļǫk men e koṃ ar [kōņaan] roñ kōn bwebwenato in."

Kiiō ej jino an kennaan, "Men eo koṃ ar kōņaan jeļā kake inaaj kwaļǫk ñan koṃ kiiō. Etan men eo, kōļowan. Ṃōñā in eaar kanooj buñbuñ an ennǫ."

Kiiō aolepān bōran em uwaņ. (Kooļan bōran im ātin im āinwōt.) Armej ro reļak lale [ejako an likao]. Ejako likao eo. Eaar likao ak [eoktak ñan] ļōļļap.

Likao eo ebar konono, "Iaar lo waan Jebrǫ." Kiiō ewōtlǫk pein rājet. "Ke rej letok kōļowan eo raar ba in jab kwaļǫk ñan jabdewōt armej."

Kiiō ewōtlǫk pein rājet. Ļadik eo ej bar konono kiiō, "Ñe inaaj kwaļǫk inaaj mej ṃōkaj. Ak wūnin an to aō mour e kōnke iaar jab kwaļǫk kalliṃur eo an Jebrǫ ñan eō. Rainin ij kwaļǫke ñan koṃ. Koṃ jāmin kalbwin eō bwe inaaj erom būñalñal.

"Ekwe lewōj aō iǫkwe koṃ." Armej ro raar pukote ak ejako.

Kiiō rōkanooj in bwilōñ em būroṃōj. Em ba, "Lale ṃōk, ke ñe eaar jab rupe kalliṃur eo enaaj kar mour ñan iien kaņe rej itok."

Āindein Ļainjin eaar kennaan.

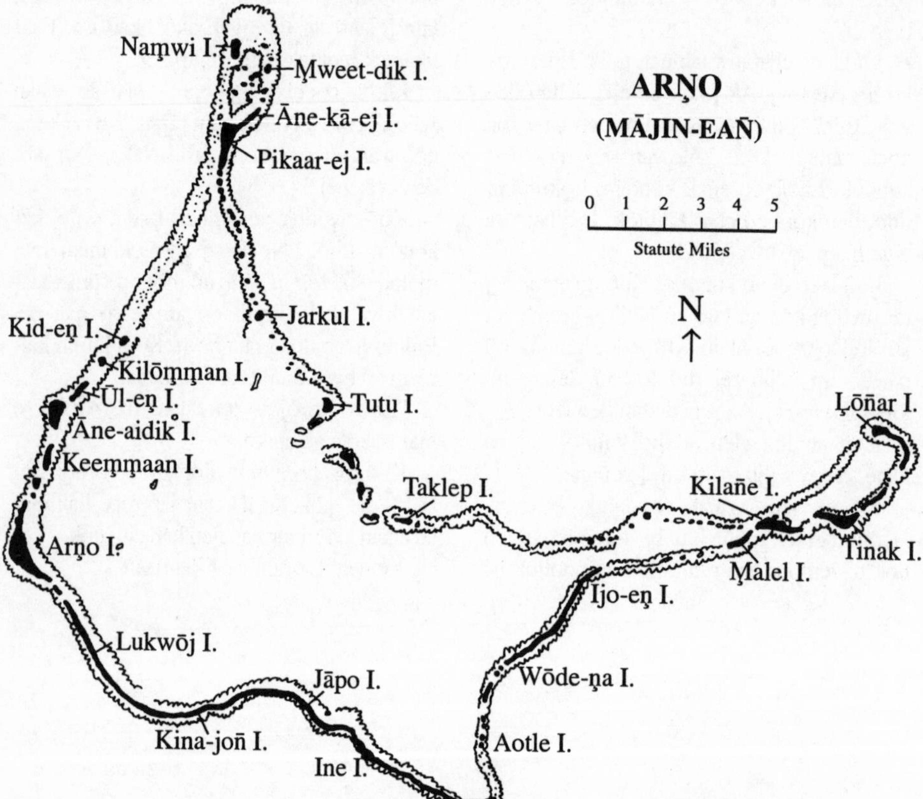

Aelōñ in Arṇo
Lagoon area: 130.77 sq. mi.
Dry land area: 5.00 sq. mi.

13: ORIGIN OF THE BANANA PLANT ON ARṂO ATOLL

As told by Ijikiel Laukōn, Wūjlañ 1955

Jọrukwōd, a magician, lived on Ļōñar Island, on Arṃo Atoll. He had two daughters. (But he was a widower.) Before he died, he made his daughters promise to bury him under the window of their house. And if anything should sprout out of his grave later, not to destroy it, but to care for it. Also, as soon as he dies, after his burial, to go to the end of the island and live with his sisters. (They were cannibals, but his daughters had not heard of them.)

They buried the father and went to see the old women. At the time they arrived at their house, the two old women were wearing mats and doing housework.

Soon after they saw the two girls, one said, "O, to be our food." The other said, "No, to be our daughters. We will adopt them."

The two women were arguing very seriously about this. The one who wanted to eat the girls won the argument. So they started preparing the *uṃ* (earth oven). But they put the girls in the storeroom and tied their hands and legs.

While the two women were busy preparing the earth oven, the two girls sang a song to notify them that they were daughters of Jọrukwōd. (They cried as they sang.)

"Jinō, jinō | Kwōn eṃṃakūt ṃōṃakūt kūtļọk jān ṃwiin | Jema ar jilōktok lio jinō | Kwōn ṃakūt jān ijin." (Mother, mother | You move, move from this house. | Father sent us here to see you mother, mother, move from here" (move us).

One of these women heard the song and went close to the girls to hear them. Finally she recognized (understood) the song and called the other woman to listen. And she also understood it.

One of the women told the other, "O, the girls are saying that they are the daughters of Jọrukwōd, who sent them in here to see his two sisters."

Finally, the two women went to ask the two girls who their father was, and why they came there. And then the two girls told them that their father was Jọrukwōd, who told them to come to see his sisters.

The girls said, "We thought we came to the right place; maybe not."

The women asked them again if it was really true that they were the daughters of Jọrukwōd, and that was why they had come. They answered, "Yes."

The women asked them again if there was anything else their father told them. The girls said, "O, yes. If anything sprouts on the grave, we must take care of it. And [we] may eat any fruit." The women let them go.

The women and the girls used to go and look at the grave. And they found the first banana *(keeprañ).* This species is called *jọrukwōd* [after the father obviously] or *keeprañ in Ṃajeļ* [Marshallese banana].

The place where the first banana grew can still be seen on Ļōñar Island. And bananas grow very well there.

I heard this story while I was on Ṃalel Island [Arṃo Atoll].

There is also a dance about this. The dance that acts out the story was invented in Japanese times to follow the old song in the legend.

The dance is very sad, and a little of the song was changed to fit the dance and make it better. Many people cried when they saw this dance.

There are many old stories with cannibals in them in the Marshall Islands.

Comments

Mr. Laukōn was from Arņo Atoll and was a trained agriculturist who worked for the government. He was in his twenties when he told me this story on Wūjlañ Atoll, where we were on an assignment.

Here is another example of the widespread motif of the origin of a food plant, a gift to mankind, through the death and burial of a person.

According to Hawaiian legend, the first taro plant sprouted from the grave of Haloanaka, the firstborn son of Wakea and Papa. Their next son, Haloa, was the progenitor of mankind (Malo 1976:244).

See Beckwith (1970:96–104) for similar legends of the origin of important plants in Polynesia and Melanesia.

The origin of corn, the important plant of the New World, from the body of a slain woman is found in the folktales of many Native American tribes, and "the gift of food to the people from the body of a slain food-goddess occurs also in Babylonian and Japanese mythology" (Leach 1949:252).

This is yet another Marshallese folktale that includes the motif of cannibalism. This indicates an abhorrence of the practice by the Marshallese, and also a recognition and the knowledge that this is done, as well as a certain fascination by the subject.

The story also illustrates the strength of kinship ties in Marshallese culture. (These overcame the hunger of the two cannibal women, and saved the girls' lives.)

This is the kind of story that was probably told to children to teach them appropriate behavior and to explain their natural environment.

Bananas, while not an important food, are enjoyed by the Marshallese. Homes, especially in the southern Marshalls, usually have several banana plants close by.

This cultivar does not do very well in the northern and northwestern Marshalls, with their scantier rainfall and thinner soils.

Anderson (1950:iv) identified two varieties of banana on Arņo Atoll: *Musa cavendishii, keeprañ, pinana,* and *Musa paradisiaca, keeprañ, pinana, ṃōkadkad.*

Stone (1951:25–26) in his discussion of the agriculture of Arņo Atoll states: "On L'anger [Ļōñar] there is a legend of how once during a period of starvation a man in chase of a rat carrying away a pandanus nut discovered a grove of bananas. This is reputedly the origin of a variety, Jorukwōr [Jọrukwōd], regarded as indigenous, and the exact spot is marked by the sleeping man—a massive piece of protruding beachrock. There are other versions of the story but discovery of this banana is common to all. The deep moist soil of this spot is regarded as the best for bananas and probably is, but very few grow there now. Nowhere on the atoll does the banana grow wild and it is probable that even the Jorukwōr was an ancient introduction. Most of the present bananas are known to have been introduced and often the circumstances attached to the introduction are remembered, as on Arņo Is. where two weeds were reputedly brought in with the soil attached to bananas introduced by German Catholic missionaries early in the century.

"*Culture:* The varieties of bananas now present on the atoll were not catalogued but they seem to be few. One or two cooking bananas are grown as well as one or more edible sorts: presumably all of these can be classed as varieties or subspecies of *Musa paradisiaca.*"

14: COCONUT DRIFTING ONTO THE SANDBAR: THE BEGINNING OF COCONUT TREES

As told by Ļamān, Mājro 1957

There were no coconut trees [*Cocos nucifera* L., *ni*] before. That man and his mother were on a sandbar. They were by themselves. He had leprosy.[1]

He slept and dreamed. He saw a human being named Audidia. He took a ripe coconut *(waini)* and said he [the man] should plant it. When he awakened, he told his mother about his dream. And his mother said, "Take the thing and plant it, if you have so dreamed."

Thus now when the ripe coconut had been planted, it grew and grew. And his mother said, "Do not touch it, so that it will grow." Now the coconut was growing; when it was older and had fronds, the young man went and tasted a fruit of it to see if it was good to eat or not.

He ate a frond *(kimej)* and it was not good to eat. His mother said, "Not now. Wait for it to grow." When it grew more, there was an *inpel* [cloth-like spathe around the base of the frond] and he tried to eat it. When he ate it, it was bad. And his mother said, "Wait." And she said, "Not now. Stay and wait. And do not move it." And they waited until the shoot *(utak)* had grown. Now the mother said, "Look, move that shoot." When he broke open the shoot, the stem *(jinnipraññrañ)* appeared. When it appeared, he went to try to eat one. It was bad.

His mother said, "Not now." When it was older and there were *kwaļinni* [tiny, young coconuts, not yet fully formed], now he went and took a *kwaļinni* and tried to eat it. Now it was bad.

Now his mother said, "Do not eat it. It should remain. Go, go, go until these things, [these] fruit are old."[2]

Now he went and took an *ublep* [young, fully-formed coconut.] He went to try to drink it. It was good. And he said to his mother, "This water is good."

His mother said that he should remain there. And the thing was to remain until the time [when it] was *urōnni* [green coconut, good for drinking].

Now he went to try to look at one and he went to husk it. Now he husked it and tried to drink the husk. Now it was bitter. It was not good. Now he again husked until the time he succeeded, until the time [when] he finished his husking. Now he discarded the *wulmōd*

---

1. Leprosy, reportedy an introduced disease in Micronesia, as in Polynesia, figures importantly in this version of the origin of the coconut tree, but this is found in no other versions. Note the analogy of the healing of a leper in this folktale with the stories in the Old and New Testaments: Naamon the leper who was healed by washing in the Jordan seven times at the direction of Elisius: II Kings 5, 1–19; the healing of the leper by Jesus as told in Matthew 8, 1–4, Mark 1 , 35–45, Luke 4, 42–44, and 5, 12–16; and the healing of the ten lepers in Luke 17, 11–19. The influence of the Bible has been strong in the Marshalls for many generations. Indeed, it was the only literature in their own language that these people had for many years.

This story apprears to be an example of syncretism—a modification and adoption of the elements from an outside source and their incorporation into the traditional folktale.

2. The stylized narrative device of repetition of a word is used to denote continuous and prolonged activity: Go, go, go. In Marshallese: Etal, etal, etal. This effective device is used in a number of Marshallese folktales.

[thin "skin" covering the eyes of the coconut]. And now the eyes of the coconut opened, and he saw water flow from the coconut. And now he tried to drink, he said to his mother that it was very good. And he drank it until the water in the coconut was finished [gone].

Now he broke it open and tried to taste the *mede* [young, jelly-like meat] inside. It was very good. And now his mother said it tasted good. Now is the proper time.

"Well, do not move it, for it should remain as *waini*" [ripe, mature coconut].

Now she said, "Break open a *utak* (shoot)." When the second shoot was also older, now he drank from the *uroor* (bunch of ripe coconuts). Many coconuts were there.

Now he put in the things first that became *waini.* Now they (those two) planted them.

Now they planted, they grew on the sandbar, which became an island because there were coconut trees. And now there were many shrubs on the sandbar. Now it was an island. Now they truly lived there.[3]

And the young man made *jekaro* [coconut toddy] from the coconut tree. And they cooked the water [liquid] of *jekaro.* And [it] became *jekṃai* [coconut syrup]. Now their leprosy was gone. Now they were healthy.

Many people came from some islands and drank from the coconut tree. And they said, "That man was a leper; here he is healthy."

Now it is ended. These two remained healthy. Their leprosy was gone.

Comments

The coconut tree and its products are very important to the Marshallese people. This was especially true in the precontact period, when they had to be self-sufficient.

This is reflected in the folklore, and in the large vocabulary that is associated with the tree. This is seen in the story, which does not, however, include all of the vocabulary used in connection with the coconut tree. See Abo et al. (1976:324–327) for details.

This, and other stories, may very well have been useful as teaching devices for Marshallese children, so that they would learn and realize the importance of the coconut trees to island geology and soils, and to their economy and life—indeed for their survival.

Compare this tale with the story of Ļakaṃ in "The Beginning of This World," (page 12) and with the story of the woman on Wōja Island, Aelōn̄ļapļap Atoll, who gave birth to a coconut, which she named Tōboļāār. This was the first coconut tree in the Marshall Islands (Buckingham 1949:4–6).

Leprosy was reported in the Marshall Islands over 150 years ago. Krämer and Nevermann (1938:242) state that: "leprosy (S. djigoa, E : jugo Ratak jogo) [is] also rare.

"Lesson's fear (*Voyage medical,* Paris 1829) that the natives would be eaten up by the leprosis has not come true." Here then is apparently another word for the disease.

The word used in this folktale is *lōba,* obviously a modification of the English word *leper.* It is used in the Marshallese language translation of the Bible, and has apparently superseded the terms reported by Krämer and Nevermann.

---

3. Note the recognition by the Marshallese, who are keen observers of their environment and natural processes, of the role of coconut trees and other vegetation as well, in soil and island formation. Island building and island erosion are ongoing processes in the Marshall Islands, of course.

An American military handbook reported that "leprosy has been present among the aborigines for many years. The disease is relatively rare and has been under control since 1900, when lepers were first segregated. In 1910 there were only twelve known cases of leprosy in the Marshall Islands, and in 1932 the leper asylum on Jālooj had only seven patients."[4]

A later official government publication states that "leprosy is rare and presents no danger to white settlers."[5]

It includes a compilation of the incidence of the more prevalent diseases in the territory. The data are from official reports, and cover the period of the last three quarters (April to December inclusive) of 1947. The statistics are based on all cases that were treated by medical officers and island health aides.

The incidence of the specific disease for each district—Saipan, Palau, Yap, Truk, Ponape, Kuwajleen, and Mājro (the Marshalls)—is listed. There is no listing for leprosy in any district (nor for Hansen's Disease, the new name for it).

The South Pacific Commision reported six cases of leprosy in the Marshall Islands in 1984, out of a population of 31,800, and seventy-one cases in the Federated States of Micronesia (Yap, Truk, Ponape, and Kosrae), out of a population of 79,300.[6]

14: NI EǪTŌK IN BOK: JINOIN NI

Ri-bwebwenato: Ļamān, Mājro 1957

Ejjeļǫk ni ṃokta. Ļeo im jinen repād ilo bok. Rej make iaer. Ļeo enañinmej, lōba.

Ej kiki im ettōņak. Ej lo juon armej. Etan Audiria. Ej bōk waini im ba en kalbwini. Ke ej ruj eba ñan jinen kōn ettōņak eo an.

Im jinen ej ba, "Kwōn bōk men [ņe] im kalbwini. Ñe kwaar tōņak āindein."

Kiiō ke eṃōj an kalbwini waini [eo] ej eddek, [im] ej eddek.

Innām jinen ej ba, "Leļǫk im jab kōṃakūti bwe en eddek." Kiiō waini [eo] ej eddek im ke erūtto im ļor kimej kiiō likao ej item edjoñ juon leen ñe ennǫ ak jab.

Ej ṃōñā kimej innām ejjab eṃṃan an kañe. Jinen ej ba, "Ejjañin kiiō. Kwōn kōttar wōt an eddek." Ke erūttoļǫk eor inpel im ej kajjeoñ ṃōñā. Ke ej ṃōñā, enana. Innām jinen ej ba, "Kōttar wōt." Innām ej ba, "Ejjañin kiiō. Kwōn pādwōt im kōttar im jab kōṃakūti." Innām rej kōttar [ñan] ke ej eddek utak eo. Kiiō jinen ej ba, "Lale kwaar kōṃakūti utak eņ." Ke ej rup utak eo ej waļǫk jinniprañrañ. Ke ej waļǫk ej ilān kajjeoñ kañe juon, im enana.

Jinen ej ba, "Ejjab kiiō." Kiiō ke erūttoļǫk im eor kwaļinni.

Kiiō ej ilām bōk juon kwaļinni im kajjeoñ ṃōñā. Kiiō enana.

4. Military Government Handbook OPNAV P22-1 (Formerly OPNAV 50-E-1) Marshall Islands. Office of the Chief of Naval Operations. August 17, 1943. United States Government Printing Office, Washington: 1946, p. 69.

5. Handbook on the Trust Territory of the Pacific Islands. Navy Department. Office of the Chief of Naval Operations, Washington, D.C. 1948. U.S. Government Printing Office.

6. South Pacific Commission Epidemiology and Health Information Services Annual Report 1984. Noumea, New Caledonia 1985.

Jinen ej ba, "Kwōn jab kijer. En pādwōt. Etal, etal, etal ñan iien erūtto men ko leen."

Kiiō ej ilān bōk juon ublep. Ej ilān kajjeoñ ilimi; ennǫ. Innām ej ba ñan jinen, "Enno dān in."

Jinen ej ba en pādwōt ijeņe. Innām ni eo ar pād ñan iien ej urōnni.

Kiiō ej ilān kajjeoñ lale juon innām iten dibōje. Ke ej dibōje ej kajjeoñ ilimi bweǫ. Kiiō emeo. Ejjab ennǫ. Kiiō ej bar dibōje ñan iien etōprak ñan iien eṃōj an dibōje. Kiiō ej joļǫk wulṃōd eo innām kiiō ej kōpeļļǫk mejān ni eo. Innām ej lale etǫǫr dān jān ni eo. Innām kiiō ekajjeoñ idaak ej ba ñan jinen eļapļǫk an ennǫ. Innām ar ilimi im ebar; emaat dān in ni [eo].

Kiiō ej rupe innām ej kajjeoñ edjoñ mede ilowaan. Ekanooj ennǫ. Innām kiiō jinen ej ba ennǫ. Ej ba, "Kiiō ejejjet iien. Atō, kwōn jab kōṃakūti bwe en pād in waini."

Kiiō ej ba, "Rup juon utak." Utak kein ka ruo ke rūttoļǫk barāinwōt kiiō idaak jān uroor eo (bwij in ni rej pād).

Kiiō, āti men ko ṃokta rej erom waini. Kiiō rej kalbwini (erro).

Kiiō rej kalbwini rej eddek ņae ilo bok eo. Kiiō bok eo ej erom juon āne bwe eor ni. Ak kiiō ejino eddek elōñ mar ilo bok eo. Kiiō ej juon āne. Kiiō rej lukkuun jokwe ie.

Innām likao eo ej jekaro jān ni eo. Im rej kōmat dān in jekaro. Innām rej erom jekṃai. Kiiō ejako an lōba. Kiiō ej mour.

Elōñ armej rej itok jān āne ko jet im bōk limeer jān ni [eo].

Im rōba ļeo ar lōba, eñeeņ emour. Kiiō ejeṃļǫk erro ej pād im mour, ejako an lōba.

15: STORY ABOUT THE BEGINNING OF PANDANUS IN THE ATOLLS OF THE MARSHALLS

As told by Ļamān, Mājro 1957

Breadfruit, pandanus, taro, arrowroot[1] came from where? We do not know. God made them. I heard a story about pandanus.

The woman of the pandanus tree, Lukjānmeto, was standing in the sea now. The woman looked after pandanus.

The pandanus tree stood in the sea. Now all of the kinds of pandanus (fruit) were on the pandanus tree, [on] the branches of the pandanus tree. One branch Annānu, one branch Jo̧ibeeb, one branch Utōttōt, one branch Lipjinmede, one branch Anperia, one branch Julele, one branch Kurajak, one branch Eki, one branch Edm̧am̧o, one branch Allorkwōm, one branch Tōbo̧tin, one branch Jolio, one branch Jo̧m̧win-jokur, one branch Rupijin, one branch Bōbijek, one branch Lo̧piñpiñ, one branch Jo̧m̧win-joñ, one branch Jo̧ilokwaar.

The pandanus tree was big and there were many kinds of pandanus [fruit] on the branches there. There was M̧ōjeel (pandanus) and there was Aujoñ.[2]

It was beside the pass of Aelōñļapļap, atoll of Rālik [the western chain of the Marshall Islands].

The name of the woman of pandanus, Lukjānmeto.

We do not know where she came from, [or] where she appeared, that woman who brought the branches.

Comments

In his discussion of the importance of pandanus to the Marshallese, Stone (1960:x) states that "during the time that elapsed between the coming of the first Marshallese inhabitants and the time of the first European contacts with the Marshallese people, there had arisen through the process of selection followed by vegetative propagation more than 130 strains of pandanus, which were grown mostly for the edible fruits, but also for leaves. A simple but effective classification had developed, and was known, in part at least, by many of the people. Today this knowledge is waning as new kinds of food become available." He notes that "Mason (1947) lists 44 cultivar names" (13).

This would seem to indicate that the story told me is a very old one. My informants were from Roñļap in the drier northwestern Marshalls, where pandanus was a very important part of the diet because of less favorable growing conditions for breadfruit and taro than in the southern atolls. The rainfall is scantier and the soils are thinner in the northern and northwestern atolls and islands.

I was given a list of the names of different varieties of pandanus in 1955 by Mr. Ijikiel Laukōn, a young trained agriculturist from Arņo. There were 48 names on the list. He told

1. *Artocarpus altilis, mā; Pandanus tectorius,* screw pine, *bōb; Cyrtosperma chamissonis, iaraj; Tacca leontepetaloides, m̧akm̧ōk.*

2. The Marshallese distinguish a large number of varieties of pandanus, each with its own name.

me that he did not know all of the different varieties of pandanus or breadfruit by sight, although he did know the names of them.

Pandanus was and, to a lesser extent, still is important to the Marshallese. The fruit provides food and the leaves provide the important material for plaiting mats, baskets, articles for sale as handicraft, and—in the old days—sails for the canoes, which were so important in the economy and the social and political organization.

The fruit was processed in different ways and preserved for future use. It was used as a food supply during long canoe voyages and stored for times of shortages, and to provide for times of threats of famine from drought and crop failure.

Mr. Laukon also gave me a list of the names of 90 varieties of breadfruit recognized by the Marshallese.

The folktale explains the origin of vegetable food in general and a specific and important one (pandanus) in particular, through the agency of a benevolent spirit, and it also explains the reason for different varieties listed.

15: BWEBWENATO IN JINOIN BŌB ILO AELŌÑ IN M̧AJEĻ

Ri-bwebwenato: Ļamān, Mājro 1957

Mā, ni, bōb, iaraj, m̧akm̧ōk rej itok jān ia? Jejaje. Anij ej kōm̧m̧ane. Ij roñ juon bwebwenato kōn bōb.

Ej pād ilo lo̧meto kiiō lio an bōb eo Lukjānmeto. Lio ej lale bōb.

Bōb ej jutak ilo lo̧jet. Kiiō aolepān wāween bōb rej pād ilo bōb. Ra ko raan bōb eo. Juon ra Annānu, juon ra Jo̧ibeeb, juon ra Utōttōt, juon ra Lipjinmede, juon ra Anperia, juon ra Julele, juon ra Kurajak, juon ra Eki, juon ra Edm̧am̧o, juon ra Allorkwūm, juon ra Tōbo̧tin, juon ra Jolio, juon ra Jo̧m̧win-jokur, juon ra Rupijin, juon ra Bōbijek, juon ra Lo̧piñpiñ, juon ra Jo̧m̧winjoñ, juon ra Jo̧ilokwaar.

Bōb eo ekilep elōñ wāween bōb ie ilo ra ie. M̧ōjāāl eor (bōb) ak Aujōñ eor.

Ej pād iturin to in Aelōñļapļap, to in Rālik. Etan lio an bōb Lukjānmeto.

Jejaje ej itok jān ia. Ej waļo̧k ia. Lieņ ej bōk ra.

16: THE STORY OF *BŌB* (PANDANUS)

As told by Ļamān, Mājro 1957

A variation of the origin of pandanus story, without naming the varieties, but with different details, was told to me by Roñļap Atoll elder Ļamān at another time, as follows.

In a place far across the ocean, there was a woman named Lukjānmeto.

There were two men (brothers) from Aelōñļapļap. They went fishing one day *(rōjep).* This is a type of fishing using a hook and line.

The younger brother paddled the canoe and the older one fished. While he put out his fishing line into the water he made a *roro.* (This is a chant; the Marshallese always do this when doing something: fishing, launching a canoe, before a battle in the old days, and so forth.)

"Ejerer a leltuñ | Ejjab leltuñ bwe ejjab a ninnin | Kwōn kiji ninnin ņe ñiōm̧ lewōj." (It is all put out on the sound of the drum | It is not a drum but a nibble | You bite with your teeth | Give it to you.)

This was chanted to the flying fish.[1] When he chanted twice and had a bite and got a flying fish, he pulled it in and took it off of the hook and put it in the canoe. And said, "There you are, brother."

Perhaps it was in the month of April that they went fishing, because it is the month of *kapiļak* (a big, short, and strong wind), which always comes in the month of April, the first week.

While the two brothers were fishing, heavy clouds arose. And the big wind arose. The two brothers could not paddle their canoe, but just drifted away in the direction of the wind. And the destination was unknown. Finally they came to a place where the *bōb* was. It was a tree with many branches, each branch with a different variety of fruit.

There was an owner of this tree who stayed at the same place. She was kind to the two brothers. They stayed with her for a while, and then went back to Aelōñļapļap, their home, with small pandanus branches for planting.

1. *Jojo,* family *Exocoetidae.*

17: A FAIRY TALE *(INỌÑ)*

As told by James (Ṃooj) Milne, Arṇo 1950

T his is the *inọñ* of the origin of lice cracking. Women crack lice with their teeth because there was once a woman who gave birth to a louse.

She hid it under a mat when she went fishing. She placed it under a clam shell in the house to keep a demon from getting it.

At low tide, she fished. One day, she forgot to hide it under the *kọnōt* shell. The louse played around under the fibers of the mat.

Then a demon *(anij)* came to the house. The louse saw the female demon; but it was too late to hide from her.

The demon picked the louse up and, "Ha, ha," she laughed. "I have been looking for you for a long, long time. And now here you are." She then picked up the louse and cracked it between her teeth.

The tide was now rising and the mother of the louse came home. She looked around and called for her louse child. No answer.

She then said, " Umm. Maybe the demon got it. I forgot to put it under the *kọnōt* shell."

So the demon then walked by (an ugly-looking female), and said: "Ha, ha. I laughed at the louse. When I bit it, it popped like this: Ummm!"

Then the mother said: "What did you say?" The demon replied: "O nothing. It is a fine day."

So when the mother started plaiting the mat again, the demon said: "Ah ha. It was funny when I picked up the louse."

She then repeated this three or four times.

Then the mother heard what the demon *really* said. She stood up and fought the demon. They fought from north to south [and] from east to west while the mother sang, *"Erei ereilikḷọk, likḷọk erei erei ar ḷọk, ar ḷọkḷọk ñan kajjien addi eṇ lik tip take, ruk!"*

Now they fought up to the *lik* (sea side of the island) and to the *ar* (lagoon side of the island.)

Then they came to the *addi* (giant clam shell) on the *lik* side.

She lifted up the demon and dropped her on the *addi*.

Then the demon died. (The sound of the demon falling and breaking was *"ruk."*)

18: STORIES OF ROÑĻAP AND ROÑDIK

As told by Tiṃa Marin, Roñļap 1957

The name of the man: Jǫlikiep;[1] he was on Aikne (an island beside the pass). He made a burning. (He burned trash.) He (opened) fire pits (like fire pits of trash). One small and one big.

The small fire pit was like Roñdik, for it was small. And the big one was like Roñļap, for it was big.[2] The reason that there are Roñdik and Roñļap, they came from the burning of Ļōjǫlikiep.[3]

Now he revealed with a word: we say a *roro* (chant). The chant said, *"Tile āne eo. | Kalakwe (Kiiō ebwil.) | Epeļļǫk menkwarar at in—kijeek in an ļeo ej kabwil."* (Burn the island. | Now it is hot. | He opens the fire pits of the man who makes the burning.)

Story of Roñdik

The name of the man was Ļajibūrbo; he was on an island of Roñdik. The name of the island, Ānewetak. Early every morning he awakened and called the woman with him. We say *rūturin* (spouse). Also his *ri-katutu* (personal attendant) awakened so that they could get his canoe, the paddling canoe of Ļajibūrbo.[4]

Now Ļajibūrbo paddled this morning. He sang (in the Ratak language [dialect], in the ancient language, *kajin etto*), *"Ļajibūrbo jerak i wa eo. | Tartawōj waan i ta ṇe. | Okok tu. | Waan i ta ṇe? Entak tu. | Waan i ta ṇe | Koṃkoṃ tu. | Wāto im ļǫk to e. | Kakōtikūt ie wa tu."* (Ļajibūrbo sails in his canoe. | What canoe goes to the east? | He picks pandanus and takes it to the west, Rālik. | What canoe? | Picks coconuts and takes to the west, Rālik. | What canoe? | Picks breadfruit and takes to the west, Rālik. | The land parcels away to the pass. | He eats many times and shits.) (The meaning of *tu* is to take to the west, Rālik.) It says go to Rālik, to the pass between Likiep and Roñdik. He ate many times and he shit and returned to his woman without

---

1. Jǫlikiep was apparently a supernatural being like Jǫbokak, the *irooj* (chief) of Bok-ak Atoll.

2. The literal translation of Roñdik is 'hole small' (small hole), and Roñļap is 'hole big' (big hole). This probably refers to the relative size of the lagoon areas, especially of these adjacent atolls. Roñdik lagoon area is 55.38 square miles and dry land area 0.65 square miles; Roñļap lagoon area is 387.77 square miles, with a dry land area of 3.07 square miles (Bryan 1946:2).

This is another explanation of the natural phenomena (relative size of two atolls) by a legend. These atolls were contaminated by radioactive fallout in 1954 during nuclear weapons testing on Pikinni Atoll. The 82 inhabitants of Roñļap, including 18 who had been on Aelōñinae, were evacuated from the atoll after the fallout occurred, and 28 American Air Force men were evacuated from neighboring Roñdik Atoll. Mr. Tiṃa Ṃarin was one of those who had radioactive materials dumped on him. He was fishing from his canoe at the time and had no shelter from the dangerous downpour. The 157 inhabitants of Utrōk Atoll to the east were also evacuated at this time. The Roñļap people were able to return to their atoll after a little more than three years. The Utrōk people returned to their atoll after three months. See Hines (1962:165–169 and passim) for a scholarly account of the disastrous nuclear weapons test (Bravo).

3. And the story explains the origin of the two atolls from the act of Ļōjǫlikiep.

4. Ļajibūrbo was obviously an *irooj,* because he had an attendant as the chiefs once had (as well as other specialists in their entourages).

food; for he was greedy. He held back the food and did not give it to people.[5]

Now when the woman went out to the canoe from the house, she said, "Is there food?"

The man said, "There is plenty of food in my house (my land parcel) on Likiep."

She said, "Why didn't you bring a little food here?" The woman said, "When will it be abundant?" (Truly plentiful—language of quantity.)

He said, "Have you looked in your house? There is a great deal of food there."

And they took the canoe to this island. And the woman spoke to the man who was in the attic. She said, "Make a fire (with a fire plow), in order to burn the hair of the baby." (In the olden days they did not cut a baby's hair until after the moon appeared in the west six times, moon/star [six months], the first haircut in the life of the baby.[6]

Now Ļajibūrbo thought about making fire. Now he brought the wood and made fire.[7]

After he made fire, the fire remained a little while, and the woman did not use it for the child's head. After five or ten minutes[8] between [intervals], she again said that he should make fire. She told the man, "Make fire so that we will go ahead (continue)." Now Ļajibūrbo again made fire.

And there was a fire there again, and it again became extinguished. Now the third time, the woman again spoke, "Make the fire."[9] Now the young man came down from the attic and made the fire.

And the woman made the fire [small torch /firebrand] and burned the head of the baby (the boy). They made it from coconut shoots, the thing to cut hair before for everyone.

And they all went. The man farthest ahead (in the lead), Riikijet,[10] took the child. Now the woman with Ļajibūrbo—the woman with Ļajibūrbo was number two. Number three, the *ri-katutu,* attendant of the child. The fourth was Ļajibūrbo, the last. (He was behind all of the people.)

Now they went to the center of the island, the place of bushes. And the *riikijet* pulled the *marpeļe* [*Ipomea tuba,* trumpet morning glory, a creeper]. (*Marpeļe* in the bush is the place of the demons, for it is crowded and overgrown.)[11]

And the two women and the *riikijet* and the baby went inside (within the bush, because it was the town of the *riikijet,* let us say, of his family).[12]

---

5. This is antithetical to the Marshallese value of sharing. A chief is especially obligated to do so. Indeed, it is a basic part of his role in society to be a redistributive leader. Also, food is of great importance to the island economy with its limited, sometimes scanty, resources. This was especially true before the advent of foreigners and the copra trade, which made food purchases possible and prevented accute food shortages and famine.

6. See the section on Postnatal Customs at the end of this story with regard to this postnatal ritual.

7. In the traditional method of making fire in the Marshalls, a piece of wood is applied against another one, and the friction produced by vigorous rubbing generates sparks that ignite tinder, usually of coconut fiber, until a fire is produced. This traditional technique is widespread, including in parts of southeast Asia, Polynesia, and elsewhere in the Pacific. It is basic, fairly easy to do, and effective (as I have witnessed on more than one occasion).

8. The English loanword *minute,* which is modified and becomes *minit* (singular and plural) is used, as is the concept of five- or ten-minute intervals.

9. Again we see the use of the ritual number three. It is also used in magic and in traditional healing techniques and formulae.

10. *Riikijet* are supernatural beings from the depths of the ocean.

11. "Bush" in the collective sense, a large, thickly overgrown area, believed to be where spirits live.

Ļajibūrbo remained there, outside of the bush. The reason was because he had done a great deal of this bad thing to the woman with him and to their children. And Ļajibūrbo again returned to Likiep.

(The meaning [and moral] of this story: the wife truly [pointedly] ignored the man and went away from him [left him], because the man ignored the woman before. We say, "Do not ignore your wife or she will ignore you."

This thing [story] is an example. Take care of the woman and do no wrong to her.

(I learned twenty or thirty stories from my *rūkorea,*[13] maternal uncle, Jepen, of the Ijjidik [clan.] He was [a] number-one captain.[14] He never drifted away [got lost.] He died in 1945. The man [Jepen] learned from Ļarunine; he was of the Ri-Kuwajleen [clan],[15] the *aļap* [lineage head, supervisor] of Jeboan *wāto* [land parcel], Roñļap *wāto*. He was a relative of Jepen. He learned from Ļatūb—a relative of the Ri-Kuwajleen clan.

Ļatūb learned from Ļainjin, [Ri-Kuwajleen] *irooj* [chief].

The stories belonged to the chiefs before. It was secret knowledge before the Germans came here, and before missionaries came to these atolls. Navigation and weather forecasting, and the like, belonged to the chiefs before.)[16]

Postnatal Customs

The ritual of burning hair of infants was described to me on Mājro in 1952. The informant was Jǫwej, a *ri-bwebwenato* and advisor to the chiefs from the northern atolls of the Ratak chain. Jǫwej explained, "The Act of Burning Hair was as follows: a woman who has given birth to a child was forbidden *(emǫ)* to sleep or eat with her husband in the same house, until the hair of the child was cut.

"It is believed that if the husband and the wife should sleep in the same house before

12. The English loanword *baamle* (from 'family') is used. Marshallese use it in addition to the traditional *bwij* (lineage) and *jowi* or *jou* (clan).

13. The mother's brother (maternal uncle), called *rukoreān* in Rālik and *wūllepān* in Ratak, is very important to his nephew *(mañden)*. They, of course, belong to the same matriclan, and the nephew may inherit his uncle's rights and authority as head *(aļap)* of their land-holding group. There is a special respect relationship therefore between these individuals, and it is reflected in the folktales.

14. The English words "number" and "captain" became *nōmba* and *kapen,* respectively. They are well integrated into the Marshallese language.

15. The Ri-Kuwajleen *jowi* was noted for the navigational skill of some of its members. Other clans had their own special skills. For example, the Ripako (shark people) were experts in bonesetting, and in warding off typhoons (using magic).

16. This is an excellent example of how important knowledge was transmitted within the lineage and clan, and the value attached to such knowledge. Note the historical events that affected this particular material, to which Mr. Tiṃa Marin referred.

See Grey (1951:76–92) for stories of two brothers, "Roñdik and Roñļap," told on Puluwat Atoll in the Western Carolines. The existence of these two uncommon names in such widely separated areas, diverse cultures, and different languages is indeed intriguing, especially in the folklore context. Were they brought to the Marshalls by ancient voyagers, perhaps the early settlers, or vice-versa? Or is it merely a linguistic coincidence?

the child's hair is cut, the husband will get sick. It is said that before the hair of the child is cut, the woman is still bleeding [vaginal bleeding]. And the husband will be poisoned by the blood and will become blind [the fear of blood-taboo contamination is widespread; see Leach 1949, 1:217].

"So before the child's haircut, the husband and his wife will sleep in different houses.

"In burning the child's hair, all of the women in the villiage have to be notified; otherwise they will be so insulted that they will start a big fight with the mother of the child and her relatives.

"When the women of the village are notified, they prepare a lot of food to bring with them when they come to the child and the mother.

"Three women are then selected to cut the child's hair. Sometimes one or two women would cut the hair. But three is the best number because it simplifies the process. One woman tends the fire. And another woman stands by with water, to put out the fire when the third woman, who actually burns the hair, gives her the word."

Another important postnatal ritual was explained to me by Jǫwej right after he had told me about the Act of Burning Hair. This is the method of disposal of the umbilical cord, and it was different for males and for females. "A male infant's umbilical cord was placed in a hole in the ground, termed *to,* right after it has been cut. (A *to* 'soaking pit' is used to soak coconut husks from which yarn is made to be used in making *eokkwaḷ* 'sennit cordage'.) It is believed that if the umbilical cord of a male infant is placed in this type of hole, he will grow up to be a good sennit maker.

"Several weeks later, the umbilical cord is taken out of the *to* and thrown into the sea. This is done so that the boy will grow up to be a good fisherman.

"The umbilical cord of a female infant is placed in a *wūnmaan̄* right after it is cut. (A *wūnmaan̄* is a bunch of pandanus closely planted together, and they are grown just for their leaves, which are used mainly for plaiting mats.) It is believed that if the umbilical cord is placed among these pandanus plants, the child will grow up to be a very good mat maker.

"A few weeks later, the umbilical cord is taken out of the *wūnmaan̄* and thrown into the sea, so that the female infant [will] be a capable fisherwoman. (This does not mean that every female infant's umbilical cord has to be thrown into the sea. Some parents will not remove the umbilical cord after it has been placed in the *wūnmaan̄.* Some would, depending on their wishes.)

"The umbilical cord of any infant will not be removed until it is good and dry of blood." As Leach (1950, 2:1149) explains, "The umbilical cord is thought to be intimately associated with the fate of the child."

The custom of special treatment, preservation of the umbilical cord, and its association with special properties or qualities of the developing individual is found in Hawai'i and elsewhere in Polynesia, and in other parts of the world as well (see Leach 1950, 2:1149). For a discussion of the Hawaiian concept and practices involved with the umbilical cord *(piko),* see Pukui, Haertig, and Lee (1972: 182–188).

Cordage made of coconut husk was essential to the Marshallese economy. It was used for lines (rigging) on the important sailing canoes, for fishing lines and nets, and for other articles in the material cultural inventory. Twine and rope were made by the men, who learned at an early age. It has become a vanishing art since the introduction of factory-made twine and rope, and with the lessening importance of sailing canoes and fishing.

There are probably not many Marshallese who can make *eokkwaḷ* today.

Fishing was extremely important in this coral atoll/island environment with its scanty terrestrial resources. The sea and lagoon reefs and waters provided the main source of protein, and different techniques of fishing were developed. The skilled fisherman was important in the community, and fishing skills were highly prized. This is also of lesser importance today with the introduction of a cash economy based on copra and employment with the government and private firms and other organizations.

Cash payments for land used by the United States government, a fairly recent factor, and payments for damage done by atomic testing have also made fishing less important for survival. Free USDA food that is provided for several communities has also lessened the incentive to go fishing.

Mat making was also important traditionally. Mats were used for sleeping, clothing, and housing, and were presented to the chief formally (as *tōl* or *ekkan*) in recognition of his authority, or given to him and others informally. They were also presented at the important *keemem* celebration (a child's first birthday) and at the wakes and funerals (*ilomej* and *eoreak*).

The pandanus leaf pounder *(dekā-in-nin)* pecked out of the inner lip of the giant clam shell (*kapwor, Tridacna gigas*) was an essential part of a household inventory, and was a prized heirloom handed down from a mother to daughter, generation to generation. They are still used, and highly valued.

The importance of this implement as well as the importance—indeed, the value—of other items of the traditional society are seen in this saying *(jabōnkennaan)* told to me on Arņo Atoll in 1950 by James (Ṃooj) Milne.

"Menin aorōk ñan ri-Ṃajeļ rej āindein: (1) jinen, (2) bwidej, (3) ok, (4) wa, (5) dekā-in-nin, im (6) wūnmaañ. Men kein rej jabōn kien, jabōnkennaan, im eļap tokjān ñan bwij eo rej āinwōt: jinen im bwidej eļaptata kab ok, wa, dekā-in-nin, im wunmañ.

Eļaptata tokjān ñan kōrā rej jinen, dekā-in-nin elabtata, kab bwidej, ok, wa, wūnmaañ eo. Im eļaptata tokjān ñan eṃṃaan rej jinen, wa, ok, bwidej, dekā-in-nin, wūnmaañ eo."

"Things that are valued by Marshallese: (1) mother, (2) land, (3) net, (4) canoe, (5) pandanus pounder, and (6) pandanus leaves.

"These are [the focus] of law and sayings. And most important to the lineage [land holding group] are as follows: mother and land are most important, and [then come] net, canoe, pandanus pounder, and pandanus leaves.

"The most important to women are mother and pandanus pounder, and [then] land, net, canoe, and pandanus leaves.

"The most important to men are mother and canoe and net. And [then] land, pandanus pounder, and pandanus leaves."

These were (and in some cases still are) the most important things in Marshallese culture. They are ranked in order of importance according to who is involved (lineage as a whole, men, or women).

The value and interdependence of these items for survival was and is obviously recognized by the Marshallese people.

This important bit of folk wisdom is known by the older Marshallese, at least. I heard it expressed a number of times over the years. I do not know to what extent the members of the younger generation know it, though.

However, a *dekā-in-nin* (pandanus leaf pounder), an *ok* (throw net), a *wa* (sailing canoe), and an island with food trees on it *(bwidej)* are depicted on the official seal of the Republic of the Marshall Islands.[17] This constitutes a certain proof of cultural conti-

17. Established in 1979.

nuity and recognition of the basic values. The traditional values of a culture are obviously reflected in its folklore, as in this *jabōnkennaan* (saying).

18: BWEBWENATO IN ROÑĻAP IM ROÑDIK

Ri-bwebwenato: Tiṃa Marin, Roñļap 1957

Etan ļeo: Jǫlikiep, ej pād ilo Aikne (āne iturin to eŋ Likiep). Ar kabwil (tile menǫknǫk ko). Ej peļļǫk melkwaarar (āinwōt wūpaaj in menǫknǫk ko). Juon edik ak juon ekilep.

Melkwaarar eo edik ej āinwōt Roñdik bwe edik im eo eļap ej Roñļap bwe ekilep. Wūnin an wōr Roñdik im Roñļap itok jān kabbwil eo an Ļōjǫlikiep.

Kiiō ej kennaan kōn juon naan, jenaaj ba roro. Roro ej ba: "Tile āne eo. | Kalǫkwe." | (Kiiō ebwil.) "Epeļļǫk menkwaarar | at in, kijeek in | An ļeo ej kabwil."

Bwebwenato in Roñdik

Etan ļeo: Ļajibūrbo, ej pād ilo juon āne in Roñdik. Etan āne eo: Ānewetak. Aolep jibboñtata ej ruj im kūr kōrā eo ippān, jenaaj ba rūturin. Barāinwōt ri-katutu eo an ej kǫruji bwe ren bōk wa eo waan, kōrkōr an Ļajibūrbo.

Kiiō ej aōŋōōŋ Ļajibūrbo jibboñin eo. Ej al (ilo kajin Ratak, kajin etto). "Ļajibūrbo jerak i wa eo. | Tartawōj waan i ta ŋe. | Okok tu. | Waan i ta ŋe. | Entak tu. | Waan ta ŋe kōṃkōṃ tu. | Wāto im ļǫk to e. | Kakōtkōt ie wa tu." (Meļeļe in "tu" ej 'bōkļǫk ñan Rālik'.) Ej ba etal ñan Rālik ñan to ikōtaan Likiep im Roñdik. Ej ṃōñā elōñ alen im epijek im rǫǫltok ñan kōrā eo im ejjeļǫk ṃōñā ippān, bwe ero ļeo [e tōr]. Edāpij ṃōñā im jab leļǫk ñan armej.

Kiiō ŋe kōrā ej ilǫk ñan wa eo jān ṃweo eba, "Eor ke ṃōñā?"

Ļeo ej ba, "Eor elōñ ilo ṃweo [wāto] i ṃweo i Likiep."

Ej ba, "Etke kwaar jab bōktok jidik ṃōñā?" Ļeo ej ba, "Enta ke ebuñpāļǫk" (lukkuun lōñ—kajin elōñ).

Ej ba, "Kwōloe ṃweo iṃōṃ ke? Kanooj in lōñ ṃōñā ie."

Innām rejro bōk wa eo ñan āniin. Innām lio ej kōnnaan ippān juon eṃṃaan ej pād ilo po eo. Ej ba, "Iti kijeek eo. Bwe en bwil kooļan bōran niñniñ eo." (Ilo raan ko etto raar jab mwijbar niñniñ ṃae eṃōj an waļǫk allōñ eo i kapilōñ jiljino alen, allōñ-iju. Mwijbar kein kajuon ilo mour eo an niñniñ eo.)

Kiiō Ļajibūrbo ej ļōmŋak [bwe] en kōṃṃan kijeek. Kiiō ŋe ej bōktok aļaļ eo im kōṃṃan kijeek.

Ṃwijin an kōṃṃan kijeek ej pād bajjek kijeek eo im lio ej jab kōjerbale ñan bōran ajri eo. Lǫkun ļalem ak joñoul minit ikōtaan ej bar ba en kōṃṃan kijeek. Ej ba ļeo, "Kwōn kōṃṃan kijeek eo bwe jekijoroor (bwe en etal wōt)." Kiiō kein karuo Ļajibūrbo ej bar kōṃṃan kijeek.

Im ar bar jǫ kijeek eo im bar kun. Kiiō kein kajilu, lio ej bar kennaan, "Kwōn iti kijeek eo." Kiiō likao eo ej to tok jān po eo im iti kijeek eo.

Im lio ej kōṃṃane kijeek eo im tile bōran niñniñ eo (ļadik eo). Rej kōṃṃan jān utak in ni, men in ṃwijbar ṃokta an aolep.

Innām ereañ rej etal. Ļeo iṃaantata ej riikjet ej bōk niñniñ eo. Kiiō lio ippān Ļajibūrbo. Ej kein karuo lio ippān Ļajibūrbo. Kein kajilu ri-katutu an ajri eo. Kein kemān Ļajibūrbo āliktata (ej pād ālikin aolep armej).

Rej ilǫk ñan lǫǫbuļōn āne, jikin mar. Im

riikjet ej kōjare marpeļe. (Marpeļe ilo mar ej jikin tiṃoŋ bwe ekkut.) Innām liṃaro ruo im riikjet eo im niñniñ eo rej deļọñ ilowaan. (Lọọbulōn mar kōnke ej jikin kweļọk an riikjit eo, jen ba baaṃle eo an.)

Ļajibūrbo ej pād wōt ijo, ilikin mar eo. Wūnin kōnke eļap an jerbal menin nana ñan kōrā eo ippān kab ajri eo nājin. Innām ej bar rọọl Ļajibūrbo ñan Likiep.

(Meļeļe in bwebwenato in: Kōrā eo ar lukkuun kōjekdọọn ļeo im etal jāne. Kōnke ļeo ar kōjekdọọn lio ṃokta. Jen ba kwōn jab kōjekdọọn lio ippaṃ ak enaaj kōjekdọọn eok.)

Menin ej juon waanjoñọk in. Kwōn kōjparok kōrā im kwōn jab kōṃṃan nana ñane.

(Iaar katak roñoul ak jiliñoul bwebwenato ippān rūkorea Jepen, Ijjidik Jowi. Nōṃba juon kapen. Ejjañin peļọk. Ar mej ilo 1945. Ļeo ar katak ippān Larunine, Ri-Kuwajleen, aļap eo an Jaboan wāto, Roñļap wāto. Ej nukun Jepen. Eaar katak ippān Ļatūb [nukun] Ri-Kuwajleen jowi.

Ļatūb eaar katak ippān Ļainjin (Ri-Kuwajleen) irooj. Bwebwenato an irooj ṃokta. Jeļāļọkjeṇ in ŋooje ṃokta Ri-Jāmne raar itok. Kab mijinede itok ñan aelōñ kein. Meto im lañ im āinwōt, an irooj ṃokta.)

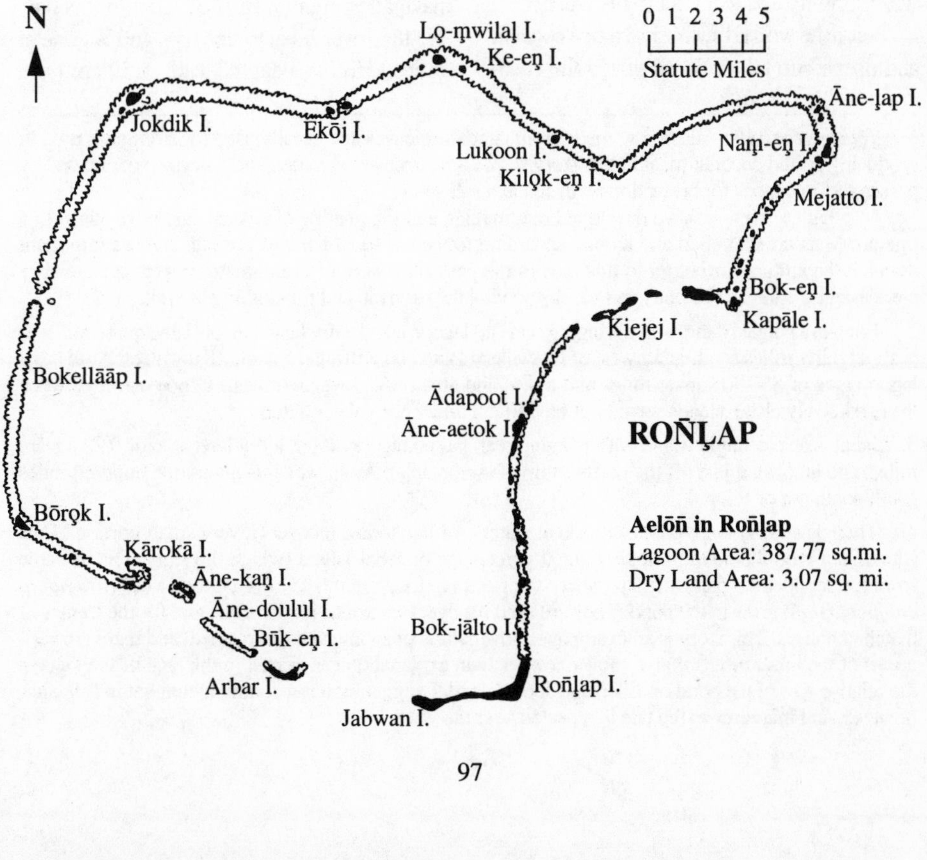

19: STORY ABOUT ELLEP IN THE DAYS OF LONG AGO

As told by Jelibōr Jam, Kuwajleen 1975

On the island of Ellep there was a man and his two girl children (daughters). The name of that man was Ļātulōn̄. Ļātulōn̄ was very industrious. Every day he left his daughters in their house—in the house area, in and around the house. And before he went to work, he enjoined the girls and said, "See that you two do not come to that place of work where I am working. But you two just play in (and around) the house."

Thus the girls obeyed their father and did not walk about but remained in the house.

After some days, the three of them ate, and the old man Ļātulōn̄ again reminded the two of them that they should not walk about. And the old man went from them because it was morning, and went out to his work.

Before he worked, he husked a ripe coconut and opened up his mat[1] and grated the coconuts. He continued grating, and he heard a sound of breaking wood. And after the girls, his daughters, broke the wood of trees (by stepping on trees in the bush area), they laughed.

At the time, he was very angry and went to punish them. But the girls fled. When they fled, he went and scooped up half of the island from the middle of Ellep.[2] And pushed it away, and took it far away from Ellep. And this island they call "Jebat."[3] (He could scoop up half of the island, because the people before [of old] were strong.)

The name from where he scooped up Jebat: Lǫkattōr—the name of the place, the place of the pool on Ellep.[4]

And Ļātulōn̄ remains on Jebat. (He is a frigate bird [*Fregata minor, ak*], and is the navigation sign *[kōkļaļ]* of Jebat to this day. He flies over Jebat to this day, and is gone at times.) His two daughters are on Ellep.

---

1. *Tōļao:* a coarsely plaited mat, made from pandanus leaves and usually used for sitting on; used in producing grated coconut meat in this story. *Tōļao* are also used in making (sun drying) copra, and by passengers in canoes for protection from sun and salt spray.

Marshallese women have developed mat making and the plaiting of baskets and other items to a fine art. Mats are classified and named according to the use to which they are put, and are important items in the cultural inventory to this day. In the past, they were of even greater importance, as they were used for sails for the outrigger canoes so vital for survival, and for clothing as well.

2. Ellep is a single island with a fringing reef (no lagoon), and a dry land area of 0.36 square miles. It is about thirty miles south-southwest of Kuwajleen Island on Kuwajleen Atoll. (Kuwajleen Atoll has a lagoon area of 839.30 square miles and a dry land area of 6.33 square miles.) Canoe travel between these relatively close islands would not be difficult under normal conditions.

3. Jebat is also a single island with fringing reef and no lagoon. It has a dry land area of 0.22 square miles, and is located just off the northern tip of Aelōn̄ļapļap Atoll, which is about one hundred miles south-southeast of Ellep.

4. There is a fairly large pool of brackish water on Ellep today. It covers a very small portion of the island, and would amount to a very small percentage of Jebat Island (which the story tells us came from the scooped up part of Ellep, where the pond is). Large numbers of mangrove trees (*Bruguiera conjugata, jon̄*) grow in the pond. They are used for dye, for various implements, and for the frames of thatched houses. This story is an example of how natural phenomena are explained, and there are variations of the basic motif. It also shows how such an explanation can persist in the face of the facts—the relative size of the pond on Ellep and Jebat Island. Exaggeration is a common element in folktales, however, and increases as the tale is repeated over the years.

(They are two fairy terns [*Gygis alba, mejǫ*], and they are the navigation signs of Ellep. They remain there to this day and are absent at times.)

After some days, a *koujinmeto* came to Ellep (a demon like a very big fire). He appeared on the ocean and came to the island and took it for his island. (Now it was the *koujinmeto*'s place, where he lived.)

There was an extremely great amount of food on Ellep at this time.

One day a man went to fish for flying fish (in the ancient language: went to *rōjep*).[5] He went from Kuwajleen. At that time, there was no food on Kuwajleen.

He was still fishing and he looked out and away. He saw a reef heron (*Demigretta sacra, kabaj*) eating a leaf of a mangrove tree (*Bruguiera conjugata, jon̄*).[6] And the man looked at the flying bird and spoke to himself, and said, "What is that in the mouth of the reef heron?"

After he was through fishing, he returned and came [back to Kuwajleen].

The next day, he again went to *rōjep* (in the ancient language: 'fish for flying fish') while it was still morning. He continued fishing for flying fish, and the bird again flew with a leaf. And the man again spoke to himself, and said, "Why is that bird flying with that leaf?"

He again said, "I say, is there an island over there to the west?" And again he returned and came to Kuwajleen and slept.

The following day, he awoke and prepared the bait for fishing, and hurried to go to fish. And he said to himself, "If I will see the bird flying, I will paddle to go see where it comes from."

When it was nine o'clock, the bird was again flying. And the man paddled away to where he saw the bird coming from.

He paddled and went; he was afraid [apprehensive] because he realized that maybe the whales would destroy his canoe.

(Whales are seen today between Kuwajleen and Ellep sometimes. Two, or three, or one. They ignore Kuwajleen and go to Ellep.)

But when he went away, out to sea, and did not see Kuwajleen, Ellep appeared.[7] And he said, "Is that an island, man?" (He spoke to himself.) Because he was tired, he drank the coconut [he had with him as] his beverage. And drifted a little, five or ten minutes. And rested.

---

5. *Rōjep* is the technique used in fishing for flying fish (family *exocoetidae, jojo*). Several hooks attached to the coconut shell floats are baited and laid out attached to long lines of coconut fiber sennit *(eokkwaļ)*.

6. This would seem to indicate that the mangrove trees have been on Ellep for some time, and that they were of importance to the Marshallese. As Fosberg (1953:17) points out, "in the Marshalls where the depressions [such as on Ellep] without outlets are commonest, there is some evidence that bruguiera may have been deliberately placed there by man. This is certainly true in some cases. . . . The fruits were used in making a dye."

7. Note the motif of the traveler/searcher alerted and informed of the presence of land by a bird. This is analogous to the dove with the green olive leaf that informed Noah that the flood water had abated (Genesis 8, 6–12), that is, the association of bird and leaf to the imparting of information. The interaction of birds, gods, and humans is a motif of Hawaiian and other Polynesian legends (see Beckwith 1970: 90–92). Birds figure in other Marshallese folktales, as, for example, in stories 33–35, "Story about Living Things (Animals) in the Marshalls" (page 151), "The Tattler and the Triton" (page 157), and "The Story of Lijebake" (page 160), and in a numbers of proverbs *(jabōnkennaan)* as well. We see the transformation of humans into birds in this and other Marshallese folktales. Flocks of birds, or single birds, are also used by Marshallese navigators as *kōkļaļ* (navigation signs) to indicate the location of the islands, by fishermen to locate schools of fish, and by seers *(rūkanaan)* and others as omens.

After a little more time (almost no time at all), he again paddled and went ahead. There were no people. But there was a great amount of food. And he picked breadfruit, picked coconuts, and hurried and paddled away, and returned to Kuwajleen.

When he arrived at Kuwajleen, his mother came to him and was very happy because of so many breadfruit and coconuts in the paddling canoe.

And his mother questioned him and said, "My son, why did you go fishing and why are there no fish but many breadfruit and coconuts?"

The boy answered his mother. "There is an island, I saw it, with an abundance of food. And tomorrow we two will go to it."

The following morning, the boy loaded his mother aboard and the two of them paddled to Ellep. And his mother went ashore. But the young man returned and came to Kuwajleen.[8]

He came to load aboard their possessions. But his mother, at the time when she went ashore, when she went, she saw the *koujinmeto* (the demon) lying down inside his house. (Now the fire had disappeared and he had become like a human being, a man [in appearance]. He could change his body into a fire or a human being.)[9]

And the woman went on to the house. When the *koujinmeto* saw her, he was very happy and delighted. And he said to the woman, "Come on in here."

And the woman, when she saw him, thought he was a real human being. And the *koujinmeto* said, "Come on in here and lie down here. For let us *inọn̄* (tell stories of the past). And you [go] first, ma'am."[10]

And the woman said to the demon, "No, you." The demon said to the woman, "You. For I want to listen to your story."

And the woman "told" an *inọn̄*. The *inọn̄* said: *"Ļokjānmeto. | Ļokjānmeto | Tūr tūr m̧ōjjāpn̄ān̄ā | Tor tor m̧ōjjāpn̄ān̄ā. Toļ, toļa | toļi, toļa likūrbala. A-A, A-A-A-A."* (This song is in the ancient language. I do not know the meaning of it.)

(The woman did this to make the demon sleep, and deeply—to make him relax.)[11]

Now the *koujinmeto* was very happy with this *inọn̄* of the woman. And the *koujinmeto,* because he was so happy to hear [the *inọn̄*], again, said, "You begin again." And the woman again began this *inọn̄* of hers.

Three times she gave the *inon.*[12] And because the *koujinmeto* liked the *inọn̄* so much, he slept, and slept very deeply.

Because the woman knew that the thing was a demon, she did not know when he would awaken and eat her. And the woman carried coconut fronds [and put them]

---

8. The shift between the words for 'boy' *(ļaddik)* and 'young man' *(likao)* is seen in this and other stories. Note also the use of the English loanword *minit* 'minute' and the introduced concept of the measuring of time to this degree.

9. Note the motif of the shapeshifter, the ability to change or transform oneself to another shape or form, as is done by the *koujinmeto* to deceive his intended victim. This motif is found in other Marshallese stories and is widespread (see Leach 1950, 2:1004–1005). Shape-shifting is a motif found in Greek and Roman mythology, as is the transformation of mortals into other forms by the gods. For example, the randy god Zeus (Jupiter) visited and impregnated Leda in the form a swan (Hamilton 1942:46) and changed himself into a beautiful bull to seduce Europa (Hamilton 1942:101). The Bible, familiar to the Marshallese for over a century, states that the devil transforms himself into an angel of light to deceive (2 Corinthians 11,14). This may have reinforced the Marshallese belief in evil shape-shifters.

10. *Inọn̄* can be translated as 'fairy tale'. The word is used as a noun or as a verb, as in this story, and can be presented as songs or chants (as in the story), or as narratives.

against the house—very many fronds. And before she set fire to the fronds, she went and looked at the demon to see if he had awakened. But he was sleeping quite soundly.

And the woman set fire to the fronds, and the house was surrounded by fire. And she ran from the house, and stood far away from it and looked to see if the *koujinmeto* would flee and come and eat [her].

When the *koujinmeto* felt the heat from the fire, he woke up and went to flee to the east. Impossible. He went to flee to the west. Impossible. Impossible to flee to the west, impossible to flee to the east, because the house was filled with fire. But he ran to the west and ran to the east inside the fire and died.

When the woman saw that he was dead, she went to the house and looked to see if he was truly dead or not. And the woman just went, for she was most apprehensive of the *koujinmeto,* lest he be alive.

And when she came close beside him, the demon was dead, truly dead. And the woman was very happy, for she would be able to stay on Ellep as long as she lived.

When her son, the young man, returned, he was very happy because his mother had made a path of good fortune for the two of them until this day.[13]

The story is ended.

---

11. The motif here is the obvious one of the heroine tricking the more powerful and dangerous evil being (demon). Her singing and chanting makes him lower his guard and become drowsy so that he falls asleep. This enables the heroine to escape and to kill him. The motif of tricking a dangerous being and killing it by burning is found in other Marshallese stories, and the motif is widespread. The Hawaiians told the legend of Kaululaau, the tricky son of Kakaalaneo, who killed off the spirits of Lanai: ". . .The remaining spirits he makes drunk in a feast house, gums up their eyes while they sleep, and then sets fire to the house" (Beckwith 1940:441). Also, in a story from Puluwat Atoll in the western Caroline Islands, evil spirits are incinerated by the hero Rongerik (Grey 1951:91–92).

12. Again we see the use of the ritual number three.

13. This story shows the loving, caring attitude of son toward mother in traditional Marshallese culture, and is also perhaps an explanation of how Ellep Island was first settled from Kuwajleen Atoll, with whose population the present inhabitants of Ellep have kinship ties. Erdland (1914:289–90) collected a similiar story about Ellep. In that version, two men follow a heron with a mangrove twig in its bill. They discover Ellep and trick and incinerate a monster. Some of the other details of the story differ.

19: BWEBWENATO IN ELLEP ILO RAAN KO ETTO

Ri-bwebwenato: Jelibōr Jam, Kuwajleen 1975

Ellep kar āneen juon eṃṃaan kab ruo nājin leddik. Etan ļeo Ļātulōñ. Ļātulōñ ekanooj in eowan. Ilo aolep raan ej likūt ledik ro nājin ŋae ṃweo imweer jel. Innām ṃokta jān an etal ñan jerbal ej kalliṃur ñan ledik ro im ba, "Lale koṃ ro ar itok ñan jikin jerbal eŋ ña ij jerbal ie. Ak koṃro ikkure wōt iṃwiin."

Āindein ledik ro raar pokake jemāer im jab etetal ak raar pādwōt iṃweo.

Ālikin jet raan rejeel ar ṃōñā innām ļōļļap eo, Ļātulōñ ej bar kakememej erro bwe ren jab etetal. Innām ļōļļap eo ar etal jān ippāer ro ke ej jibboñ wōt. Im ilǫk ñan jerbal eo an.

Ṃokta jān an jerbal eaar dibōjtok juon waini im erļǫke taļao eo an im raanke wōt ak eroñjake eddokwōjļǫk eo.

Im ļak erreiliktak ledik ro nājin rejro ettōñ. Iien eo ekanooj in ļap an illu im ilān ṃane erro. Ak ledik ro rej ko. Ke rejro ko ej etal im kōtepe jimettan āne jān lukon Ellep. Im katorlikļǫk. Im bōkļǫk ettoļǫk jān Ellep. Im eñiin rej ba, "Jebat." (Emaroñ kōtepe jimettan āne kōnke armej ṃokta rekajoor.)

Etan ijo ļeo eaar katorlikļǫk Jebat jāne: Lǫkattōr, ñan rainin. (Etan jikin eo. Jikin ļwe Ellep eo.)

Innām Ļātulōñ ej pād i Jebat. (Ej juon ak, ej kōkōļaļ eo an Jebat.) Ak ledik ro nājin rej pād i Ellep. (Rej ruo mejǫ im rej kōkōļaļ in Ellep.) Im rej pād ie ñan rainin.

Ālikin jet raan eitok juon koujinmeto. (Juon tiṃoŋ āinwōt kijeek ļapļap.) Ej waļǫk ioon lǫjet im itok ñan āne, ñan Ellep im bōke bwe en āneen. (Kiiō an koujinmeto jikin pād.)

Ellep ekanooj in ļap an lōñ ṃōñā ilo [jet] iien in.

Juon raan juon eṃṃaan eaar etal in eǫñwōd jojo. (Ilo kajin etto: etal in rōjep.) Ej etal jān Kuwajleen. Ilo iien in ejjeļǫk ṃōñā i Kuwajleen.

Ejja eǫñwōd wōt ak eļak erreilǫk, ej lo juon kabaj ej kij juon bōlōk in joñ. Innām ļeo ej lale an bao eo kātok im ekonono ippān make. Im ba, "Ta eŋ i lǫñiin kabaj eŋ?"

Ṃwijin an eǫñwōd ebar jepļaak im itok.

Raan eo juon eaar bar etal im rōjep. Ilo jibboñōn eo wōt. Ejja rōjep wōt ak bao eo ej bar kātok kōn juon bōlōk. Im ļeo ej bar kongono ippān make. Im ba, "Etke bao ŋe ej kātok kōn bōlōk eŋ?" Ej bar ba, "I ba eor juon āne ijōkaŋe i rilik?" Innām ebar jepļaak im itok ñan Kuwajleen im kiki.

Rujļǫk eo juon ej ruj em kōppojak mǫǫr in eǫñwōd. Im kaiur im etal in eǫñwōd. Innām ej ba ilo būruon, "Eļaññe inaaj lo an bao eo kātok, inaaj aōŋōōŋ in etal in lale ia in ej itok jāne."

Ke ej ruatimjuon awa bao eo ej bar kātok. Innām ļeo ej aōŋōōŋ ļǫk ñan ijo eaar lo an bao eo jādetok ie.

Ej aōŋōōŋ im etal ak ej mijak wōt kōnke ekkōl ñe enaaj rup wa eo waan ippān raj. (Raj rej pād ikōtaan Kuwajleen im Ellep jet iien rainin. Ruo ak jilu a juon. Jen jekdǫǫn Kuwajleen im etal ñan Ellep.)

Ak ke ej wanmetoļǫk em ejjab lo Kuwajleen ej waļǫk tok Ellep. Innām ej ba, "Juon ŋe āne ļōma?" (Ej kōnono ñan e make.) Kōn an ṃōk ej ilim ni eo limen. Em peļǫk jidik. Im kakkije.

Ālikin bar jidik iien (ejjeļǫk minit ṃokta) ej bar aōŋōōŋ im ļak ilǫk, ejjeļǫk armej. Ak eļap an lōñ ṃōñā. Innām eaar kōṃkōṃ mā, entak ni, im kaiur im aōŋōōŋ. Im jepļaak ñan Kuwajleen. Ke ej tōkeaktok Kuwajleen jinen ej itok ñan ippān im eļap an ṃōņōņō kōn an lōñ mā, im ni ilo kōrkōr eo.

Im jinen ej kajjitōk im ba, "Nājū, etke kwaar ilān eọñwōd? Innām etke ejjeļọk ek ak elōñ mā im ni?"

Likao eo ej uwaak jinen, "Eor juon āne, iaar loe, ebuñpeļọk kōn ṃōñā innām ilju jero naaj etal ñane."

Rujļọkin eo, likao eo ej ektake jinen im rejro aōņōōņ ñan Ellep. Im jinen ej wanāneļọk. Ak likao eo ej jepļaak im itok ñan Kuwajleen.

Ej iten ektake men ko ṃweierro. Ak jinen ilo iien eo ke ej wanāneļọk, eļak ilọk ej lo koujinmeto eo (tiṃoņ) ej babu ilowaan ṃweo iṃōn. (Kiiō ejako kijeek ak erom āinwōt armej. Emaroñ ukot ānbwin eo an ñan kijeek ak armej.)

Innām kōrā eo ej etal wōt ñan ṃweo. Ke koujinmeto eo ej loe eļap an ṃōņōņō im buñburuōn. Im ej ba ñan lio, "Kwōn deļọñ tok."

Innām lio ke ej loe ej ļōmņak lukkuun armej. Innām koujinmeto ej ba, "Deļọñ tok im babu ijōņe. Bwe jenro inọñ. Innām kwe ṃokta le."

Innām lio ej ba ñan tiṃoņ eo, "Jab, kwe." Tiṃoņ eo ej ba ñan lio, "Kwe, bwe ikōnaan roñjake aṃ inọñ."

Innām lio ej inọñ. Inọñ eo ej ba, "Ļokjānmeto, Ļokjānmeto | Tūr, tūr ṃōjjāpñāñā. | Tor, tor ṃōjjāpñāñā. | Toļi, toļa likūrbala. | A-A-, A-A-A-A." (Kajin etto al in. Ijaje meļeļe in.)

(Lio ar kōṃṃane bwe en kakiki im kattoñe tiṃoņ eo.)

Kiiō ekanooj in ļap an eṃṃōņōņō koujinmeto eo kōn inọñ in an kōrā eo. Im koujinmeto eo kōn an eṃṃan an roñ ej bar ba, "Kwōn bar jinoe!" Im lio ej bar jinoe inọñ in an. Jilu alen an inọñ. Im kōn an eṃṃan an koujinmeto eo roñjake inọñ eo ekiki im kanooj in ļap an ettoñ.

Kōn an kōrā eo jeļā ke tiṃoņ men eo ejaje ñāāt enaaj ruj im kañe. Im kōrā eo ej aljektok kimej in ni ñan ṃweo im ekanooj in lōñ kimej. Innām ṃokta jān an tile kimej ko ej etal im lale tiṃoņ eo ñe en ruj. Ak ekanooj in ļap an kiki.

Innām kōrā eo ej tile kimej ko im kapooļ ṃweo kōn kijeek. Im ettōr jān ṃweo. Im ej jutak ettoļọk im lale ñe en ko koujinmeto eo im item ṃōñā.

Ilo iien eo ke koujinmeto eo ej eñjake māāņāņ in kijeek eo im ruj eļak iten ko taļọk, eban. Eļak iten kotoļọk, eban. Eban koto, kotak kōnke epooļ ṃweo kōn kijeek.

A eaar ettōrto, ettōrtak ilowaan kijeek eo im mej.

Ke lio ej lo an mej ej etal ñan ṃweo im lale ṃool ke emej ke, ak jaab ke.

Innām lio ej etal wōt ak eļap an ekkōljaake koujinmeto eo ñe emour.

Innām ke ej tōparļọk turin, emej tiṃoņ eo, lukkun mej.

Innām lio eļap an ṃōņōņō enaaj pād Ellep towan wōt an mour.

Ke ej jepļaak tok likao eo nājin eļap an eṃṃōņōņō kōn an jinen kar kōṃṃan iiaļ in jeraaṃṃan ñan erro ñan rainin.

Ejemļọk bwebwenato.

20: STORY ABOUT ELLEP ISLAND

As told by an *aļap* on Ellep 1969

Jebat Island near Aelōñļapļap Atoll was taken from Ellep long, long ago. The large pool area on Ellep is the same shape or outline *(jekjek)* as Jebat.

The pool is salty and bottomless, and it is probably connected to the ocean.

The meaning of the name of Ellep is *el lep,* which means the nest (place) of eggs. *El* means 'nest' [and] *lep* means 'egg'.[1]

1. Jebat, the displaced island, one could call it, it is one hundred miles south of Ellep, and lies just off the northern side of Aelōñļapļap Atoll. The island is 0.22 square miles in extent and has no lagoon.

21: STORY ABOUT JEBAT ISLAND

As told by an *aļap* from Jebat, Aelōn̄ļaplap 1969

Jebat Island was first placed in the lagoon of Aelōn̄ļapļap by a powerful spirit *(ekjab).*

She became angry with the people of Aelōn̄ļapļap Atoll later, and she moved Jebat Island outside of the atoll to where it is today.[1]

1. This island movement by a powerful entity is akin to the fishing up of the islands by demi gods such as Maui in Hawai'i, and others in Micronesia, including the Marshalls (see the comments in story 71, "The Chant of Mile: Fishing Up from the Bottom of the Sea" on page 315). However, the island of Jebat was detached from another island, not fished up from the bottom of the sea as were these other islands, and anger was not the motivation for moving any of them, as was the case in moving Jebat outside of Aelōn̄ļapļap Atoll.

22: STORY ABOUT THE ATOLL OF WŌTTO IN THE OLDEN DAYS

As told by Jelibōr Jam, Kuwajleen 1975

On the atoll of Wōtto, there was a girl who was born and grew older. When she was a young girl, her mother and father died, and she did not listen to one word of advice, but went as she wanted to.

One day a bad spirit [lit. 'air'] quickly entered her body and all of her thoughts. She changed from a human being, and she took [on] the spirit of a demon.[1] The name of the demon was Likrabjel.

After some days, when the demon was in this body, it could eat canoes, eat islands, eat people, and eat similar things.

One day when she wanted to go to the ocean side, she walked first on the lagoon side of Wōtto, and she ate all of the people's canoes first.[2] Her thought was to eat the people later.[3]

At this time, she (the female *tiṃoṇ*) began to go to the ocean side and she ate from the fruit trees on the land parcel named Āne-ju; she went toward the middle of the island there.

From lagoon to ocean and not one coconut tree or pandanus or breadfruit or any bush was left standing.

She finished eating them. (There were no breadfruit, pandanus, coconuts, or grass there. It was like sand. Because the demon ate them.)

When she arrived at the ocean side, she saw a boy; the name of this boy, Ļāde.

And she saw fish inside a pool, a pool for launching model canoes—playthings. (These are few inches long. It is a sport of children.)

Ļāde looked over and saw the woman. And the demon sang: *"Kupañ luluto. | Imwiji ña. | Badet luluto. | Iṃwiji ña-a-a. | Ej je or aṃ it ke le?"*

"Kupañ [*Acanthurus triostegus triostegus* L., surgeon fish tang, or *Hopatus triostegus,* convict tang] swims ahead from side to side (*kajin ek* [fish language]). | I'm finished. Badet (a small fish) [*Abudefduf septemfascatus,* demoiselle fish] swims from side to side. | I-I-I am finished. | Do you have (*ejjeor* is the ancient language [*kajin etto*] for '*eor ke?'*) your fire board, sir?"[4] (*It* is the bottom part of the fire-making apparatus. The top part [fire stick] is called *jolǫk.*)

Ļāde now answered, "Here is the fire board."

The demon again said, "Do you have your fire stick, sir?"

Now Ļāde replied, "Here is the fire stick."

---

1. Possession by spirits, usually of a malevolent nature, is a common motif in Marshallese folklore, and there are methods of exorcising these demons when they possess individuals—as they are believed to be capable of doing even today.

2. Canoes are normally beached on the calm lagoon side of an atoll.

3. Note the motif of the ogress, a cannibal who eats other things as well—a destructive being.

4. The traditional fire-making equipment, using friction to produce a spark that ignites tinder. Two pieces of wood are used, as the informant explained. This is known as the fire plow in the anthropological literature, and is widespread. I saw it used on Wūjlañ Atoll in 1956. There was an accute shortage of matches on the atoll at the time. This method of producing fire has been supplanted by matches today, as it has been generally in the Marshalls for many years.

Now the woman came to Ļāde and ate him. And the demon said, "I ate the fire board. And I ate Ļāde! Ummm, my stomach hurts!"

Ļāde cut open her stomach with a sand clam shell [*Hippopus maculatus, jukkwe*], and appeared from the demon's anus.[5]

(She had a big mouth, and was big and tall—characteristics of demons.)

And he stood a little distance away from the demon, but the demon did not feel Ļāde going out from inside her stomach. When the demon looked around, she was surprised when she saw Ļāde outside. And she said, "Where did you come from, Ļāde?"

Ļāde replied, "In the fart that fell from your stomach."

When he finished speaking, the demon began to have increased stomach ache. And the demon said, "I ate the canoe; my stomach did not ache. I ate the island; it did not ache. I went to eat the skinny man, that lazy and sloppy, disheveled[6] Ļāde, and my stomach aches."

And she died.[7]

It is ended.

(Ļāde is on Wōtto in a piece of coral. He is on the island on the ocean side of Wōtto —on the island of Wōtto. There where he sat, there are his prints. [It is like cement on the piece of coral.] [That is, it is a formation of beach limestone, beach rocks with the mark of a man's buttocks on it. It is reportedly there today.]

The *ikid* [saga] of Ļainjin[8] also talks about this. It says, "Ļāde and Ļakne brought food to Koperwa and Liñijiļọk."

Ļāde is there to this day, but there is no story about Ļakne.

Ļāde and Ļakne are birds. They are not gone. You can see them today, seaward from Wōtto.[9]

And the prints of Ļāde are still on Wōtto.

And Liñijiļọk, a woman before, is a *kōñe* tree today [*Pemphis acidula,* ironwood]. And the *kōñe* is on Bok [Island] beside the Ujae pass. We can see it today.)

---

5. Note the motif of the escape of the hero/victim from the stomach of the demon by cutting his way out. Ļāde's reply to the demon that he came out in the fart that fell from her stomach adds a note of risqué humor to the story and enhances its entertainment value.

6. The word *apñāñā,* informant explained, is *kajin etto* (the ancient language) and means 'sloppy, lazy, disheveled'. It is used by some people today.

7. In this story, we see the motif of the human victim (or would-be victim) causing the death of the cannibal demon by using his initiative and courage. This is a widespread motif.

8. Ļainjin was the famous navigator of the Marshalls and is referred to in many folktales. He is a central figure in story 30, "Ikid eo an Ļainjin" (The Song-story of Ļainjin), page 131, which tells of his long voyage. The various navigational signs or sea markers *(kakļaļ/kōkaļļe)* are described in this "saga."

9. These are navigational signs of Wōtto. Again we see the familiar motif of humans transformed into rocks, birds, and trees, and an explanation of a natural phenomenon: the prints on the rock formation. Hawaiian mythology tells of humans and animals turned into stones (rocks) that are located on various islands of the Hawaiian archipelago (Beckwith 1970:21–22 and passim).

22: BWEBWENATO IN AELŌÑ IN WŌTTO ILO RAAN KO ETTO

Ri-bwebwenato: Jelibōr Jam, Kuwajleen 1975

Ilo aelōñ in Wōtto eaar wōr juon leddik eaar ļotak im rūttoļok. Ke ej jiroñ emej jinen im jemān. Innām ejjeļok juon naan in kouwe eaar roñ ak eaar etal wōt ñan kōņaan ko an. Juon raan eṃōkaj an mejatoto nana deļoñ ilo ānbwinnin im aolepān ļōmņak ko an. Im liin ej oktak jān armej. Ak ej bōk mejatoto in tiṃoņ. Etan tiṃoņ eo Likrabjel.

Ālikin jet raan ke ej mok tiṃoņ eo ņa ilo ānbwinnin emaroñ ṃōñā wa, ṃōñā āne, ṃōñā armej im men ko āierļok wōt.

Juon raan ke ej kōņaan wanlikļok ej etetal ṃokta iaar in Wōtto. Im kañ aolepān wa ko waan armej ro ṃokta. Ļōmņak eo an bwe enaaj kañ armej ro tokālik.

Iien eo wōt ej jino an wanlikļok im ej kañ jān keinikkan ko ilo wāto eo etan Āneju. Ej wanojļok ie jān ar ñan lik im ejjeļok juon ni ak bōb kab mā im jabdewōt mar ej jutak. Eṃōj an kañi. (Ejjeļok mā, ni, bōb, wūjooj ie. Ej āinwōt bok. Kōnke tiṃoņ ar kañi.)

Ke ej jāde ilik ej lo juon ļaddik. Etan ļaddik in, Ļāde. Innām ej loi ek ko ilowaan ļwe eo. Ļwe in bwilbwil riwut.

Ļāde ej erreiļok im loe lio. Im tiṃoņ eo ej al, "Kupañ luluto iṃwiji ña. | Badeto luluto iṃwiji ña. | Ej jeor aṃ it ke ļe?"

Ļāde ej uwaak, "It eo e." Tiṃoņ eo ej bar ba, "Ej jeor an jolok ke le?"

Kiiō Ļāde ej uwaak, "Jolok eo e." Kiiō lio ej maltok ñan Ļāde im kañe. Ak tiṃoņ eo ej ba, "Kañ iit eo im kañ Ļāde! Ummmm emetak loojiō!"

(Jekjek eo an tiṃoņ: eļap loñwiin, ñi ko [r]ekkañ; [r]ekilep im aetok.)

Ke Ļāde ej bukwe loojien ej waļok jān jikin mejļok eo an tiṃoņ. Im jutak ettoļok jidik jān tiṃoņ eo ak tiṃoņ eo ejjab eñjake an Ļāde dioij jān lowaan loojien. Ke ej erreiliktak tiṃoņ eo ej ilbōk ke ej lo Ļāde ālikin. Innām ej ba, "Kwaļok ia Ļāde?"

Ļāde ej uwaak, "Ilo jiñ eo eaar wōtlok jān loojiōṃ."

Ke ej ṃōj an ba, tiṃoņ eo ej jino an ļapļok an metak loojien im ej ba, "Ikañ wa, ejjab metak loojiō. Ikañ āne, ejjab metak loojiō. Iļak kañ ļaidikdik apñāñā ņe Ļāde, e[j] kab metak loojiō." Innām ej mej.

Ejeṃļok.

(Ļāde ej pād i Wōtto ilo juon bar. Epād eoonene ilikin Wōtto—eoonene in Wōtto. Ijo eaar jijet ie ekkal jenkwan ņa ie. Ej āinwōt jimeeņ ioon bar ñan rainin.

Ikid eo an Ļainjin ej bar bwebwenato kake. Āinwōt ba, "Ļāde im Ļakne erraņ rejro eojōk ļok ñan Koperwa em Liñijiļok."

Ļāde ej pād ñan rainin ak Ļakne [r]ejjab bwebwenato kake.

Ļāde im Ļakne rej bao. Rejjab jako. Koṃaroñ loi rainin, metoļok jān Wōtto.

Ak ioon Wōtto jenkwan Ļāde wōt ej pād.

Im Liñijiļok, kōrā eo ṃokta ej juon kōñe rainin. Im kōñe eo ej pād i bok. iturin to in Ujae. Jemaroñ loe rainin.)

23: THE STORY OF ĻABŌKJĀNWUT

As told by Mudge Samuel, Mājro 1971

Ļabōkjānwut was a boy whose mother was a rat. They lived on Mājro Island on Ṃwi-tuwaak *wāto* [land parcel]. This is at the end of Laura [Mājro] Island [the main island *(eoonene)* of Mājro Atoll].

His mother told him to stay in the area, and if he wanted to sail small model canoes *(riwut),* to do this along the lagoon side of the end of the island, and not go down the other way.

One day he disobeyed her and went down toward the middle of the island, on the lagoon side.

The waves and wind were so good for sailing his little model canoe that he disobeyed his mother. The *irooj* Jemāluut[1] called him over to his land, Eļļap *wāto.* The boy went over. Then he returned home. His mother asked him where he had been, and why he had disobeyed her. She then told him to step on her *(jura).* He did this, and pushed and pressed her down into a hole.

Then she asked him what he saw on top of her head. He said, *"Diede ṃōjālūlū"* (curly hair). She told him to keep pressing down on her head. Then she asked him again. And he replied, *"Diede arṃwe"* (long, light, straight hair). She repeated the order and asked him again. And he replied, *"Diede bōlōk"* (wavy hair, nice looking).

That was the end of that, then.

(There are three holes on Mwi-tuwaak *wāto* today from this occurrence. One of the holes is used as a well.)

Then the boy stepped away from the holes, and there was a great shining light in the sky. All of the people on the island ran out and ran around, and were greatly surprised. The boy then went back to the *wāto* of the *irooj,* and Jemāluut invited him to come in. And he did so.

End of story.

The Mājro people have this nice wavy hair today. The girls are the prettiest, on Mājro.

1. *Jemāluut* means 'rainbow' in Ratak, the eastern chain of the Marshalls, where Mājro is located. In Rālik, the western chain, 'rainbow' is *iia.*

24: ĻAIO, THE DEMON WHO STOLE FROM THE ATOLL OF MĀJRO

As told by Ļamān and Jekkein, Mājro 1955

(A man came from the real depths of the ocean, north of Pikaar Atoll.)[1]

The *irooj* (chief) of Mājro made a *jabne* to keep people away from his lands [also called *itkiju,* a magical charm of plaited coconut leaves, this is a Marshallese taboo or *emo̧* sign].[2]

Ļaio came to Mōnkōle-jāiōn̄ *wāto* (land parcel) and Mōnkōle-jāirōk *wāto* on Mājro Island. He took coconuts, breadfruit, pandanus, bananas, and taro and put them in a basket and went away to his home in the ocean, north of Pikaar.

He did this three times. On the third time, a man saw him.[3]

His basket was full and the atoll of Aur fell out. M̧aļo-eļap, Wōjjā, Aelok, and Utrōk fell out from the full basket. (These atolls had not been on the ocean before this happened.)[4]

The third time, they looked for him and one man saw him, Ļāde. He asked him, "Who are you?" The answer, "I." And Ļāde asked Ļaio, "Who are you?" The answer, "I." "Your name?" (Ļāde speaking.) The answer, "Ļaio. And your name?" Answer, "Ļāde." Now they knew each other's name.

Demon Ļaio then took a coconut from his basket and said, "This is your food." (The reason for this was, as he told Ļāde, so that Ļāde would not tell anyone about the demon.)

Ļāde took the coconut but did not eat it. The next morning the *irooj* said, "Bring out the sail and sew it up. Prepare it for use."

The *irooj* asked who saw the thief last night (the demon). One man said, "I." The *irooj,* "His name?" Answer, "I know his name. But I have forgotten it." (He was lying and had not seen the demon.)

They continued preparing the sail and the canoe.

The *irooj* said, "Who saw the demon?" Another man answered, "I." The *irooj,* "His name?" The man (who was also lying) said,

---

1. Pikaar Atoll is in northern Ratak, south of Bok-ak (Taongi), the northernmost atoll of the Ratak chain. These atolls are uninhabited. There is very little rainfall, but they are the nesting places of myriads of birds, and many turtles come ashore to lay their eggs. These two atolls have traditionally been important sources of food for the people of northern Ratak, and regular controlled expeditions were made to them to obtain the bird and turtle eggs and flesh (see Tobin 1958:47–56 for details). The regulation of the expeditions functioned to conserve these natural resources.

2. The *itkiju* or *jabne* were made of plaited coconut fronds tied to the end of a stick. Some older people still knew how to make them (as of 1951 when I was given this information). The meaning of *jabne* ('no foot') is that no foot but the chief's (the *irooj*'s) may step here. Magic *(anijnij)* was made on the *itkiju.* It is believed that if any unauthorized person takes food from the place upon which the *itkiju* is placed or even sets foot on it, he will get sick and/or die. Permission to go on the land had to be obtained from the chief (see Tobin 1958:56–57).

3. Note the use of the ritual, formulaic number three. This is found in many Marshallese folktales and is used in magical/medical formulae to this day. The importance of the number three in the introduced and well-integrated Christian religion—the Triune Godhead and the resurrection of Christ on the third day—probably confirmed the belief of the Marshallese in the efficacy of this number.

4. Note the supernatural explanation for the origin of specific atolls.

"I forgot it." The *irooj* asked the third time, "Who saw him?"

Ļāde answered. "I." The *irooj* asked, "His name?" Ļāde answered, "Ļaio."

Ļāde brought the coconut and showed it to the *irooj,* and said, "This is part of his food that he gave to me." And he told about the demon's telling him not to reveal his name.

When Ļāde told the demon's name, he [the demon] heard him and came from the ocean (from the depths). The people heard him coming and were afraid.

They picked up the sail and hid Ļāde in it. The demon came and lifted up the sail. He pulled Ļāde out and carried him away and ate him in his own place in the ocean.

Ļaio then went north of Pikaar, in the ocean, and is [now] a fish, a swordfish. He appears from the ocean, and can go up to the height of a coconut tree if he wishes to do so.

A bird, a frigate bird named Toorlōn̄, lives north of Pikaar and works against Ļaio. He prevents him from coming up and destroying canoes and people. Ļaio sees the frigate bird and is prevented from harming people.

The *roro* (chant) is: *"Eṃṃaan juon eņ ejutak wot i lukon lǫmeto Ļaio, ejede Toorlōn̄ ekwono pelle eo*[5] *eroje, an anij na kein juri Toorlōn̄ n̄an mut jerke. Jejeor bwibwi eo kabian̄."* (A man over there is just standing in the middle of the ocean, Ļaio. He looks at Toorlōn̄, he says, the wise one says, these words of the god we do not say. Toorlōn̄ pitching waves, we change course. We cast out the yolk northwest.)

The old people tell this story, but we have never seen these *kōkļaļ* (sea markers or navigation signs).[6] This is the *kōkļaļ* of Pikaar. There are many birds' eggs on Pikaar. The ocean area near Pikaar is yellowish partially, like the yolk of eggs. When you see this sign you *kapwe* (go to the right). And you will see Ron̄dik the next day.

---

5. Informant explained that *pelle eo* means the wise one in *kajin etto* (the ancient language).

6. The *kōkļaļ* are signs or sea markers—aids to navigation. Certain fish, sea animals, birds, reefs, and the like are associated with specific locations, and were important in navigation to the Marshallese. In the case of Pikaar, as told in the story, the navigational sign is discoloration of the ocean near the atoll, and there is a natural association with the abundance of birds' eggs on that atoll. This story illustrates the widespread prohibition against speaking the name of a god or other supernatural being. Ļāde disobeyed the demon and revealed its name—and was punished by being eaten. See Leach (1950, 2:782–783) for a discussion of the name taboo in other cultures. Also see Webster (1942:301–310).

25: HOW THE LARGE INLET ON WŌTTO ISLAND WAS FORMED

As told by an *aļap* on Wōtto, 1969

A *mejenkwaad*[1] who was the spouse of Ļāde[2] became angry with him when he tried to run away from her.

She pursued him to Wōtto, and stretching out her neck a very long way toward him, tried to eat him. She failed to do this, but she bit a big piece of the island instead. Her breath was so hot and so powerful that it killed the vegetation fronting the beach of the island where she had taken the piece of it with her big bite.

This is why the area is sandy and useless for growing things today.[3]

---

1. An ogress. These fearsome creatures figure in a number of Marshallese folktales.

2. Ļāde is a figure in other Marshallese stories, including story 22, "Story about the Atoll of Wōtto in the Olden Days" (page 106), and story 24, "Ļaio, the Demon Who Stole from the Atoll of Mājro" (page 110).

3. Here again we have a supernatural explanation for natural phenomena. The shallow inlet does indeed look as if might be the result of a big bite, and the area adjacent to it is barren in appearance.

26: THE BEGINNING OF THE APPEARANCE OF NAVIGATION IN THESE ATOLLS

As told by M̧ak Juda, Mājro 1972

Navigation began to appear on Nam̧dik. [There was} nn old woman and her two sons. Those people were brothers. Their mother taught them sailing and navigation.

When their teaching was completed, they began to think about sailing from Nam̧dik—to go away to Ellep. Now they planned about it and thought about it, [whether to] teach people or not?

Now, with the old woman outside, one of these men said, "We give the knowledge of navigation to the people. Do we two [say], 'Imm' or do we two [say] 'Aa'?"

In *kajin bwebwenato* (story language): *"Turin likiej i Nam̧dik | Kōjro ej 'Imm' ke? | Ak kōjro ej "Aa" ke?"* "Beside the windward side of Nam̧dik/ Do we two say 'Imm'? | Or do we say 'Aa'?"

Now they threw their mother's *dekeinnin* [pandanus leaf pounder] onto the windward side of Nam̧dik.[1]

(The meaning of this was that they could not give the knowledge of navigation to any person. They could only give it to a few clans *[jowi/jou].*)[2]

Now there are only two kinds of knowledge *(ab):* Rakinmeto ('South in the ocean') from Aelōn̄ļaplap to Epoon (in Rālik),[3] and Eañinmeto ('North in the ocean'): Nam̧o, Kuwajleen, Ujae, Lae, Wōtto, Pikinni, Aelōn̄inae, Ron̄ļap, and Ron̄dik—the western atolls [of Rālik].

(Navigators appeared only from Rālik. The Ratak people learned from them.)

Number one: There are no errors in the *ab* of Rakinmeto. It was secret. People hid it very well [kept it a secret].

Number two: Eañinmeto: Error in knowing. Never mind errors because the people who know navigation are unable to drift. They are not unable to see an island. [They cannot get lost.] They know it. There is a little difference between them [the two kinds

---

1. The *dekāinnin/dekā in nin* or pandanus leaf pounders were very important items in the Marshallese culture. They were used to prepare the pandanus leaves, process them for use in plaiting mats for household use and for clothing and for sails for the important canoes. They were considered one of the most important things for survival, as the famous *jabōnkōnnaan* (proverb) tells us. They were laboriously pecked out of the thick inner part of the shell of the giant clam [*Tridacna gigas, kapwor*], popularly known today as "the giant killer clam," and the largest bivalve known (also a good source of food). They are beautiful artifacts, highly polished through years of use and handed down from mother to daughter over the generations. Although not as necessary for survival as they were in the past, the *dekeinnin* are still used, and are still highly prized and considered to be heirlooms.

Because they were so important in the culture the throwing of the pounder onto the windward side of Nam̧dik, in the story, is highly symbolic.

2. The Marshallese see themselves as belonging to named matrilineal clans (*jowi* in Rālik, *jou* in Ratak), and matrilineages *(bwij).* These clans, which are aggregates of lineages, regulate marriage and are almost completely exogamous. They also function to support and offer hospitality to fellow clan members visiting their atolls.

3. Southern Rālik (see map of the Marshalls). The Marshalls are divided geographically primarily into two chains of atolls and single islands—Ratak, the eastern chain, and Rālik, the western chain—and are subdivided as indicated into northern, western, and southern areas, each with its specific name.

of navigation]. (The *dektile* is the *kakoḷḷe:* navigation sign of an island.)[4] They change a little between Eañinmeto and Rakinmeto. They have the same truth [correctness, accuracy], but the signs vary.

The Erroja clan knows [navigation] in Rakinmeto. And the Ri-Kuwajleen clan [knows it] in Eañinmeto. (Kabua Kabua,[5] Neimat,[6] and Ḷoani, the *aḷap* [maternal uncle] of Neimat.)

Erroja: Nelu[7] and his companions, chiefs and commoners. They knew and gave [knowledge of navigation] to a few [people], but the most famous knowledge remained with them.

They hid the teaching, but they could teach their relatives. Some chiefs appointed those whom they wished to learn.[8] They do this to this day. It [the teaching] is not really completed. They only learn a little from them.

I learned from chief Ḷaelañ. And Neimat and some others.[9]

It is ended.

4. As the informant stated, these are signs or sea markers, aids to navigation. Certain fish, birds, rocks, objects floating in the sea, and the like are associated with specific reefs, islands, or atolls, as were the navigational chants *(roro).* These helped the navigator reach his destination. They were of great importance to the Marshallese in their oceanic environment, where there were long stretches of ocean between islands in many cases.

5. Kabua Kabua (of the Ri-Kuwajleen clan) is a contemporary *irooj ḷapḷap* (paramount chief) of Rālik.

6. Neimat was the mother of Kabua Kabua.

7. Nelu (of the Irroja clan) was a chief of Rālik during the German period.

8. Note the use of the English loanword *appoint* in this story told to me in Marshallese by the elderly informant. It is also used by other non-English speakers even younger than the informant.

9. Ḷaelañ was an *irooj ḷapḷap* of lands in Rālik. He was a son of Irooj Ḷapḷap Kabua, husband of Neimat, and father of Kabua Kabua. Note how the informant identifies the knowledge of navigation with the chiefs.

26: JINOIN AN WAĻǪK METO ILO AELŌÑ KEIN

Ri-bwebwenato: Mark Juda, Mājro 1972

Jinoin an waļǫk meto ilo Naṃdik. Juon leļļap kab ruo nājin eṃṃaan. Armej rein jimjānjimjatōn, jineer ar katakin er kōn jerakrōk im meto.

Eṃōj aer katak. Rej jino ļōmņak in jerak jān Naṃdik. Ilǫk ñan Ellep. Kiiō rej ļōmņak in katakin armej. Rej pepe kake im ļōmņak kake. Katakin armej ak jaab ke?

Kiiō ippān leļļap eo ālikin ļōṃaro juon iaer ej ba, "Jej leļǫk jeļāļǫkjeņ ñan armej kōn meto. Kōjro 'imm' ak kejro 'aa' (ba)?" (Kajin bwebwenato: Tuuri likiej i Naṃdik | Kōjro ej 'imm' ak kejro ej 'aa' ke?)

Kiiō rej joļǫk dekeinnin an jineer ņae likiej in Naṃdik. (Meļeļe in ejjab maroñ leļǫk jeļāļǫkjeņ in meto ñan jabdewōt armej. Remaroñ leļǫk ñan jet wōt jowi.)

Kiiō eor ruo ab: Rakinmeto: jān Aelōñļapļap ñan Epoon (Rālik). Im Eañinmeto: Naṃo, Kuwajleen, Ujae, Lae, Wōtto, Pikinni, Aelōñinae, Roñļap, im Roñdik. Aelōñ tu rilik.

Meto ar waļǫk jān Rālik wōt. Ri-Ratak ar katak jān er.

Nōṃba juon ejjeļǫk bōd ilo ab in Rakinmeto. Ittino, eļap an armej ņooje.

Nōṃba ruo: Eañinmeto: Bōd in jeļā. Jekdǫǫn bōd kōnke armej rejeļā meto eo. Rejjab maroñ peļǫk ak jab maroñ lo āne. Rejeļā.

Jidik wōt an oktak jān doon. (Dekātile ej kakōļļan āne.) Oktak jidik ikōtaan Eañinmeto im Rakinmeto. Āinwōt juon aer ṃool ak dekātile āinjuon jidik.

An Erroja jowi rejeļā ilo Rakinmeto. Im Ri-Kuwajleen ilo Eañinmeto. (Kabua Kabua, Neimat, Ļoani, aļap eo an Neimat.)

Erroja: Nelu im ro ṃōttāer. Irooj im kajoor. Rejeļā ak rej leļǫk ñan ro jet ak buñbuñ in jeļā eo epād ippāer.

Ittino in katak bōtab remaroñ katakin nukwier. Jet irooj rej *appoint* ro rōkōņaan katakin er. Rej kōṃṃan wōt rainin. Ejjab lukkuun kōmaatļǫk. Jidik wōt rej katak jān er.

Iaar katak ippān Ļaelañ, im Neimat, im ro jet.

Ejeṃļǫk.

27: THE REASON THE KAPINMETO PEOPLE KNOW NAVIGATION: STORY OF THE BEGINNING OF THE KNOWLEDGE OF NAVIGATION

As told by Jelibōr Jam, Kuwajleen 1975

There was a woman, her name was Litarmelu. Her clan was Ri-Kuwajleen. She lived in Kipinmeto. (Kipinmeto and Kapinmeto are the same.)[1]

Now the chiefs came and took her from Kapinmeto and took her to Jālooj, and put her on an island named Piñlep. And the chiefs gave her four places, land holdings, for her home—three land parcels and one island. The name of the island was Arļap (north of Piñlep).

Litarmelu was perhaps twenty-three years old now.[2] After a few days, three men appeared. These men came up without a sail. Their ship was like a box.

And Litarmelu saw the men and brought them with her. She took them in, and took very good care of them.

Because Litarmelu was so kind to them, now they asked her, "Do you want to learn navigation so that you will be able to go to all the atolls in the Marshalls?"

And Litarmelu said, "Yes, I want to." The men said, "Tomorrow we will go to teach you navigation."[3] One of the men said, "Perhaps it will be better if we tow you by hand in the water and teach you in it."

And when it was noon, low tide, they towed Litarmelu beside Barijur (a big rock on the Piñlep reef; it is bigger than a house or a ship; it is there to this day).

As they towed her, they asked Litarmelu, "Where are we now?" Litarmelu answered, "To windward, [on the] ocean side of Barijur."

Now the man said, "Are you squinting?" Litarmelu said, "Should I sleep?" And the man said, "Yes, sleep!" (so that she should not see where they were towing her).

Now the man towed her again to the south. When he reached the south side of Barijur, the man again asked, "Where are we now?" Litarmelu said, "I do not know." The man asked, "Do you not recognize this place? Do you feel that wave that is coming into the lagoon?" She said, "Yes, I feel it." And the man said, "And the wave that is coming into the ocean?"

Litarmelu said, "Yes, I feel it again." Now the man said, "I will tow you again. Go to sleep."

(Litarmelu was on the reef between Piñlep and Barijur when the man was questioning her. One man spoke and towed her, and two just followed.)[4]

Now he towed her and circled. And he

---

1. Informant asked, "Do you know where Kapinmeto is located? Ujae, Lae, and Wōtto. Kuwajleen and Ellep are not included. They are in Eañinmeto, [together] with Pikinni, Roñļap, Roñdik, and Aelōñinae" [*Kapinmeto* means 'bottom of the ocean' or 'western atolls', and *Eañinmeto* means 'north in the ocean']."

2. Note the incorporation of the western chronology (23 years) into the folktale.

3. Note the motif of strangers who arrive in a strange craft, and who reward their benefactress (Litarmelu) with valuable knowledge. Note also the use of the loanword *bo̧o̧k* 'box'.

4. Informant clarified the situation for me, and I sketched it in my notebook following his directions. The importance of location is evident in this and other folktales, as it is to the Marshallese in their everyday life, as reflected in their language (see Carr and Elbert 1945:xx, 279–286; Tobin 1967:112–113; and Bender 1969:267–270, 279–286).

again circled (reversed) to the left and to the right.

And Litarmelu was still asleep, and kept her eyes closed. She did not know where she was being taken.

And the man returned to the east (ocean, windward) side of Barijur. And again he asked, "Where are we now?"

Litarmelu answered, "I think to the west of Barijur." The man: "Why do you say to the west?" Litarmelu said, "I think so." The man said, "O, you don't know navigation yet. Wake up and see where you are."

She woke up and saw she was to the east. Litarmelu said, "Ummm, now I understand." The man said, "Close your eyes again." Now Litarmelu closed her eyes again. He returned to the south. The man again asked, "Where are we now?" Litarmelu answered, "To the south of Barijur." Now the man said, "Why do you say to the south?" Now Litarmelu answered, "Because I feel the wave coming into the ocean from the lagoon."

Now the man asked, "And do you feel the wave coming in from the ocean?" Litarmelu said, "Yes." Now the man said, "Wake up!" Now he explained it to Litarmelu. He said, "See, the wave is coming into the lagoon now. The wave is coming here from the lagoon." He said, "Do you see how the waves strike together? Well, that is the way of the ocean."

And the first day ended. Now the second day. It was like the first day. They returned and towed Litarmelu north of Barijur. They began from the east of Barijur and towed her to the north. Now the man asked, "Where are we now?"

Litarmelu answered, "To the east of Barijur." The man said, "No. To the north. Wake up and look!" Litarmelu said, "O, I am mistaken! I thought it was to the east of Barijur." Now the man said, "Well, I will explain it again now." Now the man said, "Do you see the wave that is going into the lagoon from the ocean?"

Litarmelu answered, "Yes." The man said, "Do you see the wave that is coming into the ocean from the lagoon?" Litarmelu answered, "Yes." The man asked again, "Is it clear that your body feels the wave is coming into the ocean from the lagoon?" Litarmelu said, "Yes."

Now the man explained, "Do not say to the east of Barijur, for it is clear that these waves strike together. If it were to the east, one of those waves would be absent."

Litarmelu replied. She said, "What wave is absent?"[5] The man answered, "Waves coming in from the west are absent and there are waves coming in from the east only." The reason the waves coming in from the west are absent is because they are blocked off by Barijur. And here we are at the north. And your body is feeling all these waves."

Now the second day was ended. Now they did the same thing on all directions of the rock for four days.[6] After the fourth day the instruction was ended.

---

5. Informant explained that, "N̦o te eo . . ." 'what wave is missing' is wave language *(kajin n̦o)*. In Rālik language *(Kajin Rālik)* it is, "N̦o ta eo."

6. Informant explained that all questions are not repeated in telling the story. It is shortened, as he had done.

Now only explanation. Now he revealed these ways of explaining to Litarmelu. *"Liklaļ netinkōt."* Now Litarmelu asked, "What is *netinkōt?"* Now the man explained it. He said, "Because it is the bottom (western side) of the atoll and the waves are not high there. And they say *'netinkot'*.[7] And if at the eastern part of the atoll they say *'jurenokme'."*

The man asked Litarmelu, "Do you know what *jurenokme* is?" Litarmelu said, "I don't know." The man said, "The meaning is because it is a high wave. And it is the sign (sea marker) of the eastern part of the atoll. *Netinkōt* is the sign of the western part of the atoll. Do you understand now, Litarmelu?"

Litarmelu asked, "About what?" The man said, "*Likiej* and *liklaļ* of an atoll." Litarmelu said, "Yes, I understand now."

The man said, "Say it." Litarmelu said, "*Liklaļ, netinkōt* are like small waves. *Likiej, jurenokme* are like high waves."

Now the man said, "Well, good." Litarmelu asked, "And north and south?" The man again replied, *"Kāājinrōjep."*

"What is *kāājinrōjep?"* Litarmelu asked. Now the man said, "You will see a wave shaped like a flying-fish hook" *(Kāājinrōjep).*[8] Now that first day was finished, and he said, "Get ready, for we are going to sail. And you tell the Naṃdik people, the Epoon people, and the Aelōn̄ļapļap people—they who drifted here to Jālooj. If they want to go, they should come here, for we are going to Naṃdik, Epoon, and Aelōn̄ļapļap, when there will be a good wind.

"I will clarify the time of sailing again."[9]

After three days he said, "Tomorrow you all come and we will sail." And some Epoon people and Naṃdik people loaded aboard, and they sailed the following day.

The wind came from the east, and the weather was good, and the canoe drifted. But there was no sail.

After some time, the food was all gone, and the drinking water was all gone, and they were angry with Litarmelu. "Why did you tell us to sail? For we are hungry and thirsty. But there is no island. How will we be able to survive now?

"You said we will arrive at an island now. But many days have passed. You are lying exceedingly. If it is the same tomorrow, we will kill you."

Now at three o'clock that same afternoon, they saw Naṃdik. Now the man said to Litarmelu, "Do we *umm?* or do we *aaa?"* (The meaning of *umm:* do not reveal to people. Hide it. Do not tell. The meaning of *aaa:* reveal to the people.) Now Litarmelu said, "We *umm.*" Now the man broke apart the pandanus leaf pounder and said, "To the western, bottom side of Naṃdik."[10] That afternoon they went and stopped at Naṃdik.

---

7. Kapinmeto in this case means the 'bottom section of the atolls'. It is also called *kapin-aelōn̄-in.*

8. Informant explained the meaning of *kāājinrōjep.* These are the flying-fish hooks used in the old days. They were made from *ļat in waini* (coconut shells). They were about one inch long, like a finger. The bait was placed on the shank of the hook. They were good hooks, he said.

9. Informant sketched and labeled the waves and their names described in the story and taught to Litarmelu, in my notebook, in their relation to Kuwajleen Atoll.

10. As noted in story 26, "The Beginning of the Appearance of Navigation in These Atolls" (page 113), the pandanus leaf pounders *(deke-in-nin)* were important items of Marshallese material culture. Because they were so important in the culture, the breaking of a pounder in association with sailing to Naṃdik is highly symbolic of the importance of the action. Compare this story with that one, in which a pandanus leaf pounder is not broken, but is thrown to Naṃdik.

And the (three) men again sailed and went away. And we do not know where they went.

Litarmelu remained on Naṃdik. And she became pregnant and gave birth to many children. (We do not know who the father was or the names of the children, except for one.) The name of one of them was Ļainjin, a male, and he learned navigation from his mother. Litarmelu sailed from Naṃdik to Piñlep (Jālooj) and gave the boy, her son, to Lineo (to adopt).

Litarmelu remained for a few days and sailed to Aelōñļapļap. From Aelōñļapļap [to] Kuwajleen. The place where she stayed on was Kuwajleen. The name of the land parcel is Erļañ. (The air strip is there today.)

Now the chiefs on Jālooj wanted to sail and come to Aelōñļapļap, and they took Ļainjin and his mother aboard—his mother named Lineo). And they sailed to Aelōñļapļap but did not see Aelōñļapļap. And they drifted and did not know where they were.

Now Ļainjin (the boy, who was a child) saw a bird, just as his mother Litarmelu had instructed him. And he appeared from his mat and saw the bird and knew where they were. And the worried chiefs said if the boy knew where the island was he should reveal it.

And the mother was angry with the boy. "I said you should make a noise now. Can you reveal the island?"

The boy again made a sound and said, "Toorlōñ is at the cape of Aji-io-io | the sign of Pikaar." (It is a chant. Toorlōñ is the name of the chief of all of the frigate birds) [*Fregata minor* Gmelin, Pacific man-o'-war, *ak*, and *Fregata ariel* gray, least man-o'-war, *ak*].[11] Aji is the name of a piece of land there, at Pikaar Atoll. Now the chiefs said, "You know where the island is!" Now his mother was very angry and said, "If the island does not appear, they may kill the two of us. Well, go ahead and reveal the island."[12]

Now the boy said to his mother, "The things I am looking for will reveal the island."

His mother said, "Are you sure?" The boy said, "Yes, I am sure. Just as I think of the ocean, I am thinking of the island." (He was reassuring his mother, for she was afraid, very frightened.)

The boy said, "Well, I reveal the island to you now. Here we are, west of Pikaar. But we started for Aelōñļapļap and drifted and now we are going to Aelōñļapļap."

And they changed course, tacked, and pointed toward Aelōñļapļap.

After three days, they saw Aelōñļapļap. And they went and stayed on Aelōñļapļap. The chiefs really honored the boy. That boy stayed there and wanted to see his mother. And he said to the chiefs. "I want to see mamma." And the chiefs said, "Well, we will sail when the wind is good."

I do not know how many days, perhaps a week, and the wind was good. Now they sailed from Aelōñļapļap and came toward Naṃo. And did not see Naṃo for perhaps two weeks. (They drifted away from Naṃo.)

---

11. Chief of the Frigate Birds *(Irooj in Ak)*. The frigate birds themselves are thought to be the chiefs of birds *(Irooj in Bao)*, presumably because of their large size, strength, and skill in getting their food, and their dominance over other birds.

12. Informant explained *bōke* ('point' or 'cape') by sketching Kuwajleen Atoll for me and indicating the various capes of the atoll. He said, "Bōke in Kuwajleen: eoonene iturin jikin kālọk eo etan Būkien Kālōñ. Bōke in Ruot-Niṃur ej Bōke in Kōmļaan. Ilo aolep aelōñ eor etan bōke ko. Bareinwōt āne ko āinwōt Kōle, āinwōt turilik-rok Bōke in Tōlmọñ." (The cape of Kuwajleen: on the main island next to the airfield, the name is Bōke in Kālōñ [Cape of Kālōñ]. Cape of Ruot-Niṃur [Roi-Namur as Americans call it] is Bōke in Kōmļaan [Cape of Kōmļaan]. The names of the capes are [found] on all of the atolls, also on islands like Kōle, for example, [to the] southwest is Bōke in Tōlmọñ.)

Now they said it would be good to reveal the island again. Now the boy spoke again. He said (chanted), *"Akio | Likio | Takeo-o | Likiej jān Jinme!"* (This is in the ancient language and I do not know its meaning.)[13]

Now the chiefs said, "If you are able to reveal the island, reveal it."

Now the boy said, "Where is a good place?" The chief said, "It is up to you." And the boy said, "We are going to Naṃo."

Now they sailed to Naṃo, and many days passed. And the chiefs said, "When will Naṃo appear?" Now the boy said, "It will be clarified."

The following day, Naṃo appeared. Now the chiefs said, "It is not Naṃo." And the boy said, "Naṃo!" Now the chiefs said, "Why is it Naṃo, because they tacked to the west of it?"

The boy said, "The current took the canoe to the east."[14] He explained it. "And the canoe is slow in sailing to Naṃo. This afternoon the canoe will arrive at Naṃo."

The chiefs looked and saw that it was really Naṃo. The chiefs had not believed this.

They remained on Naṃo for two days and sailed again from Naṃo and came toward Kuwajleen and did not see Kuwajleen.

And the chiefs again questioned the boy, "Where is Kuwajleen?" The boy said, "It is under the sun." Because the sun was in the west.

Now the chiefs said, "Well, go to the west!" And the boy said, "Go to the west!" And the canoe went to the west. It went-went-went and then straight ahead, the Meik Pass. The boy said, "This is it."

That night the canoe entered the Meik Pass. Now the chiefs said, "Where are we? Kuwajleen? Or another atoll?" The boy said, "Kuwajleen." Now they went on to Kuwajleen Island, and the boy went to be with his mother.

And the chiefs decreed that the boy should remain with them. Now the mother instructed him intensively, so that he would know [it] very well. And the boy learned all of his mother's knowledge.

Now the chiefs took the boy to be with them. But his mother Litarmelu sailed to Ratak [the eastern chain of the Marshalls], Rālik Rak [the southern part of the western chain], and Eañinmeto [the northern atolls], and went to Ujae and remained there for a few months. And sailed from Ujae, coming to Lae. From Lae to Wōtto, and did not see Wōtto. But they went up north of Wōtto into the sky and have been gone to this day.

(This is an amazing thing. Can it be true?)

There is no grave of Litarmelu on the island. [Or] on any island.

The canoes that were sailed were about seventeen.

The proof of this story: one man was in the canoe of Litarmelu and was bailing and the bailer fell out. And the man jumped out after the bailer and landed in a thicket of pandanus trees on Wōtto.

Now the man was shocked and said (grunted), "Umm, why did I think that I was on the ocean? But why am I on the island?"

Now the man went to the people and told them that the fleet of canoes of Litarmelu had gone away into the sky.

It is ended.

(I do not know if it is true. But this is how I heard it from people in the past.)

---

13. Nor did informant know the location of Jinme. However, there is an island named Jinme on the eastern side of Ānewetak Atoll. "Likiej in Jinme" would be translated as 'the windward or ocean side of Jinme'.

14. Informant explained that *iaitak* means 'the current took the canoe to the east'. And *iaito* means 'the current takes the canoe to the west'. And *būkaien* or *būkain* means 'ocean' in *kajin etto* (the ancient language).

Comments

One wonders if the element of the "ship like a box" in this legend was derived from an actual historical incident. Perhaps from a Japanese or Chinese junk that had drifted to the Marshall Islands in the distant past. Such craft have indeed reached the Marshalls and have been reported in the literature.

In his important "Table of Voyages Affecting Micronesian Islands," Riesenberg (1965: 168) states: "Japan to Lae: Krämer and Nevermann, 1938:12. 1883: A Japanese junk drifted to Lae and was captured and plundered.

"Japanese to Ujae: Hambruch, 1915:227. About 1910: Three Japanese fishermen cast ashore at Ujae."

Indeed junks used by Japanese and Chinese fishermen and traders were square in shape, box-like as compared to the Marshallese outrigger canoes.

Perhaps the initial appearance of such craft, which might have occurred in the distant past, so impressed the Marshallese that it was incorporated into the folktale, without an explanation of its provenance, and without details, thus becoming an element in an important legend explaining the invaluable knowledge of navigation.

This is not to imply that the Marshallese learned navigation from such contacts. Marshallese navigation requires, as this legend and others, and the navigation chants clearly reveal, a detailed knowledge of local conditions, which outsiders would obviously not have. Nor would they be able to impart navigational information to the Marshallese, because of the language barrier.

The word *wa,* used in this legend for the strange craft means 'canoe, ship, or boat'. Obviously a vessel "like a box" would not be a canoe.

27: WŪNIN AN RI-KAPINMETO JEĻĀ METO: BWEBWENATO IN JINOIN JEĻĀĻǪKJEŅ KŌN METO

Ri-bwebwenato: Jelibōr Jam, Kuwajleen 1975

Eor juon kōrā, etan Litarmelu. Jowi eo an, Ri-Kuwajleen. Ar pād i Kipinmeto. (Kipinmeto im Kapinmeto āinwōt juon.)

Kiiō itok irooj ro im bōke liin jān Kipinmeto. Im bōkļǫk ñan Jālooj. Im doore ilo juon āne. Etan āneo Piñlep. Innām irooj ro raar leļǫk emān jikin, eṃ, ñane bwe en iṃōn. Jilu eṃ ak juon āne. Etan āneo Arļap (iōñ in Piñlep).

Bwe bōlen eor roñoul jilu an Litarmelu iiō kiiō. Ļǫkun jet raan ewaļǫk jilu eṃṃaan. Wa rej itok kake ejjeļǫk wōjļā āin wa eo āinwōt bǫǫk.

Innām Litarmelu elo ļōṃaro im bōktok er ñan ippān. Im kanooj in eṃṃan an lale er. Kōn an Litarmelu jouj ñan er kiiō rej kajjitōk ippān, "Kwōj kōņaan ke ekkatak meto bwe komaroñ etal ñan aolep aelōñ in Ṃajeļ?" Innām Litarmelu ar ba, "Aet, ikōnaan." Ļōṃaraņ rej ba, "Ilju jenaaj etal in katakin eok meto." Ļeo juon eba, "Bōlen eṃṃanļǫk ñe jenaaj atake eok ilo lǫjet im katakin [eok] ie."

Innām ke ej raelep, eibwij innām reilem atake Litarmelu iturin Barijur. (Juon dekā kileplep ioon pedped in Piñlep. Ekilep jān juon eṃ ak juon wa. Epād ie rainin.)

Ilo aer atake rej kajjitōk ippān Litarmelu, "Ia in kiiō?" Litarmelu ej uwaak, "Likiej in Barijur." Kiiō ļeo ej ba, "Kwōj erre?" Im Litarmelu ej ba, "Ak in kiki ke?"

Innām ļeo eba, "Aet, kwōn kiki!" (Bwe en jab loe aer atake.)

Kiiō ļeo ebar atake rōkeañ ļǫk. Ke ej tōpar Barijur turōk ļeo ebar kajjitōk, "Jej pād ia kiiō?" Litarmelu eba, "Ijaje." Ļeo eba, "Kwojjab kile ijin?" Ļeo eba, "Kwōj eñjake ke ņo eņ ej wanartak?" Litarmelu eba, "Aet, ij eñjake wōt." Ļeo eba, "Ak ņo eņ ej wanlikļǫk?" Litarmelu ej ba, "Aet ij bar eñjake."

Kiiō ļeo ej ba, "Ij bar atake eok. Kwōn kiki wōt."

(Litarmelu ar pād ioon pedped ikōtaan Piñlep im Barijur ke ļeo ar kajjitōk. Juon eṃṃaan ej kōnono im atake im ruo rej ļoore wōt.)

Kiiō ej atake im addeboulul. Innām bar addeboulul tuanmiiñ im tuanbwijmaroñ.

Im Litarmelu ej kiki wōt. Im kōn an kar kiki (kili) mejān wōt, ejaje rej atake ļǫk iaļǫk. Im ļeo ej bar rǫǫl ñan likiej im Barijur. Im bar kajjitōk, "Jej pād ia kiiō?"

Litarmelu e uwaak, "N̄a ij ļōmņak turilik in Barijur." Ļeo eba:, "Taunin aṃ ba turilik?" Litarmelu ar ba, "N̄a ij ļōmņak." Ļeo ej ba, "O kwōjjañin jeļā meto. Ruj ṃōk im lale ia in."

Eļak ruj ej pād turear. Litarmelu eba, "Ummm, ij kab meļeļe." Ļeo ej ba, "Bar kili mejaṃ." Kiiō Litarmelu ebar kili mejān. Kiiō ļeo ej bar atake. Bar rǫǫl ñan turōk. Ļeo ej bar kajjitōk, "Ia in jej pād ie kiiō?" Litarmelu ej uwaak, "Turōk in Barijur." Kiiō ļeo ej kajjitōk, "Taunin aṃ ba turōk?" Kiiō Litarmelu ej uwaak, "Kōnke ij eñjake an wanliktak ņo ņe jān ar."

Kiiō ļeo ej kajjitōk, "Ak kwōj eñjake ke ņo itok jān lik?" Litarmelu eba, "Aet." Kiiō ļeo eba, "Ruj." Kiiō ej kōmeļeļeik Litarmelu. Eba, "Lale ņo e ej wanartak kiiō. Lale ņo e ej itok jān ar." Eba, "Kwōj lo ke an ņo kaņe itaak ippān doon? Ekwe, wāween dein ilo lǫmeto."

Innām ejeṃļǫk raan kein kajuon. Kiiō raan kein karuo. Ejja āinwōt raan eo ṃokta. Bar etal im atake Litarmelu eañ in Barijur.

Jino jān rear in Barijur im atake niñaļǫk. Kiiō ļeo ej kajjitōk, "Ia in jej ro pād ie kiiō?"

Litarmelu euwaak, "Iturear in Barijur." Ļeo eba, "Jaab, tueañ. Ruj ṃōk im lale." Litarmelu eba, "O, ibōd! Ij ļōmņak turear in Barijur." Kiiō ļeo eba, "Ekwe, inaaj bar kōṃļeļeik kiiō." Kiiō ļeo ej ba, "Kwōj lo ņo ņe ej wanartak jān lik ke?"

Litarmelu euwaak, "Aet." Ļeo ej bar kajjitōk, "Kwōj ke loe ņo eo ej wanliktak jān ar?" Litarmelu euwaak, "Aet." Ļeo ej bar kajjitōk, "Alikkar ke an ānbwinniṃ eñjake ņo eo ej wanliktak jān ar?" Litarmelu ej uwaak, "Aet." Kiiō ļeo ej kōmeļeļe kiiō, "Kwōn jab ba likiej in Barijur bwe alikkar an ņo kein itak ippān doon. Ñe kar likiej ejako juon iaan ņo kein." Litarmelu ej uwaak. Ej ba, "Ņo ta eo ejako?" Ļeo ej uwaak, "Buñtok i rilik ņe ejako. Ak buñtok i rear ņe wōt. Wūnin an jako buñtok i rilik eo kōnke epenjak ilo Barijur. Innām ānbwinniṃ ej eñjake aolep ņo kein."

Kiiō ejeṃļǫk raan eo kein karuo. Kiiō āindein aolep raan kein ñan emān raan. Iļǫkan raan kein kemān ejeṃļǫk katak.

Kiiō kōmeļeļe wōt. Kiiō wāween kōmeļeļe kiiō ej kwaļǫk ñan Litarmelu, "Liklaļ, netinkōt." Kiiō Litarmelu ej kajjitōk, "Ta in 'netinkōt'?" Kiiō ļeo ej kōmeļeļe kiiō. Ej ba, "Kōnke kapin aelōñ innām ejjab utiej ņo in. Innām rej ba 'netinkōt', ak ñe likiej etan 'jurenokme'." Ļeo ej kajjitōk ippān Litarmelu, "Kwōjeļā ta in 'jurenokme'?" Litarmelu eba, "Ijaje." Ļeo eba, "Meļeļein kōnke 'eutiej ņo'. Innām ej kōkōļaļ in likiej in aelōñ. Netinkōt ej kōkōļaļ in kapin aelōñ. Koṃeļeļe ke kiiō, Litarmelu?"

Litarmelu e uwaak, "Kōn ta?" Ļeo ej ba, "Likiej im liklaļ in aelōñ." Litarmelu ej ba, "Aet. Imeļeļe kiiō." Ļeo ej ba, "Ba ṃōk." Litarmelu ej ba, "Liklaļ, netinkōt āinwōt edik ņo. Likiej, jurenokme āinwōt eutiej ņo." Kiiō ļeo eba, "Ekwe eṃṃan."

Litarmelu ej kajjitōk, "Ak eañ im rak?" Ļeo ebar uwaak, "Kāājinrōjep."

"Ta in kāājinrōjep?" Litarmelu ej kajjitōk. Kiiō ļeo ej ba, "Kwonaaj lo ņo eņ āinwōt kāājinrōjep in." Kiiō ejeṃļǫk raan ņe. Kiiō eba, "Kōppojak bwe jen jerak. Innām kwōn ba ñan Ri-Naṃdik, Ri-Epoon, Ri-Aelōñļapļap ro raar petok ñan Jālooj in. Ñe rōkōņaan uwe, ren itok bwe jen etal ñan Naṃdik kab Epoon kab Aelōñļapļap ñe enaaj eṃṃan kōto. Iien jerak eo inaaj bar kalikkare."

Ļǫkun jilu raan ej ba, "Ilju koṃ naaj itok jen jerak." Innām ektake jet Ri-Naṃdik, jet Ri-Epoon im jerak ilo raan eo juon.

Kōto eo ej itok jān rear, lañ eṃṃan an wa eo peļļǫk. Ak ejjeļǫk wōjļā. Ļǫkun jet iien emaat dān. Im maat ṃōñā. Innām rej lu Litarmelu, "Enta kwaar ba kemin uwe? Ke kōm kwole im maro. Ak ejjeļǫk āne. Jenaaj bōk ad mour jān ia kiiō? Koṃ ar ba jenaaj tōprak āne wōt kiiō. Ak ekanooj lōñ raan emootļǫk. Koṃ kanooj in riab. Ñe enaaj ļǫk ilju kōm naaj ṃan koṃ!"

Kiiō jilu awa raan eo ilo jota eo wōt reloe Naṃdik. Kiiō ļeo ej ba ñan Litarmelu, "Jejro 'ummm' ke? Jejro 'aaa'?" (Meļeļein "umm", 'jab kwaļǫk ñan armej'. Ņoje. Jab ba. Meļeļe in "aaa", 'kwaļǫk ñan armej'.) Kiiō Litarmelu ej ba, "Jejro ej 'umm'." Kiiō ļeo eruje dekā nin wōt im joļǫk ņa ilǫjet im ba, "Turilik, likiej in Naṃdik." Jotaan eo wōt etal im pād i Naṃdik. Innām ļōṃaro raar bar jerak im etal. Innām jejaje reetal ia ļǫk. Litarmelu epādwōt Naṃdik. Innām ebōrǫro im waļǫk elōñ nājin ajri. (Jejaje wōn ar jemān ak etan ajri ro ak juon wōt jejeļā etan.) Etan juon iaer Ļainjin, eṃṃaan. Im katak meto ippān jinen.

Innām Litarmelu ej jerak jān Naṃdik ñan Piñlep (Jālooj). Im leļǫk ladik eo nājin ñan Lineo (bwe en kōkaajiririiki). Litarmelu epād iuṃwin jet raan innām jerak ñan Aelōñļapļap. Jān Aelōñļapļap, Kuwajleen. Jikin eo epād i Kuwajleen, etan ṃweo Erlañ. (Epād ñan rainin *airstrip* eo.)

Kiiō irooj ro i Jālooj rōkōŋaan jerak in itok ñan Aelōñļapļap. Innām raar ektake Ļainjin im lio jinen. (Jinen etan Lineo.) Em jerak ñan Aelōñļapļap im jab lo Aelōñļapļap ak repeļo̧k im jaje ijo rej pād ie.

Kiiō Ļainjin (ļadik eo, āinwōt ajiri) elo juon bao āinwōt an kar jinen Litarmelu ar katak ñane. Em ej waļo̧k jān jaki eo em lo bao eo im jeļā kajjien repād ie. Im kōn an inepata irooj ro rej ba ñe ļadik eo ejeļā kajjien āne en kwaļo̧ke.

Innām jinen ej lu ļadik eo, "Iaar ba kwōn ekkeroro kiiō komaroñ ke kwaļo̧k āne eo?"

Ļadik eo ej bar kwaļo̧k ainikien im ba, "Toorlōñ e būkien Aji eō-eō-eō/ Kakōļļan Pikaar." (Ej roro. "Toorlōñ" etan irooj in aolep ak. "Aji" ej ṃōttan bwidej ie.)

Kiiō irooj ro rōba, "Kwōjeļā kajjien āneo?" Kiiō lio jinen eļap an illu em ba ñe ejjab waļo̧k āne eo, remaroñ ṃan kōjro. Ekwe kwōn etal wōt im kwaļo̧k āneo.

Kiiō ļadik eo ej ba ļo̧k ñan jinen, "Men ko iaar pukoti kein enaaj waļo̧k āne."

Jinen ej ba, "Kwōj ṃool ke?" Ļadik, "Aet, ṃool. Āin aō ļōmņak kōn lo̧jet wōt aō etetal ilo iaļ in āne."(Ej kōkajoor jinen bwe elōļñn̄o̧ñ, emijak.) Ļadik eo eba, "Ekwe, ij kwaļo̧k āne ñan koṃ kiiō. Ijin jej pād ie, Likiej in Pikaar. Ak ijo jaar ilo̧k ñane, Aelōñļapļap. Innām kiiō jej etal ñan Aelōñļapļap." Innām eitem karōk wa im jitōñ Aelōñļapļap.

Ļo̧kun jilu raan relo Aelōñļapļap. Innām reetal im pād i Aelōñļapļap. Ļadik eo, irooj ro rej lukkuun kautieje.

Ļadik ņe eaar pād innām kōŋaan lo jinen. Innām ba ñan irooj ro, "Ikōŋaan lo Ṃaṃa." Innām irooj ro raar ba, "Ekwe jenaaj jerak ñe eṃṃan kōto."

Ijaje jete raan, bōlen juon wiik, im eṃṃan kōto. Kiiō rej jerak jān Aelōñļapļap im itok ñan Naṃo im jab lo Naṃo iuṃwin bōlen ruo wiik. (Re peļo̧k ñan Naṃo.)

Kiiō rōba eṃṃan bar kwaļo̧k āne. Kiiō ļadik eo bar kōnono. Ej ba (roro), "Akio likio-o takio-o I Likiej jān Jinmi!" (Ej kajin etto. Ijaje ewi jikin eo.)

Kiiō irooj ro rōba, "Eļañn̄e komaroñ kwaļo̧k āne kwōn kwaļo̧k." Kiiō ļaddik eba, "Ia-o eṃṃan?" (Āinwōt ta eo eṃṃan?)

Irooj ro raar ba, "Aṃ wōt pepe." Innām ļaddik eo eba, "Jej etal ñan Naṃo."

Kiiō rej jerak tok ñan Naṃo im elōñ raan remootļo̧k. Innām irooj ro raar ba, "N̄āāt enaaj waļo̧k Naṃo?" Kiiō ļaddik ej ba, "Enaaj alikkar."

Raan eo juon ewaļo̧k Naṃo. Kiiō irooj ro raar ba, "Ejjab Naṃo." Innām ļadik eo ej ba, "Naṃo!" Kiiō irooj ro rej ba, "Ta wūnin Naṃo kōnke rej kabbwe ñane?"

Ļadik eo eba, "Eaetak." Ej kōmeļeļeiki, "Innām wa eo ej ruṃwij an jerakļo̧k ñan Naṃo. Jo̧teen eo wa eo etōpraktok Naṃo."

Irooj ro reļak lale ṃool ke Naṃo. Ejjeļo̧k kar kōjatdikdik ippān irooj ro ke Naṃo.

Pād i Naṃo iuṃwin ruo raan innām bar jerak jān Naṃo ñan Kuwajleen. Kiiō bar irooj ro rej kapen ejjab ļadik eo. Innām jerak jān Naṃo im itok ñan Kuwajleen im jab bar lo Kuwajleen.

Im irooj ro rōbar kajjitōk ippān ļadik eo, "Epād ia Kuwajleen?" Ļadik eo eba, "Epād iuṃwin aļ." Kōnke aļ epād i kapilōñ.

Kiiō irooj ro raar ba, "Ekwe, kabbwe!" Innām ļadik eo ej ba, "Kabbwe!" Innām ekabbwe wa eo. Etal-etal-etal im ļak jejjet to in Meik. Ļadik eo ba, "Iōñņe."

Boñōn eo wōt edeļo̧ñ toon Meik. Kiiō irooj ro rōba, "Ia in? Kuwajleen ke? Ak bar juon aelōñ ke?" Ļadik eo eba, "Kuwajleen." Kiiō reitok ñan Kuwajleen im ļadik eo etal ippān jinen.

Innām irooj ro raar kalliṃur bwe ļadik eo en pādwōt ippāer.

Kiiō jinen elukkuun katakine bwe en kanooj jeļā. Innām aolep jeļā ko an jinen eṃōj an ļadik eo būki.

Kiiō irooj ro raar bōk ļadik eo ņa ippāer. Ak jinen kiiō Litarmelu ej jerak ñan Ratak, Rālik-rak, im Eañinmeto. Innām etal ñan

Ujae im pād iuṃwin jet allōn̄. Innām jerak jān Ujae itok n̄an Lae. Jān Lae n̄an Wōtto im jab lo Wōtto. Ak reital ioon Wōtto ļọk im jako n̄an rainin.

(Menin bwilōn̄ eo in. Emaron̄ ṃool ke?)

Ejjeļọk libwin Litarmelu ioon āne. Ioon jabdewōt āne.

Wa ko eaar jerak kaki ej tarrin joñoul-jil-jilimjuon.

Menin kaṃṃool bwebwenato in ej juon eṃṃaan epād ioon wa eo an Litarmelu. Eaar āneen im wōtlọk lem eo im ļeo ekālọk jān wa eo im jok ioon juon wūnmaan̄ (bwijin bōb eo) i Wōtto.

Kiiō ekūṃṃūļọk ļeo im ba, "Uṃṃṃ, etke bōb lọjet ak etke āne?"

Kiiō ļeo etal ippān armej im bwebwenato ke inej eo an Litarmelu emootļọk im meja-toto ļọk.

Ejeṃļọk.

(Ijaje eṃool ke ak kar āindein iaar ron̄ ippān armej ro ṃokta.)

28: STORY ABOUT WEATHER: THE WAY THE OLD PEOPLE IN THE MARSHALL ISLANDS USED (FORECAST) WEATHER

As told by Jelibōr Jam, Kuwajleen 1975

The sky was cut in half. And within it, the moon began to appear from the west. They named it Taktakinae. (It is ancient language, but we do not know what it means.)

And when the moon was there at one o'clock, going down to three o'clock, they named it Limeto. When it was in the absolute middle, they named it Lipepe.

When it was in the east and the middle, they named it Limetak. And when it was in the east, they named it Tutuinae.

In these ways, the understanding of the moon began to come from the west and came to the middle of the west.

The reason they said, "Limeto" is because of big battles. (In the ancient language this is wind and rain.)

And if the canoe is going to sail at this time, when it is Limeto, you load aboard. But if it is bad weather, you off-load (do not go). Because a lot of rain and wind come up suddenly. And they call it Limeto.

And if it is to the east and middle—the meaning of their saying "Limetak" is because Limetak is 'wrap up, load aboard'.

And we again think about the canoe [about sailing].

If a canoe is going to sail and the cargo has been wrapped up and loaded aboard, but the weather is bad, you can ignore the bad weather and not unload the cargo. And you can sail because it is Lemlem Ektak. However, when there is no rain and much wind, and the moon is in the west, well, perhaps these things [rain and wind] will come down at the time when the moon is in the east, in the middle.

At this time, you will recognize that you will still not know when it will come down, rain or a big wind.

But when the moon is in the Tutuinae, well, ignore anything and you should sail, for it is the right night to sail.

It is ended.

(They use this to this day.)

28: BWEBWENATO IN LAÑ: WĀWEEN AN RITTO RO ILO M̧AJEĻ KŌJERBAL LAÑ

Ri-bwebwenato: Jelibōr Jam, Kuwajleen 1975

Lañ eṃōj bukwe ilo juon ṃōttan ruo. Innām ilowaan an allōñ jino waļǫk jān kapilōñ. Rej ŋae etan Taktakinae. (Ej kajin etto ak jejaje meļeļe eo.)

Innām ñe allōñ ej pād ilo juon awa wanlaļļǫk ñan jilu rej ŋae etan Limeto. Ñe ej pād i lukwin ioļap rej ŋa etan Lipepe.

Ñe ej pād iwetan (turear) ioļap rej ŋa etan Limetak. Im ñe ej pād i rear rej ŋa etan Tutuinae.

Wāween dein meļeļe in allōñ jino tak jān kapilōñ im itak ñan rālik in ioļap.

Wūnin aer ba, "Limeto" kōnke pata ko reļļap. (Ilo kajin etto ej kōto im wōt.)

Innām eļañe wa men eo ej iten jerak ilo iien in, ke ej Limeto, kwōj ektak. Ak enana lañ kwōn ekto. (Jab etal.) Kōnke ej jidimkij an naaj ļap kōto ak wōt. Innām rej ba, "Limeto."

Ak eļañe ej pād iwetaan ioļap. Meļeļein aer ba, "Limetak," kōnke Limetak "lemlem ektak".

Innām jej bar karkar kōn wa. (Jen ba ļōmŋak kōn wa.)

Eļañe juon wa ej jerak innām eṃōj an lemlem ṃweiuk im ektak ak enana lañ komaroñ in kōjekdǫǫn an nana. Im jab ākto ṃweiuk ak kwōn jerak kōnke "lemlem ektak." Ijoke eļañe eaar jab wōt im ļap kōto im allōñ ŋa i kipilōñ, ekwe enaaj bōlen wōtlǫk men kein ilo iien eo ñe allōñ ej pād iwetaan ioļap.

Iien jab in kwōnaaj ekkōl wōt kwōjaje enaaj wōtlǫk ñāāt, wōt ak kōto eļap.

Ak eļañe allōñ ej pād ilo Tutuinae, eokwe jekdǫǫn jabdewōt ak kwōn jerak, bwe ejejjet boñ-in-uwekan.

Ejeṃļǫk.

(Rej kōjerbal ñan rainin.)

29: ABOUT THE *IKID* (SONG-STORY) OF THE LŌRRO AND LIKAKŌJ

As told by Jelibōr Jam, Kuwajleen 1975

Ikid are *al im bwebwenato:* song-stories. They are like songs. And all of the stories in the Marshall Islands are within them. Some of the old people of Kapinmeto, the western atolls of the Marshalls, know them. *Kōkļaļ* (navigational signs [sea markers]) are within the *ikid.*

(Kabua [*irooj ļapļap*: paramount chief during the German period] forbade anyone from learning *ikid* without his permission. They were not for general knowledge. They were valuable property, and [were] used by navigators. Only a few people know *ikid* today.)

These girls were with some girls who were very obedient to their mother and father, and they were unhappy with their work. They met together and the work of one of the girls was to just laugh. And the thought of the other girl was the thought to just fly. And they met together and planned to just juggle to Wōjjā first, and to do the same to all the atolls of the Marshalls.

Because they were so unhappy, juggling was a thing to make their thought better [improve their morale.]

And they began from Ujae on a land parcel *[wāto],* the name of it, Lọ-to. They said, "We two will arrive on Lae first." And they began their *ikid* and said,[1]

"Where did the canoe run away to? *Iurileo* (*kajin etto:* ancient language) *ilikinjelañ* (*kajin bwebwenato:* legend language) to the wave sleeps the *melbo* (ancient language: color of the sky at sunrise and sunset: *mel*) laughing alight the *le* [*Diomedes immutabilis Layson,* albatross; *Diomedes nigripes* black-footed albatross]. And drifts *mekabwut* (a bird), *mennana* (a bird), the *arelōñ* (a bird).[2] Throws upward[3] here, juggles to the east, to run and take *irijiroñ* (legend language) *ininiñ* (legend language). And the boys are now gone.

"Do not sleep near the fire Mājlep [Altair: a star], fall a large wave *mōjit* (legend language) island, those islands, bring to the north, bring to the south.

"A good wind at the time of Mājlep *eaki* (legend language) *m̧urm̧ur* (legend language) *eaki* Tōrwa [Island, M̧aļo-eļap Atoll]. We see north and we see south and fly, glide like a bird (like a frigate bird) this thing. The *irooj* (chief) *rojino*

---

1. The informant explained that the girls proceeded juggling stones and singing and chanting as they went, naming the things—navigation signs and atolls and islands they saw, and on which they stopped. "They walked on land and on water. The meaning of Likakōj: it is just a name. She does not know how to be angry (she is peaceful). She is a little crazy. Lōrro (the name of that woman) is a little crazy. She is ready to fly but does not fly."

This, and all *ikid* are chanted in an almost continuous, low monotone by the narrator. They were chanted by navigators to help keep them on course, and awake and alert. (Presumably the low tone helped assure secrecy.) This is how the informant handled it, except, of course, he explained some of the obscure and special words and phrases to me, as noted later.

2. I was unable to identify these birds.

3. *Ekale* is *kajin bwebwe* (crazy language), because Lōrro is crazy. The meaning of the word is 'throw up'. There are many words in this *ikid* that are crazy language, the informant explained.

(ancient language). Wait, wait (ancient language). Flapping (like a bird's wing). Fly up, it rains on us from the ocean side of the shore.

"Juggle on the *n̗a* [rock platform], this woman, your canoe will come. Lower the sail! Raise the sail! *Dokōt* (ancient language) on the sea and arrive at Wōjjā [Atoll]; it sails from Wōdmeej [Island, Wōjjā Atoll], and sails to leeward/westward to Ļ̗olelo̧lur [the sea area between Ratak and Rālik, the eastern and western chains of the Marshall Islands]. A small rain shower, we tack at Aerōk [Island]. You are at Utrōk [Atoll]. You see Retabweta (a chief), Retabōn (a chief), Mejrōk (an island). Lower the sail, this fleet of canoes of the chief. One is going to the south, and the other chief is going to the north.

"Go ahead and tack to the north. Go ahead and tack to the south. The three waves. The four waves. (Many waves come here.) Pull the paddles from the sea. Seize it!

"We seize the steering paddle.

"It is ended now."

In another *ikid,* when they see Pikaar [Atoll] they say, *"Ļōm̧aro an irooj im jepļaak im wārōkean̄. Lo iur eo i likiej in āne jee Pikaar."* (These men of the chief return and go to the north from the south. I see a flock of birds on the windward side of this island. That island over there is Pikaar.)

29: KŌN IKID EO AN LŌRRO IM LIKAKŌJ

Ri-bwebwenato: Jelibōr Jam, Kuwajleen 1975

(Ikid rej al-bwebwenato. Rej āinwōt al ak aolep bwebwenato in M̧ajeļ rej pād ilowaan. Jet iaan rūtto ro in Kapinmeto rejeļā. Kōkōļaļ rej pād ilowaan. Rej lukkuun aetok. Juon al ekanooj aetok.)

(Kabua [irooj eo ilo iien Jāmne] eaar kamo̧ an jabdewōt armej katak ikid n̄e ejjeļo̧k mālim jāne. Ikid rejjab n̄an jeļāļo̧kjen̄ n̄an jabdewōt armej. Ikid rej menin aorōk n̄an rainin. Ri-meto raar kōjerbali. Jet wōt armej rejeļā ikid rainin.)

Ledik rein ej jet iaan ledik ro raar kanooj pokake jineer im jemāer, innām kōn an jerbal būrom̧ōj ippāerro, ro ar ioon doon im lio juon jerbal eo an ettōn̄ wōt. A lio juon ļōmn̗ak eo an ļōmn̗ak in ekkāke wōt. Innām erro ar iioon doon im likūt ļōmn̗ak in lejon̄jon̄ n̄an Wōjjā m̧oktata, kab enaaj bar aolep aelōn̄ in M̧ajeļ. Kōn an ļap aerro būrom̧ōj, lejon̄jon̄ in ej menin kōm̧anm̧an aerro ļōmn̗ak.

Innām rejro jino jān Ujae ilo juon wāto, etan in, Lo̧-to. Rejro ba, "Kōjro kōttōpar Lae m̧okta." Innām rejro jino ikid in aerro im ba, "Ekkoko wa? Iurileo ilikinjelan̄ n̄an n̗o eo kiki melbo tūn̄tūn̄ kōjokwe le eo im peto mekabūt jerka, mennana, arelōn̄ eo ekaļe[4] jon̄jon̄ takwōt kottōr im būk irijiron̄ ininin̄ a ejja jako ļadik ro.

"Kōm̧in jab eo̧wilik Mājlep bun̄i linn̗o m̧ōjit āne kein āne letak ean̄tok. Letak irōk tok.

"Jowan Mājlep eaki m̧urm̧ur eo eaki Tōrwa. Jelo iōn̄ a jelo irōk a kātok jebļā tok wōt meni. Irooj ro rejino ko jokwor, jokwor pikpik kāļo̧k eoute kōj jān lōke kappe.

"Likijarōk, ilo n̗a kōrā in waam̧ enaaj

4. Ekaļe: kajin bwebwe, kōnke Lōrro ej bwebwe. Meļeļe in naan eo ej jolin̄tak. Āinwōt elōn̄ naan ilo ikid in rej kajin bwebwe.

wawōj pone! jerake! Dokōt eoon meto in elboboļo̧k Wōjjā ejerak jān Wōdmeej em kabbweļo̧k ñan Lo̧lelo̧lur eļañin kemjeje tak i Aerōk kom̧uri ļo̧k Utrōk in kom̧ lo Retabweta eo Retabōn Mejrōk im pone inej in irooj juon eŋ ej tarōñaļo̧k a irooj juon eŋ ej tarniñaļo̧k.

"Etal ļo̧k en diaktok eañ. Etal ļo̧k em diaktok i rōk. Ŋo jilu eo. Ŋo emān eo. Eŋoŋotok, Ep! Kwōn jarke! Jej jej jarke.

"Jaarōk jebwe eo.

"Ejem̧ļo̧k."

(Ilo bar juon ikid ke rej lo Pikaar rej ba, "Ļōm̧aro an irooj im jepļaak im wārōkeañ lo iur eo i likiej in āne jee Pikaar.")

Ri-bwebwenato eo ar kōmeļeļeik bwe ledik rein lejoñjoñļo̧k dekā ko im al ke raar etal. Im ŋa etan aolep men kaŋ, kōkļaļ ko, aelōñ ko, im āne ko raar loe im pād ie.

Raar etetal ioon āne im lo̧jet.

Meļeļe in Likakōj: etan wōt. Lieŋ ejaje illu (eļap an aenem̧m̧an ippān). Ej jidik bwebwe. Lōrro (etan kōrā en) ej jidik bwebwe. Epojak in ekkāke ak ejjab ekkāke.

30: THE *IKID* (SONG-STORY) OF ĻAINJIN

As told by Jelibōr Jam, Kuwajleen 1975

The canoe is sailing from the windward side of N̄atik.[1]
The canoe is sailing from the windward side of N̄atik.

The *jabu*[2] sounds; the men should go to the east Rālik when the atoll appears.

Get off the canoe and you wake up.[3] And you wake up the people of the island.

The pilot will disembark. You[4] show and investigate the road there, south in the road there.

The rat cries out.

You make a feast to you.

Lan̄peran,[5] the *dōb*[6] cries out, child of Etao[7] *edda*[8] *wajwe.*[9] "Wake up the sunshine," it says.[10]

Koeak[11] says, "Pick pandanus!" He says, "Pick coconuts!"

Dig up the island harvest in the taro patch, provisions for the fleet of canoes. Sail!

We sail, we sail,[12] we see flying fish[13] on the windward side of N̄atik and Pohnpei.[14]

They fly over[15] the *m̧o̧le*[16] north of Koro,[17] they bring (pull) the line of[18] this canoe (maneuver the canoe).

Take the line, we tack, we see mountains, we see the mountains shaped like the sail of a canoe (the tops of the mountains seen from afar).

We go on the road of death. (Because they do not know where the canoe is going: to death or to life.) It is God's will if we live.

---

1. N̄atik, an atoll in the Eastern Carolines, west of the Marshall Islands.
2. *Jabu,* the name of the *jilel* (*Cymatiidae charonia tritonis,* triton or trumpet shell), used to signal, call, and assemble people.
3. Ancient language *(kajin etto): kolbaj.*
4. Ancient language: *bōn.*
5. Lan̄peran, the name of a person, a legendary island-fisher.
6. *Dōb*, an insect, a little bigger than a *kallep,* a black ant.
7. Etao, the trickster of Marshallese folklore, similar to Olofat (Iolofāth) of the western Carolines, Maui of Polynesian folklore, and other tricksters throughout the world.
8. Ancient language, meaning unknown to informant.
9. Ancient language, meaning unknown to informant.
10. Ancient language: *ekain.*
11. Koeak, a person's name, meaning 'fast (adj.)'.
12. Ancient language: *jeklak, jeblak.*
13. The *kōkļaļ/kōkaļļe* (navigation sign/sea marker) of N̄atik Atoll and Pohnpei (Ponape).
14. Pohnpei Island, a large island of volcanic origin north of N̄atik.
15. Ancient language: *jeorto.*
16. The navigation sign of Koro, *Siganus rostratus,* rabbit fish.
17. Koro: an island. Part of Pingelap (Pin̄lep) Atoll?
18. Ancient language: *lin.* A canoe line called *iep* today.

All of us go and scoop coconut containers of water boiling up and many coconut containers, and many coconut containers.[19]

We go running. Far up in the sky the frigate bird on the windward side of Jinme.[20]

(The frigate bird is flying like a kite. It is the navigation sign of Jinme.)

You tack, you are going where? The white foam of the sea of Ānewetak[21] goes to the north. Make provisions for this, your canoe where with Ļōkotoñorñor there.[22]

That *iṃiṃ*[23] makes magic (forecast your bone!). For I crave fish.[24]

We sail in the canoe, a log and those men,[25] they each one have an adze. They make the canoe, Ļakele[26] hits us. Wake up in the custom of the frigate bird. It flies over the coconuts of the canoe, pandanus in the canoe.[27] That flock of birds, each one brings food under its wings here.[28]

The launching ceremony was performed.

It was launched in the water and sailed on to Wōtto.[29]

He knows, he knows the sea on the canoe on the sea.

He pierces the fish, the fish ahead of the canoe.

Lōtran the man in that canoe?

Lōrro and Ļakne.[30]

They take food[31] to Koperwa[32] and Liñijiļọk.[33]

---

19. A place in the sea where fresh water boils up. Ļainjin knew where it was, but we do not know today. It is a navigation sign near Kosrae (Kusaie) Island today.

20. Jinme, an island on the eastern side of Ānewetak Atoll.

21. Ānewetak Atoll, north of Pohnpei. It is the northwesternmost of the Marshalls, and to the northeast of Wūjlañ Atoll, the westernmost. (The white foam of the sea of Ānewetak refers to the residue of of processed arrowroot [*Tacca leontopetaloides, ṃakṃōk*] floating on the ocean off Ānewetak, because there was much arrowroot there.)

22. Ļōkotoñorñor, a floating log *(kājokwā)* or a reef *(wōd),* the navigation sign of Pikinni (Bikini) Atoll: 'Beginning at Pikinni' or 'The start of Pikinni' *(Jinoin Pikinni).*

23. *Iṃiṃ, Rhinecanthus aculeatus* L., triggerfish. It has spines at the base of its tail *(di ielo)* that it uses to prevent it from being pulled out of its hole in the reef. This is another navigation sign.

24. *Ibatur* 'I crave fish'. I want to eat fish (because I have been on a canoe for a long time).

25. *Ļōṃaro* 'those men'. Birds? Fish? Informant did not know which.

26. Ļakele: The name of a person.

27. It is customary to bring coconuts, breadfruit, and pandanus to the canoe for provisions.

28. In the story, birds bring food under their wings from Pikinni, like the story where the birds fed Elija. Informant was citing 3 Kings 16, 24–17, 24. "Elias hid near the torrent Carith, where ravens brought him food." (This shows how the introduced biblical lore is used to illustrate and draw analogies in the narrative of traditional stories. Other examples are found in the oral tradition.)

29. From Pikinni they sailed to Wōtto Atoll.

30. Lōrro and Ļakne: *pejwak* [*Anous stolidus,* brown noddy.] Two birds (men of Wōtto), the navigation sign next to Wōtto Atoll.

31. Ancient language: 'they take food' (the *Anperia* cultigen of pandanus).

32. Koperwa: The name of a shark, male. He is far from land: twenty miles from Āne-Ļaṃōj.

33. Liñijiļọk: the name of a female, a *kōñe* [*Pemphis acidula*] tree. It is on the beach (sand) on Ujae and is a navigation sign of Ujae Atoll.

And the log[34] shall be the floating boat for fishing.

Thus it drifts there.

The barracuda moves like a porpoise.[35]

It points to the big pass. It tells the location of the island.

Pound this canoe[36] and the sound (of pounding) and this *aroñ*[37] comes here. This canoe goes to the south.[38]

Leap porpoise, leap porpoise,[39] complete coming porpoise.

The frigate bird[40] sails above that small cape. The *kaaļo*[41] flies over that big cape and large flock of birds over there. This thing is Pojar.[42] The frigate bird goes from side to side, diving over the flock.

You count so that[43] we count the navigation signs[44] with that log over there, with that. And the Chief of the Lagoon.[45]

The canoe arrives and anchors to the south at those shallow passes.[46]

Please awake and fold your belongings (ready to embark or disembark). You make magic with pandanus leaves (forecast with them) so that (we see) tomorrow will be good.

He wants to go now, Jowaļañ load up[47] *korej*,[48] load up.

Balooj[49] that group, all many porpoises[50]

---

34. The floating log is the navigation sign of Ujae. It is 200 miles from Āne-Ļaṃōj Island, Ujae Atoll.

35. The barracuda [*Sphyraena barracuda* Walbaum, *jure*] is the navigation sign. It lives forty or fifty miles to the south of Ujae and dives up and down in the water (like a porpoise). There is only one in the ocean.

36. Pound the canoe with wood, hand, or paddle.

37. *Aroñ* [*Hynnis cubensis,* African pompano], a navigation sign of Ujae and a method of fishing in Ujae. The fish appears when the canoe is pounded.

38. To the south of Ujae Atoll.

39. A large group of porpoises [*Delphinus reseventris, ke*] is the navigation sign of Ujae.

40. The frigate bird [*Fregata minor, ak*], the navigation sign forty or fifty miles from Ujae.

41. *Kaaļo* [*Sula leucogaster,* brown booby], the navigation sign of the big cape on the western side of Ujae Atoll. There is only one *kaaļo*.

42. Pojar, the name of a land parcel *(wāto)*.

43. Ancient language: *ep in:* so that/ in order to.

44. There are many kinds of birds there: *pejwak, kaaļo, jekad* [*Anous tenuirostris,* little noddy], *mejǫ* [*Gygis alba,* fairy tern], *mānnimouj* [a kind of tern], *keār* [*Sterna sumatrana,* black-naped tern]. There are many together and they fly off of Ujae. There is only one frigate bird, and he is the highest in the sky. These birds are in the ocean sixty or so miles seaward and are the navigation sign of Pojar. The frigate bird goes from side to side and flies over the *wūnaak* (flock of birds). This is *kajin bao* (bird language).

45. Chief of the lagoon, the giant octopus of the legend. It is a navigation sign of Ujae (all of the navigation signs are south of Ujae and to the west).

46. Mejje-kaņ, shallow pass area at the island of Ujae. It is a fishing place for *aroñ*.

47. Ancient language: *eitin.*

48. Ancient language: *korej.*

49. Balooj, name of a man/rock at Looj Island, Lae Atoll. There are two of these big rocks on Lae today.

50. The many porpoises are the navigation sign of Looj.

on the oceanside of Looj, many of those men who make pandanus leaf magic (on the island and in the ocean: porpoises).

Libake,[51] they put flower garlands on her head and neck and take her to the canoe so that Ledikdik[52] and Lejm̧aan[53] pick her up[54] and take her to the canoe.

Likerilem is angry [Likerilem is troubled and angry] with Lijinm̧ōt because she wants to go on the canoe and Lim̧am̧ōko should stay. She does not want the woman to go.

She stays and works on the island.

That Libukaje[55] slaps [beats] the drum, raise the sail.[56] It goes ahead. Jobareo[57] works in the strong current, in the strong current. The canoe moves violently from side to side on the waves, pushed over the canoe.

It is ended at Lae.

We meet to unload from the canoe, cast off Libat,[58] cast off Likerilem.[59] Lijoñan[60] should board the canoe.

Should die together[61] and wake up by pounding the canoe, with hands, to arouse Koujinmeto, Koujinmeto.[62]

That man, O that man, he does not sleep, the smart one. Feel the current toward the island,[63] it loads *kōtae,*[64] the current of the sea goes east. Lower the line of the sail.[65] Loosen the sail so that we ascertain, the group arrives here, pierce and throw away from the hard pandanus mat, this mat, mat O, mat, very hard.[66]

---

51. Libake [also Lijebake], the name of a woman. She is a turtle [*Chelonia mydas* L., green sea turtle, *wōn*]. She is in the ocean and is small and has red "skin." She is far away from Lae, forty to sixty miles southwest of Lae. It varies. I have seen her and others have seen her [informant said]. She is about three feet long.

52. Ledikdik, the name of a woman.

53. Lejm̧aan, the name of a woman.

54. Ancient language: *rōkere.* And the following paragraph: "Her troubled throat, Likerilem is angry." The throat *(bōro)* is the seat of the emotions to the Marshallese, analogous to the heart in Western cultures.

55. Libukaje, a woman.

56. The sail of the canoe.

57. Jobareo, the name of a man.

58. Libat, the name of a woman.

59. Likerilem, the name of a woman.

60. Lijoñan, the name of a woman. Libat, Likerelem, and Lijoñan are navigation signs of Ellep Island today. They are *dekā* (rocks) today. Before, they were clouds or in the ocean. It is not clear what they were, the informant explained.

61. Ancient language: *kaōiōie.*

62. Koujinmeto. It is a navigation sign of Ellep. It is a big fire-shaped demon. It approaches and makes the viewer crazy. It is on the water and is very bright at night, like the lights of Kuwajleen [the American missile base].

63. Technique of the traditional navigators *(rimeto)* to locate an island.

64. *Kōtae,* ancient language for the technique of observing the current patterns. It was used by *ri-meto.*

65. The *iep,* a special line on the sailing canoe.

Long sailing on the ocean,[67] go to the west, long sailing on the ocean, go to the west. Long sailing on the ocean, go to the west.

Big waves. Heavy clashing seas.[68]

West of Demar[69] and that island to the south. The canoe crosses to the south.

The giant octopus[70] appears higher than Anel.[71] Dekā-eņ[72] some porpoises there.

They lead to the west, fish say. On the oceanside of Nakwōpe[73] and M̧ōn-o.[74] We will prepare[75] to clap stones to chase porpoises.[76]

Startle what? Bone in the ear.[77]

Very long[78] giant eel in the sea.[79] The big net of those two, father and son. It flies up, Jikborej[80] circles over the canoe but does not alight[81] on the canoe.

Seize that forward line[82] in order to tack to the west.[83] This canoe is flying through the waves, it speeds. It arrives at Naṃdik near M̧adṃad.[84]

A very large flock of birds,[85] the pandanus leaves, the pandanus leaves, the leaves of

---

66. Ancient language, *maañin edeñij* 'hard pandanus mat', [is] the navigation sign of Naṃo Atoll, because the *maañ* (pandanus leaves) of Naṃo are hard (strong), [those] on Ļọ-eņ and on the main island of Naṃo. (Naṃdik Atoll *maañ* are also hard.) Pandanus mats [are] used on land and on ocean (voyages) [as utility mats].

67. Ancient language: *jektil ketak.*

68. Ancient language: *ajibokdede.*

69. Demar, an island of Naṃo Atoll, near Ļọ-eņ Island to the west and south. The next mentioned island is to the south a bit.

70. *Kouj,* the giant octopus that is a navigation sign of Naṃo. It is in the ocean 60 miles and sometimes 200 miles from the atoll.

71. Anel, an island of Naṃo Atoll, to the south.

72. Dekā-eņ, an island on the eastern side of Aelōnļapļap Atoll, to the south.

73. Nakwōpe: The name of a *wāto* (land parcel) on Aelōnļapļap.

74. M̧ōn-o, a land parcel *(wāto)* on Wōja Island, Aelōnļapļap. Some porpoises *(raj)* are aligned offshore with this *wāto*. It is a navigation sign of Wōja.

75. Ancient language: *wajoke.*

76. Stones are clapped underwater to drive porpoises ashore, by men in canoes and in the water. The technique is called *jibke.*

77. Refers to the ears of the porpoises, who are very sensitive to noise, and can thus be herded ashore and captured.

78. Ancient language: *eajeded.*

79. Aṃaṃ, a giant eel in the ocean. It is a navigation sign of Wōja, and is like a *dāp* [*Gymnothorax* sp., moray eel], but big[ger]. ("There is a story [*bwebwenato*] of Wōja about an *aṃaṃ* and a father and his son," the informant said.)

80. Jikborej, a bird with long tail and white feathers, a sea bird [white-tailed tropic bird *Phaethon lepturus?*]. It is a navigation sign of Aelōnļapļap.

81. Ancient language: *eliakabwitwit.*

82. Ancient language: *manilik.*

83. Ancient language: *jeboul.*

84. M̧adṃad, an island of Naṃdik Atoll.

85. A very large flock of birds (a *iur*), larger than a *wūnaak* flock. This is a navigation sign of M̧adṃad Island (on the ocean, and [with] many kinds of birds).

Ṃadṃad, and the pandanus leaves[86] of Wūndik.[87] And Woman, pierce[88] the porpoises, Lijinej, Lijoñal, and Lijenṃaļokļok.[89]

It (the wave) strikes the cape at Lelō[90] and points to Naṃdik, it goes to Taij[91] and Lejpel,[92] *Joor ko*[93] on the island, turtles in the sea, ocean side, east side of Leltiñ and Jabad.[94]

Many canoes[95] sail together, they sail to the southeast. Libujen[96] blows against the canoe, they all deceived Jutōkwa, Jutōkwa.[97]

The man sails away from the island,[98] the frigate bird lands, "Liṃaakak, my child Inedel,[99] and what kind of fish do you eat?" Inedel: "We two, my father, dive, dive down into the sea. Dive down into the fish trap. Bring up the fish trap. Bone of a fish, top part of a breadfruit." "And what else?"[100]

"Alle-dikdik[101] is my food from my mother and father."

"Why don't you come here and we two will fly?"[102]

"I am just afraid of you, for you are a demon."[103]

---

86. There is a large supply of pandanus [*Pandanus tectorius* var.] leaves *(maañ)* on Naṃdik Atoll, and of very good quality for thatching houses, and the like.

87. Wūndik, the name of a land parcel *(wāto)* on Ṃadṃad. The navigation sign of the island, of Ṃadṃad, is the large quantity of pandanus leaves *(maañ),* and [the navigation sign] of the sea is the very large flock of birds of many kinds *(iur).*

88. Pierce with a spear *(ṃade).*

89. Lijinej, Lijoñal, and Lijenṃaļokļok: They are navigation signs. They were women (human beings) originally, and God turned them into rocks. They are from Kusaie (Kosrae) to Naṃdik.

90. Lelō Island, adjacent to Kosrae Island. It is on the principal harbor and is the main settlement.

91. Taij, a "rock" with two coconut trees on it, between Ṃadṃad and Naṃdik Islands (Naṃdik Atoll).

92. Lejpel, a *dekā* (rock) on Naṃdik.

93. *Joor ko:* Pillars, posts. Navigation signs.

94. Leltiñ and Jabad, the names of two land parcels *(wāto).* Informant did not know where they are located, but they are not on Naṃdik, he said. (Perhaps Kosrae?)

95. Ancient language: Five to ten, twenty, or thirty canoes. Many canoes that sail together: *elitoab teltel.*

96. Libujen, a woman—a wind that comes from the northwest.

97. Jutōkwa, a man—admiral of the fleet. Because they did not know sailing directions, he was the admiral.

98. They refer to the people in the canoe, and he refers to Jutōkwa.

99. The Epoon story of Inedel is quoted partially in this *Ikid.* Liṃaakak is the kite, the shape of Didi Island, and the *ak* (frigate bird) high in the sky is a navigation sign of Epoon. The informant explained the meaning of the story to me: the father who neglected his son, Inedel; the stepmothers who mistreated him; the dead mother who appeared to her son in the shape of a demon; and his reaction and end.

100. Informant explained that the *ṃak* (top portion of the breadfruit) is the bad part. The rest of the breadfruit, the middle section *(wutwut)* and the bottom section (*ajibōk* [Rālik], *ṃokta* [Ratak]) are the good parts. The stepmother mistreated the boy by withholding food from him, and giving him inferior food. This is a breach of Marshallese custom, and it is a breach of familial responsibilty as well.

101. *Alle-dikdik,* a fish, member of the wrasse family. It is small and not good for food, the informant explained. *Dikdik* means 'very small'.

102. Mother speaking.

103. Son speaking.

She pinches him with her fingertips, pinches with the flesh between her fingers, flies off.

I eat, for I ate *lo,*[104] the cape of Epoon, Aelo.[105]

I am happy with my dessert, the branch of *būkien.*[106] The branch of pandanus, Letkonimen,[107] comes on board the canoe, and ornaments the canoe platform.

We anchor at the sandbank.[108] We make food and put it in the attic.

(Now they are between Epoon and the Gilbert Islands.)[109]

Those people, from where?[110] We do not recognize them. You place with what? A shellfish gives me a little home. I do not give you a little home because I am afraid of my mother Lokjenmeto.[111] She said she will return and make an earth oven. In order to eat me.

Whale leaping up (like a porpoise) in the water!

We are afraid they will kill us.[112] We launch the canoe and flee from this island.

Who is going to be the captain? Ļekōj? Ļoktō[113] knows the location of Jikut[114] and Rukut[115] and what?

The fresh water, the drink of Etao. The *toul*[116] is high in the sea. Two curlew fly apart.

---

104. Another person speaks. Informant explained that *lo* [*Thalassoma vitidum,* wrasse] is like *mao* and a member of the wrasse family. It is about six inches to a foot long.

105. Aelo, possibly the name of an island or land parcel *(wāto)* on Epoon?

106. Būkien, a kind of pandanus (a pandanus cultigen).

107. Letkonimen, a navigation sign. It is a big *imen* (ray), black on top, with a white underside and a long, barbed tail. It also lives in the lagoons. Informant has seen them at Kuwajleen Atoll. The ray is kind and does not hurt people. *Jeṃjọ, imen,* and *letkonimen* (manta) [are respectively] the smallest size ray, the middle size ray, and the biggest ray. They are one family, informant explained. If you see a manta ray between Nauru Island (west of Nauru) and Epoon, you will see an island. This thing cannot hurt you. It is kind. The canoe may even touch the manta, he said.

108. A sandbar on ocean side of Epoon. The A-frame type of traditional house had a small attic *(po),* used primarily for storage.

109. The Gilbert Islands (Kiribati), *Aelōñ in Pit* or *Kilbōt* in Marshallese. They were known to ancient Marshallese through castaways whose canoes had gone adrift. Most of these Gilbertese landed on Epoon, Mile, and other southern islands in the Marshalls. Those who were not killed were absorbed by the Marshallese and the women founded the clan called Ri-Pit in the Marshalls today. Canoes and boats have continued to drift up into the Marshalls and other parts of Micronesia from the Gilberts and the Ellice Islands (Tuvalu), which lies south of the Gilberts. Porpoise *(raj)* are navigation signs between Nauru and Epoon, to the north of Nauru. The porpoises are eight to ten feet long and are black. They are a sign to and from Nauru.

110. Ri-emwa: is this ancient language? Gilbertese? or Nauruan? [the informant asked himself].

111. Lukjānmeto, a woman. It is the name of the mother, [who] was a demon, like a very big fire.

112. Is this a reflection of actual experience with cannibals to the south of the Marshalls, and their escape from them?

113. Ļōktō, the name of the captain.

114. Jikut, the name of a star (constellation). It was used in the traditional system of counting and means 200. Also *Jukut, Jikūt.* See appendix E concerning the old Marshallese method of counting, on page 389.

115. Rukut, the name of a star (constellation), [which also] means 400 in the traditional system of counting. Also *Rukūt.*

116. Toul, a shellfish. It is like the *jukkwe* [*Hippopus maculatus* Lamarck, sand clam], but it is round and the *jukkwe* is long, the informant explained.

One bird speaks in Ratakese.[117] One speaks in Gilbertese. Some other curlews are together[118] in a flock and fly to the west, those our graves. If it is good[119] and that magic[120] is forecast, the atoll of Mile will appear. The island, the tops of the trees will appear (like hairs bristling on an arm).

What canoe sails? The canoe of movement.

The canoe sails.

Sail to the south of Mile and sail to the south of Mile to encircle with a net. Mackerel to the southwest of N̦adikdik.[121] We cast off the canoe bailer the *mao*[122] eats it. The mao at the oceanside of Kilañe.[123] Smear the forehead with oil. The forehead is shiny. Pull in the tuna,[124] food of the turnstone[125] here.

It is of very good appearance,[126] the tip of its lateral fin, you cannot see its face.[127] Where men?

East of the sunrise, the *Ikid* of L̦ainjin is ended.

The *Ikid* is ended.

(L̦ainjin went around to all the atolls/islands in the Marshalls, as the old people said, but I only learned this one [The Ikid].

I learned when I was a child from my father, Jam, a man of Kapinmeto, western Rālik. He learned from his father and his uncle, and others. He could forecast weather, including typhoons, and would warn people to prepare for them so that they would not be damaged.)

---

117. The Marshallese spoken in the Ratak chain of the Marshall Islands. There is a slight dialectical variation between Ratak and Rālik, the western chain of the archipelago, and there are local variations, especially noticeable on Ānewetak/Wūjlañ, the westernmost of the Marshalls, and long isolated.

118. *Kowak* [*Numenius tahitiensis,* bristle-thighed curlew]; these two birds are a navigation sign, as is another flock of curlews, additional curlews. We do not know how many, the informant said. Four? or six? We do not know.

119. Ancient language: *kibroitaken.*

120. This implies using divination with pandanus-leaf folding *(bubu in maañ).* The navigation sign of Mile Atoll is many fish and many birds. "The fish flow *(ek tọọr).*" Mackerel [*Scomber japonicus* Houttuyn, *ṃōlṃōl*], albacore *(kawakawa)* [*Euthynnus a. yaito, ļooj*], and yellowfin tuna [*Neothunnus a. macropterus, bwebwe*]. Many kinds of fish. Mile is the only place in the Marshalls where there are so many, the informant stated.

121. N̦adikdik (Knox) Atoll, a small atoll just south of and very close to Mile Atoll. It is [considered] part of Mile and is used as a source of fish, turtles, birds, and other foods. It was believed to be the place where the spirits of the departed went before going to Jibuinemōn in the land of the dead. A qualifying test had to be passed first to determine whether or not the spirit could continue its journey. (This motif is found throughout the world.) The spirit leaps across a channel in the reef in which a horrible monster lurks . If the spirit has sinned in life it will fall, to be devoured by the monster. The navigation sign of N̦adikdik is the *ṃōlṃōl* (mackerel).

122. *Mao* [*Cheilinus* sp., wrasse; or *Scarus jonesi,* blue parrotfish]. I am not sure which fish the informant meant.

123. Kilañe, an island on the eastern side of Arņo Atoll (Mājin-eañ) and east of the large pass. Arņo is the atoll just north of Mile Atoll. The navigation sign of Kilañe is the schools of *mao.*

124. The navigation sign of Arņo is a single tuna [*Neothunnus macropterus, bwebwe*], the chief of the tunas *(irooj in bwebwe).*

125. And a single turnstone [*Areneria interpres, kōtkōt*] is the navigation sign, [together] with the tuna.

126. Ancient language: *Ejurjur.*

127. This is because the fish is so long, and because it is so bright and beautiful. It is like the sunrise, the informant said. [This may or may not symbolize the arrival of the voyagers at the east, the place of sunrise *(takinaļ).*]

Comments

Krämer and Nevermann (1938:245–246) refer to "The Ikid of Ļainjin" as follows: "The song of Laindjin, the great seafarer of Lae. I got this epical song through Ladāp Lanbulien of Lae." [The Marshallese text with German translation is recorded: 276.]

"Although the Rālik text remained inexplainable, I nevertheless learned something about its contents. According to that it deals with the story of Djibuke, cf. Erdland (1914: 211–220) under the title of 'The jealousy of the Pleaides of Jubuge's wife.' Jabro, Jubuge's brother and beautiful women—Lang in Jiarel (taboo rain). His soul eaten."

"Song of Jibuke when he went to get the lightning," "Song of Linkaro," and "Songs of Laindjin" are included in this ethnographic report (pp. 276–301 and passim).

The Carolinians (Micronesians to the west of the Marshall Islands) also use sea marks/signs as navigational aids. These include fish, whales, porpoises, birds, and other phenomena as in the Marshallese navigational system and in "The Ikid of Ļainjin." See Gladwin (1970:205–208) and Riesenberg (1972:19–56 and passim) for details of the seamarks in the Central Carolines especially. The system is still used in the Carolines.

Lewis (1972:114–115, 316–320 and passim) discusses the use of seamarks by Gilbertese navigators in some detail. These include "directional marks ashore" stone pillars. Compare this with the named rocks *(dekā)* and the *joor ko* stone pillars or posts used by Marshallese navigators, as described in "The Ikid of Laijin." (Could this be an analogous function?)

Lewis's evaluation is applicable to the use of *kōkļaļ/kōkaļļe* (seamarks/navigation signs) by the Marshallese navigators. He states, "Magic and shrewd observation are in all probability combined in certain Gilbertese betia or 'seamarks'. What is one to make of the following instance? 'Between Tarawa and Maiana were porpoises in pairs whose heads always pointed in the direction of the passage into Tarawa lagoon at the place called Bairiki.' Grimble evidently thought it could be a valid observation, because he added in the parentheses that it was 'quite probable that these porpoises would be feeding on some sort of food swept out of Bairiki passage by the tide race of the lagoon at falling water' (Grimble, n.d. (a)."

Compare this with the *kōkļaļ/kōkaļļe* in "The Ikid of Ļainjin" as recorded in this story (see footnote 74 on page 135), the porpoises in the ocean aligned with M̧ōn-o *wāto* (land parcel) on Wōja Island, Aelōn̄ļapļap Atoll. The same feeding opportunities may very well exist there.

"The Gilbertese Sea marks and manifestations" *(betia)* are listed and described in Grimble (1972: 137–141). Lewis's comments concerning the habits of seabirds, as known to Gilbertese and other Pacific Islanders, are obviously pertinent to the *Ikid.* Marshallese knowledge of the habits of seabirds and other creatures is seen in the *Ikid*, and has become part of the oral tradition.

Lewis states,"Not surprisingly, since the coconut palms of an atoll come into view seventeen kilometers from the deck of a canoe, land-locating signs are considered of primary importance in the Pacific. Their order of importance naturally varies according to local conditions, but most are known everywhere.

"Birds take pride of place in the navigators' repertoire in groups as remote from each other as the Tuamotus and the Carolines. Terns, noddies, and boobies are the most important species, for they all roost ashore, flying out to the sea each day to fish and returning home each evening. Their habits vary according to locality, but terns and noddies generally congregate up to forty kilometers offshore, while flocks of boobies may confidently be expected at sixty. The sighting of a substantial number confirms the proximity of land, but only their morning and evening flight-paths indicate its direction" (1977:36–37).

Lewis notes traditional knowledge of the Marshalls by Gilbertese (1972:320–321).

Compare this with "The Ikid of Ļainjin": the *kōkļaļ* that points toward Mile; the two curlews that fly apart, one speaking Ratakese, the other speaking Gilbertese; and the mention of the location of Ļainjin's canoe between Epoon Atoll and the Gilberts.

Krämer and Nevermann (1938: 224–225) report that: ". . . Chamisso had heard that there dwelt people from *Repith-Urur,* that is *ri Bit urur* (Gilbert Islanders), who are killed on some of the islands.

"Also the fact that the drinking of palm syrup and palm wine was only introduced by the Gilbert Islanders, and the occurrence of several words from their language *(jārik, jigū, jēibi)* indicates frequent, if involuntary acquaintance."

See Knight (1982:273–279) for an *ikid* that he calls a "poem." It is in English and agrees in a number of details (e.g., the beginning at N̄atik) with the version of "The Ikid of Ļainjin" that was told me.

30: IKID EO AN ĻAINJIN

Ri-bwebwenato: Jelibōr Jam, Kuwajleen 1975

Kajeke wa in jān likiej in N̄atik. Kajeke wa in jān likiej in N̄atik.

Edjon̄jon̄ jabu eo erwōj m̧ōm̧aan in tak Rālik n̄e ebelaļ aelōn̄ in.

Kotoktok in koļbaj ri-āne eo.

Enaaj to jineet eo. Bōn ekine iiaļ kā rōk in iiaļ kā.

Ettōn̄ļǫk kijdik eo.

Kokwōjkwōj wōj.

Lan̄peran, ekōjan̄ dōb eo nājin Etao edda wajwe. Eruj kwonaļ ekain̄ Koeak ej ba, "Okok." Ej ba, "Entak."

Rekbij āne eo retto ilo bōl m̧ōre inij eo ep en jerak!

Jeklak, jeklak jeloe jojo ko i likiej en N̄atik im Poonpe. Rej jeorto m̧ǫle eo ean̄in Koro en rebuk ņa lin wa in. Buk ņa lin ep jān jejtak jeloi toļ ko jeloi i baļ ko jetal ilo iiaļ in mej ilo kilaan Anij n̄e jemour.

Jej ilān itok bōke buļuļļuļ an elōn̄ bōkā, a elōn̄ bōkā jej ettōr. Etto ak eo likiej in Jinme.

Kwojeje ep kwōn jek ta? Lim̧lim̧ in Ānewetak in eļļa ļǫk iaan wa in kwǫmuri wa in waam̧ ia? Ippān Ļōkōton̄orn̄ōr ian̄.

Im̧im̧ eņ ejuok am̧ ielu! Bwe ibatur.

Kōm tartem lo kājokwā kab ļōm̧aro rejro kajjo an māāl. Rejro jekjek i wa eo Ļakele in em̧an kōj. Iruj in m̧anit in ak eo ej piktak ni in wa, bōb in wa. Jar in rej wōj kajjo em abjāje tok. Ar kamennuwawa.

Ebwil i lǫjet en kāļǫk em kajōke ļǫk Wōtto.

Epel meto jeļā eo. Eawie ek eo ikōn wa eo.

Ļōtran m̧aan in wa eņ?

Ļeddo im Ļakne. Rejro eǫjōk ļǫk n̄an Koperwa em Lin̄ijiļǫk. Ak kājokwā waad wapepe.

En̄eņ ej peļǫk wōt ijeņ.

Ej wurtak jure eo ejitōn̄ toļap ej ba kajjien āne eo.

Kwōn pikir wa in im kaluje epitōk aron̄ in. Eleļǫk i rōk wa in. Bwijin ke, ketak ke, m̧okta ke.

Eto ak eo. Būke eo edik in. Ej ketak kaaļo eo būke eo eļap eŋ ak bao jok āne. Meni Pojar in eokwa.

Kobōnbōn ep jen kajje kōkōļaļ kōn eiō kājokwā uweo kōn eiō. Kab Irooj in Ar. Ej jikirōk wa in etōkeak i kipin mejje kaŋ.

Jouj ruj im ṃweakdik eṃṃan bwe en ilju.

Ekijerjer Jowaļañ eiten kọrej eiten Balooj. Jar eŋ rejwōj jibketak wōt likin Looj in jaran kamaañ eo in.

Libake eŋ rej eneke em lemeto bwen Ledikdik im Lejṃaan rōkere em bōk ŋa i wa eŋ.

Eññūr būruon Likrilem ej illu kōn Lijinṃōt ebwe en to Liṃaṃōko ejjab kōrā in iuwe in etal. Ej pād in jo āne.

Wa eo tartak irōk tak. Libukaje eŋ ej pā pinnen kotak baļ in. Ej tarṃaan Jōbareo em jo ilo ae eo ekōt a ekōt lijarawi ilo ŋo ko juri.

Ejeṃļọk. Ejeṃļọk i Lae.

Kōm pepe ep jān ekabil joļọk Libat joļọk Likarelelem. En iuwetok Lijoñan. En kaōiōie kab pinektake kōj.

Koujinmeto, Koujinmeto—Ļeō-e—ļeō. Ejjab kiki jeļā eo. Ej junmeto ej ekatok kōtae eaetak bokā in door ļọk iep in koṃin jopāl ep jān kakōlkōl jar eo ejikrōk tōbe, tōbe jān maañin edeñij edde ŋa eddo o edde ñijñij. Jektil ketak ilo meto kā irilik.

Jektil ketak ilo meto kā irilik, jektil kātok ilo meto kā irilik.

Ajibokdede. Eliṃaajŋoŋo kapin Demar in kab eneŋ irikin eļļā ļọk irōk wa in.

Ejetake kouj eo utiej jān Anel Dekā eŋ raj jet kā. Rej wor tok ek ko raar ba. Ilikin Nakwōpe em Ṃōn-o. Kōm naaj wajoka em jebroñ koṃ ta? Di eŋ lọjiliñin.

Eajeded amān eo ṃwieo ļap eo aerro jemān eŋ. Ekkāke Jikborej eliakabūtbūt ioon wa. Keare mānilik ŋe bwe en jeboul ebūtbūt wa in ib ekonel. Ejikrōk Naṃdik epaak Ṃadṃad iur ļapļap eo, maañ eo, maañin Ṃadṃad, a maañin Wūndik, a le, dibwiji raj ko Lijinej em Lijoñal kab Lijenṃaļokļok.

Ej kōj wōt bikien Leļļō em ejitōñļọk Naṃdik ej kaitok Taij em Ļejpel joor ko i āne, wōn ko i meto likiej in Leltiñ im Jabad.

Elitaob teltel ej teltel tok irōk tok eañin tok Libujen renwōj bukbukwōj Jutōkwa, Jutōkwa. Ļeo ejed āne eo, eto ak eo. "Liṃaakak nājū Inedel a kokañ ikōt, Inedel?"

"Kōmro jema tulọk, tupā, tulojo di in ek juon ṃak in mā juon." "Kab bar ta?" "Alle dikdik e kijō jān jinō im jema." "Kwōjjab itok kōjro kāļọk?"

"Ibaj mijak eok bwe kwe anij." "Kinji, apiji, kāļọk."

"Iṃōñā ep iaar kañ lo eo i būkien Aelo. Ilaļtata aō kaṃaulaļ ra eo i Būkien raan bōb." Letkonimen eŋ ej uwetok ijaļapļap em kaibojooj erein. Kōm ļak po ļọk Bok eo eṃōj ubuk ŋa i po. (Kiiō rej pād ikōtaan Epoon im aelōñ in Kilibōt.)

Ri-Emwa raŋ ke jejjab ikile er. Koṃ dok kōn ta? Jukwe juon iuriur jikini, iuriur jikini. Ijjab iuriur jikini bwe imijak jinō Lukjānmeto. Eaar ba jepļaakin eō eouṃwin eō bwe en kañ eō. "Boñool, boñoolñol raj!"

Jelōļñọñ rōba ṃan kōj. Jen bwil im ko jān āniin. Ļōt eŋ ej iten Ļekōj? Ļōktō ejeļā kajjien jikut im rukut kab ta?

Aebōj eŋ limen Etao. Toul eo eutiej i lọmeto. Kowak ruo eo rej kā jān doon ej kajiratak juon. Ej rukweia juon. Bar jet kā rej jep koļan im kāto, wūliej ko ad kaŋe. Kibroitaken em bwe eŋ, aelōñ in Mile. Āneo eddoñ ŋe a eouwe.

Waan ta eŋ ke ejerak? Waan jo. Eouwe irūkin Mile a eouwe irūkin Mile a ekōļ-jabļeļe. Ṃōlṃōl ko irūkin Ŋadikdik kōm ļak joļọk lim eo, mao ekañe. Mao in lo Kilañe eŋ ilik in kapit deṃān. Jetōltōl daṃ. Ekọjōk ejmeme eo kijōṃ kōtkōt eiō.

Ejurjur jabōn pein. Eikṃōjṃōj mejān. Ea ļōṃa?

Arļap in takōnaļ.

E jeṃļọk ikid eo an Ļainjin.

(Ļainjin ej kapooļ aelōñ in Ṃajeļ. Āinwōt rūtto ro ar ba. Ak men eo wōt iaar katak.

Iaar katak ippān jema Jam ke iaar ajri. Ļeo eaar juon eṃṃaan in Kapinmeto. Im Jam eaar katak ippān jemān im aļap eo an. Im ro jet armej. Emaroñ in lale lañ, ta eo naaj itok, kab taibuun. Im emaroñ kakil armej bwe ren kōppojak ñan taibuun bwe ren jab jorrāān.)

EPOON

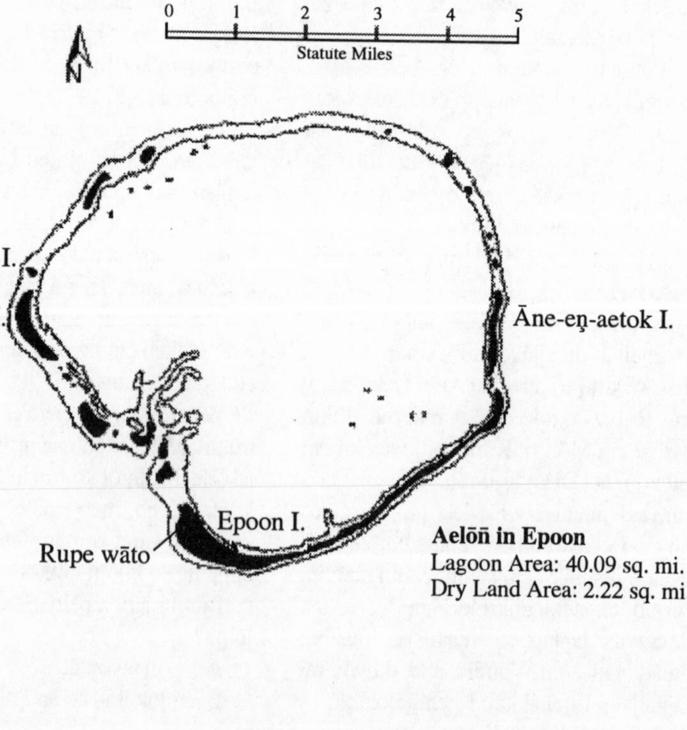

Aelōñ in Epoon
Lagoon Area: 40.09 sq. mi.
Dry Land Area: 2.22 sq. mi.

31: OUR MOTHER FOREVER, OUR FATHER AND THE FATHER OF OTHERS

As told by Jobel Emos, Kuwajleen 1975

The reason we Marshallese follow and honor our mothers, is because of her clan and *aļap* [lineage head.] Not your father's. They say, "*Ninnin im bōtōktōk,*" breast and blood.

There is a *jabōnkōnnaan,* a proverb, about this. It says, "*Jined ilo kōbo, jemād im jemān ro jet.*" The meaning of this is that we know who our mothers are but not our fathers.[1]

We get our addresses[2] from our mothers. "*Kōbo*" means *'ṃool ilo ṃool', 'lukkuun ṃool',* correct, true; absolutely, positively correct, true.

The title[3] of this story is "Jined ilo Kōbo. Jemād im Jemān Ro Jet."

This story is a story of Epoon [Atoll], about a young man, his name was Inedel. His father took two women after the mother of the boy (Inedel) died. The women did not take good care of him (the boy).[4]

His mother finished turning into a bird and returned to come to the young man to help him. Perhaps she was like a person but she flew like a bird. (Perhaps she was like an angel.)[5]

The two of them, father and son, fished on the canoe; they had not yet pulled up the fish trap [pulled it up in the morning to reset it].

Now his father jumped [into the sea] and revealed [pulled up] the fish trap. During the time his father was gone, disappeared into the sea, his mother appeared like a bird. She questioned the boy, and said, "Inedel, what kind of fish did you eat for your food?"

Now the boy said, "We two, my father and I, Inedel, dive toward the fish trap, dive and go."

Now he said, "Bones of one fish and the top part of two breadfruit" [*Artocarpus altilis, ma*].[6] Now the woman said, "And what else?"

Inedel said, "The *alle dikdik*" (the very small *alle*) [*Thalassoma* sp., wrasse]. (*Alle dikdik* is a very small fish—one inch long maximum.)

His mother said, "Why don't you come and we two will fly away?"

Now the boy [said], "I am afraid of you because you are a demon."[7]

---

1. This proverb is well known in the Marshalls, and expresses the attitude toward one's mother and one's identity in relation to her—clan and lineage membership, rank, and land-use rights.

2. The informant, who spoke English well, although he told me all of the stories in Marshallese, used this English word rather than the Marshallese equivalent.

3. Again an English word was used in a legend told in Marshallese.

4. The father was obviously of chiefly *(irooj)* rank, as only they were able to practice polygyny. Here we see the cruel stepmother, loving mother, and neglectful father—motifs found in the folktales of other cultures.

5. Note the motifs of a person transformed into an animal after death, and returning to guard and help the child. Note also the use of the English word and concept 'angel' *(enjel).* This appears to be an example of the syncretism of traditional and Christian beliefs. One can see the resemblance to the traditional belief in *lōrro* (flying women).

6. The *ṃak* (top part of the breadfruit, near the stem—and the least desirable to eat).

7. Again we see the concept of people turning into harmful spirits after death, and the use of the modified English loanword *demon (tiṃoņ)* in the Marshallese narrative.

Now his mother came and pinched him (with her nails on his arms). She pinched him with two fingers, and flew away.

Now his father appeared. He finished throwing the fish inside the canoe and dived down again. He put down the fish trap [set it in position] again (with a rock) and returned to the boy.

He said to the boy, "Inedel, why are you crying?"

Inedel said, "The fish bones, my food, pierced my hand."

His father said, "That is not your food, fish. It is the food of the women on the island."

And they argued. (They repeated thus two more times.)[8]

Because his father maintained [its being] the food of the women.

Now the two of them paddled away to the island. The father called the women that they should carry the canoe. And when they carried the canoe, the man and the two women were on one side and the boy was on one side [the other side].[9]

When they finished, they put the canoe on the shore.[10] And the man and the women went and slept. The boy took fish, and went and cooked fish. And now he went and picked breadfruit, [and] picked coconuts [*Cocos nucifera, ni*]. And when the breadfruit and fish were cooked, they were ready to eat. Now he went and woke up his father. Now his father woke up the women and called them so that they would come and divide the food, so that they would eat. Now the women divided. They gave the top part of the breadfruit, *alle dikdik* [the tiny fish], and the partial covering on the husked coconut, the "skin" over the eyes of the nut, to the boy.[11]

The women ate real food: real breadfruit, real fish, real coconuts.

Now they ate. When they were finished, they slept [until] when the day would come, [until the next day].

Now they again did everything (for three days) [that is, repeated the actions, division of food, eating, and sleeping—three days in all].[12]

Now came the fourth day, and the boy's father wanted to change his thinking. He wanted to know why the boy was crying all the time. Now those two went paddling again to the place where the fish trap was.

Now his father did not dive but remained beneath the outrigger platform. Now he heard the song, the sound of the mother's song: "Inedel, what kind of fish do you eat?"

Now Inedel answered his mother. He said, "We two, my father and I, Inedel, dive toward the fish trap, dive and go."

His father heard this. Now his father appeared from beneath the outrigger platform. He questioned Inedel again, the same as before, "Why are you crying?"

Now Inedel changed his thinking, because he wanted to go with and follow his mother.

Now Inedel answered his father, "The

---

8. Three times in all. This is the ritual number in magical/medical treatments—the number of basic ingredients in a potion or ointment, and the number of times taken.

9. The boy was made to bear more of the burden than was fair. His father and stepmothers mistreated him—again.

10. *Ioon kappe,* the informant explained, is the end of the water, the beach. It is next to the water (ocean or lagoon). The *kappe* is, he said, where the last of the water comes beside the island, that is, the high-water mark.

11. Here is a violation of the Marshallese ethic of sharing and generosity in the distribution of food (further mistreatment of the boy by the greedy and cruel stepmothers in their withholding of food).

12. Here again is the use of the ritualistic, formulistic number three *(jilu)*.

bones of that fish are the food of those women on the island."

His father said, "It is not the food of those women, but [it is] your food."

(He said it again three times.)

Now it was the boy's food. Now they again paddled to the island. Now the man, the boy's father, called to his wives. And they came to the canoe.

Now when they took the canoe, his father said, "You two there on that side. We two, the boy [and I], on this side."[13]

When they put the canoe on shore, he told those women to take the fish and cook them, while the man, [the boy's] father, went to pick breadfruit and coconuts.

Now all the work was finished and they were ready to eat. The man called the boy, because he had gone to sleep. Now the boy came and his father said, "Divide the food."

Now the boy gave the food to one of the women and said, "Mother, [this] is your food here, for you should plait my loincloth." (The meaning of *ōr* in *kajin etto,* the ancient language, is *kaļ* 'loincloth'.)[14]

Now he spoke like this to the other woman. He again spoke like this, "For you should plait my skirt."[15]

Now he gave to his father and said, "Your food here, father, for you should just make my kite."

Now they finished their making [of the articles of clothing] and the kite and gave them to the boy, and he put the clothes on. And the three of them returned and slept. But the boy went and played with the kite and looked for his mother. And he sang when he went, when he seized the kite, as it went up.

He sang and went. Now *"Liṃaakak eo eaar iañōkoto | Jouj aluje nejū | Tujeljel iañ | Jāt ie | Tujeljel a etu"* (ancient language: dive down and stay). (The kite went up to the north | Please look at it my child [the kite] | It rolls up to the north | Comes up to the south | Up in the sky | Under the water | Dive down | Dive down and stay.)

Now the people called him to make *ekkan* with them [presentation of food][16] to his father, for his father was a chief.

And they said, "Look at the *tōl* [the food presented], and wait for the *tōl.*"

And Inedel took one coconut and one breadfruit from the *tōl* and went away, saying he would take them to his father.

Now Inedel went. The people went and reported to his father, "The boy, your son, will shortly reach the end of the island, so that he can get to where his mother is."

Now the father awoke and looked out and saw the boy, his son. The father ran to overtake his son. And the son hurried to sing so that he would go faster.[17]

Now when he was just about to reach his son, his son jumped in a hole in front of the island. And his mother grabbed him. (The name of the island is Tōkā.)

13. The father repents his mistreatment of his son, and apparently tries to make up for it, to correct his mistakes.

14. Loincloth *(kaļ)* made of finely plaited pandanus matting, worn by men.

15. Skirt *(in)* made of coconut leaves or shredded hibiscus bark [*Hibiscus tiliaceus* L.] worn by men. These articles of wearing apparel have not been used for many years in the Marshall Islands, but, as we see, knowledge of them survives in the folklore, the oral tradition. German ethnographers described these and other items of material culture of the Marshallese at the time of the administration of Micronesia by the German Empire.

16. See the comments on page 147 for a discussion of the formal presentation of food.

17. A magical song/ formula is used to hasten flight, to escape a pursuer here. This is seen in other Marshallese folktales, and in the tales of other cultures as well.

Now they disappeared and went under the ground inside the hole. And those two, mother and son, remained inside the hole.

Now his father dug in order to find those two. Now he dug, dug, dug, and cried out and said, *"Kwōj jemei ikōb, kōb, kōb ļọk ia ļe?"* (In the ancient language—he asked, "Where are you?")

"You, *jemei,* I dig, dig, where, sir?"

(The name of the *wāto* (land parcel) today is Jemeikōbkōb.)[18]

Now these two replied, the boy and his mother, "We two are here."

Now the man made five holes, and he asked the question five times. And those two replied again five times. Now the man was tired, because it was a lot of work, and he wanted to "prepare," to defecate. And he went to the ocean side of the island and sat on a rock and defecated. And a shrub was beside him, *ut-ilo-mar* [*Guettarda speciosa,* a creeper]. Now he grabbed leaves to wipe himself with.

He wiped himself and got shit on his hand. And died. But the boy remained with his mother.

The things that prove the story are: the shrub that the man grabbed remains to this day on Tōkā on the land parcel, and the five holes that he dug [as well].

Now all the leaves on the shrub are halves, because half is gone. (But all the good ones do not have half missing.)

[That is: one shrub/plant of *utilomar* has only half leaves. All other *utilomar* have whole leaves. You can see this to this day.]

And five holes remain. And people put rubbish, or coconut husks—all kinds of rotten things—in them. But they do not ever fill up.

All of the rotten things disappear and again appear and remain. (There is drinking water inside. It is not brackish. You can drink it or bathe with it.)

The story is ended.

(The story is of Epoon. It teaches the reason we say, *"Jined ilo kōbo. Jemād im jemān ro jet."*) I learned this story and others from my grandfather.

Comments

See Erdland (1914:170) "Jiner ilo Kobō, Jemer im Jemen Jet" for a brief explanation of the proverb. The parallel texts are in Marshallese and German. Several other proverbs were recorded by the German ethnographer.

Japanese folklore is replete with stories of ghosts and benevolent and malevolent spirits, some of which take the form of animals, as in this and other Marshallese folktales. See Piggot 1975:61–84 and passim, and Leach 1950(2): 539–540.

One wonders how much, if any of this folklore was told to Marshallese by Japanese during their stay of over a generation in the Marshall Islands (or similiar tales by their German predecessors).

If this were done, it would probably tend to reinforce Marshallese beliefs.

Similiar stories from the Bible, known to the Marshallese for over a century, have undoubtedly had this effect.

A Japanese physician, Dr. I. Ishoda, who was practicing medicine in the Marshalls,

18. This is an example of the origin of some of the *wāto* (land parcel) names: in legends. The informant voluntarily sketched a map of Epoon and Tōkā for me to be sure that I understood it completely.

translated 51 of the anthropomorphic *Aesop's Fables* into Marshallese.

These *Bwebwenato an Aesop* were printed in booklet form in 1929 and distributed in the Marshalls. How widely they were circulated and read I do not know. They were reprinted at the Marshall Islands Intermediate School in the early 1950s, when I obtained one of them.

Concerning the presentation of food, the formal presentation of food and other valued items to the chiefs *(irooj ro)* was an important part of the Marshallese custom *(m̧antin M̧ajeļ),* the traditional culture. Indeed it still is. The act of formal or even informal presentation of goods is one of recognition of the rank and authority of the one who is honored, as it is in other cultures. Informants have explained the different ways of giving to the chief *(wāween leļo̧k ñan irooj).* These include:

Nibarbar: When the chief comes to an island. This is a community effort.

Ekkan: Given by the community later in the visit of the chief, and while he is on the island as a visitor or resident.

Tōl: Given by a section of the island or atoll, or by a group in the community.

To̧o̧r pata: Goods (money and the like) received from sources other than the land. For example, valuable items that were brought by the sea to an island, such as lumber, logs, turtles, and so forth. These things were taken by the *aļap* to the *irooj* for his use or disposal.

Kamaatat: Given to individuals, such as the *aļap* or *irooj edik* (secondary or subchief, literally 'little chief'), and to the *irooj* and *irooj ļapļap / irooj eļap* (paramount chief). This includes money nowadays, and *menin aorōk* (things of value).

31: JINED ILO KŌBO, JEMĀD IM JEMĀN RO JET

Ri-bwebwenato: Jobel Emos, Kuwajleen 1975

Wūnin kōm, ri-Ṃajeļ, ļoor im kautiej jined kōnke jowi im aļap eo an. Ejjab jemām. Rej ba, "Ninnin im bōtōktōk."

Im eor juon jabōn kōnnaan kake. Meļeļein ej jejeļā wōn ej jinen eo ad. Ak ejjab jemān.

Jej bōk *addresses* ad jān jined. "Kōbo" ej ṃool ilo ṃool. Lukkuun ṃool.

Title eo an bwebwenato in ej, "Jined ilo Kōbo, Jemād im Jemān Ro Jet." Bwebwenato eo ej juon bwebwenato in Epoon. Kōn juon likao etan Inedel.

Jemān ar bōk ruo kōrā ālikin jinen ļadik eo (Inedel) ar mej. Kōrā ro ejjab eṃṃan aer lale (ļadik eo).

Jinen eṃōj an oktak ñan āinwōt bao im ro̧o̧l in itok ñan likao ilo jipañ. Bōlen ej āinwōt armej ak kāļo̧k āinwōt bao. (Bōlen āinwōt enjel ke.)

Erro jemān rej eo̧ñwōd ioon wa, rejjañin ebbwā u.

Kiiō jemān ej kāļo̧k im kwaļo̧k u eo. Kiiō iien eo jemān ej jako, ilo lo̧jet ļotļo̧k, jinen ej waļo̧k āinwōt bao. Kiiō ej kajjitōk ippān ļadik eo. Ej ba, "Kokañ koṃōñā ek rot?"

Kiiō ļadik eo ej ba, "Inedel kōmro jema tulo̧k, tu bwā, tu lojo." Kiiō ej ba, "Di in juon ek, ṃakan mā ruo."

Kiiō lio ba, "Kab bar ta?" Inedel ej ba, "Alle dikdik eo kijō jān jinō im jema."

Jinen ej ba, "Kwōj itok. Kejro kāļo̧k?"

Kiiō ļadik eo, "Ij mijak eok bwe kwe anij (tiṃo̧ŋ)."

Kiiō itok jinen im kinji. Kiiō ej apiji. Kinji, apiji im kāļo̧k.

Kiiō ewaļo̧k jemān. Eṃōj jo̧ļo̧k ek ilowaan wa im bar tulo̧k. Kiiō ebar likūti u eo (kōn dekā). Ero̧o̧l ñan ļadik eo.

Eba ñan ļadik eo, "Inedel etke kwōj jañ?"

Inedel ej ba, "Di ko [di]in ek [kā] kijō rej lōke peiū."

Jemān ej ba, "Bōta kijōṃ. Kijen kōrā ro āne."

Innām rej akwāāl. (Rej bar ba āindein ruo alen.) Kōnke jemān eļap an kajoor kijen kōrā ro.

Kiiō erro aōŋōōŋ ļo̧k āne [āne ļo̧k]. Jinen [Jemān] ekūr kōrā ro bwe ren bōk wa eo. Innām ke rej bōk wa eo ļeo kab kōrā ro juon (irājet) tu jimettan in wa eo. Kiiō ļadik eo epād irājet.

Eṃōj rej likūt wa ioon kappe. Innām ļeo im kōrā ro rej etal im kiki. Ļadik eo ej būki ek ko im etal im kōmat ek. Im kiiō ej etal im kōṃkōṃ mā, entak ni. Im eļaññe emat mā im ek, kiiō repojak in ṃōñā. Kiiō etal im ko̧ruj jemān. Kiiō jemān ej karuji kōrā ro im kūr tok er bwe ren itok im ajeej ṃōñā, bwe ren ṃōñā. (Kiiō kōrā ro rej ajeej. Releļo̧k ñan likao eo ṃak in mā, alle dikdik, im wūlṃōd in ni.)

Kōrā ro rej ṃōñā lukkuun ṃōñā: lukkuun mā, lukkuun ek, lukkuun ni. Kiiō rej ṃōñā. Eṃōj, rej kiki ñe raan eo naaj itok. Kiiō rej bar kōṃṃane aolep men (jilu raan).

Kiiō raan eo kein kemān kiiō. Kiiō jemān ļadik eo kōŋaan ukot an ļōmŋak. Ekōŋaan jeļā ta wūnin ļadik eo ej jañ aolep iien. Kiiō erro reetal bar aōŋōōŋ ñan jikin eo u eo ej pād ie.

Kiiō jemān ejjab tulo̧k ak pād iuṃwin ere eo. Kiiō ej roñjake al eo, ainikien jinen al eo, "Inedel a kokañ ikōt?"

Kiiō Inedel ej uwaak jinen. Eba, "Inedel ke kōmro jema tulo̧k tu bwā tu lojo."

Jemān ej roñjake wōt. Kiiō ewaļo̧k jemān jān iuṃwin ere eo. Bar kajjitōk ippān Inedel āinwōt ṃokta, "Ta wūnin kojañ [aṃ jañ]?"

Kiiō Inedel ej uwaak jemān. Kiiō, "Di in ek kā kijen liṃaro i āne."

Jemān ar ba, "Ejjab kijen liṃaro ak kijōṃ." (Ej bar ba ruo alen.) Kiiō kijen ļadik eo.

Kiiō rej bar aōņōōņ ñan āne. Kiiō ļeo, jemān ļadik eo, ej kūri kōrā ro ippān. Innām rej itok ñan wa eo.

Kiiō rej bōk wa jemān ar ba, "Koṃro ijōņe irājet. Im kōm ro ļadik eo, irājet."

Ke rej likūt wa eo ioon kappe eba liṃaro [ren] būki ek ko im kōmatti. Eļañne ļeo jemān ej ilān kōṃkōṃ mā im entak ni.

Kiiō eṃōj aolep jerbal ko im rej pojak in ṃōñā, ļeo ej kūr ļadik [eo], bwe ar ilān kiki. Kiiō ļadik eo ar itok im jemān ar ba, "Kwōn ajeej ṃōñā ko."

Kiiō ļadik eo ej leļọk ṃōñā ñan kōrā eo juon im ba, "Jinō ieo kijōṃ ijo, bwe kwōn āje ōr eo aō." (Meļeļein "ōr" ilo kajin etto ej 'kaļ'.)

Kiiō ej ba āinwōt ñan kōrā eo juon. Ej bar ba āinwōt, "Bwe kwōn āje in eo aō."

Kiiō ej leļọk ñan jemān im ba, "Kijōṃ ijo jema bwe kwōn kab kōṃṃane limakaak eo nājū."

Kiiō eṃōj aer kōṃṃane im leļọk ñan ļadik eo im ekōņake. Im erjel rọọl im kiki. Ak ļadik eo ej etal im ikkure kōn limakaak eo im pukotļọk [ñan ippān] jinen.

Innām ej al ke ej etal ke ej jibwe limakaak eo, wanlōñļọk. Ej al im etal. Kiiō, "Liṃaakak eo eaar iañōkto. | Jouj aluje nājū. | Tujeljel iōñ. | Takjeljel irōk. | Lañ ie. | Jāt ie. | Tujeljel a etu." (Kajin etto: tulọk im pād.)

Kiiō armej rej kūri in rej ekkan ñan jemān, bwe jemān irooj. Im rej ba lale tōl ak kōttar tōl e. Innām Inedel ej bōk jān tōl eo juon ni im juon mā im ej etal wōt. Im ba būki wōt ñan jemān.

Kiiō Inedel ej etal wōt. Kiiō armej reetal im kōnnaanļọk [ñan] jemān, "Ļadik eo nājiṃ ṃōttan jidik enaaj jeṃļọk āne bwe en tōpar ijo jinen ej pād ie."

Kiiō jemān eruj im reilọk, loe ļadik eo nājin. Ej ettōr jemān im kōttōparļọk nājin. Im nājin eṃōkajļọk an al bwe en ṃōkaj an etal. Kiiō ṃōttan jidik bwe en tōpare nājin ak nājin ej kāļọk ilowaan juon roñ iṃaan āne eo. (Etan āne eo Tōkā.)

Kiiō rej jako im etal iuṃwin bwidej ilowaan rọñ eo. Innām erro jinen im nājin repād ilowaan rọñ eo.

Kiiō jemān ej kōb bwe en loe erro. Kiiō ej kōb, kōb, kōb ej laṃōj im ba, "Kwōj jemei ikōb, kōb ļọk ia ļe?" (Kajin etto: ej kajitōk kwōj pād ia?)

(Etan wāto rainin ej Jemeikōbkōb.)

Kiiō erro rej uwaak, ļadik im jinen, "Kōmro e ije."

Kiiō ļeo ej kōṃṃane ļalem rọñ. Im ej kwaļọk kajjitōk ļalem alen. Im erro rej bar uwaak ļalem alen. Kiiō ļeo eṃōk, bwe eļap an jerbal. Kiiō ekōņaan kōppojak, mejļọk. Im ar etal ñan lik im jijet ioon juon dekā im pijek. Im juon ut ej pād iturin, utilomar. Kiiō ej jibwetok bōlōk in kwiir.

Ekwiir im potak im kūbwebwe pein. Im mej. Ak ļadik eo pād ippān jinen.

Kein kaṃool ñan bwebwenato: Ut eo ļeo ej jibwe ej pādwōt ñan rainin. Ioon Tōkā ioon wāto eo. Kab roñ ko ļalem eaar kūbwiji.

Kiiō ut eo aolep bōlōk rej jimettan. Kōnke ejako jimettan. (Ak aolep rōṃṃan ejjab jako jimettan.) Koṃaroñ loe ñan rainin.

Im ļalem rọñ rej pād. Im armej releļọk menọknọk, ak bweọ rej ṃor ak rejjab penjak.

Aolep men rej ṃor im rejako im rej bar waļọk im pādwōt roñ. Eor dān in aebōj ilowaan. Ejjab kaļaebar. Koṃaroñ idaak ak tutu ie.

E jeṃļọk bwebwenato.

(Bwebwenato ej an Epoon. Ej katak wūnin jej ba, "Jined ilo Kōbo. Jemād im Jemān Ro Jet.") Iaar katak bwebwenato in im ko jet ippān jiṃṃaō.

32: STORY ABOUT INEDEL

As told by M̧ak Juda, Mājro 1968

Inedel was a boy, the son of an *irooj* (chief).[1] His mother had died. The father's other wife hated the boy. She did not feed him well. She just gave him *m̧ak in mā* (the inedible top part of the breadfruit) and *diin ek* (fish bones).

His father played with the boy. He tied him to a kite and released the kite, holding on to the string of the kite as it went up into the air.

The other wife cut the kite string, and the boy was lost in the sky.

The island of Didi, near Tōkā Island in Epoon Atoll, has the shape of a kite.

---

1. See Grey (1951, vol. 2:15–20) for another version of the legend of Inedel. This also includes the motif of the kite and its association with Didi Island. This association of a topographic feature and folktale helps to keep the tale alive, and is seen in other Marshallese stories and in the folklore of other cultures as well—Polynesian and Native American, for example.

This story also tells us that kite flying was a form of recreation in the Marshall Islands in the distant past. Grey's version of the story may be derived from that of Buckingham (n.d.:30–33).

33: STORY ABOUT LIVING THINGS (ANIMALS) IN THE MARSHALLS

As told by Jelibōr Jam, Kuwajleen 1975

On Wōtto there was a canoe; these living things tried to see who could launch it into the water.[1]

And they began with the *kaaļo* [*Sula dactylatra,* brown booby] [and told him] that he should launch the canoe. And Kaaļo could not do it.

And they told the *kowak* [*Numenius tahitiensis,* railbird] that he should go to launch the canoe. And *Kowak* said, "The *kaaļo* is not strong, he did not try. He is weak."

And Kaaļo was very angry with the *kowak,* and said, "Well, just continue. Are you tired?" The *kowak* replied, "When I will go, all will see, for that canoe will be in the water."

And the *kaaļo* said, "If you are lying, I will never stay with you again later on."

And *Kowak* went to launch the canoe. The canoe did not move even a little bit.

And the *kowak,* because he himself trusted the *kaaļo,* separated from him, and they dislike each other to this day. (And as it is today, their being together is bad.)[2]

And they told the *kako* [*Gallus gallus,* rooster] that he should go launch the canoe. And it did not move.

And they told the *ak* [*Fregata minor,* frigate bird] that he should launch the canoe. And it did not move. They were the largest of the birds, but the canoe did not move.

And they called to each bird, one by one, that each should come to launch the canoe. But it did not move. And some of the living things said, "Is this all of the birds there are?"

And they said, "There is one, but he is worthless, for his legs are very thin. And he is very small."

"O-O." Some of the birds said. "Who could that be?" And they replied, "The *annañ*" [*Puffinus tenurostris,* small slender-billed shearwater]. And they said, "Bring him here!"

Some asked, because they did not know him, "Where is he? The very small *annañ.* He should come to launch the canoe!" (In *kajin etto,* the ancient language, *enten* means *iten*: come in order to do something.)

And some of the birds said, "The rooster should go and look for the *annañ.* For he should hasten here."

And the rooster was angry. And said, "It is useless for me to look for the *annañ,* because he cannot move the canoe. Look here, when the canoe did not move with those very big birds [pushing it], how can it truly move with the *annañ* [pushing it]?"

Some of the birds said, "Nevermind, but go tell him that he should come here!"

And the rooster went. When Rooster reached the *annañ,* he said to the *annañ,*

---

1. In this story, the animals interact with one another and not with humans or supernatural beings, as in other Marshallese stories. They are anthropomorphized, however, and speak and behave as humans might—a worldwide folktale motif. The story tells about different animals (mostly birds) and describes their attributes. It also explains somewhat their appearance and behavior today, another widespread folktale motif.

2. Here we see the explanation of the behavior of these birds, and its attribution to the incident of the folktale. The alleged mutual avoidance may be due to differential feeding and nesting patterns.

"But you are very small—is it true that you can launch that canoe? Please note that you are all covered with soil and are very dirty." ([That was] because he [*annañ*] was making a taro patch.) "You get up here; we two are going!" (Hurry up!)

And the *annañ* said, "Well, you go on ahead quickly!"

And the rooster went quickly. Then when the *annañ* was leaving his taro patch, he chanted toward the lagoon side and said, *"Kako eo eaar iten jōjōiki eō. | (Ej dike eō kōnke ña ettoon im dik.) Ionni bōli eņ aō ebōli. | Ebōli ke wa eo!"*

(This is an ancient chant. I do not know what it means.)

When he finished uttering this chant, he stamped his feet (to remove the mud). And when he finished stamping, he flew from there and again alighted about twenty feet away.[3] And again said, *"Kako eo eaar iten jōjōiki eō. | (Ej dike eō kōnke ña ettoon im dik.) Ionni bōli eņ aō ebōli. | Ebōli ke wa eo!"*

And he again stamped his feet. When the birds saw the sand of Wōtto moving (from the stamping of the *annañ*), they were startled and said, "Why is this island moving?"

And they did not know why, for they did not see the *annañ*. And the *annañ* again chanted a third time and said, *"Kako eo eaar iten jōjōiki eō. | (Ej dike eō kōnke ña ittoon in dik.) Ionni bōli en aō ebōli. | Ebōli ke wa eo!"*

And he again stamped his feet. And they saw him again and were astonished at it.

And when the *annañ* came to the canoe, he said, *"Neen an annañ. Iio likō doore?"* (He was talking to himself in the ancient language, like, "Where is the pounding, pounding, placing?" [a partial translation].)

And he dragged the canoe and went, went [until] it was in the water.

When it was in the water, he cried out and said: *"Kōbre iō bwe iit iunniñ jemen ikwōl"* (ancient language). And it means, "You did not believe I could launch a canoe, because I am small."

And the birds were surprised because his legs were as thin as coconut sennit [small cord], and he was very small.

And they said, "It is clear that he alone is the strongest of all the birds."[4]

The *annañ* said, "Everyone come; let us get on board this canoe."

And all of the birds got aboard. And the hermit crabs *(oņ)* boarded and went inside the canoe.[5] And the crabs *(baru)*.

And they loaded aboard two *wat* [*Tetradon* sp., puffer (blowfish)] so that they would bail [the canoe].[6]

And the canoe went seaward, and sailed. When it sailed, the crabs and the hermit crabs ate the sennit fastenings of the canoe, and the canoe came apart. The birds were very angry with the pufferfish. For they had not cleared out the water within the canoe and thrown it away.

Because there were no fastenings of the canoe, it sank and all the birds and living things [animals] there were angry with the hermit crabs and the crabs. And all swam, but

---

3. Note the use of the English loanword and the measurement *feet.* It has been incorporated into the language (see the Marshallese text of this story).

4. Here we see triumph of the weak and scorned individual (in this case the little bird) after larger individuals have attempted to accomplish a task that requires strength, and have failed—in other words, the underdog wins. This is a motif in other Marshallese folktales, and it is widely distributed throughout the world and is of considerable antiquity (see Leach 1949:[1]115: Unpromising hero/heroine). The stories are obviously exemplary and didactic.

5. The hulls of the traditional Marshallese canoes were very deep and of large capacity.

the *kijdik* (rat) did not know how to swim. And he told the pufferfish that it should take him on its back and swim with him.

But the pufferfish did not want to do it (refused). And the rat said to the rooster, "Can you swim with me on your back?"

The rooster replied, "I cannot do it, because I do not know how to swim."

But when the *kweet* (octopus) appeared [from within the canoe], he said to the rat, "Why are you crying, friend?"[7]

The rat replied, "Because I do not how to swim. And when I told these men that they should take me on their backs, they refused!"

And the octopus said, "Well, come here friend, I will take you on my back." The rat said, "Thank you very much, friend. I will never forget your kindness to me!"

And the rat went and sat on the octopus's head. And the octopus swam toward the island carrying the rat.

About nine feet from the island he said, "Jump [off] now. And go ashore!"

The rat replied, "Not here, for I am afraid of the *pako* (shark). For the shark is eager to eat me. Go ahead again toward the island a little more [farther]." And the octopus replied, "Well, we will go toward the island again a little more."

And when he was six feet from the island, the octopus said, "Jump off my head now, and go ashore!" The rat said, "Friend, a little bit more."

And the octopus again moved slowly toward the island a little [farther]. And the rat said, "Your kindness is extremely great, friend. I will never forget this thing that you did for me. Well, I will jump now and go ashore."

As the rat jumped from the octopus's head, he defecated on the octopus's head and jumped off and went ashore. [Informant laughed.] But the octopus did not know it [that the rat had defecated on him]. And the octopus said, "Goodby, friend!"

The rat reached the middle of the sand [beach]. The rat cried out and said, "A-A-A, look at that rat shit on that octopus's head!"

The octopus replied, "What is that you said, friend?"

The rat answered, "I said, look at those small fish beside you."

And the octopus again went seaward a little bit.

The rat cried out again, "A-A-A, look at that rat shit on that octopus's head!"

And the octopus heard it and was angry with the rat and went to the island. And the octopus said, "What did you say friend? Won't you come here?" And the octopus came on the island, and reached the rat, and grabbed him.

---

6. The pufferfish sucks in water and inflates its body as a defensive measure to frighten predators, so it was used by the birds in lieu of a canoe bailer. Note the observation and the use of the characteristic behavior of the pufferfish as part of this story. Canoe bailing is essential, due to the nature of the construction of Marshallese canoes. The upper parts of the hull are lashed together with coconut sennit and caulked with coconut fiber and breadfruit sap, in the traditional method of construction, and leakage is the norm. The men who bail out the canoe perform a vital function.

Land was sometimes given by a chief to a man who sailed with him and bailed out his canoe, as this was an extremely arduous task and necessary to keep the canoe afloat and enable it to stay underway while engaging in warfare, and also during ordinary times. The term of this type of land is *kwō-dailem* (see Tobin 1958:39 for details).

7. The rat and octopus interaction was recorded by Erdland (1914:245–246) in the tale of *Der Verhexte Brotfruchtbaum* (The Enchanted Breadfruit Tree). The parallel texts of this and other folktales are in Marshallese and German.

And the rat fled, and went inside a *debakut* (a kind of pandanus tree that has many pandanus leaves there—old leaves). And the octopus returned toward the sea, and said, "As long as I live, I will never again love this rat, for he deceived me greatly. But my kindness to him was great, and I saved his life."

It is ended.

The meaning of this thing: [There are] two meanings within it. The first: Because the rat did not return the kindness of the octopus, it was a very bad thing, and people should return kindness to those who are kind to them.[8]

When I was a child, they told me, "Do not be like the rat who lied."

Second: Because they had no confidence in the *annañ*—it is bad if we do not have confidence in a person.

And you can see the rat-shit on the octopus to this day. It is black on its head.

And that rat is evil to this day. It steals and destroys, for it defecated on the head of its friend.[9]

33: BWEBWENATO IN MENINMOUR KO ILO ṂAJEĻ IN

Ri-bwebwenato: Jelibōr Jam, Kuwajleen 1975

Ilo Wōtto eor juon wa, mennin mour kein rej kōmmaroñroñ in bwillọke ñan lọjet. Innām raar jino kōn kaaļo eo bwe en bwillọke wa eo. Innām kaaļo eo eaar bane. Innām rej ba kowak eo en etal in bwillọke wa eo. Innām kowak eo eaar ba, "Jebab ṃool kaaļo eo ak eṃōjṇọ." (Ejjab kajoor, ejjab kajjeoñ ak kate, eṃōjṇọ.)

Innām kaaļo eo eļap an illu ippān kowak eo. Im ba, "Ekwe baj kwe ṃōk?" Kowak eo eouwaak, "Eļaññe inaaj etal aolep naaj lale. Bwe wa eo enaaj pād ilọjet."

Innām kaaļo eo ej ba, "Eļaññe koriab ijjāmin bar pād ippaṃ tokālik."

Innām kowak eo ilām im bwillọke wa eo. Wa ejjab eṃṃakūt ñan jidik.

---

8. The motif of the helpful octopus and ungrateful, malicious rat is found elsewhere in Oceanic folklore. The story is told in Polynesia, Micronesia, and Melanesia. The returning of bad for good is basic to the story, and is an example, especially for children, of antisocial behavior. The story is told in Micronesian Kiribati (the Gilbert Islands) just south of the Marshalls (Luomala 1975:246–247). In this version, the octopus revenges himself on the rat for the latter's nasty action of defecating on his head. (Birds in a canoe are also elements in the story from Kiribati.) The story is also found in the Polynesian culture of Tuvalu (Ellice Islands), which lies south of Kiribati.

In the story collected by Gittens (1977:82–84), the rat is carried by the squid. He nibbles the squid's head and leaves a bald spot. The rat is later killed by the squid in this version of the story. The rat and octopus story is also told by the Samoans, another Polynesian group, whose islands are located southeast of Tuvalu (Wright 1981:42), and in Polynesian Tonga, which is south of Samoa (Gifford 1924:206). This is an example of diffusion and change in details of basic stories. Variations can be seen within the individual cultures as well, for example, within the Marshall Islands.

9. Note the explanation of the coloration of octopuses, and of the destructive behavior of the rats in the story recorded by me in the Marshall Islands. In Kiribati, the story of the Rat and Octopus explains the reason for the enmity between these animals (Luomala 1975:246). Note: My translation of the chant of the *annañ* is: The rooster came and loathed me. | (He disliked me because I am dirty and small.) Inside that taro patch of mine it launches. | It launches the canoe!" The words for taro patch and launch sound somewhat alike, and the informant explained that *ioonni* means 'inside', in the ancient language. This translation makes sense in the context of the story.

Innām kowak eo kōn an kar lōke e māke kaaļo eo eaar jepel jān eō im rejro dike doon ñan rainin. (Im āinwōt kiiō enana aer pād ippān doon.)

Innām raar ba kako eo en etal in bwillọke wa eo. Innām eaar jab eṃṃakūt.

Innām rej ba ak eo en ilān bwillọke wa eo. Eaar jab eṃṃakūt. Kōnke bao ko rōļļaptata kein iaan bao ak eaar jab eṃṃakūt wa eo.

Innām rej kūr ñan kajjojo bao bwe ren iten bwillọke wa eo. Ak ar jab eṃṃakūt. Mennin mour ko jet rej ba, "Emaat ke bao?"

Innām rej ba, "Eor juon ak ejjeļọk tokjān bwe ekanooj in aidik neen. Kab kanooj in unniñ."

"O-O." Bao ko jet rej ba, "Kar wōn kwe?" Innām rej uwaak, "Ak annañ eo." Innām rej ba, "Pukōt tok!"

Jet rej kajjitōk bwe rejaje kajjien, "Bwe epād ia? Annañ wunniññiñ eo? Entōn bwillọke wa eo!" (Kajin etto: iten.)

Innām bao ko jet rej ba, "Kako eo en etal in pukot annañ eo. Bwe en ṃōkaj tok." Innām kako eo ej illu. Im ba, "Ejjeļọk tokjān aō etal in pukot annañ bwe eban eṃṃakūt wa ṇe. Lale ṃōk ke eaar jab eṃṃakūt wa ṇe ippān bao kaṇe rōļļap ak ta ṃool ke enaaj eṃṃakūt ippān annañ nana eo?"

Bao ko jet rej ba, "Jekdọọn ak kwōn etal in ba en itok!" Innām kako eo ej etal. Ke kako eo ej tōpar ļọk ippān annañ eo ej ba ñan annañ eo, "A kokanooj unniñ ak ta ṃool ke komaroñ bwillọke wa eṇ? Lale ṃōk, ke kokanooj bwidejdej im ettoon." (Kōnke ej kōṃṃan juon bōl in iaraj.), "Kwōn jerabtok, jerro etal!"

Innām annañ eo ej ba, "Ekwe, kwōn iwōj eṃṃōkaj wōj!"

Innām kako eo ar eṃṃōkaj in etal. Innām ke annañ eo ej eṃṃakūt jān bōl eo an ej roro ar ļọk im ba, "Kako eaar iten jōjōiki eō. | (Ej dike eō kōnke ña ettoon im dik.) Ionni bōli eṇ aō ebōli. | Ebōli ke wa eo!"

(Roro in etto. Ijaje meļeļein menin.)

Ke eṃōj an ba roro in ej doorōk kōn neen. Im ke ej eṃōj an doorōk ej kāļọk jān ijo im bar jokļọk tarrin roñoul *feet* im bar ba, "Kako eo eaar iten jōjōiki eō. | Ionni bōli eṇ aō ebōli ke wa eo!"

Innām ej bar doorōk.

Ke bao ko rej lo an eṃṃakūtkūt bokin Wōtto (jān doorōk an annañ eo) rej ilbōk im ba, "Ta wūnin, an eṃṃakūtkūt āniin?"

Innām rejaje ta wūnin bwe rejjab loe annañ eo. Innām annañ ej bar roro (kein ka jilu) im ba, "Kako eo eaar iten jōjōiki eō. | Ionni bōli eṇ aō ebōli. | Ebōli ke wa eo!"

Innām ej bar doorōk. Im rej loe im kanooj bwilōñ kake. Ak ke annañ eo ej itok ñan ippān wa eo ej ba, "Neen an annañ eo. Iiao likō doore." (Ej kōnono ñane make. Im ilo kajin etto.)

Innām eaar bwillọke wa eo im etal, etal epād i lọjet.

Ke ej pād i lọjet ej ļaṃōj im ba, "Kōbre eō bwe iet iunniñ jemānni-kwōl" (kajin etto).

Innām bao ko rej bwilōñ kōnke aidik neen wōt eokkwaļ aidik ak ekanooj in niñ. Innām rej ba, "Alikkar ke ej make wōt kajoor jān aolep bao."

Annañ eo ej ba, "Aolep tok bwe jen uwe i wa e."

Innām rej uwe aolep bao. Im oṃ ko rej uwe im etal ilowaan wa eo. Kab baru. Im rej ektake ruo wat. Bwe ren kab āneen. Innām ej pemetoļọk wa eo. Im jerak. Ke ej jerak baru ko kab uṃ ko rej kañe eaṃ ko, eaṃ an wa eo. Im ej mejaļjaļ ļọk wa eo. A wat ko eļap an bao ko illu ippāerro. Bwe rejjab kōmaate dān eo jān lowaan wa eo im joļọke.

Kōn an ejjeļọk eaṃ an wa eo ej douj im aolep bar im menninmour ko ie rej illu ippān oṃ kab baru ko. Innām aolep raar aō ak kijdik eo ejaje aō. Innām ej ba ñan wat eo bwe en aō kake. Ak wat eo eṃakoko. Innām kijdik eo ej ba ñan kako eo, "Kwōj maroñ ke in aō kake eō?"

Kako eo ej uwaak, "Ijjab maroñ bwe ijaje aō."

Ak ke kweet eo ej waļǫk lōñtak ej ba ñan kijdik eo, "Etke kwojañ ļe jera?"

Kijdik eo ej eouwaak, "Kōnke ijaje aō. Ak iļak ba ñan ļōmaraņ ke ren aō kake eō reṃakoko!"

Innām kweet eo ej ba, "Ekwe, itok jera. Ña in aō kake eok." Kijdik eo ej ba, "Kokanooj in eṃṃool jera. Ijāmin meļǫkļǫk jouj in aṃ ñan eō!"

Innām kijdik eo ej etal im jijet ioon bōran kweet eo. Im kweet eo ej aō āne ļǫk kake kijdik eo.

Im tarrin ruatimjuon *feet* āneļǫk ej ba, "Kāļǫk kiiō. Im wōnāneļǫk."

Kijdik eo ej uwaak, "Ejab ijin bwe imijak pako eo. Bwe ña eļap an pako kōņaan kañ eō. Innām kwōn bar wōnānewōj jidik."

Innām kweet eo ej uwaak, "Ekwe, kejro wōnāneļǫk jidik."

Innām ke ej jiljiljino *feet* āneļǫk kweet eo ej ba, "Kāļǫk jān bōrā kiiō. Im wōnāneļǫk."

Kijdik eo ej uwaak, "Jera, bar ṃōttan jidik."

Innām kweet eo ej bar tōbal āneļǫk jidik. Innām kijdik eo ej ba, "Eļap wōt aṃ jouj ļe jera. Ke ña iban meļǫkļǫk menin kwaar kōṃṃane ñaneō. Ekwe inaaj kāļǫk kiiō im wōnāneļǫk."

Ke kijdik eo ej kāļǫk jān bōran kweet eo. Ej pekate bōran kweet eo im kāļǫk wōnāneļǫk. Ak kweet eo ejaje. Innām kweet eo ej ba, "Iokwe eok jera!"

Innām kijdik eo ej ba, "Iokwe eok jera!"

Ke kijdik eo ej tōpar lukkuun eoon bok kijdik eo ej laṃōj im ba, "A-A-A, lale kūbwe in kijdik ioon bōran kweet eņ!"

Kweet eo ej uwaak, "Ta in kwōj ba ļe jera?"

Kijdik eo ej uwaak, "Ij ba lale ek jidik kaņe ituruṃ."

Innām kweet eo ej bar wōnmetoļǫk jidik.

Kijdik eo ej bar laṃōj. Im ba, "A-A-A, lale kūbwe in kijdik eņ i bōran kweet eņ!" Innām kweet eo ej roñjake im ej illu ippān kijdik im wōnāneļǫk. Im kweet eo ej ba, "Ta in kwōj ba ļe jera? Kwōn itok ṃōk." Innām kweet eo ej wōnāneļǫk. Im kōtōparļǫk kijdik eo. Im jibwe.

Innām kijdik eo ej ko. Im deļǫñ ilowaan juon debakut. Innām kweet eo ej jepļaak metoļǫk. Im ba, "Towaan wōt aō mour ijāmin bar iǫkwe kijdik in. Bwe eļap an ṃoņe eō. Ak eļap aō kar jouj ñane. Im kōjparok mour eo an."

Ejeṃļǫk.

(Meļeļe in menin: Ruo meļeļe ilowaan.

1. Kōn an kijdik eo jab ukot jouj eo an kweet eo ñane. Juōn men ekanooj nana. Im armej ren ukot jouj ñan ro rej jouj alikkar.

Ke iaar ajri rej jiroñ tok eō im ba, "Kwon jab āinwōt kijdik eo eaar riab."

2. Kein ka ruo: kōn aer pere annañ eo. Innām enana ñe jej pere juon armej.

Innām kwōnaaj loe kūbwe in kijdik eņ ioon bōran kweet eņ ñan rainin. Ej kilmeej ioon bōran.

Im kijdik eņ ej kanooj in nana ñan rainin. Ej kǫǫt im kǫkkure bwe eaar pekate bōran jeran.)

34: THE TATTLER AND THE TRITON: A PARABLE ABOUT THE COMING OF THE MISSIONARIES TO EPOON

As told by Jobel Emos, Kuwajleen 1975

The story is short but the explanation/meaning is good. It is like a prophecy.[1] Now the beginning:

The triton [*Cymatiidae charonia tritonis* l., triton/trumpet, *jilel*] was underneath a coral head. (The name of the coral head was Barļap [lit. trans. 'big coral head'].) The coral head was on the sand, but when it was high tide, the water came on it.

The name of the land parcel that is on the ocean side is Rupe (the place of the missionaries). At the time there were no missionaries.

Now the triton turned upside down. The light [shine] *(meram)* of the triton did not appear, and it was low tide—no water. Now the tattler [*Heteroscelus incanus, kidid*], the bird, flew there, and the triton asked, "Can you come and take me (the triton), so that we two [may] fly around the Marshalls?"

And the tattler said, "Good." The tattler seized the triton, and the two of them flew.

Now they sang. The triton sang first. Now the song said, *"Jilel etūt kaaļo̧ tillo elel buke iōñ.* | *Elel buke rōk.* | *Elel wōt iju raan eņ bar eañ ilik.* | *Jepjep in ņa eņ ilik bar eņ.* | *Jui-jui-jui.* | *Raan-raan-raan-raan eo.* | *Epād tok, ilikin ia, in ia in ke-ke-e-e?* | *Ilikin Roñļap-o-o meram Roñļap kiiō."*

This song is partly in the *kajin etto* (ancient language).

In the language of today, the meaning is, "Triton is showing the light now. | He comes to the north. | He comes to the south. | He comes to the morning star and again to the north ocean. | Piled up big rock pile on the ocean reef.[2] | Calling-calling-calling the dawn (day) dawn-dawn the dawn. | It is coming. On the ocean side of where (what island)? | Where-where is it? | On the ocean side of Roñļap O-O. | The dawn is rising on Roñļap now."

The tattler now. He sang, *"Kidid, kidid ukokōj ņa.* | *Ukokōj raan eo. Ukokōj raan eo.* | *Raan eo, raan jeeded eo, raan ņweeded eo.* | *Raan eo epādtok ilikin ņa in ia in ke?* | *Ilikin Mile O-O. (Ijuweo)."*

(This song is also partly in the ancient language.)

In the language of today, the meaning of the song is: Tattler, tattler turn over (discover) the rock pile to find the light. | Turn over the dawn, turn over the dawn. | The dawn, it is dawn already *(jeeded eo).* | The dawn is the color of sunrise. | The day is here on the ocean side. | On the ocean side of where . . . ? | On the ocean side of Mile O-O. (Over there)."

(Now thus they went around to all the Marshalls from the song of the Tattler and the Triton.)

Now the *Morning Star* (the ship of the

---

1. The informant changed his initial description of the story from that of *parable* to *prophecy.* (He used the English word *prophecy.*) The story obviously contains elements of both. The English loanword *būrabōļ* is also translated as *waan joñok* 'example' (lit. 'frame for measuring'), which, of course, is what a parable is essentially. Certain individuals, both male and female, were and still are considered to be able to foretell the future through dreams. They are known as *ri-kanaan* (prophets). Spirit possession was and still is sometimes involved.

2. The *ņa* are places on the fringing reef and shore of an island where high tides have deposited rocks. Piles of these rocks are used as fishing platforms.

missionaries) came. It came to the place where the tattler and the triton were. And the *Morning Star* went around and revealed the light (gospel) like the tattler and the triton went around.

The Epoon people knew the story before the *Morning Star* came. So it is regarded as a prophecy, not a parable. Like Isaiah said that Christ will come.[3]

The meaning of this story: The triton is shiny (like the gospel). And cannot move around. So the tattler carried it around the Marshalls, as the *Morning Star* carried the gospel.

The Epoon people were surprised, and accepted the gospel because of the story.[4]

I learned this story on Epoon from the old people.

[The Protestant missionaries came to Epoon in 1857, and established their mission on Rupe *wāto* (land parcel). And the church is there to this day.]

34: KIDID (PEDO) IM JILEL: BŪRABŌĻ IN AN ITOK MIJINEDE ÑAN EPOON

Ri-bwebwenato: Jobel Emos, Kuwajleen 1975

Bwebwenato in ekadu ak eṃṃan meļeļe. Āinwōt *prophecy.* Kiiō jinoin:

Jilel eo ej pād iuṃwin juon bar. (Etan bar eo Bōrļap.) Bar eo ej pād ioon bok ak ñe ibwijtok itok dān.

Etan wāto eo ej pād ilikin ej Rupe (jikin an mijinede). Ilo iien eo ejjeļọk mijinede.

Kiiō jilel eo ej pedo. Ejjab waļọk meram eo an jilel eo. Innām kiiō epāāt ejjeļọk dān. Kiiō ej kātok kidid eo, bao eo. Kiiō jilel ej kajjitōk, "Komaroñ [ke] itok im bōke eō. Bwe kōjro kāļọk im rawūn i Ṃajeļ in?"

Innām kidid eo eba eṃṃan. Innām kidid eo ej kiji im erro kāļọk. Kiiō rej al. Jilel ej al ṃokta. Kiiō al ej ba, "Jilel e tit kaaļọ tillo Elel buke iōñ. | Elel buke rōk. | Elel wōt iju-raan en pād eañ ilik. | Jep jep in ṇa en ilik bar eṇ. | Jui-jui-jui. | Raan-raan-raan-raan eo. | Epād tok, ilikin ia, in ia in ke-ke-e-e? | Ilikin Roñļap O-O-emeram Roñļap-kiiō." (Ṃōttan kajin etto al in.)

Ilo kajin raan kein meļeļe in al eo ej: "Jilel ej kwaļọk meram kiiō. | Ej itok tu iōñ. | Ej itok tu rōk. | Ej itok ñan iju-raan. | Im bar itok ñan lọmeto tu iañ. | Ejoujik dekā eṇ ioon pedped ilik. | Kōre-kōre-kōre raantak (raan)-Raantak, raantak, raantak eo. | Ej itok. Ioon lik in ta? | Ta āne? | Ioon lik in Roñļap. | (Etak-aļ ioon Roñļap kiiō.)"

Kidid eo kiiō. Ej al, "Kidid, kidid ukokōj ṇa. | Ukokōj raan. | Ukokōj raan eo. | Raan eo raan jeeded eo, raan ṃweeded eo.

---

3. The informant was referring to the Hebrew prophet Isaiah and the book of Isaiah. Note the explanation of a historic event foretold by a prophecy in the Epoon story.

4. Thus a folktale (parable/prophecy) may have facilitated the introduction and acceptance of a new religion and its bearers. Birds figure prominently in a number of Marshallese folktales and are usually anthropomorphic (human characteristics, such as speech in this story, are ascribed to them), and they are invariably helpful to humans. These creatures were, in real life, important in the island economies as sources of food, indicators of schools of fish for fishermen, and as navigational aids.

Mr. Emos sketched a map of Epoon Atoll, including Rupe *wāto,* in my notebook and showed me where the events in the story had occurred.

| Raan eo epād tok ilikin ŋa in ia in ke? | Ilikin Mile O-O."

(Epād ṃōttan kajin etto al in.)

Ilo kajin raan kein meļeļe in al eo ej, "Kidid, kidid ukōttok ŋa eo in kappok meram eo. | Ukōttok raantak eo. | Ukōttok raantak eo. | Raantak eo, e raantak kiiō wōt (jedeed eo). | Raantak eo ej uno in raantak. | Raan eo epād ijin ilikin./ Ilikin ia? | Ioon ilikin Mile O-O (ijuweo)."

(Kiiō āindein [aerro] rawūn in aolep aelōñ in Ṃajeļ jān al an kidid im jilel.)

Kiiō tokālik ej itok *Morning Star* (wa eo waan mijinede ro).[5] Ej itok ilo jikin eo kidid eo im jilel eo rej pād ie. Im *Morning Star* ej rawūn ilo Ṃajeļ im kwaļọk meram (*gospel*). Āinwōt jilel im kidid rej rawūn.

Armej in Epoon raar kar jeļā bwebwenato in ṃokta [jān an] *Morning Star* kar itok. Āindein rej ļōmņak ke āinwōt kanaan. Ejjab būrabōļ. Āinwōt Isaiah ej ba Christ naaj itok.

Meļeļe in bwebwenato eo: Jilel eo ebōlōl (āinwōt *gospel*). Im ejjab maroñ ṃakūtkūt āindein kidid eaar bōkļọke im rawūn ilo Ṃajeļ. Āinwōt *Morning Star* eaar bōkļọk *gospel* eo.

Ri-Epoon raar bwilōñ im raar bōk *gospel* kōnke bwebwenato eo.

Iaar katak bwebwenato in i Epoon jān rūtto ro.

5. Mijinede ro raar itok ñan Epoon ilo 1857.

35: THE STORY OF LIJEBAKE

As told by Titōj, Mājro 1956

A young girl named Nemejowe lived on M̧akin Atoll in the Gilbert Islands with her mother and father. One day her mother and father went away from the house. Before they left, the mother put out her mats to sun and air. She told the girl to be sure and watch them so that they would not be ruined by rain.

After the parents left, Nemejowe became drowsy and fell asleep. While she slept, the different kinds of rain came and had a meeting. They said, "Let us go and rain on the mats there while the girl is sleeping." They asked each other, "Who will go and rain on the mats while the girl is sleeping?"

They said, "You, Wōtdikdik there (small, light shower). He said, "Not I. For I will lightly shower and awaken the girl there."

They said to another one, "You go, Uttajō (rain that falls in slow drops)." He said, "Not I. For I will rain slowly and awaken the young girl there."

They said to another one, "You go, Mijeljel (large and intense rain)." He said, "Not I. For I will rain heavily and intensely and awaken the young girl there."

They said, "You go, Wutwo (cloudburst type of rain, sudden and heavy)."

He said, "Well, I will." And he rained and ruined the mats.

Nemejowe's parents returned and the mother became very angry with her daughter, because the mats were ruined. She uttered a curse *(kanijnij).*

"Pikpikūr kapin uliej in jem̧am̧." ("Pat the back of the head of your father.")[1]

"Ta eo iaar ba ñan eok!" ("What did I say to you!")

This was an extremely harsh and cruel thing to say. And the daughter cried. She went out on a sandspit and cried.

Lijebake appeared in the shape of a sea turtle [*Erethmachelys imbricata,* Hawksbill turtle, *jebake*].

A demon had entered the turtle, as demons entered the Gandarene swine in the Bible story. It enters and goes like a human being. It may enter people *(kakkonono armej),* and birds, rocks, and so forth. It is a turtle today.

She spoke to her granddaughter and asked her what the trouble was. After Nemejowe told her, Nemejowe became a seabird [*Thalasseus bergli,* crested tern, *keār*],[2] and flew away, flying above her grandmother Lijebake, who was swimming.

They traveled like this until they reached Mile, and Lijebake asked Nemejowe, "Nemejowe, where are you going to live?"

Nemejowe replied in a chant *(roro)*:

"*Ejjab ijo in* (not in this place),

Bwe epaake aelōñ eo (because it's close to the atoll [M̧akin]).

Kwon tulo̧k jān mañinpit eiō (you dive from this pandanus leaf here)

ej petok (which is drifting this way),

Bwe kwōnaaj loe (for you will see it)."

The pair continued their journey northward, arriving at Arņo, Aur, Aelok, and Utrōk.

---

1. A most taboo act in Marshallese culture.

2. Or *Sterna sumatrana* 'black-naped tern'. *Keār* is the generic term. It is used in this story and in story 30, "The *Ikid* of Ļainjin" (page 131), and in other stories. The specific terms *keār ļap* 'big *keār*' for *Thalasseus bergii* and *keār dik* 'little *keār*' for *S. sumatrana* were not used.

At each atoll the same conversation was held. They finally arrived at Pikaar, where they stopped. This is the reason for the large number of turtles at Pikaar.

The grandmother, the turtle Lijebake, and granddaughter, the seabird Nemejowe, can be seen between the atolls of Pikaar and Mājeej to this day.

The brother of Nemejowe became very heartsick when she left M̧akin. So he came to look for her in the shape of another seabird, the *ak* [*Fregata minor*, frigate bird].

He finally arrived at Pikaar and saw her there. He could not stay there with her because of the taboo relationship between brother and sister. So he went north to Bok-ak Atoll.

This atoll was round when he saw it. But when he decided to stay there he changed it so that it was shaped like an *ak* with wide-spread wings. He can be seen above Bok-ak today. He is a very large *ak* and flies so high above the atoll that he almost cannot be seen.

The end of the story.

Comments

Lijebake also figures in Marshallese legend, according to Krämer and Nevermann (1938:253-255), as the mother of Etao, the trickster of many incidents in Marshallese folktales.

The versions of the legend of Lijebake collected by Krämer and Nevermann, Erdland (1914:193), Buckingham (1949:8–9), and by me all differ in some of the details, including the itinerary of the bird and the turtle. However, Pikaar is the destination of the travelers, and the home of Lijebake in all of the versions of the legend.

This is, of course, another example of variation in a folktale in a culture.

The motif of a transformation of humans into birds is found in a number of Marshallese folktales. In this case, it is the transformation of a young girl into a tern.

Another chant of Lijebake was given to me by Ļakōm̧, an elderly *aļap* on Mājro in 1956. We were discussing the traditional Marshallese system of navigation at the time.

"Kwōj wālok ia ļọk jibū?

Likin ia in ia? Likin ia in ia?

Likin Mile jujin.

Jab bwe ilok reitem lale maañ-in-pit kom pej ko bwiin lio rā petōm eọtōk.

Jabwil erer wawōj, wawōj wōt!"

(Where are you going grandmother?

Sea side of what place is this? The sea side of what place is this?

The sea side of Mile. Stay here.

Not this place. Because I look this way and see these pandanus leaves and old keys of pandanus of the women from the Gilberts.

Drift and drift on shore.

Roll on and go on and just go on!)

Marshallese Turtle Lore

Turtles are part of the food supplied by the bountiful marine environment. They were highly prized by the Marshallese. An ancient chant refers to "the food-bearing turtle." Their habits were observed and taken advantage of in order to gather their eggs and to capture the turtles themselves, on land and in the water. Special techniques were developed to do this.

Older Marshallese have told me that they consider these creatures to be quite intelligent.

The story of Lijebake, the anthropomorphic turtle mother who spoke to and helped Nemejowe and who traveled from M̧akin in the Gilbert Islands through the Marshall Islands to Pikaar Atoll in the north of the archipelago, reflects the importance of these animals in traditional Marshallese culture.

There are large numbers of turtles and sea birds at Pikaar and Bok-ak atolls, which are uninhabited by man.[3] They were an important resource for the people of northern Ratak.

Elaborate rituals were associated with the first food-gathering expeditions of the year, which occurred in summertime, and were led by the chief *(irooj)*. Homage was paid to the spirits *(ekjab)* of each atoll: Ļāwūn Pikaar and Jo̧-Bok-ak. See Tobin (1958:47–56) for details. Permission of the chief had to be obtained to visit the atolls and exploit their resources.

The rituals associated with the visits to Pikaar and Bok-ak and other bird islands *(ānen bao)* ceased sometime after the Marshallese accepted Christanity.

One of the most knowledgeable Marshallese in the lore of turtles and customs *(m̧anit)* associated with them was Raymond DeBrum of Likiep Atoll and Jāmo̧ Island.

He gave me the following information on Mājro in 1956: "There was a special way of distributing the turtle flesh according to our custom. The turtles would come ashore on a land parcel *(wāto)* on the island. The lineage head *(aļap)* would take the turtle and cook it in the earth oven *(um̧)*. He would take the shell, the four flippers, and some of the intestines *(m̧ōjñal)* that had been previously cleaned and washed. All of the rest of the meat was put in a basket and taken to the chief *(irooj)*.

"The most important part of the turtle was the frontal portion *(aerā)*. If that was not brought to the chief as well as the rest of the

3. Although there is not enough water to support a permanent population on Pikaar, a small supply is reportedly available if one knows how to locate it. As M̧ak Juda told me on Mājro in 1970, when discussing his visits to Pikaar and Bok-ak during the early Japanese period: "I went up on Irooj Ļaelañ's sailboat for a survey trip. We stopped at Aur and discussed the trip with Jajua, Irooj Eļap. Then we went over to M̧aļoeļap. . . . At Pikaar a small boat went ashore with the party. . . . We found a source of freshwater coming out on the reef near the island. It welled up through a small channel (*iaļ in m̧aj* 'road of the eel'), so-called because it was so crooked and winding. This water was available no matter how high the tide was. It was perfectly fresh, not salty or brackish. The party of eight Marshallese used this source of water for over a week and a half. There was no other source of water on the atoll. . . . There is no source of water on Bok-ak as on Pikaar. . . . Later I accompanied Irooj Jeim̧ata on a Japanese ship on a survey trip to Pikaar. Jeim̧ata showed me the underground source of freshwater. It must be dug for. It is on the edge of the beach on the southwest end of the island. This is a *kōkļaļ* (navigation sign) known only to the *ri-meto* (navigators)."

In discussing Pikaar and Bok-ak and the other "bird islands" *(ānen bao)* on Mājro in 1952, Raymond DeBrum explained: "On visiting Pikaar to hunt for turtles and birds, which are many on the island, the preparation to worship is the same method as they did on Jāmo̧. At the middle of the island near a *kōņo* tree [*Cordia subcordata*], Ļāwūn Pikaar, is a well of fresh water covered with a white stone. And to uncover this well water, one must know the secret way the *irooj* or their navigators know. First, from the trunk of the tree, face the sun and start to count your footsteps sideward from the sun about in the direction of southeast about six feet, and then face the sun and take some six feet toward the sun. And then dig the hole. Two or more feet deep, the white stone will be seen, and clean water underneath. This well was last seen by Laeberber before the typhoon of 1890. Ļāwūn Pikaar, or the *kōņo* tree, was washed away by the typhoon. And now no one can tell the point from which to start for water."

parts reserved for him, he might become angry and throw the people off the land.

"The layer inside the belly *(kọọj),* the head *(bar)* also, the portion of the body fat *(tañinṃur)* near the hips, and very hard portion of the very thin fat inside the shell *(wiwi);* it is rolled out and cooked. The small intestine *(kauwe)* is softer and better to eat. The heart was given to the chief, but not the liver or lungs. The eggs inside the turtle *(kọọj lep niddik)* and the bottom *(ḷokwan)* also go to the commoners *(kajoor).*

"If a person saw a turtle come ashore, he had to report it to the *aḷap.* (It is true today also.)

"After the turtle is cooked, the hip *(ṃur)* is given to the person who reported the landing of the turtle as a reward. This is the custom, no matter what the age, rank, or sex of the person reporting the landing. People have been thrown off their land for not obeying the custom of giving to the chief.

"When the turtle was brought to the chief, he called all his *aḷap*[s] and selected one of them to be his Distributor of Food [steward] *(ri-kōṃōñā).* This was done in turn.

"Each *aḷap* got his share of the turtle—no matter how small the pieces it had to be divided into. The meat is highly prized because of the strong smell.

"The saying is *'Wōn ajjuwōnwōn'* (strong smell of the turtle). And this makes even a small portion sufficient.

"These customs are followed on some atolls, for instance, on Aelok, Utrōk, and a few other places. On Mājro and Arṇo today, this distribution is not done. It began changing in Japanese times and accelerated in American times. If people wish to give, they will."

36: STORY ABOUT A KAKWŌJ

As told by Reverend Ernej,[1] Wūjlañ 1955

This story is about this *kakwōj.* It was on Wūjlañ [Atoll] on a coral head on the lagoon side of Kilǫkwōn Island.

A *kakwōj* is a kind of living thing in the sea. And its shape is like that of a human being's. Legs, head, arms: all of its body is like that of a human being's. However, its skin is like that of a fish. It has a bad, bad odor, the odor of the exposed reef.

It can live in the sea and on an island. We say that this thing is almost like a *ņooniep.*[2] People do not know if it can really speak, but in this story the two men who saw the *kakwōj* said that it spoke.

At the time of long, long ago, two men sailed to gather *mejānwōd* [*Tridacna maxima* (Roding), fluted clam] on the lagoon side of Kilǫkwōn. And one of the men spoke jokingly about this *kakwōj.* They both knew there was a coral head of *kakwōj;* however, they had not yet seen it. Because this thing only appeared at times when people just said its name.[3]

These days we say the name Kakwōj on Kilǫkwōn, but in the olden days it was absolutely forbidden.[4]

When these men finished gathering *mejānwōd,* they got ready to return. Then this Kakwōj called out and told them to wait. These men waited and the thing came to the man who joked about its name.

This *kakwōj* caused the man to fall out of the canoe [pulled him out], and they fought down into the sea. The man suffocated to death.

The other man hurried to flee to the island, to Kilǫkwōn, and told all of the people that they should go and look for the other man, for the *kakwōj* had fought with them [the two men].

The people took ripe coconuts with them to *kōjeļae,* to smooth the surface of the sea to search now on the sea, so that they could see clearly into the water.[5] When they found the place where they [the two] had fought, they saw the man was rolled up below on that female [the *kakwōj*]. They were sorry about it and wanted to dive down, but no one could dive down, because they were afraid of the *kakwōj.*

After this time, the *kakwōj* has not appeared again to present days.

This story has been passed down to this day.

---

1. Reverend *(rōplen)* Ernej (Anej) was a descendant of the *irooj ro* (chiefs) of the original Wūjlañ Atoll people, and of Ānewetak Atoll ancestors as well. He was probably the best informed person in the community concerning the history and customs of Wūjlañ, and was very well informed about the history and customs of Ānewetak Atoll, too. Although he was an ordained Christian minister, he never denigrated or criticized the traditional beliefs or practices in his discussions with me.

2. The *ņooniep* are described by the Marshallese as supernatural humanoid creatures similar to the *rimmenanuwe* (the little people) in their actions, if not in appearance. They are usually benevolent, and figure in a number of Marshallese folktales.

3. This is an example of the widespread belief in the power of a name—in this case, the appearance of a harmful entity.

4. Note the prohibition/restrictions against using (uttering) a name in certain circumstances—a specific location in this case. This is a widespread belief/practice (see Webster 1942:301–310).

Comments

Long-isolated Wūjlañ Atoll is relatively small, with a lagoon area of 25.47 square miles, and a dry-land area of only 0.67 square miles (Bryan 1946:2).

It is the place to which the displaced Ānewetak Atoll people were moved in 1947, after their atoll was taken by the United States government for use as an atomic weapons testing site (after having taken Pikinni Atoll for the same purpose).

They were able to move back recently (while continuing to maintain Wūjlañ), after Ānewetak had been rehabilitated as much as deemed possible, in terms of the land, by the American authorities. (Some parts of the large atoll had been completely destroyed, and others were devastated and contaminated). New homes and community buildings were constructed by the Americans, and coconut, breadfruit, and pandanus trees were planted. The agricultural program continues.

Unfortunately, Reverend Ernej and other older people did not live to see the return for which they had yearned for so long.

It should be noted that the *kakwōj* have been described by Marshallese outside of Ānewetak and Wūjlañ as "legendary cruel sea men with long fingernails" (Abo et al. 1976:129).

One wonders if this Wūjlañ *kakwōj* tale is based upon an incident involving a strange, fearsome, and dangerous marine animal that appeared in the Wūjlañ lagoon in the far distant past. Such an incident would have undoubtedly reinforced the belief in *kakwōj* by the Wūjlañ people. Or it could have been the genesis of the belief. Details could have been added or changed or forgotten as the *kakwōj* story was told over many years (as happens in the narration of tales).

This is speculation on my part, of course, but it is not outside the realm of possibility. One such arrival occurred on Pohnpei Island, 224 nautical miles to the southwest of Wūjlañ Atoll, several years ago. A large saltwater crocodile, probably from the Solomon Islands or New Guinea, was discovered in the mangrove swamps of the island. These aggressive and dangerous amphibians are capable of traveling long distances from their natural habitat. "Exceptionally venturesome individuals have showed up on the Cocos-Keeling Islands, which are separated by more than 600 miles of empty ocean from the south coast of Sumatra, and on Rotuma Island, which is about the same distance from the Solomons, although the latter individual could have come by way of Fiji, which could have involved a mere 260-mile swim" (Minton 1973:19). Belew (Palau), far to the west of the Marshalls, is the only marine crocodile habitat in Micronesia.

---

5. *Kōjeļae* was explained in more detail to me by Ļaijea on Jālooj Atoll in 1957, as follows: "*Kōjeļae* means to throw grated coconut on the surface of the sea. The oil in the grated coconut smoothes out the surface. And you can see where to dive better when you dive for *mejānwōd.* It is done mainly for *kamejānwōd* [gathering/collecting *mejānwōd*]." This technique was also practiced by Hawaiian and other Polynesian fishermen. See Beckwith (1970:431) for mention of this useful technique for fishing in Hawaiian folktales, using *kukui* nut oil, and in folktales of New Zealand and the Marquesas (433): "A few similar incidents [to those in Hawaiian folktales] are found in other groups based on common customs or common tradition. The use of oil to clear waters is noted in New Zealand. Compare also the incident in Marquesan stories of emptying a gourdful of oil into the sea in order to look into the sea bottom, or into Hawai'i."

36: BWEBWENATO IN JUON KAKWŌJ

Ri-bwebwenato: Rev. Ernej, Wūjlañ 1955

Bwebwenato in kakwōj in ej pād ilo Wūjlañ ilo juon wōd iarin āne eo Kiļǫkaŋ.

Kakwōj ej juon kain menninmour in lǫjet im jekjekin āinwōt bar armej. Neen, bōran, pein, aolepān ānbwinnin āinwōt armej. Ijokwe kilen āinwōt ek. Bwiin eļap an ibbwilwōdwōd.

Emaroñ in mour ilo lǫjet kab ilo āne. Jen ba men in enañin barāinwōt ŋooniep. Armej rejjab jeļā eļañne emaroñ lukkuun kōnono ak ilo bwebwenato in ļōmaro ruo raar lo kakwōj eo, rej ba eaar kōnono.

Ilo iien ko etto im etto ruo emmaan raar jerak in kōmejānwōd iar in Kiļǫkaŋ. Im ļeo juon ej kōnono kōjak kake kakwōj in. Erro jeļā jiṃor ke ewōr wōd in kakwōj bōtab erro ejjañin loe. Bwe menin ej waļǫk ilo iien wōt armej [rej] ba etan bajjek.

Ilo raan kein jej ba etan kakwōj ilo Kiļǫkaŋ ak ilo etto emo ñan jidik.

Ke eṃōj an ļōṃaro kōmejānwōd rejro pojak in rǫǫl. Ļak lale kakwōj in laṃōj im ba erro en kōttar. Ļōṃarein rejro kōttar im men eo ej itok im erro ļeo eaar kōjjak kōn etan ire.

Kakwōj in enaaj kǫwōtļǫk ļeo jān wa eo. Im erro ej ire lāļļǫk ilo lǫjet. Ļeo ej jabjab menwan im mej.

Ļeo juon enaaj ṃōkaj in ko āneļǫk ñan Kiļǫkaŋ im jiroñ ļǫk armej ro wōj ke ren ilān pukot ļeo juon bwe erro kakwōj eo kar ire.

Armej ro rej ebbweik waini ippāer kein aer kōjeļae im pukot ļeo. Ke rej kōjeļaeik [ijo er]ro ar ire ie rej lo ej eddāpilpil ilaļ ioon lieŋ. Raar būroṃōj kake im kōŋaan tuuri ak ejjeļǫk juon emaroñ tuuri bwe remijak kakwōj eo.

Ālikin iien in kakwōj eo ejjañin bar waļǫk tok ñan raan kein.

Bwebwenato in raar bwebwenato liktak ñan rainin.

37: ĻŌPPEIPĀĀT (LOW TIDE)

As told by Jobel Emos, Kuwajleen 1975

Now a woman went to the lagoon and saw that the reef was exposed (very low tide), and she said, "O-O-O. It is low tide!"

Now the octopus (its name was Leppeipāāt) answered and said, "What low tide? For it is I." Now the octopus again spoke, "Why don't you cook me in the earth oven and eat me?"[1]

Now the woman asked, "What kind of firewood should I use?" The octopus said, *"Marjej"* [*Wedelia biflora,* a small plant] (very small leaves). The woman again asked, "What kind of rocks should I use?" The octopus answered, *"Tilaan"* [pumice]. Now the woman again asked, "What kind of leaves should I use?" The octopus said, *"Atat"* [*Triumfetta procumbens* Forst., a plant].

Now the woman covered the earth oven. When she was finished, the woman returned to her house and waited until it was finished [ready]. Then she returned and opened up the earth oven.

She opened up the earth oven and there was no octopus. The octopus was gone. There was nothing in the earth oven.

This trickery happened three times. And the woman was deceived three times by the octopus.[2] And now the woman realized that the octopus had lied and she changed her mind and no longer believed the octopus.

Now she again went to the lagoon at nine o'clock. She went to the lagoon and it was again low tide. The reef was exposed. And she again called the octopus, "O-O-O. It is low tide!"

Now it again said, "What low tide? For it is I."

Now it said, "Why don't you cook me in the earth oven and eat me?"

Now the woman said, "What kind of firewood should I use?"

Now the octopus again said, *"Marjej."* Now the woman began to make an earth oven. Now she did not use *marjej* as the octopus said. (She said to herself, "It is lying.") And she used *kōn̄e* [*Pemphis acidula,* ironwood tree].

(The woman was deceiving the octopus, but the octopus thought the woman was obeying its word.)

Now the woman again asked, "What kind of rocks should I use?"

The octopus said, *"Tilaan."*

Now the woman said (to herself), "It is lying," and she put large boulders in the earth oven.

Now she again asked, "What kind of leaves should I use?"

---

1. Note the attribution of human characteristics (anthropomorphism) to the octopus. This also occurs in the "Story about Living Things (Animals) in the Marshall Islands" (story 33, page 151), where an octopus is benevolent in its behavior (it helps a rat and is defecated upon in return for its efforts). Animals communicate and interact with one another and with humans in other Marshallese stories as well. This is an ancient and widespread motif in folktales.

2. Here again we see the use of the ritual, formulaic number three, and the motif of attempted deception of the human by the animal.

Now the octopus said, *"Atat."* Now the woman said (to herself), "It is lying, but I will use *kiden*" [*Messerschmidia argentia,* a tree].[3]

Now she placed *(take)* the octopus inside the earth oven (in cooking language: *take* is like *likūti* 'put or place something') and covered it up.

Now the octopus cried out, and said, "Take me out! Take me out!" (In the ancient language *juk eō* is the same as *jukok* in the language of today. Earth oven language is 'Take me out! Take me out!'), "I will be cooked! I will be cooked!" (In the ancient language, *inamat* is the same as *inaaj mat* in the language of today: 'I will be cooked'.)

Now the woman said, "It is lying! It is lying! Cover it up! Cover it up!"

Now she went to the earth oven to wait until it was finished [ready].

She went to take it out, and the octopus was cooked. Dead and cooked.[4]

Now she went to make grated coconut for the side dish to eat it with the octopus. She was just eating, and she heard a song. The mother of the octopus, the giant octopus said—the giant octopus appeared from the ocean and came over: "There she is coming | There she is coming from the northwest | To the cooking place | Under the *kiden* on the oceanside | *Kiden* what? What *kiden*?" (and it sang the song three times).[5]

Now the woman heard it and did not understand very well what it was saying in the song. And when the giant octopus neared the woman's house, the woman understood the words in the giant octopus's song.

Now the woman knew what she had to do. She stood by with a knife (a big knife of the people of long ago; they made them from clam shells).

Now the woman continued singing and said, "Give me the tentacle (ancient language), the tentacle | So that I can cut it | So that I can cut it | So that I can throw it away."

And she repeated the song six times (the chant).

Now the woman cut off a tentacle each time she sang the song, and the giant octopus died.[6]

The legend is ended.

(I have seen the earth oven of the octopus on the main island of Ujae. It is on the southernmost end of Ujae. It is on the ocean side of the island.

If the earth oven is destroyed, it will appear again. The earth oven cannot be destroyed permanently.)[7]

---

3. The Marshallese audience of the *ri-bwebwenato* (storyteller) would know that the woman was being lied to by the octopus, and that the materials it told the woman to use to prepare the earth oven *(uṃ)* to cook it would not do the job, but that those she did use would. This enhances audience involvement, of course, and adds an element of humor to the story and to its entertainment value.

4. The motif of the intended victim turning the tables on the one who tried to deceive her (or him) is seen here, and in other Marshallese folktales. It is a widespread motif.

5. The motif of mother love and attempted revenge for the killing of an offspring is seen in the appearance of the angry giant octopus and its threat to the woman's life.

6. The triumph of good over evil, human over monster, is seen in this tale, and is a motif that runs through Marshallese folklore and that of many cultures.

7. A feature of the local landscape (earth oven of the octopus) is explained by the folktale. This helps to keep the tale alive, of course.

Comments

The informant introduced the story by explaining that an *inọñ* is not a true story but that a *bwebwenato* is. (This is an *inọñ,* he said, not a true story. The story about Inedel is true. It is a *bwebwenato,* he concluded.)

He laughed when he told of the woman putting large boulders into the earth oven to deceive and kill the octopus. Indeed, so did I. Such were his skills as a raconteur.

Mr. Emos voluntarily sketched a map of Ujae Island for me, with the location of the earth oven and the village.

For the next few days after telling me the story, whenever the ebullient and jocular Mr. Emos met me on the island, he would call out to me: *"Kaneūṃ kaneūṃ ta?"* (What kind of firewood should I use?) And I would reply: *"Marjej."* Then he would ask, *"Dekeūṃ dekeūṃ ta?"* (What kind of rocks should I use?) My reply would be, *"Tilaan."* And he would ask, *"Bwilkōṃ bwilkōṃ ta?"* (What kind of leaves should I use?) And I would reply, *"Atat."*

It became a running and inside joke between us.

37: ĻŌPPEIPĀĀT

Ri-bwebwenato: Jobel Emos, Kuwajleen 1975

Kiiō juon kōrā ej wōnarļọk im ej lale epāāt ṃōņakņak innām ej ļaṃōj im ba, "Je ļōppeipāāt" (o-o-epāāt).

Kiiō kweet in (etan Ļōppeipāāt) ej uwaak im ba, "En ta pāāt eo ke ña e ije." Kiiō kweet eo ej bar ba, "Kwōjjab item uṃwin eō, me kañe eō?"

Kiiō kōrā eo ej kajjitōk, "Kaneūṃ kaneūṃ ta?" Kiiō kweet eo ej ba, "Marjej." Kōrā eo ej bar kajjitōk, "Dekeūṃ dekeūṃ ta?" Kweet eo ej uwaak, "Tilaan." Kiiō kōrā eo ebar kajjitōk, "Bwilkōṃ bwilkōṃ ta?" Kweet eo ej ba, "Atat." (Kanooj edik bōlōk.)

Kiiō kōrā eo ej kobale uṃ eo. Kiiō ej ṃōj kōrā ar bar rọọl ñan ṃweo iṃōn im kōttar an mat. Kiiō erọọl im jukok.

Eļak jukok uṃ eo ejjeļọk kweet. Ejako kweet. Uṃ eo ejjeļọk kobban.

Ar kōṃṃane jilu alen an riab, an ṃoņe kōrā eo. Im kiiō kōrā eo eṃōj an lo an kweet eo riab innām kiiō enaaj ukot an ļōmņak jān kweet eo kiiō. Kiiō ej bar etal, wōnarļọk ruatimjuon awa. Innām eļak wōnarļọk im bar pāāt ṃōņakņak. Innām ej bar kūri kweet eo, "Je ļōppeipāāt!" Kiiō ebar ba, "Enta pāāt eo bwe ña e?"

Kiiō ej ba, "Kwojjab iuṃwin eō me kañ eō?"

Kiiō Kōrā eo ej ba, "Kaneūṃ kaneūṃ ta?"

Kiiō kweet eo ej bar ba, "Marjej." Kiiō kōrā eo ej jino kōṃṃan uṃ. Kiiō ejjab kōṃṃan marjej āinwōt an kweet eo ba. (Lio ej ba ñane make, "Ej riab.") Ak ekōṃṃane kane kōñe. (Lio ej ṃoņe kweet eo ak kweet eo ej ļōmņak lio ej pokake naan ko an.)

Kiiō kōrā eo ej bar kajjitōk, "Dekeūṃ dekeūṃ ta?"

Kweet eo ej ba, "Tilaan."

Kiiō kōrā eo ej ba (ñane make), "Eriab." Im elikūt dekālọļ ilo uṃ eo.

Kiiō lio ej bar kajjitōk, "Bwilkōṃ bwilkōṃ ta?" Kiiō kweet eo ej ba, "Atat." Kiiō kōrā ej ba (ñane make), "Eriab, ak inaaj illik kōṃṃan kiden." Kiiō ej taake kweet eo (likūti) ilowaan uṃ (kajin kōmat: taake ej āinwōt likūti) innām kobale.

Kiiō kweet ej ļaṃōj im ba, "Juk eō! Juk eō!" (Kajin etto ej āinwōt jukok ilo kajin rainin. Kajin uṃ ej, *"Take me out! Take me out!")* "Inamat! Inamat!" (Kajin etto ej āinwōt "inaaj mat" ilo kajin raankein.)

Kiiō kōrā eo ej ba, "Ej riab! Ej riab! Kobale! Kobale!"

Kiiō eļak etal ñan uṃ eo ṃōj an kōttar an mat. Eļak jukok, emat kweet eo. Emej im emat.

Kiiō ej ilān jiraal. Ej ja ṃōñā wōt ak eroñjake juon al. Jinen kweet, kouj eo ej ba (kouj ej waļọk jān lọjet im itok). "Uweo takale | uweo takajen kapilōñ iōñ ijo | Re uṃwine ek eo ie. | Atiti ek eo ie. | Ioṃwin kiden eņ ilik. | Kiden ta? | Ta kiden?" (Im ej bar al jilu alen.)

Kiiō kōrā eo ej roñjake im ejjab kanooj meļeļe ta eo ej kōnono kake ilo al eo. Innām ke kouj eo ej epaaktok ñan ṃweo iṃwōn kōrā eo emeļeļe kōn naan ko ilo al eo an kouj eo.

Kiiō kōrā eo ejeļā aolep ta eo an kōṃṃane. Kiiō ej *stand by* kōn juon jāje (juon bakbōk kileplep an rūtto ro—rej kōṃṃane jān di).

Kiiō kōrā eo ej al tok wōt im ba, "Letok joko eo (kajin etto) joko eo | Bwe in jeke | Bwe in jeke | Bwe in joļọk."

Innām ej bar al jiljino alen (roro eo in).

Kiiō kōrā ej jeke joko kajjo alen ilowaan al im emej kouj eo.

Ejeṃļọk inọñ eo.

Iaar loe uṃ in kweet [eo] ioon eonene in Ujae. Epād jabōn tata turōk in Ujae.

Ñe uṃ eo ej jorrāān, enaaj bar waļọk. Eban jorrāān uṃ eo.

38: TWO WOMEN

As told by Jelibōr Jam, Kuwajleen 1975

There were two women from Ujae. I do not know the names of the women. The two were sleeping and they awoke and the tide was very low. And one of the women went and processed pandanus leaves.[1]

The other woman cried out and said, "O-O-O. The very low tide!"

The octopus said, "Never mind the low tide, for it is I. Why don't you come and cook in the earth oven and eat me?"[2]

Now the woman went to the ocean and seized the octopus and brought it to the island from the ocean and came and dug an earth oven. And said to the octopus, "What kind of firewood should I use?" The octopus said, *"Marjej"* [*Wedelia biflora*, a small leafy plant].

The woman asked, "What kind of rock should I use?" The octopus replied, *"Tilaan"* [pumice].[3]

The woman asked, "What kind of leaves should I use?" The octopus answered, *"Atat"* [*Triumfetta procumbens* Forst., a small leafy plant].

Now the woman made the fire, and used *marjej* for firewood, and used *tilaan* for the rocks. And when the earth oven was finished [prepared for cooking], she raked the [heated] rocks in the oven to the side and put the octopus inside the oven, and covered it with *atat* leaves, and covered it over (with sand and earth). When she had finished covering it over (with sand and earth), she went to the house, and said to the [first] woman, "Bring our food, the coconut meat and grate it; for the earth oven in which the octopus is cooking is almost finished" [cooking the octopus].

When it was a little later, the woman said, "Well, ma'am, that octopus is cooked now. I will just go and uncover the earth oven." And she went, and the earth oven was uncovered. The octopus was gone.

Now the woman was surprised, and said to herself, "Why is the octopus gone? Why, I do not understand it." Now she called the [first] woman, "Where are you, ma'am?" The [first] woman said, "Here I am."

The woman again spoke, "Bring that coconut meat, our food, so that we can just eat from inside the earth oven. But the octopus is gone!"

And the [first] woman brought the coco-

---

1. The leaves of the *Pandanus tectorius* (screw pine, or *maañ in bōb*) were very important materials in the plaiting of mats for wearing apparel and household use, and for the manufacture of sails for the sailing canoes, vital to the Marshallese survival. The material was laboriously processed: outer spines were removed, and the leaves softened by pounding and rolled up for later use by the women. This is still done.

2. See footnote 1 on page 167.

3. *Tilaan:* igneous rock, or pumice, which washes ashore in the Marshalls occasionally. Perhaps it originates in Hawai'i, where volcanoes are still active. (Indeed some Marshallese have told me that they believe *tilaan* does come from there.) This light substance is obviously unsuitable for use in the earth oven *(uṃ)*, which is the point of the narrative, of course. Any Marshallese listener would be cued for the ultimate result of the octopus's deception. This also applies to the other deceptive directions the clever octopus gave to the cook. The plants for firewood and lining the earth oven were also unsuitable (as the listeners would also know, and savor the anticipation of failure, perhaps).

nut meat and the two of the them sat and were very surprised.

The next day they awoke when it was just morning. They looked out and the tide was very low. And the [second] woman again cried, "O-O-O. The very low tide!"

The octopus again answered the woman, "Never mind the low tide. For it is I. Don't you want to come and cook me in the earth oven? And eat me?"

And the woman did as before.

The woman asked the octopus, "What kind of firewood should I use?"

The octopus said, *"Marjej."* The woman again asked, "What kind of rock should I use?" The octopus again answered, *"Tilaan."*

The woman asked, "What kind of leaves should I use?" The octopus again answered, *"Atat."* Now the woman discarded the previous earth oven and dug a new earth oven.

And she made it as the octopus said. And when the earth oven was depressed (ready), she put the octopus in it and covered it with *atat,* and covered it (with sand and earth) and again went to the [first] woman and told her that she should grate copra, so that they would have a side dish with the octopus.[4]

A short while later, the [first] woman said, "This octopus is cooked now. Go and uncover the earth oven. And when you have finished uncovering the earth oven, call me so that I can bring our side dish (of coconut meat)."

The [second] woman went to uncover the earth oven, and the octopus was gone again. And she called to the [first] woman, "Well, the octopus is gone." The [first] woman was angry. She said, "You do not know how to cook with an earth oven. If the octopus appears tomorrow, I will go and the two of us will cook it in the earth oven."

And the [second] woman said, "It will be good if it is only you. You cook it in the earth oven."

And the [first] woman said, "It will be better if it is only me."

And they slept fitfully that night (anxious for it to be morning). And when it was morning, they went together toward the lagoon, and it was low tide.

And they again said, "O-O-O. The very low tide!" The octopus answered, "Never mind the low tide, for I am here. You two come here and take me and cook me in the earth oven and eat me."

Now they went and brought the octopus and made a new earth oven. And again questioned the octopus, "What kind of firewood should I use?" The octopus said, *"Marjej."* Now the [second] woman replied, "He is lying. He is lying. Real firewood."

Now the [first] woman again asked, "What kind of rocks should I use?" The octopus answered, *"Tilaan."* The [second] woman replied, "He is lying. He is lying. Real rock."

The [first] woman again asked, "What kind of leaves should I use?" And the octopus answered, *"Atat."*

And the [second] woman again replied, "He is lying. He is lying. Real leaves."

And they dug the third earth oven and made a fire and used real firewood, and brought real rocks and real leaves.

When the earth oven was depressed, they raked aside the rocks in it and placed the octopus inside the earth oven, and put rocks (on the octopus). And the octopus cried out, "Throw off the rocks and leaves again and take me out. I will be cooked! I will be cooked!"

(*Inamat* in the ancient language is 'I will be cooked'.)

The [second] woman said, "He is lying!

4. Informant explained that only coconut meat *(waini)* is *jiraal.* All other vegetables and meat or fish are *jālele.*

He is lying! Cover it up! [the earth oven] Cover it up!"

The octopus again called out the second time, "Throw off the rocks and leaves again and take me out. I am cooked! I am cooked!"

The [second] woman again said, "He is lying! He is lying! Cover it up! Cover it up!"

The octopus went to cry out the third time. It could not cry, for it was burnt.

And the [first] woman completed covering up the earth oven and went to the house and rested a little. And the [second] woman said, "Well, the octopus should be done now. It cannot possibly flee now."

Now the [first] woman replied, "Well, you are right. For it spoke and we did not hear its voice. Well, I am going to husk coconuts to prepare our side dish of coconut meat."

The [second] woman said, "Do you think the earth oven is finished [ready] now?"

The [first] woman answered, "Go and see if it is. And stand on it. For if it is warm, [it is] hot. Well, it is finished."

Now the [second] woman went—went and came to the earth oven and stretched out her leg and stepped on the earth oven. She felt the warmth on her leg and cried out, "The earth oven is finished."

The [first] woman replied, "Well, uncover it, for I am grating coconuts."

As she grated she sang, "Spread on | Step on around the base of the coconut tree | Many coconuts falling down at one time | Many, many here!"

The woman who was grating coconuts said, "This is enough for our side dish, ma'am. Where is the octopus?"

The [second] woman replied, "Here it is. Bring the coconut meat! We will eat beside the earth oven."

And she brought the coconut meat. And they ate some of it.

And they pulled out the octopus from within the earth oven, and each woman took a tentacle and ate it. And not all the tentacles were eaten, but they were finished eating. And they hung the octopus in a *kiden* [*Messerschmidia argentia,* a tree] outside of the house, and they just went to lie down. They had just lain down and they heard a sound that was coming from the west. The sound was the voice of the mother of the octopus that they had killed and eaten.

The voice said, "From over there it comes, ma'am | It comes here from the west | To those who made the earth oven there | Smoke the fish beneath that *kiden* on the oceanside | *kiden* | what *kiden?"* (In the ancient language *ua tok le* means 'from over there it comes, ma'am' [used in above chant].

When they heard the octopus singing, the [first] woman said, "But ma'am, what is this thing?" The [second] woman said, "It is the sound of the waves. It is the sighing of the wind. And you just work!"

And the octopus again sang. And when they both listened, it was clear to them. And they planned what they should do. And they said, "We will cut pandanus leaves from the pandanus tree (outside the house) and bring them into that loft.[5]

And the [second] woman said, "Look and see if it will be good for us to stay in that loft!"

5. The traditional Marshallese houses, which were shaped like A-frame houses of today, had a loft *(po)* at the rear of the house *(eṃ* or *ṃweo).* This was used as a storage area. The *irooj* (chiefs) and their offspring the *bwidak*(s) are said to have had more elaborate houses, with side walls, and they were larger than those of the *kajoor* (commoners), including the *aļap*[s] (lineage heads). This is recalled by some of the Marshallese. For example, Ṃak Juda explained this to me on Mājro in 1968, and illustrated it with sketches of the living structures of traditional Marshallese culture.

And the [first] woman made magic (with pandanus leaves) to see if it would be good.[6] She saw that it was very good, and she said to the [second] woman, "Let us go to that loft. When the big octopus comes, it will destroy us."

The [second] woman replied, "And ma'am, are you sure?"

The [first] woman said, "It will be clear."

When the octopus came close, they climbed up into the loft and made ready in case the octopus was coming to kill them, for the octopus was very angry about her child the octopus.

They just remained there and the big octopus stretched out her tentacle.

And the women seized the pandanus leaves that they had made ready in the loft and said (chanting), "Give me the tentacle | The tentacle | So that I can cut it | So that I can throw it away."

The women sang, and they cut off the octopus's tentacle and threw it away.

Now the octopus reached out another tentacle. And the women again chanted, "Give me the tentacle | The tentacle | So that I can cut it | So that I can throw it away."

And they again cut the second one and threw it away.

And they did thus until all of the tentacles of the octopus were finished [cut off]. And when they were finished, they dug a huge earth oven and cooked her. And the earth oven remains there to this day. The two earth ovens of the small octopus are also there.

It is ended.

But there are many octopuses on Ujae. And the kind of coconut that they grated is also there to this day.

The name of the coconut is *pia.* It has been grated, prepared inside the shell. If you open the coconut shell, it will be as if (the coconut meat) had been grated. It is not ungrated coconut meat. Many coconuts are like this to this day.[7]

The earth oven is on Maratak land parcel on the main island of Ujae. One earth oven is on Mwijit-eņ land parcel.

Three earth ovens are there to this day. And they are very large. They are as big as the snack bar on Kuwajleen.[8]

---

6. *Bubu in maañ:* divination by means of folding pandanus leaves. The shape of the final folding foretells the future outcome or event. Divination is also done by knotting coconut leaves *(bubu in kimej in ni).* See Krämer and Nevermann for a description of this technique, and see Lessa (1968: 188–210) for a discussion of the technique as practiced in the Western Carolines. These techniques are still known to a few of the older Marshallese, and they have been demonstrated to me. *Bubu in maañ* is also known as *kwojerip.* And *bubu in kimej in ni* is also known as *kajare bouj.* The technique of forecasting the future by means of counting out beach pebbles *(ļā)* is called *boļā,* and was demonstrated and explained to me by the *ri-meto* (navigator) Jo̧wej at Mājro in 1952.

7. Here we see the explanation of natural phenomena as part of the story. This is another common motif in Marshallese folktales.

8. Note the incorporation of an introduced and contemporary cultural item, the snack bar, into the story by way of explanation. The informant worked in the Kuwajleen Missile Base snack bar as janitor/clean up man, and we were sitting a short distance away from it, after work, when he told me this story. So it was a natural and convenient analogy for him. This is an example of the changes that may and do occur over the years in the narration of folktales.

38: RUO KŌRĀ

Ri-bwebwenato: Jelibōr Jam, Kuwajleen 1975

Ruo kōrā jān aelōñ in Ujae (ijaje etan kōrā ro). Ro ar kiki im ļak ruj ekanooj pāāt. Innām lio juon ej item kōmaañ. Ak lio juon ej laṃōj im ba, "O-O-O. Ļōppeipāāt!"

Kweet eo eba, "Enta pāāt eo, baj ña e. Kojab item uṃwin eō ma kañe ña?"

Kiiō lio ej wōnmetoļǫk im jibwe kweet eo im bōk ānetak jān lǫjet em item kūbwij juon uṃ. Im ba ñan kweet eo, "Kaneūṃ kaneūṃ ta?" Kweet eo eba, "Marjej." Lio ej kajjitōk, "Dekeūṃ dekeūṃ ta?" Kweet eo ej uwaak, "Tilaan." Lio ej kajjitōk, "Bwilkōṃ bwilkōṃ ta?" Kweet eo ej uwaak, "Atat."

Kiiō lio ej kōjǫ kijeek eo. Im kōṃṃan kane, marjej. Im kōṃṃan dekā tilaan. Innām ke ej ṃōj uṃ eo ej tokrake uṃ eo im likūt kweet eo ņa ilowaan uṃ eo. Im kalbubuuk kōn bōlōk in atat. Innām kobalōke. Ke ej ṃōj an kōbalōke ej etal ñan ṃweo im ba ñan lio juon, "Bōktok kijerro waini im raanke bwe enañin mat uṃwin kweet eņ."

Ke ej meļanļǫk jidik lio ej ba, "Eole emat kiiō kweet eņ. Ña ij etal in jukok." Etal im ļak uṃ eo eļak jukok. Ejako kweet eo. Kiiō lio ekūṃṃūļǫk, im make kōnono ippān, "Ta wūnin ejako kweet eo? Etke ijjab meļeļe?" Kiiō ej kūr tok lio juon, "Ewi kwe le?" Lio juon eba, "Ña e."

Lio ej bar kōnono, "Kwōn bōktok waini ņe kijem bwe jenro ṃōñā bajjek ilowaan uṃ e. Ak ejako kweet eo!"

Innām lio juon ej bōkļǫk waini eo im rejro jijet im kanooj in bwilōñ.

Raan eo juon rōbar ruj ke ej jibboñ wōt. Ļak bar erreilǫk ekanooj ļap an pāāt. Innām lio ej bar laṃōj, "O-O-O. Ļōppeipāāt."

Kweet eo ej bar uwaak kōrā eo, "Enta pāāt eo ke ña e. Kwōj jab itok im uṃwin eō? Im kañe eō?" Innām lio ej bar kōṃṃan āinwōt ṃokta.

Lio ej kajjitōk ippān kweet eo, "Kaneūṃ kaneūṃ ta?" Kweet eo ej ba, "Marjej." Lio ej bar kajjitōk, "Dekeūṃ dekeūṃ ta?" Kweet eo ej uwaak, "Tilaan."

Lio ej bar kajjitōk, "Bwilkōṃ bwilkōṃ ta?" Kweet eo ej uwaak, "Atat." Kiiō lio ej joļǫk uṃ ṃokta im bar kūbwij juon uṃ ekāāl. Im kōṃṃan āinwōt [an] kweet eo ba. Innām ke ej ṃōj uṃ eo ej likūt kweet eo im kalbubuki kōn atat. Im kobale im bar etal ippān lio juon im ba en raanke waini. Bwe ren ro kab jiraale kweet eo.

Meļan ļǫk jidik lio juon ej ba, "Emat kweet eņ kiiō. Kwōn ilān jukok. Innām ñe eṃōj aṃ jukok kwōn kab kūr eō bwe in bōkwōj jiraal e arro."

Lio juon eļak jukok ebar jako kweet eo. Innām ej ikkūrļǫk ñan lio juon, "Eole, ejako kweet eo." Lio juon ej illu. Im ba, "Kwe kojaje uṃuṃ. Ñe enaaj waļǫk kweet eo ilju inaaj iwōj kejro uṃwini." Innām lio juon ej ba, "Eṃṃan ñe baj kwe wōt. Kwōn uṃwini."

Innām lio juon ej ba, "Eṃṃan ļǫk ñe ña wōt."

Innām rejro kiki boñōn eo im kijerjer bwe en raan. Innām ke ej jibboñ wōt rejro jiṃor wōnarļǫk im ļak ilǫk epāāt.

Innām rejro raar bar ba, "O-O-O. Ļōppeipāāt!" Kweet eo ej uwaak, "Enta pāāt eo? Ke ña e. Koṃin ro itok im bōke eō. Im uṃwin eō. Im kañe eō."

Kiiō rejro ilām bōktok kweet eo im kōṃṃane juon uṃ kāāl. Im bar kajjitōk ippān kweet eo, "Kaneūṃ kaneūṃ ta?" Kweet eo ej uwaak, "Marjej." Kiiō lio ej uwaak, "Ej riab! ej riab! Lukkuun kane."

Kiiō lio ej bar kajjitōk, "Dekeūm̧ dekeūm̧ ta?" Kweet eo ej uwaak, "Tilaan." Lio ej uwaak, "Ej riab! ej riab! Lukkuun dekā."

Lio ej bar kajjitōk, "Bwilkōm̧ bwilkōm̧ ta?" Ak kweet eo ej uwaak, "Atat." Lio ej bar uwaak, "Ej riab! Ej riab! Lukkuun bōlōk."

Innām rej kūbwij um̧ eo kein kajilu im kōjo̧e im kōm̧m̧an lukkuun kane. Em bōktok lukkuun dekā bōktok lukkuun bōlōk.

Ke ej mej um̧ eo rejro tokrak innām likūt kweet eo ņa ilowaan um̧ eo. Innām jinikeike. Innām kweet eo ej ļam̧ōj, "Juki eō! Juki eō! (Āinwōt bar joļo̧k dekā im bōlōk. Im kwaļo̧ke.) Inamat! Inamat! (Inamat ilo kajin etto ej imat ak inaaj mat.)

Kōrā ro rej ba, "Ej riab! Ej riab! Kobale! Kobale!"

Kweet eo eaar bar lam̧ōj kein ka ruo, "Juk eō! Juk eō! Inamat! Inamat!"

Kōrā ro rej bar ba, "Ej riab! Ej riab! Kobale! Kobale!"

Kein kajilu alen kweet eo eļak iten lam̧ōj. Eban lam̧ōj bwe ebwil. Innām kōrā ro rejro kōmwijļo̧k aerro kobale um̧ eo im etal ñan m̧weo im kakkije jidik. Im lio juon ej ba, "Iole, enaaj mat kweet eņ kiiō. Ejāmin ko kiiō."

Lio juon ej uwaak, "Ekwe kwōj m̧ool. Bwe eaar kōnono innām kōjro jab roñ ainikien. Ekwe ij ilān eddōb tok arro jiraal."

Lio juon eba, "Kwōj ļōmņak emat ke um̧ eņ kiiō?"

Lio juon ej uwaak, "Kwōn etal im lale m̧ōk. Im juur ioon. Bwe eļañne emāņāņ, ebwil. Ekwe emat."

Kiiō lio juon ej etal. Etal im ļak um̧ eo eleļo̧k neen em juur eoon um̧ eo. Im eñjake an bwil neen ak ej lam̧ōj im ba, "Emat um̧ e."

Lio juon ej uwaak, "Ekwe, kwōn jukok bwe ña ij raanke."

Innām ke ej raanke ej al, "Bwijibwiji debini | M̧ōram̧rōm̧ waini | ñore | ñōōōre/ Elōñ ijōņe!"

Kōrā eo eaar raanke ej ba, "Ebwe arro jiraal le. Ewi kweet eo?"

Lio juon ej uwaak, "Eñe, kwōn bōktok waini ņe! Kōjro m̧ōñā iturin um̧ e."

Innām ej bōkļo̧k waini eo. Innām rejro jiraal bajjek. Innām rejro katuwe kweet eo jān lowaan um̧ eo em kajjo kijen ko im m̧ōñā. Innām ejjañin maat ko ko kijeerro ak remāt. Innām rejro totoik kweet eo ņa ilo kiden eo ilikin m̧weo. Innām rejro iten babu bajjek. Rejro ja babu wōt ak rej roñjake juon ainikien ej itok jān kapilōñ. Ainikien, ainikien kweet eo jinen kweet eo ro ar m̧ane im kañe. Ainikien eo ej ba, "Ua taka le | Ua tokijān kapilōñ | Ijo um̧winak eo ie ratiki ek eo ie ium̧win kiden eņ ilik. | Kiden | Ta kiden?"

(Ilo kajin etto meļeļe in "ua taka le" ej 'jān ijuweo ej itok le'.)

Ke rejro roñ an kweet eo al lio juon ej ba, "A le, ta men in le?" Lio juon ej ba, "Lijiņo im anij. [Ñilli ņo 'm anij.] Kwōn jerbal wōt!" (Āinwōt ainikien mejatoto im ainikien ņo.)

Innām kweet eo ej bar al. Im ke ro jim̧or roñjake alikkar aerro roñ. Im rejro pukpukot ta eo renaaj kōm̧m̧ane. Innām rejro ba, "Ekwe kōjro jekjek tok maañ in bōb ņa ilo po eo."

Innām lio juon ej ba, "Kwōn m̧ōk lale em̧m̧an ke bwe en arro pād ilo po eņ." Innām lio juon ej bubu (kōn maañ) im lale em̧m̧an ke. Eļak lale ekanooj in em̧m̧an. Innām ej ba ñan lio juon, "Jero naaj pād ilo po eņ. Ñe enaaj itok kweet eņ eļap in ko̧kkure kōjro." Lio juon ej uwaak, "A le, kwōj m̧ool ke le?"

Lio juon ej uwaak, "Enaaj alikkar."

Ke ej epaaktok kweet eo rejro tallōñ ļo̧k ñan po eo im kōppojak ñan ñe ebaj itok kweet eo im m̧ane er, bwe eļap an kweet eo illu kōn kweet eo nājin.

Rejro ja pādwōt ak kweet eo kilep ej kapeļļo̧k koon. Innām kōrā ro rej jibwetok maañ ko raar kōpooji tok ņa ioon po eo im ba, "Letok joko eo joko | Bwe in jeke | Bwe in joļo̧ke."

Kōrā ro rej al im rej bukwe koon kweet eo im joļǫke.

Kiiō kweet eo ej bar leļǫk juon koon. Im kōrā ro rej bar al, "Letok joko eo joko | Bwe in jeke | Bwe in joļǫke."

Innām rejro bukwe koon kweet eo kein ka ruo im joļǫke.

Āindein aerro kōm̧m̧an ñan maatin koon kweet eo.

Innām ke ej maat rejro kubwij juon um̧ kileplep im um̧wini. Im um̧ eo ej pād ñan rainin. Im ruo um̧ an kweet edik rej bar pād.

Ejem̧ļǫk.

Ak elōñ kweet i Ujae. Innām waini eo erro ar raankeiki ej barāinwōt pād ñan rainin.

Etan waini in "pia." Em̧ōj raankeiki. Kadede ŋa ilowaan ļat eŋ. (Ñe kwōj kōpeļļǫk ļat enaaj āinwōt em̧ōj raanke, ejjab waini. Elōñ ni rej āinwōt ñan rainin.)

Um̧ [eo] ej pād ioon wāto in Maratat ioon eonene in Ujae.

Juōn um̧ epād ioon wāto in Mwijit-eŋ. Um̧ ko jilu repād ie ñan rainin. Im rej lukkuun ļap. Joñan wōt jināk bar [*snack bar*] eo ioon Kuwajleen.

39: STORY ABOUT A WOMAN ON KŌLE ISLAND[1]

As told by Jelibōr Jam, Kuwajleen 1975

This woman had five boy children [sons]. The one boy was two years old. One boy was three years old. And one boy was five years old. And one boy was six years old. And one boy was seven years old.

These boys went all the time to fish beside Kōle.[2] When they returned, their mother quickly made a fire (with a fire plow).[3] And bathed the youngest child. She did this for the youngest boy daily.

It continued this way and later one time, a woman named Lijoṃanet came. She came and talked with her during the day. And the boys returned from fishing. When the boys returned, Lijoṃanet quickly left. But the woman began to become ill. And did not make a fire. And did not quickly bathe the youngest boy.

And the next day the boys again went to fish, and Lijoṃanet came and said to the woman, "What, ma'am, are you ill?"

The woman replied, "Yes, I am ill."

Lijoṃanet said, "And may I enter you?"

The woman replied, "Yes."[4]

When Lijoṃanet entered, she entered within the body of the woman. And the woman became a *mejenkwaad.*

When the boys, her sons, came from their fishing, the woman called to the youngest boy, and said, "Hurry up with my fish." And the youngest boy was quick to bring them to her.

At that time, this woman took the fish from the boy and ate it. And grabbed the boy and ate him, too.

After eating the boy and the fish, she was restored to health, and came and again made a fire and cooked fish.

But the boys did not know that she had eaten the youngest boy.

The next day the boys again went to fish. When the youngest boy was missing, they questioned their mother and said, "Where is the little boy?" Their mother replied, "He is staying [here], for he is cold."

And the boys again went to fish. When it was evening, they returned. And the mother came and called out to the boys, "Hurry up with my fish." And the youngest boy brought it. And the mother took the fish, and ate it. And grabbed the boy, and ate him [again ate a son].

That night when they slept, the boy appeared and spoke to the three boys. "The reason the youngest boy is missing, our

---

1. The word *aelōñ* 'atoll' is used for Kōle, although it is a single island without a lagoon—instead of *āne* 'island, islet'. The latter is used for an islet of an atoll.

2. Kōle is in the southern Marshalls, in the Rālik chain, about thirty miles southwest of Jālooj Atoll. It is where the displaced Pikinni Atoll people were relocated after their home atoll was taken for the testing of nuclear weapons after World War II. Kōle is 0.36 of a square mile in extent, while Pikinni has 2.32 square miles of land area and 229.20 square miles of lagoon.

3. In the fire-plow method of making fire by friction, one piece of wood is rubbed vigorously against another that has been placed on the ground. The resultant sparks ignite the tinder of dried coconut husks.

4. Note the spirit possession. In this case, rare in Marshallese folklore, it is with the permission of the victim, and as requested by the spirit (demon). Spirit possession is a widespread motif in folklore and in alleged occurrence. The biblical stories of spirit possession may well have reinforced the traditional Marshallese beliefs.

mother ate him. And she also ate me." When they awoke, the boys questioned their mother. "Where are the boys?"

Their mother lied and said, "They are still sleeping. And if you want to go to fish, go."

The boy who was a little younger than the two boys said, "Let's go, the three of us, and sail to fish! And not return here. For see here, the two boys are missing."

The oldest boy replied, "Don't you see that the two boys remain with their mother? And don't you believe that this is a dream?"

And the three went to fish. When it was night, they returned and the mother again did as before. And they brought the fish and their mother grabbed the boy and the boy cried out.

At the time when he called out, the oldest boy and the other boy ran from the canoe. And saw what he had heard. When he went away, their mother was eating the boy. And the boy [the oldest] hurried to return to the canoe to the other boy. And said to him, "See here, our mother has eaten [our] younger brother." He said, "Look, there were five of us, and two were missing before, and now she has eaten another. Well, what are the two of us going to do?"

The other boy replied, "We two will sail from this island."

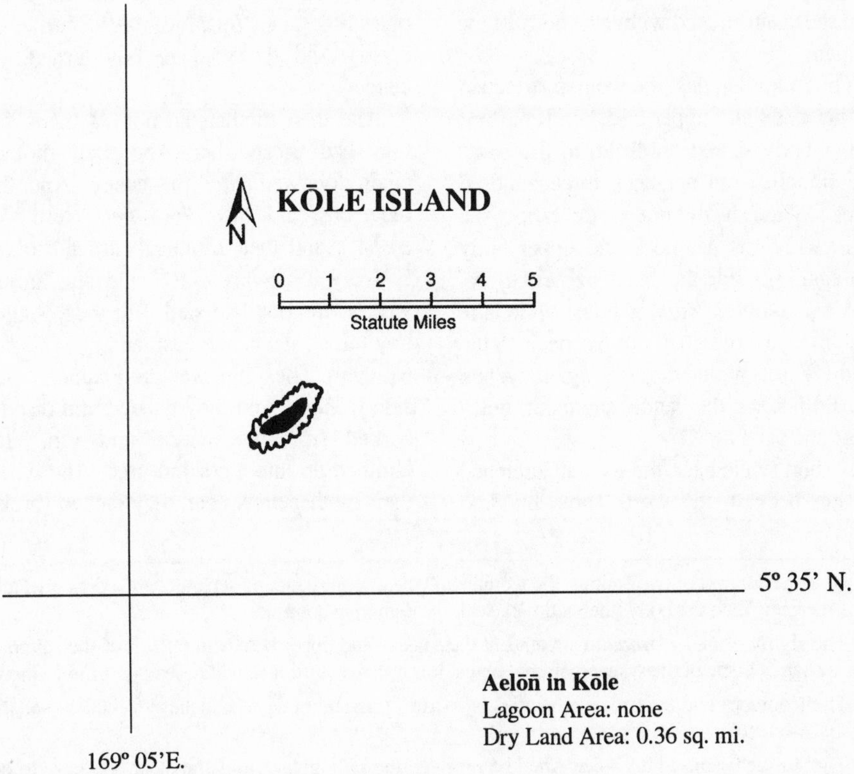

Aelōn̄ in Kōle
Lagoon Area: none
Dry Land Area: 0.36 sq. mi.

And their mother, when she finished eating the boy and the fish, made the fire and cooked the fish, the boys' catch. And she said to herself that she would eat again [next time], the two boys.

The next day the boys hurried to go to fish. And they fished a little beside the island. When it was past sunset, they sailed and ran [went] to the north. Their mother looked for and hunted the boys' canoe in the night. But she did not find it. And she returned and slept. When she slept, Lijoṃanet again appeared from within the body of the woman. And the two of them (the woman and she) talked with each other.[5] And the woman said, "Tomorrow I will look for the canoe."

Lijoṃanet said, "I will go with you." And she again entered within the body of the woman.

The following day, the woman stretched out her neck and upper body, with the rest of her body seated on Kōle, to the east.[6] She stretched out her neck three hundred miles.[7] When she did not see the canoe, she again withdrew her neck and upper body and again became the same size as before. And sat a little. After a little while, the woman again stretched out her neck to the south. Three hundred miles again. When she did not see the canoe, she again withdrew, and sat a little.

A short while later, the woman stretched out her neck to the west. Three hundred miles to the west. But she did not see the canoe. She again withdrew. She sat a little, and rested.

After a few minutes [had passed], she stretched out her neck to the north three hundred miles.

At this time, the older boy was seated on the outrigger platform, and looked out and away. The sky had darkened in the south, because the woman was coming.

And the older boy said to the younger boy, "When I say *'bwābwe'* (turn east / to windward!), you just turn the canoe west / to leeward. And when I say *'kabbwe'* (turn the canoe west!), you just turn the canoe east."

And when their mother drew near them, the older boy said, "Get ready, sir!" When their mother was coming to eat them, the older boy said, *"Bwā-bwe-e-e!"* (turn ee-e-e-ast!) And the younger boy turned the canoe west.

And their mother did not eat them, for they had tricked her. And their mother again followed after the canoe. And the older boy said, *"Kab-bwe-e-e!"* (turn we-e-e-st!), and their mother heard the older boy say, *"kab-bwe-e-e!"*[8] and she turned west as the boy had said. But the younger boy turned the canoe east, and she did not eat them. Thus they went and came alongside Roñdik. And they hurried and disembarked from the canoe and ran, and climbed up into a coconut tree. And when their mother drew near, they picked (broke

5. Note the concept of two entities, the woman and the evil spirit, acting separately in a dialogue, and then "merging" into the body (the victim's), with the demon in control.

6. The ability of *mejenkwaad* to stretch out their necks and upper bodies in pursuit of their human prey is characteristic of these supernatural beings. It is a shape-shifting, a widespread motif in folklore.

7. The loanword and concept *ṃail* 'mile' is used in this and other Marshallese folktales (see the Marshallese text).

8. The storyteller raised his voice when he repeated the sailing directions the older boy gave to his brother, and he prolonged the words as one would do while sailing a canoe. This narrative device enhanced the dramatic quality of the story, which would add to the entertainment afforded the audience by this horrifying and suspenseful story.

off) a midrib of a coconut frond and threw it [like a spear] to the west.[9]

And their mother chased the midrib of the coconut frond. About six hundred miles to the west, she ate the midrib of the coconut frond and again returned to go eat the boys.

When she drew near, she ate the canoe.[10]

After she ate the canoe, she stretched out her neck to eat the boys. And they again broke off a midrib of a coconut frond and threw it to the east. And the woman followed the midrib of the coconut frond and stretched out her neck six hundred miles to the east. She ate the midrib of the coconut frond, and again returned to eat the boys.

When she came this time, she had opened her mouth and stretched [her lower jaw and mouth] under the water. And her upper jaw stretched up with the clouds.

And the boys again broke off a midrib of a coconut frond and threw it to the south. And the woman again followed the midrib of the coconut frond to the south six hundred miles. And ate it. And again returned.

When she neared, they again broke off another midrib of a coconut frond and threw it to the north. And the woman again followed the midrib of the coconut frond six hundred miles. And ate it. And again returned.

When she came, she was very angry, and she opened her mouth very wide. When she came close to the boys, they broke off a sprout of the coconut[11] and threw it up to the sky.

And the woman followed it. And she did not return again. (All of her body went up into the sky.)

It is ended.

(The meaning of this story: From knowledge you will live. From your intelligence. Like the boys.)

---

9. This is an example of a widespread motif of tricking (and halting and slowing down) a pursuing entity by casting down objects in its path—the obstacle flight or magic flight motif.

10. The destruction of the canoe in which the intended human victims are fleeing is another motif found in other Marshallese folktales, and adds a graphic element of suspense to the narrative. It is a danger to which the Marshallese were able to relate easily.

11. *Tūrijibake:* the stage of development just before the *pāp*, the midrib of the coconut frond. It is in the middle and above on all coconut trees, the storyteller explained. This story obviously had a didactic as well as an entertainment function, as the storyteller has indicated in his conclusion: one must use one's intelligence and initiative, and cooperate with one's sibilings, as the boys did. The dramatic, suspense-filled story should have impressed the value of such behavior upon a young audience.

39: BWEBWENATO IN JUŌN KŌRĀ ILO AELŌÑ IN KŌLE

Ri-bwebwenato: Jelibōr Jam, Kuwajleen 1975

Kōrā in eor ļalem nājin ļaddik. Ļadik eo juon ej ruo an iiō. Ļadik eo juon ej jilu an iiō. Im ļadik eo juon ej ļalem an iiō. Im ļadik eo juon ej jiljino an iiō. Im ļadik eo juon ej jiljilimjuon an iiō.

Ļadik rein aolep iien rej ilān eọñwōd iturin Kōle. N̄e rej rọọltok jineer ej ṃōkaj in kōjọjo kijeek (kōn it). Im katutu ļadik eo edik. Āindein an kōṃṃan ñan ļadik eo edik ilo raan ko.

Pād em ļak juon iien eitok juon kōrā etan Lijoṃanet. Ej itok im bwebwenato ippān iuṃwin raan eo. Ak ļadik ro remootļọk in eọñwōd. Ke Ļadik ro rej rọọltok Lijoṃanet ej ṃōkaj in etal. Ak kōrā eo ej jino an nañinmej. Im kōṃṃan kijeek. Ak ejjab ṃōkaj in katutu ļadik eo edik.

Raan eo juon ļadik ro rej bar etal in eọñwōd innām Lijoṃanet ej itok im ba ñan kōrā eo, "Ta le ko nañinmej?"

Kōrā eo ej uwaak, "Aet, inañinmej."

Lijoṃanet ej ba, "Ak ij maroñ ke deļọñ ñan ippaṃ?" Kōrā eo ej uwaak, "Aet."

Ke ej deļọñtok Lijoṃanet ej deļọñ ilowaan ānbwinnin kōrā eo. Im kōrā eo ej erom mejenkwaad.

Ke ej itok ļadik ro nājin jān ke raar eọñwōd liin ej laṃōj ļọk ñan ļadik eo edik. Im ba, "Kwōn ṃōkaj tok kōn juon kijō ek." Im ļadik eo edik ej ṃōkaj in bōkļọk.

Ilo iien eo kōrā in ej bōk ek eo jān ļadik eo im kañe. Im jibwe ļadik eo im bar kañe.

Ṃwijin [an] kañ ļadik eo kab ek eo. Ej mour im itok im bar kōṃṃan kijeek im kōmatti ek ko.

Ak ļadik ro rejaje ke eṃōj an kañ ļadik eo edik.

Raan eo juon ļadik ro rej bar etal in eọñwōd. Ke ej jako ļadik eo edik rej kajjitōk ippān jineer im ba, "Ewi ļadik eo edik?" Jineer ej uwaak, "Ej pādwōt, bwe ekōŋaan piọ."

Innām ļadik ro rej bar etal im eọñwōd. Ke jota ļọk rej bar rọọl. Im jineer ej itok im ikkūrļọk ñan ļadik ro, "Ṃōkaj tok kōn juon kijō ek." Im ļadik eo edik ej bōkļọk. Im jinen ebōk ek eo, im kañe. Im jibwe ļadik eo. Im bar kañe.

Boñ in eo ke rej kiki ļadik eo ej waļọk im kōnono ñan ļadik ro jilu, "Wūnin an jako ļadik eo edik, jinedeañ eaar kañe. Innām ña eaar bar kañe." Ke rej ruj ļadik ro rej bar kajjitōk ippān jineer, "Erki ļadik ro ruo?"

Jineer ej riab im ba, "Rej kiki wōt. Ak eļañne koṃ kōŋaan eọñwōd, koṃin etal."

Ļadik eo edikļọk jidik jān ļadik ro ruo ej ba, "Jel etal im jerak in eọñwōd! Im jab bar rọọltok. Bwe lale ṃōk, rejako ļadik ro ruo."

Ļadik eo erūttotata ej uwaak, "Kwōj jab lale ke ļadik ro rej pādwōt ippān jined? Ak kwōjjab pokake ettōŋak in?"

Innām erjeel ilān eọñwōd. Ke [ej] boñļọk rej rọọltok im jineer ej bar kōṃṃan āinwōt ṃokta. Im rej bōkļọk ek eo im jineer ej jibwe ļadik eo im ļadik eo ej laṃōj.

Ilo iien eo ke ej laṃōj ļadik eo erūtto ej ettōr jān wa eo, im ļadik eo juon. Im lale ta eo eaar roñjake. Ke ej ilọk jineer ej kañ ļadik eo. Innām ļadik eo eṃōkaj in rọọl ñan wa [eo] ippān ļadik eo juon. Im ba ñane, "Eoļe ļadik eo edik eṃ jinerro ej kañe." Ej kōnono, "Lale ṃōk ke kar kijeañ ļalem ak ar jako ruo ṃokta ak kiiō eṃōj an bar kañe juon. Ekwe jero naaj et?"

Ļadik eo juon ej uwaak, "Jero naaj jerak jān āniin."

Innām jineer ke ej ṃōj an kañ ļadik eo im ek eo ej kōṃṃane kijeek eo im kōmatti ek ko, koņan ļadik ro. Ak ej ba ilo būruon ke enaaj bar kañ ļadik ro ruo.

Raan eo juon ļadik ro rejro ṃōkaj in etal in eo̧ñwōd. Im ro ar eo̧ñwōd bajjek iturin āne eo. Ke [ej] tulo̧k aļ ro ar jerak im ettōr niñaļo̧k. Jineer eaar kālik-keaar im pukot wa eo waan ļadik ro ilo boñōn eo. Ak ejjab loe. Innām ej jepļaak im kiki. Ke ej kiki Lijoṃanet ej bar waļo̧k jān ilowaan ānbwinnin kōrā eo. Im rejro (kōrā eo im e) rej bwebwenato. Innām kōrā eo ej ba, "Ilju inaaj pukot wa eo."

Lijoṃanet ej ba, "Inaaj iwōj ippaṃ wōj." Im kiiō ej bar deļo̧ñ ilowaan ānbwinnin kōrā eo.

Rujlo̧kin eo kōrā eo ej mōōbōb taļo̧k ñan rear. Mōōbōb taļo̧k jilubuki ṃail. Ke ej jab lo wa eo ej bar jentok. Im jijet jidik. Ālikin jidik iien kōrā eo ej bar mōōbōb rōñaļo̧k. Im pād tarrin jilubuki ṃail. Ke ejjab lo wa eo ej bar jintok. Im jijet jidik.

Meļan ļo̧k jidik kōrā ej mōōbōb toļo̧k. Jilubuki ṃail toļo̧k. Ak ej jab lo wa eo. Ej bar jintok, jijet jidik. Im kakkije.

Mootļo̧k jet minit ej mōōbōb niñaļo̧k jilubuki ṃail.

Iien in ļadik eo erūtto ej jijet ioon petak eo. Im ļak erreilo̧k, emaroktok lañ tu jab in irōk. Kōnke kōrā eo ej itok.

Innām ļadik eo erūtto ej ba ñan ļadik eo edik, "Eļañe inaaj ba 'Bwābwe' kwōn kab kabbwe. Im ñe inaaj ba kabbwe kwōn kab bwābwe."

Innām ke ej epaak tok jineerro, ļadik eo erūtto ej ba, "Pojak ļe!" Ke jineerro ej iten kañe ļadik eo erūtto ej ba, "Bwā-bwe-e-e-e!" Innām ļadik eo edik ej kabbwe.

Innām jineerro ejjab kañe [er]ro bwe erro kar riab ñane. Innām jineer ej bar ļoor ļo̧k wa eo. Innām ļadik eo erūtto ej ba, "Kab-bwe-e-e-e!" Im jineer eroñjake an ļadik eo erūtto ba kab-bwe-e-e-e. Im ekabbwe āinwōt ļadik eo ba. Ak ļadik eo edik ej bwābwe. Innām ejjab kañe erro. Āindeo ļo̧k innām ro tōkeak i Roñdik. Im kaiur erro im to jān wa eo im ettōr. Im tallōñ ilo juon ni. Im ke jineer ej epaaktok rejro ej ļote juon pāp in ni im wiake toļo̧k.

Innām jineer ej lukworkwore pāp eo. Tarrin jiljino ṃail toļo̧k ej kañ pāp eo im bar jepļaaktok in iten kañ ļadik ro.

Ke ej epaaktok ej kañ wa eo.

Ṃōjin an kañ wa eo ej mōōbōb in kañ ļadik ro. Im rejro bar ruje juon pāp im wiake taļo̧k. Im lieņ [lio] ej ļoorļo̧k pāp eo im mōōbōb jiljinobuki ṃail taļo̧k. Ej kañ pāp eo. Im bar jepļaak tok in kañ ļadik ro.

Ke ej itok ilo iien jab eo, eṃōj an walañi im itōke lo̧ñi i lo̧jet. Ak lo̧ñi[in] tulōñ ej itok ippān tok.

Innām ļadik ro rej bar ruje juon pāp im wiake rōñaļo̧k. Innām lieņ [lio] ej bar ļoorļo̧k pāp eo rōñaļo̧k jiljinobuki ṃail. Im kañe. Im bar ro̧o̧ltok.

Ke ej epaaktok rejro ļote pāp eo juon im wiake niñaļo̧k. Im lieņ [lio] ej bar ļoorļo̧k pāp eo jiljinobuki ṃail. Im kañe. Im bar jepļaak tok.

Ke ej itok eļap ļo̧k an illu. Im ekanooj eļap an walañi loñi[in]. Ke ej epaaktok ļadik ro rej ļote tūrjepake eo im wiake lōñļo̧k ñan lañ.

Innām lieo ej ļoorļo̧k. Innām eaar jab bar ro̧o̧ltok.

Ejeṃļo̧k.

(Meļeļe in bwebwenato: Jen jeļāļo̧kjeņ kwōnaaj mour. Kōn aṃ jiṃaat. Āinwōt likao ro.)

40: STORY ABOUT A MEJENKWAAD

As told by Jelibōr Jam, Kuwajleen 1975

A woman was drifting eastward and drifted ashore. People had wrapped her up with mats and tied it [the bundle] and cast it adrift.[1]

It was not clear where the woman had come from. But when she drifted ashore on an island—the name of the island was Alle, on Ujae Atoll—not a single person saw her drift ashore. And she remained on a coral head on the beach [at the water's edge] for a long time.

One day, two men sailed from Āne-Ļaṃōj in Ujae Atoll to go to *rōjep* (fish for flying fish) [family *Exocoetidae,* flying fish, *jojo*].

(The method of *rōjep* is to use twelve fathoms of line made of *arṃwe* [*Pipturus argenteus,* a tree] on the canoe, and there can be five coconut containers (*bōkā)* and a hook in [each] container.[2] This is not fishing with lines.

They do not use *rōjep* these days, but they did during the Japanese times.

They make hooks from coconut shells, and throw them into the water one by one.

And when the flying fish eat it [the baited hook], people collect them.

When there are no coconut containers, they use lines.[3] The name of this fishing with coconut shell containers is *kōbbōkāke.*)

Because it was low tide, they were quick to launch their canoe and the two of them sailed to Alle. (Because Āne-Ļaṃōj is treacherous. There are many coral heads there, like the lagoon of Mājeej.)

The reason for their sailing was that two of them went to obtain crabs for bait, coconut crabs [*Birgus latro, barulep*].

When they arrived at Alle, one of the men promptly looked for crabs, while the other man was picking coconuts.[4]

When the man had found lots of crabs, he needed to cook crabs for their food. The other man finished picking coconuts. He brought the coconuts, and said to the other man, "Drink coconuts, sir! And if there are cooked [crab] claws, give me one for my food., so that I may eat."

And the other man said, "Here is a coconut for you to drink!"

And the one man sat at the east end of the fire. And the other man sat at the north of the fire. And ate crabs.

The two of them continued to eat, and they saw that a shadow was beside the fire. The sun was to the east, and the shadow was very clear. (It was about eight o'clock or so in the morning.)

When they saw it, they were surprised. And were very much afraid. At this time, the

---

1. This was one of the traditional methods of disposal of corpses. It is no longer practiced by the Marshallese. The dead are now all interred, and the funerary rites today are a combination of the traditional and the introduced (Christian). This is another example of religious syncretism.

2. The *bōkā* were used for drinking-water and coconut-oil storage and transportation in the old days. They have long been replaced by Western-style containers.

3. The loanword *ļain* (from English *line*) is used in this story, as well as the traditional word for the same object, *eo.* They are both part of the Marshallese vocabulary today.

4. The special term *entak* is used only for picking coconuts. For picking breadfruit, *kōṃkōṃ* is used, and for picking pandanus, *okok.*

shadow revealed [made] a sound and explained her name.

And she sang and said, *"Eotōktok ilikin Alle. | Im bwiji āneo. | Kajabuk likin āne. | Likin āne. | Likin āne-e-e!"*

(In the ancient language, *bwiji āne* is 'set foot on the island'. And *kajabuk* is 'land on the island'.)

"Drift ashore on the ocean side of Alle and set foot on the island. Land on the ocean side of the island. | The ocean side of the island. | The ocean side of the island-e-e!"

And the men stood apart and and ran to their canoe and sailed. And they did not look back, for they were frightened. And they did not speak to each other.

When they reached the canoe, they hurried and cut the line at the front of the canoe and sailed and went to Āne-Ļaṃōj.

When they reached Āne-Ļaṃōj, the men there and the women came to them to get flying fish. And they asked, "Do you have a catch?" They answered, "Nothing." And the people said, "Why? For the water was very good."

And the two said, "There is a very tough demon, and she appeared to us." The people did not believe [them]. But they said, "Because you are not men!"

And the young men were angry, but there was nothing they could do. And they said that tomorrow two or three men should go to Alle. The time [was set for] early in the morning.

And the next day, three men went and launched the canoe and sailed to Alle.

When they reached Alle, the two men made a fire, as before.

And the other man was picking coconuts. A short while later, they did not see the shadow of Likināne (a female).

But they heard a sound. It said:

"Eotōktok likin Alle. | Im bwiji āne eo. | Im kajabuk Likināne." ("Drift ashore on the ocean side of Alle. | And set foot on the island. | And land on the ocean side of the island.")

The other man said, "See what you have done, men. This is Likināne" [lit. the ocean-side of the island].

The reason he said Likināne was because he did as the sound [had] said. But they did not know the name of the woman.

But the reason they understood was because the sound made it clear.

The other young man became frightened and crazed, and was very ill.

And the two men took the other young man and went to the canoe and returned to Āne-Ļaṃōj.

When the canoe was going seaward, the crazed young man said, "I am going to eat you two in only a little [while]!"

And the two men became afraid. And the crazed youth said, "Won't you two look at the island, as there are many people there."

And the two young men looked away to Alle, and saw a great many women walking on the sand.

And the young man who was crazed said, "Well, my name should be Likināne.[5]

"You two hurry up, for when the sun is in the middle [of the sky], truly I will eat you two. And eat this canoe!"

And the [one] young man was frightened but tried hard. He seized the crazy young man, for he was going to leap into the water. The other young man said, "It is is clear that that thing is a *mejenkwaad!* And male *mejenkwaad* are difficult to cure."[6]

---

5. Note the possession of the human by the evil spirit. This is a motif found in a number of other Marshallese folktales, and has, it is said, occurred in real life. The Marshallese have developed techniques for exorcising these interlopers, as have other cultures as well.

6. Note the sex differentiation. Perhaps this reflects the relative attitudes toward men and women in the culture.

The young man said to himself, "Who says he should live?"

And the three of them reached Āne-Ļaṃōj. And the crazed young man called ashore and said, "I'm going to eat [someone or something]!"

And all of the people said, "It is clear that the young men were right before!"

And the two young men brought the crazed young man ashore, and came to [be among] the people on Āne-Ļaṃōj.

That evening, the crazed young man said he wanted to eat fish, but [that] they should not cook it. And they brought a *bwebwe* [yellowfin or bluefin tuna] later that very evening. When they brought it, the crazed young man arose (sat up) and said they should bring the fish [to him]. And they brought it to him, and gave it to him. When he grabbed the fish, he did not discard anything from [it], but ate the fish from the head to the tail.

And all of the people at that time were surprised. For he did not discard one bone from the fish, but ate the bones. And the fish bones inside were very soft, and he ate them.

And the people said, "What will happen when night comes? Where will we flee to? When we do not know the medicine" [for curing the *mejenkwaad*].

Some of the people said, "We will treat the possessed *mejenkwaad*. We will just try!"

When he had finished the fish, the crazed young man said, "I am hungry for [crave] a pregnant woman."

And the people tried to bring the number one medicine for *mejenkwaad*.

But it did not cure the crazed youth. After just two days, he died. And later when he appeared to people, they became ill.[7]

And they spread the word from Āne-Ļaṃōj to Ujae and some other islands that a young man died on Āne-Ļaṃōj from having gone to Alle.

And there was a demon on Alle. The name of this demon inside [Alle] revealed her name herself as Likināne. And we say that no canoes should go to Alle.

And young men from the main island of Ujae heard and did not believe. And they said, "We will go to Alle tomorrow and [or] the day after tomorrow."

And after three days, a canoe sailed from Ujae, [with] six men [aboard]. When the canoe was far from Alle, they saw people walking on the sand. And they said, "Those people came from Āne-Ļaṃōj. It is clear that what they talked about was false." When they came closer, they did not see any of those people.

And the men in the canoe said, "Those people are in the interior of the island." When they arrived, they disembarked but did not see people. But they heard a sound. It said, *"Eotōktok ilikin Alle. | Im bwiji āne eo. | Kajabuk likin āne."* ("Drift ashore on the ocean side of Alle. | And set foot on the island. | Land on the ocean side of the island.")

And the young men hurried to sail. And they now knew that it was true. No one was ill.

And a canoe sailed from Epāju, [with] five men, and went to Āne-Ļaṃōj. When they drew alongside Alle, they saw people walking on the sand.

And when the canoe came closer to Alle, they did not see any people walking. But at this time, a young man on the canoe became crazed.

When he was crazed, the young man said, *"Eotōktok ilikin Alle. | Im bwiji āne eo. | Kajabuk likin āne."* ("Drift ashore on the ocean side of Alle. | And set foot on the island. | Land on the ocean side of Alle.") The young man said, "My name is Likināne."

(If [there are] two [people], she [the demon] does not damage [them]. If three,

7. When his spirit returned.

she damages one. If four, she does not damage. If five, she damages one. If six, she does not damage one. If seven, she can damage one. I do not know why, but it is like this. As it says in the stories.)

And they went and reached Āne-Ļaṃōj. And the people on Āne-Ļaṃōj said, "That young man there who was gone is dead."

And they said, "Will there be a way that he will live?"

And some of the people on Āne-Ļaṃōj said, "We have treated [a] *mejenkwaad,* but he did not live."

And they hurried to sail to the main island. And the crazed person said, "If there were only four people in the canoe, well, I would never have damaged the young man. But when five, well, I would eat one!"

And they reached the main island and they used divination to find what the best medicine would be (pandanus-leaf divination).[8] And they found three green, [and] three red leaves of the *kañal* [*Pisonia grandis,* a tree.]

They [had] just found the medicine, but the crazed young man was dead.

Later a man went [away] from the main island of Ujae. The name of that man was Bōrraan. And two young men [went] with him. And the canoe sailed, just when it was morning, and went to Epāju. And Bōrraan took three red [and] three green leaves of *kañal* and crushed them by rubbing them between the palms of his hands.

When the leaves were in small pieces, he called the young men to him and massaged them with the *kañal* leaves, and massaged himself. When Bōrraan was finished, he said, "You two sail, but I am remaining to see if the *mejenkwaad* they said is on the island is for real [actually exists]."

And the two men sailed to Āne-Ļaṃōj, but Bōrraan remained.

And he [had] heard about what the men had done before.

And Bōrraan did the same again, for he wanted Likināne to appear. Bōrraan now made a fire. And Likināne appeared to Bōrraan.

And this time, when the woman appeared, Bōrraan was quick to take three coconut shoots and set fire to one. And he waited for Likināne to come to him (for she was far away). When she neared Bōrraan, he took the heated coconut shoot and stood and burned Likināne. Then Likināne fled, and Bōrraan pursued her.

[He] pursued [her] away, and Likināne went under a piece of coral that had drifted and come ashore there. And Bōrraan lifted the piece of coral.

When he lifted the piece of coral and rolled it away from where it had been, Bōr-

---

8. The traditional pharmacopoeia is extensive. Preparations of plant materials are used; these are ingested or applied externally according to the specific illness or need. Massage, usually with coconut-oil-based preparations, is often performed. Special treatment has been developed for prenatal and postnatal care. Magical formulae, chants, and songs may be part of the treatment of illnesses, and they are still used by *ri-wūno* (medicine men/women). Such treatment gives psychological support, in addition to the physiological benefits that the patient may receive. The patients have confidence in the ability of the specialists and in the traditional method of healing.

The adaptable and pragmatic Marshallese may use three methods to help the patient: traditional medicine, Western medicine, and religion (prayers, Bible reading, and hymn singing). The latter also give psychological support. These methods may be, and often are, combined.

The medical authorities in the Marshalls have wisely not tried to prevent access to the traditional methods of healing, and the Nitijeļā (the Marshallese legislative body) has officially recognized the value of Marshallese medicine: Nitijeļā resolution number 28, 1971, "Requesting that the department of Health Services in the Marshall Islands seek ways by which Marshallese medicine could be applied on patients at the hospital" (adopted 4/8/71).

raan saw bones, the bones of Likināne. And he took the coconut shoots and laid them down on the bones, and set fire to them. And [he] brought many coconut fronds and burned the bones.[9]

And he went from there when the bones were finished [burned up] and gone. And he went to lie down a bit, and rested a short while [before] the canoe came. And he boarded it and told the men that he had finished burning up Likināne.

And Likināne lost her power and [now] only appears. However, a big wind blows the woman like [a piece of] cloth because she has no bones.

It is ended.

(And when she appears, she does not eat people. Women only become ill, but they do not die.

But men do not become ill, even a little bit.[10] But women take medicine from the leaves of the *kañal:* three red and three green. And [when] treated, they become well.

People see her [the demon] on Alle to this day.)

There are many *mejenkwaad* in a few atolls [islands] in the Marshalls—in all of the atolls of the Marshalls.

There is one on Mājro named Limejobren. And there is one on Wōtto named Likrabjel. There are *[mejenkwaad]* on some places and each has a name. They have bones, but only on Ujae do they not have bones.

There are some *mejenkwaad* that can stretch out their necks and chests and eat pregnant women only.

---

9. We see the destruction of the evil spirit by burning, and the victory of the hero—the triumph of good over evil. This is a common theme in Marshallese folktales, and in other cultures as well. The incineration of the threating evil entity has a dramatic quality to it, and means final and complete removal of the dangerous being, or loss of power, as in the story. The hero, Bōrraan, figures in other tales, including story 1, "The Beginning of This World" (page 11), and story 2, "Story about Bōrraan" (page 37).

10. The distinction is made between the sexes in regard to acquisition of the illness, and immunity from it. The *mejenkwaad* concept may be based upon anxieties of women (and their relatives) during pregnancy. The mortality rate of both mothers and babies may have been quite high. This would be especially true if complications developed. As Pukui, Haertig, and Lee (1972, vol. 2: 7–8) have correctly pointed out, "Anxieties during pregnancy are common. Pregnant woman have both vague anxiety feelings and quite specific fears that they may die during delivery, and that the coming child may be abnormal or deformed or stillborn." While this was in reference to women in contemporary Hawai'i, it might very well be applicable to Marshallese culture as well.

The ability of the *mejenkwaad* to stretch out their necks and chests for long distances has an analogue in Hawaiian mythology. "Kana is a famous stretching kupua or wizard who can extend himself to the sky and who has five alternate, nonhuman bodies. [He is a shapeshifter.] His adventures are varied and extravagant, and Kana's stretching contest with a magic hill is told in several versions" (Kirtley and Mookini 1979:67). Reference is made to Beckwith (1970: chap. 33, "The Kana Legend").

Belief in predatory female shapeshifters exists in the Philipines, far to the west of the Marshalls. "For weeks, the slums of Manila's Tondo district have been abuzz with the rumors that a 'manananggal', a supernatural creature similar to the vampires of European mythology, has been terrorizing the area. According to Filipino folklore, a 'manananggal' appears as a woman who can cut her body in two. The top half flies around at night searching for babies to devour. The top half must return before daybreak to move around like regular folks" (*Honolulu Advertiser,* May 8,1992; Robert H. Reid, Associated Press, Manila).

40: BWEBWENATO IN JUON MEJENKWAAD

Ri-bwebwenato: Jelibōr Jam, Kuwajleen 1975

Juōn kōrā ar petok im eọtōk. Armej raar kūtim kōn jaki. Im lukwōje im kōpeļọkwe.

Kōrā eo ejjab alikkar ijo ej itok jāne. Ak ke ej eọtōk tok ilo juon āne etan āne eo Alle, ilo aelōñ in Ujae, ejjeļọk juon armej ar lo an eọtōk. Ak etto an pād iuṃwin juon boñ ipārijet.

Juōn raan ruo eṃṃaan rejro jerak jān Āne-Ļaṃōj ilo aelōñ in Ujae in etal in rōjep (eọñwōd jojo).

(Ke rej kōjerbal rōjep rej kōjerbal joñoul ñeñe in eo arṃwe eoon wa [eo] emaroñ ļalem bōkā im juon kāāj ilo juon bōkā. Ejjab eọñwōd kōn eo.

Rejjab kōjerbal rōjep raan kein. Ak raar kōṃṃan ilo iien Jepaan.

Kāāj rej kōṃṃan jān ļat in ni. Im joļọk juon im juon.

Innām ke jojo rej kañe, armej rej aini.

Ke ejjeļọk bōkā rej kōjerbal ļain. Etan eọñwōd kōn bōkā kōbbōkāke.)

Kōn an pāātļọk rejro ṃōkaj in bwillọke wa eo waerro; innām rejro jerak ñan Alle. (Kōnke Āne-Ļaṃōj ekanooj nana. Eļap wōd āinwōt ar in Mājeej.)

Wūnin aerro jerak rejro etal in kappok mọọrerro baru (barulep).

Ke rejro poļọk Alle ļeo juon ej ṃōkaj in kappok baru ak ļeo juon ej entak ni. Ke ļeo ej lo elōñ baru ej aikuj kōmat kijeerro baru. Ļeo juon eṃōj an entak im ej bōktok ni ko. Im ba ñan ļeo juon, "Idaak ni ļe! Ak eļañne eor addi eņ emat letok juon kijō. Bwe ña in ṃōñā. Ak lew[ōj] juon liṃōṃ ni im idaak!"

Innām ļeo juon ej jijet iwetaan kijeek eo. Im ļeo juon ej jijet ituiōñ in kijeek eo. Im ṃōñā baru.

Rejro ja ṃōñā wōt ak rejro lo juon annañ in armej ej pād iturin kijeek [eo]. Aļ epād turear im annañ [eo] ekanooj in alikkar. (Bōlen rualitōk im men awa ilo jibboñ.)

Ke rejro loe reilbōk. Im mijak eļap ippāerro. Ilo iien in annañ in ej kwaļọk ainikien im kalikkar etan. Im ej al im ba, "Eotōktok ilikin Alle. | Im bwiji āneo. | Kajabuk likin āne. | Likin āne. | Likin āne-e-e!" (Ilo kajin etto "bwiji āne" ej 'juuri āne eo', im "kajabuk" ej 'le-ānetak': bwidej ilo āne eo.)

Innām ļōṃaro rejro jutak jān doon im ettōr ñan wa eo waerro im jerak. Ak rejro jab erreilik bwe remijak. Ak rejjab kōnono ñan doon. Ke rejro tōpar wa eo rejro kaiur im jek to eo iṃaan wa eo im aōņōōņ metoļọk im jerak. Im etal ñan Āne-Ļaṃōj.

Ke rejro tōparļọk Āne-Ļaṃōj eṃṃaan ro ie kab kōrā ro rej itok ñan ippāerro im kappok jojo. Innām rej kajjitōk, "Eor ke koņamiro ļōṃa?" Rejro uwaak, "Ejjeļọk." Innām armej ro rej ba, "Ta wūnin ke ekanooj eṃṃan lañ?"

Innām rejro ba, "Eor juon tiṃoņ kijoñjoñ eaar waļọk ñan kemro." Armej ro rejjab tōmak. Ak rej ba, "Kōnke koṃro ejjab eṃṃaan!"

Innām likao ro rej illu ak ejjeļọk aer maroñ. Innām rejro ba, "Ilju en ṃōk etal ruo ak jilu eṃṃaan ñan Alle. Awa eo jibboñtata."

Innām raan eo juon jilu eṃṃaan rej etal im bwillọkwe wa eo im jerak ñan Alle. Ke rej tōprak Alle ļōṃaro ruo rej kōṃṃan kijeek āinwōt ṃokta.

Ak ļeo juon ej entak ni. Meļan ļọk jidik rejjab lo annañ in Likināne. Ak juon ainikien rej roñ. Ej ba, "Eotōktok likin Alle. | Im bwiji āne eo. | Im kajabuk Likināne."

Ļeo juon ej ba, "Eoļe Likināne in!" Wūnin an ba Likināne ej kōṃṃan āinwōt ainikien eo ba. Ak raar jaje etan kōrā in. Ak wūnin aer jeļā kōnke ainikien eo ej kalikkare.

Likao eo juon ej mijak im udeakeak. Im ekanooj in ļap an nañinmej.

Im ļōmaro ruo rej bōk likao eo juon im etal ñan wa eo im jepļaak ñan Āne-Ļaṃōj.

Ke ej wōnmetoļoķ wa eo likao eo ebwebwe ej ba, "Inañin kañ koṃro wōt jidik!"

Innām likao ro ruo rej likūt mijak ņae ippāerro. Innām likao eo eudeakeak ej ba, "Koṃro lale ṃōk āne. Ke ekanooj lōñ armej ie."

Im likao ro ruo rej erreiloķ ñan Alle. Im ļak lale ekanooj lōñ kōrā rej etetal ioon bok.

Innām likao eo ebwebwe ej ba, "Ekwe ña eņ eta Likināne, Likināne. Koṃro kaiur koṃro bwe ñe aļ epād ioļap, ṃool inaaj kañ koṃro. Im kañ wa in!"

Innām likao eo juon ej mijak ak ej kate wōt. Im dāpiji likao eo ebwebwe bwe ej ilān kāļoķ loјet. Likao eo juon ej ba, "Alikkar ke mejenkwaad men ņe!"

Innām mejenkwaad in eṃṃaan ej baj pen unoke. Likao ej make kōnono ippān, "Wōn ej ba en mour?"

Innām rej tōprak Āne-Ļaṃōj. Innām likao eo ebwebwe ej ikkūr āneļoķ im ba, "Inaaj kañ!" Im aolep armej rej ba, "Alikkar ke likao ro ṃokta raar ṃool!"

Innām likao ro ruo rej bōk āneļoķ ļeo ebwebwe im rej itok ñan ippān armej ro i Āne-Ļaṃōj.

Jotaan eo wōt likao eo ebwebwe ej ba ekōņaan ṃōñā ek. Ak ren jab kōmat.

Im rej bōktok juon bwebwe jotanļoķ eo wōt. Ke rej bōktok likao eo ebwebwe ej jerkak im ba ren bōktok ek eo. Im rej bōktok ñan ippān. Im leļoķ ñan ippān. Im leļoķ ñane. Ke ej jibwe eaar jab joļoķ jidik jān ek eo. Eaar kañ ek eo jān bōran im etal ñan ļokan.

Im aolep armej ilo iien eo rej bwilōñ. Bwe eaar jab joļoķ juon di jān ek eo ak kañ di ko im rekanooj in pidodo ilowaan kañe di ko.

Innām armej ro rej ba, "Enaaj kōjkan ñe eboñ? Jenaaj ko ñan ia? Ke jejaje unoke."

Jet iaan armej rej ba, "Jenaaj unokan mejenkwaad e ṃōk. Jenaaj baj kajjeoñ!"

Ilo wōt iien eo ke ej mat ek eo likao eo eudeakeak ej ba, "Ijol bōrǫro!" Innām armej ro rej kajjeoñ bōktok unokan mejenkwaad eo kein ka juon.

Ak eaar jab mour likao eo eudeakeak. Ālkin wōt ruo raan emej. Innām ilowaan likao eo waļoķ ñan armej, armej rej nañinmej.

Innām rej kōnnaanļoķ jān Āne-Ļaṃōj ñan Ujae im āne ko jet. Ke emej juon likao i Āne-Ļaṃōj itok jān an kar etal ñan Alle.

Innām ewōr juon tiṃoņ i Alle. Etan tiṃoņ in ilowaan kwaļoķ etan make, Likināne. Innām kemij ba bwe en ejjeļoķ wa eņ, en etal ñan Alle.

Innām likao ro jān eonene in Ujae rej roñ im jab tōmak. Ak rej ba, "Jenaaj ṃōk kajjeoñ in etal ñan Alle ilju im jōkļaj."

Innām ļokun jilu raan ejerak juon wa jān Ujae, jiljino eṃṃaan. Ke ej etoļoķ wa eo jān Alle rej lo an armej etetal ioon bok. Im rej ba, "Armej raņ rej itok jān Āne-Ļaṃōj. Alikkar ke riab men eo raar ba kake." Ke wa eo ej epaakļoķ ejjeļoķ armej rej loe.

Innām ļōṃaro i wa eo rej ba, "Armej ro repād ibuļōn āne." Ke rej po ļoķ rej to im etetal ak rejjab ellolo armej. Ak rej roñ ainikien, ej ba, "Eotōktok ilikin Alle. | Im bwiji āne eo. | Kajabuk likin āne."

Innām ļōṃaro rej kaiur er in jerak. Innām rej kab jeļā ke ṃool. Ejjeļoķ enañinmej.

Innām ejerak juon wa jān Epāju, ļalem eṃṃaan. Im iloķ ñan Āne-Ļaṃōj. Ke rej etal iturin Alle ļoķ rej lo an armej etetal ioon bok.

Im ke rej epaakļoķ Alle ejjeļoķ armej rej lo an etetal. Ak iien eo wōt eṃōkaj an udeakeak juon likao i wa eo.

Ke ej udeakeak likao eo ej ba, "Eotōktok ilikin Alle im bwiji āne eo. | Kajbuk likin āne." Likao eo ej ba, "Eta in Likināne!"

(N̄e ruo ejjab kọkkure, n̄e jilu ekọkkure juon. N̄e emān ejjab kọkkure. N̄e ļalem ekọkkure juon. N̄e jiljino ejjab kọkkure juon. N̄e jiljilimjuon emaron̄ kọkkure juon. Ijaje ta wūnin ak āinwōt. Āinwōt ej ba ilo bwebwenato.)

Innām rej etal wōt im tōprak Āne-Ļaṃōj. Innām armej ro i Āne-Ļaṃōj rej ba, "Ejja mej eo an likao eo ejako wōt ṇe."

Jet iaan armej i Āne-Ļaṃōj rej ba, "Kem ar unokan mejenkwaad ak ejjab mour."

Innām rej ṃōkaj kake in jerak n̄an eonene. Innām armej eo eudeakeak ej ba, "Eļan̄n̄e kar emān wōt armej i wa eo. Ekwe ijāmin kar kọkkure likao in. Ak ke ļalem. Ekwe inaaj ṃōn̄ā juon!"

Innām rej tōpar eonene im rej bubu ta uno eṃṃan. (Bubu in maan̄.) Im rej lo, jilu maroro, jilu būrōrō bōlōkin kan̄al.

Rej kab lo uno eo ak emej likao eo eudeakeak.

Tokālik ej etal juon eṃṃaan jān eonene in Ujae. Etan ļein Bōrraan. Kab ruo likao ippān. Im eaar jerak wa eo ke ej jibbon̄ wōt im etal n̄an Epāju. Innām Bōrraan ej bōk jilu burōrō, jilu maroro in bōlōkin kan̄al. Im itieoi ṇa ilo pein.

Ke ej tipdikdik bōlōk ko ej kūrtok likao ro ruo im kapiti erro kōn bōlōkin kan̄al ko.

Im kapiti e make. Ke ej ṃōj Bōrraan ej ba, "Ren jel jerak n̄an Alle." Ke rej poļọk Alle ej ba, "Koṃro jerak, ak n̄a ij pādwōt in lale ke mejenkwaad eo raar ba ioon āniin."

Innām ļōṃaro ruo rej jerak n̄an Āne-Ļaṃōj ak Bōrraan ej pādwōt. Innām eaar ron̄ kōn wāween ko ļōṃaro ṃokta raar kōṃṃane.

Innām Bōrraan ej bar kōṃṃan āinwōt bwe ekōṇaan bwe en waļọk Likināne. Bōrraan ejja kōṃṃan wōt kijeek, Likināne ej waļọk tok n̄an ippān Bōrraan.

Iien eo ke lio ej itok n̄an ippān Bōrraan, Bōrraan ej ṃōkaj in bōk jilu utak. Im tile eo juon. Im kōttar tok Likināne. (Bwe ej ettoļọk.) Iien eo ke ej epaake Bōrraan, Bōrraan ej bōk utak eo, ebwil im jutak im tile Likināne. Iien eo ke Likināne ej ko. Innām Bōrraan ej lukọrkọre Likināne.

Lukọrkọre ļọk innām edeļon̄ Likināne iuṃwin bar eo eaar petok im eọtōk ie. Innām Bōrraan ej ukōj bar eo.

Ke ej ukōjļọk bar eo im dāpilļọk jān ijo eaar pād ie, Bōrraan ej lo di ko di in Likināne. Innām ej letok utak ko, im likūti ṇa ioon di ko, im tili. Im bōktok elon̄ kimej im tile di ko.

Im etal jān ijo ke ej maat di ko, im jako. Im ilān babu jidik. Im kakkije meļan ļọk jidik ej itok wa eo im ej uwe ie im ba n̄an ļōṃaro ke eṃōj an tile Likināne.

Innām Likināne ejako an kajoor ak raan kein ej waļọk wōt. Ijoko kōto eļap uki lieņ āinwōt nuknuk kōnke ejjeļọk di.

Ejeṃļọk.

Ak ṃōṃaan rejjab nan̄inmej n̄an jidik. Ak kōrā rej bōk uno jān bōlōkin kan̄al jilu bōrōrō im jilu maroro im unoke rej mour.

Armej ro rej lo ilo Alle wōt n̄an rainin.

Eor elon̄ mejenkwaad ilo [ko] jet aelōn̄ in Ṃajeļ; ilo aolep aelōn̄ in Ṃajeļ. Eor i Mājro etan Limejōkraņ. Innām eor ilo Wōtto etan Likrabjel. Eor ijoko jet jikin in eor kajjo etāer.

Eor di ippāer ak ilo Ujae wōt ejjeļọk di.

Eor jet mejenkwaad remaron̄ kaitokļọk kōnwaer im ubweer im kan̄e kōrā bōrọro wōt.

41: MEJENKWAAD STORY FROM ĀNEWETAK

As told by Irooj Joanej, Wūjlañ 1955

Mejenkwaad are female demons (*tiņoņ*). They affect (possess) women during pregnancy and after they have given birth.

There have been many cases of this in the Marshall Islands. A mouth can open up at the base of the affected person's neck. [He indicated the location of the *medulla oblongata.*] The neck can expand and stretch out to another island. And she can eat people: anyone, any sex or age, especially her husband.

Possession will take place in a pregnant woman or up until her child's *keemem* [the important celebration of the child's first birthday, and of its surviving the crucial first year of life]. And it will take place if the woman is alone.

It is worse at night. Several people of any age or sex should be with her, preferably of the age of fourteen or fifteen years and upward.

The symptoms of *mejenkwaad* sickness *(nañinmej in mejenkwaad)* are as follows: Blood flows from between the teeth of the affected person. The eyes are wild and insane looking. The place at the back of the neck moves as if it is breathing.

If medicine is not applied, another mouth appears. Then it is too late, because the sick person goes out of her mind.

However, she may be cured by magical chants. But medicine *(wūno)* is useless.

All persons who die in childbirth become *mejenkwaad* and will even harm children.

Mejenkwaad medicine *(wūno in mejenkwaad)* is made from the roots of the *nen* [*Morinda citrifolia* L., a tree.] The medicine is drunk by the patient three times a day for three days, and is repeated if the patient is not well by then.

[Three is the ritual number in the Marshall Islands. And medical/magical treatments are done in series of threes.]

The patient is forbidden to leave her house during the course of the treatment.

The people of Ānewetak knew the medicine, but they learned it from a Marshallese castaway before the white men arrived. Ļato was his name.

The doctor (*ri-wūno*) used a frond of a coconut tree, like the kind we use to decorate our canoes. He waved it and sang a magical song. This is the second stage of the treatment *(ekkōpāl).*

The Marshallese also did this. [A man from Arņo Atoll who was present at the discussion confirmed this.]

This worked against any demon. This was done a little, day or night.

The doctor stands over the patient, who is covered with a mat. The frond is waved over the afflicted one, and the doctor chants: [a short four-line chant followed].[1]

Magic *(ekkōpāl)* is done if the patient becomes worse, and it is done in conjunction with the medicine.

The patient goes to sleep. Several songs may be sung. The patient is visited by the doctor two or three times a day until she becomes well.

A woman died in childbirth, with the baby inside her, on Ānewetak Island, years

1. I recorded the magical chant but do not include it in this presentation. It would not have been appropriate to do so.

ago. And she was buried in the evening and was seen the next day. She was seen day and night for one month. This was in the time of Chief Pita.

All of the people gathered in the house of the chief, because they were afraid at night. They could hear the demon clearing her throat.

The chief was not afraid. He stood outside all night, blowing the *jilel* [*Charonia tritonis,* trumpet shell] and chanting. The demon finally went away.

Any demon may enter a person, pregnant or with a small child. The woman may dream of a demon first, then treatment follows.

If she acts crazy and blood flows, treatment must be given immediately. This has happened in the past, but not very often. (The old power *[mōmō]* is disappearing. Demons do not show up very often nowadays.)

But women who do not know the magic must be very careful.

When the demon enters the woman, she is called a *mejenkwaad.* If she dies while carrying the child or after giving birth, she is called *mejenkwaad.*

Any woman who dies in childbirth is *mejenkwaad,* whether she was possessed by a demon or not.

Mejenkwaad always try to possess a pregnant woman or one with a baby. After the possessed woman dies, she is known as a *mejenkwaad.*[2]

2. There are similar hostile, dangerous, and aggressive supernatural female figures in Mexican folklore. "In Yucatan the wicked woman is the *x-tabai,* a demon of the woods. She appears at times young, beautiful, finely clad, with loose flowing hair, to lure a man into the bush. If he cannot get away from her after she has revealed her true self, she chokes him to death. And the Llorona (La Llorona, the wailing woman) roams the streets of Mexico City, wailing for her children (whom she had murdered) and revenging herself on men. "No doubt the legend of the Llorona had its origin in some of those that have come down from the pre-Conquest days, in which the goddesses Cihuapipíltin, those who died when their first child was born, return to earth to harm children and adults. The Llorona also haunts all the other big cities of the Republic" (Toor 1950:531–532). The similarities between the goddesses Cihuapipíltin and the *mejenkwaad* are obvious. And the *x-tabai* also resemble some of the demons *(tiṃoṇ)* of Marshallese folklore.

42: MEJENKWAAD STORIES

As told by a Jalooj *aļap,* and others, Kuwajleen 1975

There have been many *mejenkwaad* in the Marshall Islands. They entered women during the Japanese times, but not in the American times, as far as I know. I saw this happen on Jebwad [Island], Jalwōj [Atoll] during the Japanese times.

The woman's mouth spits blood. The old man who knew said, "Give her *uno in mejenkwaad jān kañal*" [*mejenkwaad* medicine made from *kañal—Pisonia grandis,* a tree].

This was done, and the *mejenkwaad* was driven out of the woman. And she became as well as she was before the *mejenkwaad* entered her.

I think the reason for [there being] no *mejenkwaad* during the American times is that we go to church more nowadays.

There are no *mejenkwaad* on Epjā [Ebeye Island, Kuwajleen Atoll] that I know of.

Another informant, a young man living on Epjā and working on the Kuwajleen Missile Base, but originally from Aelōñļapļap Atoll, stated, "I have heard that there have been many *mejenkwaad* in the Marshall Islands, including during the American times. But I have never seen one."

An informant from Aelok Atoll, a Trust Territory employee, age fifty, stated: "There are no *mejenkwaad* or *lōrro* today because the Americans brought enlightenment. But there were in Japanese times and before. But many people believe in them today. Many people, including a minister and his wife whom I know, believe in demons."

I learned from Reverend Sasser [an Assemblies of God missionary] that demons are afraid of God and can be driven away by prayers.

The informant then referred to the incident described in the Bible when Jesus drove demons from a man who had been possessed by them into swine, thus healing him.[1]

This, the informant explained, is proof of the power of God to exorcise demons.

---

1. Mark 5:1–20, and also Matt. 8:28–34, expulsion of the devil in Gerasa (the Gerasene demoniac). Other instances of spirit possession and exorcism are narrated in the Bible. The transmission of Judeo-Christian beliefs in evil spirits by the missionaries may very well have reinforced the traditional Marshallese beliefs in malevolent supernatural entities. In the absence of scientific information, traditional beliefs in the Marshall Islands and elsewhere have functioned to explain misfortunes for which there was no apparent cause, and methods have been developed to cope with them. Exorcism, whether practiced in the Marshalls or the United States (as it is today) or elsewhere, obviously functions to relieve stress and in some cases feelings of guilt, and to alleviate psychosomatic illnesses.

43: A MEJENKWAAD ON ARŅO

As told by an Arņo man, Mājro 1955

My mother died in childbirth in 1947 on Arņo, and she tried to attack (in a dream) her sister about one month later. (The sister had given birth two weeks before the attempted attack.) She told her mother about the dream.

And my grandmother took water from the tops of beer bottles and decorated her (my mother's) grave,[1] and moistened the sister's forehead with it. She did this once a day for three days. The sister recovered.

The first night after my mother's burial, my father dreamt that she came to him and asked, "Why do you sleep well instead of looking after the baby?" And then she sang this song to him, "*Atitūñañ tūñañ i ilo iaļ in jerata in aō* | *buñ kūtuon aō walkeke to irōk to.* | *Ijako ilo iaio im melan ko ie.*" ("Baby hinting for food from mother's sister after mother died | wind blowing the sail when sailing to southern Ņadikdik[2] | I am away from the place, [my] home area, and the good times there.") (The tune came from a known song, but the words were originated from the demon.)

After singing the song she said, "Name the baby Atitūñañ." (This means 'eating little food', and is used when people come and eat after one another. *Tūñañ:* people hint for food by looking at it. One may call and say, *"Kwōn jab etal im tūñañ,"* an instruction to children. It is bad to *tūñañ.*)

My father was awakened by people who heard him groaning. If they had not awakened him, he would have been possessed by the *mejenkwaad (tūtiṃōņṃōņ)* and gone out of his mind. He then told the dream and sang the song, and everyone cried.

The baby was given another name, though. It died one year later. People thought that the baby had some of the mother's sickness. The child could not be a demon. Anyone who does not know sex *(men ko in laļ in)*[3] cannot be a demon.

This belief is from the Bible. But the custom or belief before the missionaries came was also that children could not be demons.

If any father had been possessed by the demon, a different kind of medicine *(wūno)* would have been used.

---

1. Empty bottles are placed upside down in the ground around graves to outline and decorate them.

2. Ņadikdik (Knox) Atoll, a small atoll adjacent to Mile in southern Ratak, was believed to be the final destination of the spirits of deceased Marshallese. They had to jump across a channel in the reef as a test of their worthiness to go to the other world *(Ep).* If they were worthy and not weighted down by their sins, they were able to pass the test. If not, they fell into the sea and were devoured by a monster. The motif of a special place of departure for the souls of the dead (a "leaping place") is found among other island people in the Pacific. See Beckwith (1970:144–163) for a discussion of this belief in Hawai'i and elsewhere in Polynesia. The belief in testing or judgment of souls is an ancient and widespread one and is part of the belief systems of major religions of today.

3. Translation: "things of this world," that is, worldly things (the theme of the innocence or purity of children). This belief is found in many other cultures. For example, in her discussion of traditional Mexican funerary rites and and associate beliefs, Toor (1950:160–163) explains that "the wakes for children are different. . . . This derives from the Catholic belief that young children are free from sins, and go straight to heaven. . . . The corpses are called angelitos, little angels. . . ." The Catholic burial mass for young children is called "The Mass of the Angels," and Islam teaches that all children who die before reaching the age of discretion go to Paradise.

44: MEJENKWAAD STORY AND LŌṂKEIN STORY

As told by Raymond DeBrum, Mājro 1952

Mejenkwaad means dead in childbirth. (Eaten up baby. The baby has been eaten by the mother.) They are always dangerous and will return to haunt people. They will cause people to become insane.

They are wandering demons *(wōneṇak)*. They are not stationary and may not be avoided.

Doctors may cure the effects of this; special Marshallese doctors *[ri-wūno]*. *Mejenkwaad* are found all over the Marshall Islands. The doctor must be of the same *bwij* [lineage] or *jowi/jou* [matriclan] as the *mejenkwaad*.

Mejenkwaad may be heard crying at night. They will attack day or night. They strike part of the body—slap it. The part hit will become sore.

Lōṃkein was thrown into the sea after *bubu* [divination with folded pandanus leaves] was made, and which said not to bury her on land because she would hurt people.

She was taken out in a canoe ten miles from land. Rocks were tied to her. She floated on the surface until three in the afternoon.

Her son spoke to the corpse and told her that they were tired and hungry. So she sank.

E. and J. [two young Marshallese males] saw two *mejenkwaad*, Lōṃkein and Wōdejebato, one hour apart.[1]

These *mejenkwaad* had lived on Ujae and on Roñļap Atoll, and died with their child inside them.

The men talked to themselves. They were frightened and were out of action for the next day. They yelled and screamed, and tried to run outside and chase the spirits. It took four people to hold them down.

1. During the early part of the American administration of the islands.

45: STORY OF LŌM̧KEIN

As told by Jelibōr Jam, Kuwajleen 1975

Lōm̧kein was a chiefess who looked after all her commoners and lineage heads very well. She had three or four children. And later she was again pregnant, and at the time when she went to give birth, because some of the chiefesses talked against her, they made magic against her so that she could not deliver her child.

And she was prevented from delivery by magic, for maybe six months. And one night she went to die. And she arose and again lay down and went to sleep. And when she slept, a child was born and died. At that time, because she had suffered so long, they said that Lōm̧kein was dead. And they looked and were surprised that she had arisen and eaten her child (only part of the child).[1]

And some of the old women made medicine for her. (In the ancient language, the meaning of *rupik* is 'to make medicine'.)[2] They fled. They stood up and ran. They were frightened. But some of them grabbed the child [of Lōm̧kein] from her, and laid it down on the ground, for it was dead. And Lōm̧kein stood and spoke and menaced the people. (She wanted to eat them.) At this time, blood flowed from her mouth and nose, and eyes, and ears.

And the people were very frightened. When it was after sunrise, Lōm̧kein lay down, for she died.

The people just sat in the house. And the spirit of Lōm̧kein departed, but her body remained inside the house.

Lōm̧kein spoke to one man; the man's name was Ļakatau. She said, "If you bury me, I will eat all the people in the Marshalls.[3] And from when it will be sunrise you will see me everywhere—on the branches of the breadfruit trees, and the branches of the coconut trees, and the branches of the pandanus trees. And anyone I want to kill, I will just kill them right away."

And Ļakatau replied, "O, do not harm your people. For they should not be destroyed."

And Lōm̧kein went away from Ļakatau. And she did not appear again from morning until after sunset, when the darkness had set in.

They just sat near the body, and Lōm̧kein walked on the road. And she frightened those who were walking in the night at this time and who saw her.

Because of their fear, none of the people walked in the night. And those who sat inside the house beside the body heard the voice say, "I will eat you! When I kill you."

And right on that day, she killed the

1. Note the cannibalistic motif, specifically the highly abnormal act of eating one's child. This enhances the dramatic quality of the story and adds a note of horror that audiences everywhere seem to enjoy. The motif of a cannibalistic ogress is a widespread one (see Leach 1949:816 for description and distribution).

2. This story illustrates the use the Marshallese made of sorcery (black magic) and magic to counteract the harmful magic. Magic to obtain a favorable result was also practiced. Special rituals including oral formulae, usually chanted, were performed. Such attempts to use the supernatural to attain one's desired result are still made, apparently, but probably to a much lesser degree than in times past.

3. Note the incorporation of the modern name M̧ajeļ (Marshall) in this story—in the Marshallese narration and text that follow.

women. And they died. When it was after noon, Ļakatau made magic with pandanus leaves *(bubu kōn maañ)*[4] and sought where would be a good place to bury her (Lōm̧kein). But all of the places were bad. And they again made magic to cast her adrift on the sea. But it was not good (the magic revealed).

When it was three o'clock, she again ate a child.

And that evening they made the pandanus leaf magic to see if it would be good or bad to tie a rope around her and cast her adrift in the sea.

And there was nothing that they could do (the pandanus leaf magic said). But they went out and cast her adrift.

And they loaded her aboard a canoe and rowed seaward from Lae [Atoll] about thirty or twenty-five miles to sea.

When it was four o'clock, they had reached there, perhaps five miles, or twenty, or thirty miles. And they tied a thirty pound rock around her neck.[5] (They wrapped up Lōm̧kein in a mat.)

They tied the rock to her. And they put it down into the sea.[6] They then looked and saw that she did not sink. But she just floated like the canoe.

And the men jumped over onto Lōm̧kein and stood on her. But she did not submerge. And when the sun was setting, about six feet above the water, Ļakatau said, "What are you doing now, my child?"—he asked Lōm̧kein. "For the sun will set in just a little while. And the island is very far away, and when it becomes dark we will never see the islands, for a cloud is coming down from the sky. There will be a great deal of wind and rain."

And Lōm̧kein circled at the opposite side of the canoe [the side without the outrigger].

A short while later she stopped and went down, head first.

They looked at her and she was gone. And when they returned toward the island, it began to rain; there was a lot of wind. And Ļakatau spoke again , "My child. Look here, there is a lot of wind, and we will never reach the island.

"What will happen now? For it is dark, and we cannot see the islands."

A short while later, they saw a fire that appeared across from the island.

And a short while later, the wind lessened, and the rain lessened, and they went straight to the fire.

When they saw the island, the fire was gone, and there was a lot of rain. The wind was right, and when they reached the island—the name of the island was Looj, on Lae—the wind was extremely strong and the rain was very heavy. And they went ashore and slept, perhaps one or two hours that night. When they were sleeping, Ļakatau spoke, and those next to him heard him speaking with Lōm̧kein. For Lōm̧kein said, "Did you see the fire last night?"

And Ļakatau said, "Yes, I saw it."

Lōm̧kein again said, "Did you see the wind decrease and the rain decrease? Well, I made the fire for a navigation sign to the island. And when the wind decreased, it was I again who made it decrease. And the rains, when they decreased, it was I who made

4. *Bubu in maañ:* divination, foretelling the future by means of folding pandanus leaves and interpreting the resulting folds according to an established code. See footnote 6 on page 174.

5. Note the use in this and other Marshallese folktales of English loanwords for measuring and weighing objects and for reckoning time. They are easily recognizable in most cases. For example, *bo̧un* (pound), *batōm* (fathom), *awa* (hour)—eight o'clock is literally "eight hour" *(ruwalitōk awa),* etc.

6. Burial at sea was one of the traditional methods of disposal of a corpse (see Krämer and Nevermann 1938:308–213 for traditional Marshallese funerary rites).

them decrease. And you just come here tomorrow, very early in the morning, and pull me out from within that pool on the ocean side. For I am very cold."

When it was morning, Ļakatau awakened, and some of the young men rowed seaward. And they said to Ļakatau, "You were very fast in awakening and getting up and standing up and going out to the well."

Ļakatau replied, "[That was] because I heard a voice last night. It said 'Be speedy in going to the ocean side.'"

The young men said, "We will go with you there." And Ļakatau said, "Well, I will go fast. But you go slowly!"

And Ļakatau went toward the ocean side. When he got there, Lōm̧kein was sitting inside the pool and combing her hair with her hands. (She had cast off the mat.)

And Ļakatau stood and was very surprised. And called the young men, his companions, to come and see Lōm̧kein inside the pool. And the young men came and stood and saw Lōm̧kein within the pool. And they were also surprised. And Ļakatau said to the young men, "You just stand there! For I am going to speak with Lōm̧kein."

And Ļakatau went toward the ocean. When he was going, Lōm̧kein turned around and looked toward the ocean.

And Ļakatau continued on. He was very frightened. Even though he was frightened, he persevered and went on. When he stood close to Lōm̧kein, he said, "My child, why are you like this? For we are greatly afraid of you now. For you [have] changed into a demon, and you are a demon now."

And Lōm̧kein changed into a stone, and floated inside the pool. She did not go to the bottom. There was a lot of water, and she just floated.

And Ļakatau took the stone, and went to the island with it. He put it on the branch of a *ut* [*Guettarda speciosa,* a tree], and went to the house. And the young men, his companions [went with him].

And they talked about the way Lōm̧kein had appeared to the three of them.

When the three of them had just reached the house, they looked at the branch of the breadfruit tree, [and saw] an octopus crawling up it.

And the men were surprised. And one of them ran and brought people there so that they would come and see the octopus. For this was the first time that they had seen such a thing.

And the man said to the people, "Come and see the octopus on the branch of the breadfruit tree." And the people said, "There is not one thing of the sea that can climb up a branch of a breadfruit tree, or pandanus, or coconut tree. You are lying."

And the man said, "For this is the first time you will see this kind of thing. Come here!"

And the old people remained there. But the young women and young men ran with the man, and when they got there, the octopus was still on the branch of the breadfruit tree.

And some of the girls again returned and told the people that they should go to see it. And when they got there, the octopus was still there, from morning until noon.

Some of the young men went to bring the octopus and eat it.

When they reached the octopus, they saw that it only had six tentacles and a small head; very long tentacles (perhaps one and a half fathoms long), but a small head.

Because this was the first time that they had seen anything like this, they were afraid to eat it. So that they did not eat it. And it remained there until it would leave on its own.

When it was sunset, it was still there. And they watched to see when it would leave.

When the sun rose, in the morning, it was still there. They watched it closely to see where it would go. When it was eight o'clock or so, they did not know where it went. And they did not know that it was Lōm̧kein.

And Lōm̧kein did not cease talking to Ļakatau, but she did not speak to the people.

Later that evening, the octopus walked about and frightened people, and spoke to them when they were asleep. (It made the people dream.) "When you see the octopus, you will know that it is I, Lōm̧kein. And cats[7] and any kind of animal: pigs, dogs, and other such creatures.

"And I will harm the people with poison coral."

(Lōm̧kein lives on poison coral and likes to rub this on people. The name of the coral is *wōdidid* 'rubbing coral'.[8] There is much of this coral in the Marshalls: Lae, Ujae, and Kuwajleen. It is brownish-yellow and burns the skin, and one cannot speak.

The Marshallese believe that Lōm̧kein causes this sickness.[9] There is Marshallese medicine against this sickness.)

And none of the people on Lae walked about in the evening. In the daytime, not even one person walked about alone. But they had to go out two by two. Even though two of the people were walking in the daytime, Lōm̧kein could harm both of them.

And only one person made the people well on Lae. His name was Ļakatau. (He did not administer medicine, but he just took hold of them and they became well.)

Six nights later, Lōm̧kein began to walk about on the atoll of Ujae, and again harmed people. At this time, Ļakatau worked hard to cure people. After some time, she told Ļakatau that she would go to all the atolls in the Marshalls. Also, that she would be on every canoe that sailed on the ocean or on the lagoon.

And Lōm̧kein obeyed one more person, the *irooj* (chief) Jipe. (She obeyed Ļakatau and Jipe only, to this day.)

And Jipe finished making medicine, and gave it to all of the atolls in Rālik. However, it was not effective for those for whom it was not appropriate to take medicine of Lōm̧kein. But the medicine of Lōm̧kein was effective for those for whom it was appropriate to take this medicine [for the sickness caused by Lōm̧kein].

And Lōm̧kein said, "I will walk about on all of the atolls in Ratak and the atolls in Rālik anytime."

The story is ended.

In 1907, Lōm̧kein was very strong in damaging people. She appeared as a real human being. She appeared in all of Ratak and Rālik. And all of the people did not see her.

These days, she does not appear. But there is sickness that comes from her. The name of the sickness is *lennab* (rash or hives). And there is medicine for *lennab.*

There were children of Lōm̧kein. The name of the oldest male was Ļakalep, a real human being.

When Lōm̧kein was a human being, she gave birth to him. He was not a demon. And there is the medicine of Ļakalep. It came from him. And he taught the people.

My grandfather learned medicine against the sickness of Lōm̧kein. He learned this medicine from Jipe who was a chief in Rālik, [and] who lived before Kabua.

---

7. Note the use in the story of the cat *(kuuj),* an animal introduced to the islands relatively recently.

8. Perhaps this is *Millepora alcicornia* Linn., stinging or fire coral. According to Halstead (1959: 32), "This false coral is generally found living among true corals along reefs in the warm waters of the tropical Pacific."

9. Here is another example of the attribution of the etiology of an illness to the supernatural, in the absence of scientific information. Folklore functions to explain, and traditional medicine enables those affected by the illness to cope with it.

45: BWEBWENATO IN LŌM̧KEIN

Ri-bwebwenato: Jelibōr Jam, Kuwajleen 1975

Lōm̧kein eaar juon lerooj ekanooj in em̧m̧an an lale aolep kajoor kab aļap ro an.

Eor jilu ke emān nājin. Innām tokālik eaar bar bōrǫro im iien eo ke iten keotak kōn an lerooj ro jet bane raar jerake ñan nājin.

Im eaar kajjin im eñtaan ilo iien keotak eo an, iom̧win bōlen jiljino allōñ. Innām ilo juon boñ eaar iten mej. Innām eaar jerkak im bar babu im kikiļǫk. Ke ej kikiļǫk eļotak ajiri eo im mej. Liin kōn an to an eñtaan rej ba emej Lōm̧kein. Ak reļak ilbōk ej jerkak im kañ ajiri eo (m̧ōttan ajiri wōt).

Innām jet iaan leļļap ro rej rupik ñane. (Ilo kajin etto meļeļe in rupik ej kōm̧m̧an uno.) Rej ko. Rej jutak im ettōr. Remijak. Ak jet rej jibwetok ajiri eo (nejin Lōm̧kein) jāne. Im kababu ņa ioon laļ bwe emij. Ak Lōm̧kein ej jutak im ekkōnono ñan armej ro. (Ekōņaan kañ er.) Iien in ej tǫǫr bōtōktōk jān lǫñin im bǫtin kab mejān, kab lojilñiin.

Innām armej [ro] rekanooj in mijak. Ke [ej] joraanļǫk, Lōm̧kein ej babu bwe emej.

Armej ro rej jijet kake wōt ilowaan m̧weo. Ak an Lōm̧kein emootļǫk ak ānbwin ej pādwōt ilowaan m̧weo.

Lōm̧kein ej kōnono ñan juon em̧m̧aan; etan ļeo Ļakatau. Ej ba, "Eļañne kom̧ naaj kalbwin eō inaaj kañ aolep armej in M̧ajeļ in. Innām jān ñe enaaj tak aļ kom̧ naaj lo eō ilo jabdewōt jikin. Iraan mā, ak iraan ni, ak iraan bōb. Im jabdewōt eo ikōnaan m̧ane bwe āinwōt inaaj m̧ane."

Innām Ļakatau ej uwaak, "O, kwōn jab kǫkkure armej raņe am̧, bwe ren jab jorrāān."

Innām Lōm̧kein ej bar etal jān Ļakatau. Im ejjab bar waļǫk jān ke ej jibboñ [ñan] ke ej tulǫk ļǫk aļ. Im jok mārok eo.

Rej jijet wōt iturin wōt ānbwin eo ak an Lōm̧kein ej etetal ioon iiaļ. Im ro rej etetal in boñ iien eo rej loe ej kaamijak er.

Kōn aer mijak ejjeļǫk armej eaar etetal ilo boñ eo. Ak ro rej jijet ilowaan m̧weo iturin ānbwin eo rej roñjake ainikien an ba, "Inaaj kañ kom̧! Ña ijja m̧an kom̧!"

Innām ilo wōt raan eo eaar m̧an ruo kōrā. Im remej. Ke ej raelepļǫk Ļakatau ej bubu kōn maañ im pukot ijo ej em̧m̧an an kalbwine ņae. Ak enana eoļap jikin. Innām rej bar bubu ñan aer kōpeļǫke. Ak ejjab em̧m̧an. (Bubu ej ba.)

Ke ej jilu awa ebar m̧an juon ajiri.

Innām jotaan eo rej bubu im lo bwe em̧m̧an ak enana aer lukwōje im kōtalke.

Innām ejjeļǫk aer maroñ. (Bubu ej ba.) Ak rej ilǫk wōt im kōtalke.

Innām raar ektake ņae juon wa. Im aōņōōņ metoļǫk jān Lae, tarrin jilñuul ak roñoul-ļalem m̧ail metoļǫk.

Ke ej emān awa rej tōprakļǫk, bōlen ļalem m̧ail, ak roñoul, ak jiliñoul m̧ail. Innām rej lukwōj juon dekā jiljinoñoul bǫun eddoon. (Rej limi Lōm̧kein kōn jaki.) Rej lukwōj dekā ņa ippān. Im rej doorļǫk ņae ilǫjet.

Ļak lale ejjab pelaļļǫk. Ak ej eppepe wōt āinwōt wa eo. Innām ļōm̧aro rej kālǫk ñan eoon Lōm̧kein im jutak. Ak ejjab wōnlaļļǫk. Innām ke eiten tulǫk aļ, tarrin juon ñeñe aļ jān lǫjet, Ļakatau ej ba, "Kwōj et wōt nājū?" (Ej kajjitōk ippān Lōm̧kein.) "Ke enañin tulǫk aļ wōt jidik. Ak ettoļǫk āne innām ñe emarok kem jāmin lo āne ko. Bwe juon e kōdǫ ej pādlōñtak. Enaaj kanooj ļap kōto im wōt."

Innām Lōm̧kein ej errǫlǫǫl ikōjaan wa eo.

Meļan ļǫk jidik ej bōjrak im wōnlaļļǫk tubōran.

Raar lale ļǫk innām ejako. Innām ke rej rǫǫl ñan āne eo ejino an wōt im ļap kōto. Innām Ļakatau ej bar ba, "Nājū, lale ṃōk ke eļap kōto im kem jāmin tōprak āne.

"Enaaj kōjkan kiiō? Ke emarok im kem ejjab ellolo āne?"

Meļan ļǫk jidik rej lo juon kijeek ej waļǫk ikijjien āne eo. Innām edikļǫk jidik kōto. Kab edikļǫk wōt. Innām rej anōk kijeek eo.

Ke rej lo āne eo ejako kijeek eo. Ak eļap wōt. Ak kōto ej dik wōt. Innām ke rej tōprak āne, etan āne eo Looj (i Lae), ekanooj ļap kōto kab ļap an wōt. Innām rej wōnāneļǫk im kiki. Bōlen juon im ruo awa boñōn eo. Ke rej kiki ļǫk Ļakatau ej ekkōnono im ro iturin rej roñjake an kōnono ippān Lōṃkein. Bwe Lōṃkein ej ba, "Kwaar lo ke kijeek eo boñ?"

Innām Ļakatau ej ba, "Aet, iaar loe."

Lōṃkein ej bar ba, "Kwar lo ke an dikļǫk kōto kab dikļǫk wōt? Ekwe kijeek eo ña ij kōṃṃan kakōļļe ñan āne. Im ke edikļǫk kōto eo. Bar ña ij kōṃṃan bwe en dikļǫk. Kab wōt ko, ke ej dikļǫk ña eo ij kōṃṃan bwe ren dik. Innām kwōn kab itok ilju ej jibboñtata im kaatwe eō jān ilowaan ļwe eŋ ilik. Bwe eļap aō piǫ."

Ke ej jibboñ wōt Ļakatau ej ruj kab ro iaan likao ro raar aōŋōōŋ metoļǫk kake. Innām rej ba ñan Ļakatau, "Enañin ṃōkaj aṃ ruj im jutak im diwōj ñan aebōj."

Ļakatau ej uwaak, "Kōnke iaar roñ juon ainikien boñ. Ej ba, 'Kwōn kab eṃṃōkaj in wōnliktak.'"

Likao ro rej ba, "Kemij ro [kem ro ej] iwōj ippaṃ wōj." Innām Ļakatau ej ba, "Ekwe, ña ij eṃṃōkaj. Ak koṃro ej ebbat tok wōt!"

Innām Ļakatau ej wōnlikļǫk. Ļak ilǫk Lōṃkein ej jijet wōt ilowaan ļwe eo im kūrij bōran kōn pein. (Eṃōj juļǫk jaki eo.) Innām Ļakatau ej jutak im bwilōñ. Im kōttartok likao ro ṃōttan bwe ren iten lo Lōṃkein ilowaan ļwe eo. Innām likao ro rej itok im jutak im lo Lōṃkein ilowaan ļwe eo. Im rej bar bwilōñ. Innām Ļakatau ej ba ñan likao ro, "Koṃro jutak wōt ijōŋe! Bwe ña ij etal in kōnono ippān Lōṃkein."

Innām Ļakatau eaar wōnmetoļǫk. Ke ej etal, Lōṃkein ej oktak im jujālmetoļǫk.

Innām Ļakatau ej etal wōt. Ekanooj in mijak. Jekdǫǫn ñe emijak ak ej kate wōt im etal. Ke ej jutak iturin Lōṃkein ej ba, "Nājū, etke kwōj āinwōt ŋe? Ke kem kanooj mijak eok kiiō? Bwe eṃōj aṃ oktak ñan tiṃoŋ. Innām kwe kamanij kiiō."

Innām Lōṃkein ej erom juon dekā. Eļap dān ak ej eppepe wōt.

Innām Ļakatau ej bōk dekā eo. Im wōnāneļǫk kake. Im door ŋa iraan juon ut. Im etal ñan ṃweo. Kab likao ro ṃōttan.

Im rej kōnono kake wāween an waļǫk Lōṃkein ñan erjel.

Ke rejel tōprakļǫk wōt ṃweo ak reļak lale raan mā eo, juon kweet ej tōbal lōñļǫk ie.

Innām ļōṃaro rej bwilōñ. Innām juon iaer ej ettōr im pukot armej ro wōj bwe ren iten lale kweet eo. Bwe ej kab juon alen aer ellolo āinwōt in.

Innām ke ļeo ej ba ñan armej ro, "Koṃin itok in lale kweet eŋ iraan mā eŋ." Innām armej ro rej ba, "Ejjeļǫk juon menin lǫjet emaroñ tallōñ iraan mā, ak bōb, ak ni. Kwōj riab!"

Innām ļeo ej ba, "Bwe et ej kab juon alen ami naaj ellolo men rot in ke. Koṃin itok!"

Innām rūtto ro rej pādwōt. Ak jiroñ kab likao rej ettōr ippān ļeo im ļak ilǫk kweet eo ej pādwōt iraan mā eo.

Innām jet iaan kōrā ro rej bar jepļaak im bar ba ñan rūtto ro wōj bwe ren iten lale. Innām reļak ilǫk kweet eo ej pādwōt; jān ke ej jibboñ ñan ke ej raelep.

Jet iaan likao ro raar ilān pukot kweet eo im ṃōñā.

Ke rej tōparļǫk kweet eo reļak lale jiljino wōt koon. Ak edik bōran. Ekanooj aetok koon (bōlen juon jimettan ñeñe aetokan). Ak edik bōran.

Kōnke rej kab ellolo āinwōt rej mijak in

ṃōñā. Innām raar jab ṃōñā. Ak ej pādwōt ñan iien eo ej make etal.

Ke ej tulọk ḷọk aḷ ej pādwōt. Innām rej lale enaaj etal ñāāt. Ke ej iten tak aḷ jibboñ eo, ej pādwōt. Eḷap aer lale enaaj etal iaḷọk. Ke ej rualitōk im men awa rejaje etal iaḷọk. Innām ejjeḷọk aer ḷōmṇak bwe Lōṃkein eo.

Ak Lōṃkein ejjab jeṃḷọk an kōnono ippān Ļakatau ak ejjab ba ñan armej.

Joteenḷọk eo kweet eo ej etetal im kamijak armej. Im ej ba ñan armej ilo iien aer kiki. Ej kattōṇak armej. Im ba ñan er, "Eḷaññe koṃ naaj lo kweet eṇ, koṃin jeḷā bwe ña Lōṃkein. Kab kuuj, kab jabdewōt kain meninmour: piik, kidu, men ko ej pād ilowaer kein.

"Kab inaaj wōdikūr."

(Lōṃkein ej jokwe ioon wōd ej karōk im ekōṇaan ir men eo ioon armej. Etan wōd eo wōd-idid. Elōñ ilo Ṃajeḷ: Lae, Ujae, im Kuwajleen. Ej ṃōṇakṇak im iaḷo, im eḷap an bwil. Im jejab maroñ kōnono.

Ri-Ṃajeḷ rej ḷōmṇak Lōṃkein ej kōṃṃane kain nañinmej in. Ewōr uno in Ṃajeḷ [ñan] juṃae nañinmej in.)

Innām armej otemej ioon Lae rej jab etetal in jota. Ilo raan juon armej ejjab make iaan in etetal. Ak ej aikuj ruo iaan ruo iaan. Jekdọọn ruo iaan armej ej etetal ilo raan ak Lōṃkein ej maroñ in kọkkure er ruo aolep.

Innām juon wōt ej kemour armej ioon Lae. Etan Ļakatau. (Ejjab leḷọk uno ak ej jibwe wōt im emour.)

Ļọkun jiljino boñ Lōṃkein ej jino etetal ioon aelōñ in Ujae. Im bar kọkkure armej. Ilo iien eo eḷap an Ļakatau jerbal in kemour armej. Elkin jet iien ej ba ñan Ļakatau ke enaaj etal ñan aolep aelōñ in Ṃajeḷ. Barāinwōt enaaj pād ioon jabdewōt wa ko rej jerak i lọmeto ak i loṃaḷo.

Innām bar juon eo armej in Lōṃkein ej pokake, irooj eo Jipe ñan rainin (ej pokake wōt Ļakatau im Jipe).

Innām eṃōj an Jipe kōṃṃan an uno. Im leḷọk ñan aolep aelōñ in Rālik. Ijoke ro ejjab ekkar aer bōke uno in Lōṃkein ej jab pokake er.

Innām Lōṃkein eaar ba, "Inaaj etetal ioon aolepān aelōñ in Ratak im aelōñ in Rālik jabdewōt iien."

Ejeṃḷọk bwebwenato.

Ilo 1907 Lōṃkein ekanooj in kajoor in kọkkure armej. Ej waḷọk āinwōt lukkuun armej. Ej waḷọk ilo Ratak im ilo Rālik. Im aolep armej raar jab loe.

Raan kein ejjab waḷọk. Ak eor nañinmej ej waḷọk jāne. Etan nañinmej eo: lennab. Im eor uno in lennab.

Eor nājin Lōṃkein. Etan ḷeo erūttotata Ļakalep; lukkuun armej.

Ke Lōṃkein ej armej ej keotak. Ejjab tiṃoṇ. Im eor uno an Ļakalep. Ej waḷọk jāne. Im eaar katakin armej.

Jimmaō eaar katak uno jumae nañinmej in Lōṃkein. Eaar katak uno eo jān Jipe. Eo eaar juon irooj in Rālik ar mour ṃokta jān Kabua.

46: STORY ABOUT LŌM̧KEIN

As told by a Mājro *aļap*, Mājro 1972

The word *katok* means to make offerings to a demon *(tim̧oņ)*.

Emo̧ņmo̧ņ is a strong and aggressive class of demon. These demons can appear night or day.

For example: Lōm̧kein. She is in Rālik [the western chain of the Marshalls] and in Ratak [the eastern chain] and travels all over the Marshall Islands. People have seen her. She is like a real person *(lukkuun armej)*, and is *mo̧ņmo̧ņ* (possessed of supernatural powers).

Lōm̧kein was not buried when she died because people believed that she would destroy everyone if they did so. So she was thrown into the ocean.

She had died because her older sister had made magic that stopped her womb, and prevented the birth of her child. So she died.

She was able to become a *mejenkwaad* in life. And she had a mouth in the back of her head. She had a very long neck and could bite people at a long distance.

She is in a *pukor*, a rock that floats in the ocean.[1]

If you pick it up and set it aside, it will be gone. It will disappear the next day. *Mejenkwaad* is a type of sickness affecting pregnant women. Lōm̧kein brought this sickness. It appears when a pregnant woman's husband is absent.

Lōm̧kein affects men, women, and also children. Women from other islands than Kapinmeto [the northwestern Marshalls] did not sleep on these islands for the fear of being affected by Lōm̧kein [during stops at these islands on board ship].

However, local women could do it without harm.

At the pass into Ujae Atoll, people threw food into the water to appease Lōm̧kein, so that the weather and sea conditions would be good. That is *katok:* offerings, appeasement.

If they did not do this, they would be in trouble.

1. Perhaps this is a type of pumice *(tilaan)* found in the Marshallese waters occasionally.

47: STORY OF TWO BROTHERS ON JĀLOOJ

As told by Rhine Brain, Mājro 1970

This is a story of Jālooj Atoll, the story of two brothers who lived on the island of Jālooj, long, long ago.

One brother went to the eastern half of the atoll, and the other brother went to the western half of the atoll.

One day a huge *tiṃoṇ* (demon) appeared. We do not know where she came from. And she ate up all the *rijerbal* (workers) of the brother in the west. He alone was left. And then the demon disappeared. We do not know where she went.

So from then on, everything attempted on both sides went wrong. The people could not work as well together, or for one another, as they had before the demon came.[1] However, the Jālooj people worked well with the Germans and the Japanese, and they have worked well with the Americans to this day.

The brothers became two big rocks. They were located on the lagoon side of Jebwad Island.[2] They were there before the big typhoon [of 1958], but I do not know if they are there today or not.

---

1. The informant and I were talking about community development projects on Jālooj Atoll, and this elicited the story of the two brothers. Here again, we see a supernatural explanation for human behavior, as well as for natural phenomena, by means of a folktale. This story may be based on a historical incident in the far distant past, shrouded in the mists of time—perhaps a political schism and internecine warefare. This has occurred a number of times in various parts of the Marshalls. The demon and her actions may symbolize the war and destruction that ensued.

2. Jebwad Island became the trading center for foreigners, and later, the administrative headquarters for the German government of the Marshall Islands, and its successor, the Japanese government. Because of this, the Jālooj people had more sustained and intensive contact and interaction with the foreigners than any other Marshallese community in the pre-World War II period. Davenport (1950:32–33) was told a more detailed and lengthier version of this story. The demon in this version was a *mejenkwaad.* The informant, James (Ṃooj) Milne, a student at the University of Hawai'i at the time, explained that "this proves that younger brothers should always obey their older brothers, otherwise a *mejenkwaad* will eat them." The didactic function of this version of the story is obvious.

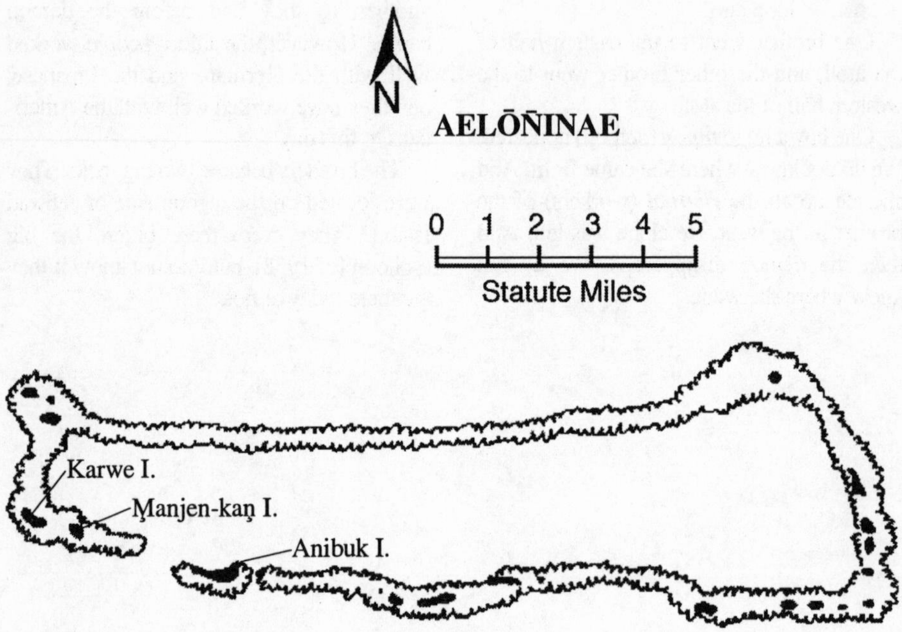

Aelōñ in Aelōñinae
Lagoon Area: 40.90 sq.mi.
Dry Land Area: 1.08 sq.mi

48: ABOUT A WOMAN WHO HAD TEN BOYS

As told by Jelibōr Jam, Kuwajleen 1975

The boys had only one arm, only one leg, only one eye, [and] only one ear.

The woman lived on an island named Jenkaņ [M̧anjen-kaņ] in Aelōn̄inae [Atoll]. When the boys were older, they made a plan to go to an island named Karwe. And one day, there was a very low tide. Now the boys waded from Jenkaņ and went out on the reef toward Karwe.

When they went ashore on Karwe they had a very big catch of langusta and they cooked them.

And they had just cooked them [when] a demon sang to them. She said, "The sound of the tapping, sound of falling, Likarwe | She cries O-O | She cries to the north | She cries to the south | She cries on the branches of that *kubōk* [*Instia bijugata,* a tree].

"The place | Your place of *n̄ōrn̄ōr*[1] | Throw here my food, a person | And throw here my food, a langusta."

Now she went to wait for them to go to sleep. And she ate them. And the boys did not return [to their home on Jenkaņ Island].

When it was evening, their mother was very worried about the boys, her sons, not having returned. And the sun set.

The next day, the boys had not returned, and the woman was very worried.

Later she again gave birth to ten more sons ([with] only one arm, only one leg, only one eye, only one ear).

And the boys, when they were older, planned to go over to Karwe, to play. After a while, one day, the tide was very low and the weather was good. The boys went to the other island. And before they went, their mother said, "Where are you going, my sons? For your older brothers went and did not return. How will it be if the same thing happens to you?"

The boys replied, "What about our older brothers, are they not men?" (They asked if those men were cowards. And they ridiculed them because they went and did not return. If they were real men, they would return.)

Their mother said, "Maybe there is a shark between these islands. And if you go, do not sleep on the island, but hurry back here.

"And if you see that it is high tide, well wait until it is low tide. And if it is low tide, come here, for it is bad for you to sleep on that island."

The boys replied, "Well, if we go and see a shark, we will seize it and kill it. And if we go and see a demon, we will burn it up.

"And do not worry, for we will return and you will see us."

Their mother said, "Well, go." And she was very hopeful concerning the words of the boys, her sons.

And when the boys went, their mother came and watched them wading and going. And when they were gone, their mother returned and waited for them.

When they went ashore on Karwe, they had a very big catch of langusta and they cooked them. And they had just cooked them [when] a demon sang to them. She said, "The sound of tapping, sound of someone falling, Likarwe | She cries O-O | She cries to the north | She cries to the south | She cries on the branches of that *kubōk* | The place | Your

---

1. *N̄ōrn̄ōr* 'the sound of grating coconut meat or removing skin of cooked breadfruit (*raanke waini* or *jukkwe mā*)'.

place of *n̄ōrn̄ōr* | Throw here my food, a person | Throw here my food, a langusta."

Now she went to wait for them to go to sleep, and she ate them.

The boys had not returned [after] a long time, but it was high tide.

And their mother spoke to herself and said, "Maybe they will return when it is low tide, in just a little while."

When it was low tide, she prepared the boys' food, but the boys did not return. And the woman went to the end of the island and looked to see if the boys would be returning. She remained there until it was the highest tide. And she returned, and she was very worried.

Later she again give birth to ten boys. Nine of the boys had only one arm, only one leg, only one eye, only one ear. But the youngest one, number ten, was like a regular human being: two arms, two legs, two eyes, two ears.

When they were older, their mother very sternly instructed them that they should not go to the island, to Karwe, for there were twenty of her sons who went there and did not return. The boys thought about this as they grew older.

One day the boys said to their mother, "Why haven't the older boys returned?"

Their mother replied, "I do not know."

The boys said, "Maybe there is something good on the island, and we want to look for our older brothers. Do not hold us, for we are going to see what is on that island."

Their mother cried very much and said, "It will be bad if you do not return." The boys said, "We will be able to do anything if danger appears to us. And tomorrow we will go."

Because the boys strongly insisted, their mother did not speak again, but she just cried.

The next morning, the boys prepared to go, and the youngest boy said, "Am I going?" And the older boys said, "You can not come. You stay here." But the youngest boy did not want to stay; he just wanted to go with them.

And the boy who was a little older than him said, "Well, come, for I will protect you from harm."

But the older boys said, "You just stay here, for you are crazy." The reason they said crazy was because he had two legs, two arms, two eyes, two ears. And they said, "crazy." But all his brothers had only one leg, one arm, one eye, one ear. And they said that they were real human beings.

Because the younger brother begged insistently, they said, "Well, come, but no one is going to protect you from danger."

And they began to wade from their island and went away to the other island.

When they reached the island and came up on the beach, the older boys prepared their food. But the youngest boy walked on the beach, and when he saw some *mejān jidduul* [lit. eye of the *jidduul:* operculum of *turbo* sp., cat's eye], he treasured them. And he thought about *mejān jidduul* because they were almost like the eyes of human beings.

And he went to his older brothers, and the boys said, "What are those things you bring here?"

The youngest boy said, "These things are treasured by me, for they are like eyes of human beings."

And because it was high tide, they waited for low tide so they could get langusta. And they said, "Why is there nothing to harm us on this island? And why didn't our older brothers return? Well, it will become clear!"

When it was low tide, they waded on the reef to get langusta. And at the time of low tide, they could not see any langusta.

A short while later, it was high tide and langusta appeared with the waves. And the boys put langusta in the baskets and returned to Karwe, and cooked them.

They had just cooked the langusta and a demon appeared. And all of the boys heard the demon sing. She sang, "The sound of tapping, sound of someone falling | Likarwe | She cries to the north | She cries to the south | She cries on the branches of that *kubōk.* | The place | Your place of *n̄ōrn̄ōr* | Throw here my food, a person | And throw here my food, a langusta." (She wanted to eat the langusta and the people.)

And the older boys were greatly afraid, and did not know what they should do. And they hurried to go to sleep. And they waited for what the demon was going to do to them. But the youngest boy prepared the demon's food and came out next to her.

And the demon said, "Greetings to you, friend." And the boy said, "Sit here, for I am just cooking our food, these langusta."

The demon said, "Hurry up, for I am very sleepy. And how about you?"

The boy replied, "I am also sleepy, and when we are finished eating, I will sleep."

The demon said, "And I also, friend." And the two ate their food, langusta and coconut meat (as a side dish). And the demon said, "I have just finished eating, friend, so that I am about to go to sleep."

And the boy said, "Well, me too. I will sleep too." And the two of them lay down next to each other.

And the boy, because he was frightened, took *mejān jiduul* and put them on his eyes and slept.

But the demon did not sleep. And after a little while, the demon raised up and looked at the boy, so that if he was sleeping, she would eat him. And she looked over and saw the *mejān jidduul* and she thought that the boy was awake.[2]

And the demon lay down again. A short while later she raised up again and looked at the boy. She saw that the boy was not asleep. And she said to the boy, "Friend, why are you not sleeping?"

The boy startled and awakened and said, "Because those ants bit me." The boy said, "And you, friend? Why do you not sleep? I know about you. The reason you do not sleep is because you are thinking of eating us boys, my older brothers. And you go away from us, for if you remain, I will burn you up!"

And the demon was embarrassed and she went away from them.[3]

It is ended.

The meaning of this story is: They say that we should not ignore those younger than us.

There are two versions of this story. One is from Pin̄lep, Jālooj. And one from Aelōn̄inae.

The demon on Jālooj, at the time when she said, "Throw here my food, a human being, and throw here my food, a langusta," now the youngest boy pulled a big boulder out of the fire and threw it at the demon. And the demon ate the boulder, and her mouth was very full. And she died.[4]

There are no cat's eyes in the story from Jālooj.

On Jālooj they went from Pin̄lep to Take and Arļap. And today there is a sandbank named Bokelikarwe.[5]

It is located next to Take and Arļap.

---

2. The deception by use of cat's eyes *(mejān jiduul)* is a graphic and believable tactic (if one stretches one's imagination a bit), and is found elsewhere in Marshallese folklore. Etao (the Marshallese trickster) used them to simulate a wakeful condition, and thereby prevented his human and demon enemies from killing him.

3. The triumph of the neglected and scorned youngest sibling over others—his older brothers or an evil supernatural being—is another motif found in several Marshallese folktales, and is found in the folklore of other cultures as well (the Male Cinderella motif).

48: KŌN JUŌN KŌRĀ EOR JOÑOUL NĀJIN ĻADDIK

Ri-bwebwenato: Jelibōr Jam, Kuwajleen 1975

Ļadik ro juon wōt pā, juon wōt ne, juon wōt māj, juon wōt lọjilñi.

Kōrā in ej pād ilo juon āne etan in Jenkaņ ilo Aelōñinae. Ke ļadik ro rej rūtto ļọk rej ļōmņak in etal ñan juon āne etan Karwe. Innām juon raan eļap an pāāt. Kiiō ļadik ro rej tuwaak jān Jenkaņ im etal ioon pedped ļọk ñan Karwe.

Ke rej atoļọk ekanooj in lōñ koņaer wōr innām rej kōmatti wōt.

Innām rej kōmatti wōt ak tiṃoņ eo ej al tok ej ba, "Jirjir eo bōke Likarwe. | Ejañ O-O. | Ejañ tuiōñ | Ejañ turōk | Ejañ ilo raan kubōk eņ | Jikin jikūṃ ñōrñōr | Jotok juon kijō armej juon | Jotok juon kijō wōr juon."

Kiiō ej iten kōttar aer kiki in kañ er. Innām ļadik ro rejjab bar rọọl.

Ke ej boñļọk jineer ekanooj in inepata kōn an ļadik ro nājin jab rọọltok. Ak etulọk aļ.

Rujlọkin [raan] eo juon ļadik ro rejab rọọltok innām kōrā eo ekanooj ļap an inepata.

Tokālik ebar kemmour joñoul ļaddik (juon wōt pā, juon wōt ne, juon wōt māj, juon wōt lojilñi.)

Innām ļadik ro ke rej rūttoļọk rej bar likūt ļōmņak in ikkure ļọk ñan Karwe. Pād im ļak juon raan ekanooj in ļap an pāāt ak eṃṃan lañ. Ļadik ro rej bar etal ñan āneo juon. Innām ṃokta jān aer etal jineer ej ba, "Koṃij ilọk ñan ia? Nājiimmān. Ke jeimi immān raar etal im jab bar rọọltok. Enaaj kōjikan ñe barāinwōt koṃ?"

Ļadik ro rej uwaak, "En ta ļōṃa jeirro ejjab eṃṃaan ļōṃaro?" (Rej kajjitōk ñe ļōṃaro rej pikōt ke. Im rej kajjirere [kake] er kōnke raar etal im jab rọọl tok. Innām rejjab lukkuun eṃṃaan. Im rej likūt ajiri ak kōrā kōnke rejab rọọl tok. Ñe rej lukkuun eṃṃaan renaaj rọọl.)

Jineer eba, "Bōlen eor juon pako ikōtaan āne kein. Innām eļaññe koṃij etal koṃin jab ilān kiki ak koṃin ṃōkaj tok. Innām eļaññe koṃij lale bwe eibwijtok, ekwe koṃin kōttar an pāātļọk. Im ñe enaaj pāāt koṃin itok bwe enana ami kiki āneņ."

Ļadik ro rej uwaak, "Ekwe eļaññe kem naaj etal im lo juon pako kem naaj jibwe im ṃane. Ak eļaññe kem naaj etal im lo juon tiṃoņ kem naaj tile. Innām kwōn jab inepata bwe kem naaj rọọl tok im kwōnaaj lo kem."

Jineer ej ba, "Ekwe, koṃ etal." Innām eļap an kejatdikdik kake ennaan ko an ļadik ro nājin.

Innām ļadik ro ke rej etal, jineer ej itok im lale aer tuwaak im etal. Innām ke rej mootļọk, jineer ej jepļaak im kōttar er.

Ke rej atoļọk Karwe ekanooj loñ kwoņāer wōr innām rej ja kōmatti wōt ak tiṃoņ eo ej altok. Ej ba, "Jidjid eo bokwe Likarwe | Ejañ O-O. | Ejañ tuiōñ | Ejañ turōk | Ejañ ilo raan kubōk eņ | Jikin jikūṃ ñōrñōr

---

4. The killing of a demon by means of trickery, by outwitting it, is another widespread motif. Among the methods used by the heroes and heroines of Marshallese folktales are (1) false steering commands shouted out for the benefit of the pursuing demons (to confuse them), (2) trapping the demon in a house and burning it up, and (3) causing it to ingest a harmful object, such as in this story.

5. Here again we see explanation of a geographical feature and name by reference to a folktale. This is also widespread, and is found in many Hawaiian and other Polynesian folktales (see Beckwith 1970: passim).

| Jotok juon kijō armej juon | Ak jotok juon kijō wōr juon."

Kiiō ej itok im kōttar aer kiki im kañe er.

Etto an ļadik ro jab jepļaak ak eibwij. Innām jineer ej kōnono ippān make im ba, "Bōlen renaaj jepļaak tok ñe enaaj pāāt, kiiō ļǫk jidik."

Ke ej pāātļǫk ej kōppojak kijen ļadik ro ak ļadik ro rejjab rǫǫltok. Innām kōrā eo ej etal ñan jabōn āne eo im lale ñe ļadik ro ren rǫǫl tok. Eaar pād ijo ñan ke ej ibwijtok. Innām ejepļaak im kanooj inepata.

Tokālik ebar kemmour joñoul nājin ļaddik. Ļadik ro ruatimjuon ej juon wōt pā, juon wōt ne, juon wōt māj, juon wōt lojiliñin. Ak diktata eo, kein kajoñoul ej āinwōt armej: ruo pā, ruo ne, ruo māj, ruo lojiliñin.

Ke rej rūttoļǫk jineer ej kanooj katakin er bwe ren jab etal āneļǫk ñan Karwe bwe eor roñoul nājin ļaddik raar etal ṃokta im jab bar rǫǫltok. Innām ļaddik rein rej likūti ļōmņak in ippāer ilo aer rūttoļǫk.

Juōn raan ļadik ro rej ba ñan jineer, "Ta wūnin an jab jepļaak tok ļadik ro ṃokta?"

Jineer ej uwaak, "Ijaje." Ļadik ro rej ba, "Bōlen eor juon men eo eṃṃan ej pād i āne eo. Innām kem kōņaan pukot ļadik ro jeim. Innām kwōn jab dāpij kem, bwe kemin ṃōk etal in lale ta eņ i āneņ."

Jineer ej kanooj jañ im ba, "Enana eļañne koṃ jab rǫǫl tok."

Ļadik ro rej ba, "Kem naaj maroñ kōṃṃan men otemjej eļañne jorrāān naaj waļǫk tok ñan kem. Innām ilju kem naaj etal."

Kōn an ļadik ro akweļap, jineer ejjab bar kōnono, ak ej jañ bajjek.

Rujļǫkin eo juon, ļadik ro rej kōppojak in etal ak ļadik eo ediktata ej ba, "Ña ij iwōj ke?" Innām ļadik ro rōrūtto rej ba, "Kwojjab itok. Kwōn pādwōt." Innām ļadik eo edik ejjab kōņaan pādwōt ak ekōņaan etal ippāer. Innām ļadik eo erūttoļǫk jidik jāne ej ba, "Ekwe, kwōn itok bwe inaaj lale eok jān jorrāān." Ak ļadik ro rōrūtto rej ba, "Kwōn pādwōt bwe kwe bwebwe." Wūnin aer ba "bwebwe" kōnke ruo neen, ruo pein, ruo māj, ruo lojiliñin. Innām rej ba, "bwebwe." Ak aolep ļadik ro jein rej kajjo ne, kajjo pā, kajjo māj, kajjo lǫjiliñin er innām rej ba er lukkuun armej.

Kōn an ļadik eo edik akweļap rej ba, "Ekwe, itok ak ejjeļǫk enaaj lale eok jān jorrāān."

Innām rej jino aer tuwaak jān āne eo āneer im ilǫk ñan āne eo juon.

Ke rej atoļǫk ļadik ro rōrūtto rej kōṃṃan kijeer. Ak ļadik eo ediktata ej etetal ioon bok, im ke ej lo mejān jidduul ko ekanooj in kaurōki. Innām ej ļōmņak kaki mejān jidduul ko kōnke enañin āinwōt mejān armej.

Innām ej etal ippān ļadik ro jein, im ļadik ro jein rej ba, "Enta kaņe kwōj būkitok?"

Ļadik eo edik ej ba, "Men kā reṃṃan ippa, bwe āinwōt mejān armej."

Innām ke ej ibwij rej kōttar an pāātļǫk bwe ren kǫwōr. Innām rej ba, "Etke ejjeļǫk menin kǫkkure inin? Ak ta wūnin ļadik ro jeidiañ kar jab jepļaak, ļōṃa? Ekwe, enaaj alikkar!"

Ke ej pāāt, rej tuwaak im kǫwōr. Innām ke ej pāāt ejjeļǫk wōr eņ rej loe. Meļan ļǫk jidik eibwijtok innām elekā wōr. Innām ļadik ro rej ātet wōr ko ņa ilowaan iiep ko im jepļaak ñan Karwe. Im kōmat. Rejja kōmat wōr ak juon tiṃoņ ej waļǫk tok. Ak aolep ļadik ro rej roñjake an tiṃoņ eo al tok. Ej ba, "Jidjid eo bokwe Likanwe | Ejañ O-O | Ejañ tuiōñ | Ejañ turōk | Ejañ ilo raan kubōk eņ | Jikin jikōṃ ñōrñōr | Jotok juon kijō armej juon | Ak jotok juon wōr juon."

(Ekōņaan ṃōñā wōr im armej.)

Innām ļaddik rōrūtto rekanooj in mijak em jaje ta eo ren kōṃṃane. Innām rej [kō]kairir im kiki. Im kōttar ta eo tiṃoņ eo enaaj kōṃṃane ñan ereañ. Ak ļadik eo edik ej kōppojak kijen tiṃoņ eo im kajijettok ņa iturin. Innām tiṃoņ ej ba, "Iǫkwe eok ļe jera." Innām ļadik eo ej ba, "Jijet ijōņe, bwe ij ja kōmat wōr kā kijerro."

Tiṃoņ eo ej ba, "Kaiur eok bwe ñā ikanooj mejki. Ak baj kwe?" Ļadik eo ej uwaak, "I bar mejki ak ñe eṃōj arro ṃōñā inaaj kiki."

Tiṃoņ eo ej ba, "Kab ña ļe jera." Innām rejro kajjo kijen wōr im jiraal (ippān waini) bajjek. Ak tiṃoņ eo ej ba, "eṃōj aō ṃōñā ļe jera, bwe ij ja kiki." Innām ļadik eo ej ba, "Ekwe, barāinwōt ña. Ij bar kiki." Innām rejro babu iturin doon.

Innām ļadik eo ke ej mejki, ej letok mejān jidduul ko im likūti ņa ioon mejān im kiki. Ak tiṃoņ eo ejjab kiki. Ak ej riab in kiki. Innām ālikin jidik iien tiṃoņ eo ejjerkak im lale ļadik eo bwe ñe ekiki enaaj kañe. Ak eļak erreitok im lale elo mejān jidduul ko im ej ļōmņak ļadik eo ej erre.

Innām tiṃoņ eo ej bar babu. Meļan ļọk jidik ej bar jerkak im lale ļadik eo. Eļak lale ejjab kiki. Innām ej ba ñan ļadik eo, "Jera, etke kwōjjab kiki ļe?" Ļadik ejjab uwaak, kōnke eļap an kiki. Tiṃōņ eo ej bar jibwe ļadik eo im ba, "Jera etke kwojjab kiki, ļe?"

Ļadik eo ej ilbōk im ruj im ba, "Kōn an kallep kā kiji eō." Ļadik eo eba, "Ak kwe ļe jera. Etke kwojjab kiki? Ña ijeļā kake eok. Wūnin kwojjab kiki, kōnke kwōj ļōmņak in kañ kimeañ ļaddik rā jeiū. Innām kwōn etal jān kōmeañ! Bwe eļañne kwōj pādwōt inaaj tile eok."

Innām tiṃoņ eo ej jook im etal jān er. Ejeṃļọk .

Meļeļe in bwebwenato in: Rej ba jen jab kajekdoon ro reddik jān kōj.

Eor ruo bwebwenato. Juōn ilo Piñlep, Jālooj. Im juon ilo Aelōñinae. Tiṃoņ eo ilo Jālooj ilo iien eo ke ej ba, "Jotok juon kijō armej ak jotok kijō wōr juon." Kiiō ļadik eo ediktata ej katuwe dekādọļ jān lowaan kijeek eo im kadkad ļọk im kade tiṃoņ eo. Innām tiṃoņ eo ej kañ dekā eo im ekanooj booļ lọñi eo. Im emej.

Ejjeļọk mejān jiduul ilo bwebwenato in Jālooj.

Ilo Jālooj rej etal jān Piñlep ñan Tōkā im Arļap. Im rainin eor juon bok etan Bokwā-Likarwe. Epād iturin Tōkā im Arļap.

(Ri-bwebwenato eaar kōmļeļe kake naan eo ilo bwebwenato in: jidjid. Eaar ba jidjid ej juon ainikien ak jejaje ej waļọk jān ia. Āinwōt lōñ ekilep [tapping sound]. Jet roñ ilo āne ko edik. Ikōņaan roñ ilo Epjā jet iien. Eaar ba.)

49: STORY ABOUT ELEVEN BOYS

As told by Jobel Emos, Kuwajleen 1975

The eleventh boy, they said he was crazy. The reason they said crazy—the youngest man, they put down the name Crazy [named him Crazy]—was because he had two eyes, two nostrils, two arms, two legs—like a human being

Because those men had only one arm, only leg, only one nostril. Not like a human being—half a human being.

Now, every day, they went to pick breadfruit. The breadfruit tree [*Artocarpus altilis, mā*] was in the sea, far from the island—only one breadfruit tree. And the breadfruit belonged to a *kidu in lọjet,* an "animal of the sea."[1] The name of the animal: *kidudujet.* (The meaning of this thing, 'some are of the sea'.)

The breadfruit belonged to the animal. Now these men went to steal the animal's breadfruit. Now at the time they went, early in the morning, the ten men wanted to run away from the youngest, and they said "Crazy." They did not want him to ride with them and pick breadfruit. But the boy went first, before the rooster crowed (at three o'clock).[2]

He went, and went inside the canoe and hid himself to wait for the time the canoe would sail.

Now the ten men came and said, "Let us go and sail now to pick breadfruit, for the crazy boy is still sleeping."[3]

Now they sailed, and Crazy knew that the canoe was sailing. Now when they neared the breadfruit in the sea, Crazy appeared from inside the canoe.[4]

Crazy appeared just as they were coming up to the breadfruit tree. And none of them made a noise, so that the animal would not awaken and eat them.

Only Crazy cried out. He said, *"Ketak O-O! Ketak laḷ!"* ("Hit O-O! Sound of hitting below!")

(The meaning of this is that the ten brothers had gone without him before and had picked breadfruit three times, and the animal did not wake up.

Crazy did not go with them previously.)

Now the crazy man cried out and all the young men were afraid.

At the time, the animal had not awakened. He continued to sleep.

Now they climbed up the tree and positioned themselves [lined up] from top to bottom. The oldest man was highest, the second (oldest) was below him. Thus they completed their positioning downward [toward the ground], and the crazy one farthest

---

1. The word *kidu* means 'dog', and also 'animal', exclusive of cats and rats. However, *menin mour* (living thing) is more commonly used for animals in general. *Kidu in lọjet* can be translated as 'dog or animal of the sea'. The latter seems more appropriate in this story, because of the extremely large size of the monster.

2. Informant used the modified English loanword *awa* 'hour'and the introduced system of marking passage of time. In the Marshallese text: *jilu awa* 'three o'clock'. This is found in other Marshallese folktales as well.

3. Note the shift from the use of "boy" and "boys" to "man" and "men." This is not unusual in Marshallese narrative style, and is done in a number of folktales, and in ordinary discourse as well.

4. Traditional Marshallese sailing canoes had very deep hulls, and one could easily hide inside a hull.

below was on the canoe. Because he was the youngest.[5]

Now the highest man [in the tree], the oldest man, began to twist off the breadfruit and gave it to the man below [him], his younger brother. He gave it to him and said, whispering, "E-O-O" ("Here it is"), and handed it to him.

Now they all followed, and each one handed [the breadfruit] downward [to the man below him]. And the last man, the "crazy" who was on the canoe, they handed it to him (this fellow, the real human being).

Now he grabbed the breadfruit and cried out in a loud voice. *"WO-O-O. Ekilep wōt!"* ("O-O-O. It is big!")

Then all of the men jumped onto the canoe, because they were afraid about the shouting of Crazy. And they hastened to sail to the island. One breadfruit was obtained, but it was enough, because it was big.

Now they took it to their mother so that she would cook it. The old woman, their mother was cooking. There were fish.

Now their mother was cooking it. The boys went to play a little and wait while their mother cooked. The crazy boy and his mother just stayed and cooked.[6]

The boy cooked six boulders (rocks from the mountain).[7]

They were like balls—the size of a ball.[8]

Now the foods were cooked, and the mother called them to come and eat.

Now they looked toward the east. They saw half of the east was blocked off because the animal [had] awakened and appeared. (He was very large.) Now he came to see who stole the breadfruit, in order to eat them (the thieves).

And when the boys and the mother saw him, they were afraid. And they died the kind[9] [of death] that is fainting. [They fainted and became unconscious, dying from fear.]

Only Crazy did not die. He readied [himself] with the rocks that he had cooked, because now the rocks were like fire [red hot].

Now he went and took the leaves of those *ut* [*Guettarda speciosa,* a tree] for seizing the rocks, so that he would not damage his hands. Because the rocks were like the bullets of a gun.[10]

Now the animal drew near, and the boy threw [the rocks]. Now when the rocks were all gone, the animal was dead.[11]

When it died, the boy went to divide up the food, because the men who had died [and] just fainted had not yet awakened. He finished dividing eleven shares [of food].[12] Now the eleventh was the share of his

5. Note the explanation in terms of the importance of seniority in Marshallese culture, that is, among brothers. Perhaps this was didactic in this story. It is a common motif in Marshallese folklore.

6. Marshallese men help the women in cooking, usually performing the more arduous tasks, such as preparing the earth oven, as illustrated in this story (although women also do this).

7. Note that there are no mountains or hills in the Marshalls. This is an example of accretion of knowledge—post-contact or as a result of an early voyage to one of the islands of volcanic origin to the west of the Marshalls, Pohnpei, or Kosrae, perhaps. Or actual boulders may have been brought in from these high islands as ballast in ships from Europe or North America, or embedded in the roots of large trees that drifted ashore, as they still do.

8. Storyteller used the English loanword *bǫǫļ* 'ball', which, with the artifact, has been incorporated into the culture.

9. Storyteller used the English loanword *kain* 'kind', which has also been integrated into the Marshallese language.

10. Note the English loanword and introduced concept and artifact: *joot in bu* 'shot or ammunition for a gun'.

mother, but he did not make food [for himself], because while they slept, he ate.

Now he put a little diarrhetic shit on the food, on the shares of the men who had fainted. But on the share of his mother alone he did not [put] it.[13]

Now when he finished making the food, he awakened them and his mother. And they awakened and ate. And when they ate, these men said, "What is the smell in these foods?"

Now Crazy replied, "Well [you] just eat, because you were frightened. Perhaps birds came and shit on it while you were sleeping."

When he had said this, the men were angry with him, but there was nothing that they could do.

The story is ended.[14]

(At the time when the boy finished cooking the rocks, he sang. Now Crazy sang. He said, *"N̦o jetak, jetak | N̦o in kidu | Pinej turin lan̄."* (The wave comes in, comes in | The wave of the *kidu* | It covers the side of the sky.)[15]

The reason Crazy sang was because they saw a wave, a wave of the animal. And they died (these men who fainted), because they knew the wave was the wave of the animal.

When I asked the informant, Mr. Jobel Emos, what the meaning of the story is, he replied: "The meaning of this story is that some brothers do not love each other. And their thinking is not the same. and will be damaged from the thing [the lack of consensus]. But with the mother it is all the same. Only one level.[16]

"And if they took on the thinking of their mother, everything would be good. And there would be no damage.

"I learned this story on Epoon from the old people. *Inon̄* are not true, like the *bwebwenato* of Inedel is true. But [the story of] Lippeipat is not true. It is an *inon̄."*[17]

---

11. This is a widespread motif. The underdog hero defeats an evil attacker's threat or overcomes obstacles, while his older brothers fail to act, or fail in the attempt—the Male Cinderella motif, which is found in other Marshallese folktales.

12. Food is carefully divided into shares for distribution, especially at formal presentations or celebrations *(keemem).* The principle of sharing and reciprocity is a leitmotif of Marshallese culture and a major positive value. Generosity is respected and appreciated by the Marshallese, who are a most generous and hospitable people.

13. Note the motif of the triumphant hero tricking his brothers in revenge, but being dutiful and respectful toward his mother, as is the ideal behavior in Marshallese culture. This attitude toward one's mother is also found in other Marshallese folk tales.

14. This conclusion emphasizes the motif of the underdog outwitting his neglectful brothers, and the triumph of the Male Cinderella. The trickster motif is also seen (the use of feces in the food offered another). The Marshallese trickster Etao does this in several stories, as does the Polynesian trickster Maui in Polynesian folktales.

15. The informant explained that the animal was so big that it blocked out the sky in the direction from which it advanced on the island. (This obviously enhances the dramatic quality of the story.)

16. Note the use of the English loanword *ļābōļ* 'level' instead of the Marshallese *jepaan wōt juon* or *eon̄ wōt juon* in the Marshallese text, and the explanation of the story, which emphasizes the attitude toward one's mother in Marshallese culture.

17. *Inon̄* can be translated as "fairy tale," and *bwebwenato* as "narrative." However, there is overlapping in the folktales. For a discussion of the distinction made by Marshallese, see Davenport (1952:iii–viii). As he correctly points out, "any classification of cultural data is a strained one, for sharp distinctions are seldom made" (iii).

49: BWEBWENATO IN ĻADIK RO JOÑOULJUON

Ri-bwebwenato: Jobel Emos, Kuwajleen 1975

Kein joñouljuon rej ba bwebwe. Wūnin rōba bwebwe: ļeo ediktata, rej likūti etan bwebwe: Wūnin aer ba bwebwe kōnke ruo mejān, ruo roñ in bǫtin, ruo pein, ruo neen: āinwōt armej.

Kōnke ļōm̧aro jet juon wōt pā, juon wōt ne, juon wōt roñ in bǫti. Aolep men ippāer juon wōt, ejjab āinwōt armej: jimettan in armej.

Kiiō aolep raan rej ilān kōm̧kōm̧ mā. Mā ej pād ilo lǫmeto ettoļǫk jān āne; juon wōt mā. Innām mā eo ej an kidu in lǫjet. Etan kidu eo: Kidudujet. (Meļeļein menin 'kidu in lǫjet': "jet" ej 'lǫjet'.)

An kidu [eo] mā eo. Kiiō ļōm̧aro joñouljuon rej iten kǫǫt mā an kidu. Kiiō ilo iien eo rej etal, ilo jibboñtata, ļōm̧aro joñouljuon rōkōņaan ko jān ļadik eo ediktata im rej ba bwebwe. Rejjab kōņaan bwe en uwe ippāer im kōm̧kōm̧ mā. Ak ļadik eo eaar etal wōt m̧oktata, m̧okta jān kako eo ikkūr (ilo jilu awa). Ej etal im deļǫñ ilo wa eo im kūttilek im kōttar iien eo wa [eo] naaj jerak.

Kiiō ļōm̧aro joñoul rej itok im rej ba, "Jen etal im jerak kiiō ilān kōm̧kōm̧ bwe ļadik eo bwebwe ej kiki wōt."

Kiiō rej jerak. Kiiō bwebwe [eo] ejeļā kiiō wa eo ej jerak. Kiiō ke rej epaaktok mā eo i lǫmeto. Kiiō ewaļǫk bwebwe jān lowaan wa eo.

Kiiō waļǫk bwebwe [eo] im kiiō rōtōpar mā eo. Innām aolep rej jab keroro bwe enjab ruj kidu eo im kañ er.

Kiiō bwebwe [eo] wōt ej lam̧ōj. Ej ba, "Ketak O-O. Ketak laļ." (Meļeļe in ej likao ro joñoul raar etal ñan mā eo m̧okta im raar jab bōkļǫk bwebwe eo. Im raar kōm̧kōm̧ mā jilu alen im kidu eo eaar jab ruj.)

(M̧okta bwebwe [eo] ejjab pād ippāer.)

Kiiō ļeo bwebwe ej lam̧ōj im aolep likao ro remijak. Iien eo kidu ejjañin ruj. Ej kiki wōt.

Kiiō rej tallōñ im ekkar. Ļeo erūtto epād ilōñtata, im ļeo kein karuo laļtok. Em̧ōj āindein aer ekkar laļtak im bwebwe eo ilaļtata epād ioon wa eo, kōnke ediktata.

Kiiō ļeo ilōñtata, ļeo erūttotata ej jinoin iñti mā eo im leļǫk ñan ļeo ilaļtak, ļeo jatin. Ej leļǫk ñane im ba, unoojdikdik, "E-O-O." Im leļǫk ñane.

Kiiō aolep rej ļore im leļǫk kajjojo laļ ļǫk. Innām ļeo āliktata, bwebwe eo, ej pād iwa eo, rej leļǫk ñane. (Kijak eo lukkuun armej eo.)

Kiiō ej jibwe mā eo im lam̧ōj kōn eļap ainikien, "WO-O-O. Ekilep wōt!"

Innām aolep em̧m̧aan rej kāļǫk ioon wa eo kōnke remijak kōn an bwebwe eo lam̧ōj.

Innām rej m̧ōkaj im jerak ñan āne eo. Etōprak juon mā ak ebwe kōnke ekilep.

Kiiō rej bōkļǫk ñan jineer bwe en kōmat. Leļļap eo jinen ej kōmat. Eor ek.

Kiiō jinen ej kōmatte. Ļadik ro rej ilān ikkure bajjek im kōttar an jineer kōmat. Ļadik eo bwebwe im jinen rej pādwōt im kōmat.

Ļadik eo ej kōmatti jiljino dekā dǫl (deka jān toļ). Rej āinwōt bǫǫļ. Dettan wōt bǫǫļ.

Kiiō emat m̧ōñā ko. Im jinen ej kūrtok er bwe ren itok im m̧ōñā.

Kiiō rej erreilǫk. Rej loe epenjak jimettan in rear kōnke kidu eo eruj im waļǫk. (Eļap in kilep.) Kiiō ej itok in lale wōn eaar kǫǫt mā, bwe en kañ er.

Innām ļadik ro joñoul im jineer rej loe remijak. Innām remej. Kain eo ej ļotļǫk.

Kiiō bwebwe wōt ejjab mej. Epojak kōn dekā ko ar kōmatti. Bwe kiiō dekā ko rej āinwōt kijeek.

Kiiō ej ilām bōktok bōlōkin ut kein an jibwi dekā ko bwe enjab kọkkure pein. Kōnke dekā ko rej āinwōt joot in bu.

Kiiō epaaktok kidu eo. Kiiō ļadik eo ej kade. Kiiō ke ej mat dekā ko, emej kidu eo.

Ke ej mej, ļadik eo item ajeej ṃōñā eo bwe ļōṃaro rej mej rej ļotļọk wōt, rejjañin ruj. Kiiō ṃōjin ajeej joñouljuon kōj. Kiiō kein joñouljuon ej kijen jinen. Ak e ejjab kōṃṃan ṃōñā. Bwe ke rej kiki ej ṃōñā. Kiiō ej leļọk jidik ṃwi ioon ṃōñā ko kijen ļōṃaro raar ļotļọk. Ak ioon kijen jinen eo wōt ejjab kōṃṃane.

Kiiō ke eṃōj an kōṃṃan ṃōñā eo ej kọruj er im jinen. Im rej ruj im ṃōñā. Im ke rej ṃōñā ļōṃaro rej ba, "Ebwiin ta ṃōñā kein?"

Kiiō bwebwe ej uwaak, "Ekwe kwōn ṃōñā wōt bwe kwaar lōļñọñ. Bōlen bao ko raar itok im pekati ke kwaar kiki."

Kiiō eṃōj an ba men eo ļōṃaro rej illu ippān ak ejjeļọk aer maroñ.

Ejeṃļọk bwebwenato.

(Ilo iien [eo] ke ļaddik ej ṃōj an kōmatti dekā ej al. Kiiō bwebwe ej al, ej ba, "Ņo jetak, jetak. | Ņo in kidu. | Pinej turin lañ."

Wūnin ej al bwebwe eo kōnke rej lo juon ņo; ņo in kidu, im emej [ļotļọk ļōṃaro].

Kōnke rejeļā ņo ej ņo in kidu.)

[Ke iaar kajjitōk ri-bwebwenato eo Mr. Jobel Emos, ta meļeļein bwebwenato in, eaar uwaak āindein:, "Meļeļein bwebwenato in ej jet jōṃjānjōṃjātin rejjab iọkwe doon. Im ejjab juon wōt aer ļōmņak. Innām renaaj jorrāān jān men eo. Ak ippān jinen joñan wōt juon. Juōn wōt *level.*

"Innām ñe renaaj bōk ļōmņak eo an jinen enaaj eṃṃan jabdewōt. Im ejjeļọk jorrāān.

Iaar katak bwebwenato in i Epoon ippān rūtto ro.

"Inọñ rejjab ṃool ak bwebwenato rej ṃool, āinwōt bwebwenato an Inedel ej ṃool ak Ļōppeipāāt ejjab ṃool, ej inọñ."]

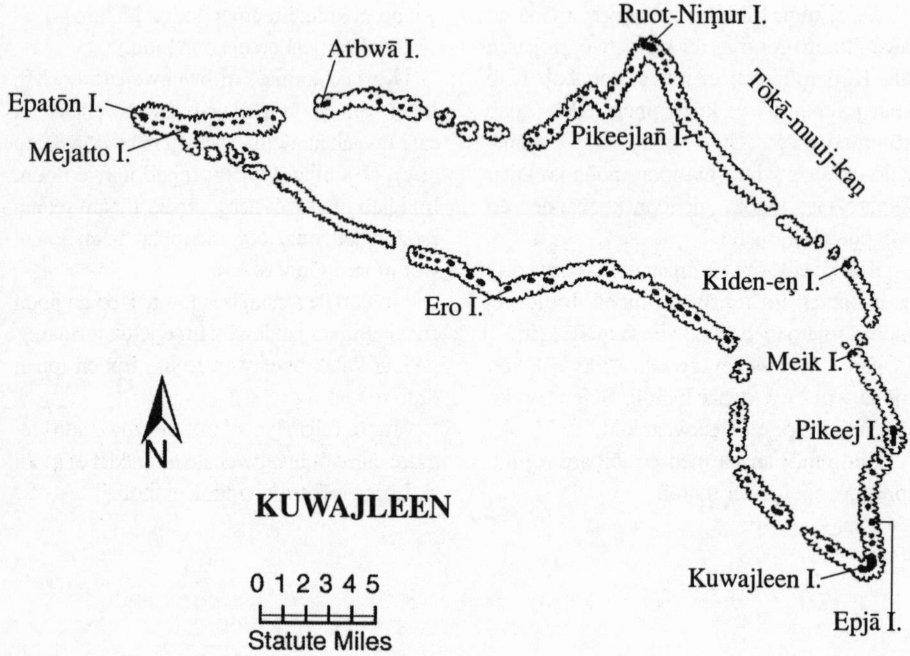

Aelōñ in Kuwajleen
Lagoon Area: 839.30 sq. mi.
Dry Land Area: 6.33 sq. mi.
(before additional land
added by dredging)

50: STORY ABOUT TWO EPATŌN WOMEN

As told by Jelibōr Jam, Kuwajleen[1] 1975

One of the women had six or seven sons. Every day the boys played, and they looked out for each other very well.

Their mother trusted them greatly, for the older boys took care of the younger boys.

One day, the boys went out again and played from morning until night. Their mother hoped that they were still playing and were about to return soon, for it was night. But they did not return.

Not like the days before. For they were accustomed to returning when the sun was still up.

But that day the sun set and the old woman began to worry and said to herself, "How is it that the boys have been accustomed to returning promptly? But why do they not return promptly now?

"What is it? Because of rain? And a big wind? And thunder? And lightning?

"Perhaps they will appear here when it is finished thundering and lightning and raining.

"I will just wait a little longer, for if they do not return I will go and look for them."

A little while later she went and looked for them. She went out and a woman was just eating. And that woman said to her (the woman who was looking for her children): "What are you walking about for, woman? For it is quite dark, and it is raining and thundering."

The woman answered, "I am walking about looking for my children, Kinukne (the name of the oldest son) and Kānukne (the second son) and Kājooneañ (the third) and Kājoonrak (the fourth) and Kājoonjat (the fifth) and Kājoonlañ (the sixth) and Kājoonmeja-to-o-to-o (the seventh)."

Now the woman said, "I did not eat Kinukne and Kānukne and Kājooneañ and Kājoonrak and Kājoonjat and Kājoonlañ and Kājoonmeja-to-o-to-o." (As Ļainjin said to the chiefs.)[2]

"O," the woman said. "O, thank you." "You are welcome" (the old woman said).

She continued on again and met with another old woman now. The old woman said, "What are you walking about for, woman? For it is very dark, raining, and thundering."

"I am walking about looking for my children, Kinukne and Kānukne and Kājooneañ and Kājoonrak and Kājoonjat and Kājoonlañ and Kājoonmeja-to-o-to-o."

Now the other old woman answered again, "I did not eat Kinukne and Kānukne and Kājooneañ and Kājoonrak and Kājoonlañ and Kājoonmeja-to-o-to-o!"

Now she again went ahead and came upon an old woman who was washing her hands and mouth. Now that old woman asked her, "What are you walking about for woman? For it is very dark, raining, and thundering."

---

1. Epatōn (Ebaden) is a rather small but fertile island (0.52 sq. mi. of dry land area) on the northwest tip (cape) of Kuwajleen Atoll, the largest atoll in the world (839.30 sq. mi.). The main island *(eonene)*, after which the atoll is named, is at its opposite (southeastern) extreme, some 80 miles away.

2. Ļainjin was the famous navigator whose name and deeds appear in many Marshallese folktales (see story 30, "The *Ikid* of Ļainjin" on page 131). His name is also used as a formula to conclude stories: "as Ļainjin said," or "as Ļainjin told the chiefs," and the like.

The old woman (the mother) said, "I am walking about looking for my children, Kinuke and Kānukne and Kājooneañ and Kājoonrak and Kājoonjat and Kājoonjat and Kājoonmeja-to-o-to-o!"

That old woman who was washing her hands and mouth said, "I ate Kinuke and Kānukne and Kājooneañ and Kājoonrak and Kājoonjat and Kājoonlañ and Kājoonmeja-to-o-to-o!"[3]

Now the old woman (the mother) leaped at the other one, and they fought. They fought. They fought to the ocean and they fought to the lagoon. To the place of the clamshell.

(In the ancient language *tiptake* means to pick it up and throw it down. And *ruk* is the sound of breaking.)[4]

The demon died, she who ate the children. And the woman stomped on the stomach of the demon, and the children appeared (from the mouth of the demon).[5]

They came out dead. Now the woman squeezed the children's stomachs with the sprout of a coconut tree, and massaged them, and they all came to life.[6]

To this day, the boys are the names of land parcels on Epatōn.

Thus Ļainjin told the chiefs.

---

3. Here we see motifs of mother love, of a mother searching for her lost children, and of cannibalism.

4. (The mother picked up the clam shell and threw it down and it broke.)

5. Note the theme of good (represented by the mother) and evil (represented by the demon) fighting to the death, and the triumph of good over evil. These are found in a number of other Marshallese folktales, and indeed those of other cultures.

6. Note the widespread theme of resurrection. In this case, a sprout of the very important coconut tree, and massage, are used in bringing the sons back to life. Both are used today in treating illness by the Marshallese *ri-wūno* (medicine people). Note also the use of repetition, alliteration, duplication, and rhythm in the dialogue. The storyteller smiled when he recited the line, "Kinukne and Kānukne and Kājooneañ and Kājoonrak and Kājoonjat and Kājoonlañ and Kājoonmeja-to-o-to-o."And he chuckled afterward. He obviously enjoyed telling it. This is characteristic of Marshallese narrative style, of the *ri-bwebwenato,* and it certainly enhances the stories.

I checked with the Office of Land Management of the Marshalls at Mājro report of October 15,1959 of the names of the land parcels *(wāto)* and could not find the names of the boys of the story. Perhaps they were named after the boys years ago and have been changed. Changes do occur in the names of the land parcels but these are usually a result of division of the land, and reflect this with a geographical designation (north or south, or middle) added to the original name. The present-day names are: Jeņrōk, Ṃōn-aidik, Ṃōn-alooj, Addi-eņ, Kājoni, Ļobōlǫk-rāirōk, Ļobōlǫk-rāiōñ, Mejatin-wōn, Ṃōn-tain, Ṃōn-kūtak, Ṃōn-aļ, Ṃōn-bar, Ṃōn-wūjooj, Lo-ran, Akadik-eņ, Wātoon-aļ, Apatutu, Lo-kabbwil, Denijo, Kineprōk, Wōte-jabuk, Ṃwin-kino, Lik-ioļap, Jen-iōñ, Batin-kañal, Nokwat, Nukut, and Likin-bōn, 28 in all. As an *aļap* (lineage head) of Epatōn Island explained to me on Kuwajleen in 1975, "the meaning of the names of *wāto*s on Epatōn in 'The Story of Two Epatōn Women' is that Kinukne and Kānukne are there. They are like *ņooniep* [supernatural beings of a specific kind]. Perhaps they were the sons of the *irooj* (chief) before. They are not demons. And they did not give their names to the *wāto*s. Maybe they are the sons of the chief. Those men do not harm people."

50: BWEBWENATO IN RUO KŌRĀ IN EPATŌN

Ri-bwebwenato: Jelibōr Jam, Kuwajleen 1975

Kōrā eo juon eor jiljino ak jiljilimjuon nājin ļaddik. Aolep raan ļadik ro rej ikkure im kanooj in eṃṃan aer lale doon. Jineer ej kanooj in lōke er kōn ļadik ro rōrūtto kōjparok ļadik ro reddik.

Ļak juon raan ļadik ro raar bar etal im ikkure jibboñ ñan boñ. Kōn an jineer kejatdikdik bwe rej ikkure wōt em nañin rọọl bwe eboñ. Ak rejab rọọl. Ejjab āinwōt raan ko ṃokta. Bwe rekōn rọọl ñe ej or wōt al.

Ak raan eo etulọk aļ im leļļap eo ej jino inepata em ba ippān make, "Etke ļaddik rekōn ṃōkajtok? Ak kiiō etke rej jab ṃōkaj in rọọltok? Ta, kōn an wōt ke? Em ļap kōto? Em jourur? Em jarom? Bōlen renaaj waļọk tok ñe eṃōj an jourur im jarom im wōt.

"Ijja bar kōttar jidik bwe ñe rejab itok inaaj ilān pukot er."

Ļọkun jidik iien ej etal im pukot er. Eļak ilọk juon kōrā ej ṃōñā bajjek em kōrā i ne ej ba ñane (lio ej pukot ajiri ro nājin), "Kwōj etetal in ta le? Ke enijōk marōk, wōt, jourur."

Ke lio ej uwaak, "Ij etetal in pukot [ļōṃaro] nājū Kinukne (etan ļeo nājin erūtto) Kānukne (ļeo nājin kein karuo) em Kājooneañ (kein kajilu) em Kājoonrak (kein kemān) em Kājoonjat (kein kaļalem) em Kājoonlañ (kein kajiljino) em Kājoonmeja-to-o-to-o (kein kajiljilimjuon)."

Kiiō lieṇ eaar ba, "Iaar jab kañ Kinukne em Kānukne em Kājooneañ em Kājoonrak em Kājoonjat em Kājoonlañ em Kājoonmeja-to-o-to-o." (Āinwōt Ļainjin ej ba ñan irooj ro.)

"O," kōrā eo eaar ba, "O, koṃṃool!"

"Kōn jouj," leļļap eo eaar ba.

Ar bar etal im bar iioon juon leļļap kiiō. Leļļap ej ba, "Kwo etetal in ta le? Bwe enijōk marok, wōt, jourur."

"Ij etetal in pukot nājū Kinukne em Kānukne em Kājooneañ em Kājoonrak em Kājoonjat em Kājoonlañ em Kājoonmeja-to-o-to-o."

Kiiō bar uwaak leļļap eo juon, "Iaar jab kañ Kinukne em Kānukne em Kājooneañ em Kājoonrak em Kājoonjat em Kājoonlañ em Kājoonmeja-to-o-to-o!"

Kiiō bar etal [im lo] juon leļļap ej aṃwini pein im lọñiin. Kiiō leļļap ṇe ej kajjitōk ļọk ippān, "Kwōj etetal in ta le? Ke enijōk marok, wōt, jourur."

Leļļap eo (jinen) ej ba, "Ij etetal im pukot nājū Kinukne em Kānukne em Kājooneañ em Kājoonrak em Kājoonjat em Kājoonlañ em Kājoonmeja-to-o-to-o!"

Leļļap eo eaar aṃwini pein im lọñiin, eba, "Iaar kañ Kinukne em Kānukne em Kājooneañ em Kājoonrak em Kājoonjat em Kājoonlañ em Kājoonmeja-to-o-to-o!"

Kiiō leļļap eo (jinen) ekāļọk im ro ire. Ire, ire likļọk im ire arļọk kajjien aded eo in tiptake ruk!

(Ilo kajin etto "tiptake" ej 'kotake im kawōtlọke'. Im "ruk" ej 'ainikien rup'.)

Emej tiṃoṇ eo, lio [ekar] kañ ajiri ro. Innām lio ej juur lọjien tiṃoṇ eo em ewaļọk ajiri ro (jān lọñiin tiṃoṇ). Waļọk remej.

Kiiō lio karọọl jepake eo ñan ļadik ro nājin ioon lọjieer im kapiti er. Em aolep mour.

Ñan rainin ļadik ro rej etan ṃōkaṇ Epatōn.

Āindein Ļainjin ar ba ñan irooj ro.

51: ABOUT A WOMAN WHO HAD A BOY CHILD

As told by Jelibōr Jam, Kuwajleen 1975

Perhaps they stayed on Epoon Atoll, but it is not very clear.

The island the two of them stayed on, there was no food there. And all of the people were worried and walked around to look for their food.

But the boy had a paddling canoe. His father had made it and died from it. (The boy was his son.)

When the boy was older and his mother and he met the hunger [became hungry], he walked out, leisurely and saw the canoe that his father had made. And now he planned to finish the canoe just so that he could go fishing every day.

And he hurried to finish the canoe.

One day he went and just walked around on the lagoon side [of the island]. And he saw a ripe coconut that had drifted in, and he went and got it and took it away to his mother.

And their breakfast on the following day was the ripe coconut [*Cocos nucifera*, coconut tree, *ni;* ripe coconut, *waini*].

Right after they [had] finished their breakfast, the boy said to his mother: "My mother, I have finished the canoe of my father. And I would just [like to] go to the islands over there to the north, and see if there is food there. For if there is much [food], I will load my canoe and bring it here for us."

And his mother said: "Be careful in your journey. For who says that it is not a demon island? I have never seen anyone go to that island."

And the boy said: "I would just like to try going."

And his mother said: "Well, go! And hurry back." And the boy took the paddling canoe and paddled.

When he reached the island, he smelled the sweet odor of breadfruit [*Artocarpus altilis, mā*] and the sweet odor of pandanus [*Pandanus tectorius* Park, *bōb.*] And the boy said to himself: "It is clear that this island is loaded with food; very much food. Well, I will just see."

And he took the canoe ashore and went toward the middle of the island. When he went, many breadfruit were falling to the ground. (Some had fallen a little in the past and some when he saw them.) Many pandanus, many coconuts, many taro [*Cyrtosperma chamissonis, iaraj*], many papayas [*Carica papaya, keinabbu*], many bananas [*Musa* sp.]—*kōḷowan* is *pinana,* banana in *kajin etto,* the ancient language. Any [and all] foods. ([I do] not [use the word] *kain* [kind] [here] because *kain* is in *kajin pālle* [the white man's language, English].)[1]

And the boy loaded his canoe with breadfruit, coconuts, bananas, *kōḷowan.* And it was full of food. But not one person did he see on the island.

When he returned, his mother was just sitting under the coconut trees near the lagoon side of their house. For she was looking for the boy, her son.

And the woman said: "My son, you are late already. Is there any *mọọr*?" (in the ancient language, food).[2]

The boy said, "[There is] a lot. Come

1. Here is another linguistic evaluation by the informant. The English noun *kind* was borrowed by the Marshallese as *kain*, and although it is well integrated into the language, he made the distinction that he did.

2. Note the close similarity to *mour* (life, living, alive, well-being, welfare). Food, of course, sustains life.

here! We will carry the food to the island from the canoe."

When his mother went to the ocean and saw that there was much food there, she was happy, and called the people near them so that they would come and get their food, and help the two of them carry [the food] onto the island.

When they finished their carrying, they took the canoe onto the island and they said, "*Wa in kōjōban kōj*" (ancient language: 'the canoe that makes us fortunate': *jeraaṃṃan kōj*).

At the time, the people were very happy, but they had no canoes that they could paddle to the other island. But the boy would again go to the island on the morrow. The next day he again took his canoe seaward and said to his mother, "I will hurry up now, for there is a lot of food and I will quickly load this canoe."

And he took his paddling canoe and paddled and reached the other island and went onto the island and harvested taro (*eto* is *kajin iaraj,* taro language for 'to harvest', and is used only for taro), took bananas, picked breadfruit, and hurried and returned. When he came, his mother and the people again came to the canoe and saw that there were several different kinds of food from the food before. And they said, "Whose food is the great big taro there?"

The young man replied, "Food within the mouths of the greedy ones there, but you ask. Well, take those things to the island [with you]."

But another woman leaned toward the inside of the canoe and saw the banana, and said, "And whose food is this?—that big banana there."

The boy answered in the Ratak dialect,[3] "O, food within the mouths of the greedy ones. But you ask. Let us all hurry" (*wok* is *O* in the Ratak dialect).

And they hurried and took the things; they were just finished and they took the canoe onto the island and again said, *"O-O-O, wa in kōjōban kōj."* ("O-O-O, this canoe makes us fortunate.")

And they divided [the food] among themselves, and went to their houses and stayed there.

The following day, the boy went and met the Etao[4] who was beating [processing] coconut husk fiber, *bweo̧*.

(The *kein dōn̄dōn̄,* tool for slapping [processing] *bweo̧,* is made from a piece of *kōn̄e* wood [*Pemphis acidula* Forst., ironwood] and is thin and about one and one-half feet long.)

And he [the boy] said, "You will be slapping out until when?"

The Etao replied, "Only until my coconut husk fibers are finished."

"And are you a little hungry?" [the boy asked].

The Etao replied, "O, yes. I am hungry, but what can be done about it? There is no food in our house."

The boy said, "Well, I will go bring us food here from that island to the north."

Etao replied, "What, sir? Friend. How will you be going there?"

The boy replied, "A canoe that I have. And I am going to paddle now, for I am leaving."

The Etao called to him, "I will wait for you here!"

---

3. The Ratak (eastern chain of the Marshalls) dialect is used in this story, as indicated by the storyteller, even though he said that he thought the locale might be Epoon Atoll, which is in the Rālik (western) chain. He himself is from the western part of Rālik.

4. Etao is the trickster/hero figure of the Marshalls, and is comparable to Olofat (Iolofāth) and Nareau of other Micronesian folktales, to Maui (under his various names) of Polynesia, and to the tricksters of other cultures. See Leach (1950 vol. 2:1123–1125) for an overview of these interesting characters.

The boy turned around [toward Etao] and said, "I will hurry now." And he went and got the canoe and paddled. And when he reached the island, he took the canoe and got baskets, and got his implements for picking breadfruit. And he went in to the island and picked breadfruit.

He was just picking breadfruit [when] he heard a voice. But he did not see people. And he ceased picking, because he was frightened.

The voice cried, *"Bwiin armej jādwa juon in!"* (In the ancient language *jādwa* is "and canoe.") ("Odor of a human being in this small canoe!")

And the boy hurried to descend from the branch of the breadfruit tree and loaded his baskets and took them to the canoe and paddled.

When he reached the other island, he remembered the Etao and took his food, breadfruit, to him. And said to the honorable Etao, "O, sir, friend. I heard a voice that said *'Bwiin armej jādwa juon in!'* ("Odor of a human being in this small canoe!") And I hurried and came.

"There would have been many breadfruit for you to eat, but because I was afraid of the voice, [I] hurried back. And that is the reason for the few breadfruit, your food there."

Etao said, "You will go again tomorrow. For if you meet with harm, I will help you."

The boy said, "Thank you. During the past days, I never saw people at that time—just heard a voice. And I just heard a voice today. And I will go again tomorrow, as you say."

The boy returned and went to the canoe and took breadfruit to his mother.

And said, "[There are] few breadfruit there. For I was frightened by a voice that I heard. Never mind, I will go again tomorrow."

His mother replied, "Do not go back there, for we do not know whose island that is" [who is on that island].

The following day the boy again went and took his canoe and paddled. But his mother did not know, for she had restrained him and said that he, the boy, should not go.

And the boy looked for people when he first arrived on the island. But he did not see even one. And he climbed [a tree] and again picked breadfruit.

After he finished picking breadfruit, he carried breadfruit and ripe coconuts to his canoe. When he went to paddle, he saw that the demon was running after him [chasing him]. And the boy hastened to paddle with all his might.

When the demon (a male demon) saw the boy hastening to paddle, he cried out and said, "Never mind if you go, but you and your canoe are my food!"[5]

Now the boy paddled and said a *roro* (chant) for paddling. *"Kartak jān lo naṃ no | Wea | Wea | Wea ea-e | Kiped eo | Jeña. | Lim eo jeña | Wa eo kartak | Kartak O-O-O | Rujri | Rujurjur wōj!"* (He chanted the paddling *roro* to himself.) ("Paddle from that little lagoon over there | Paddle fast | Paddle fast | Paddle fast-t-t | The paddle | The bailer with me | The canoe paddle | Paddle O-O-O | Over there | Over there to you!")

Now the demon hurried with all his might and grabbed the sternpiece of the canoe and ate it.

At that time the boy moved forward to the bow of the canoe and sat and paddled.

And again said, *"Kartak jān lo naṃ no | Wea | Wea | Wea ea-e | Kiped eo | Jeña. | Lim eo jeña | Wa eo kartak | Kartak O-O-O | Rujri | Rujurjur wōj!"* ("Paddle from that little lagoon over there | Paddle fast | Paddle fast | Paddle fast-t-t | The paddle | The bailer

5. The motif of the pursung demon or evil spirit is found in a number of Marshallese folktales. It is a widespread motif that adds to the dramatic quality of a narrative, as does the motif of cannibalism.

with me | The canoe paddle | Paddle O-O-O | Over there | Over there to you!")

The canoe continued to go [run] and beached on the sand on the other island.

And the boy jumped off and ran. But the demon came ashore and ate the canoe and ate the breadfruit, and again cried out to the boy and said, "You flee, but I will catch you. I will eat you.[6]

"Now I know who went to eat that food that time on my island. It was you. I will catch you!"

And the boy ran and came to where Ļe-Etao was working.

When Etao saw the boy, the boy was almost dead from being almost out of breath and panting.

The Etao said, "Why are you almost out of breath and panting, sir, friend?"

The boy replied and said, "I am fleeing from that demon." The Etao said, "Well, I will help you. Come here, and go under my coconut fiber."

Because, at that time the Etao was slapping [processing] coconut fiber, the boy went under the coconut fiber of the Etao and hid. The Etao just continued making his fiber and the demon came. And Etao said to the demon, "Why are you almost out of breath and panting, sir?"

The demon replied, "Because I am chasing the *kolej* [*Pluvialis dominica,* golden plover], my pet, in this direction.

"Have you seen it running near here?"

Etao replied, "I did not see it, but come here, and the two of us will go to my house for you to rest a little. I will just tell you *inọn̄* (legends). And you just tell legends to me."

And the demon obeyed the Etao and thought to himself, and said (to himself), "I will eat that person Ļe-Etao when he goes to sleep."

But Etao spoke to himself and said, "When that demon sleeps deeply, I will burn him up."

(The demon was tall. He could become as short as a finger [six inches]. He could change his shape in any manner.)[7]

(Etao is a man, and is very proficient in lying. He is a human being, not a demon.)

Thus were the thoughts of the two, [kept] from each other, at the time when they went to the house.

The demon said to Ļe-Etao, "See here, friend, you will begin telling legends to the two of us." And the Etao said to the demon, "But you, sir [you go first]."

The demon replied, "[You go first] because I am still out of breath, and because I want to hear your legends, for they say they are good."

Etao said, "Well, I will tell the best legend."

And the two of them went inside the house. And Etao gave a piece of coconut fiber to the demon and said, "Take this, sir. I give you this, your material for sennit. And listen to my legend."

(They made coconut sennit, *eokkwaļ,* by rolling and twisting the prepared coconut husk fibers, *bweọ,* on their thighs. And they

6. Here again we see the motif of the pursuit of a canoe by an evil entity in an attempt to kill those fleeing from it. This obviously enhances the suspenseful quality of the story. The degree of destruction of the canoe varies among the Marshallese stories that I have recorded, from complete destruction, as in this story, to partial destruction, and none whatsoever. But the intended victims always escape.

7. This is another example of shape-shifting. Which is "an important mechanism in the folklore of all peoples. A shape-shifter is a creature or object [that] is able to change its shape either at will or under special circumstances. Shape-shifting may be evil or benign . . ." (Leach 1950, vol. 2:1004–1005). This motif is found in other Marshallese stories, as, for example, the *mejenkwaad* who can stretch their necks out for miles in pursuit of their victims, the *kojinmeto* who can assume different shapes to deceive their victims, and other spirits who can assume the guise of humans and of animals.

told stories as they did this. This is the Marshallese custom, *m̧antin M̧ajeļ*, and is like the coffee of the white man [that is, helps to fight boredom, fatigue, and sleep].)[8]"

The demon said, "Thank you, sir. Well, tell a legend."

And Etao began to tell a legend. And said, "*Rōkōjañ dōb eo nājin Etao | Rōkōjañ dōb eo nājin Etao | Edda wōj wie | Edda wōj wie | Rōkōjañ mejān dejjōñ | Edejōñjōñ.*"

(Rōkōjañ is *kajin aje*: drum language or *tiin* [empty metal container: large biscuit container, etc.]. It means 'beat'. In the ancient language, *dōb* is drum.[9] *Edda wōj* is 'close your eyes'. *Dejjōñ* is 'heavily'. And *edejōñjōñ* is 'really heavy'. He chanted this so that his [the demon's] eyes would not open, so that he would sleep really deeply.)[10]

("Beat the drum, child of Etao. | Beat the drum, child of Etao. Close your eyes. Close your eyes. Close your eyes heavily. | Really heavily.")

When Etao was ending his legend, the demon began to be sleepy, and said to Etao:

"I say that you are bewitching me, sir, friend!" *(Anji* is 'to bewitch', *kanijnij* in the ancient language.)

The Etao replied, "No, but it is because you have enjoyed listening to this legend very much."

The demon said, "O, sir, it is true, sir, I enjoyed listening to this legend very much. Repeat it one and two times more so I can listen again, for I have greatly enjoyed listening."

The Etao now again repeated his *inoñ*. "*Rōkōjañ dōb eo nājin Etao | Rōkōjañ dōb eo nājin Etao | Edda wōj wie | Edda wōj wie | Rōkōjañ mejān dejjōñ | Edejōñjōñ.*" ("Beat the drum, child of Etao. | Beat the drum, child of Etao. | Close your eyes. | Close your eyes. | Beat your eyes heavily. | Really heavily.")

Now the demon began to yawn (a sign of drowsiness) and his eyes became heavy. And he did not make a noise now because he became sleepy. And his eyes were pressed down. (In the ancient language *ewetok* is 'came [became]'.)

And Ļe-Etao, when he saw that the demon was dozing off and starting up (a sign of sleepiness), again began [to chant] his legend to make the demon sleepier.

When the demon heard the legend, he leaned over and lay down. And slept, and deeply. The Etao called out one and two times but the demon did not move at all! Because he slept soundly.

At that time, the Etao went and brought the boy, his friend, so that the two of them could carry coconut fronds, the kind that are old, to the house so that the two of them could set fire to it. This was the plan of Etao earlier.

When there were a great many coconut fronds, Etao set fire first to the west [side] of the house. And set fire to the south [side]. And the boy set fire to the north [side] of the house, and to the east [side] last of all. And they stood and watched the house burning.

A short while later the demon felt heat and went to flee to the west, [but] there was fire. And he did not know which way to go, for the whole area [of the house] was on fire. And he burned up and died.[11] And the Etao spoke to

8. Note the incorporation of the analogy of white men drinking coffee into the narration of this traditional tale. This is another example of how folktales change in details in the telling over the years, reflecting new experiences and culture change, and creativity on the part of the storytellers as well.

9. The informant described and sketched the traditional drum (*aje*). It is hourglass-shaped, made of breadfruit wood, and the drumhead is made from the stomach of a shark, he explained.

10. Note the use of a magical chant to control the demon. Chants (*roro*) were and still are used in connection with magic and medicine (healing), and for other purposes as well.

the boy, his friend, and said, "Go and find our mother, for you have been here a long time [that is, gone from your mother]."

When the boy went to his mother and told her about how the demon had gone to eat him, his mother was very sad.[12] And the boy said, "Get ready, for we two will go to that island and stay there. For the demon whose island it was is gone."

The mother replied, "When will we two go?"

The boy replied, "Tomorrow." The following day they prepared their canoe and went. And the Etao spoke truthfully[13] to the boy and the old woman their mother, and said, "You two go now." And they went and remained on the island to this day. (But I do not know where it is.)[14]

It is ended.

(The meaning of this thing: If you strive to attain something, and if there are people to help you, you will attain your goal.

That is, if there is something you want or need, but you do not know the way to go about it [to obtain it], and if there is a person who helps you, you will reach it.

If Etao had not helped the boy, it would have been impossible [for the boy to have reached his goal], and he would have died. But Etao helped him.

Sometimes Etao [is] good. Sometimes [he is] bad. Etao lies a great deal.)

---

11. The motif of the destruction of the evil spirit by burning is found in other Marshallese folktales, and in the folktales of many other cultures. It has the obvious dramatic quality of complete destruction. The motif of trapping an evil, threatening spirit or spirits in a house, then setting fire to the house and thus killing the dangerous occupants, is found in Hawaiian folklore. For example, see Beckwith (1970:444) "Story of Hanaaumoe."

12. The sadness was presumably because of the danger, the close call that her son had experienced.

13. Here we see the trickster Etao in his benevolent aspect. His veracity at times (when it suits him) is recognized in this story.

14. Note the motif of the island of much food. Compare this with the Marshallese story of the young man from Kuwajleen who found a great deal of food on Ellep Island. He also took care of his mother, who killed a demon (a shape-shifter), and lived happily ever after (story 19, "Story about Ellep in the Days of Long Ago, page 98).

The informant explained the meanings of the words in the canoe-paddling chant that are in the ancient language (*kajin etto*) or that are seldom used today: "*karkaak* is 'paddle', *lo* is 'that', *no* is 'there', *wea* is 'paddle fast', *kiped* is 'the paddle', *jeña* is 'with me', *rujri* is 'over there', and *rujurjur wōj* is 'over there to you'."

The Marshallese are very odor-conscious, and have a number of words for specific odors, pleasant and unpleasant, including those emanating from various parts of the body, and from various objects and conditions. Some of these do not have English counterparts.

Sweet-smelling flowers are prized and are used as garlands or leis (*ṃarṃar*) for neck and head, especially for festive occasions, and are presented to guests of honor and visitors to the island, as is done in other Pacific Island cultures.

Marshallese will say appreciatively, and to provoke amusement: "*O, ennọ bwiin. Bōlen juon lerooj ej etetal bajjek!*" (O, a delicious smell. Maybe a chiefess is just walking by!) The presence of an attractive woman on an island is poetically said to be announced by the sweet odor of pandanus fruit or of flowers. This is how a chief, in an important speech on Mājro in 1973, before a large gathering, described how he found the chiefess who later became his wife.

51: KŌN JUŌN KŌRĀ EOR JUŌN NĀJIN ĻADDIK

Ri-bwebwenato: Jelibōr Jam, Kuwajleen 1975

Bōlen rej pād i aelōñ in Epoon, ak ejjab kanooj in alikkar.

Āneo eo rejro pād ie, ejjeļọk ṃōñā ie. Innām aolep armej rej inepata im etetal in kappok kijeer ṃōñā.

Ak ļadik eo eor juon waan kōrkōr. Jemān eaar kōṃṃane, im mej jāne (ļadik eo nājin).

Ke ļadik eo ej rūttoļọk im rejro jinen iioon kwōle eo, ej ikkureļọk im lo wa eo jemān eaar jeke im kiiō ej ļōmņak in kaṃōjļọk wa eo. Bwe en kab eọñwōd ek aolep raan.

Im ej kaiuri in kaṃōjļọk wa eo.

Ilo juon raan eaar etal im etetal bajjek iaar. Im loe juon waini ej petok im eaar ilām bōke im bōkļọk ñan ippān jinen.

Im ṃabuñ eo aerro ilo rujļọkin eo waini eo.

Ṃwijin wōt aerro ṃōñā ļadik eo ej ba ñan jinen, "Jinō, eṃōj wa eņ waamro jema. Innām ña ijja ṃōk etal ñan āne eiō eañ ṃōk. Im lale eor ke ṃōñā ie. Bwe ñe elōñ inaaj kanne wa eo waō kōn ṃōñā im ebbōktok kijerro."

Innām jinen ej ba, "Lale aṃ etal bwe wōn ej ba ejjab āne anij (tiṃoņ)? Āneeņ ke ejjeļọk eņ inañin lo an etal ñane."

Innām ļadik eo ej ba, "Ij baj kajjeoñ in etal."

Im jinen ej ba, "Ekwe etal! Kab ṃōkaj tok." Im ļadik eo ej bōk kōrkōr eo ñan lọjet im aōņōōņ.

Ke etōparļọk āne eo ej āt bwiin tañal in mā kab bwiin tañal in bōb. Innām ļadik eo ej ba ilo būruon, "Alikkar ke āniin ebuñ-pāļọk kōn ekkan. Ekwe ijja ṃōk in lale."

Innām ej bōk kōrkōr eo āneļọk im wōnoojļọk. Ke ej ilọk elōñ mā remābuñ. Elōñ bōb, elōñ ni, elōñ iaraj, elōñ keinabbu, elōñ kōļowan (kajin etto: pinana). Elōñ aolep jabdewōt ṃōñā.

(Jet mootļọk jidik im jet ke ej loe ie.)

(Ejjab, "kain." Kōnke, "kain" ej kajin pālle.)

Innām ļadik eo eaar kanne wa eo waan kōn mā, bōb, ni, pinana, kōļowan. Innām eboļ kōn ṃōñā. A ejjeļọk juon armej eloe ilo āne eo.

Ke ej jepļaak eļak ilọk jinen ej jijet wōt iuṃwin ni ko i jabar in ṃweo iṃwerro. Bwe ej pukot ļadik eo nājin.

Innām kōrā eo ej ba, "Nājū konañin ruṃwij. Eor ke ṃọọr (kajin etto: ṃōñā)?"

Ļadik eo eba, "Elōñ. Kwōn itok! Kōjro aljōk āne wōj, ṃōñā jān wa e."

Ke jinen ej wōnmetoļọk im loe an kanooj lōñ ṃōñā, ej eṃṃōņōņō im kūrtok armej ro repaake erro bwe ren iten ebbōk kijeer. Im jipañ erro aljōk āneļọk. Ke ej ṃōj aer aljōk rej bōk wa eo āneļọk im rej ba, "Waan kōjōban kōj (kajin etto: kōjeraaṃṃan kōj)."

Ilo iien eo, eļap an armej ro eṃṃōņōņō. Ak ejjeļọk wa ippāer bwe ren aōņōōņ ñan āne eo juon. Ak ļadik eo enaaj bar etal ñan āne eo ilo raan eo ilju. Ej raan wōt ak ej bar bōk metoļọk wa eo waan im ba ñan jinen, "Inaaj ṃōkaj tok kiiō bwe eļap an lōñ ṃōñā im enaaj jerab ṃōkaj aō kanne wa in."

Innām ej bōk kōrkōr eo an im aōņōōņ im tōprakļọk āne eo juon im wōnāneļọk im etto iaraj. Ebōk pinana, kōṃkōṃ mā. Im ṃōkaj im jepļaak. Ke ej ilọk, jinen kab armej ro rej bar itok ñan wa eo im lo bwe jet wōt ko wāween ṃōñā jān ṃōñā ko ṃokta. Im rej ba, "Kijen wōn iaraj kileplep ņeņe?"

Likao eo ej uwaak, "Kijen lowae lọñiin tōrtōr ņeņe a kwōj ejitōk. Ekwe, koṃin būki men kaņe ānewōj."

Ak bar juon kōrā ej ṃaltok ñan lowaan wa eo im lo pinana eo. Im ba, "A kijen wōn, pinana kileplep ņeņe?"

Ļadik eo euwaak ilo kajin Ratak, "Wok, kijen lowae loñiin tōrtōr. A ejitōk. Kemimen ṃōkaj."

Innām rej ṃōkaj. Im būki men ko; ej ṃōj wōt ak rej bōk wa eo āneļọk im bar ba, "O-O-O waan in kōjōban kōj." Im rej wōj ajeej ñan doon. Im etal ñan ṃōko iṃweer im pād ie.

Rujļọkin eo juon ļadik eo ej etal im iioon Etao eo ej dōñdōñ an bweọ. Im ej ba ñan Etao eo, "Kwonaaj dōñdōñ ṃae ñāāt?"

Etao eo ej uwaak, "Iien eo wōt emaat bweọ ko aō. Ak kwōj kwōle ke bajjek?" likao eo ej kajjitōk.

Etao eo ej uwaak, "O, aet. I kwōle ak enaaj kōjkan ke ejjeļọk ṃōñā iṃwiin iṃōrro."

Ļadik eo ej ba, "Ekwe, inaaj ṃōk etal in ebbōktok kijerro jān āne ṇe iōñ."

Etao ej uwaak, "Ta ļe, jera? Kwōnaaj etal iaaļọk?"

Ļadik eo ej uwaak, "Juon eṇ wa ippa. Innām ña ij etal in aōṇōōṇ kiiō. Iọkwe eok bwe ña imootļọk."

Etao eo ej ikkūrļọk, "Inaaj kōttar eok ije."

Ļadik eo ej oktaklik im ba, "Inaaj ṃōkaj tok wōt kiiō." Innām ej etal im bōk wa eo im aōṇōōṇ. Im ke etōparļọk āne eo ej bōk wa eo im bōk kilōk ko im bōk kein kōṃkōṃ eo an. Im wōnāneļọk. Im kōṃkōṃ.

Ejja kōṃkōṃ wōt a ej roñ juon ainikien. Ak ejjab ellolo armej. Im eṃōj an kōṃkōṃ bwe eor an mijak.

Ainikien eo ej ba, "Bwiin armej jādwa juon in!" (Ilo kajin etto jādwa ej 'kab wa'.)

Innām ļadik eo ej ṃōkaj in to jān raan mā eo im ebbōkļọk kijen mā. Im ba ñan Ļe-Etao eo, "A ļe jera, iroñjake juon ainikien ej ba, 'Bwiin armej jādwa juon in!' Innām iaar ṃōkaj im itok. Enaaj kar lōñ kijōṃ mā, ak kōnke imijak ainikien eo, im ṃōkaj tok. Innām wūnin an iiet kijōṃ mā ṇe."

Etao eo ej ba, "Kwonaaj ṃōk bar etal ilju. Bwe ñe kweioon jorrāān inaaj jipañ eok."

Ļadik eo ej ba, "Koṃṃool jera. Ilo raan ko remootļọk ijjañin kar ellolo armej iien eṇ. Kab roñjake ainikien. Ak ij kab roñ wōt rainin. Innām inaaj bar etal ilju āinwōt aṃ ba."

Ļadik eo ej jepļaak im etal ñan wa eo im bōkļọk mā ko ñan jinen.

Im ba, "Eiiet mā ṇe bwe imijak. Kōn juon ainikien iaar roñjake. Jekdọọn ak inaaj bar etal ilju."

Jinen ej uwaak, "Eṃōj aṃ etal bwe jejaje āneen wōn āneeṇ."

Rujļọk eo juon ļadik eo ej bar etal im bōk wa eo waan im aōṇōōṇ. Ak jinen ejaje. Bwe eaar dāpiji im ba en [kab] jab etal ļadik eo.

Innām ļadik eo jinoin an tōprakļọk āne eo ej kappok armej. A ejjeļọk juon ej loe. Innām ej tallōñ im bar kōṃkōṃ.

Ṃwijin an kōṃkōṃ. Ej aljōk mā im waini ñan wa eo waan.

Ke ej iten aōṇōōṇ ej lo tiṃoṇ eo ej ettōrļọk ñan ippān.

Innām ļadik eo ej kamaat an maroñ in aōṇōōṇ.

Ke tiṃoṇ eo ej lo an ļadik eo kaiuri in aōṇōōṇ ej laṃōj im ba, "Jekdọọn ñe kwōj ko ak kijō kwe kab wa ṇe waaṃ!"

Kiiō ļadik eo ej aōṇōōṇ im ba (ej roro in aōṇōōṇ).

"Kartak jān lo naṃ no | Wea | Wea | Wea ea-e | Kiped eo | Jeña. |

"Lim eo jeña | Wa eo kartak | Kartak O-O-O | Rujri | Rujurjur wōj!"

(Ej roro in aōṇōōṇ ñane make.)

Kiiō tiṃoṇ eo ej kamaat an maroñ im jibwe jiṃ eo iļọkan wa eo im kañe.

Iien in ļadik eo ej keṃaanļọk ñan ṃaan wa eo im jijet im aōṇōōṇ. Im bar ba, "Kartak jān lo naṃ no | Wea | Wea | Wea ea-e | Kiped eo | Jeña. |

"Lim eo jeña | Wa eo kartak | Kartak O-O-O | Rujri | Rujurjur wōj!"

Wa eo ettōr in deo im pāāte ṇa ioon bok in āne eo juon. Innām ļadik eo ej kāļọk im ettōr. Ak tiṃoṇ eo eatotok im kañ kōrkōr eo im kañe mā ko, im bar laṃōj ñan ļadik eo im ba, "Kwōj ko wōt ak kopo. Inaaj kañ eok.

"Jebba ta eŋ ekōŋaan kañi mōña kaŋ iañ eŋ āne eŋ āne eō. Ak kwe. Kwōj kab po!"

Innām ļadik eo eaar ettōr im kattōparļǫk ijo Ļe-Etao ej jerbal ie.

Ke etao ej lo ļadik eo, ļadik eo enañin jako kōn an ikkijeļǫk.

Etao ej ba, "Etke kokkijeļǫk ļe jera?" Ļadik eo ej uwaak, im ba, "Ij ko jān tiṃoŋ eŋ." Etao eo eba, "Ekwe inaaj jipañ eok. Kwōn itok. Im deļǫñ iuṃwin bweǫ kā aō."

Kōnke iien eo Etao eo ej dōñdōñ bweǫ. Innām ļadik eo ej deļǫñ ļǫk iuṃwin bweǫ ko an Etao eo im tilekek. Etao eo ejja kōṃṃane bweǫ ko an wōt ak ej itok tiṃoŋ eo. Im Etao eo ej ba ñan tiṃoŋ eo, "Etke kokkijeļǫk ļe?"

Tiṃōŋ eo ej uwaak, "Kōnke ña ij lukwarkware koleej eo nājū tok ijintok. Kwaar baj lo ke an ettōrtok ijōkein tok?"

Etao eo ej uwaak, "Ijjab loe ak kwōn iwōj jero etal ñan ṃweeŋ iṃō bwe kwōn kakkije jidik, bwe in kab inǫñ ñan eok. Innām kwōnaaj baj inǫñ ñan eō."

Innām tiṃoŋ eo ej pokake Etao eo im ļōmŋak ilo e make. Im ba (ñan e make), "Inaaj kañ kijoñe Ļe-Etao ñe ekiki."

Ak Etao eo ej kōnono ippān make im ba, "N̄e ettoñ tiṃoŋ ŋe inaaj tile."

(Tiṃōŋ aetok, emaroñ ekadu lukkuun āinwōt addi in pein [jiljino inij]. Āinwōt emaroñ ukot jekjek eo an jabdewōt wāween. Etao ej eṃṃaan. Ak lukkuun mālōtlōt ilo riab. Ej armej, ejjab tiṃoŋ.)

Āindein ļōmŋak ko aerro jān doon. Ilo iien eo ke rejro etal ñan ṃweo.

Tiṃōŋ eo ej ba ñan Ļe-Etao, "Eoļe, jera, kwōnaaj jino inǫñ ñan kōjro." Innām Etao eo ej ba ñan tiṃoŋ eo, "Ak kwe ļe."

Tiṃōŋ eo ej uwaak, "Kōnke ij ikkijeļǫk wōt, kab ke ikōŋaan aṃ inǫñ. Bwe rej ba eṃṃan."

Etao ej ba, "Ekwe, inaaj kwaļǫk inǫñ eo eṃṃantata."

Innām rejro deļǫñ ilowaan ṃweo. Im Etao eo ej leļǫk juon bweǫ ñan tiṃoŋ eo im ba, "Eowaj ļe, lewōj eieo aṃ kein eokkwaļ kab roñjake aō inǫñ."

(Rej kōṃṃan eokkwaļ kōn iñiñ ioon wūnin ne ko aer ke rej bwebwenato. Ej ṃantin Ṃajeļ. Āinwōt kǫpe an ripālle.)

Tiṃōŋ eo ej ba, "Koṃṃool ļe. Ekwe inǫñ ṃōk."

Innām Etao eo ej jino an inǫñ. Im ba, "Rōkōjañ dōb eo nājin Etao | Rōkōjañ dōb eo nājin Etao | Edda wōj wie | Edda wōj wie | Rōkōjañ mejān dejjōñ | Edejōñjōñ."

(Ilo kajin etto "dōb" ej aje. "Edda wōj wie" ej 'kilōk mejān (eddo) ñan eok'. "Dejoñ" ej 'eddo'. Im "edejōñjōñ" ej 'lukkuun eddo', bwe enjab peļļǫk mejān. Bwe en lukkuun kiki.) (Ilo roro eo Etao eo ej ba kilōk mejān tiṃoŋ eo. Ak tiṃoŋ eo ejaje ta eo ej roro [kake].)

Ke ej jeṃļǫk an inǫñ Etao eo, tiṃoŋ eo ej jino an mejki. Im ba ñan Etao ej, "I ba kwōj anji eō ļe jera!" (Kajin etto: "anji" ej 'kanijnij'.)

Etao eo ej uwaak, "Jab, ak kōnke eļap an eṃṃan aṃ roñjake inǫñ in."

Tiṃōŋ eo ej ba, "A ļe, ṃool ļe, ekanooj in eṃṃan aō roñjake. Bar jerak ṃōk juon im ruo alen bwe in bar roñjake. Bwe eļap an eṃṃan aō roñ."

Etao eo kiiō, ej bar jerak inǫñ eo an, "Rōkōjañ dōb eo nājin Etao | Rōkōjañ dōb eo nājin Etao | Edda wōj wie | Rōkōjañ mejān dejjōñ | Edejōñjōñ."

Kiiō tiṃoŋ eo ej jino an mebbōļa im eddo tok mejān. Ak ejjab ekkeroro kiiō bwe eouwetok mejki eo im joon mejān. (Kajin etto: "eouwetok" ej 'itok'.)

Im Ļe-Eetao ke ej lo an tiṃoŋ ej ejjabwel (kakōlle in mejki) ej bar jino inǫñ eo an im kakiki ļǫk tiṃoŋ eo.

Ke tiṃoŋ eo ej roñjake wōt inǫñ eo, eoļǫk im babu. Im kiki, im ettoñ. Etao ej laṃōj juon em ruo alen ak tiṃoŋ eo ejjab ṃakūtkūt ñan jidik! Bwe eļap an kiki.

Ilo iien eo Etao eo ej etal im āñintok ļadik eo jeran, bwe ren ro aljōktok kimej rot eŋ eṃor ñan ṃweo bwe ren ro tile. Āinwōt kar ļōmņak eo an Etao ṃokta.

Ke ej kanooj lōñ kimej Etao eo ej tile ṃokta rālik in ṃweo. Innām tile rōk. Ak ļadik eo ej tile eañ in ṃweo im rear āliktata. Innām rejro jutak im lale an bwil ṃweo.

Meļan ļǫk jidik tiṃoŋ eo eñjake an māņāāŋ im eļak iten ko tulǫk, eor kijeek. Innām ejaje ijo ej ilǫk ieļǫk bwe aolepān peļaak in kijeek wōt. Innām ebwil im mej. Im Etao eo ej ba ñan ļadik eo jeran, im ba, "Kwōn etal in pukot jinerro bwe etto aṃ jab etal."

Ke ļadik eo ej etal ippān jinen im kōnnaan kōn an kar tiṃoŋ etal in kañe, eļap an jinen būroṃōj. Im ļadik eo ej ba, "Kwōn kōppojak bwe jenro etal ñan āneeŋ im pād ie. Bwe ejako tiṃoŋ eo kar āneeŋ."

Jinen ej uwaak, "Jero naaj etal ñāāt?"

Ļadik eo ej ba, "Ilju."

Rujļǫkin eo juon rejro kōṃṃane wa eo waerro im etal. Im Etao eo ej kōnono ṃool ñan ļadik eo kab leļļap eo jineerro im ba, "Koṃro etal kiiō." Im rejro etal im pād i āne eo ñan rainin. (Bōtab ijaje ia.)

Ejeṃļǫk.

(Meļeļe in menin: Rej ba ñe kwōj kōttōpar im enaaj or rijipañ eok, kwōnaaj tōprak.

Āinwōt ñe eor juon men kwōj kōņaan ak aikuj ak kwōjaje wāween etal ñane, im ñe eor rijipañ eo, kwōnaaj tōpare.

Ñe Etao ejjab jipañ ļadik [eo] eban tōprak im enaaj kar mej. Ak Etao [eaar] jipañ e.

Jet iien Etao eṃṃan. Jet iien enana. Etao eļap an riab.)

[Ri-bwebwenato eo eaar kōṃeļeļe jet naan in kajin etto im jet naan armej rejjab kanooj in kōjerbale raan kein. Āinwōt in: "Kartak" ej 'aōņōōŋ'. "Lo" ej 'jeŋe', "No" ej 'ijo'. "Wea" ej 'aōņōōŋ in ṃōkaj'. "Kiped eo" ej 'jebwe eo'. "Jeña" ej 'ippa'. "Rujri" ej 'eñŋe'. Im "rujurjur wōj" ej 'eñŋe wōj'."]

Rej pād ilo roro in aōņōōŋ eo an ļadik eo.

52: ABOUT A MAN NAMED JEMERKINENE

As told by Jelibōr Jam, Kuwajleen 1975

He had a wife and some young sons (boys). The place where he lived, the name of the land parcel, was Mōjankwal.[1] The island where it was located was Iṃroj, on Jālooj Atoll.

This man was a fisherman and every morning at five o'clock he sailed from Iṃroj and went out to the western side (bottom) of Take and Arḷap (north of Piñlep) and fished there. He fished for one week. Then one day he did not go fishing, for he had made a big catch the previous day. When he awoke very early in the morning, he called his wife to him and said, "See that you do not go and wash your face and hands in the pool inland."

The following day, the man awoke when it was morning and said to his sons, "Come here, for we are going to fish." And the canoe sailed and went again to where he wanted to fish (between Arḷap and Take).

That afternoon, he returned again to Iṃroj. He had a great many fish. He again instructed his wife, "See that you do not go and wash your face and hands in that pool."

Now the woman said, "Why, when it is only drinking water and for bathing? And I do not see any reason why it is bad."

And Jemerkinene did not comment, but said to the woman, "Bring that water in a container,[2] so that I can wash my hands and drink." And he said, "Spread out my mat so that I can sleep. For tomorrow, just before dawn,[3] I will go fishing again. And I again admonish you that you do not go to wash yourself in that pool."

When the man woke up the following day, he sailed just before dawn. And the woman arose when it was sunrise and brought the fish that was left over from their evening meal. She warmed it up a little so that it would not smell bad, and ate a little and put it away again. And the woman stood up and went to the pool. She went to the pool and scooped up water with the container and drank. When she finished drinking, she again scooped up water with the container and washed her hands. She finished washing her hands and she clapped her hands three times.

She had just finished clapping her hands when a woman appeared from within the pool and said, "Greetings to you, madam, friend."

The woman was very surprised and she said, "I am afraid to become friends with you."

The other woman said, "Why, madam, when we two will look out for each other very well?" The woman said, "Are you telling me the truth, madam?"

Now the woman said, "Really, truly." And the woman said, "Well, come, we two are going." And the two of them went lagoonward to the house.

In the afternoon (perhaps three or so o'clock), Jemerkinene and his sons returned

1. The term *ṃweo* 'the house' (from *eṃ* 'house') is also used for 'land parcel' *wāto*. All such parcels are named, and their names are known to the islanders.

2. Coconut shells were used as containers (*bōkā*) for carrying and storing drinking water, and for *pinniep* 'coconut oil', which is used for grooming and massage (for healing and magical purposes). In battle, women were *ri-bōk bōkā* 'water carrying people', who stayed behind the line of battle with the water supply and went to succor the warriors. They were, in effect, the auxiliaries.

3. *Jimmarok* 'the time when there is a little light in the east, not yet sunrise'.

from their fishing. Jemerkinene disembarked from the canoe and went to the house.

He looked ahead and saw two women inside the house. And he said to himself, "It is clear that that woman washed her hands in that pool, for why are there two women in the house there?"

He went to the house and said, "What did I say? Why did you not obey me? Now which of you two is the human being and which is the demon? Because you two have an identical appearance."

Now the demon said, "I am a human being." The woman said, "That woman is lying. I am a real human being." Jemerkinene said, "I do not know which is the demon and which is the human being."

Now the women argued and said, "I am a human being and she is a demon!"

Because their arguing was great, Jemerkinene said, "Stop your arguing, for it will be proven by your work." And Jemerkinene said to the demon, "Make a fire." And the demon said, "Both of us will go to make a fire."

And when they went together to make the fire, Jemerkinene watched their work. And the demon did not know how to make a fire.

And Jemerkinene again asked, "Which is the demon and which is the human being?" Now the demon argued greatly. And it was not clear which of the two was the demon.

Now Jemerkinene seized the woman with him and took her to the lagoon side and brought a log and put her inside it—the log was hollow—and the two small boys. And the woman was beginning her pregnancy. But Jemerkinene did not know about it, because the demon was arguing so much. And Jemerkinene said, "The human being should stay here."

But the woman drifted away. And drifted and landed on Kōle. And the boys made a canoe.

And Jemerkinene remained (on Jālooj), and one day he again took the older boys and sailed and went fishing.

Then they came upon a canoe that had sailed there from Kōle. The younger boys were accustomed to fishing in their father's fishing place. And Jemerkinene said to the older boys, "Ask them what canoe that is?"

And the older boys called out, "What canoe is that?"

Now the younger boys called out to their father's canoe and said, "*Eañijen-Rōkijen* (From-north-and-from-south)."[4]

Now the older boys were surprised and said, "Why are you evasive with your words?"

Now the younger boys replied, "What can we do?"

Now the older boys said to themselves, "Why can't we hear them?"

The younger boys said, "And why can't you hear us? For we hear you."

Now the older boys said, "You are evasive with your words. Do you know where Jemerkinene is?"

The younger brothers now said, "He is on the island. He is on the canoe. He is in the cabin[5] here." (In the ancient language *ejimin* means 'is on'.)

Now the older boys talked briefly. They whispered and said, "How do they know where he is?"

Now the younger brothers said, "And

4. *Eañjen-Rakjen* was the name given the large schooner of *Iroojļapļap* (Paramount Chief) Kabua in the late nineteenth century (during the German period).

5. The *pelpel* 'cabin' was a small structure (a thatched hut) placed on the sailing canoe platform. It was used to shelter passengers (mostly the women, older people, and children) against the elements. It was also used to protect perishable goods. The *pelpel* are no longer used, and have not been used for many years, as most of the travel between nearby atolls and within atolls has been with motor-powered boats.

why do we not know where he is?"—they argued with the older ones.

Now the older brothers again said, "Why do they hear us?"—because they were not speaking loudly.

Now the younger brothers again said, "And why do we not hear?"

The older brothers said, "Bring your canoe close to us, so that we can see what canoe that is."

Now the younger brothers tacked and said, *"Bōkjel | bōkjel | bōkjel | bōk. | Lipperalua jarōm jatel jako."* (This chant *[roro]* is in the ancient language. We do not know what it means.)

The canoe was gone quickly. The older boys looked for it; it was gone. They did not know where it had gone.

And the older boys and their father returned to Imroj and took their catch of fish to their mother so that she could cook it. And the demon tried to cook it. And Jemerkinene hid and watched her cooking. Now Jemerkinene said to himself, "Maybe that is the demon."

And when she was finished cooking, she called Jemerkinene and the boys to eat breakfast. And when they finished eating, Jemerkinene lay down and said to the woman: "Come here with me." And the woman went to him and lay down with him.

Now she said, "Delouse me." And she said, "See that you delouse the front part of my head"—not the back part. And Jemerkinene just deloused the front of the woman's head. And when the woman was asleep, he deloused the back of her head. As he deloused the back of her head, a mouth smiled at him (at the back of her head).[6]

Jemerkinene said, "Ummm . . . this is a demon! What shall I do? Kill her? Not kill her?" He continued delousing her. She smiled much more than before! Now he planned to kill the woman. And he seized the fire and burned the house, and looked to see if the demon was dead.

Because he did not know whether she was dead or not, he again carried palm fronds and stood them against the doors and windows (in the white man's language, windows) and brought many, many palm fronds, and stood up again and looked.

Then the demon arose and went to flee, but she could not. And she burned up and died.[7] Now Jemerkinene was very sorry about the woman that he had caused to drift away with his sons.

He stayed there, and then one morning before dawn, he woke up his sons so that they would go out fishing again.

They had just gotten to their fishing place when they again saw the canoe coming and they called to the canoe. And Jemerkinene said, "Say to them, 'What canoe is that?'" The younger boys answered, *"Eañijen-Rōkijen."*

Now the older boys said, "Do you know where Jemerkinene is?"

Now the younger boys [said], "He is on the island. He is on the canoe. He is in the cabin there."

Now the older boys said to themselves, "Why do they know where he is?"

Now the younger boys said, "And why don't we know?"

The older boys said now, "Well, bring that boat close to us."

Now the younger boys said, *"Bōkjel | bōkjel | bōkjel bōk. | Lipperalua jarōm jatel*

6. The informant grinned broadly, showing all of his teeth, to demonstrate the frightening and unexpected act of the demon.

7. Again we see the widespread motif of the intended victim outwitting and killing a demon by burning her or him up.

jako." (Perhaps this was a chant for going away, fleeing.)[8]

Now the older boys looked for the canoe. It was gone. The older boys said, "Where is the canoe? Why did it go away so quickly? Well, what shall we do now?"

Jemerkinene said, "It will be good if we wait here for daybreak."

Now they all remained there a short time, and when dawn was breaking, they saw the wake of the canoe.

Now Jemerkinene said, "Let us follow that wake." Now they went after the wake. They went, they went, and they saw Kōle. When they went ahead, the younger brothers had beached the canoe.

Now the older brothers said, "There is a canoe now. Well, let us go and see what canoe that is. Perhaps it is *Eañijen-Rōkijen."*

Jemerkinene said, "Well, take our canoe to the island. Let us see what canoe that is."

Then the youngest boy (with whom the mother had been pregnant) was bathing next to the younger boys' canoe. And Jemerkinene said to the boy, "What is the name of that canoe, sir?" The boy did not answer. Now Jemerkinene again asked, "What is the name of your mother, sir?" The boy did not answer.

Jemerkinene again asked, "Where is your mother, sir?" The boy replied, "She is in the house."

Jemerkinene again questioned the boy, "What is the name of your father, sir?" The boy replied, "The name of my father is Jemerkinene."

Now Jemerkinene said to himself, "Who is the woman? She whom I cast adrift?" And he again questioned the boy. "Do you have older brothers?"

"I have." The boy answered.

Jemerkinene asked, "Where are they?" The boy answered, "They are in that house."

Jemerkinene again asked, "Will you repeat the name of your father?" The boy replied, "The name of my father is Jemerkinene."

Jemerkinene said, "I am he. Come here. We two are going to your mother."

And the boy went and rode astride his father's hip. They went, and saw the woman and the two boys.

And Jemerkinene said to the younger boys, "You go and tell your older brothers to come and see their mother."

And the younger boys hurried and ran to their older brothers and said, "Jemerkinene said, 'You come!'" And the older brothers disembarked from the canoe and went with the younger boys to the house and their father said, "Your mother is alive."

The older boys ran and greeted their mother (seized her hands and kissed her).

And to this day Jemerkinene and his family are on Kōle (as Ļainjin said).[9]

(The reason this story appeared is because we should be truthful [lit. keep and obey the truth].)

---

8. This *roro* 'chant', the informant explained, is in *kajin etto* (the ancient language), and the meaning is unknown.

9. When I asked Jelibōr Jam what the form was that Jemerkinene and his family had assumed, whether as demons (spirits), rocks, reefs, or coral heads, or in plots of ground, or something else, he said that he did not know. Kōle is a small (0.36 sq. mi.) single raised coral island with a narrow fringing reef, and it is the home in exile of the displaced Pikinni Atoll people.

52: KŌN JUŌN EṂṂAAN ETAN JEMERKINENE

Ri-bwebwenato: Jelibōr Jam, Kuwajleen 1975

Eor juon koņaan kōrā em jet nājin ļaddik. Jikin eo ej pād ie etan ṃweo Ṃōjaankul. Āne eo ej pād ie Iṃroj ilo aelōñ in Jālooj.

Ļein ej juon eṃṃaan in eọñwōd innām aolep jibbon̄ ļalem awa ej jerak jān Iṃroj em ilọk ñan kapin Tōkā im Arļap (iōñ in Piñlep) im eọñwōd ie. Ioṃwin juon wiik in an eọñwōd. Ļak baj juon raan eaar jab ilām eọñwōd bwe eļap an kar lōñ koņaan ek raan eo juon. Ke ej ruj jibboñtata ej kūrtok kōrā eo em ba, "Lale kwōn jab etal in aṃwin eok ilo ļwe eņ iooj."

Raan eo juon ļeo eruj wōt ke jibboñ em ba ñan ļadik ro nājin, "Koṃ itok jen etal in eọñwōd." Innām ejerak wa eo em bar etal ñan ejja ijo wōt ekōņaan eọñwōd ie (ikōtaan Arļap im Tōkā).

Jọten eo ebar rọọltok ñan Iṃroj. Ekanooj lōñ ek. Ej bar kalliṃur ñan kōrā eo, "Lale bwe kwōn jab etal in aṃwin eok ilo ļwe eņ."

Kiiō kōrā eo ej ba, "Ta wūnin ke ej make wōt dān in idaak kab tutu? Ak ijjab lo wūnin an nana."

Innām Jemerkinene ejjab kōnono ak ej ba ļọk ñan kōrā eo, "Letok dān ņe ilo bōkā bwe in aṃwin peiū kab idaak." Innām eba, "Kwōn erak jaki bwe in kiki. Bwe ilju ej jimmarok inaaj bar etal in eọñwōd. Ak ij bar kalliṃur bwe kwōn jab etal in aṃwin eok ilo ļwe eņ."

Ļọk ruj ļeo raan eo juon ejerak wōt ke ej jimmarok. Ak lio eruj ke ej tak aļ em bōktok ek ko ṃōttan aereañ kōjota. Em kāmāņāāņi jidik bwe en jab ekkōrōōr. Em ṃōñā bajjek em bar kọkūņi. Ak lio ejutak em etal ñan ļwe eo. Etal im ļak itōke bōkā em idaak. Ke ej ṃōj an daak ebar itōke bōkā eo im aṃwin pein. Ej ṃōj an aṃwin pein ak kabokkļọk pein jilu alen.

Ej ṃōj wōt an kabokkoļọk pein ak ewaļọk juon kōrā jān lowaan ļwe eo em ba, "Iokwe eok le, jera."

Eļap an ikkūṃļọk kōrā eo em ba, "Iṃakoko in jeraik eok."

Lio juon eba, "Ta wūnin le, ke ekanooj eṃṃan arro naaj lale doon?"

Kōrā eo eba, "Kwōj ṃool ke le, luweo?" Kiiō lio eba, "Lukkuun ṃool." Innām kōrā eo eba, "Ekwe itok jerro etal." Innām ro wōnarļọk ñan ṃweo. Em bar iṃweo ļọk. Jotaan eo (bōlen jilu men awa) erọọltok Jemerkinene kab ļadik ro nājin jān ke raar eọñwōd.

Jemerkinene eļak to jān wa eo em etal ñan ṃweo. Ej erreilọk em lo ruo kōrā ilowaan ṃweo. Im ej ba ilo būruon, "Alikkar ke lieņ eaar aṃwini pein ilo ļwe eņ, bwe etke ruo kōrā eņ imweeņ?"

Etal em ļak ṃweo eba, "Ta eo iaar ba? Etke kwaar jab pokake eō? Kiiō ewi armej eo ak ewi tiṃoņ eo iaamiro? Ke iaamiro wōt juon."

Kiiō tiṃoņ eo eba, "Ña armej." Kōrā eo eba, "Ej riab lieņ. Ña lukkuun armej." Jemerkinene eba, "Ña ijaje. Ewi tiṃoņ eo ak ewi armej eo?"

Kiiō kōrā ro rej akwāāl im ba, "Ña armej ak lie tiṃoņ!" Ke ej ļap aerro akwāāl Jemerkinene ej ba, "Eṃōj amiro akwāāl bwe enaaj alikkar kōn jerbal ko amiro." Innām Jemerkinene eba ñan tiṃoņ eo, "Kwōn kōjọ kijeek eņ." Innām tiṃoņ eo eba, "Kemro aolep kemij ro ilān kōjọ kijeek eņ."

Innām ke rejro jiṃor ilān kōjọ kijeek eo Jemerkinene ej lale aerro jerbal. Innām tiṃoņ eo ejaje kilen kōjọjo kijeek.

Innām Jemerkinene ej bar kajjitōk, "Ewi tiṃoņ eo ak ewi armej eo?" Kiiō tiṃoņ eo eļap an akweļap. Innām ejjab em alikkar tiṃoņ eo iaarro.

Kiiō Jemerkinene ej jibwe kōrā eo ippān em bōkļọk ŋa iar em bōktok juon kājokwā em door kōrā eo ŋae. (Ejjeļọk kobban kājokwā eo.) Em ļadik ro ruo reddik. Ak lio ejino in iten bōrọro ak Jemerkinene ejaje kōn an ļap an tiṃoŋ eo akweļap. Innām Jemerkinene ej ba, "Armej eo en pādwōt." Ak lio ilām kōpeļọke. Em epeļọk em eọtōk i Kōle. Em ļadik ro rej jekjek wa.

Ak Jemerkinene epād (i Jālooj) im ļak juon raan ebar bōk ļadik ro rōrūtto em jerak em etal em eọñwōd. Ļak ilọk rej iioon wa eo ej jeraktok jān Kōle. Ļadik ro reddik remminene kōn aer eọñwōd ilo jikin eọñwōd eo an jemāer. Innām Jemerkinene ej ba ñan ļōṃaro rōrūtto, "Koṃin kajjitōk 'Waat ŋe?'"

Innām ļadik ro rōrūtto rej ikkūr ļọk, "Wa ta ŋe?"

Kiiō ļadik ro reddik rej ikkūr ļọk ñan wa eo waan jemāer em ba, *"Eañijeŋ-Rōkijen."* Kiiō ļōṃaro rōrūtto rej ikkōṃļọk em ba, "Etke koṃij ililet ami kōnnaan?" Kiiō ļadik ro reddik rej uwaak, "A kemin et?" Kiiō ļadik ro rōrūtto remake ba, "Etke renañin roñļọkijeŋ?" Ļadik ro reddik rōba, "A etke koṃij jab roñļọkijen. Ke kōm roñļọkijeŋ?"

Kiiō ļadik ro rūtto ba, "Ke koṃij ililet ami kōnnaan koṃij jeļā Jemerkinene epād ia?"

Ļadik ro reddik kiiō, "Ejimin āne. Ejimin wa. Iōñŋe ilo pelpel ŋe." (Ilo kajjin etto, meļeļe in "ejimin" ej 'epād'.)

Kiiō ļadik ro rūtto jidik wōt aer kōnnaan, rej unoojdikdik em ba, "Etke renañin jeļā kajjien?" Kiiō ļadik ro reddik, "A etke kemin jaje kajjien?" (Rej akwāāl ñan ro rōrūtto.)

Kiiō ļadik ro rūtto rōbar ba, "Etke renañin roñļọkijen?" (Kōnke ejjab ļap aer kōnono.)

Kiiō ļadik ro reddik raar ba, "A etke kemin jab roñļọkijen?" Ļadik ro rōrūtto rōba, "Kepaaktok wa ŋe jen ṃōk lale wa ŋe. Wa rot ŋe."

Kiiō ļaddik ro reddik rej ŋatoon em ba, "Bōkjel | bōkjel | bōkjel | bōk. | Lipberalua jōrom jatel jako." (Kajin etto roro in. Kem jaje meļeļe.)

Eṃōkaj an wa eo jako. Ļadik ro rōrūtto rōļak pukote, ejako. Rejaje etal iaļọk. Innām ļadik ro rōrūtto im jemāer rej bar rọọl ñan Iṃroj im bōkļọk ek ko koŋāer ñan kōrā eo bwe en kōmat. Innām tiṃoŋ eo ej kate wōt em kōmat. Ak Jemerkinene ej kōjjade im lale an kōmat. Innām eļak lale ejjab kanooj in jeļā kōmat. Kiiō Jemerkinene ej make ba, "Bōlen tiṃoŋ eo eŋ."

Innām ke ej ṃōj an kōmat ej kūrtok Jemerkinene kab ļadik ro bwe ren ṃōñā in jibboñ. Innām ke ej ṃōj aer ṃōñā Jemerkinene ej babu em ba ñan lio, "Kwōn itok ippa ije." Innām lio ej etal ñan ippān em baj babu ļọk ippān.

Innām lio eba, "Kwōn ākūti bōra." Im ba, "Lale kwaar ākūt tok ñan kapin bōra." Innām Jemerkinene ākūt wōt iṃaan bōran kōrā eo, em ke ej kiki kōrā eo ak ākūt ikipin bōran. Eļak ākūt ikipin bōran juon lọñi ej ettōñ tok ñane (ilo kipin bōran).

Jemerkinene ej ba, "Ummm . . . tiṃoŋ eo in! Eaar kōjkan? Ta in? Ṃane ke? Jab ke?" Eļak bar ukot tok. Ekanooj ļap an ettōñ ļọk jān ṃokta! Kiiō ej ļōṃŋak in ṃan kōrā eo. Innām ej jibwetok kijeek eo em tile ṃweo. Em ettōr jāne, em lale en mej ke tiṃoŋ eo.

Kōn an jaje en mej ke jab ke ej bar aljōk tok kimej em kajutok ŋa ikijjien kōjām kab rōñōl ko (i kajin pālle, wintō) em kanooj kalōñlōñ tok kimej in ni, em bar jutak em lale.

Eļak erreilọk tiṃoŋ eo ej jerkak em ļak iten ko; eban. Ak ebwil em mej. Kiiō Jemerkinene eļap an būroṃōj kōn kōrā eo eaar kapeļọk wōt ŋa ippān ļadik eo nājin.

Pād em ļak juon jimmarok ekọruj ļadik ro nājin bwe ren etal in eọñwōd. Ejja ijo wōt jikin aer eọñwōd ke rej ilọk rej bar lo wa eo ej itok em rej ikkūrļọk ñan wa eo. Em Jemerkinene ej ba, "Koṃin ba 'wataŋe?'" Ļadik ro reddik rej uwaak, "Eañijeŋ-Rōkijeŋ."

Kiiō ļadik ro rōrūtto rej ba, "Koṃij jeļā Jemerkinene epād ia?"

Kiiō ļadik ro reddik, "Ejimin wa, ejimin āne. Eñōņe ilo pelpel ņe."

Kiiō ļadik ro rōrūtto rej ba ñan er make, "Etke renañin jeļā kajjien?" Kiiō ļadik ro reddik, "A etke kemin jaje?"

Ļadik ro rōrūtto kiiō, "Ekwe kepaaktok wa ņe."

Kiiō ļadik ro reddik rej ba, "Bōkjel | bōkjel | bōkjel bōk | Lipperalua jarom jatel jako." (Bōlen roro in ko.)

Kiiō ļadik ro rōrūtto reļak pukot wa eo. Ejako. Ļadik ro rōrūtto rōba, "Ewi wa eo? Etke enañin ṃōkaj an jako? Ekwe, jijet kiiō?"

Jemerkinene eba, "Eṃṃan ñe jeañ pād [im] karraan ṃokta ijin."

Kiiō ereañ pād jidik iien em ke ej iten tak aļ relo aode in wa eo.

Kiiō Jemerkinene ej ba, "Jen ṃōk ļoor aode ņe." Kiiō reetal ippān aode ļǫk. Etal, etal im lo Kōle. Ke rej ilǫk eṃōj an ļadik ro reddik ārōk wa eo.

Kiiō ļadik ro rōrūtto rej ba, "Juōn ņe wa. Ekwe jen etal in lale waat eņ. Bōlen Eañijeņ-Rōkijeņ."

Jemerkinene ej ba, "Ekwe le-ānewōj wa ņe. Jen lale ṃōk wa ta ņe." Ļak ilǫk ļadik eo ediktata em jinen, eaar bōrǫroiki, ej tutu iturin wa eo waan ļadik ro reddik. Im Jemerkinene ej ba ñan ļadik eo, "Etan wa ņe ļe?" Ļadik eo ejjab uwaak. Kiiō Jemerkinene ej bar kajjitōk, "Etan jinōṃ ļe?" Ļadik eo ejjab uwaak.

Jemerkinene ej bar kajjitōk, "Epād ia jeṃaṃ ļe?" Ļadik eo ej uwaak, "Epād iṃwiin."

Jemerkinene ej bar kajjitōk ippān ļadik eo, "Etan jeṃaṃ ļe?" Ļadik eo ej uwaak, "Etan jema Jemerkinene."

Kiiō Jemerkinene ej ba ñane make, "En ta ke kōrā eo? Eo eaar kōpeļǫke?" Innām ej bar kajjitōk ippān ladik eo, "Eor ke jeiṃ?" "Eor," ļadik eo ej uwaak.

Jemerkinene ej kajjitōk, "Erri?" Ļadik eo ej uwaak, "Repād iṃweeņ."

Jemerkinene ej bar kajjitōk, "Bar ba ṃōk etan jeṃaṃ?" Ļadik eo ej uwaak, "Etan jema, Jemerkinene." Jemerkinene eba, "Ña e. Kwōn itok. Kōjro etal ippān jinōṃ."

Innām ļadik eo ej etal em jaja ippān jemān. Reetal, im lo kōrā eo kab ļadik ro ruo. Im Jemerkinene ej ba ñan ļadik ro reddik, "Koṃro etal in ba ñan jeimiro bwe ren itok in lo jineer."

Innām ļadik ro reddik rej ṃōkaj im ettōr ñan ippān ļadik ro jeier im ba, "Jemerkinene ej ba, 'Koṃro itok!'"

Innām rejro to jān wa eo em etal ippān ļadik ro reddik ļǫk ñan ṃweo em jemāer ej ba, "Jinemiro ej mour wōt."

Ļadik ro rōrūtto rej ettōr em iǫkwe jineer ro (jibwe pein em mejenmaiki).

Innām ñan rainin Jemerkinene kab jinukun eo an ej pād i Kōle ñan kiiō. (Āinwōt Ļainjin ar ba.)

(Wūnin an waļǫk bwebwenato in kōnke jen kanooj kōjparok ṃool eo.)

53: A STORY OF TWO MEN IN RATAK, ON WŌJJĀ ATOLL, ISLAND OF MĀJJEN

As told by Jelibōr Jam, Kuwajleen 1975

These men worked during the day and then in the evening they went to fish for goatfish [*Mulloidichthys auriflama, jo*] (*karjo*: fishing for *jo* with a pole).

Three days later,[1] the two of them worked all day, and after three o'clock[2] they finished their work and went and prepared their bait of sand crab [*karuk:* white sand crab].

When it was finished, the one man went ahead. But the other man was slow.

And the one man, when he went, he pounded crabs for the bait, and began to throw it to the fish [chum the fish]. (*Anan* is *kajin ek*, fish language and animal language, *anan* 'so that they would come'.)

But the other man, when he came, was in a hurry and prepared the bait.

And he came and fished [he chummed the fish, then went to the fish with his pole].

On the island, there was a fishing law, that if we fish, it is bad to look behind our back—to look back at the fish that we have pulled back with our pole.

(*Kubōle* is *kajin lebwā*, fishing language, for pulling back one's pole.)

And the man who was slow spoke to himself, and said, "Why is it forbidden to look back at the fish behind us that we pull back with our pole, sir? Why do I not see the meaning of that? Tomorrow I will just look back to see why it is forbidden."[3]

And the two of them fished apart from each other—one here, one there. When they were finished, they went to their canoe and paddled.

When they paddled, the other man [the one who was slow] said, "Why is it forbidden for us to look back when we pull back a goatfish, sir?"

The other man replied, "I do not know. For it is a law from long ago."

And the other man said, "Well, tomorrow we two will come in only one canoe. And I will look back when I catch a fish."

The following day, they again prepared to go to paddle to the other island to fish. They only paddled one canoe. When they arrived, the one man said, "See that you do not look back. For it has been thus from long ago. When our grandmothers and our grandfathers said to us that we should just tell our children and our friends when they would come to fish in this fishing place."

---

1. Again we see the use of the ritual/magical number three—three days in this case. Dosages of traditional medicine or the application of healing techniques are normally prescribed for three times a day, usually for three-day periods, and for magic as well.

2. In the Marshallese text of this story, the English loanword (and concept of measurement of time) is used. The English word *hour* becomes *awa.* It is well integrated into the Marshallese language.

3. *Mọ* means 'taboo, forbidden', and was used in a manner analogous to the Polynesian equivalent *tapu* (*taboo,* or in Hawai'i, *kapu*). For example, access to and exploitation of certain fishing or bird and turtle nesting areas was forbidden at certain times to the common people. This functioned as a form of conservation of natural resources. The person and prestige of the *irooj* (chief) was usually involved in the prohibitions, as was also true at other places where they were imposed. In this story, of course, one of the characters does not understand the reason for the taboo, and breaks it.

The other man said, "Well, I am not eager to look back now, but if I have a very big catch, I will just try."

And the two of them fished. And they had extremely large catches of fish.

The one man finished fishing and went onto the island and collected his catch of fish and took them and went. And he said to the other man, "Just hurry up, for I am going to wait for you and see if you look behind your back!"

And the other man, because he had a very large catch of fish, tried to pull the fish back with his pole, and looked back behind [that is, he broke the taboo].

When he looked back, he saw a woman and she was gathering together the fish on the island.

When he saw the woman, he was startled and he became a little crazy[4]—not very much—that is, he could not think well, and he could turn into a crazy person—and he was very frightened, because he knew that he had broken the law. And he hurried and ran.

When he went away, the canoe was gone. The one man had paddled away because he was tired of waiting for him.

And when it became darker [later at night] he thought what would be good for him to do. And he saw that he should roll up inside a *kaōnōn* [*Cassytha filiformis,* a creeper]. (This is a kind of vegetation, *mar*, that is common on an island.) And he rolled up onto the middle of the sandy beach, and slept there.

When it was about eight o'clock, the *kwōlej* [*Pluvialis dominica,* golden plover] flew [there] and landed on the man and cried, "*Kwōlej*! *Kwōlej*!"[5] The man was lying down.

When it landed on him, it became a demon. When the man saw it was like this, he closed his eyes (because he was afraid).

A little while later, he woke up and saw that the woman was leaning over him, and peering into his face. And the man again hastened to sleep.

When he slept, the demon came down from on top [of him] and moved him [the roll of vegetation] with her hands, unrolling him, toward the sea.

When the demon had moved him toward the sea, she said to the man, *"Emao in tue eok | Emao in jejetake, Ļakareo | Jelakļǫk wōt! | Jelakļǫk wōt!"* (In the ancient language it is: "I am ready to eat you." The meaning of *emao* is 'I am ready', and *tue* is 'eat'. In the ancient language, *jejetak* is 'open it up

4. People become crazed in folktales, just as they do in real life in the Marshalls. They become afflicted with *būroṃōj* (an acute melancholia type of illness) and with *ļaro,* an analogous affliction that causes the victim to become a *lōrro* and "fly away." These are apparently psychosomatic illnesses. There are traditional methods of curing or attempting to cure the victims. Magical chants and magical acts are used with massage and ingestion of botanical-based medicines. The usual cause of these afflictions is the loss or the absence of a loved one, or, as in this case, for breaking a taboo (which probably functioned as a form of social control). The man became *bwebwe.*

5. The name of the bird and its distinctive cry sound the same to the Marshallese. They compare a person who puts his name and himself forward inordinately, and boasts a great deal (that is, a pushy self-promoter) with the *kwōlej,* which is seen everywhere, and whose cry is heard everywhere, they say. Such a person is said to be "*āinwōt kwōlej*" 'like the *kwōlej*'. The *kwōlej* were thought to be ghosts and harbingers of death. See Leach (1949 vol. 1:142) for such folk beliefs in the United States and Europe.

The Hawaiians call the golden plover *kolea* and attribute special powers to them. They are thought to be messengers of the gods. And there is also an analogous reference to them and to certain undesirable human personality traits. Pukui and Elbert (1971:150) note: "*kolea* . . . Fig. to repeat, boast; one who comes to Hawaii and becomes prosperous and then leaves with his wealth. . . . One who claims friendship or kinship that does not exist."

[uncover it]', and Ḷakareo is the name of this man. And *jelakḷọk* is 'open it up [uncover it]'.)

She finished (unrolling it), but she again rolled it up (with the man inside) toward the island, toward the island. (She knew that it was a human being, but she wanted to play a little. She was toying with the man.)

[That is, the demon was playing a cat-and-mouse game with the man.] And she again went up onto the man and sat and combed her hair with her fingers.

(In the ancient language, *kōrbar* means to comb one's hair with one's fingers. There were no combs before the white men came. The Marshallese used their fingers and the word *kōrbar*. Today we use *kuuṃ* [comb], and not *kōrbar*.)

A short while later, she [the demon] again flew off, and descended from above the man and again said, *"Emao in tue eok | Emao in jejetake, Ḷakareo | Ekaḷa kuuk! | Jelakḷọk wōt! | Jelakḷọk wōt!"* ("I am ready to eat you. | I am ready to open it up, Lakareo. | It is here, bite! | Open it up! | Open it up!")

The demon moved the man (in the bundle of vegetation) unrolling toward the sea, and almost all of his body appeared from the *kaōnōn* into which he had rolled his body.

At the time, the man was very frightened. He thought the demon was going to eat him, and he did not wake up but continued to sleep (pretended to sleep and closed his eyes tightly).

The demon did not move or make noise. But she stood a short distance away from the man.

[When] the man did not know where the demon was, he awakened and looked for the demon beside him. For the man thought that the demon was gone, but when the man awakened, the demon was standing beside the water and smiling. Because the demon said to herself, "When I roll him (in the vegetation) toward the water and again loosen him [uncover/unroll him], I will eat him."

And because the man was afraid of the demon, he again pretended to be asleep. And the demon came and rolled him toward the island. (The young man was rolled up as within a mat.)

When she got to the place on the island, the demon jumped over onto the boy and again sat.

At this time, the man began to lose his fear, and now he was angry, and said to himself, "When the demon opens (unrolls) me toward the sea, at that time I will get up."

A short while later, the demon again flew from above the man and said, *"Emao in tue eok | Emao in jejetake, Ḷakareo | Ekaḷa kuuk! | Jelakḷọk wōt! | Jelakḷọk wōt!"* (In the ancient language *Ekaḷa kuuk* means 'it is here, bite!') ("I am ready to eat you. | I am ready to open it up, Lakareo. | It is here, bite! | Open it up! | Open it up!")

At the time, half of the body of the man was uncovered. Now the demon was very happy, because [she thought] she was going to eat him right then. (In the ancient language, *kakkōnono* is 'she is happy' [because half of the man's body was uncovered].)

When the man woke up and saw the demon staring at his face, he called out and said, "What are you looking at?"

And the demon was startled and went to run away. When the man saw the demon starting to run away, he hastened to get up, and stood up and said, "What kind of woman there tried hard to eat me, men?"

And the demon turned before him and went away.

And the man pursued the demon and said (to the demon—no one else was around), "For a long time the woman endeavored to eat us. This time, you will be gone from here." (*Annen* is this time. This word is not used very much today.)

When the demon heard this, she did not

remain again, but ran and flew beyond the edge of the reef. And she is gone to this day. It is ended.

(The meaning of this thing: If your resolve or strength is weak, you will be harmed, and arrive at a thing of temptation. Like Adam and Eve.) [If your resolve is weak, you will fall into temptation.]

53: JUON BWEBWENATO AN RUO EM̧M̧AAN I RATAK ILO AELŌÑ IN WŌJJĀ, ĀNE IN MĀJJEN

Ri-bwebwenato: Jelibōr Jam, Kuwajleen 1975

Ļōm̧arein rejro jerbal ilo raan im ļak jota rejro etal in kadjo (eo̧ñwod kōn bwā).

Ļokun jilu raan raar jerbal aolep raan eo im ļak jilu awa em̧ōj aerro jerbal ak rejro etal im kōm̧m̧an mo̧o̧reerro karuk.

Ke ej m̧ōj ļeo juon em̧ōkaj. Ak ļeo juon ej ebbattok. Im ļeo juon ke ej iļo̧k ej no baru ko mo̧o̧ren. Im jino an anan. (Anan ej kajin ek im menninmour. Anan bwe ren itok.) Ak ļeo juon ke ej itok ej kaiuri wōt in kōm̧m̧ane mo̧o̧r eo mo̧o̧ren. Em itok, im eo̧ñwōd.

Ilo āne eo eor juon kien eo̧ñwōd ie. Bwe ñe jej eo̧ñwōd, enana erreilikļo̧k iļo̧kan ek en kwaar kubōle. ("Kubōle" ej kajin lebwā.)

Innām ļeo eaar ebatļo̧k ej kōnono ippān make, im ba, "Ta wūnin an mo̧ erreilikļo̧k ek eñ jej kubōle ļōm̧a? Etke ijjab lo meļeļeen? Ilju inaaj m̧ōk baj erreilikļo̧k in lale ta wūnin an mo̧."

Innām rejro eo̧ñwōd jān doon. (Juon ijo, juon ijo.) Ke ej m̧ōj rejro etal ñan wa ko waerro im aōņōōņ.

Ke rejro aōņōōņ ļeo juon ej ba, "Etke emo̧ ad errālikļo̧k ñe jej kubōl juon jo ļe?"

Ļeo juon ej uwaak, Ijjab jeļā. Bwe kien in jān etto.

Innām ļeo juon ej ba, "Ekwe ilju jero naaj itok ilo juon wōt wa.

"Innām inaaj erreilikļo̧k ilo iien ñe eko̧jōk juon ek ippa."

Rujļo̧kin eo juon rejro bar kōppojak in etal in aōņōōņ ñan āne eo juon in eo̧ñwōd. Juon wōt wa eo rejro aōņōōņ kake. Ke rejro tōprak ļo̧k ļeo juon ej ba, "Lale bwe kwōn jab erreilikļo̧k. Bwe ekar āindein wōt jān etto. Ke jibūrro im jim̧m̧aro raar ba ñan kōjro. Bwe jenro kab jiroñ ro nājū ak jerad ro ñe renaaj iten eo̧ñwōd ilo jikin eo̧ñwōd in."

Ļeo juon ej ba, "Ekwe ijjab kijer in erreilikļo̧k kiiō, ak ñe eļap an lōñ koņa inaaj kajjeoñ m̧ōk."

Innām rejro eo̧ñwōd. Im kanooj lōñ koņaerro.

Ļeo juon ekam̧wij an eo̧ñwōd im wōnān-etak im aini ek ko koņan im būki im etal. Ak ej ba ñan ļeo juon, "Kab m̧ōkajtok bwe ij ilān kōttar eok ak lale kwaar erreilikļo̧k!"

Innām ļeo juon kōn an lōñ koņan ek ej kajjeoñ kubōl ek eo im erreilikļo̧k iļo̧kan ļo̧k. Ke ej erreilikļo̧k eļak lale juon kōrā ak ej aini ek āne in. Ke ej lo kōrā eo, eilbōk im ļo̧kjāņan. Im kanooj in mijak bwe ejeļā ke eaar ko̧kkure kien eo. Im ej kaiur [im] ettōr.

Ke ej iļo̧k ejako wa eo. Em̧wij an ļeo juon aōņōōņ bwe em̧ōk in kōttare.

Ak ke ej bon̄ļo̧k ej ļōm̧n̄ak ta em̧m̧an bwe en kōm̧m̧ane. Innām eaar lo bwe en etal in lemlem ilo juon kaōnōōn. Innām ej dāpil ļo̧k ñan lukwōn eoonbok. Im kiki ie.

Ke ej rualitōk im men awa koleej eo ej kātok im jok ioon ļeo im jañ ("Koleej! Koleej!")

Ke ej jok ioon erom juon tim̧oņ. Ke ļeo ej

loe an āinwōt eo ej kiil mejān (kōnke e mijak).

Meļanļǫk jidik ej ruj im ļak lale lio ej allimōmō ioon. Im lale tok mejān ļeo. Im ļeo ej bar kaiuri im kiki.

Ke ej kiki tiṃoŋ eo ej to jān eoon im kōjabwil metoļǫk. Ke tiṃoŋ ej kōjabwil metoļǫk ej ba ñan ļeo, "Emao in tue eok. | Emao in jejetake, Lakareo. | Jelakļǫk wōt. | Jelakļǫk wōt!"

(Ilo kajin etto "emao" ej 'ipojak', "tue" ej 'kañe', "jejetake" ej 'kōpeļļǫke' im "jeļakļǫk" ej 'kōpeļļǫke'. "Ļakareo" ej etan ļeo in.) Ej ṃōj ak ej bar lime āneļǫk, āneļǫk. Im bar kālōñtak ioon ļeo em jijet. Im kūrbar. (Ilo kajin etto "kūrbar" ej kuuṃ kōn addiin pā. Jejab kanooj in kōjerbal naan in rainin. Jet wōt iien. Kar ejjeļǫk kuuṃ ṃokta ripālle raar itok. Ri-Ṃajeļ raar kōjerbal addiin peier im naan eo "kūrbar.")

Ej meļanļǫk jidik ej bar kāļǫk. Im to jān eoon ļeo im bar ba, "Emao in tue eok. | Emao in jejetake, Ļakareo. | Ekaļa kuuk! | Jerakļǫk wōt! | Jerakļǫk wōt!"

Tiṃōŋ eo eaar kajabwil metoļǫk ļeo im enañin waļǫk aolepān ānbwinnin jān kaōnōōn eo eaar pǫpuut ānbwinnin kake.

Ilo iien eo ļeo eļap an mijak im ej ļōmṇak tiṃoŋ eo enaaj kañe. Im ejjab ruj ak kiki wōt. Tiṃōŋ eo ejjab eṃṃakūtkūt ak ekkeroro. Ak ej jutak ettoļǫk jidik jān ļeo.

Ke ļeo ejjab jeļā tiṃoŋ eo epād ia ej ruj im pukot tiṃoŋ eo iturin. Bwe ļeo ej ļōmṇak tiṃoŋ eo emootļǫk, ak ke ej ruj ļeo, tiṃoŋ eo, ej jutak imetoon im ettōñdikdik. Kōnke tiṃoŋ eo ej ba ippān make, "Ñe inaaj lim āneļǫk im bar jeļat metoļǫk, inaaj kañe."

Innām kōn an ļeo mijak tiṃoŋ eo ej bar riab kiki. Innām tiṃoŋ eo ej itok im bar lime āneļǫk. (Likao ej limi āinwōt ilowaan juon jaki.)

Ke tōparļǫk ijo i āne tiṃoŋ eo ej kālōñtok ioon ļeo im bar jijet.

Iien in ļeo ej jino an joļǫk an mijak ak kiiō ellu. Im ba ñan ippān make, "Ñe tiṃoŋ eo enaaj jeļat eō metoļǫk iien eŋ inaaj jerkak."

Meļan ļǫk jidik tiṃoŋ eo ej bar kāļǫk jān eoon ļeo im ba, "Emao in tue eok | Emao in jejetake, Ļakareo | Ekaļa kuuk! | Jelakļǫk wōt! | Jelakļǫk wōt!"

(Ilo kajin etto "ekaļa kuuk" ej 'epād ijo'.)

Iien eo emmat jimettan in ānbwinnin ļeo. Kiiō tiṃoŋ eo ej kakkōnono in kañ ļeo ilo iien eo. (Ilo kajin etto kakkōnono ej lukkuun ṃōŋōŋō, kōnke ļeo ej emmat jimettan in ānbwin.)

Ke ļeo ej ruj im lo an tiṃoŋ eo kalimjōk tok mejān, ļeo ej laṃōj im ba, "Ta ŋe kwōj lale?"

Innām tiṃoŋ eo ej ilbōk im iten ko. Ke ļeo ej lo an tiṃoŋ eo iten ko ej kaiuri jerkak im jutak im ba, "Kōrā rot ŋe ekōŋaan kātōke ļōṃa?"

Im tiṃoŋ eo ej rǫǫl iṃaan im ko. Innām ļeo ej lukworkwore tiṃoŋ eo im ba (ñan tiṃoŋ eo—e wōt ej pād ie). "Etto wōt an lien ekōŋaan iten kātōke ñan kōj. Annen eo kwōj jako ie in." ("Annen eo" ej 'iien in'. Jejab kanooj in kōjerbal naan in rainin.)

Ke tiṃoŋ eo ej roñ eaar jab bar pād ak eaar ettōr im kāļǫk ilikin baal. Im ejako ñan rainin.

Ejeṃļǫk.

(Meļeļe in menin: ñe enaaj ṃōjŋǫ atōm, kwōnaaj jorrāān. Im po ilo menin kapo. Āinwōt *Adam* im *Eve*.)

54: STORY ABOUT A YOUNG MĀJEEJ GIRL

As told by Jelibōr Jam, Kuwajleen 1975

The name of this young girl: Limedwetip. As in the custom of the old people of long ago, when she was fifteen years old, they brought all the best smelling things, and annointed her as in the custom of the old people.[1]

They annointed her for twelve days. In the ancient language it is called *kajiroñroñ* 'introduce to girlhood'.

On the twelfth day, a man appeared. He was very tall. He came up from the ocean. The reason he came was to seek the sweet smell there that came from her (the young girl).

As he came, he sang a song. The song said, "I come from the little lagoon, my house in the ocean, *likōmkōmļǫk, likōmkōmtok* | Big wave, north of Mājeej here | O-O-O Limedwetip."

(The words of the song of the demon, he who was tall, *"likōmkōmļǫk," "likōmkōmtok,"* and *"ai-eo"* are in the ancient language. I only know the meaning of *"ai-eo."* It is 'big wave'.)

He sang the song three times. The fourth time, an old woman heard it and told the chief. And the women with Limedwetip said to the old woman, " Do not make noise. You just lie down. For you are an old woman. And you are not telling the truth."

They were surprised when the demon appeared. Now they looked for where they hid Limedwetip. (They all hid.)

When they saw the male demon, they dug a hole and put all of the people in it, within the hole. The demon came and went to where they dug the hole. And he did not know where the entrance to the hole was.

Now he really looked for it. He pulled up grass. He threw off rocks. He threw off pandanus leaves. He threw off coconut leaves. The hole appeared. (Because they had put a coconut shell on the entrance of the hole to cover it.)

He saw the hole. And he grabbed all of the people, throwing them by one up into the air. And as they fell down, he ate them.

Everyone was eaten, but he seized Limedwetip and put her behind his ear (like a pencil).[2] And returned to the little lagoon, the place in the ocean.

Today, if you see a golden plover [*Pluvialis dominica*] on the ocean to the north of Mājeej, you will know that it is Limedwetip, the sign (sea marker) of Mājeej. (It is a long distance from Mājeej—thirty or fifty miles.)

It is on the ocean nowadays.

Because Ļainjin knew and revealed it to the chiefs in the Marshalls. Because the chiefs wanted to keep Ļainjin (a real person). Because he knew navigation—he knew the signs of the islands.[3]

Before Ļainjin appeared, the chiefs used the magic of pandanus leaves [divination by means of interpretation of various folds of pandanus leaves, called *bubu in maañ*].

---

1. *Kapti*, massage with coconut oil (*pinniep*), usually perfumed with sweet-smelling flowers, was and still is done in the Marshalls. It is done for grooming and for medical treatment. Magic and magical chants/songs were used in conjunction with healing or to gain benefits from the massage.

2. An English loanword and artifact, *pinjeļ* (pencil), is incorporated into the folktale, reflecting changes in the culture.

But Ļainjin learned from his mother Litarmelu (a real person.) And he taught the chiefs.

The chiefs in the Marshalls kept it and hid the teachings (knowledge) from the commoners.

54: BWEBWENATO IN JUŌN JIROÑ IN MĀJEEJ

Ri-bwebwenato: Jelibōr Jam, Kuwajleen 1975

Etan jiroñ in, Limedwetip. Āinwōt ilo ṃanit an rūtto ro etto ñe ej joñoul ļalem iiō rej bōktok aolep men ko reñajtata. Em kapit jiroñ in āinwōt ilo ṃanit ko an rūtto ro.

Ioṃwin joñoul ruo raan in aer kapti. Ilo kajin etto, "Kajiroñroñ." Raan eo kajoñouljilu ewaļǫk juon eṃṃaan. Ekanooj aetok. Ej itok i lǫjet tok. Wūnin an itok ej pukot ijo ñaj eo ej ilǫk jāne. (Jiroñ eo.)

Ilo an itok ej jarōk juon al. Al eo ej ba, "Ij itok jān naṃ e iṃō i lǫmeto likōmkōmļǫk, likōmkōmtok / Ai-eo iañ in Mājeej in / O-O-O Limedwetip." (Al eo an tiṃoņ eo, ļeo ej aetok. "Likōmkōmļǫk, likōmkōmtok" im "Ai-eo" rej kajin etto. Ijeļā wōt meļeļe in "Ai-eo". Ej 'eļap no'.)

Jilu alen an al. Kein kemān juon leļļap eroñ em ba ñan irooj eo. Innām kōrā ro ippān Limedwetip rej ba ñan leļļap eo, "Kwōn jab ekkeroro. Kwōn baj babu wōt. Bwe kwe leļļap. Innām kwōj riab."

Reļak ilbōk e ewaļǫk ļeo. Kiiō rej pukot ijo rej ņooje Limedwetip. (Aolep reņooje.) Ke rej lo tiṃoņ eṃṃaan rej kōb roñ em door aolep armej ņa ie. Ilowaan roñ eo.

Tiṃōņ eo ej itok im etal ñan ijo raar kūbij rǫñ [eo] ie. Innām ejaje kajjien mejān rǫñ eo.

---

3. The *kōkļaļ* or *kakōļļe* (signs or sea markers) are aids to navigation. Certain fish, birds, marine mammals, objects, sea conditions, and the like are associated with specific geographical points and were very important to the Marshallese navigators in reaching their landfalls. As the story tells us, this knowledge and the knowledge of divination by folds of pandanus leaves (*bubu in maañ*), as well as other methods of foreseeing the future, were valuable information and were highly prized. Retention of this information obviously enhanced the prestige and authority of the *irooj* (chiefs).

The rite of passage called *kajiroñroñ* (introduction to girlhood) was explained to me by a knowledgeable middle-aged male *aļap* (lineage head) of chiefly lineage from western Rālik and Kapinmeto, on Mājro in 1973. "*Kajiroñroñ* was a menstrual ceremony to celebrate the onset of menses (at ten to eighteen years of age). The *jukun* was the menstrual hut where the premenstrual girls were sequestered. A *kajiroñroñ* feast was held to celebrate the event. It was forbidden (*emǫ*) to go fishing when this happened.

"Bōrraan, an *irooj* of Aelōñļapļap, who was an *Etao* (rascal) type, would damage the *jukun*: take things from them. He disobeyed the chief and went fishing. He went off in a canoe for weeks and months (meaning Bōrraan went adrift). Iroojrilik (a spirit) caused the island of Ep to appear.

"There is a large tree on Wōja, Aelōñļapļap, a *kōñe* [*Pemphis acidula,* ironwood]. It is twisted, and it is there today. It was used by Bōrraan to make his fishing equipment.

"The reason the girls were good in the days of old was because there were *jukun*."

Note the elements also found in the long folktale "Story about Bōrraan" (story 2) on page 37. See Krämer and Nevermann (1938:187–189) for a description of "puberty ceremonies of the girls," in which are described the use of special huts in which the girls were sequestered, the massage with special ointments, and the magical chants. Leach (1950:[2]706–707) discusses the beliefs and customs associated with menstruation in other cultures.

Kiiō ekanooj in pukote. Ej tūm̧tūm̧ wūjooj. Ej joļǫk dekā. Joļǫk maañ in bōb. Joļǫk kimej in ni. Ewaļǫk rǫñ eo. (Kōnke raar door ļat eo i mejān rǫñ bwe en pineje.) E lo rǫñ eo. Em jibwe ne in armej. Im juurlōñļǫk. Em ej wōtlǫktok ak kañe.

Ej maat aolep ak ej jibwe Limedwetip em dieke em jepļaak ñan nam̧ eo, jikin i lǫmeto.

Rainin ñe kwōj loe juon koleej ej pād i lǫmeto, tuiōñ in Mājeej, jeļā ke ej Limedwetip, kōkļaļ in Mājeej. (Etoļǫk jān Mājeej: jiliñuul ak lemñoul m̧ail.) Epād i lǫjet rainin. Kōnke Ļainjin ejeļā em ej kwaļǫk ñan irooj ro in M̧ajeļ. Kōnke irooj ro rej kōŋaan dāpiji Ļainjin (lukkuun armej). Kōnke ejeļā meto, ejeļā kajjien kōkļaļ in āne kaŋ.

Kar m̧okta jān Ļainjin ar waļǫk, irooj ro rej kōjerbal bubu in maañ. Ak Ļainjin ar katak ippān jinen Litarmelu (lukkuun armej) em ļeo ej katak ñan irooj ro.

Irooj ro in M̧ajeļ rej dāpiji im ŋooje katak jān kajoor.

55: THE GIRLS FROM EP

As told by Jelibōr Jam, Kuwajleen 1975

These girls circled the world and saw a tree with flowers that pleased them very much.[1] This tree was the tree of a chief [an *irooj*]. (It is not clear what the name of the chief was.)

And when the girls saw the tree, they came from the atoll of Ep[2] every time when the rooster crowed in the morning, before it was daytime. They came and plucked flowers from the branches of the tree.

They plucked the flowers for many days, but the chief whose tree it was did not know that they were doing this.

It continued thus, and one morning the chief awakened and went to see this tree.

The girls had gone away and had broken some branches—and had taken flowers from the branches.

At the time, the chief was very angry and he killed people who were near his house. The following mid-day, he said that all of the people should meet with him, so that he could tell them that it was forbidden for any person to come to this tree with flowers. For it was precious to him, and any person whom he would see [at the tree], he would kill.

And they all told the people who had not come. That night, many old men came and watched the tree, to seize people if they should come to damage the tree [that is, they acted as watchmen for the chief].

When it was after midnight, all of the people were asleep.

When the rooster crowed, the girls first began coming to the tree and plucking flowers. And they said, "*Pit pit wōj i kio jab ņe.* | *N̄a i kio jab e, diō diō, pāllū pāllū.* | *Jenro pikkeļǫk kālimako.*" (They sang—just played.) "Make flower garlands from the *kio* flowers over there. | I put that *kio* flower garland over my ear, over my ear. | On my head, on my head. | We two are ready to fly away." [Informant explained the different ways of wearing garlands and their nomenclature.][3]

When they had finished their song, they again returned to Ep.

That day, when it was sunrise, the chief and the old men went to the tree and saw that it was more damaged than before. At the time, the chief began [a] war and all of the people of the island fought. And the number of those who died equaled the number of those who were left alive. (One hundred fought and fifty lived and fifty died.) (People today do not know the above word.)

At the time, the chief was very angry, and said, "It will be like this again tomorrow. We will kill [fight] each other if that tree here is damaged again."

---

1. The informant explained: The name of the tree with flowers is *kio* [*Sida fallax.*]. It is a little low but very big. And the color of the flower is a little orange. There are many *kio* on Pikaar and Bok-ak [the uninhabited northernmost atolls of the Ratak Chain]. There are *kio* on all of the atolls of the Marshalls. This tree is very good.

2. The informant did not know if this is the famed island of Marshallese legend, the home of the two supernatural beings, the females Liwātuonmour and Lidepdepju, who came to Naṃo and to Aur, and who founded the *irooj* clans.

3. The informant explained that *diō* refers to the flower garland (lei) or *ṃarṃar* when it is worn on one's head over one ear. One refers to it as *pāllū* when it is worn on the head and above both ears, even with the forehead, and as *ṃarō* when it is worn around the neck.

And all of the *aḷap*[s] (elders) and the young men of the group of the chief decided to make *bwinnen im mej*[4] that night.

When it was late evening, they all came to the chief's house, outside of it, and just ate and watched the tree so that no one would go to it. Because there was so much food, the people ate a great deal in the night, and when they were finished, they slept soundly.

At the time when it was just *raan eņ an irooj* (the daylight of the chief),[5] the chief awakened and looked at the tree. He did not see people. And he came and saw the group of people [who] were trying their best to closely watch and guard the tree.

When they saw it was day, they slept. At the time, the chief again went inside the house and lay down and slept. When he was sleeping away, the rooster crowed on the early side. And the chief heard the rooster crow and got up and went outside and looked at the tree.

When he did not see people, he again went inside and lay down. He lay down and slept soundly. When he was sleeping soundly, the rooster crowed a second time.

And the girls again appeared at the tree and again sang, "*Pit pit wōj i kio jab ņe.* | *N̄a i kio jab e, diō diō, pāllū pāllū.* | *Jenro pikkeļok kālimako.*"

"Make flower garlands from the *kio* flowers over there. | I put that *kio* flower garland over my ear, over my ear. | On my head, on my head. | We two are ready to fly away."

When the song was finished, the girls again returned. The girls returned and the rooster crowed a third time.

When the old men and the young men awakened, they went to the tree and saw that it had again been damaged. And they said to each other, "Who has damaged this tree, men? We will be in continual fear now. For perhaps the chief will again make war. Sir, how will it be? When we do not know who of us will be gone now."

When it was sunrise, the chief awoke and went out to the tree and saw that it had again been damaged.

And he again brought war to all the people of the atoll.

This time it was the same as before, the number of the dead, and the living.

When it was after mid-day and the sun was west of the middle of the sky, all of the *aḷap*[s] of the chief met and decided that they should end their war, because many people had died but there was no reason for their deaths, and there would be fewer of the chief's group [they would be diminished].

And they said, "It will be better if we make a great deal of food and stay awake from evening until sunrise (stay awake—just eat and do not sleep). For they should not fight again and reduce the people of the chief's group. But they should see [watch] and if they will see the person [who has damaged the tree], well, the person, that one, should die."

---

4. *Bwinnin in mej,* Jelibōr Jam explained, is the custom of eating a full meal before a battle. Food is eaten so that one does not go to sleep. The group of men in this story observed this custom to help themselves stay awake so that they could watch (guard) the chief's tree.

5. *Raan eņ an irooj*, 'daylight of the chief', the informant explained, is just before dawn, a little light in the east. The *irooj* wake up then and eat and awaken all the others. Some *irooj* do this today, and tell the people what to do: clean up trash or weeds, or sail or go fishing, and so forth. [This is an example of the traditional role of the chiefs as planners and organizers of economic activities.]

When the chief heard the decision, he said, "Well, that is really a good decision, men. I will sleep well now while this decision is thus."[6]

Later in the evening, they brought a great deal of food so that they could *bwinin im mej:* eat and stay awake during the night. And they took everyone of a good age, and all the old men, so that they would all stay awake together in the night, and not sleep.

They stayed awake from the evening to midnight; all of them did not sleep, but they hid in those places out of sight.

When the rooster crowed the first time, they saw the girls come to the tree and they said, "We just say, who is that wants to come to damage that tree, and [it is] those girls."

Now the girls began their song and said, "*Pitpit wōj i kio jab ņe. | N̄a i kio jab ņe.*" Their song was not ended, but all of them [the chief's group] ran up and seized the girls.

When they seized the girls, they took them to the chief, and the chief took them inside his house and said to them, "Where did you come from?"

The girls answered, "We come from Ep. But can you release us two so that we can return to our mother and our father?"

The chief answered, "What I see is only that you two are very beautiful, and I will release you. I do not want to release you, for you are human beings inside my house."

The girls replied, "We are not human beings, but people of the sea. We are just demons. And release us."

Now the chief replied, "What are you doing? Telling a lie? Why do you say 'demons' when you are talking so well to me?"

The girls said, "We are demons, not people."

The chief replied, and said, "The three of us will remain a little while, and in the days to come, we three will go to your mother and father."

It was a short while later, and the girls again asked to return. And the chief said, "Well, you get ready, for we will go to your island so that you can see the old people. Then we three will come back here again."

The girls said, "Well, good." And they prepared a canoe for their sail to Ep.

The following day, when it was early in the morning, they launched the canoe and sailed to Ep. When they were nearing Ep, the girls changed the chief's thoughts into the thoughts of the people of Ep [that is, they "brainwashed" him].

When the way of thinking of the chief had been changed, he saw the atoll of Ep—an island that was so long that we could not see from one end to the other. And the lagoon had a very sandy bottom (no coral heads, a very good place). And it was a very beautiful atoll. A short while later, they (the people of Ep) took the canoe ashore, and when it was finished, the girls led the chief to their house, to their elders. And the elders spoke to every-

---

6. This illustrates the decision-making power of the *aļap*[s] (lineage heads), subject to the approval of the *irooj* (chief), and their position vis-à-vis their chief. The position of the lineage heads, the leaders from the ranks of the commoners *(kajoor)*, was illustrated when another informant, M̧ak (Mark) Juda, explained the meaning of the word "*nitijeļā*" to me on Mājro in 1971. The *Nitijeļā* is the name given the legislative body of the Marshall Islands. The late *Irooj ļapļap* Ļōjjeiļañ Kabua is said to have given it this name. The *nitijeļā* was a pit dug for an arena for cock fighting, using *kōtkōt* [*Arenaria interpres,* ruddy turnstone] as combatants. This was done by the *irooj* in the past. The term was also used in *kajin etto* (the ancient language) to indicate the meeting place of the wise people (*nit* 'place', *in jeļā* 'of knowledge'). The *aļap*[s] met there in a circle around the *irooj,* the informant explained, and sketched a circle with the *aļap*[s] around their *irooj* in the middle, analogous to the pit with the cocks in it and the spectators around it.

body on Ep and said, "There is a new human being who came here with the girls to Ep."

After three days,[7] the people of Ep wanted to eat the human being, the chief. (All of the people of Ep were demons, but the girls had changed into human beings and loved the chief, for he had taken good care of them.)[8]

And the people of Ep all decided to make food, so that they would bring the chief and the girls their food, and at the time of bringing food, they would eat the chief.[9] But there was one small reason why the food and the people of Ep would come slowly, because the island was very long. And the people of Ep said, "Hurry up!" and said, "*Kōto jein, kōto jein, kōto je wa!*" ([It was] in the ancient language: "The canoe will sail. For this wind is good!")

Some of the people cried out and said, "*Kaiber O-O. Kaiber, bwe ejja jako ri-bukwōn jeiuweo em ri-bukwōn jekoko; dettolok!*" (*Kaiber* is 'wait' in the ancient language.) ("Wait O-O. Wait, for the people of that *bukwōn* [district/division of an island or atoll] over there [fairly close], the people of that *bukwōn* way over there [can still see them], and the people of that *bukwōn* far, far over there [out of sight] are not present, they are far away!")[10]

But because the girls were also people of Ep and knew all the thoughts of the people of Ep, they hurried up and led the chief to the canoe, so that the three of them could sail.

But when they went to where the canoe had been, the people of Ep had hidden the canoe, and it was gone.

And the girls said, "*Jejjab mijak anij kiiō* | *Jekki linno* | *Jekki linno* | *Rumļǫk, ṃōnļǫk, ṃōnļǫk ļǫk* | *Waļǫktok, batbat eo* | *Ej waļǫktok kōn jouj in wa eo.*" (In *kajin timōn*, demon language, *jekki linno* is 'hurry up!') ("We are not afraid of demons now. | Hurry, hurry. | Go down inside, you cannot be seen [out of sight]. | Appears the hermit crab | It appears with [in] the bottom part of the canoe.")[11]

And the people of Ep were very anxious to eat the chief, but because the island was very long, the people were delayed in their [coming] to eat the chief. And the girls again said to the crab, the name of the crab, *batbat*, that he should hurry up and show all of the trees, the trees that should be for the canoe.

And the crab said, "*Jejjab mijak anij eiō* | *Jekki linno* | *Jekki linno* | *Ṃōnļǫk, em ļak, waļǫktok batbat eo* | *Ej waļǫktok kōn jiṃ ko.*" ("We are not afraid of demons over there. | Hurry, hurry. | Go down inside and the crab appears, he appears with the end pieces.")

And he again said, "*Jejjab mijak anij eiō* | *Jekki linno* | *Jekki linno* | *Ṃōnļǫk, em ļak,*

7. Note the ritual number and period of three days.

8. Note the motif of cannibals/cannibal islands. Cannibalism did exist to the southeast, south, and southwest of the Marshalls, in parts of Polynesia and Melanesia, but not in Micronesia, either historically or in the oral tradition as a reported culture trait. The occurrence of cannibals and cannibalism in Marshallese folktales may indicate contact with cannibalistic groups by the Marshallese enroute to their present location, or at a later period.

9. The custom of making and bringing food to visitors and to their chiefs was, and is, very important, and it was done in a specified manner by the community. Special terms are used for the different types of presentation.

10. The Marshallese are quite conscious of relative spatial positions and distances; this is reflected in the language, as in part of this story, and in others. See Carr and Elbert (1945:xx, xxiii), Tobin (1967:112–113), and Bender (1969:267–270 and 279–286) for details.

11. The informant sketched a canoe hull in my notebook and indicated the component parts. These included the *jouj*, the bottom part above the keel or *erer*, and the attached end sections fore and aft, *jim*, which figure prominently in this graphic presentation of the frightening pursuit.

waḷọk tok batbat eo | Ej waḷọk tok kōn rā ko." ("We are not afraid of demons over there. | Hurry, hurry. | Go down inside and the crab appears | He appears with the boards [upper portion of the hull].")

Thus the crab worked [used] the parts of the tree that should be used for the canoe.[12] And when everything was ready, the girls said, "Make two fishing poles from *ut*" [*Guettarda speciosa* L., a tree.] (This is good for making fishing poles, houses, and fish spears, breadfruit-picking implements, implements for digging the earth, canoes, and all kinds of tools like that. The name of it is *ut*.)[13]

When it was finished, they launched the canoe and hurried up and sailed. When they had gone a little way, the people ran up, the people of Ep (the demons) to eat everyone who was in the canoe.[14] And they flew to the canoe of the girls and the chief, so that they could eat those three.[15]

Then the girls said (to the chief), "Give me one of your fishing poles of *ut*, and one to that little girl, so that when the people of Ep come, we will use the poles at the stern of this canoe."

At that time, there were one hundred or two hundred women and men; they flew behind the canoe to come and eat all of them. (Demons know how to fly like birds.)

And the girls said (they sang): *"In kat bwā ut eo | Ri-Ep kātok | O-O | Jilib! Jilib! Piruk! | Kañe wōt pako!"* ("Hold, hold fast, the fishing pole of *ut*, ready to fish, and move from side to side. | The people of Ep they fly overhead O-O. | The sound of something hitting the water! | The sound of something hitting the water! | The sound of something heavy hitting the land! | Sharks eat!")[16]

All of the people of Ep who had come ahead fell, and the sharks ate them. But about twenty [demons] came to eat them—the three people in the canoe.

And the girls again said, *"In kat bwā ut eo | Ri-Ep kātok | O-O | Jilib! | Jilib! Piruk! | Kañe wōt pako!"* ("Hold, hold fast, the fishing pole of *ut*, ready to fish, and move from side to side. | The people of Ep they fly overhead | O-O | The sound of something hitting the water! | The sound of something hitting the water! | The sound of something heavy hitting the land! / Sharks eat!")

Thus it went until the time when all of the people of Ep who had flown to the canoe were finished. (All the demons died, eaten by sharks.)[17]

---

12. The motif of the helpful anthropomorphic animal, in this case the crab, is a widespread one. For example, the story of the helpful octopus and the ungrateful, malicious rat is told in the Marshall Islands and in many other parts of Oceania.

13. We see the versatility of this valuable tree, and the inventory of traditional material culture that is described.

14. Here again is the widespread and dramatic motif of pursuit by evil beings. This adds to the suspense of the tale, and to audience enjoyment. It is found in a number of other Marshallese stories.

15. Note the exciting and very threatening motif of pursuit of the intended victims by means of flying. This gives the evil pursuers the advantage over their desired prey and makes escape seem doomed to failure, thereby accentuating the danger in the situation.

16. The informant explained the meanings of the onomatopoetic words *jilib* and *piruk*. *Jilib* is the sound of something hitting the water *(ijjiliblib),* the hook in this case. It is the sound of the water, he said. And *piruk* is a heavy sound on land *(ippirukruk),* like the thud of a coconut falling to the ground.

17. This is imitative magic to ward off evil. The "magical chant/song/spell destroys enemies" motif is clear. In this case it was the magical chant that caused the pursuing demons to fall into the sea to be eaten by sharks.

When they were finished, the canoe of the chief reached the atoll from which he had sailed. And the girls of Ep did not return to Ep, but remained with the chief and showed him anything at all that he could do for all of the people of his group who were angry with the chief at the time that he made war on the atoll, when he was angry about the tree, this tree. (They told the chief to make things good and to help all of his people.)[18]

Thus the chief "threw away his mistake" [apologized] and did good to the people of his group.

It is ended.

(The meaning in this: I do not understand it very much, but the chief was angry about a simple tree and made war. It was of no importance [as a reason for making war].[19]

But the girls lived with the spirit and revealed the thought [idea] to the chief, so that people would change and love the chief.)[20]

55: LEDIK RO JĀN EP

Ri-bwebwenato: Jelibōr Jam, Kuwajleen 1975

Ledik rein raar kapooļ laļ im lo juon ut ekanooj eṃṃan ippāerro. Ut in ej make ut eṃṃantata ilo aer kar loe.[21]

Ut in ej ut in juon irooj. (Ejjab alikkar etan irooj.) Ak ke ledik ro rejro lo ut eo rejro itok jān aelōn̄ in Ep ilo aolep iien ņe n̄e ej ikkūr kako in jibbon̄, ṃokta jān an raan. Rejro itok em irrur.[22]

Ebaj lōn̄ wōt raan emootļǫk in aerro rur jān leen ut eo ak irooj eo utin ut eo ejaje ennaan.

Pād im ļak juon jibbon̄ irooj eo ej ruj im etal in lale ut eo ut in.

---

18. The motif here is the ancient and widespread one of the teaching of correct interpersonal behavior to mortals by a supernatural being (in this case, by more than one).

19. We see the motif of remorse for misbehavior, and the guide for proper behavior of a chief toward his people.

20. Is this a reflection of the introduced Christian doctrine of the power of the Holy Spirit to change one's life? It sounds as if it is. The word *jetōb* or spirit in this story was used only once as quoted, and is used in the Marshallese translation of the Bible as Holy Ghost/Holy Spirit: *Jetōb Kwojarjar.*

There is an analogy to the Marshallese Land of Ep in Hawaiian mythology. Beckwith (1970:67-80) discusses "Mythical Lands of the Gods." Her reference to "Kuaihelani . . . the land of the deified dead" is reminiscent of this Marshallese tale, "The Girls from Ep." Beckwith writes, "It lies to the west, for two chiefesses who travel thence voyage eastward to Hawaii; after a voyage of forty days, the sweet smell of kiele flowers hails their approach to its shores. It is called in chant 'the divine home land | the wonderful land of the setting sun | going down into the deep blue sea,' and a migration from Kuaihelani is described as 'the ali'i (chiefs) thronging in crowds from Kuaihelani | on the shoulders of Moanaliha (Ocean).'" And Beamer (1984:59) writes, "Aukele and the Sky Islands: mysterious islands of Kua-I-Helani (Far-away-Helani) so often mentioned in the chants. . . ."

21. Ri-bwebwenato eo ej kōmmeļeļe: ut eo etan kio. Ettā jidik, ak lukkuun kilep. Elōn̄ rej pād ilo juon wōt jikin. Im ut wūno in oran, dik. Elōn̄ i Pikaar im Bok-ak. Eor ilo aolep aelōn̄ in Ṃajeļ. Eṃṃan ut in.

22. Ri-bwebwenato eo eaar bar ba ejaje epād ia āne in Ep eo. Im eaar ron̄ kake ilo bwebwenato wōt.

Eļak ilǫk eṃōj an ledik ro ruje jān raan. Kab būki ut ko iraan.

Iien eo wōt eļap an illu irooj eo im ṃan armej ro repaake ṃweo iṃōn. Raeleb in ļǫk eo ej ba bwe aolep armej ren kweļǫk tok ñan ippān. Bwe en kōnnaanōk er bwe emǫ an jabdewōt armej itok ñan ut eo ut in. Bwe eaorōk ippān. Innām jabdewōt armej eo enaaj loe enaaj ṃane bwe en mej.

Innām rejwōj kōnnaanōk armej ro raar jab itok. Ilo boñōn eo elōñ ļōļļap rej itok im lale ut eo im kappok armej ñe ren itok im kǫkkure ut eo.

Ke ej mootļǫk lukwōn boñ aolep armej im kiki.

Ke ej ikkūr kako eo, ṃoktata ledik ro rej jino aer itok ñan ut eo im irrur. Im rejro ba, "Pit pit wōj i kio jab ņe. | Ña i kio jab e, diō diō, pāllū pāllū. | Jenro pikkeļǫk kālimako." (Rej al, ikkure bajjek.)

Ilo iien in ke ejeṃļǫk aerro al, rōbar jepļaak ñan Ep.

Raan eo wōt ke ej tak aļ irooj eo kab ļōļļap ro rej etal ñan ut eo ļak lale ej kab baj jorrāān ļǫk jān ṃokta. Iien eo irooj eo eaar kabuñ an pata. Im aolep ri-āne rej wōj tariņae.

Im oran eo emej wōt eo emour. (Jibuki raar tariņae im lemñoul raar mour im lemñoul raar mej.)

(Armej ro kiiō rejaje naan eo ilōñ.)

Ilo iien eo eļap an illu irooj eo, im ba, "Enaaj āindein bar ilju jenaaj ṃan doon ñe ebar jorrāān ut e."

Innām aolep aļap ro kab likao ro doon irooj eo rej wōj pepe im kōṃṃan bwinnin emmej ilo boñ eo.[23]

Ke ej jotaļǫk rej wōj itok ñan nabōj in ṃweo iṃwōn irooj eo im kōjota bajjek im lale ut eo bwe en ejjeļǫk eņ ej etal ñane. Kōn an lōñ ṃōñā ekanooj in ļap an armej ro ṃōñā iuṃwin boñōn eo im ke rej mat, rekiki im ettoñ.

Ilo iien eo ke baj raan eņ an irooj,[24] irooj eo eruj im lale ļǫk ut eo. Ejjab ellolo armej. Innām ej itok im lale armej ro doon ke raar kate er im emmijrake ut eo.

Ke rej lo an raan, rekiki. Ilo iien eo, irooj eo ej bar deļǫñ ñan lowaan ṃweo im babu ļǫk im kiki. Ke ej kiki ļǫk ej ikkūr kako eo iṃaantata. Innām irooj eo eroñjake an kako eo ikkūr im jerkak im wōnnabōjļǫk im lale ļǫk ut eo ut in.

Ke ejjab ellolo armej ej bar deļǫñtok im babu. Ej babu ļǫk wōt ak ettoñ. Ke ej ettoñ ej ikkūr kako eo kein karuo alen.

Innām ledik ro rejro bar waļǫk tok ñan ut eo im bar al.

"Pit pit wōj i kio jab ņe. | Ña i kio jab e, diō diō, pāllū pāllū. | Jenro pikkelǫk kālimako."

Ilo iien eo ke ej jeṃļǫk al eo ledik ro rōbar jepļaak. Ledik ro rej jepļaak wōt ak ekkūr kako eo kein kajilu alen.

Ke ej ruj ļōļļap ro kab likao ro rej etal ñan ut eo im ļak lale eṃōj bar kǫkkure. Innām rej ba ñan doon, "Wōn eaar kǫkkure ut in, ļōṃa? Jej kab naaj mijak kiiō. Bwe bōlen irooj in enaaj bar kōṃṃan tariņae. Ļe, enaaj kōjkan? Ke jejaje wōn enaaj jako iadeañ kiiō."

Ke ej tak aļ irooj eo ej ruj im ilǫk ñan ut eo ut in im ļak lale ebar ṃōj kǫkkure.

Im ej bar kōṃṃan tariņae ñan aolep armej in aelōñ eo.

Ilo iien eo ejja āinwōt ṃokta, oran eo emej wōt eo emour.

Ke ej raelepļǫk im pād aļ rilik in ioļap ej

23. "Bwinnin im mej" ej ṃōñā armej kañe bwe rej jab kiki. Im bwe remaroñ waj wōt. Kōnke ren waj im lale ut eo an irooj eo.

24. Raan eņ an irooj ej ṃokta jidik raantak eo. Eor jidik wōt meram ilo rear. irooj ro ruj im ṃōñā im karuji aolep armej. Ej ṃantin irooj in etto. Jet rej kōṃṃan rainin. Im rej ba ñan armej ta eo rej aikuj kōṃṃane: rara, rejak, eǫñwod, im āinwōt.

kwaļọk tok aolep aļap ro an irooj eo im pepe, bwe en ṃōj aer tariņae bwe elōñ wōt armej ro remej ak ejjeļọk wūnin aer mej, im eiietļọk doon irooj eo.

Innām rej ba, "Eṃṃanļọk ñe jenaaj kōṃṃan elōñ ṃōñā im itok im emmej jān jota ñan ñe etak aļ. (Ṃōñā wōt. Im jab kiki.) Bwe ren jab bar tariņae in kaiietļọk armej ro doon irooj eo. Ak ren loe im ñe renaaj lo armej eo, ekwe armej eo en mej deeo."

Ke irooj eo ej roñjake pepe eo ej ba, "Ekwe, ejet in pepe eṃṃan ļōṃa. Inaaj kiki eṃṃan kiiō ñe āindein pepe in."

Ilo iien eo ej boñļọk elōñ ṃōñā rej bōktok bwe en bwinnen emmej ilo boñōn eo. Im rej bōktok aolep ro eṃṃan dettāer, kab aolep ļōļļap ro bwe ren wōj jiṃor emmej ilo boñōn eo. Im jab kiki.

Raar emmej jān jotaan eo ļọk ñan lukwōn boñōn eo aolep rej ruj im jab kiki ak rej tilekek ijoko rōttino.

Ke ej ikkūr kako eo ṃokta rej lo an ledik ro itok ñan ut eo innām rej ba, "Jebaj ba wōn ņe ekōņaan itok in kọkkure ut ņe, ak ledik raņ e."

Kiiō ledik ro rej jino aerro al im ba, "Pit pit wōj ikio jab ņe | Ña ikio jab e." Ejañin jeṃļọk wōt al eo aerro ak rej wōj ettōrtok im jibwe ledik ro.

Ke rej jibwe ledik ro rej bōkļọk erro ñan ippān irooj eo im irooj eo ej kadeļọñ itok erro ņae lowaan ṃweo imōn im ba ñan erro, "Koṃwinro itok jān ia?"

Euwaak ledik ro, "Kemijro itok jān Ep. Ak kwōj maroñ ke kōtļọk kemro bwe keminro jepļaak ñan ippān jinemiro im jemāmiro?"

Irooj eo ej uwaak, "Ta ij lale wōt ke koṃro kanooj in deeọ ak inaaj kōtļọk koṃro. Ijjab kōņaan kōtļọk koṃro bwe koṃro armej in lowaan mwiin iṃō."

Euwaak ledik ro, "Kimro ejjab armej ak ri-lik im bōk anij bajjek. Innām kwōn kōtļọk kōmro."

Kiiō irooj ej uwaak, "Koṃijro et? Kōnono riab ke? Etke koṃro ba 'anij'? Koṃro ke ekanooj in eṃṃan amiro kōnono tok ñan eō?"

Ledik ro rej ba, "Kemro anij. Ejjab armej."

Irooj eo ej uwaak. Ej ba, "Jejel ja pād jidik innām ilo raan kaņe rej itok jel naaj etal ippān jinemiro im jemāmiro."

Ej baj meļan ļọk ak ledik ro rej bar kajjitōk aer jepļaak. Innām irooj eo ej ba, "Ekwe, koṃro kōppojak bwe jenaaj etal ñan āne eo ānemiro. Bwe koṃwinro lo rūtto ro. Innām jel naaj bar jepļaak tok."

Ledik ro rej ba, "Ekwe eṃṃan." Innām rej kepooje juon wa ñan aer jerak ñan Ep.

Rujļọkin eo ke ej jibboñtata rej bwillọkwe wa eo im jerak ñan Ep. Ke rej tōprak ļọk Ep, ledik ro rej ukot an irooj eo ļōmņak ñan mejatoto in armej in Ep.

Ilo iien eo ej oktak mejatoto eo an irooj eo ej lo aelōñ in Ep. Juōn āne ekanooj aetok im jejjab lo jabōn tu jeņ im tu jeņ. Ak ekanooj kabokbok arin. (Ejjeļọk wōd ekanooj in eṃṃan jikin eo.) Im juon aelōñ ekanooj in erreo. Meļan ļọk jidik rej (armej in Ep) bōk āneļọk wa eo im ke ej ṃōj, ledik ro rej ukwe irooj eo ñan ṃweo i mwerro ñan ippān rūtto ro. Im rūtto ro rej kōnnaanōk jabdewōt armej in Ep im ba, "Eor juon armej kāāl eaar itok ippān ledik ro tok ñan Ep."

Ļọkun jilu raan, armej ro ilo Ep rōkōņaan kañ armej eo, irooj eo.

(Aolep armej in Ep rej tiṃoņ wōt ak ledik rej kar oktak ñan armej im rej iọkwe irooj eo bwe eṃṃan an kōjparok er.)

Innām armej in Ep rejwōj pepe in kōṃṃan ṃōñā bwe ren bōktok kijen irooj eo kab ledik ro, naaj ilo iien in aer bōktok ṃōñā renaaj kañ irooj eo. Ak jidik wōt wūnin an ruṃwij tok ṃōñā ko kab armej ro in Ep. Kōnke eļap an aetok āne eo. Innām armej ro ilo Ep rej ba, "Ṃōkajtok!" Im ba, "Kōto jein, kōto jein, kōto je wa!"

(Kajin etto: "Enaaj jerak wa eo. Bwe eṃṃan kōto in!")

Jet iaan armej rej laṃōj, im ba, "Kaiber O-O. Kaiber, bwe ejja jako rūbukwōn jeiō im rūbukwōn jeiuweo em rūbukwōn jekoko; rettoļǫk!" ("Kaiber" ej 'kōttar' ilo kajin etto.)

Ak kōnke ledik ro bar armej in Ep rejeļā aolep an armej ro ilo Ep ļōmņak. Rejro kaiur [em] ro im ukwe irooj eo im etal ñan wa eo bwe renjel jerak.

Ak ke rej ilǫk ñan ijo wa eo eaar pād ie eṃōj an armej in Ep ņooje wa eo im ejako.

Innām ledik ro rej ba, "Jejjab mijak anij kiiō | Jekki linno | Jekki linno | Ruṃļǫk, ṃōnļǫk, ṃōnļǫk ļǫk | Waļǫktok, batbat eo | Ej waļǫktok kōn jouj in wa eo." (Ilo kajin tiṃoņ "jekki linno" ej 'kaiuri'!)

Ak armej in Ep eļap aer kijerjer in kañ irooj eo ak kōnke eļap an aetok āne eo im eruṃwij tok armej ñan aer naaj kañ irooj eo. Ak ledik ro rejro bar ba ñan baru eo, etan baru eo batbat, bwe en kaiur in kwaļǫk tok aolep wōjke ko wōjke in wa eo.

Innām batbat eo ej ba, "Jejjab mijak anij eiō | Jekki linno | Jekki linno | Ṃōnļǫk, em ļak, waļǫk tok batbat eo | Ej waļǫktok kōn jiṃ ko."

Innām ej bar ba, "Jejjab mijak anij eiō | Jekki linno | Jekki linno | Ṃōnļǫk, em ļak, waļǫk tok batbat eo | Ej waļǫk tok kōn rā ko."

Āindein an batbat eo jerbale tok wōjke in wa eo. Im ke ej dedeļǫk jabdewōt, ledik ro rej ba, "Jektok ruo bwā ut." (Eṃṃan ñan kōṃṃan bwā, eṃ, ṃade in eǫñwōd, kein kōṃkōṃ, kein kōbwe bwidej, wa, im āinwōt. Etan 'ut'.)

Ke ej ṃōj rej bwillǫkwe wa eo im kaiur im jerak.

Ke rej mootļǫk jidik, ej ettōrtok armej ro, armej in Ep (tiṃoņ ro) im kañ aolepān ijo wa eo eaar pād ie. Im kāļǫk ñan wa eo waan ledik im irooj eo, bwe ren kañ erjel.

Ilo iien eo ledik ro rej ba (ñan irooj eo), "Kwōn lewōj juon aṃ bwā ut, ak juon an ledik ņe edik bwe ilo iien eņ ej itok armej in Ep koṃro naaj toore ņa iļǫkan wa in."

Iien eo wōt eor jibuki ak rubuki kōrā ak eṃṃaan rej kātok iļǫkan wa eo in itok in kañ ereañ. (Tiṃoņ rejeļā kāļǫk āinwōt bao.)

Innām ledik ro rej ba (rej al), "In kat bwā ut eo ri-Ep kātok-O-O / Jillib! Piruk! / Kañe wōt pako!"

Aolep ro raar itok iṃaantok iaan ri-Ep ro aolep in wōtlǫk ņa i lǫjet im pako e kañe er. Ak ebar kātok roñoul im men (tiṃoņ) im itok in kañ er, armej ro iwa eo.

Innām ledik ro rej bar ba, "In kāt bwā ut eo ri-Ep kātok-O-O. Jillib! Piruk! / Kañe wōt pako!"

Āindeo aer kōṃṃan ñan iien eo ej maat aolep armej in Ep ro raar kātok ñan wa eo. Ke rej mat etōpraktok ļǫk wa eo waan irooj eo ilo aelōñ eo eaar jerak jāne. Im ledik in Ep ro raar jab jepļaak ñan Ep ak raar pādwōt ippān irooj eo im kwaļǫk jabdewōt men ko en kōṃṃane ñan armej otemjej ro doon im raar illu ippān irooj eo ilo iien eo eaar kōṃṃan tariņae ilo aelōñ eo, ke ej illu kōn ut eo ut in.

Āindein irooj eo eaar joļǫk an bwōd im kōṃṃan eṃṃan ñan armej ro doon.

Ejeṃļǫk.

(Meļeļe in: Ijjab kanooj in meļeļe ak irooj eo ej illu kōn juon ut wōt im kōṃṃan tariņae. Ejjeļǫk tokjān.

Ak kiiō ledik ro rej mour kōn jetōp in kwaļǫk ļōmņak ñan irooj bwe armej ren oktak im iǫkwe irooj eo.)

56: LIJIBOKRA

As told by Lore Kejibuke, Pikinni 1969

Lijibokra is a female *ekjab* [spirit], not a *tiṃoṇ* [demon.] She came to Pikinni long ago and poisoned *(karkar)* the fish there.

Then Wōdejebato, a male *ekjab*, chased her away. She went to the west. Wherever she went, she poisoned the fish. This included the fish on Ronđik Atoll.

I do not know where she is today.

Comments

Lore Kejibuke was the magistrate of the Kōle/Pikinni people when he told me about Lijibokra. She figured in the more recent history of the people of Pikinni Atoll, when the Pikinni people were uprooted from their atoll and relocated on Ronđik Atoll in 1946. Pikinni Atoll had been taken from them by the United States for the testing of atomic (and later nuclear) weapons.

The resettlement was a failure. The Pikinni people claimed that the fish were poisonous, and that they did not have enough to eat as a consequence—unlike Pikinni, where the fish and other marine resources were plentiful and edible.

They blamed the condition of the fish and of Ronđik Atoll as a whole on the evil actions of Lijibokra. This negative factor and that of the scanty land resources on the small atoll led to their final relocation by the government on tiny Kōle Island.

Wōdejebato was believed by the Pikinni people to still dwell in a reef under the water of the Pikinni lagoon. The reef is located just off of the main landing-beach on Pikinni Island (the main island of the atoll).

Containers of water were taken from the dwelling place of Wōdejebato in the reef, and were brought to the homes of the Pikinni people for protective use, much as holy water is used elsewhere.

It should be noted that *ciguatera*, fish poisoning, exists in a number of areas in the Marshalls. Attributing it to a supernatural spirit was the Marshallese explanation of the problem, in the complete absence of scientific information.

Explanation of phenomena of this kind is of course one of the important functions of folktales, and has obvious psychological value. See Halstead (1959:117–131) for a discussion of *ciguatera*-producing fishes: "Ciguatera is a type of poisoning produced by a large variety of tropical reef or shore fishes. More than 300 different species have been incriminated to date. Apparently, any marine fish, under the proper circumstances, may become involved with this type of poison, since all of the species listed as poisonous are commonly eaten in some localities, and considered as good food fishes. It is, therefore, believed that these fishes become poisonous because of their food habits. . . . Ciguatera is a serious problem in certain tropical areas such as the central and south Pacific Ocean and the West Indies" (117).

The Lijibokra and Wōdejebato legend was recorded by the German ethnologist Erdland. "Wurijibādo (*wur*—fresh pandanus cone, *i*—of, *jabādo*—to throw into the sea; it was forbidden to throw what was left of food into the sea)—a coral reef on the side of the lagoon of

Bigini [Pikinni]. At W's time a leprous woman lived in Bigini called Lijbukra: the discharge of her wounds formed a glossy strip on the water (*ļae*). Every fish using that as food turned poisonous. W., being angry at it, expelled the woman from the atoll to Rongerik [Roñdik]; since that time there are no poisonous fish in the lagoon of Biginni, whereas they occur almost everywhere else. W. himself, having come from the west, was considered a son of Wullep" (Erdland 1914:336).

Other older Pikinni men also told me that there were no poisonous fish (*ek kadek*) on Pikinni Atoll, and that there never have been to their knowledge. (They all knew the legend.)

This information was given to me on Kōle Island in the early 1950s, and on Pikinni in 1969 and 1970, where the men were fishing and eating their catches, and sun-drying some of the fish for shipment to their families on Kōle.

The magistrate and other representatives of the community were on Pikinni as advisors and workers in the first phase of the Pikinni rehabilitation program—cleanup of debris, clearing and replanting of the atoll, and construction of homes and other facilities. The goal is the resettlement of the Pikinni people on their home atoll, which was finally returned to them, albeit in a ravaged condition.

Another story of Wōdejebato was told to me by Raymond DeBrum on Mājro in 1953. "Wōdejebato and his sister Liwajjoto came up from the west on a log of redwood and landed at the lee of Pikinni. On account of Liwajjoto's mats [her wearing apparel] [having] all rotted off through continual soaking, she stayed behind while Wōdejebato went to the main island and took a wife, Lijurilōñ by name, from another man. On account of the long trip, the log got watersoaked, so in order to render it buoyant again, she made magic (*anijnij*) called *Bokeppen*.

"After Liwajjoto's mats rotted off, Wōdejebato forced incest on his sister, which caused the log to become waterlogged quicker than it should have, therefore she had to charm the log.

"Wōdejebato is now a large bunch of sea grass in a *naṃ* (secondary lagoon) in Pikinni. Liwajjoto is now a large *dimuuj* (clam) in the lee reef, and Lijurilin̄ is a rock shaped like an *aje* (drum) shorewards from Wōdejebato."[1]

1. *Ņam*: 'shallower part of lagoon between beach and secondary reef'.

57: STORY ABOUT LŌRRO

As told by Jelibōr Jam, Kuwajleen 1975

On Roñļap Atoll, there were two old people. Their [life] being together was very good. The man was gone one day, and the woman was very sad and did not eat and did not drink. And she did not talk with people, but just meditated. After six days, people looked around again to go to feed her. She was gone, and they searched for her all day long. But they did not find her.

That night, they again searched for her. They did not find her. They searched for almost two weeks.[1] But they did not find her. And they ended their search.

But she was not there, because she had flown to Wōtto and turned away to where there was a group of people on Wōtto.

And the woman appeared to all of the people on Wōtto. And the people looked for where she would land there.

But she did not land. And the people on Wōtto looked for her, and she was gone.

The same day at three o'clock or so, this woman came to Ujae and appeared to twenty some men who were making *m̧akm̧ōk* [*Tacca leontepetaloides,* arrowroot— that is, they were processing it].[2]

This woman landed on Ujae and disguised herself and showed herself to two of the women who were cooking in the earth oven.

And one of those women, the Ujae woman, thought she was part of the women who came to bring leaves. And [she] said, "Women, feed that woman, for she has not eaten yet."

And the other woman went to feed the woman, the *lōrro*.

The *lōrro* hurried up and hid herself in the coconut tree [*Cocos nucifera, ni*], and the Ujae woman spoke to the other woman and said, "Why is it that the woman was gone so fast from here, when you were going to feed her, she was gone?"

The other woman replied, "She hid herself in that coconut tree."

After only five or more minutes,[3] children who were bathing in the lagoon cried out and said, "Look at that *lōrro!*" And they looked and she was gone.

When it was five o'clock, still the same day, the *lōrro* came to Lae. As she came to Lae, a canoe was in the Lae lagoon. And all the men in the canoe saw her, but because the *lōrro* came to the island and landed in almost two minutes [ahead of them] near the church, some of the people thought that she was another Lae woman—because she had disguised herself. When the Lae people spoke to her, she did not reply. But she flew away quickly. And they said, "Look at that

1. Note the introduced Western concept of time and the loanword *wiik* from English *week.* See the Marsallese text "Bwebwenato in Lōrro" on page 263.

2. The arrowroot (*Tacca leontopetaloides* L.) tubers are processed to make them edible and suitable for storage. The tubers are grated and the bitter substance they contain is removed by several washings with fresh water. The resultant material (starch) is sun dried, packed in pandanus leaf containers (traditionally), and is used as needed. It is usually mixed and cooked with other foods such as coconut meat or pandanus fruit or juice. It was stored for times of food shortages as well, and was especially important on the drier northern and northwestern atolls of the Marshalls, where soils are poorer and the rainfall is scantier than on the southern atolls.

3. Note the use of the English loanword *minit* 'minute' and the Western concept of reckoning time.

lōrro!" They looked around and went to search for her. The sun had set. But they only saw her flying.

On the morning of the next day, the *lōrro* flew down to Epatōn, Kuwajleen, and appeared to some of the people on Epatōn.

On the morning of the same day, the *lōrro* came to Ruot and Nim̧ur [adjacent islands in northeastern Kuwajleen Atoll]. And men who were fishing saw her, and she just flew to Enm̧aat and those there saw her, and the *lōrro* did not stop, but just flew to the main island of Kuwajleen. And she circled Kuwajleen one time.[4]

And from the smallest to the biggest, everyone saw her. At that time, the people were very surprised, because they had just seen a *lōrro* [for the first time]. Previously they had only heard about it, but [now] they [had] just seen the *lōrro* and verified that the woman was flying.

However, many of the people said, "Soul of a person" (the thing that is inside of people).

And she continued to fly, and went to Nam̧o [Atoll], and some of the people on Nam̧o saw her. The same day, this *lōrro* continued and went to Aelōn̄ļapļap. Some people saw her on Wōja and talked about the sighting. "At the time we saw the *lōrro,* it was ten o'clock. And she was gone." And people were surprised, but some were not afraid.

This *lōrro* flew and landed on the sandbar in front of Buoj, and slept. But four men, one of these men a Lae man, were paddling with two canoes, and went to fish. When they arrived near the sandbar, they saw the *lōrro*, [who] was lying down. And they said, "[There is] a log over there on that sandbar." And the two men in the other canoe approached the sandbar, and the man, the Lae man, said, "That thing is not a log. But why is it like a person?" The other men looked at it and recognized (knew) that it was a human being.

And the two of them thought that it was dead and had drifted here in the ocean and drifted ashore. And the two of them called to the [other] two men and said, "That is a person on the sandbar. Maybe it drifted ashore last night!" At the time that the two of them shouted, the *lōrro* raised up and sat. And continued to fly to Aerōk, and some [people] saw her and talked about it. And the four men witnessed [attested to them] that they had seen her again. But many people did not believe it.

The *lōrro* continued to go, and some of the people on Jebwad [Jālooj Atoll] and all of the men in the canoes on the sea saw her.

And she continued flying and landed on an island named Petkio. (It is in Ratak [the eastern chain of the Marshalls], but I do not know where it is located.)[5]

And the women there said, "Go to Āne-kaņ-lik." And she continued to go and then landed on Āne-kaņ-lik.

Six women were plaiting flower garlands [leis]. The flowers they picked were long, and measured from their wrist joints to their finger tips. That was the size of their flowers.

4. The word *rawūn* (from English *round*) is used as a verb meaning 'to circle or make a round trip'. It is also used to describe a field trip or other voyage that makes a round trip. The field trip ship is called *wa in rawūn* or *waan rawūn*.

5. One of the islands of Bok-ak (Taon̄i) Atoll, the northernmost atoll of the Ratak chain, is called Petkio. Bok-ak is uninhabited due to lack of potable water and adequate soil. But it is the nesting place for large numbers of seabirds and sea turtles, and it functioned as a game reserve and valuable source of food for the people of the northern Marshalls (see Tobin 1958:47–56). It was believed that the *ekjab* (spirits) Jo̧-Bok-ak and Ļāwūn-Pikaar dwelt on Bok-ak and Pikaar, respectively, and homage was paid them. Bok-ak and the atoll of Pikaar to the south (also uninhabited) are claimed as *mo̧* (taboo) lands by the *irooj eļap* (paramount chiefs) of Northern Ratak, who have controlled their resources.

There were very many [of them]. And they [the women] said to the *lõrro*, "Where have you come from? And again, where have you come from?"

And the *lõrro* replied, "I came here from Roñļap." And the women said, "Where were you? And again where?"

The *lõrro* answered, "I just came on the road to here. I was on Jebwad. And I came to Petkio. And the people on Petkio said [that] I should come!"

The women replied, "Well, enter here, and again, enter here."

At the time when the *lõrro* was going to enter, an old man leaning on a cane came up to her. But the women said to the *lõrro*, "Here is something for you to eat!"

And the *lõrro* came and just seized the food, but the old man hit the *lõrro*'s hand with his cane.

At this time, the *lõrro* went and looked at the side of the house. It was very steep alongside.[6]

When the *lõrro* looked at it and saw the steepness of the side of the house, she said to herself, "If I fall, perhaps I will never see my relatives [again]."

But the old man insisted and said, "The *lõrro* should return from the house." When he spoke to her, the *lõrro* flew away, and came back to Jebwad, and just came, and continued on to Roñļap.

One night, two men went to fish. And they talked along the way.

One of the men said, "Why has the woman been gone so long that we are tired of looking for her but do not see her?"

The two of them continued talking, but they saw a shadow—a big shadow—and they searched beneath the moonlight.

Because the shadow was so big, they did not think that it was the shadow of a bird. But they said, "Sir, what is this the shadow of?" The other man said, "That's the shadow of a person!"

And the other man said, "Well, you go north on that road. And I will go south on this road here."

And they looked, and the shadow was coming down the road.

When the shadow approached them, they easily recognized that it was a human being. And they both got ready, apart from each other, for when she came down, they planned to seize her together. And when she was two feet high [above the road], they put down [suppressed] their fear. Although they told [themselves it was a] demon, their thought of seizing the *lõrro* was greater than their fear.

And they leaped from the north and from the south and both seized her at the same time. And one of the men seized the top part of her head, and the other man seized her legs. At the time they seized her, she weighed two pounds,[7] and later she died.

And they hurried to the old women who knew how to make the soul return to the body.[8] When they brought the *lõrro,* they cried out and said, "The woman was gone,

---

6. The traditional Marshallese houses (*eṃ* or *ṃwe*) were of the A-frame type. The sides rested on the ground, and were obviously steep, as the story tells us. The houses of the chiefs *(irooj)* and their offspring (*bwidak*) were larger, with rather low sides that raised the roofs off of the ground. There were apparently no large community structures or meeting houses, such as the Gilbertese *maneaba* or the men's houses of Palau (Belau) and Yap, or the feast houses of Truk (Chuuk) and Ponape (Pohnpei).

7. The English loanword *bọun* 'pound' and the associated concept of weighing are used here.

8. The concept of soul loss is a widespread one. It has been described as "absence of the soul from the living body resulting in sickness, and eventually death, if it is not regained. . . . Soul-catching, or the restoration of the soul to the living body, is a complicated and detailed ritual requiring the services of a highly specialized shaman" Leach (1950[2]:1052).

for many weeks and months. Maybe she came back."

And people ran and woke up the young men. And they said, "Look for the old women, for they should come and treat her and pat her on the chest."[9]

When it was three o'clock, [getting on] toward dawn, all the people stayed awake near the *lōrro*. They heard a sound. It was not clear what the sound was, but they heard it stop near the house.

At that time, the *lōrro* came alive and arose and flew up to the skylight in the house.[10] And the people seized her. When they seized her, she was again dead. And they put her down on the ground again and treated her. After a little while, the people again heard the sound coming to the side of the house.

And some of the women who were treating the *lōrro* said, "The sound is coming and looking for that *lōrro* to take her away."

And they seized the *lōrro,* and at that time, the *lōrro* went to get up, but they seized her. And she laid down again.

When it was sunrise, the *lōrro* came to life, and all the people recognized that she was the woman who was missing. And the women who were treating her said to each person that they should not come to the *lōrro* (approach her) until after six days had elapsed. For it is bad to talk with her. But later, everyone can come and question the *lōrro* about all of the roads that she took on her journey [—her itinerary].

It had been many months earlier that they had seen her come in the air.

And all of the people waited until the end of six days.

When six days had passed, the women who treated her said, "All of the people should stay in their houses, for we will walk with the *lōrro* and come to your houses."

And that day, while it was still morning, the *lōrro* awoke to comb her hair, and cleaned up a little outside the house [picked up leaves and other trash],[11] and washed her face. When she was finished, she entered and got ready, and the women brought her to the houses of the people of Roñļap.

And when the women went inside the first house, all the people inside the house stood and came and greeted the *lōrro* and asked her, "Where have you been?"

And the *lōrro* explained [to them] all of the islands where she had gone, and had continued [on] to her old home, the home of the *lōrro*.

And the *lōrro* said to them, "If the old man had not sent me from one island named Āne-kaņ-lik, I would have gone in with the women who were making flower garlands and stayed with them forever. And you never would have visited me."

And the *lōrro* went from the first house and went in with the people at the second house, and greeted them. And the people ran up to her, and they were very sad and happy

---

9. *Pikūr ubōn*: This is a healing technique using the hands, a form of massage, and magical chants or songs. Coconut oil (*pinniep*) is sometimes used, as are medicines made from plants and their juices.

10. The informant explained that the *demāju* were skylights in the thatched roofs of the old-style houses. They admitted light and air, and were at the front of the houses, about three feet square in size.

11. This is the normal daily routine of Marshallese women, except at the housing areas at the urban centers.
Erdland (1914:270, 332) discusses the Marshallese belief in flying women. It is obviously similar to the belief in flying witches that existed in Europe and early Colonial America, and elsewhere. As Leach (1950[2]:1179) points out, world folklore almost universally reports witches as having the ability to fly. Although the Marshallese *lōrro* are not witches and are not malevolent, they obviously share this amazing ability. The alleged sightings of flying women by groups of people have apparently been cases of mass hallucination.

that the *lōrro* had again returned. And they asked her, "Where were you?" And the *lōrro* explained her itinerary. And the people said, "When you began your departure, where did you start your trip from?" The *lōrro* replied, "I slept, and at the time when I was very troubled, I do not know whether I awoke or I was dreaming. And when I woke up, I was trying to leave the house. At the time when I did not see people, my trouble became greater, and I did not know where I was. "But I thought it would be good to run at the time, when I began to fly. And I went to Wōtto and appeared to the men who were making [processing] arrowroot. And I went to Ujae and saw the women who were cooking in an earth oven and appeared to some of them, and went to Lae and again appeared to some of the Lae people. From Lae, I came to Epatōn and Ruot and Niṃur and Kuwajleen, and went [continued to go] to Naṃo. And went to Aelōñļapļap. At this time I was very tired, and I slept on a sandbar. The reason I awoke was because young men were noisy, and I was startled and woke up and flew and went to Aerōk [Aelōñļapļap]. And went to Jebwad [Jālooj] and appeared to men who were in the canoes. And went and landed on Petkio [Bok-ak]. And the women said I should go first to Āne-kaŋ-lik.

"When I went, the women were plaiting flower garlands of *ut-kio* [*Sida fallax*]. And they said, 'Come in, and again, come in.' When I was slow for the time being, an old man came and said I should go. And he pushed me, and said, 'Do not come in, but return.' And thus I am before your eyes [in your presence] today."

And the *lōrro* went to all of the houses on Roñļap and spoke these same words that she had said to the people of the other houses.

And all of the Roñļap people reported it and the people on Wōtto Atoll confirmed it—some of them because they saw her.

Also those who saw her on Ujae Atoll. Like those to whom she appeared on Lae Atoll. And those on Kuwajleen Atoll: Epatōn, Ruot, and Niṃur, and on the main island of Kuwajleen. And four men on Aelōñļapļap, Buoj, and some of those on Wōja and Aerōk.

And they again brought these words to Jālooj Atoll. And those on Jebwad, those who had seen her and those in the canoes confirmed that the woman flew like a bird. But all of those who did not see her said it is a lie.

And it is ended.

(The *lōrro* flew during the Japanese times. The middle part. And people saw her and confirmed it. I heard the story from Roñļap people who saw and seized the *lōrro*—the name of the man was Jeban—he is dead now—at the time she returned from Petkio.

And there are some who are *būroṃōj* [afflicted with an acute melancholia-like condition], and they run, and people seize them, before they can fly away.)

57: BWEBWENATO IN LŌRRO

Ri-bwebwenato: Jelibōr Jam, Kuwajleen 1975

Ilo aelōñ in Roñļap eor ruo rūtto. Ekanooj in eṃṃan aerro pād ippān doon. Ļak baj juon raan ļeo ejako innām lio eļap an būroṃōj im ejjab ṃōñā ak ejjab idaak. Ak ejjab bwebwenato ippān armej ak kōļmānļọkjeņ wōt. Ļak baj ālikin jiljino raan armej ro reļak bar etal in naajdik ļọk, ejako. Innām rej pukote iuṃwin juon raan eiieo. Ak raar jab loe.

Boñon eo rej bar pukote. Rejjab loe. Raar pukot iuṃwin tarrin ruo wiik ak raar jab loe. Innām ej bōjrak aer pukote.

Ak ejjab wōt ke eaar kāļọk ñan Wōtto im ļak ilọk rej jar i Wōtto.

Innām eaar waļọk kōrā in ñan aolepān armej ro i Wōtto. Im armej ro i Wōtto rej ettōr ñan ippān. Im lale ijo enaaj jok ie. Ak eaar jab jok. Ak armej ro i Wōtto raar lale ļọk im ejako.

Ak eaar jab jok. Ak armej ro i Wōtto raar lale ļọk im ejako.

Raan eo wōt ilo jilu men awa kōrā in eaar itok ñan Ujae im waļọk ñan joñoul jiṃa eṃṃaan rej kōṃṃan ṃakṃōk.

Kōrā in eaar jok i Ujae im kōjakkōlkōle ñan ruo iaan kōrā ro rej uṃuṃ.

Innām lio juon iaan kōrā ro, kōrā in Ujae ej ļōmņak ṃōttan kōrā ro raar etal in ebōktok bōlōk innām ej ba, "Lio kwōn naajdik kōrā ņe bwe ejjañin kar ṃōñā."

Innām kōrā in Ujae eo juon eļak iten naajdik kōrā eo lōrro. Lōrro eo ej kaiuri [im] penjak ilo ni eo im kōrā in Ujae eo ej ba ñan lio juon im ba, "Etke enañin ṃōkaj an jako kōrā eo ije ke iļak ba men ko kijōṃ ko, ejako."

Lio juon ej uwaak, "Eaar penjak wōj ilo ni ņe."

Ļọkun wōt ļalem im men minit ajiri ro rej tutu iar rej laṃōj im ba, "Lale lōrro eņ!" Innām raar jāleļọk im ejako.

Ke ej ļalem awa ejja raan eo wōt. Lōrro eo itok ñan Lae. Ļak ilọk ñan Lae juon wa ej pād iar in Lae. Innām aolep ļōṃaro ioon wa eo raar loe ak ej ke āneļọk lōrro eo im jok tarrin ruo minit iturin ṃōn jar eo jet iaan armej ro rej ļōmņak bar kōrā in Lae. Kōnke ej kōjakkōlkōle. Ke armej in Lae ro rej kōnono ñane ejjab uwaak ak ej ṃōkaj in kāļọk. Innām rej ba, "Kala lōrro eņ!" Reļak iten pukote, etulọk aļ. Ak raar lo wōt an kāļọk.

Jibboñ in raan eo juon lōrro eo ej kātok ñan Epatōn, Kuwajleen im waļọk ñan jet iaan armej ro ilo Epatōn.

Jibboñ in raan eo wōt lōrro eo ej itok ñan Ruot im Niṃur. Im ļōṃaro rej eọñwōd raar loe im eaar kātok wōt ñan Enṃaat im ro ie raar loe im lōrro [eo] ejjab bōjrak ak itok wōt ñan eonene in Kuwajleen. Im rawūni Kuwajleen juon alen.

Im jān diktata ñan eļaptata [rūttotata] aolep raar loe. Ilo iien in eļap an armej bwilōñ bwe rej kab ellolo lōrro. Ak ṃokta rekin roñjake wōt. Ak rej kab ellolo. Im kaṃool ke kōrā ej kāļọk.

Ijoke elōñ jet iaan armej rej ba, "An armej." (Men ej pād ilowaan armej.)

Innām eaar kāļọk wōt im etal ñan Naṃo im jet iaan armej in Naṃo raar loe. Raan eo wōt lōrro in eaar kāļọk wōt im etal ñan Aelōñļapļap. Jet armej raar lo i Wōja im kōnnaan kake, "Ke kem ar lo juon lōrro kiiō ej joñoul awa. Im emootļọk." Im armej ro rej bwilōñ ak jet rejjab tōmak.

Lōrro in eaar kāļǫk im jok ilo bok eŋ iṃaan Buoj im kiki. Ak emān eṃṃaan, juon iaan ļōṃarein eṃṃaan in Lae, raar aōŋōōŋ kōn ruo kōrkōr in ilān eǫñwōd. Ke rej tōparļǫk turin bok eo rej lo lōrro eo ej babu. Im rej ba, "Juōn ŋeŋe kājokwā iraan bok ŋe!" Innām ļōṃaro ruo ilo wa eo juon rejro kepaakļǫk bok eo im ļeo, eṃṃaan in Lae, ej ba, "Ejjab kājokwā men ŋe. Ak etke āinwōt armej?" Ļeo juon eļak erreilǫk ekile ke armej.

Innām rejro ļōmŋak emej im eaar petok im eǫtōk. Innām rejro ikkūr ñan ļōṃaro ruo im ba, "Armej men e ioon bok eŋ. Bōlen eaar eǫtōk boñ!" Ilo iien ke rejro laṃōj lōrro eo ej jerkak im jijet. Im kāļǫk im etal wōt ñan Aerōk im jet raar loe im bwebwenato kake. Im ļōṃaro emān rej kaṃool er bwe raar bar loe. Ak armej ro jet rejjab tōmak.

Lōrro in ar etal wōt im jet iaan armej ro ilo Jebwad raar loe kab aolep ļōṃaro ioon wa ko i meto.

Innām eaar kāļǫk wōt im jokļǫk ioon juon āne etan Petkio. (Epād i Ratak ak ijaje ia.[12])

Im kōrā ro ie rej ba, "Kwōn etal wōt ñan Āne-kaŋ-lik." Innām eaar etal wōt im ļak jokļǫk ioon Āne-kaŋ-lik.

Jiljino kōrā rej ļōļō ut. Aitkwan ut ko rej ļōļō joñan ut jān kōbļǫk in pā ñan ṃaan addi. Joñan ut ko de kein.

Ekanooj in lōñ. Innām rej ba ñan lōrro eo, "Kwōj itok jān ia? Im bar itok jān ia?"

Innām lōrro ej ba, "Ij itok jān Roñļap." Innām kōrā [ro] rej ba, "Kwaar pād ia? Im bar pād ia?"

Lōrro eo ej uwaak, "Ij itok wōt ilo iiaļ eo tok. Iaar pād Jebwad. Im itok ñan Petkio. Im armej ro ilo Petkio raar ba, 'In itok'."

Kōrā ro rej uwaak, "Ekwe, deļǫñ tok im bar deļǫñ tok."

Ilo iien eo ke lōrro eo ej ilān deļǫñ juon ļōļļap ej jokoŋkoŋtok ñan ippān. Ak kōrā ro rej ba ñan lōrro eo, "Lewōj men ŋe kijōṃ!"

Innām lōrro eo ej itok im jibwe ṃōñā eo wōt ak ļōļļap eo ej deñļǫk pein lōrro eo kōn jokoŋ eo jokoŋan.

Iien in lōrro eo eļak erreitok ñan turin ṃweo, ekanooj jirūṃle turin.

Ke lōrro eo ej erreitok im lo an jirūṃle turin ṃweo. Ej ba ippān make, "Ñe inaaj wōtlǫk bōlen ijāmjin lo ro nukū."

Ak ļōļļap eo ej akweļap im ba, "Lōrro eo en jepļaak jān ṃweo." Ke ej kōnono ñane lōrro eo ej kāļǫk. Im jepļaaktok ñan Jebwad im itok wōt im etal ñan Roñļap.

Ilo juon boñ ruo eṃṃaan rejro ej etal in eǫñwōd. Im rejro bwebwenato ilo iiaļ eo.

Ļeo juon ej ba, "Etke enañin baj ļap an jako kōrā eo ke jeṃōk in pukot ak jejab loe?"

Rejro ja bwebwenato wōt ak rejro lo juon annañ. Annañ eo eļap. Im rejro pukot ikijjin meram in allōñ.

Annañ eo kōn an ļap rejro jab ļōmŋak bwe annañin bao.

Ak rejro ba, "Ļe enaaj annañin ta in." Ļeo juon ej ba, "Annañin armej men ŋe."

Im ļeo juon ej ba, "Ekwe, kwe iōñin iiaļ ŋe. Ak ña irōk in iiaļ e."

Innām rejro lale an annañ eo itok ilo iiaļ eo tok.

Ke ej epaaktok annañ [eo], eļap aerro kile ke armej. Innām rejro kōppojak jān doon bwe eto laļtak rejro jiṃor ļōmŋak in kab jibwe. Innām ke ej ruo *feet* utiejān rejro likūt mijak ippāerro. Kōnke rej ba tiṃoŋ, ak ļōmŋak in jibwe lōrro eo eļap jān aerro mijak.

Innām rejro kātok jān eañ kab jān rōk im jepaan wōt juon aerro jibwe. Im ļeo juon ej jibwe jabbōran. Ak ļeo juon ej jibwe neen.

---

12. Eor juon āne etan Petkio. Epād ilo aelōñ in Bok-ak, aelōñ eo eañtata an Ratak. Ejjeļǫk armej rej jokwe ie. Ak elōñ bao im wōn rej pād ie. Rūtto ro raar ŋae etan, "Mǫ in Irooj." Kab aelōñ in Pikaar im aelōñ in Jāmǫ barāinwōt.

Iien eo ke rejro jibwe ruo bo̧un eddo im tokālik emej.

Im rejro m̧ōkaj kake ñan leļļap ro rejeļā kajok an.

Ke rejro bōkļo̧k lōrro [eo] rejro lam̧ōj im ba, "Kōrā eo eaar jako, ium̧win elōñ wiik im allōñ ko remootļo̧k. Bōlen eñe emoottok."

Innām armej ro rej ettōr im irujļo̧k ñan ippān likao ro. Im rej ba, "Pukot tok kōrā ro bwe ren itok in unoke im pikūr ubōn."

Ke ej jilu awa joraantak aolep armej ro rej emmej iturin lōrro eo. Rej roñjake im jem̧ļo̧k iturin m̧weo.

Iien eo lōrro eo emour im jerkak im kelōñļo̧k ñan demaju in m̧weo. Innām armej ro rej jibwe. Ke rej jibwe ebar mej. Im rej bar doore ņa ilaļ im unoke. Ālikin jidik iien armej ro rej bar roñjake ainikien ej itok ñan turin m̧weo. Im jet iaan kōrā ro rej uno[ok] lōrro eo rej ba, "Ainikien in ej itok in pukot lōrro ņe im bōke ñan ippāer."

Innām rej dāpiji lōrro eo im iien eo ej bar iten jerkak lōrro eo, ak rej dāpiji. Im ej bar babu.

Ke ej tak aļ iien eo lōrro eo emour im armej otemjej rej kile ke kōrā eo eaar jako. Innām kōrā ro rej unoke rej ba ñan kajjojo armej bwe ren jab itok ñan ippān lōrro in ñan ñe eļo̧k jiljino raan. Bwe enana kōnono ippān. Ak tokālik aolep armej remaroñ itok im kajjitōk aolepān iiaļ ko lōrro eo eaar etal ieļo̧k.

Ke elōñ allōñ ko remootļo̧k ak reļak loe ej itok i mejatoto tok.

Innām aolep armej rej kōttar wōt ñan ļo̧kun jiljino raan.

Ke ej ļo̧k jiljino raan kōrā ro raar unoke rej ba, "Aolep armej ren pādwōt i m̧ōko im̧weer bwe lōrro e kem naaj etetal ippān im iwōj ñan m̧ōko im̧ōmi."

Im raan eo ke jibboñ wōt lōrro eo eaar ruj in kūrbar. Im rarō jidik inabwij in m̧weo. Im kwaļ mejān. Ke ej m̧ōj ej deļo̧ñ im kōppojak im kōrā ro rej āñini ñan m̧ōko im̧ōn armej in Roñļap.

Im ke kōrā ro rej deļo̧ñ tok ilowaan m̧weo m̧okta aolep armej ilowaan m̧weo rej jutak im itok im io̧kio̧kwe lōrro eo im kajjitōk ippān, "Ia ko kwaar pād ie?"

Innām lōrro eo ej kōmeļeļe aolepān āne ko eaar pād ie im ilo̧k wōt ñan jikin eo jikin lōrro.

Im lōrro eo ej ba ñan er, "Eļañe ļōļļap eo eaar jab jilkinļo̧k eō jān juon āne etan in Āne-kan̄-lik inaaj kar deļo̧ñ ippān kōrā ro rej ļōļō ut im pād ñan indeo. Im kom̧ jāmjin kar lotok eō."

Innām lōrro ej etal jān m̧weo m̧okta im deļo̧ñ ļo̧k ippān armej ro ilo m̧weo kein karuo. Im io̧kio̧kwe er. Im armej ro rej ettōr tok ñan ippān. Im kanooj in būrom̧ōj im m̧ōn̄ōn̄ō bwe lōrro eo ej bar jepļaaktok. Im rej kajjitōk ippān, "Kwaar pād ia?" Im lōrro ej kōmōļeļe iiaļ ko an im armej ro rej ba, "Kar baj jino in am̧ etal kwaar jino etal ia ļo̧k?" Lōrro eo ej uwaak, "Iaar kiki innām iien eo ke ej ļap aō inepata ijaje ke iruj ak iaar ettōn̄ak im ļak ruj iaar kajjioñ dioj jān m̧weo. Ilo iien eo ke ijjab ellolo armej eļap ļo̧k aō inepata im ijaje ia [eo] ij ilo̧k ieļo̧k. Ak ij ļōmn̄ak em̧m̧an bwe in ettōr iien eo iaar jino kāļo̧k im ilo̧k ñan Wōtto im waļo̧k ñan ļōm̧aro rej kōm̧m̧an m̧akm̧ōk. Im ilo̧k wōt ñan Ujae im lo kōrā ro rej um̧um̧ im waļo̧k ñan jet iaer. Im etal ñan Lae im bar waļo̧k ñan jet iaan armej in Lae. Jān Lae iaar itok ñan Epatōn im Ruot im Nim̧ur im Kuwajleen. Im etal wōt ñan Nam̧o. Im etal ñan Aelōñļapļap. Iien in eļap aō m̧ōk. Im iaar kiki ioon juon bōk. Wūnin aō ruj likao ro rej ekkeroro. Innām iaar ilbōk im ruj im kāļo̧k im etal wōt ñan Aerōk. Im etal ñan Jebwad im waļo̧k ñan armej ro rej pād ioon wa ko im etal wōt im jokļo̧k Petkio. Innām kōrā ro rej ba in etal m̧okta ñan Āne-kan̄-lik.

"Ke ij etal kōrā ro rej ļōļō utkio. Im rej ba, 'Kwōn deļo̧ñ im bar deļo̧ñ.' Ak ke ijja rum̧wij ej itok juon ļōļļap im ba ña in etal. Innām ej iuun ļo̧k eō. Im ba, 'Kwōn jab deļǫñ ak kwōn jepļaak.' Im eñiin ña ipād iṃaan mejāmi rainin."

Innām lōrro eo ej etal ñan aolep ṃōko in Roñļap im kōnono ejja ennaan ko wōt ṃokta eaar ba ñan rūṃōko jet.

Innām aolep ri-Roñļap rej kōnnaan im armej ro ilo aelōñ in Wōtto rej kaṃoole, jet iaer bwe raar loe.

Barāinwōt ro raar lo ilo aelōñ in Ujae. Āinwōt ro eaar waļǫk ñan er ilo aelōñ in Lae. Kab ro ilo aelōñ in Kuwajleen: Epatōn, Ruot, im Niṃur. Kab eonene in Kuwajleen. Kab emān eṃṃaan ilo Aelōñļapļap, Buoj. Kab jet iaan ro ilo Wōja. Kab Aerōk.

Innām raar bōkļǫk ennaan kein ñan aelōñ in Jālooj. Im ro ilo Jebẉad ro raar loe kab ro ioon wa rej kaṃool ke kōrā ej ekkāke in āinwōt bao. Ak ro otemjej raar jab loe rej ba riab.

Innām ejeṃļǫk.

(Lōrro ej ekkāke ilo iien ko an ri-Jepaan. Ilo lukōn. Im armej raar loe im kaṃoole. Rūbwebwenato ar roñjake bwebwenato jān ri-Roñļap ro raar loe im jibwe lōrro eo.

Etan ļeo Jeban [emej kiiō]. Iien eo ej rǫǫltok jān Petkio.

Im eor jet rej būroṃōj im rej ettōr im armej rej jibwe er ṃokta jān aer ekkāke.)

58: TWO JĀLOOJ WOMEN (LŌRRO)

As told by Jelibōr Jam, Kuwajleen 1975

A woman on Jālooj named Lukure flew away and returned again. I did not see that woman, but I heard about it. She flew away during the German time [the period of German rule].

The name of the other woman was Lijuka. She went to Japan. I was a student on Jebwad [Jālooj Atoll] and heard about it.

She returned again and reported to the people stories about Japan, and some of the Japanese [on Jebwad] said the stories were true.

I do not know if the people saw her when she flew. That woman is alive today.

Men Who Are Būroṃōj

There are men who are *būroṃōj* and eat excrement, and throw off their clothes and are naked. They change to crazy [become crazy] from *būroṃōj*. Some are blind from *būroṃōj*. If they are treated [with traditional Marshallese medical treatment: *uno in Ṃajeḷ*], they become well. I saw it during the Japanese time. They were *būroṃōj* because their women left them or died. I have not seen it during the time of the white men [the American period]. There have been many like this.

Comments

The word *būroṃōj* itself means 'sorry; sorrow, sadness; mourn', and is probably derived from *bōro* (throat) and *ṃōjņọ* (weak). The throat is the seat of the emotions to the Marshallese, analogous to the heart in other cultures.

Būroṃōj may result from the prolonged absence or loss of a loved one (as has been indicated in the Marshallese stories of its occurrence). The affected person becomes deeply depressed. It would probably be classified as a psychoneurosis.

Hysterical blindness is apparently one manifestation of *būroṃōj*. I heard of a case of this in 1952. A homesick/lovesick young Marshallese male high school student on Truk was afflicted, and was sent back to his home on Mājro. He recovered shortly thereafter, following traditional treatment.

It was diagnosed as hysterical blindness by an American physician on Truk who answered my query about it. This was apparently the youth's culturally acceptable way of escaping from what he felt to be an impossible situation.

58: RUO KŌRĀ IN JĀLOOJ (LŌRRO)

Ri-bwebwenato: Jelibōr Jam, Kuwajleen 1975

Juōn kōrā i Jālooj etan Lukūre ej kāļọk im bar rọọl. Iaar jab loe liin ak iaar roñ kake. Eaar kāļọk ilo iien Jāmne.

Etan kōrā eo juon Lijuka ar etal ñan Jepaan. Iaar rijikuuļ i Jebwad im iaar roñ. Ar bar rọọltok im kennaan ñan armej bwebwenato in Jepaan. Innām jet iaan ri-Jepaan raar ba ṃool an bwebwenato.

Ijaje ñe armej raar loe ke ar kāļọk.

Liin ej mour wōt rainin.

Ṃōṃaan Rebūroṃōj

Eor ṃōṃaan rej būroṃōj im ṃōñā kūbwe. Im joļọk nuknuk eo aer im rej koļeiat.

Rej oktak ñan bwebwe, jān būroṃōj. Jet rej pilo jān būroṃōj. Ñe rej uno rej eṃṃan.

Iaar loe ilo iien Jepaan. Rej būroṃōj kōn an jako kōrā ak mej. Ijañin ellolo ilo iien Pālle. Ekar wor eloñ āinwōt.

59: A LŌRRO STORY FROM ARŅO ATOLL

As told by an Arņo youth, Arno 1953

I and many people on Ine Island on Arņo Atoll saw a *lōrro* in 1950. This *lōrro* was a woman whose husband had gone away to northern Ratak (*Aelōñ Kaiōñ*).

This woman suffered from lovesickness (*būroāōj*) and she flew away to the north to join her husband. She flew with her arms extended over her head. (which they say is the way *lōrro* fly).[1]

---

1. The women who claimed to have flown away may indeed have believed it, or they may have lied in some cases to gain attention, which they obviously received. And the alleged sightings of flying women can be attributed to culturally conditioned misperceptions or delusions, and to crowd psychology.

60: A LŌRRO STORY FROM ĀNEWETAK ATOLL

As told by Irooj Joanej, Wūjlañ 1955

Būroṃōj (lovesickness) affects women. They want a man, are sad, and may fly away (really fly away). The woman who is *būroṃōj* becomes crazy and then flies away. When she flies, she is called *ledik raṇ* or *lōrro*. She flies like a bird and then returns to her island.

Some fly away to their lover. Some fly like Lianjepel to Ṇadikdik.[1] She flew carrying her baby Lino. Lianjepel was lovesick for Leddiklañ, an *irooj* of Ānewetak. She had been cast off by him when he tired of her.

This happened during the German times.

After she returned to Ānewetak from Ṇadikdik, she was taken back by him.

This is the only case of this kind in the history of Ānewetak, and it is known by all of the Ānewetak people.

Men who become *būroṃōj* may become crazy, and they sometimes become ill. They cannot think (*obrak ļōmņak*). They cannot fly, though.

No man ever became *būroṃōj* on Ānewetak or on Wūjlañ.

1. A small atoll next to Mile Atoll in southernmost Ratak. It is 670 nautical miles to the southeast of Ānewetak Atoll, and is the legendary leaping-off place for the spirits of the dead.

61: ABOUT A WOMAN ON UJAE NAMED LIBWINER

As told by Jelibōr Jam, Kuwajleen 1975

And there were three men. The name of one man: Jowaļañ (as Ļainjin said in his *ikid* song/story [saga]).[1] The name of one man: Ļatarbwin. The name of one man: Koperwa.

Jowaļañ was on Ujae, on the main island of Ujae. Ļatarbwin was on Bok [Island] on Ujae. Koperwa was on Epāju [Island] on Ujae.

One day, Ļatarbwin sailed to the main island of Ujae. When he landed, this woman (Libwiner) came out and met the canoe of Ļatarbwin. And Ļatarbwin said, "Do you want to ride with me to Bok? There are very many flying fish [*Exocoetidae, jojo*] and many tuna [*Gymnosarda nuda,* dog-tooth tuna, *jilo*] and every kind of food."[2]

And Libwiner answered and said, "Well, if you will take good care of me, as Jowaļañ does, I will go with you."

Ļatarbwin said, "Your stay with me will be better than [with] Jowaļañ."

And the woman replied, "Well, when are you sailing?" The man (Ļatarbwin) answered, "I wanted to sail a long time ago. Although I asked you if you would be happy to come with me, and it was clear that you were happy and would not delay me, but you alone were slow. (That is, he was waiting for her to come, but she delayed.)

"If you are ready, well, let us go now."

And the two of them went and sailed to Bok, and stayed there. One day Jowaļañ was worried and saw Ļatarbwin taking a walk, and he threw a rock at him. And he did not hit him. (*Lel:* 'hit', is *kajin joot,* language of the shot [bullet][3] from a gun, of spearing fish, and of people, with the fist.)

And he again took a rock, a second one. But it did not hit him. The third rock hit Ļatarbwin and passed to the north and decapitated Ļatarbwin, as it went north.[4] And Koperwa, when he heard that Ļatarbwin was dead, went and took [loaded] Libwiner on the canoe with him (*ektaketok: kajin wa:* canoe language). And the two of them stayed on Epāju.

One day, they sailed to Ujae, the main island. And at the time, when they had disembarked, it was evening, and they were very cold. And Koperwa said, "Go bring some fire here for the two of us. For let us stay (lie) near the fire" *(ewilik: kajin kijeek,* is fire language only, for 'to stay near or next to the fire').

And the woman went and saw Jowaļañ

---

1. Jowaļañ, the storyteller explained, is a *kōkļaļ,* a navigation sign today (for Ujae).

2. The word *kain* 'fundamental nature or quality', a loan from English *kind,* is used in the Marshallese text.

3. The loanword *joot,* from English *shot* (bullet for a gun [*bu*]), is used in the Marshallese text. The Marshallese formerly used slingshots (*buwat*) in warfare. The beach pebbles used in them were called *bu.* Birds were also brought down by slingshots (see Krämer and Nevermann 1938:88). They also threw rocks at their enemies.

4. Throwing rocks at houses to show dislike/disapproval of the dwellers, and directly against one's enemies, is done today by the Marshallese, and has increased markedly, especially in the urban centers of Mājro and Epjā (Ebeye), Kuwajleen. Boys and young men seem to be the principal offenders, as reflected in the police reports published in *The Marshall Islands Journal,* a weekly newspaper. This antisocial behavior is also practiced on Pohnpei, Yap, Chuuk (Truk), and Belau (Palau). Motor vehicles are also targets these days.

pounding taro [*Cyrtosperma chamissonis, iaraj,* the native taro of the Marshalls].[5]

And when he saw Libwiner coming, he was very happy, and he said, "Libwiner, hurry and come here."

When the woman went to him, he gave her a little pounded taro for her food. And he said to her, "What kind of food did you have with Ļatarbwin, ma'am?"

The woman replied and said, "The very best of things."

Jowaļañ said, "Is there no taro on Bok?" The woman answered, "Why? Is that thing over there not also an island?"

[And Jowaļañ asked,] "And what are you doing now?" [The woman replied,] "I came to get fire." And she lit fire to a coconut [shoot] and took the fire and returned to Koperwa. When she had gone and was about thirty feet away, she extinguished the fire,[6] so that she could again talk to Jowaļañ.[7] And [she] again returned, because she enjoyed watching the body movements[8] of Jowaļañ while he was pounding [taro].

And that woman again returned and lit the coconut shoot. And Jowaļañ again said, "Why have you returned here so quickly, ma'am?"

The woman replied, "Because I went over there, over there a little distance. I extinguished the fire, and I am again returning and lighting the coconut shoot and I am hurrying to go."

When she finished lighting the coconut shoot, she again said, "*Iọkwe eok* [Greetings], sir, Jowaļañ."

Now Jowaļañ said, "I again give you your food, a little pounded taro." And Jowaļañ gave her the pounded taro and said, "*Kepaak ña karean.*" (In *kajin etto,* the ancient language, it is, 'come close to me'.)

And Libwiner stood up and went. And again extinguished the fire, because she wanted very much to see Jowaļañ pounding [the taro].

And she again lit her fire. And Jowaļañ said, "Why have you returned here so quickly, ma'am?"

The woman replied, "Because my thing for carrying fire was no good" (the coconut shoot).

And she again lit the coconut shoot and returned and went. When she went, she very much wanted to return, but she was determined to go to Koperwa.

When she reached Koperwa, it was almost daybreak.

And Koperwa said, "Why are you so slow with that fire, ma'am? For the rooster has crowed, and we will sail now, just before sunrise."

The woman said, "Because I am tired of looking for my thing for bringing fire (the coconut shoot) and everything is wet—because it rained when we brought it here, and that is the reason for my slowness in bringing the fire."

---

5. Taro was pounded with stones found on the reefs. They are not used today. *Iaraj* is grown and used today on Ujae, the informant said. Most of it is grown on the main island where Jowaļañ pounded taro. The name of the land parcel (*wāto*) is Bat-eņ. There are many taro patches (*bōl*) there today.

6. Note the use of the introduced method of measurement, but with the Marshallese word for 'foot' (*ne*) in the Marshallese text.

7. *Lekōto* (lit. 'give or use wind') 'engage in light (flirtatious) conversation between young people of the opposite sex'.

8. *Buñten* 'body actions: dancing, walking, and so forth—their manner, method, technique', a word seldom used today, the informant explained, but obviously germane to this story.

When it was not yet sunrise, the woman prepared their belongings and they launched their canoe and sailed to Epāju, and remained there.

After some days, the man Koperwa brought many crabs and many fish. And they cooked [them] for eating in the evening.

And the woman thought about[9] the time she was with Ļatarbwin before on Bok, because she had not eaten the things she had eaten with Ļatarbwin for a long time.

And she said to Koperwa, "O, sir, I liked it when I used to eat flying fish and eyes of tuna with Ļatarbwin on Bok before." (She remembers her past actions.)

Koperwa replied, "O, ma'am, don't you know? *Aelōn̄ kōmālij*?[10] [On] some islands there are many kinds [of food]. But other islands are not like that.

"And I say to you that the flying fish are only goatfish. The testicles of crab are the eyes of tuna on Epāju.[11] So do not worry."

The following day, they again sailed to the main island. When they landed, Jowaļañ came, and said that they should get the taro, their food for the evening.

And the man sent the woman in order to bring their fire.

The woman went and got the fire and the thing for the two of them to eat. When she returned, she was quick in taking the taro [for] their food. But because she wanted to return to Jowaļañ again, she extinguished the fire and just carried away the taro and gave it to Koperwa. And the man said, "Why didn't you bring the fire here with you, ma'am?"

Now the woman said, "Because my thing for bringing fire in—a coconut shoot—was no good—it was wet. And it was not good for me to bring fire in. But I am going to return again and bring fire."

Koperwa replied, "And hurry back now. I am coming with you to select a dry coconut shoot for you to bring fire in, for I am very cold. You just hurry up."

Libwiner replied, "Yes sir, Koperwa, the greatest one within my throat."[12] And she went to bring fire. When she went, Jowaļañ finished preparing [grooming] himself and sat down beside his place of pounding taro. (He put on a flower garland and a new grass skirt, so that Libwiner would love him.)

---

9. *Emļọkwe* means 'to think about', in *kajin etto*, the ancient language.

10. Jelibōr Jam explained that *aelōn̄ kōmālij* refers to some islands where certain foods such as tuna or breadfruit are not found, or where they are scarce. This is true of breadfruit for Pikinni, Bok-ak, and Pikaar.

11. Fish eyes and crab testicles were delicacies and *kijen irooj* (food of the chiefs) in the old days, the informant explained. The commoners (*kajoor*) may also eat them today. Before, when there was good food, it was taken to the chief. The eyes of *jilo* [*Gymnosarda nuda*, dog-toothed tuna] and of *bwebwe* [*Neothunus macropterus*, tuna] are a special delicacy because they are big and tasty, more so than of other fish. They are eaten cooked (not raw). "There are no *jilo* on [off of] Epāju to amount to, only a few," the informant explained.

12. The throat (*bōro*) is the Marshallese seat of emotions, analogous to the heart of Western cultures. For example, a person may be described as "*utiej bōro*" or 'high throated', which means haughty. Conversely, "*ettā bōro*" 'low throated', means humble, and is a value in Marshallese culture. The translation in Western terms would be "Koperwa, you are the first in my heart."

Libwiner said, "*Iokwe eok*[13] [greetings], sir, Ļōjwaļañ. Give me a little fire if you can."

Ļōjwaļañ said, "O ma'am, Libwiner, that is fire just for you there. You take it!"

Libwiner lit the coconut shoot and, when it was burning, she took the fire and went. When she went a short distance away, within eyesight of Jowaļañ, she extinguished the fire and again returned. And again said, "*Iọkwe eok*, sir, Ļōjwaļañ. It is still no good, for the fire went out."

Jowaļañ said, "What happened that it went out?" (The woman replied,) "Because my thing for carrying fire is no good."

"Are you coming again to get it?" Jowaļañ asked.

Libwiner replied, "O, yes, for the old man, my husband, is colder."[14]

Jowaļañ said, "Well, you take all of that fire and carry it away. But don't you want to wait for this pounded taro for your food?"

Libwiner replied, "I want to very much, but I am just hurrying with the fire, for Ļōkoperwa is colder. I will return."

And she took the fire and went. But because she did not know how to cast out Ļōjwaļañ from her throat [from her heart: stop thinking about him—she was obviously infatuated with him], she again extinguished the fire and again returned.

But it was just a few minutes before the morning star. All of the night during that night she went back and forth and got fire, because she did not want to go back to Koperwa, but she only wanted to stay with Jowaļañ. But Koperwa was waiting for Libwiner and he was tired. And when sunrise came, he sailed and returned to Epāju.

When Libwiner went to Jowaļañ, Jowaļañ gave her his food, the pounded taro and said, "You just remember me when you will see your things of good fortune from Koperwa. (Do not forget me.) Now maybe you have finished your coming to get fire, for it is past sunrise. And you two go and sail!" (you two: Libwiner and Koperwa).

When Libwiner took her food, the pounded taro, and returned, Koperwa was gone. And she went to go to Jowaļañ; Jowaļañ was gone. And she did not know where to go because she thought Jowaļañ loved only her like before when she was with him.

---

13. Literally: Love [to] you, sir. It is the Marshallese greeting to a person, analogous to the Hawaiian word *aloha,* and in English, to both *hello* and *goodbye*. Suffixes are used to indicate the number of persons who are addressed. (This usage is adhered to scrupulously.) The origin of the greeting was revealed to me by Mark (M̧ak) Juda, a most knowledgeable older man from Rālik. He explained that *iia* means rainbow in the Rālik Chain (Western Marshalls), while in Ratak (the Eastern Marshalls) the word is *jemāluut*. He went on to explain that *iia kwe* means 'rainbow on you', and is a greeting of honor. That is, the rainbow (a thing of beauty) is with (or on) you. This has been contracted to *iọkwe* (*yokwe*). (He gave me this interesting etymological information in the course of a rather casual conversation, which is how I obtained a great deal of information about Marshallese language and culture.) This conversation was held on Mājro in 1967.

Note also in this part of the story the occasional use of the male prefix (referred to in note 7 of story 2, "Story about Bōrraan," page 38) with the names of the two men: Ļōjwaļañ for Jowaļañ, and Ļōkoperwa for Koperwa. See also note 1 of story 75, "The War between the Ri-M̧wejoor and the Ļajjidik and Raarņo" for further information concerning the female prefix.

14. *Ļōḷḷap jeiū:* 'the old man, my older brother', referring to 'my husband'; 'my wife' would be *leḷḷap jeiū,* 'the old woman, my older sister'.

And Libwiner thought a little. And she did not know what to do. She lost out.[15] She wasn't staying with Koperwa and she wasn't staying with Jowaļañ.

She became a rock, to this day.

(In *kajin etto*, the ancient language, *juroñjatok* means 'become a rock'. Libwiner became a rock because of her bad actions.)

It is ended.

(The rock is on the island of Ujae and it just sits on the lagoon side. I have seen it.)

When I asked about the meaning of this story, the storyteller and informant, Jelibōr Jam, replied: "The meaning of this story is, 'Do not carry the fire of Libwiner.' That is, do not deceive people who want to help you."

Comments

Humans being changed into rocks or other material objects by supernatural beings is an ancient and widespread motif. This occurs, for example, in Greek and Roman mythology. See Hamilton (1942:114–116 and passim) for stories of such transformation from ancient Greece. She retells the old stories of transformation by the gods as acts of compassion and punishment. Leach (1950:1122) discusses transformation as punishment, as in the Marshallese story of Libwiner. The story of the punishment of Lot's wife (Genesis 19, 24.26) by turning her into a pillar of salt has been familiar to Marshallese for many generations. This is another example of an introduced concept and story coinciding with traditional beliefs and tales, perhaps making the new belief system more comprehensible and acceptable, and perhaps also reinforcing traditional beliefs, consciously or subconsciously. (This probably never occurred to the American missionaries.)

The so-called grass skirt or *in* was made of coconut leaves or hibiscus fiber, and was worn by males. They also wore a loincloth type of garment made of finely plaited pandanus leaves, called a *kaļ*. Females wore finely plaited pandanus mats (*ed*). Two overlapping mats were worn from the waist to above the ankles. They were usually attractively decorated with various designs. Nothing was worn above the waist except for garlands of flowers (*ṃarṃar*) worn by both sexes, usually on festive occasions.

Special necklaces (*ṃarṃar in irooj*) were worn by the *irooj* (chiefs). These were made of *likajjid* shells, a small white cowrie [*Cypraeidae*], with fiber of hibiscus (*ļǫ*).

I saw and sketched one of these necklaces that belonged to Irooj Ļapļap Tōbo of Arṃo Atoll (he was chief of approximately one-half of the large atoll). It was hanging on the living room wall of his frame house, and I was given information about it at the time, in June of 1950. I was told that only the *irooj ļapļap* (paramount chief) may wear this kind of necklace all of the time. It is given to him when he assumes office. The highest *leatoktok* (leader) performs this ceremony, and "talks to him" (gives him advice). Tōbo explained that the *irooj edik* (subchiefs) may

15. Note the word *luuj* meaning 'lose', an English loanword. It has even been integrated into the proverb or saying (*jabōnkōnnaan*) "*Illu, luuj,*" literally: "Angry, lose," said of one who loses his or her temper. In other words, "Stay cool." The traditional Marshallese word for 'lose' is *jako*. To lose in war is called *jipǫkwe*. An *irooj* (chief) who was defeated in war was called *irooj jipǫkwe*, and this usually entailed loss of land. I have heard people referred to as *irooj jipǫkwe*. It was explained to me that their ancestor had been defeated in a war by another *irooj*.

wear a chief's necklace only in time of war—that is, one of this special kind of necklace. The chief wore his own, of course.

Another special type of permanent necklace—as opposed to flower garlands or leis *(ṃarṃar)*—was described to me by Mark Juda on Mājro in 1972. "They are called *kejibul* in Rālik, and are made from *pejao,* a red clam shell. The old men of long ago made them as *ekkan* (tribute) to the *irooj* and *irooj edik.* The ordinary people did not wear them. But if the *irooj* ordered one of the people (a man) to dance, the dancer wore a *ṃarṃar* necklace made of the *libbukwe* cowrie, a shell like the *dimuuj* clam.

"There are none of these necklaces today, but there were close to this time, during Japanese times. People lost them with their other possessions at Jebwad [on Jālooj], when it was destroyed by bombing.

"Women only were able to use them. And the chief did not need to allow this or give permission to them, as for the men. Men needed to obtain permission (as we say, 'the chief needed to point out to them').

"*Alu* [*Ellobiidae*] necklaces, of the small shells, are used today. They were not restricted to use by the chiefs formerly. They were not items of tribute to the chiefs."

61: BWEBWENATO IN JUON KŌRĀ I UJAE, ETAN LIBWINER

Ri-bwebwenato: Jelibōr Jam, Kuwajleen 1975

Im eor jilu eṃṃaan. Etan ļeo juon, Jowaļañ. (Āinwōt Ļainjin ar ba. Ilo ikid eo an.) Etan ļeo juon, Ļatarbwin. Etan ļeo juon, Koperwa.

Jowaļañ ej pād Ujae. Ilo eonene in Ujae. Ļatarbwin ej pād i Bok ilo Ujae. Koperwa ej pād i Epāju ilo Ujae.

Juōn raan Ļatarbwin ar jerak ñan eonene in Ujae. Ke ej poļǫk kōrā in (Libwiner) eaar ilǫk in wōnṃae wa eo waan Ļatarbwin. Im Ļatarbwin eaar ba, "Kwōj kōņaan ke iuwe ippa ñan Bok? Ekanooj lōñ jojo kab jilo kab jabdewōt kain ṃōñā."

Innām Libwiner eaar uwaak im ba, "Ekwe, eļañne enaaj eṃṃan aṃ lale eō im āinwōt Jowaļañ inaaj iuwe ippaṃ."

Ļatarbwin ej ba, "Enaaj emōnļǫk aṃ pād ippa jān ippān Jowaļañ."

Innām lio ar uwaak, "Ekwe ñāāt in kwōj jerak?" Ļeo ej uwaak, "Iaar kōņaan jerak wōt etto. Ak kōnke ijja kar kajjitōk ippaṃ ñe koṃōņōņō in itok ippa im alikkar ke koṃōņōņō im ejjeļǫk ruṃwij ippa ak kwe wōt ņe koruṃwij.

"Eļañne kopojak, ekwe kiiō."

Innām rejro etal im jerak ñan Bok. Im pād ie. Ilo juon raan Jowaļañ eaar inepata im lo an Ļatarbwin etetal bajjek im ej kade kōn juon dekā. Innām ar jab lel.

Ej bar bōk juon dekā kein ka ruo. Ar jab lel. Dekā kein ka jilu, elel Ļatarbwin im woļǫk niñaļǫk im jekarļǫk bōran Ļatarbwin. Innām Koperwa ke ej roñ ke emej Ļatarbwin ej ilām ekataketok Libwiner ñan ippān. Im rejro pād i Epāju.

Juōn raan rejro jerak ñan Ujae, eonene. Im ilo iien eo, ke rejro toļǫk, ejota im eļap aerro piǫ. Im Koperwa ej ba, "Kwōn etal in ebbōktok arro kijeek. Bwe jenro eǫwilik."

Innām lio ej etal im lo Jowaļañ ej jukjuk iaraj.

Innām ke ej lo tok Libwiner ej kanooj in ļap an eṃṃōņōņō im ba, "Libwiner kwōn ṃōkaj tok."

Ke lio ej ilǫk ippān ej leļǫk jidik kijen jukjuk in iaraj. Im ej ba ñane, "Ta eo kijōm̧ ippān Ļatarbwin le?"

Lio ej uwaak im ba, "Men ko rennǫtata."

Jowaļañ ej ba, "Ta ejjab ejjeļǫk iaraj i Bok ke?" Kōrā eo ej uwaak, "Ta wūnin an ejjeļǫk ke bar āne men eņ?"

(Im Jowaļañ ej kajjitōk,) "Innām kwōj et kiiō?" (Lio ej uwaak.) "Iaar iten ebbōk kijeek." Innām ej tile utak eo im bōk kijeek eo, im jepļaak ñan ippān Koperwa.

Ke ej etal im ettoļǫk tarrin jiliñoul ne ej kune kijeek eo, bwe ekōņaan bar lekōto ippān Jowaļañ. Im bar jepļaak. Kōn an kanooj em̧m̧an an lale buñtōn an Jowaļañ jukjuk.

Innām lien ej bar jepļaak im tile utak eo. Im Jowaļañ ej bar ba, "Etke enañin m̧ōkaj am̧ jepļaak le?"

Lio ej uwaak, "Kōnke iaar ilǫk emļak ijjiōtok jidik. Ekun kijeek eo. Im ij bar jepļaaktok in tile utak e in m̧ōkaj kake in etal."

Ke em̧ōj an tile utak eo ej bar ba, "Iǫkwe eok ļe Jowaļañ."

Kiiō Jowaļañ ej ba, "Ij bar lewōj kijōm̧ jidik jukjuk." Innām Jowaļañ ej leļǫk jukjuk eo im ba, "Kepaak ña kōraeņ." (Ilo kajin etto ej 'kwōn kepaaktok ñan eō'.)

Im Libwiner ej jutak im etal. Im bar kune kijeek eo im jepļaak. Bwe eļap an kōņaan lo an Jowaļañ jukjuk.

Innām ej bar tile kijeek eo an. Im Jowaļañ ej ba, "Etke enañin m̧ōkaj am̧ jepļaaktok le?"

Lio ej uwaak, "Kōnke enana kein ebbōk kijeek ie aō" (utak eo).

Innām ej bar tile utak eo im jepļaak im etal. Ke ej etal eļap an kōņaan bar jepļaak ak ej kate wōt in etal ippān Koperwa.

Ke ej tōparļǫk ippān Koperwa enañin raan wōt jidik.

Innām Koperwa ej ba, "Etke konañin rum̧wij kōn kijeek ņe, le? Ke ejako ekkūr kako im jero naaj jerak wōt kiiō ñe eiten tak aļ."

Lio ej ba, "Kōnke im̧ōk in kappok aō kein ebbōk kijeek bwe aolep men otemjej im tutu. Bwe ar wōt ke jejro ej potok. Innām wūnin aō rum̧wij in bōktok kijeek e."

Ke ejjañin tak aļ lio ej kōppojak men ko m̧weiero im rejro bwillǫkwe wa eo waerro im jerak ñan Epāju. Im pād ie.

Ālikin jet raan ļeo Koperwa ej bōktok elōñ baru kab elōñ ek. Im rejro kōmat im m̧ōñā ilo jǫteen eo.

Im lio ej emļǫkwe[16] iien eo eaar pād ippān Ļatarbwin m̧okta ilo Bok. Kōnke etto an jab m̧ōñā men ko eaar m̧ōñā ippān Ļatarbwin.

Im ej ba ñan Koperwa, "A ļe, iǫkwe ke ikōn baj m̧ōñā jojo kab mejān jilo ippān Ļatarbwin i Bok m̧okta."

Koperwa ej uwaak, "A le kojaje ke? Aelōñ kōmālij.[17] Jet āne elōñ jet wāween. Ak jet āne ejjab āinwōt āne ko jet.

"Innām ij ba ñan eok ke jojo wōt jo. Mejān jilo wōt rǫǫn barulep.[18] Innām kwōn jab inepata."

Rujļǫk eo juon rejro bar jerak ñan eonene. Ke rejro bwillǫk ej itok Jowaļañ. Im ba ren kab itok in bōk iaraj eo kijeerro jǫteen eo.

Innām ļeo ej jilkinļǫk kōrā eo bwe en ilān bōktok aerro kijeek.

Lio ej etal im ebbōk kijeek kab men eo kijeerro. Ke ej jepļaak eaar m̧ōkaj in bōkļǫk iaraj eo kijeerro. Ak kōn an bar kōņaan jepļaak ñan ippān Jowaļañ eaar kune kijeek eo im iaraj eo wōt ej bōkļǫk im leļǫk ñan

---

16. *Emļǫkwe* ej 'ļōmņak kake' ilo kajin etto.

17. Aelōñ kōmālij ilo kajin etto: jet aelōñ ko me ejjeļǫk ak eiiet wōt m̧ōñā rot kein ie, jilo, barulep, mā, iaraj im m̧ōñā ko jet barāinwōt.

18. Rǫǫn barulep rej mejān jilo ioon Epāju. Rǫǫn barulep ej juon m̧ōñā eo ennǫ, kijen irooj ilo kar raan ko m̧okta. Ilo tōre ko ñe ej ennǫ juon m̧ōñā, rej bōkļǫk ñan irooj eņ an aelōñ eņ.

Koperwa. Im ļeo ej ba, "Etke kwaar jab bōktok kijeek eo ippaṃ tok le?"

Kiiō lio ej ba, "Kōnke enana kein ebbōktok kijeek eo aō juon utak a etutu. Innām ejjab eṃṃan aō ebbōktok kijeek kake. Ak ij bar jepļaak in ebbōktok kijeek."

Koperwa ej uwaak, "Kab ṃōkajtok kiiō. N̄a ij iuwōj in kālet juon utak eo eṃōrā bwe en aṃ kein ebbōktok kijeek bwe eļap aō piọ. Kwōn kab ṃōkajtok."

Libwiner ej uwaak, "Aet ļe, Koperwa eo eļaptata ilowaan buruō." Innām ej etal im bōktok kijeek. Ke ej etal eṃōj an Jowaļan̄ kakōṃṃanṃōn im jijet iturin jikin jukjuk iaraj eo an.

Libwiner ej ba, "Iọkwe eok ļe, Ļōjwaļan̄. Letok jidik aō kijeek n̄e komaron̄."

Ļōjwaļan̄ ej ba, "A le, Libwiner aṃ wōt kijeek ŋe. Kwōn bōke!"

Libwiner ej tile utak eo im ke ej bwil ej bōk kijeek eo im etal. Ke ej penjakļọk jidik Jowaļan̄ ej kune kijeek eo im bar jepļaak. Im bar ba, "Iọkwe eok ļe, Ļōjwaļan̄. Enana wōt ke ekun kijeek eo."

Jowaļan̄ ej ba, "Ebajet im kun le?" (Lio ej uwaak), "A kōn an nana kein ebbōk kijeek e aō." Innām, "Kwōj bar iten ebbōk?" Jowaļan̄ ej kajjitōk.

Libwiner ej uwaak, "O, aet bwe epiọļọk ļōļļap jeeŋ."

Jowaļan̄ ej ba, "Ekwe kwōn kōmaat kijeek ŋe im bōke. A ta, kwōjjab kōŋaan kōttar jukjuk in iaraj in kijōṃ ke?"

Libwiner ej uwaak, "Eļap aō kōŋaan, ak ijja ṃōkajļọk kōn kijeek e bwe epiọļọk Ļōkoperwa. Inaaj bar rọọltok."

Innām ej bōk kijeek eo im etal. Ak kōn an ļap an jiktok Ļōjwaļan̄ i būruon ej bar kune kijeek eo im bar jepļaak.

Ak ejako etak ijuran eo. Aolepān bon̄ōn eo, bon̄in wōt an jepļaak im ebbōk kijeek, kōnke ejjab kōŋaan jepļaakļọk n̄an ippān Koperwa ak ekōŋaan wōt pād ippān Jowaļan̄. Ak Koperwa eaar kōttar Libwiner im ṃōk. Ak ke ej iten tak aļ ej jerak im rọọl n̄an Epāju.

Ke Libwiner ej ilọk ippān Jowaļan̄, Jowaļan̄ ej leļọk jukjuk eo kijen im ba, "Kwōn kab kememej wōt eō n̄e kwōnaaj lo menin jeramman ko aṃ jān Koperwa. Kiiō bōlen eṃōj ṃokta aṃ itok in ebbōk kijeek bwe ejako etak aļ.

"Ak kwōn etal, koṃro jerak!"

Ke Libwiner ej bōk jukjuk eo kijen im jepļaak, emootļọk Koperwa. Innām eļak iten jepļaak n̄an ippān Jowaļan̄, ejako Jowaļan̄ innām ejaje ijo ej ilọk ieļọk kōnke eaar ļōmŋak Jowaļan̄ ej iọkwe wōt āinwōt ṃokta ke eaar pād ippān.

Innām Libwiner eaar ļōmŋak bajjek. Innām ejaje en et. (Eaar jab jeļā ta eo en kōṃṃane. E luj. Ejjab pād ippān Koperwa im ejjab pād ippān Jowaļan̄.)

N̄an rainin erom jurōnjatōk.

(Ilo kajin etto: ej 'erom juon dekā'. Libwiner ej erom dekā kōnke nana an jerbal.)

E jeṃļọk.

(Dekā eo ej pād ioon āne in Ujae ejijet iar bajjek. Iaar loe.)

Meļeļe in bwebwenato in, "Kwōn jab ebbōk kijeek in Libwiner." (Āinwōt kwōn jab ṃoŋe armej ro kōŋaan jipan̄ eok.)

62: THE STORY OF ĻAÑINLUR

As told by Jǫwej, with Konto Sandbergen as interpreter, Mājro 1952

The act of marrying: *mare* or *koba*: A long time ago, no one should know that two people are planning to be married, especially the sisters and brothers of the couple. (No one should see them together until they are permitted to live together.)

There lived a man on Jāmǫ Island named Ļañinlur. He was the son of Ļāwūn Jāmǫ, the *irooj* (chief) of Jāmǫ Island.[1]

He had paddled his canoe from Jāmǫ to Aelok Atoll to marry a beautiful woman he loved. But he had failed, in spite of the numerous *kūtde* (gifts),[2] many turtles. (This proves that Jāmǫ has plenty of turtles.) He failed because the older sister of the woman on Aelok was still unmarried and felt insulted for having her younger sister get a husband before she did. And through embarrassment, [she] had gone away from Aelok Island to stay on the *tōkā,* a reef extending from an island connecting that island with the next island (usually). (It is the custom, although it is not recognized by the people nowadays that an older sister should be married before her younger sisters.)

Finally, the relatives and Ļañinlur decided that the best thing for Ļañinlur to do was to go home without his loved one. Otherwise, Nioṃajid, the older sister, would not come back to Aelok again. And so, with a broken heart, Ļañinlur paddled his canoe back to Jāmǫ Island.

At Jāmǫ, Ļāwūn Jāmǫ, the father was trying everything to make his son happy, but he just could not do it. So, he figured that what he could do was to have his son marry the woman he loved, in spite of everything. And when he heard that Nioṃajid had not gone back to Aelok, after the return of his son, he told his son to take more *kūtde* with him, and go to Aelok and bring back his bride.

On his second voyage, Ļañinlur succeeded in bringing back his bride.

It is said that when Ļañinlur was paddling his canoe toward Aelok, he had sung a chant. That chant is as follows: *"Lijjuplili ko ke, malkan jobweņ wa eo, | Ekar bul ip en koren Lolurenono, | Kwoje ta wōj, malkan kipedped, kipedped, | Kiper ko an, Likapijwewe."* ("Whirlpools here are paddle prints of a canoe, | That was launched to paddle toward Loluren's wave, | Going eastward, prints of paddling, paddling | The paddles of the whirling pools.")

---

1. Jāmǫ is a small (0.06 square-mile) island with a fringing reef and no lagoon. It lies between Likiep and Aelok atolls in Northern Ratak. According to tradition, it was the residence of the spirit (*ekjab*) Ļāwūn Jāmǫ, the High Chief of Jāmǫ, who dwelt in a huge *kañal* tree (*Pisonia grandis*) from which he sometimes emerged to walk around the island. On these occasions, he is said to have appeared as a strong, handsome chief. In the past, people who visited the island to gather seabirds and sea turtles and their eggs paid homage to Ļāwūn Jāmǫ (Tobin 1958:49–56). In this folktale, the father of the protagonist is identified as "Ļāwūn Jāmǫ, the *irooj* (chief) of Jāmǫ Island." The supernatural figure was apparently incorporated into the folktale as a human being. There is no indication that he is other than human.

2. *Kūtde* (newer word: *anbōro*). This is the general term for presents of things of value given by a man to a woman before and/or after he marries her. Taro patches have sometimes been given as *kūtde* (Tobin 1958:40).

63: ABOUT A CHIEF ON EPATŌN, KUWAJLEEN

As told by Jelibōr Jam, Kuwajleen 1975

He sailed from Epatōn;[1] the wind was very good. And his steward,[2] because he was so very high in the chief's favor, thought he could do anything he wanted to.

And when the canoe sailed, he was fast in seizing the steering paddle.

When he grasped the steering paddle, he thought it would be good to sing. (I am going to explain it to you. If you traveled in a chief's canoe, it was bad for any person to sing. And only the chief should sing. But the man was high in the chief's favor, and he thought that it would be good [permissible] for him to sing.)

Now he began to sing. The song he sang said, "Where is the pandanus, the fish, your food Lijinde? | Just eat a little while you can, for you may die." (Lijinde was the name of the chief's wife.[3] And the meaning of the song is to eat a little food for if there is anything such as war or anything that kills you, never mind for you have eaten.) [That is, eat while you can, for you may die. An old custom before battle.][4] The man seized the steering paddle and sang. He sang many times.

Now when the chief's wife heard her name in the song she strained to listen from the cabin,[5] her place, and she smiled at the

---

1. See footnote 1 of story 50, "Story about Two Epatōn Women" (page 219).

2. The *ri-kaṃōñā* ('people who make food' or stewards) were men of achieved status who served the *irooj ļapļap* | *irooj eļap* (paramount chiefs). Their function was explained to me by *Irooj eļap* Ļañṃooj Raaņņo, of northern Ratak, at his residence on Mājro in 1951. Dwight Heine interpreted for us. We had been discussing the traditional Marshallese social structure, and ascribed and achieved status. Ļañṃooj said: "I will tell you about the *ri-kaṃōñā*. He was a man chosen from the *aļap*[s] [lineage heads] to take care of the *ṃōn kijdik* (rat house). This house was used to store the food of the *irooj eļap*. It was built on high posts with a raised roof. The other houses were just roofs placed on the ground [similar to A-frame houses].

"The *ri-kaṃōñā* was a steward. This position was one in which *aļap*[s] from any lineage *(bwij)* could be chosen by the chief. This was not a hereditary position. They redistributed (*ajej*) food— gave food to the people after the *ekkan* [presentation of food to the chief] had been made. They also distributed (*kabwijrak*) food the chief had ready to give in return for *ekkan*. The *ri-kaṃōñā* were in charge of all issuing of food. There are no regular *ri-kaṃōñā* now. They are chosen when they are needed; for special occasions, and are hired and fired at will.

"Long ago, the food was produced locally and had to be stored—taken care of to prevent it from being spoiled. A specific man was needed for this job. Nowadays, much of the food taken from the land and bought from the trading ship or retail stores is stored by the people in their houses—or stores, if they have them. And the chief has his own food supply at home and people bring food to him. The only time the *ri-kaṃōñā* is called upon nowadays is for a feast (*keemem*) and other occasions when food must be distributed. Today, a man with a western education is used as a sort of *ri-kaṃōñā*. He is called the 'supercargo'. He must know bookkeeping methods, writing, and so forth. All of the chiefs have one of these men with them. They are paid regular salaries [and] are like a business manager. They were very powerful in the Japanese times—got into politics, and so forth." [This discussion illustrates the feudalistic nature of traditional Marshallese society and the important role of the *irooj ļapļap* / *irooj eļap* as conservator of the food resources of the group, and as a distributive chief. The adaptation to the changing economy by chiefs and the people, and the role of the *ri-kaṃōñā* are also seen.]

3. The wife of the chief was called the *lejeļā*. And the corresponding name of the spouse of a chiefess was *irooj eṃṃaan*. Sexual intercourse with them was regarded as a serious transgression against their chiefly spouses, and was punished—hence the danger the steward in this story courted by his acts.

man. When the man had sung many times, the chief looked over at the cabin and saw his wife smiling. And he did not think well of this. The younger brother was steering the canoe. (The man who was singing was the older brother.)

The younger brother saw that the chief was troubled. He said, *"Ruje ukōt eo."* (The meaning in the ancient language is 'cease your singing'.)

Because of his haughtiness due to the chief's wife smiling at him, he did not listen to what his younger brother told him. And the chief was troubled and kept it to himself.

When the canoe arrived on the lagoon side—downwind side of Kuwajleen (southwest on the main island, where the missile site is)—when the canoe arrived, it was evening, and the chief said to his steward, "You remain on the canoe there and take care of everything there. It is up to you to do what you wish" (because the man was very high in position, but had a poor character). "If there is food there that you want to eat, well, just eat as much as you are able to. This evening when it is high tide, you will come here from that canoe, so that I will give my decision to you."

Now the man said, "All right." Now he went to the canoe and remained there. (The canoe was next to the beach, partly on the beach and partly in the water. But the canoe was not anchored.) He waited there until high tide; he launched the canoe and threw over the anchor (a rock) and anchored it.

When he finished anchoring the canoe, he jumped overboard and swam to the island, and went and changed clothes and went to the chief. And the chief said, "Have you finished eating, sir?"

The man replied, and said to the chief, "I have finished eating all the most delicious things in that canoe, and I ate all of the food of the chiefess, your wife." (He showed his haughtiness by doing this: eating the food of the chief and the chief's consort without asking the chief first.)

And the chief said, "Well, come here and I will reveal my decision. This is my decision: that all of the Kuwajleen men shall make a surround-net. It shall be very long. And tomorrow, very early in the morning, we will sail to go fishing. My only wish is to reveal the fishing place. Is this decision good with you?" he asked.

The chief again spoke, "If it is good with you, well, we will go fishing. But if it is not, well, we will not go fishing."

The man replied, "This decision is good with me!" Now the chief spoke to him, "Well, go and tell all the people of the island that they should make a surround-net for tomorrow morning before daybreak [and go fishing with it]."

Now when the man went, it was night time, and he went and awakened all of the people in the houses, so that they would wake up and make a surround-net as the man told them.

When it was just before daybreak, they launched the canoes. They divided the net with the same length given to each of the canoes. And all of the Kuwajleen men boarded the canoes and sailed.

The chief's canoe went ahead. They sailed and went—went and came to Tōkā-

---

4. *Bwinnen in mej:* see footnote 4 on page 248.

5. The small structure (hut) called the *pelpel.* It was placed on the sailing canoe platform and used to shelter passengers (mostly women, old people, and children) against the elements. They are no longer used, and have not been for many years. The wives of the chiefs were supposed to stay in the *pelpel* during the voyages.

muuj-kaņ (the part of Kuwajleen Atoll where there are many passes—it is at the northeast in the atoll).[6]

They tacked and sailed directly to the island, and set the net. And the chief said to his steward, and the man younger than him that they should jump overboard and seize the forward part of the net and secure it on the reef.

And the two of them jumped overboard and stood on the reef and seized the net. Now they set it to the south and returned to Kuwajleen.

When the net on the chief's canoe had been set, the chief said, "Bring another net here from one of those canoes." And another canoe came and again set a net. Thus the canoes set the net. (There was only one net, a very long one.) And when the net was set out from all of the canoes, the chief said "Let us go to Kuwajleen!"

Now the canoes were gone, and only the steward and his younger brother, the two of them, were left standing on the reef.

The two of them waited for the canoes, but they did not return. Then the older brother said, "What is the reason that the canoes did not return, man?"

Now the younger brother replied, "Perhaps you did something bad."

When they had stood there a long time, the high tide came in and they had no place to stand (because of the water covering the reef). And they thought they were about to die, because if they swam northward, there was a pass to the north. If they swim southward, there was another pass to the south.

Now they said, "What is [a] good [course of action]? For the island is very far from us. Maybe we will just die here."

A short while later the net said, "You two climb along, hand-over-hand, with me to the south."

And the two of them did as the net told them to do.

They climbed along the net and came to the end of it. The net said, "Well, you two stand here, for I am going to Anbwe (a big coral head that was located in the pass) over there. And you pull me in."

Now they pulled the net to where they stood. And the net began to move and went to Anbwe—[the] Anbwe to which the net had referred previously.

When the net reached Anbwe, it encircled and tied up to Anbwe, and said to the youths, "Well, you climb along me here again."

Now they climbed along and went again. And when they reached Anbwe, the net said, "Well, you two pull me in again."

Now they pulled it in again, and it reached to where they stood. The net again went to the south.

Thus the three made their way to Meik. And the net said, "Bring the line to the island and hang me on the branch of that pandanus tree. And place one-half of me on the ground below, and you cover up with half and rest on half."

Now they lay down and rested on half and covered up with half. At that time, they were hungry, but because it was night and they were cold, they did not move about, but they slept.

---

6. Tōkā-muuj-kaņ, as Elle Malolo, a Kuwajleen *aļap* (lineage head), explained in more detail to me later, is the part of Kuwajleen Atoll where there are many passes. It is to the northeast of the atoll and distant from the islands of Kiden-eņ and Pikeejlañ. It is in the middle. Niṃur and Ruot islands are to the north in Tōkā-muuj-kaņ. (Niṃur is to the north of Pikeejlañ Island.)

When it was just before dawn, a demon came up from the water. The two men were very frightened. And the net flew from the branch of the pandanus tree and went toward the ocean.

When it was daytime, the net said, "You two go now to Kuwajleen, and I will stay here."

And the two came to Pikeej and launched a log and swam with it to N̄en̄e, and rested a little and took as their food sprouted coconuts and just drank coconut water. And came to Kuwajleen.

And the chief was very surprised when he heard that the steward and the young man, his younger brother, were on Kuwajleen. And he told his people to look for them. When they saw the two of them, they said, "The chief wants you two." And the two of them went to the chief. And the chief said, "You come and sleep in this house tonight." And they went away from the chief and again came to the people who were their relatives.

Now the people, their relatives, asked them, "What did the chief say?"

Now they said, "He said that we are to sleep with him tonight." Now their relatives said, "And are you going to?"

They replied, "Yes, we will go. For the chief said so." When it was evening, they went as the chief had said.

When the chief saw them he said, "You two come here and eat first. And when you two have finished, you will go and put your sleeping mats in the *wūliej*" [a special restricted place in a house].[7]

And they went to place their sleeping mats and lay down and slept.

When it was morning of the next day, the chief awakened them so that they would rise and eat first.

And when they were eating, the chief said, "When you have finished eating, you are to go and launch that paddling canoe so that those young men can take you out to that reef in the ocean so that you can collect shellfish[8] as food for my wife and us this evening."

And the youths prepared their equipment for gathering shellfish. When everything was ready, they went and launched the paddling canoe. And a few young men went and took them to the reef.

And the chief had ordered the young men who put the steward and his younger brother there, that they should tell the two of them that they should just wait for the canoe that would come and load the two of them aboard from the reef.

And the young men took them out to the reef and returned. And the youths collected shellfish and waited for when the canoe would arrive to load the two of them aboard.

7. *Wūliej*: The word is used for 'head, grave, or chief's taboo place'. Special respect must be shown toward all of these in varying degrees. The head, especially of an *irooj*, must not be touched disrespectfully. Nothing should be hung or placed above the head of the chief—a widespread custom throughout the Pacific Islands. The grave of a chief is especially taboo, and one was supposed to avoid it, unless one was related to the chief.

The storyteller explained the taboo place in the houses (*jikin irooj wōt*, lit. 'the place of the chief alone'). It was located at the center, rear of the house. People sat next to the door opposite. Hence the common term and association for three things: head, grave, and chief's place. They are still respected today.

8. *Mejānwōd*: *Tridacna maxima* (Röding), fluted clam, lit. "eye of the reef." They generally live in small holes in the reef (obviously the reason for their name), and attach themselves to the reef. They are common on Kuwajleen and are from one to eighteen inches in length.

They remained there, and the tide came in until it became high tide. They stood on the reef a little while. They just stood a short time, and they looked out and saw a dorsal fin of a shark that was the size of canoe sails.

When it was far away from them, they thought it was the canoe that was coming to load them aboard.

When it came close, they said, "Oh sir, that thing is a shark!" And the shark swam and maneuvered up on the reef and reached the two of them in the middle of the reef, and swallowed them up and returned to the ocean.

And the young men were gone.

As Ļainjin said.

The story is ended.

(This is to say we should not be haughty to people of high rank.)

Now there is a pass at the western end of Kuwajleen. The name of the pass, 'reef pass'. When they [the Americans] lengthened the island, the pass disappeared. But whenever the moon rose from the west, that shark appeared, because at the time the moon rises (every month), the tide is very low. The shark appeared previously, but does not appear now.

Comments

The informant explained: "The *pako tọrtọr* (pushing/sweeping-away shark)[9] pushes and sweeps against canoes and throws people off and eats them and anything that is on the canoes, Marshallese canoes, with its tail. And returns and eats. They do this many times.

"I was in a canoe between Lae and Ujae when one attempted to capsize the sailing canoe. If it had been a paddling canoe, it would have been destroyed. The tail of this shark was narrow but long. Those sharks are considered to be extremely dangerous by the Marshallese."

There is a story that I heard on Mājro in 1951, of Marshallese canoes being attacked by a large school of thresher sharks.

The Marshallese were, it was said, fleeing from the Japanese, and were enroute to Mājro from Aur Atoll. This was during World War II.

Marshallese fishermen and others used preventive magic to protect themselves against shark attack. This was done when the fishermen went diving in deep water, and in the main passes where sharks are prevalent. People who had to ford the shallow passes between the islands at high tide (a dangerous time) also used this supernatural protection.

Special belts made of knotted coconut sennit (*eokkwaḷ*) were worn. These are called *kañūr in pako* (shark belt) or *irōk in pako*. *Irōk* is the older name for belt. The kind of belt that is knotted all the way is the most powerful, because it is the most complete.

Magical chants called *al in joloba* and *al in kelni* were recited by the one seeking protection against the shark attack.

This practice was explained to me by Ļorak, an elderly *aḷap* who was an expert in medicine (*uno*) and magic (*bubu*) on Mājro in 1957, and by another elderly *aḷap*, Ṃak Juda, on Mājro in 1970.

Both informants stated that one must

9. *Alopias vulpinus,* common thresher shark, and big-eye thresher shark, *Alopias superciliosus,* thought to be a deep-water variety, the best known of thresher sharks (Kato, Springer, and Wagner 1967:17–18).

believe in the efficacy of the belts and chants in order to be protected by them (which would explain any failure, one might suppose).

Ļorak made one of each kind of shark belt for me. He recited the chants and told me what they meant. He instructed me to don a belt and recite the chants before entering water where sharks might be present. He assured me that they would protect me from shark attack, no matter where I ventured.

A younger informant told me, on Mājro in 1970, that his grandmother knew magic to protect one against sharks. She would make the sign of the cross with leaves over the chest of the would-be fisherman, and recite a chant. This invoked a demon to stay with the supplicant and protect him. This only had to be done one time, and the protection was permanent. This magic was also performed by older men, the informant explained. This is an obvious example of religious syncretism.

The magic and wearing of special belts to protect against shark attack presumably gave psychological support to those putting themselves in harm's way—and gave them the courage to do so.

It would not be appropriate to present the magical chants here.

63: KŌN JUŌN IROOJ ILO EPATŌN, KUWAJLEEN

Ri-bwebwenato: Jelibōr Jam, Kuwajleen 1975

Eaar jerak jān Epatōn, ekanooj eṃṃan kōto. Innām Ri-kaṃōñā eo an kōn an kanooj in utiej ippān irooj eo an ej ļōmņak emelim men otemjej.

Innām ke jerak wa eo ej kotake an jibwe jebwe eo.

Ke ej jibwe jebwe eo ej ļōmņak eṃṃan bwe en al.

(Inaaj kemeļeļeik eok. N̄e kwōj uwe ilo waan irooj enana al an jabdewōt armej. Ak irooj wōt en al. Ak utiej ļeo ippān irooj eo an ej ļōmņak eṃṃan bwe en al.)

Kiiō ej jino an al. Al eo ej al kake ej ba, "Bōb in ea ekañe ek ko kijōṃ ko Lijinde? I Ṃōñā em denbwijrok." (Lijinde etan kōrā eo an irooj. Im meļeļe in al eo ej ṃōñā bajjek wōt bwe ñe eor men eo āinwōt tariņae ak jabdewōt eo ej ṃane eok, jekdọọn bwe eṃōj aṃ kañi ko kijōṃ. Ļeo ar jebwe[bwe] im al, elōñ alen ej al.)

Kiiō ke lejeļā eo ej rōñ etan ilo al eo ej emmō jān pelpel eo jikin em ettōñdikdik ļọk ñan ļeo. Ke ebaj lōñ alen an ļeo al, irooj eo eļak erreilọk ñan pelpel eo, ej lo lejeļā eo ettōñdikdik. Innām ejjab kanooj eṃṃan an ļōmņak, ke ļōṃaro jatin ej jebwebwe. (Ļeo ej al ej ļeo erūtto.)

Rej lo an inepata irooj eo im rej ba, "Ruje ukot eo." (Meļeļe eo ilo kajin etto ej 'kabwijrak aṃ al'.)

Kōn an utiej būruon kōn an lejeļā eo ettōñ ļọk ñan e ejjab roñjake an ļōṃaro jatin kōnnaan ñane. Innām irooj eo eaar likūt wōt inepata in an ņa ilo būruon.

Ke ej po wa iar in jittoeņ Kuwajleen—(turōk turilik in eonene, jikin mijeļ)—ke wa eo ej po tok ej jota innām irooj eo ej ba ñan ri-kaṃōñā eo an, "Kwōn pād i wa eņ em lale aolep men kaņ ie. Aṃ wōt pepe men eo kokōņaan kōṃṃane." (Kōnke kanooj utiej ļeo ak enana būruon ļeo.) "N̄e eor ṃōñā eņ kokōņaan kañe, ekwe kwōn ṃōñā joñan wōt aṃ maroñ. Jotanin ibwijtok in kwōnaaj itok jān wa ņe, bwe in kwaļọk juon aō pepe ñan eok."

Kiiō eba, "Ekwe." Kiiō ļeo ej etal ñan wa eo im pād ie. (Wa eo ej pād iturin perijet: ṃōttan ioon perijet im ṃōttan i lǫjet. Ak ejjab añkō wa eo.) E pād ie ñan ke ej ibwijtok, ej bwillǫke wa eo im joļǫk kadkad (dekā) eo em emeje.

Ke ej ṃōj emeje wa eo, ej kāļǫk em aō āneļǫk. Im etal im kōṃrāiki innām etal ippān irooj. Innām irooj ej ba, "Eṃwij ke aṃ ṃōñā ļe?"

Ļeo e uwaak im ba ñan irooj eo, "Eṃōj aō ṃōñā aolep men ko rennotata i wa eŋ. Em kar kijen lejeļā ŋe eṃōj aō kañi." (Āinwōt eaar kwaļǫk an utiej būruon kōn an kōṃṃane āindein: kōn eaar [an] kañ kijen irooj eo im lejeļā eo im eaar jab kajjitōk ippān irooj eo ṃokta.)

Innām irooj eo eba, "Ekwe itok. Ña in kwaļǫk pepe eo aō. Eñiin pepe eo bwe aolep eṃṃaan in Kuwajleen in, ren ujaak ṃwieo en kanooj in aetok. Innām ilju ej jibboñtata jenaaj jerak in ilān eǫñwōd. Koŋaō wōt kwaļǫk jikin eǫñwōd eo. Eṃṃan ke pepe in ippaṃ?" Ej kajjitōk.

Irooj eo ej bar ba, "Ñe eṃṃan ippaṃ, ekwe jenaaj ilān eǫñwōd. Ak eļañīe enana, ekwe jejemān ilān eǫñwōd."

Ļeo ej uwaak, "Pepe in ekanooj eṃṃan ippa!" Kiiō irooj eo ej kōnono ñane, "Ekwe kwōn etal in ba ñan aolep riāniin, bwe ren ujaak ṃwieo ñan ilju ej jimmarok."

Kiiō ke ļeo ej etal, eboñ ej ilām kǫruj aolep ri-eṃ bwe ren ruj in ujaak ṃwieo.

Kiiō rej ruj im etal im ujaak ṃwieo āinwōt an ļeo ba. Ke jimmarok wōt rej bwillǫke wa ko im ajeej ṃwieo dettan wōt juon ŋa ioon wa ko. Em aolep eṃṃaan in Kuwajleen em iuwe ioon wa ko em jerak.

Wa eo waan irooj eo ej etal iṃaan ļǫk. Raar jerak em etal etal em ļak Tōkāmujkaŋ. (Ṃōttan aelōñ in Kuwajleen eo me repād elōñ to ie. Epād turear im eañ.)

Diak em tarānetak. Em katoto ṃwieo. Innām irooj eo ej ba ñan Ri-kaṃōñā eo an, kab ļeo edikļǫk jāne bwe ren ro kāļǫk in jibwe ṃaan ṃwieo eo ŋa ioon wōd eo.

Innām rejro kāļǫk im jutak ioon wōd eo im jibwe ṃwieo eo. Kiiō rej katoto rōñaļǫk im jepļaak ñan Kuwajleen.

Ke ej jeṃļǫk ṃwieo eo i wa eo waan irooj eo irooj eo ej ba, "Bōktok bar juon ṃwieo jān wa kaŋe jet." Innām ej itok juon wa im bar katoto ṃwieo. Āindein an wa ko katoto ṃwieo. (Eor juon wōt ṃwieo, kanooj in aetok.) Im ke ej maat ṃwieo jān aolep wa irooj eo ej ba, "Jen etal ñan Kuwajleen!"

Kiiō wa ko remootļǫk ak Ri-kaṃōñā eo kab likao jatin erro wōt ruo em jutak ioon wōd eo.

Ro ar kōttar wa ko ak rejab rǫǫltok. Innām ļeo erūtto ej ba, "Ebajet ke ejjab itok wa ko ļe?" Ļeo edik ej uwaak, "Bōlen eor meneŋ enana im kwaar kōṃṃane."

Ke etto aerro jutak ej ibwijtok em ro likjab. Innām ejjeļǫk ļōmŋak in mour ippāerro.

Kōnke ro ļak iten aō niñaļǫk eor juon to eañ. Ro ļak iten aō rōñaļǫk ebar eor to i rōk.

Kiiō rejro ba, "Ta in eṃṃan? Ke ettoļǫk āne jān kōjro. Bōlen kōjro naaj mej wōt ijin."

Meļanļǫk ṃwieo eo eba, "Koṃin ro in pitto ippa rōñaļǫk." Innām rejro kōṃṃan āinwōt an ṃwieo ba ñan erro.

Ro pitto ļǫk em ļak jeṃļǫk ṃwieo eo. Ṃwieo eo eba, "Ekwe, koṃro jutak ijin bwe ij etal ñan Anbwe (juon wōd eļap epād i to eo) iuweo innām koṃin ro tōbwetok eō."

Kiiō rejro tōbwetok ṃwieo eo ŋa ijo rejro jutak ie. Ak ṃwieo eo ej jino an eṃṃakūt im etal ñan Anbwe eo. Anbwe eo eaar ba ṃokta.

Ke ṃwieo eo ej tōpar Anbwe eo ej pouti Anbwe eo. Em ba ñan likao ro, "Ekwe, koṃro bar pitto ļǫk ippa tok."

Kiiō rejro pitto im etal. Im ļak tōpar Anbwe eo ṃwieo eo eba, "Ekwe koṃro bar tōbwetok eō."

Kiiō rejro bar tōbwetok. Ļǫk tōprak ijo rejro jutak ie. Ṃwieo eo ebar etal wārōñaļǫk. Āindein aerjel kōṃṃan ļǫk ñan Meik. Innām ṃwieo eo eba, "Koṃin ro kab tāik eo āne wōj im totoik eō ņa iraan bōb ņe. Innām likūt jimettan ņa i laļ innām komro naaj kǫǫjooj kōn jimettan ak komro im kineek eō kōn jimettan."

Kiiō rejro babu im kineek jimettan ak rejro kǫǫjooj kōn jimettan. Iien in rōkwōle, ak kōnke eboñ im repiǫ rejro jab emmakūtkūt ak rōkiki.

Ke ej iten raan ej itok timoņ jān lǫjet. Rōkanooj in mijake. Innām mwieo eo ej kāļǫk jān raan bōb im wōnmetokļǫk. Innām timoņ eo eko.

Ke ej raan, mwieo eo eba, "Komin ro etal kiiō ñan Kuwajleen ak ña ij pādwōt ije." Innām rejro itok ñan Pikeej em bwillǫke juon kājokwā em aō tok kake ñan ñeñe em kakkiji jidik em kōmman kijeerro iu em idaak ni bajjek. Innām ilǫk ñan Kuwajleen.

Innām irooj eo ke ej roñ ke Ri-kamōñā eo kab likao eo jatin repād ioon Kuwajleen, eļap an bwillōñ. Im ba ren pukōttok erro. Ke rej lo erro rej ba, "Irooj eo aikwiji komro." Innām rejro etal ippān irooj eo. Im Irooj eo ej ba, "Komro itok in kiki imwiin buñinin." Innām rejro diwōj jān ippān irooj eo im bar itok ñan ippān armej ro nukierro.

Kiiō armej ro nukierro rej kajjitōk ippāerro, "Ej iaan irooj eņ?"

Kiiō rejro ba, "Ej ba kemin ro kiki ippān boñinin." Kiiō armej ro nukier ro rej ba, "Innām komin ro etal ke?"

Rejro uwaak, "Aet, kemro naaj etal. Bwe irooj eņ ej ba." Ke ej jota ļǫk rejro etal āinwōt an kar irooj eo ba.

Ke irooj eo ej lo erro ej ba, "Komin ro itok in mōñā mokta. Innām ñe emōj komro naaj etal in kōmman kinemiro jaki ņa ijjien wūliej." Innām rejro ilān kōmman kineerro jaki im babu im kiki.

Ke ej jibboñ in raan eo juon irooj eo ej kǫruj erro bwe ren ro ruj in mōñā mokta. Innām ke rejro mōñā irooj eo ej ba, "Ñe emōj amiro mōñā komro naaj etal bwillǫke kōrkōr eņ bwe likao rā ren kab likūt ļǫk komro ñan wōd eņ i meto bwe komin ro kōmejānwōd tok kijedeañ lejeļā eo ñan jǫtenin."

Innām likao ro rej kōppojak aerro kein kōmejānwōd. Ke ej pojak jabdewōt rejro etal em bwillǫke kōrkōr eo. Innām likao ro jet rej ilām likūtļǫk erro ñan wōd eo. Im irooj eo ej kallimur ñan likao ro rej likūtļǫk Ri-kamōñā eo kab likao eo jatin bwe ren ba ñan erro ke ren ro kab kōttar wōt wa eo enaaj ilān ekōtake erro jān wōd eo.

Innām likao ro raar likūtļǫk er rej jepļaak. Ak likao ro rej kōmejānwōd em kōttar wōt ñan ñe enaaj waļǫk tok wa eo ej iten ekōtake erro.

Ro ar pād innām eibwij ñan ke ej ibwijleplep. Jidik wōt aerro juur eoon wōd eo. Rejro ja jutak wōt ak rōļak erreļǫk rej lo juon ūl in pako dettan wōt wōjļā in wa kaņ.

Ke ej ettoļǫk wōt rejro ļōmņak wa eo ej itok in ektake erro eo.

Kiiō ej epaaktok rejro ba, "A ļe pako men ņe!" Innām pako eo eitem ikdeelel ioon wōd eo im kattōpar ļǫk erro ņa ilukwōn wōd eo im āt erro i lǫñin im rǫǫl. Innām ļōmaro rejako.

Āinwōt Ļainjin ar ba.

Ejemļǫk bwebwenato.

(Āinwōt ba jān jab kautiej buruwōd ñan ro rōutiej.)

Kiiō eor juon to i jabōn Kuwajleen turilik, etan to eo, "To pedped." Ke emōj an kaitokļǫk āne eo (ri-Amedka ro), to ejako. Ak aolep takinallōñ i kapilōñ ej waļǫk pako eņ. Kōnke ilo takin allōñ i kapilōñ kanooj in ibwij. Mokta pako ar waļǫk ak kiiō ejjab waļǫk.

64: STORY ABOUT TWO YOUNG MEN AT WŌJA, AELŌÑĻAPĻAP

As told by Jelibōr Jam, Kuwajleen 1975

These young men were brothers and they looked out for each other very well. They were there and one day they decided that each one should make a fish trap.[1]

They plaited the traps (with coconut sennit) and the older man said, "We two will look to see if there will be a big catch of fish.[2]

"And you be diligent making your fish traps."

And the younger man replied, "I think there will be a big catch in my fish trap, for the entrance [to the trap] I am thinking of making is very good. The name of the entrance is *liā*" (*liā* means 'so full the contents come out [of a stomach, box, or fish trap], as if they would vomit out').

The older man again spoke, "Well, make the fish trap (with coconut sennit). Let's (the two of us) go to place it in the water on the bottom and see if there will be a big catch of fish."

(All food from the sea is classified as *ek* (fish), including turtles [*Chelonia mydas* L., green sea turtle, *wōn*[3] and *Eretmochelys imbricata,* Hawksbill turtle, *jebake*], clams [*Tridacnidae, kabwōr*], and *dimuuj* [medium-sized tridacna, clam], and the like, and whales and porpoises. Just as Ļainjin separated them.)[4]

After three days,[5] they finished their fish traps.

And they said, "If it is low tide, we will go to place these fish traps in the water." And they rested a little, and waited for low tide.

When the sun was in the middle of the sky [at noon], it was good that the youngest boy[6] should go and place the fish trap in the ocean. (He had made magic of the leaves of pandanus [divination],[7] and it revealed what would be good.)

But the older man said, "I believe, sir, that it is not good to place my fish trap in the water today. I do not know when it will be good. But at a good time, I will go place it in the lagoon" (one man in the ocean and the other man in the lagoon).

---

1. Fish traps *(u)* were important in the traditional subsistence economy. They were made in several shapes. *Pemphis acidula,* ironwood, *kōñe* was commonly used for the frames, which were tied with coconut sennit *(eokkwaļ).* Stone weirs *(me)* were also constructed for permanent use. These fish-trapping techniques are rarely used today.

2. The noun *koņan* ('his/her catch') is used for fish and birds, the storyteller explained.

3. Marshallese use the word *wōn* specifically for the green sea turtle, and generally to include all species of turtles. However, they are also specific when they feel it necessary, and use the words for the hawksbill and leatherback turtles, *jebake* and *wōn atoļ* (*Chelonia mydas* and *Dermochelys coriacea,* respectively).

4. Note the reference to the famous navigator and culture hero Ļainjin, who is referred to in a number of these tales, most notably in story 30, "The *Ikid* (Song-story) of Ļainjin," page 131.

5. The ritual number three is used here. This is a frequently occurring element in Marshallese folktales and in the culture, especially in the areas of magic and healing.

6. Note the narrative style: the shift in usage from young man to boy. This is found in other folktales of the Marshalls as well.

And when it was late afternoon, the older man took his fish trap,[8] and went and placed it within the thicket of pandanus trees[9]—hid it.

The older man hurried, for the younger man was just arriving and saw that he had placed his fish trap within the pandanus thicket. And he hurried to go to the lagoon, and remained there until the time when he knew that his younger brother would return, after he had placed his fish trap in the ocean.

The older man went to the house, and saw his younger brother and said to him, "Have you finished placing your fish trap in the water, sir, my younger brother?" he asked.

The younger man replied, "It is finished." The younger man asked. "And for you, is it finished?"

The older man replied, "Didn't you see it? I had just come from the lagoon, when I placed my fish trap in the lagoon."

The younger man again asked, "When will we go to bring up the fish trap?" (This word, *ebbwā,* is *"kajin u,"* 'fish trap language' used for fish trap work only.)

The older man replied, "After three days." The younger man said, "I think my fish trap will be full after two days, and I will go again and see."

The older man said, "No, we should both go and look at the same time."

And the younger man obeyed his older brother.

When three days had passed, the older man said to his younger brother, "You go first, for I will wait for the time being, until the tide becomes a little lower."

And the younger man went and got the paddling canoe and paddled away to his fish trap. And went to look at it. When he went, the fish trap was truly full with many fish. But the older man climbed up into the attic in their house, and caused the house to fly. He made the house go up into the air like an airplane. The house posts remained in place, but the rest of the house went up into the air.

The older man made the house fly away—it was thirty miles to the west (from the lagoon side to sea). He returned to the island.

(He moved the house back again to land on the island. He wanted to hide from his brother.)

After he flew to the ocean side of Wōja, the young man, his younger brother, appeared above where he had placed the fish trap.

He looked up at the house—it was coming down slowly toward him, and he was extremely frightened.

And the young man inside the house that was flying toward him said, "What kind of fish are those?" The man replied, "Jọwe"

---

7. *Bubu in maañ* or *kwōjerip*: the technique of foretelling the future by folding the leaves *(maañ)* of the *Pandanus tectorius,* screw pine, *bōb,* and reading the results of the folding. The specialists in this and other techniques of divination were called the *ri-bubu.* They were called upon before any serious undertaking was begun. See also footnote 11 on page 355. The technique of *bubu in maañ (kwojerip)* was, in this story, known by a nonspecialist, apparently.

8. The storyteller explained that *jota dikdik* is from three to six p.m., and is followed by *jota* (evening), then *boñ* (night), and *lukwōn boñ* (lit. 'waist or middle of the night: midnight'). Both traditional and introduced concepts and measurements of time are used in Marshallese folktales. English loanwords such as *minit, awa, wiik,* and so forth, have been incorporated into the language and are used in ordinary conversation.

9. *Wūnmaañ: Pandanus fischerianus.*

[*Plectropomus truncatus,* bass]. The older lad said, "Throw it to me!"

The older lad again said, "What kind of fish are those?" The younger lad replied, "Aroñ" [*Hynnis cubensis,* African pompano.] The older lad said, "Throw it to me. And all those fish inside the canoe!"

Now the fish inside the canoe were all gone, and the older lad flew away from the canoe—he was inside the house, and the house flew away from the paddling canoe—and landed on the posts, the posts of the house. And the older lad hurried and took the fish and carried them away into his fish trap. And he returned and lay down for a little inside the house.

A short while later, the young man, his younger brother, came. And the older lad was pretending that he was asleep. And the young man, his younger brother, came and woke him up. And the older lad awoke, and asked the younger lad, his younger brother, "Do you have a catch of fish, sir, younger brother?"

The younger man replied, "O, sir, nothing. For there was a very surprising thing." The older young man replied, "What was that, sir?"

The younger man said, "O, sir, a house. It flew to me and took all of my catch of fish."

The older young man said, "What, sir, are there houses that can fly?"

The younger young man replied, "Yes. That thing came and took all of my catch of fish, and carried them away."

"And what kind of fish [were they]?" the older lad asked.

The younger lad said, "I do not know. For I was very much afraid."

The older lad said, "You are lying. You did not have any fish. It is clear that not a single fish can enter that fish trap of yours there."

And the younger young man said, "It was full of fish. And it will be clear tomorrow. It will not be good if the fish trap is placed in the water to soak for three days, for there will be no place for the fish to enter. And one night will be best (because it will be full of fish, and no fish will be able to enter).

And the older man said, "Well, that would be fine with me, too, if only for one night. My fish trap will be full again."

And the younger lad said, "And your fish trap, do you have a big catch of fish?" The older lad said, "Well, just wait, for I must go to see first."

And he went to the center of the island to the interior of the pandanus thicket.

And he returned and said to the boy, his younger brother, "Bring that basket here. We will go and bring it and just cook and eat (the fish)."

And the two of them went. When they arrived at the fish trap, the younger lad stood beside the fish trap, and the older lad threw off the coconut fronds with which he had covered the fish trap.

After they were thrown off, the younger lad was surprised. And he said, "Why are there so many fish inside [it] when it was on the island—the place where it is there?"

And the older lad answered, "Because I know how to make a fish trap. Fish came from the water and came inside." (He was lying.) "But do not be surprised. And put [the fish] inside [the basket], for we are going."

And the boy put [the fish] inside [the basket], and they returned to the house. And the surprise of the younger boy was not ended.

The next day, the younger boy spoke to the young man, his older brother. And said, "Look here, my older brother, I will hasten to go to lift the fish trap out of the water. For when it is past noon, the house will come again and take my catch of fish."

The older young man said, "Well, you hurry up and go and come back and we will lift up my fish trap."

And the younger boy hurried and went, and took the paddling canoe to the water, and paddled away to where the fish trap was.

And he dived down and brought up the fish trap; it was full of fish! [Informant raised his voice for emphasis.]

And he again dived down and set it with stones on top of it [to anchor it]. And he came up and sat and rested a little.

And the older man again flew with the house as before, and flew above the paddling canoe, the canoe of the younger boy. And said, "What kind of fish are those? If bass, throw them! It is better that you give me those fish!"

And the younger boy gave all of his catch of fish. And was just sad. And he was afraid.

And the older man again hurried and flew and again landed [the house] on the posts. And took the fish and carried them away to his fish trap.

When the younger man came, the older lad again asked, "Do you have a catch, sir, my younger brother?"

The younger lad answered, "Nothing, sir, my older brother. Because that thing came again to take them."

"What was that, sir?" the older lad asked.

The younger lad said, "O, sir, a house."

The older lad said, "What kind of a house, sir?"

The younger lad said, "It was truly like a house. And it said that I should give it all of my catch of fish!"

And the older lad said, "Well, we will go look at my fish trap in the middle of the island. Bring that basket. We will go see if there are any fish there."

And the two of them went into the middle of the island. When they reached the fish trap, the younger lad just stood. But the older lad threw off the coconut fronds with which he had covered the fish trap.

When the fronds had all been thrown off, the younger lad looked over at the fish trap; it was full of fish. But the younger lad remembered that he had had a catch of bass.

And when he saw the bass inside the fish trap of the older man, he began to think badly [unfavorably] of his older brother. And said to himself, "I say this man flew with his house, our house. Well, it will be clear tomorrow."

When it was late evening, after they had eaten, he (the younger man) went and laid down beneath the attic. (The older brother slept outside of the house, elsewhere.) And just came in order to bring some black soil in order to go to put the soil [mark] beneath the floor of the attic in their house.

And the older man said, "Why are you still lying down? It is clear that you do not know how to make a fish trap.

"Because every time you go and pull up your fish trap and come and deceive me and say there is a thing that comes to you and takes those fish, your catch."

The younger man said, "I did not deceive you, my older brother. And I am really being truthful with you. I will go out tomorrow again and look at my fish trap, to see if there is a catch. However, I will go after noon, now. Because I went before noon and the thing came.

"Each day I went in the morning and the house came again. But now I will go in the evening."

And they slept. In the morning, the younger boy came again and brought a coconut husk of the sort that had already been scorched with a fire (in order to weaken it).

And he came and again marked under the attic.

The shape of the mark was like an X. And when it was late afternoon, the younger boy took the paddling canoe and went. But the older man prepared to fly again with the house.

When the younger man reached the fish

trap, he just looked around on the horizon, to see whether the house would come again. When he did not see it, he dived down [into the water] and brought up the fish trap. It was full of fish. After he took the fish from the contents of the fish trap, he again dived down and set it [the fish trap] on the bottom of the water. When he came up, he examined his catch of fish very closely so that he would know what kinds of fish were in his catch.

When he went to paddle, the house again flew to him.

Because it was night, the older man hurried out and said, "Give me all of those fish inside that canoe."

The younger man looked up to the house in order to look for the mark that he had marked with an X beneath the attic. When he saw the X, he said, "O, sir, why is this just like our house, my older brother?"

Simply because of this query, the older man was ashamed, and flew down, and has not returned to this day.

And the younger man took his catch of fish and returned. When he went away, he did not see the house. And he wanted to see his older brother. But because his older brother had done this bad thing, he was ashamed (*āliklik* 'more than ashamed, chagrined, embarrassed, afraid—with a feeling of unworthiness and inferiority') with his younger brother.

The younger brother needed to see his older brother so that he might clear up the interchange they [had] had with each other.

But he did not see his older brother.

It is ended.

[I asked Jelibōr Jam what the meaning of the story was. And he replied: "The meaning of this story: Because we should not do bad [things] to each other. Because it will ruin our living place."]

Comments

Jelibōr Jam was unsure about a detail in this story, and he wanted to make sure that he was telling me the story as he had been told it years ago. He told me that he would refresh his memory with his *wa in keemem* on Ebeye that evening. He explained that a *wa in keemem* is one who knows Marshallese lore, and has been so designated by a mutual teacher. Kōnnel, he said, was his *wa in keemem.*

One can see where this would be a practical method of preserving the stories, especially the details, in a preliterate society—and even after the introduction of writing, as in this case.

The word *wa* means 'canoe, ship, boat, or vehicle in general'; *keememej* means 'to remember'. Hence *wa in keemem* would be 'vehicle of remembering', a graphic, accurate, and poetic term, indeed.

The conscientious informant checked with Kōnnel and others when he was not absolutely certain of a detail of a story. This happened very rarely, however.

64: BWEBWENATO IN RUO LIKAO ILO WŌJA, AELŌÑĻAPĻAP

Ri-bwebwenato: Jelibōr Jam, Kuwajleen 1975

Likao rein rejro jimjānjimjātin ekanooj in eṃṃan aerro lale doon. Pād em ļak juon raan ro pepe, bwe renro kajjo u in kōṃṃan.

Rejro [eọ]eo u wōt ak ļeo erūtto ej ba, "Kōjro lale in enaaj lōñ koŋan ek. Innām kwōn kanooj in kōṃanṃan u ŋe aṃ."

Innām ļeo edik ej uwaak, "Ij ļōmŋak enaaj kanooj lōñ koŋan u e aō. Bwe ekanooj in naaj eṃṃan bōro e ña ij ļōmŋak in kōṃṃane. Etan bōro e, liā." (Joñan obrak bwe koppan rej etal jān lowaan lọjien, bōk, u. Āinwōt emmwij jān lowaan.)

Ļeo erūtto ej bar ba, "Ekwe, [eọ]eo u ļọk bwe jenro etal in jooni in lale eo enaaj lōñ koŋan ek. (Aolepān ṃōñā jān lọjet rej ŋa etāer, "ek." Āinwōt ek, wōn, kapoor, mejānwōd, im āinwōt; im raj im ke. Āinwōt Ļainjin ar kōjpel er.)

Ālikin jilu raan eṃōj u ko aerro. Innām rejro ba, "Ñe epāāt kōjro naaj etal in jooni u kein." Innām raar kakkiji jidik. Im kōttar an pāātļọk.

Ke aļ ej pād ioļap eṃṃan bween an ļadik eo edik etal in joon u eo an ŋa ilik. (Eaar kōṃṃan bubu in maañ. Im eaar kwaļọk ta eo naaj eṃṃan.)

A ļeo erūtto ej ba, "Ña ļe enana bween aō joon u eo aō rainin. Ijaje enaaj eṃṃan ñāāt. Ak iien eo eṃṃan inaaj ilān joon ŋa iar." (Ļeo juon ilik im ļeo juon iar.)

Innām ke ej jota dikdikļọk ļeo erūtto ej bōk u eo an. Im ilām joon ŋa ilo unmaañ eo.

Ļeo erūtto ej kaiuri wōt bwe enañin itok ļeo edik. Im lo an door u eo an ŋa ilowaan unmaañ eo, im ṃōkaj in etal ñan ar. Im pād ie ṃae iien eo ejeļā ke ļeo jatin erọọltok jān ke eaar joon u eo an ŋa ilik.

Ļeo erūtto ej etal ñan ṃweo. Im lo ļeo jatin. Im ba ñane., "Eṃōj ke joon u eo aṃ ļe jatū?" (Ej kajjitōk.)

Ļeo edik ej uwaak, "Eṃōj." Ļeo edik ej kajjitōk, "Ak kwe, eṃōj ke?"

Ļeo erūtto ej uwaak, "Kwojjab lale ke? Ij kab itok jān ar. Ke iaar joon u eo aō ŋa iar."

Ļeo edik ej bar kajjitōk, "Jero naaj ilān ebbwā ñāāt?"

Ļeo erūtto ej uwaak, "Ļọkun jilu raan." Ļeo edik eba, "Ña ej ļōmŋak enaaj booļ u eo aō, ļọkun ruo raan. Innām inaaj ṃōk etal im lale."

Ļeo erūtto eba, "Jab, en jepaan arro ilān lale wōt juon." Innām ļeo edik ej pokake jein.

Ke ej ļọk jilu raan ļeo erūtto ej ba ñan ļeo jatin, "Kwōn iwōj ṃokta, bwe ña ijja kōttar an pāātļọk jidik."

Innām ļeo edik ej ilām bōk kōrkōr eo im aōnōnļọk ñan ippān u eo. Im ilān lale. Ke ej ilọk, e lukkuun booļ u eo kōn [lōñ] ek. Ak ļeo erūtto ej tallōñ ilo po eo, ilo ṃweo iṃwerro. Im kāļọk kake ṃweo. (Eaar kātoļọk ṃweo āinwōt juon baļuun. Joor ko rej pād ak ṃōttan ṃweo ar wōnlōñļọk ñan lañ.)

Ļeo erūtto eaar kātoļọk kake ṃweo, ej jiliñuul ṃail toļọk erọọl im kātok ñan āne eo.

Ļak kātok ñan lik in Wōja likao eo jatin ej waļọk lōñtak jān ke eaar joon u eo an. Eļak erreilōñ ļọk ilo ṃweo ej jokadikdik laļtak ñane. Innām eļap an abinmake (mijak).

Ak likao eo ilowaan ṃweo ej kātok ñan ippān im ba, "Ikōt ŋeŋe?" Likao eo uwaak, "Jọwe." Likao eo erūtto ej ba, "Jotok!"

Likao erūtto ebar ba, "Ikōt ŋeŋe?" Likao eo edik e uwaak, "Aroñ." Likao erūtto ej ba, "Jotok. Kab aolep ek kaŋe ilowaan wa ŋe!"

Kiiō emaat ek ilowaan wa eo. Innām likao erūtto ej kāļọk jān wa eo. (Ej pād ilowaan ṃweo im ṃweo ej kāļọk jān kōrkōr eo.) Im jokļọk ioon joor ko, joor in ṃweo. Im likao erūtto ej kaiuri im būki ek ko em bōkļọk ñan lowaan u eo an. Im bar rọọltok im babu bajjek ilowaan ṃweo.

Meļan ļọk jidik, ej itok likao eo jatin. Im likao eo erūtto ej riab kiki. Innām likao eo jaten ej itok im kọruje. Innām likao erūtto ej ruj. Im kajjitōk ippān likao eo jatin, "Eor ke kwoņaṃ ek ļe jatū?"

Likao edik ej uwaak, "A ļe, ejjeļọk. Bwe eor juon men ekanooj kabwilōñlōñ." Likao erūtto ej uwaak, "Taje eo ļe?"

Ļeo edik ej ba, "A ļe juon eṃ. Ej kātok ñan ippa im būki aolep ek ko kwoņa."

Likao eo erūtto ej ba, "Ta ļe, eor ṃweeņ [eṃ] emaroñ ekkāke?"

Likao eo edik ej uwaak, "Aet. Eñeo eaar item kōmaati ek ko kwoņa. Im būki."

"A ek rot ko?" Likao erūtto ej kajjitōk.

Likao edik ej ba, "Ijjab jeļā. Bwe eļap aō mijak."

Likao erūtto ej ba, "Koriab. Kojoda. Alikkar ke. U eņ aṃ eban deļọñ juon ek ie."

Innām likao edik ej ba, "Eaar booļ kōn ek. Ak enaaj alikkar ilju. Enana ñe jilu boñ in an jojo u in. Bwe enaaj ejjeļọk jikin an ek deļọñ. A eṃṃan wōt juon boñ." (Kōnke enaaj booļ kōn ek im ejjeļọk ek maroñ deļọñ.)

Innām ļeo erūtto ej ba, "Ekwe, ebar eṃṃan ippa ñe juon wōt boñ. Enaaj bar booļ u eņ aō."

Innām likao edik ej ba, "Ak u eo aṃ, elōñ ke koņan ek?" Likao erūtto ej ba, "Ekwe, kōttar ṃōk. Bwe in etal in lale ṃokta."

Innām ej wōnoojļọk ñan ilowaan unmaañ eo. Innām ej jepļaaktok im ba ñan ļadik eo jatin, "Ioļe, ebooļ u eo aō kōn ek. Kwōn bōktok kilōk ņe. Jero etal im bōktok. Im kōmat bajjek im ṃōñā."

Innām rejro ej etal. Ke rejro tōparļọk u eo. Likao eo edik ej jutak iturin u eo. Ak likeo eo erūtto ej joļọk kimej ko eaar kalbubu u eo kake.

Ļak juļọk. Ebwilōñ likao eo edik. Im ba, "Ta wūnin an lōñ ek ilowaan ke eoon āne. Ijo ej pād ie?"

Innām likao eo erūtto ej uwaak, "Joñan aō jeļā kōṃṃan u. Ek ej itok jān lọjet im deļọñ ilowaan. Ak kwōn jab bwilōñ. Ak kwōn ātet ļọk bwe jero etal."

Innām ļadik eo ej ātet ek im rejro rọọl ñan ṃweo. Im ejjab jeṃļọk an ļadik eo edik bwilōñ.

Rujļọk eo juon ļadik eo edik ej ba ñan likao eo jein. Im ba, "Eoļe jeiū inaaj ṃōkaj in etal in ebbwā. Bwe ñe raelep ļọk enaaj bar itok ṃweo im bar būki ek ko kwoņa."

Likao [eo] erūtto ej ba, "Ekwe kwōn jerabļọk. Bwe kwōj itok wōt ak jero bar etal in ebbwāiki u eņ aō."

Innām ļadik eo edik ej ṃōkaj im etal. Im bōk kōrkōr eo ņae lọjet.

Im aōņōōņļọk ñan ijo u eo ej pād ie.

Im etulọk im bōklōñtak u eo; ebooļ kōn ek!

Innām bar tulọk kake im jone kōn dekā. Im ej waļọk lōñtak im jijet im kakkije jidik.

Ak ļeo erūtto ej bar kāļọk kōn ṃweo āinwōt ṃokta. Im kātok ñan eoon kōrkōr eo waan ļadik eo edik. Im ba, "Ikōt ņeņe? Eļañne jọwe jotok! Emōnļọk kwōn litok ek kaņe!"

Im ļadik eo edik ej liļọk aolep ek ko koņan. Im būroṃōj bajjek. Ak e mijak.

A ļeo erūtto ej bar kaiuri im kāļọk, im bar jok ioon joor ko. Im būki ek ko. Im bōkļọk ñan u eo an.

Ke ej itok ļeo edik likao erūtto ej bar kajjitōk, "Eor ke koņaṃ ļe jatū?"

Likao edik ej uwaak, "Ejjeļọk ļe jeiū. Kōn an men eo ej bar item būki. "Taje eņ ļe?" likao erūtto ej kajjitōk.

Likao edik ej ba, "A ļe juon eṃ." Likao erūtto ej ba, "Ian eṃ ļe?" Likao edik ej ba, "Elukkuun āinwōt eṃ. Ak ej ba in kōmaat ļọk aolep ek ko kwoņa!"

Innām likao erūtto ej ba, "Ekwe jero ṃōk etal in lale u eo aō ijōņe iooj. Bōktok kilōk ņe. Jero etal in lale eor ke ek ie."

Innām rejro wōnoojļǫk. Ke rejro tōparļǫk u eo likao edik ej jutak bajjek. Ak likao erūtto ej joļǫk kimej ko eaar kalibubu u eo kaki.

Ke ej maat kimej ko likao eo edik eļak erreilǫk ñan u eo; ebooļ kōn ek. Ak likao eo edik ej kememej wōt ke kar juon eo koņan jǫwe.

Innām ke ej lo jǫwe eo ilowaan u eo an ļeo erūtto e jino an ļōmņak nanaiki ļeo jein. Im ba ippān make, "I ba ļein ej kātok kōn mweeņ, iṃōmmero. Ekwe, enaaj alikkar ilju."

Ke ej jotaļǫk, ṃōjin wōt aerro ṃōñā. Ej (ļeo edik) eitem babu, iuṃwin po eo. Em eitok wōt bwe en etal in bōktok juon bwidej kilmeej. Bwe en iten bwideje iuṃwin po eo ilo ṃweo iṃweerro.

Innām ļeo erūtto ej ba, "Etke kwōj babu wōt ļe? Alikkar aṃ jaje kōṃṃan u. Bwe aolep iien kwōj ilām baik u eņ aṃ im itok im ṃoņe eō im ba eor juon men ej iwōj im būki ek kaņ koņaṃ."

Ļeo edik ej ba, "Ijjab ṃoņe eok jeiū. Ak ij lukkuun ṃool ñan eok. Inaaj bar etal ilju in lale ṃōk u eo aō. Elōñ ke koņan. Ijoke inaaj etal ālikin raelep, kiiō. Bwe iaar etal ṃokta ilo raelep im eaar itok men eo.

"Raan wōt juon iaar etal ilo jibboñ im eaar bar itok ṃweo. Ak kiiō ij etal in jota."

Innām rejro kiki. Jibboñōn eo juon ļadik eo edik ej bar itok im bōktok juon bweǫ rot ņe eṃōj tile kōn kijeek. (Bwe en ṃōjņǫ.) Im itok im bar kakōlleik iuṃwin po eo. Wāwen kakōlle eo āinwōt ākōj. Innām ke ej jota dikdikļǫk ļadik eo edik ej bōk kōrkōr eo im etal. Ak ļeo erūtto ej kōppojak in bar kāļǫk kōn ṃweo. Ke ļeo edik etōprak ļǫk u eo ej erre bajjek iturin lañ. Im lale ñe ṃweo en bar itok. Ke ejjab loe, ej tulǫk im bōklōñtak u eo. Ebooļ kōn ek. Ṃōjin an būke ek ko jān kobban u eo, ej bar tulǫk kake, im joone.

Ke ej waļǫk lōñtak ej kanooj in kalimjōk ek ko koņan bwe en jeļā wāween ek rot ko koņan.

Ke ej iten aōņōōņ, ṃweo ej bar kātok ñan ippān.

Kōn an boñ ļeo erūtto ej kaiuri im ej ba, "Litok aolep ek kaņe ilowaan wa ņe."

Ke ļeo edik ej erreilōñļǫk ñan ṃweo bwe en pukot kakōlle eo eaar ākōje ņa iuṃwin po eo. Ke ej lo ekōj eo ej ba, "A ļe, etke āinwōt baj ṃweo iṃōrro ļe jeiū?"

Jen wōt ennaan in, ejook ļeo erūtto im ļak kar kātoļǫk, eaar jab bar rǫǫl tok ñan rainin.

Ak ļeo edik eaar būki ek ko koņan im jepļaak. Ke ej itok ejjab lo ṃweo. Im ekōņaan lo ļeo jein. Ak kōn an ļeo jein kar kōṃṃane nana in, ejook, āliklik, mijak, eppat kōn ļeo jatin.

Ļeo jatin aikuj in lo ļeo jein ñan an kare-oki naan in aerro ñan doon. Ak ejjab lo ļeo jein.

Ejeṃļǫk.

[Iaar kajjitōk ippān ri-bwebwenato eo, Jelibōr Jam, "Ta meļeļe in bwebwenato in ļe?" Euwaak, "Meļeļe in bwebwenato in: Kōnke jen jab nana ñan doon. Bwe enaaj jipeļļǫk jukjuk im pād in ad."]

65: STORY ABOUT A BOY NAMED DEELELPO JĀPO

As told by Jelibōr Jam, Kuwajleen 1975

This story came from Jāpo Island [Arn̗o Atoll].

A woman named Lijiwi gave birth to a boy. When the boy was born, he was the same size as older people. And his father was frightened and planned to kill him. After five or six days, the father said to the mother, "It will be good if I take our son to be tattooed." The mother now replied, "Is he a good size for tattooing?" The boy's father replied, "He is a very good size, for when he becomes older, his tattoo will be very good." And the mother said, "Take him when it is morning."

And the boy's father took him and brought him to the men who were tattooing, and said that they should cut up the boy so that he would die. And the boy's father returned to the boy's mother and said, "The tattooing of our son is going well."

Now the boy's mother was very happy when she heard the words that the father said to her, and she came in and sang. The song said, "Deelelpo Jāpo | Do not move under the tattooing instrument."

(*M̧ōm̧akūtkūt* is Ratak language and *em̧m̧akūtkūt* is Rālik language for 'move'. *N̄i* is 'tattooing instrument'. It was made from the beak of the frigate bird, which was used only for tattooing. If they did not have a frigate bird's beak, they used a shark's tooth. They set the shark tooth in a wooden handle. But they did not use a wooden handle with a frigate bird beak. They used the beak alone.)[1]

Now the boy answered his mother, and just sang and said, "How can I move when

1. Tattooing was practiced extensively in the Marshall Islands. Elaborate designs were made. But only the male members of the chiefly *(irooj)* class were allowed facial tattoos—an obvious mark of rank that enhanced their status and prestige. Krämer (1906:58–62) describes the method of tattooing, the tattoo designs, and the limited extent to which women were tattooed. Some of the songs that accompanied tattooing are also presented. Also see Krämer and Nevermann 1938:69–75. The Protestant missionaries who began their efforts at Epoon Atoll in 1857 proscribed tattooing, and it has not been practiced in the Marshalls for many years. The art of tattooing was said to have been brought to mankind by supernatural beings, and is an important element of several Marshallese folktales. As Alkire (1977:17) points out, "tattooing was important in most of Micronesia. The same geometric designs incised on house rafters and beams were often seen as tattoos on arms or legs. In the Central Carolines, the whole of a man's torso, front and back, might be covered with symmetrical fields of a grand design—a reflection of his high status in some communities." The plaiting and ornamentation of mats was developed to a fine art in the Marshalls. And, as Krämer (58) states, "With tattooing, it is like with the mats. Also here there seems to prevail a certain order with the Rālik-Ratak Islanders, while the ornaments seem to be inserted at random and are often identical to those of the mats. Here, the order seems mainly restricted to three parts on the chest and three parts on the back." Tattooing was also practiced extensively in Polynesia, the culture area that forms a vast triangle to the northeast, southeast, and south of the Marshalls. As Buck (1966:296) points out, "the tattooing art prevailed throughout Polynesia, except in Niue and some atolls. A Maori myth states that Mataora was tattooed in the underworld by his father-in-law Uetonga to replace his transient face painting with a permanent design. On his return to the human world, Mataora taught the craft of Uetonga, the craft *(mahi)* of tattooing *(ta moko)*." (This is comparable to the teaching of tattooing to mankind by supernatural beings, in Marshallese legends.) The class or rank aspect of tattooing is also seen in Maori culture. Buck (299) reports that "tattooing was a chiefly decoration and its social importance encouraged the acquirement of skill by experts, who were well rewarded for their services."

they have cut me up into little pieces?" (The boy had been cut up into little pieces just as the father had ordered.)

Now the man who tattooed the boy suppressed the boy's singing and raised his voice loudly and said, "Eat it and eat it" (meaning pieces of the boy—*kanjo* is Ratak language and *kañejo* is Rālik language for 'eat it').

And the old woman, the boy's grandmother [his maternal grandmother], heard the song of the man when he said, "Eat it and eat it!" And the old woman thought and said, "Why are they saying, 'Eat it and eat it!' when it is bad to eat when they tattoo?"

And the boy's father was going to their son, and he spoke to the mother and said, "Well, I am just going to see what they did to that boy."

When he went away, he went and took a little piece of the boy's flesh and brought it to the boy's mother and said, "Where are you, madam? Come out and see the raw meat, your food." And the woman said to her mother, "Put that raw meat in that basket, and hang it on the branch of that pandanus tree outside."[2]

And her mother took the raw meat and went and hung it on the branch of the pandanus tree. And she [the mother] went inside again, and she remained within the house and again sang, "Deelelpo Jāpo | Do not move under the tattooing instrument."

Deelelpo again sang, "How can I move when they have cut me up into little pieces?"

Now the man who had tattooed cried out in a loud voice, and said, "Eat it and eat it!"

It was a few minutes later, and the flesh within the basket sang and said, "Lijiwi and Ļaṃao and Ļakorōk | He cut me up and hung me outside Jāpo | Jāpo | Lijiwi." (Ļaṃao was the name of the boy's father and Ļakorōk was the man who had cut the boy up.)

The old woman, the mother of the woman, heard the song from within the basket, and said (to the young woman, her daughter), "Do not make noise, for let us see what I hear from within that basket."

After one or two minutes, the flesh again sang, "Lijiwi and Ļaṃao and Ļakorōk | He cut me up and hung me outside Jāpo | Jāpo | Lijiwi."

Now the two of them heard it very well and understood it. And the young woman spoke to the boy's father and said, "Go and see why they have cut the boy up thus."

And the boy's father said to the woman, the boy's mother, "How do you know?" And the boy's mother said, "Why does that raw meat sing within that basket?"

The boy's mother said to his father, "Make haste and go and look [find out]!" And the father went and again returned, and said, "The tattooing of our son is going well. Don't worry!"

Now the flesh again sang from the basket. And the boy's mother ran when she heard the flesh singing. She understood it very well.

---

2. Food was customarily hung in baskets from rafters of the houses, or as in this case, from trees next to the house. This was done to protect the food from animals. It is still done except by those mainly on Ebeje, Kuwajleen, and at the capital, Mājro, who have electricity (and refrigerators). The storyteller explained that the basket in the story was a *bannennor,* a container made of coconut leaves *(kimej in ni)* and used for food. There are large ones and small ones, one to three feet in size, and not as large as a *kilōk.* (He sketched one for me in my notebook.) This was typical of Jelibōr Jam's relationship with me in telling me stories and other aspects of Marshallese culture. And it was the same with other Marshallese who gave me information. They wanted to be sure that I understood what they were telling me, and were glad to answer any questions I might have.

And the woman said to her mother, "Come here, we two will go and look again."[3]

And the woman's mother stood up and went. And they hurried and went toward the ocean. They went, and the man who cut the boy up did not see the two of them. And he put flesh of the boy inside the basket and took it away and hung it on the branch of a *ut* [a tree: *Guettarda speciosa* L.].

And when the man saw the two of them, he hurried and washed his hands. And the women knew he had cut the boy up. And they took the flesh in the basket and went toward the ocean on reefs in the ocean. And placed the flesh in a pool there. And they put the flesh together (reconstructed the body). And sang, "I want to sleep awhile | sleep awhile and awake | and awake my eyes | grow the head. | I want to sleep | sleep and awake my eyes | grow the hands. | I want to sleep | sleep and grow eyes | grow all of this body!" (*Anji* in the ancient language means 'to put together' and *jaruk* is 'awake'.)

They again looked inside the pool. All of the boy's body was reconstructed. Now they took hold of the boy and raised him up.[4]

When the boy went to eat them (because he was a demon now), they twisted a coconut sprout. (We say that they made magic.)[5] And the boy recovered and came to life. He became a human being again.

And the boy went inland, away from the two of them, and cut down two *ut* in order to make two drums[6]—one for his mother and one for his grandmother. And he said that the three of them should go toward the lagoon and look for his father. And he said that the two of them should beat the drums. And the three of them went, and the women beat the drums and said, "Cut the implement of coconut tree and the implement of pandanus tree | the tallest ones, my older brother. | The sound of something moving through the air appears on the ocean side. | The sound of something moving through the air appears on the lagoon side. | The sound of something moving through the air appears in the middle of the island O-O-O-O."

Thus they again said, "Cut the implement of coconut tree and the implement of pandanus tree | the tallest ones, my older brother. | The sound of something moving through the air appears on the ocean side. | The sound of something moving through the air appears on the lagoon side. | The sound of something moving through the air appears in the middle of the island O-O-O-O." [Informant

3. Note the motif of the murdered person talking/singing to the living, and seeking help. Note also the role of a close relative, usually as in this case the mother, helping him/her.

4. Note the motif of a murdered person's cut-up body being reconstituted and resurrected. This is an ancient and widespread motif, and is found in Egyptian mythology in the story of Isis and Osiris (Lons 1975:58–62 and passim). See Beckwith (1970:153–154) for specific stories from Polynesia of chopping up of a murdered person's body and reconstitution and resurrection. The story from Anaa in the Tuamotos includes the element of placing the remains in a basket, as in the Marshallese story. See also Alpers 1970 for other stories of resuscitations and resurrections from Polynesia, and see Grey (1951:92) for a version from Puluwat in the Western Caroline Islands. The concept of resurrection is, of course, known to the Marshallese as it is to other Christians, and is a basic element in their belief system, as it has been for generations.

5. Leaves and other parts of the coconut tree are used in divination, healing, and in benevolent and malevolent magic.

6. The traditional Marshallese drums *(aje)* were hourglass-shaped. The drumheads were made of shark stomachs, and were used for signalling in warfare and for dancing. There are some older men today who know how to make these unique drums. See Krämer and Nevermann (1938:213–314) for a description of Marshallese drums and drumming.

explained archaic language in the song.][7] (He used the pandanus and coconut trees as weapons, spears. The boy was really tall; ten feet tall or thereabouts.)

And all of the people (on the island) fled, for they were afraid. And the boy stood before his father and said to his mother, "My mother, shall I kill my father?" His mother said, "It is your decision, my son."

His father said, "Do not kill me my son, for I am your fisherman."

And the boy said, "O, I am the fisherman. But why did you kill me?"

His father said, "I was not the one who killed you, but it was the man who tattooed you." And his father said, "Do not kill me, my son."

The boy again questioned his mother and said, "What shall I do with father? Kill him, or not kill him?"

His mother said, "It is your decision, my son."

And the boy speared his father with an implement of coconut tree and cast him off his spear and threw him away. And the boy and his mother and the old woman, his grandmother, remain on Jāpo to this day.[8]

And the *ut* trunks cannot grow tall there to this day on the ocean side of Jāpo,[9] because the boy carved drums there.

It is ended.

(The meaning of the story is: Do not destroy things that are given to you, as the boy's father destroyed the boy, his son.)

---

7. In the ancient language *(kajin etto),* Jelibōr Jam explained, it is like *jeiū tiuñ eriblǫk ilik:* my older brother the sound of something moving in the air (like the wind or an airplane appears). *Tipen kenato:* the tallest ones. [*Jeiū* and *ilik* mean 'my older sibling' and 'on the ocean side', respectively, in present-day Marshallese.]

8. The informant told me, in response to my question, that he does not know in what form the boy, his mother, and the old women are: demons, rocks, or what.

9. There may be a more prosaic explanation for the alleged poor growing conditions on Jāpo Island. Hathaway (1953:5), in his discussion and evaluation of soil conditions on Arņo Atoll, states: "As Stone (1951) and Wells (1951) pointed out, typhoons occur about four per century at Arno, and have left their mark on the islands in many ways. The washing away of entire islets is a spectacular consequence of typhoons, but windthrow and partial inundation have affected soil and vegetation. In certain local areas on Kilange Island, for example, nearly every large breadfruit tree was blown down in the typhoon of 1918 and large quantities of soil were thus disturbed. In other places, considerable amounts of sand and rock had been suddenly dumped on low land, or the surface layers had been washed out. Such areas were often characterized by low organic and nutrient content of the surface horizons. The more superstitious believed such land to be inhabited by malignant spirits [that] hinder the growth of plants. Stories of hallucinations caused by these demons were common." Stone (1951:4–6) reports the serious damage done to land (and soils) by typhoons: "On Arņo, the typhoon of 1905 was clearly the most destructive of perhaps a century. . . . The narrow land between Ine Village and [Jāpo] was reduced in width and the effects are plainly visible in the condition of the narrower parts of the island from [Jāpo] west to Lukwōj. The 1918 typhoon was less destructive but left some effects. . . . The narrower land northwest of [Jāpo] was repeatedly washed over for the second time by this typhoon and, at a point where the seaward reef is indented, the land was again trenched through to the reef rock below." The washing away of the fragile soils and the addition of a saline content to the soil, higher than normal, would obviously inhibit plant growth. And there may have been much more destructive typhoons in the past that devastated Jāpo and other islands in Arņo Atoll. This is suggested in the story of the inundation of Tutu Island, as told in story 2, "Story about Bōrraan," beginning on page 37.

Comments

We see the underlying theme in this story of the attitudes of mother, father, child, and grandmother toward one another.

The strong emotional relationship between mother and child is stressed here, as in other Marshallese stories and proverbs or sayings *(jabōnkōnnaan).*

Addenda: M̧ak Juda, another elderly *aļap* from Rālik, explained to me in 1967 on Mājro that "the Marshallese people used to tattoo *(eo̧).* Different designs were used. Only the chiefs *(irooj)* were allowed to have their faces tattooed. Tattoos were a sign of beauty to the people.

"The paint [ink] for tattooing *(uno in eo̧)* was made from *pedo̧ļ,* a low scrub [*Euphorbia chamissonis,* spurge]. Liquid from the *pedo̧ļ* that looks like milk was mixed with black dirt, and the mixture was burnt in a large clam shell. This produced a substance like lampblack.

"The tattooing instruments *(kein eo̧)* were made from the bones of birds, any seabird. I have seen *kein eo̧.*

"The missionaries tried to stop tattooing. But they did not succeed completely.

"There was a taboo *(mo̧)* location on some islands. For example, on Mājrwirōk Island on Jālooj Atoll, part of the land parcel *(wāto),* the tattoo place Loloñ. Near the house of the chiefs was a taboo place. It was used for sleeping, bathing, and tattooing. Only a few clans *(jowi)* could go there. For example, the M̧akauliej *(armej i wuliej,* 'people in the graveyard') could go there. The *ri-katutu* (bathing people), whose ancestors bathed the *irooj,* also could go there. (*Enen ato* means 'to come ashore to bathe'.) It is a kind of land given.

"This custom is not followed today. When I was younger, it was followed."

At the time Mr. Juda gave me this information, he was well over sixty years old.

Jo̧wej, an elderly *aļap* and *ri-bwebwenato* and navigator from Ratak, told me in 1951 on Mājro that "in Ratak, they tattooed mainly with large frigate bird *(ak)* bones, which were plentiful on Bok-ak and Pikaar atolls. People went there to gather them, to get the bones for tattooing.

"Human bones were also used—after death or when graveyards had been washed away by storm waves, exposing the skeletons."

65: BWEBWENATO IN JUŌN ĻADDIK, ETAN DEELELPO JĀPO

Ri-bwebwenato: Jelibōr Jam, Kuwajleen 1975

Bwebwenato ej waļọk jān āne Jāpo [aelōn̄ in Arņo].

Juōn kōrā etan Lijiwi eaar kemmouri ļaddik in. Ke ļadik eo ej ļotak dettan wōt rūtto raņ. Innām jemān emijake im likūt ļōmņak in ippān en ṃane.

Ļọkun ļalem ak jiljino raan jemān ej ba n̄an jinen, "Eṃṃan n̄e ibōk ļaddik ņe nejierro bwe in ilān eọuki?"

Jinen kiiō ej uwaak im ba, "Eṃṃan ke dettan n̄an an eọ?" Jemān ļadik eo ej uwaak, "Ekanooj eṃṃan dettan, bwe n̄e erūttoļọk enaaj kanooj eṃṃan eo eo an." Innām jinen ej ba, "Kwōn bōke kiiō ke e ja jibbon̄."

Innām jemān ļadik eo ej bōke im bōkļọk n̄an ļōṃaro rej eọ. Im ba ren bukwe ļadik eo bwe en mej.

Innām jemān ļadik eo ej rọọl n̄an ippān jinen ļadik eo. Im ba, "Eṃṃan wōt eọọtōn ļaddik eņ nājirro."

Kiiō jinen ļadik eo ke ej ron̄ naan eo jemān ej ba n̄ane eṃṃōņōņō em deļọn̄ im al. Al eo ej ba, "Deelelpo Jāpo | Kwōn jab ṃōṃakūtkūt iuṃwin n̄i ņe."

(Ṃōṃakūtkūt ej kajin Ratak im eṃṃakūtkūt ej kajin Rālik. N̄i ej kein eọ. Raar kōṃṃane jān n̄i in ak eo. Raar kōjerbale n̄an eọ wōt. N̄e ejjeļọk n̄i in ak ippān raar kōjerbal n̄i in pako eo. Raar likūt n̄i in pako ņa ioon juon aļaļ. Ak n̄i in ak eo rejjab kōjerbal aļaļ. Raar kōjerbal n̄i eo wōt.)

Kiiō ļadik eo ej uwaak jinen im baj al im ba, "Etke in jab ṃōṃakūtkūt ke rej bukbukwe eō em ṃōtta wōt jijidikdik?"

Kiiō ļeo ej eọuki ļadik eo ej jurļọk eo an ļadik eo im kōļap ainikien im ba, "Kanjo im kanjo!" (Ṃōttan kanniōk in ļadik eo. Ilo kajin Ratak, "kanjo" ej 'kan̄e' ak 'ṃōn̄ā' im ilo kajin Rālik ej 'kan̄ejo'.)

Innām leļļap eo jibwin ļaddik [jinen jinen eo an] ej ron̄ al eo an ļeo ke ej ba, "Kanjo im kanjo!" Innām leļļap eo ej ļōmņak im ba, "Etke ta wūnin aer ba, 'Kanjo im kanjo!'? Ke enana ṃōn̄ā n̄e rej eọ?"

Innām jemān ļadik eo ej etal n̄an ippān ļadik eo nājierro im ba n̄an leļļap eo jinen im ba, "Ekwe ijja etal in lale ṃōk rej itene ļadik eņ."

Ke ej ilọk ej ilām bōk jidik kanniōk in ļadik eo em bōkļọk n̄an ippān jinen ļadik eo im ba, "Ewi kwe le? Kwōn dioij tok im lale ukoode kijōṃ."

Innām kōrā eo ej ba n̄an jinen, "Kwōn door ukood ņe ņa ilo baninnor ņe. Em totoke ņa iraan bōb ņe inabwij."

Innām jinen ej bōk ukood eo em ilām totoke ņa iraan bōb eo. Ak ebar deļọn̄ tok em pād ilowaan ṃweo em bar al:

"Deelelpo Jāpo | Kwōn jab ṃōṃakūtkūt iuṃwin n̄i ņe."

Deelelpo ej bar al, "Etke injab ṃōṃakūtkūt ke rej bukbuke eō em ṃōtta wōt jijidikdik?"

Kiiō ļeo ej eọ ej laṃōj kōn eļap ainikien, im ba, "Kanjo im kanjo!" Ej meļan ļọk jidik ak kanniōk eo ilowaan baninnor eo ej al im ba, "Lijiwi ak Ļaṃaō ak Ļakorōk | Ebukwe eō em toto eō ņa ilikin Jāpo | Jāpo | Lijiwi." (Ļamaō etan jemān ļadik eo im Ļakorōk ļeo eaar bukwe kijakieņ.)

Leļļap eo jinen lio ej ron̄ al eo jān lowaan baninnor eo. Im ba (n̄an jiron̄ eo nājin), "Kwōn jab ekkeroro bwe jen ro lale ṃōk ta in ij ron̄ jān lowaan baninnor eņ."

Ļọkun juon minit im ruo ej bar al kanniōk eo, "Lijiwi ak Ļaṃao ak Ļakorōk | Ebukwe eō em toto ņa ilikin Jāpo | Jāpo Lijiwi."

Kiiō kanooj eṃṃan aerro roñjake im meļeļe kake. Innām jiroñ eo ej ba ñan jemān ļadik eo im ba, "Kwōn ilǫk ṃōk lale etke āinwōt rej bukwe ļadik eo."

Innām jemān ļadik eo ej ba ñan kōrā eo, jinen ļadik eo, "Ta wūnin aṃ jeļā?" Innām jinen ļadik eo ej ba, "Etke ukood eņ ej al ilowaan baninnor eņ?" Jinen ļadik eo ej ba ñan jemān, "Kwōn ṃōkaj in etal in lale ṃōk!" Innām jemān ej etal, im bar rǫǫl tok. Im ba, "Ekanooj eṃṃan eǫ [eņ] an ļaddik eņ nājirro. Kwōn jab inepata!"

Kiiō ej bar al kanniōk eo jān baninnor eo. Innām ej ettōr jinen ļadik eo im keroñjake an kanniōk eo al ļǫk kanooj in meļeļe kōrā eo. Ej ba ñan jinen, "Itok, kōjro etal im lale ṃōk." Innām jinen kōrā eo ej jutak im etal. Innām rejro ṃōkaj im wōnlikļǫk. Ro ļak etal, ļeo ej bukwe ļadik eo ejjab lo erro ak ej āti kanniōk in ļaddik ilowaan juon iep em bōkļǫk em toto ke ņa iraan juon ut. Innām ke ļeo ej loe erro ej kaiuri im aṃwin pein. Ak kōrā ro rej jeļā ke ļadik eo eo eṃōj bukwe. Innām rejro bōk kanniōk eo ilo baninnor eo im wōnmetoļǫk ñan eoon bar ko em door kanniōk eo ņa ilo juon ļwe.

Innām rejro anji kanniōk eo im al, "Ikōņaan likōn | likōn kiki jidik em ruj | Im ļak jaruk meja eddōk bōran. | Ikōņaan likōn, likōn im ļak jaruk meja, eddōk pein. | Ikōņaan likōn, likōn im ļǫk jaruk meja, eddōk aolepān ānbwinnin!"

("Ani" ilo kajin etto ej 'kōṃṃane aolep ṃōttan jiṃor āinwōt ṃokta'. Im "jaruk" ej 'ruj'.)

Rōļak erreitok ñan lowaan ļwe eo eiio aolep ānbwinnin likao eo. Kiiō rej jibwe im kōjerkake ļadik eo.

Ke ļadik eo ej iten kañe [er]ro (kōnke ej tiṃoņ kiiō) rejro kōrǫǫle jebake eo (jen ba rōkōṃṃan bubu). Innām emour ļadik eo. Eoktak ñan armej.

Innām ļadik eo ej wōnāneļǫk jān erro. Em jiktok ruo ut bwe en kōṃṃane ruo aje. Juōn ñan jinen im juon ñan kōrā eo jibwin. Innām ej ba renjel wōnarļǫk in pukot jemān.

Innām ej ba renro kab pikri aje ko. Innām rejel etal im kōrā ro rej pikōr aje ko im ba, "Jekjektok kein ni im kein bōb | Tipen kenato, jeiū. | Tiuñ errūbļǫk ilik. | Tiuñ errūbļǫk iar. | Tiuñ errūbļǫk i luujien āniin O-O-O-O."

Eñiin rej bar ba, "Jekjektok keinni im keinbōb | Tipen kenato, jeiū. | Tiuñ errūbļǫk ilik | Tiuñ errūbļǫk iar | Tiuñ errūbļǫk i luujien āniin O-O-O-O." (Ilo kajin etto meļeļe in "tiuñ" ej 'ainikien ak juon iien eṃṃakūt ilo mejatoto eo āinwōt kōto eo ak juon baļuun'. Im "tipen kenato" ej 'aetoktata'.)

(Ej kōjerbal bōb im ni āinwōt kein tariņae, ṃade. Ļadik eo elukkuun aetok, joñoul ne ak āinwōt.)

Innām aolep armej (ioon āne eo) rej ko bwe remijak. Ak ejutak ļadik eo iṃaan mejān jemān im ba ñan jinen, "Jinō, ij ṃan ke jema?" Jinen eba, "Aṃ wōt pepe nājū."

Jemān eba, "Kwōn jab ṃan[e] eō nājū, bwe aṃ ri-eǫñor."

Innām ļadik eo eba, "O, ña e ri-eǫñor. Ak etke kwaar ṃan[e] eō?" Jemān eba, "Ejjab ña eo eaar ṃan[e] eok, ak ļeo eaar eǫǫt [eǫuk] eok." Innām jemān eba, "Kwōn jab ṃane eō nājū."

Ļadik eo ej bar kajjitōk ippān jinen im ba, "Ij et ñan jema? Ṃan ke ak jaab?" Jinen eba, "Aṃ wōt pepe nājū."

Innām ļadik eo ej wekare jemān kōn juon keinni im tōbe im joļǫk. Innām ļadik eo im jinen kab leļļap eo jibwin rej pād ioon Jāpo ñan rainin.

Innām likin Jāpo ejaje aetok lōñļǫk ut kaņ ie ñan rainin. Kōnke ļadik eo ejekjek aje ie.

Ejeṃļǫk.

(Meļeļe in bwebwenato in ej: Jab kǫkkure menin leļǫk eo. Āinwōt jemān ļadik eo ej kǫkkure ļadik eo nājin.)

66: STORY ABOUT ŅOONIEP

As told by Jelibōr Jam, Kuwajleen 1975

The *ņooniep* lived like human beings. However, human beings were not able to see them at some times. But sometimes they appeared to human beings and human beings saw them.

The *ņooniep* were scattered over the Marshall Islands.[1]

And their *irooj* [chief] was named Kabua.[2] The place where he stayed was on Pikinni Atoll. He stayed there, and after some days, the chief decided with all of his young men that they should build canoes to sail to all of the atolls of the Marshalls, because he wanted to see his *ņooniep* subjects on each atoll (his *ņooniep).*

And when these canoes were completed, he had another idea, that they should make a model canoe in order to race it at any atoll at which they would arrive, to see which atoll had the fastest canoe.

For if there was a faster canoe than the chief's canoe, he would reward it, give it a prize [lit. 'thing to help / assistance'].

And they sailed from Pikinni, and came to Roñdik, and spent three days there. And raced, and the Pikinni canoes were fastest. And they sailed from Roñdik to Roñļap, and saw their relatives there, and raced, and the Pikinni canoes were again fastest.[3]

And after three days, they came to Wōtto and again raced there, and a Wōtto canoe was fastest. And the chief took the canoe, and after three days came to Ujae, and again raced there. The Wōtto canoe was fastest. The Ujae canoes were only faster than the Pikinni canoes.

After the chief saw the speed of the Ujae canoes and the Pikinni canoes, he remained on Ujae for many days.

And raced on all of those days.

And it was clear that the fastest canoe was the canoe from Wōtto, and two of the Pikinni canoes, and one from the Ujae canoes.

And the chief took the fastest canoes, and came to Lae.

And raced again. There were no canoes from Lae (for they did not make them). And they only raced with two canoes from Ujae and two from Pikinni and one from Wōtto. After three days, they came to Epatōn, Kuwajleen. They stayed there a long time, because he did not know which was the fastest of these canoes. And the chief took all of the canoes and sailed and came to Naṃo, and again made a race. And a canoe from

1. The *ņooniep* are supernatural humanoid beings who figure in a number of Marshallese folktales. In the grammar of the language, they are treated more like animals than humans: the particle *ko,* which follows words for animals, plants, and inanimate objects to pluralize them, is also used for the *ņooniep.* (A different particle, *ro,* is used for human beings.)

2. Kabua was an *irooj ļapļap* (paramount chief) of Rālik (the western chain of the archipelago). He lived in the late-nineteenth century and is described in the German literature of the Marshalls. One of his descendants, Kabua Kabua, is currently an *irooj ļapļap* of Rālik, and the name Kabua is borne by many of the extended family as a family name. The name of this historical figure was apparently incorporated into the folktale as the chief of the supernatural beings (*ņooniep*). It should be noted that the *ņooniep* are usually benevolent and nonthreatening, so the use of the name of a historical chief was not a form of criticism or protest by the narrators of the story.

3. Note the historical connections and kinship ties between the people of Roñļap and the people of Pikinni exemplified in this story about the *ņooniep.*

Naṃo was fastest. And he again spent three days, and came to Aelōn̄ļapļap, and again raced and no canoe was faster there. Now he spent many days and made happiness [furnished entertainment] to all the *ṇooniep* on Aelōn̄ļapļap.

And the chief again made races on the final days. And he took eight of these canoes: two from Pikinni, and one from Wōtto, and two from Ujae, and one from Epatōn, and two from Aelōn̄ļapļap.

And he said to his captain that he should sail to Epoon.[4]

For the chief was going to Epoon to race. And he would say to the Epoon people that he [the chief] would give a prize to any atoll that had a faster canoe than the canoe of the chief.

And the captain sailed, but the chief remained on Aelōn̄ļapļap: Je and Mejel [two islands of the atoll].

After a few days, the captain returned and the chief said, "Get ready, for we will sail from this atoll to Epoon."

And the following day, they sailed to Epoon.

When they arrived (beached) at Epoon, they saw many people racing with canoe models.

When the chief disembarked, he said, "Tomorrow will be the day to watch the races."

And they brought eight canoes from Eañinmeto ('North in the sea'), the fastest canoes.

And from Rakinmeto ('South in the sea'), they brought the fastest canoes.[5]

(Eañinmeto is the atolls to the north in the Marshalls: Kuwajleen, Pikinni, Lae, Ujae, Wōtto, Ron̄ļap, Ron̄dik. [There are] two land parcels *[wāto]* on Wōja Island, Aelōn̄ļapļap Atoll. One is [named] Kobalraiiōn̄ [to the north], and one is Kobalrairōk [to the south].

Eañinmeto is from Kobalraiiōn̄, and Rakinmeto is from Kobalrairōk.

Ujae, Lae, and Wōtto are in Kapinmeto ['west in the sea / bottom of the sea'].

Kobal are living things/animals living beside a sandbank [named] Tarej.)[6]

When it was morning, they brought food and began their preparation of the canoes. And when they put the canoes in the water and released the canoes, they ran the canoe from Pikinni and the canoe from Wōtto, and the canoe from Epoon won![7]

They did it two times to prove the winner, and the canoe from Wōtto was fastest. The canoe from Pikinni was number two.

And the canoe from Epoon was number three.

And the chief was very happy because of the canoe from Wōtto being fastest. And he gave Je and Mejel on Aelōn̄ļapļap to the *ṇooniep*[s] on Wōtto Atoll.

And he gave Epāju [an island] on Ujae to the *ṇooniep*[s] on Pikinni.

And he gave Jā [an island] on Aelōn̄ļapļap to the *ṇooniep*s on Epoon.[8]

---

4. Note the use of the English loanword *captain*, modified to *kapen* (in the Marshallese text). This has been well integrated into the Marshallese language as have many other English loanwords, and a few from the Japanese language.

5. The name *Eañijen-Rōkijen* was given to the large schooner of Irooj Ļapļap Kabua Kabua, which was used by him to visit the atolls and islands that he ruled, and for transportation in general. (He was chief of lands in the north and in the south of Rālik.) The name of the schooner was appropriate.

6. According to Abo et al. (1976:151), Kobal is the name of two navigational signs—turtles off Wōja Islet of Aelōn̄ļapļap.

7. Note the use of the English loanword *nōṃba* 'number' in the Marshallese text *bōk nōṃba juon,* 'took number one', that is, 'won the race'.

At the time that they launched with model canoes on the main island of Ujae, when they raced, they (the chief and the people) said—we say they chanted:[9]

"O-O-iolokare. | Ñijiri im bōk wain. | Iar in Lipi lein." ("O-O-one-two-three together. | Chant together and take the canoe oceanside of Lipi [*wāto*, land parcel], men.")

On Epāju, they again launched the model canoes and said, *"Kwōn rantok man dik in Eoweņo ne lejiniriañ in iip en kabōk aiman in."* ("You put up the pandanus [sail] from Eoweņo [land parcel] on the fire. | Put up the sail because the wind is in it.")

At the time when they launched at Wōtto, they said, *"Iturin iip jen kare wōjlā wa eo eṃōkaj ņe pello ņe."* ("At the end of Wōtto [the north end] | Let us combine that the sails fast above made of *pello*" [*pello, Ipomea tuba,* trumpet morning-glory].)

At the time that they launched at Epatōn, they said: *"Iten kajer kubaak ia? | Liok in bōb en apran ledik raņ."* ("Go and pull out the outrigger where?/ The root of the pandanus tree. The place where the girls lean against.)

At the time that they launched at Epoon, they said: *"Bwilibwili ia i Rupe? | Wa eo eṃōkaj eo eļļaeoeo."* ("Launch them where on Rupe [land parcel]? | The very fast canoe.")

I forget the chants of all of the places of this story.[10]

66: BWEBWENATO IN ŅOONIEP

Ri-bwebwenato: Jelibōr Jam, Kuwajleen 1975

Ņooniep āin an mour wōt bar armej. Ijoke armej ejjab maroñ in lo er ilo jet iien. Ak jet iien rej waļọk ñan armej im armej ej lo er. Ņooniep eaar barāinwōt ejjeplōklōk ilo aelōñ in Ṃajeļ in.

Innām irooj eo aer etan Kabua. Ijo eaar pād ie ilo aelōñ in Pikinni. Pād innām jet raan remootļọk irooj in eaar pepe ippān aolep likao ro jet ṃōttan. Bwe ren kōṃṃan wa in jerak ñan aolep aelōñ in Ṃajeļ. Kōnke ekōņaan lo ņooniep ro doon ilo kajjojo aelōñ (ņooniep eo an).

Innām ke ej tōprak wa kein eaar bar lo juon ļōmņak bwe ren kōṃṃan riwut bwe jabdewōt aelōñ eo renaaj tōprak ie ren kab iaekwōj im lale waan aelōñ ta eo eṃōkaj. Bwe ñe eo eṃōkaj wa eo waan irooj in enaaj kōṃṃane juon menin jipañ ñane.

Innām raar jerak jān Pikinni. Im itok ñan Roñdik. Im joļọk jilu raan. Im iaekwōj im wa ko waan Pikinni raar ṃōkaj. Im raar jerak jān

8. This reflects the customs of the chiefs giving land to their subjects as reward for services rendered.

9. The *roro* or chants were used for various purposes to stimulate those involved in the particular activity. They were used in combat to challenge the enemy and animate the warriors, and while performing strenuous activities such as canoe launching or beaching, as in this story. They are still used to a certain extent by Marshallese.

10. The storyteller explained the meaning of the chants to me as best he could. But in some cases the ancient language *(kajin etto)* with hidden (*ṃwilaļ*, lit. 'deep') meanings that he did not know, were used. Hence my English translation seems obscure in places.

Ron̄dik n̄an Ron̄ļap im lo ro nukier ie im iaekwōj im eaar bar ṃōkaj wa ko waan Pikinni.

Im ļọkan jilu raan raar itok n̄an Wōtto im bar iaekwōj ie im eaar ṃōkaj juon wa in Wōtto. Innām irooj eo eaar bōk wa eo im ļọkan jilu raan ar itok n̄an Ujae im bar iaekwōj ie. Waan Wōtto eṃōkaj. Waan Ujae ko ṃōkaj in wōt waan Pikinni ko.

Ke irooj eo ej lo an ṃōkaj waan Ujae ko kab waan Pikinni ko. Ej pād Ujae iuṃwin elōn̄ raan. Im iaekwōj ilo aolep raan kein. Innām alikkar an ṃōkaj wa eo jān Wōtto kab ruo iaan waan Pikinni ko im juon jān waan Ujae ko.

Innām irooj in eaar būki wa ko reṃōkajtata. Im itok n̄an Lae. Im bar iaekwōj ie. Ejjeļọk wa jān Lae. (Bwe raar jab kōṃṃan.) Ak rej iaekwōj wōt kōn wa ko ruo jān Ujae im ruo jān Pikinni im juon jān Wōtto. Ļọkun jilu raan rej itok n̄an Epatōn, Kuwajleen. Ijin etto an pād ie. Kōnke ejaje kake ewi wa in eṃōkaj iaan wa kein. Innām irooj eo eaar būki aolep wa ko im jerak im itok n̄an Naṃo. Im bar kōṃṃan iaekwōj ie im eaar ṃōkaj juon wa jān Naṃo. Innām eaar bar joļọk jilu raan. Im itok n̄an Aelōn̄ļapļap. Im bar iaekwōj ie im ejjeļọk wa eo ar ṃōkaj ie. Kiiō ej joļọk elōn̄ raan im kōṃṃan ṃōn̄ōn̄ō n̄an aolep ņooniep ro ilo Aelōn̄ļapļap.

Innām irooj eaar bar kōṃṃan iaekwōj ilo raan eo āliktata. Innām eaar bōk rualitōk wa iaan wa kein. Ruo jān Pikinni im juon jān Wōtto im ruo jān Ujae. Im juon jān Epatōn im ruo jān Aelōn̄ļapļap.

Ak ej ba n̄an kapen eo an bwe en jerak n̄an Epoon. Bwe irooj in enaaj etal n̄an Epoon im iaekwōj ie. Innām en ba n̄an ri-Epoon ke jabdewōt aelōn̄ eo enaaj ṃōkaj wa eo [jān] waan irooj in enaaj leļọk menin jipan̄.

Innām eaar jerak kapen eo ak irooj eo ej pādwōt ilo Aelōn̄ļapļap; Je im Mājel. [Ruo āne ie.]

Ālikin jet raan ej rọọltok kapen eo im irooj eo ej ba, "Kōppojak bwe jenaaj jerak jān aelōn̄ in n̄an Epoon." Innām rujļọk in eo juon rej jerak n̄an Epoon.

Ke rej poļọk Epoon rej lo ekanooj in lōn̄ rejwōj iaekwōj kōn riwut.

Ke irooj eo ej toļọk ej ba, "Ilju enaaj raan in āļooj iaekwōj."

Innām rej bōktok rualitik wa jān Eañinmeto, wa ko reṃōkajtata. Im jān Rakinmeto rej bōktok wa ko reṃōkajtata.

(Eañinmeto ej aelōn̄ tu ean̄ ilo Ṃajeļ: Kuwajleen, Pikinni, Lae, Ujae, Wōtto, Ron̄ļap, Ron̄dik. Ruo eṃ [wāto] i Wōja [juon āne ilo Aelōn̄ļapļap]. Juōn kobalean̄ [tu iōn̄]. Im juon kobalrairōk.

Eañinmeto ej jān Kobalean̄. Im Rakinmeto ej jān Kobalrairōk. Ujae, Lae, im Wōtto rej Kapinmeto.

Kobal rej mennin mour ioon bok [dekā] iturin āne in Bok, Tarej.)

Ke ej jibbon̄ wōt raar ebbōktok ṃōn̄ā im jino aer karōke wa ko. Innām ke rej doori wa ko ņa i lọjet im kōtļọki wa ko rej ettōr wa eo jān Pikinni kab wa eo jān Wōtto kab wa eo jān Epoon rej bōk nōṃba juon.

Raar kaṃool ruo alen innām wa eo jān Wōtto eṃōkaj. Wa eo jān Pikinni nōṃba ruo. Wa eo jān Epoon, nōṃba jilu.

Innām irooj in eaar kanooj in eṃṃōn̄ōn̄ō kōn an wa eo jān Wōtto ṃōkaj. Im leļọk Je im Mājel ilo Aelōn̄ļapļap n̄an ņooniep ko ilo aelōn̄ in Wōtto.

Im eaar leļọk Epāju [juon āne] ilo Ujae n̄an ņooniep ko ilo Pikinni.

Im eaar joļọk Jā ilo Aelōn̄ļapļap (juon āne iturin Je im Mājel) n̄an ņooniep ko ilo Epoon.

Ilo iien eo rej bwilbwil kōn riwut ko ilo eonene in Ujae ke rej iaekwōj rej ba (irooj im armej), "O-O ioļọkade. I N̄ijiri im bōk wain I Iar in Lipi lein." [Lipi ej juon wāto.]

Ilo Epāju rej bar bwilbwil kōn riwut ko im ba, "Kwōn ran̄tok maan̄ dik in Eoweņo ņe lejinirian̄ in iip en kappok aiman in." [Eoweņo ej juon wāto.]

Ilo iien eo rej bwilbwil i Wōtto rej ba, "Iturin iep jen kāre wōjļā wa eo eņōkaj ne pello ņe."

Ilo iien eo rej bwilbwil i Epatōn rej ba, "Iten kōjar kubaak ia? / Lieok in bōb eņ apran ledik raņ."

Ilo iien eo rej bwilbwil i Epoon rej ba, "Bwilibwili ia i Rupe? / Wa eo eņōkaj eo eļļaeoeo." [Rupe ej juon wāto ioon eonene in Epoon.]

(Imeļoķļoķ roro an aolep jikin ilo bwebwenato in.)

67: ŅOONIEP STORIES FROM ĀNEWETAK ATOLL

As told by Reverend Ernej, Wūjlañ 1955

One man on Ānewetak, years ago, saw a *ņooniep*. The *ņooniep* told him, "Do not tell anyone you saw me."

Later on, the man forgot this warning and told the people that he had seen a *ņooniep* who had given him fish and food and other things to make him fortunate.

Shortly after this, the man died, because of breaking his word to the *ņooniep*.

One time, some people on Jeptaan Island [Ānewetak Atoll] saw a big log with fish-ing line and hooks on it. They brought it ashore and put it in a house. But the *ņooniep*[s] stole it during the night.

68: STORIES ABOUT ETAO

ETAO'S FAMILY

As told by Raymond DeBrum, Mājro 1953

According to my father, Joachim DeBrum, Etao's family was as follows: 1. Etao's mother was Lijm̧an. She was a big eel *(dāpļap)* [family *Muranidae Gymnothorax* sp.] who lives on Jāmǫ Island.

2. Etao's wife was Leŋkade.
3. Etao's son was Limjabeo.
4. Etao's son was Kolorao.
5. Etao's son was Kurañ.

WHY *WŌT* IS BITTER

As told by Ijikiel Laukōn, Wūjlañ 1955

The Marshallese explain the bitter taste of this species of taro [*Alocasia macrorrhiza*, dry-land taro] with the following story:

Etao wanted to play a trick on some people. So he urinated on the *wōt*. And from that day to this, the plant (tuber) has a bitter taste, and it is only eaten when the rest of the food supply has been exhausted.

[Botanists and agronomists attribute the bitter taste in this plant to the presence of calcium oxalate crystals.] [1]

A STORY ABOUT ETAO

As told by M̧ak Juda, Mājro 1968

Kwōn jab kiki in Etao. (Do not pretend to sleep, bluff.)

This *jabōnkōnnaan* (proverb) is from a *bwebwenato* (story) about Etao known to most people.

Etao wanted to sleep but was afraid that he would be caught, attacked, and killed. So he put *mejān jidduul* [operculum of *Turbo* sp., cat's eyes] on his closed eyes,

1. The people of Rennell Island, a Polynesian outlier in Melanesia, tell a similar story to explain a natural phenomenon (as well as to entertain): The trickster Mauitikitiki (a local variant of Maui) urinates on a shark. This is the reason shark meat smells so strongly of urine (Elbert 1965:118–119). See Chambers (1972:118) for the story of "Etao's adventure in Oklahoma." This has a sexual motif, as do a number of other Etao stories. The incorporation of the trips to America in the adventures of the traditional Marshallese trickster shows how motifs and details of folktales may change as a culture changes, and as new information is acquired.

and went to sleep. (It looked as if he were lying there with his eyes open, awake.)

A group of men came upon him, saw that his eyes were open, and did not attack him because they thought that he was awake. Thus, the saying *(jabōnkōnnaan): "Kwōn jab kiki in Etao."*

ETAO'S TRIP TO AMERICA [OR, ETAO UPDATED]

As told by a man from Mājeej, Kuwajleen 1971

Etao made the rounds of the Marshall Islands. And he ended up on Ļōñar Island, Arņo Atoll [site of the "sex school" for young women in the old days, still joked about].

He did a lot of bad things: stole, took women, and so forth. The people on the island were going to harm him. So he fled.

He went to America, but could not do anything there because the Americans were too smart. (They knew how to make electricity, airplanes, and so forth.)

I heard this story from the *aļap*[s] [older men or lineage heads] long ago on Mājeej.

This Etao happening [trip] was before the Americans came to the Marshall Islands.

THE CHANT OF MĀJEEJ, SUNG BY ETAO

As told by Jǫwej and interpreted by Konto Sandbergen, Mājro 1952

Ekear tak i Eleo,
ejor em ko.
A eatuwe ļǫk Mājeej.
Rej kūrrin wa eake em iruj
Ibnon tok oṃ eo, ajen pepei iru eo,
Tarkiļañ a ān et ņe, ibnon tok oṃ eo,
Āneo ānen Irooj Etao, ej pelpel buwatte.
Ejaata ļǫk oṃ ko, ajan pepei Mājeej eo.

It flew across to the lagoon at Eleo, it escaped and ran away, and it went ashore at Mājeej.

They shout: sail ho, and get excited by it.

The approaching hermit crab, irregular formation of flock of birds.

On the horizon O, what land is that approaching hermit crab.

Protecting the baby northward O.

It is the land of Irooj Etao, he is slinging it continuously.

Hermit crabs are dying away, irregularity, this is Mājeej.

Comments

Etao (Ļe-Etao or Ļetao) is the trickster figure of Marshallese, and is the subject of many stories and a character in others. He is both helpful and mischievous.

A rascally or tricky person is called *"etao"* by the Marshallese, and the word is used among friends in jest as well—reflecting perhaps the ambivalent attitude toward Etao and his dual personality.

Etao is comparable to Olofat (Iolofāth) of the Western Carolines,[2] and Nareau of the Gilbert Islands (Kiribati)—both also Micronesian cultures—and to Maui (in his role of trickster), famed in Polynesian legends.[3]

Counterparts of Etao are also found in the folklore of the Native Americans. These include Manabozho, and the animal-human (transformer) tricksters: Raven, Blue Jay, Mink, and Old Man Coyote.[4]

African folklore is rich in stories of tricksters.[5] Anansi or Spider and other trickster stories were brought by African slaves to the New World, and are told in the West Indies today, as are animal trickster stories of Carib and Arawak Indian origin.[6]

Analogous characters are found in other cultures throughout the world.

It has been suggested that "psychologically the role of the trickster . . . permits the satisfactions of an obvious identification to those who recount or listen to these tales."[7]

A number of stories of Etao have been recorded by early German ethnographers and later American reseachers.[8]

---

2. Lessa 1961:18-26.
3. Luomala 1949, 1950:38, and 1955:85–98.
4. Thompson 1966:53–77.
5. Abrahams 1983: passim.
6. Sherlock 1966: passim.
7. Leach 1950 vol. 2:1123.
8. Erdland 1914:184–209 passim; Krämer 1938:253–264; Krämer and Nevermann 1938:238; Davenport 1952:50–53 and 1953:219–237; Chambers 1969:16–21, 31–33, 39–41, and 1972:107–128.

69: MAUI ON MĀJEEJ, AND WŌNEŅAK STORIES

As told by Jǫwej and interpreted by Konto Sandbergen, Mājro 1952

MAUI ON MĀJEEJ

I have only heard one story about Maui on Mājeej. This is it:

Maui was the *irooj* (chief) of the people of the Land of the Sunrise, Takinaļ. The *irooj* on Mājeej (Ļowajele) wanted to see the people of Takinaļ.

He had great magical power and when he said, "I wish I could see the people of Takinaļ," Maui and a few people from Takinaļ appeared.

These people stayed on Mājeej happily for quite some time without any trouble. Then Maui and a Gilbertese man started arguing about who had more magical power, until one day they went out to the ocean beach and started making magical incantations.

The Gilbertese told Maui to plug his ears up. Then he called on the thunder which came down and roared beside them, but Maui was not disturbed. He just looked at the thunder. (He had not plugged up his ears.)

The thunder roared for a while and then the Gilbertese sent it back. Then he asked Maui, "Well, what do you say about that?" But Maui said, "About what? That little noise that it made? Do you have a last word to say to your relatives?" he asked the Gilbertese.

The Gilbertese said, "Well, I will see." Then Maui murmured some words. He brought his hand back of his head, then brought it forward. And pulled it back.

At this instant the ocean reef started cracking. Then the Gilbertese saw what was happening and when the crack reached the middle of the ocean reef, he begged Maui to stop.

From that time on, everyone on Mājeej was afraid of Maui, and the people were wondering what they could do to destroy him.

This Gilbertese and Maui were very good friends. And they were always competing with one another in a friendly way. But when the Gilbertese saw that Maui had greater power than he had, he wanted to destroy him. So one day, he told Maui to climb a pandanus tree that held a ripe pandanus.

While Maui was leaning out on a branch, the Gilbertese took a rock and aimed it at the branch and threw it. As the branch was breaking and while Maui was falling down with it, the Gilbertese hit him on the head with another rock. Maui hit the ground and was finished by the Gilbertese and a few others who beat him to death.

When Maui's countrymen learned of his death, they all came to pay their respects (*ilo mej,* lit. 'at death', a formal wake) and to bury him *(kallib).*

While they were mourning over the grave, people of Mājeej tried to capture them. But when they suspected this, they scattered and ran eastward on the surface of the water, and disappeared into Hawai'i.

MOURNING CHANT OF RI-TAKINAĻ

Ikwe Maui ke ekar jab mej i aelōñ ko an. | A eitok im mej ņa ilo aelōñ kūbwe rap-rap-rap kein. (Too bad about Maui, for not dying on his home lands. | But he had come here and died on these shit-soiled lands.)

People of Mājeej think that the *ri-takinaļ* were *wōneņak,* demons of the bush *(tiņoņ ilo mar).* Some of them have no heads. Most of them are seen without heads. Some merely look like human beings, and may be talked to. Some can turn themselves into parasitic plants and roll onto anyone who may see them. They harm people—make them become insane. People have died from this. I know of many during the Japanese times.

A man who is still living, named Ļajer at Wōdmeej, Wōjjā, almost died from it. (He is the oldest brother of Lōke.) This *wōneņak* looked like a person. It did not have a head and was curled up in a plant. Ļajer had run away from it. He reached home and lost his mind. He was treated for it, and recovered.

TREATMENT FOR SICKNESS FROM WŌNEŅAK (UNO IN NAÑINMEJ IN WŌNEŅAK)

I have seen this treatment and it is as follows [the storyteller said]: The patient lies, sprawled out on the ground, prone or supine, and is covered with mats. People hold the mats on top of him. He is completely covered. He is shivering. The *ri-wūno* (medicine man or woman) in this case a female, Lipepidik [her name], took a new coconut frond *(juubub in ni)* or "penis of coconut tree" and made it into a *jabwi* or magical frond, and tapped the top of the mats (over her patient) while she chanted the magical song. And Ļajer became well.

A WŌNEŅAK STORY FROM KAPEN, ṂAĻOEĻAP ATOLL

There is a man named Tenje, who treated Ļaje for the attack of a *wōneņak* upon him. This Ļaje is older than I am. [Storyteller Jọwej is over seventy years of age.] Ļaje saw this *wōneņak* (a headless one). Ļaje had gone to a house which was not his, and without anyone telling him to do so. And fed some chickens.

Then he went back along the path. On the side of the road was a small bush, *marjej* [*Wedelia biflora*]. When he came abreast of it, something pulled his cane. He turned around and saw a woman, naked from the waist up, wearing old-style mat clothing.[1] He tried to pull his cane away but without success. Suddenly another woman appeared, wearing the same type of costume. Then they both vanished. And Ļaje became ill.

---

1. The traditional costume of Marshallese women consisted of two finely-plaited ankle-length, overlapping mats, and with nothing worn above the waist, except when necklaces or flower leis were worn around the neck or on the head.

70: MAUI ON MĀJEEJ

As told by Liaj, Mājeej 1952

Maui came to Mājeej from the east and contested the *irooj* (chief) Ļoajļe of Mājeej in feats of magic.

Maui caused the island to split apart (as it is today).

The chief became worried and conceded defeat, and asked Maui to return from whence he came.

He walked along the path and saw a large pandanus fruit [*Pandanus tectorius* sp., *bōb*]. And the chief asked Maui to get it, so Maui climbed up the tree.

The chief told his aide to hit Maui with a rock. And he did it.

Maui was hit in the testicles and died on Mājeej.

[There is a deep crevice on the reef, where the island started to split according to the story.]

Comments

The Maui name and character may have been introduced into the Marshalls by Hawaiian sailors and others in the nineteenth century or the early part of the twentieth. That he came from the east, *takinaļ* (the sunrise), might be a clue to Maui's provenance, as Hawai'i lies to the northeast of the Marshall Islands.

In any event, Maui does not appear to be indigenous to the Marshalls. There seem to be very few stories about him in these islands. I have only heard the two presented here.

The trickster of Marshallese folklore, Etao, is the well-known counterpart of Maui of Polynesian reknown.

The Gilbertese character in the story 69 version of "Maui on Mājeej" indicates knowledge of the Gilberts, either through contacts with castaways from these islands to the south of the Marshalls,[1] and far south of the northern island of Mājeej, or, perhaps through post-European contact with Gilbertese sailors on European or American ships.

1. See footnote 109 on page 137 (story 30), and also note that Ṃakin in the Gilberts is the first location in story 35 on page 160.

71: THE CHANT OF MILE: FISHING UP FROM THE BOTTOM OF THE SEA

As told by Jǫwej and interpreted by Konto Sandbergen, Mājro 1952

Bukonmar eo eain eoon Mile I
Mile kōtļǫk I
Bukonmar eo lik likit ļǫk O elur I
Li eo inin baaj e-e I Kaoeoe I
Detak tok Lañinperan I Kwoj kaje I
En jab kāāj in eañ I Kāāj in rak I Kāāj in Nabu I
Oware kāāj in Pit eo I Liklǫke I
Ede joñjoñ bwe ekkōt eoon i Mile I
Jen ro kijbadbad I Kijbadbad I Kijbad ke I
Ān eo Mile in I
Ioon wōd e jepo.

Bukonmar[1] gathered Mile up I
The released Mile I
Bukonmar is lowering (the fishing line) O, It is calm I
Lady North of the sheet cleats O-yell I
Climb aboard Lañinperan I Hello.
It shall not be the hook of the north I The hook of the south I The hook of Nabu I
Beg for that Gilbertese hook I O, lower it.
It is taut I Because of Mile's great resistance on the line I
Let us try hard I Try hard to reach it I
That land of Mile it is I
Your land and my land I Our land I And that is all I
On top of this reef, O, lower our sails.

Comments

The story of the fishing up of an island by a culture hero/trickster is widespread in Polynesia, where Maui/Mauitikitik performed this feat (Luomala 1950a:45 and 1955:86). Beckwith (1970:308–310) also tells of the fishing up of the Hawaiian Islands by "the great fisherman Kapuhe'euanui (the large-headed octopus)." Stories of this amazing feat are also found in Micronesia with different characters involved (see Lessa 1961:290–325).

In the Marshalls, the basic and perhaps prototypical story of island fishing is narrated briefly in the Marshallese creation story (story 1, "The Beginning of This World," page 11), and in the other story of the fishing up of Mile by a character named Lañinperan, after the island (atoll) had been overturned and sunk by the trickster Etao. See Chambers (1969:54–63 and 1972:128–129) for discussion and analysis of the story and associated chants in the versions he collected (pp. 31–33 and 36–37), and those collected by Krämer and Nevermann (1938: 61–62), and Davenport (1952). After Jǫwej had told me the story of Maui on Mājeej, and the chant of the *ri-takinal,* he chanted "The Chant of Mile: Fishing Up from the Bottom of the Sea."

It was not done within the context of a story, however, and the role of Etao in the sinking of the atoll was not mentioned. This might have been because I was unaware of the story of Etao's sinking of Mile, and

1. Bukonmar and Lañinperan are called *ri-bwe* (invisible people).

because I had told Jo̧wej I was interested in chants, and did not ask about Etao and Mile.

Jo̧wej followed up this chant with the one at the end of story 68, "The Chant of Mājeej, Sung by Etao," page 310. The association, at least in narrating stories, of the two tricksters, Maui and Etao, is tantalizing, as is that of Bukonmar and Lañinperan who, like Maui, fish up an island/atoll. The Gilbertese hook element is also intriguing. These stories are perhaps symbolic of the discovery of these islands and atolls.

72: ABOUT A WOMAN WHO WAS ON ROÑDIK

As told by Jelibōr Jam, Kuwajleen 1975

The woman was very industrious. When she saw that the thatch on her house there was rotten, she began to make thatch[1] for her house, during perhaps two or perhaps three months.

And she began to prepare the pandanus leaves by removing the spines, during one night, six or seven sections.[2]

During the following week, the moon began to rise from the west, and when she saw the moon, she said to herself, "It will be good if I make two sections during one evening. For if the moon will be in the east, well, I will make this amount before the moon sets." And she made two sections during one evening. At the time when the moon was in the east, she began her work [and worked] until the moon set in the west. This continued, and two nights from the time when it was *jetmar* [the night after the full moon, *jetñōl*], she began to work to the day [until daybreak]. She almost did not sleep because she was very anxious about her work—[that] it should be finished quickly.

On the third night, she ate a little and went and removed spines from the pandanus leaves—she had just gone to remove spines [when] her eyes became heavy and she fell asleep beside the spine-removing equipment. When the moon was in the middle of the sky, the woman began to dream. In her dream, she saw a very white thing, and it fell down to her from the moon.

And it came and stayed beside her. And she heard a sound that came from the white thing. The sound said, "I am M̧ōjo̧liñōr. I come from [the] cold."

The woman was startled, and she went to wake up; it was as if her eyes were pressed down, and she could not wake up.

And the sound again appeared [occurred], the second time from the white thing. It said, "I am M̧ōjo̧liñōr. I come from [the] cold."

And the old woman tried to get up. When she got up, she changed her thinking and became quite crazy.

When she screamed out many times about the dream that she had seen, people woke up near her.

And when they picked her up, she could

---

1. Thatch is made from the leaves of *Pandanus tectorius,* screw pine, *bōb.* The long, hard-surfaced and sharp-edged leaves are called *maañ.* The leaves of this important and hardy tree are used for other purposes as well, for mats, containers, and handicraft today—and for wearing apparel and canoe sails in the past. The fruit of the edible varieties is also used raw, and is prepared in a number of ways.

2. The thatching material is prepared as described in the story. The sharp spines are removed, and the processed leaves are rolled up for storage and future use. The material is further processed to make it suitable for the finer work of plaiting mats and the like. The sections of thatch are called *jiņ* in Rālik and *tap* in Ratak. Thatched roofs and thatched siding have been almost entirely superseded by imported building materials: corrugated metal roofing and lumber. Plywood is especially favored for siding, because it is relatively cheap and easy to use in construction. Metal roofs are certainly more practical as a means of collecting water to run off into adjacent concrete cisterns and metal drums. They provide a more abundant and cleaner water supply. However, they make the house interiors much hotter than do the thatched roofs, and they require a cash outlay initially and for replacements, which the traditional thatching materials do not. The construction of the traditional types of houses and the making of thatch sections and pandanus leaf panels may very well become a lost skill in the not-too-distant future.

not reveal a word about it. But here she said, "I am only M̧ōjǫliñōr. I come from [the] cold." And the old woman was ill for one year. They treated her until they were exhausted. But she did not become well. When she became a little better, she told [them] the name of her sickness: M̧ōjǫliñōr, to this day. And the name of this sickness appeared, it came from [the] cold.

It is ended.

(The meaning of this thing: Girls from young to old, also, "Do not sleep beneath the sky at the time when the moon is full; for you will [contract] M̧ōjǫliñōr." The different phases of the moon: quarter, half-moon, up to the full moon are not harmful.

In other words, they must sleep inside their houses or under trees such as *kiden* [*Messerschmidia argentia*] or pandanus [*Tectorius* vars., *bōb*] or *kōņņat* [*Scaevola frutescens* L.] or just *ut* [*Guettarda speciosa* L.]. But they should not sleep in the open space.

The Marshallese obey this to this day. And they should not sleep beneath the sky if the moon is in the east [full moon]. It is bad; big cold[ness] comes, and they cannot be well. There is no Marshallese medicine that can cure them.

I saw a woman who got M̧ōjǫliñōr on a boat during the Japanese time.

She did not want to use a blanket or go inside the boat [go below], because she was seasick. And she became like crazy, and trembled, and could not speak. And after some days she became better. But she was not like before.

And she could not speak or walk right. She stuttered, stammered, and staggered, to the time that she died.

When she became sick, she was a girl, and she had not married yet. And when she died she was sixty. She could not work; she only ate.

She lived on Ujae. The name of that woman was Jorbit. She died during the Japanese time, before the war.

Marshallese doctors [*ri-uno:* traditional practitioners] treated her, and she became a little better, but not very much. It was impossible to cure her.

I only heard about that [one] woman who got the M̧ōjǫliñōr sickness.

Marshallese believe this to this day. If you sleep under the full moon, cold[ness] can enter you.

I do not know if it is a demon or what.)[3]

3. The belief that sleeping under the light of the moon is dangerous is found in other cultures, and is apparently quite old. Leach (1950 vol. 2:744) states: "Sleeping in the light of the moon is bad. In Egypt, Greece, Armenia, Brazil, and many other places, sleeping with the moonlight in one's eyes weakens the sight. In Europe generally, sleeping in the moonlight often results in insanity; the lunatic is so-called because he is moon mad [from the Latin *luna* 'moon']. Throughout the world the moon is an evil principal or body as compared with the good sun." We hear of the effect of the full moon on the minds of some people: "There is a full moon tonight. A lot of crazies will be out," and the like. This is part of American folklore, and has been reported by law enforcement and hospital emergency-room personnel. Jelibōr Jam drew pictures in my notebook to explain the shapes (phases) of the moon relative to *M̧ōjǫliñōr*, and said, "Quarter-moon and half-moon and such as that are not bad. You can sleep beneath the sky and in the open places. But when there is a full moon or if the moon is in the east, you cannot." This is apparently an old belief in the Marshall Islands. For example, it was reported by German ethnologists who worked in the Marshalls during the German period. "[M̧ōjǫliñōr]: resulting from the influence of the moon on somebody sleeping in the open" (Krämer and Nevermann 1938:244). They state that "evil spirits *(anjilik)* cause certain diseases" (246).

72: KŌN JUŌN KŌRĀ EAAR PĀD ROÑDIK

Ri-bwebwenato: Jalibōr Jam, Kuwajleen 1975

Kōrā eo ekanooj in eowan. Ke ej loe an m̧weo im̧ōn m̧or aj ko ie, ej jino an eppel aj in m̧weo im̧ōn ium̧win ruo ke ak jilu allōñ.

Innām ej jino an karere im kōm̧m̧an ilo juon boñ jiljino ak jiljilimjuon jim̧.

Ilo wiik eo juon ej jino an tak allōñ i kapilōñ im ke ej lo allōñ, ej ba ñane make, "Em̧m̧an ñe inaaj kōm̧m̧ane ruo jim̧ ilo juon jo̧ten. Bwe ñe allōñ enaaj pād i rear, ekwe inaaj kōm̧m̧an joñan wōt an jab tulo̧k allōñ." Innām ruo jim̧ ej kōm̧m̧ane ilo juon jo̧ten. Ñan iien eo ke allōñ ej pād i rear ej jino jerbal joñan wōt an tulo̧k allōñ i kapilōñ. Pād im ļak mootļo̧k ruo boñ jān iien eo ke ej jetmar ej jino an jerbal ñan raan. Enañin jab kiki kōn an kanooj inepata kōn jerbal ko an, bwe ren m̧ōkaj in tōprak.

Boñōn eo kein ka jilu eaar m̧ōñā bajjek innām etal im karere, ej kab ja iten karere wōt ak eddotok mejān im kiki ŋa iturin wōt karere eo. Ke allōñ ej pād ioļap kōrā in ej jino an ettōŋak. Ilo ettōŋak eo an ej lo juon men ekanooj mouj ak ej wōtlo̧k tok jān allōñ. Im item pād iturin. Im ej roñ juon ainikien ej itok jān men eo emouj. Ainikien eo ej ba, "Ña M̧ōjo̧liñōr itok jān pio̧."

Ke leļļap eo ej ilbōk. Im iten ruj, āinwōt ñe ren joon mejān im eban ruj.

Innām ainikien eo ej bar waļo̧k kein ka ruo jān men eo emouj. Ej ba, "Ña M̧ōjo̧liñōr itok jān pio̧."

Innām leļļap eo ej kate im jerkak. Ke ej jerkak eoktak an mejatoto im eļap an bwebwe.

Ke ej ellam̧ōjm̧ōj elōñ alen kōn ettōŋak eo eaar loe, armej ro rej iruj̧lo̧k ñan ippān. Im ļak kotake, ejjeļo̧k ennaan emaroñ in kennaan kake. Ak ijo ej ba, "Dein ke ña M̧ōjo̧liñōr itok jān pio̧."

Innām leļļap in eaar nañinmej ium̧win juon iiō. Raar unoke im m̧ōk. Ak eaar jab mour. Ke ej em̧m̧anļo̧k jidik ej ba etan nañinmej eo an, M̧ōjo̧liñōr ñan rainin.

Im ej waļo̧k etan nañinmej jab in, itok jān m̧ōļo.

Ejem̧ļo̧k.

(Meļeļe in menin: jiroñ ļo̧k ro reddik em rūtto barāinwōt, "Kwōn jab kiki ium̧win lañ ilo iien ñe [eor] ekilep allōñ bwe kwōnaaj m̧ōjo̧liñōr."

Āinwōt rej aikuj kiki ilowaan m̧weo im̧weir ak ium̧win wōjke; āinwōt kiden ak bōb ak kōŋŋat ak ut bajjek. Ak ren jab kiki i meļaaj.

Ri-M̧ajeļ rej pokake ñan rainin. Im rej jab kiki ium̧win lañ ñe allōñ epād tu rear. Enana itok m̧ōļo in eļap in reban mour. Ejjeļo̧k uno in M̧ajeļ emaroñ kemour[i].

Iaar loe juon korā ej bōk m̧ōjo̧liñōr ioon wa ilo iien Jepaan.

E m̧akoko ko̧o̧joj ak deļo̧ñ ilowaan wa. Kōnke eļļao. Innām ej erom āinwōt bwebwe, im wūdiddid. Im ejjab maroñ kōnono. Im ālikin jet raan ej em̧m̧anļo̧k. Ak ejjab āinwōt m̧okta.

Ak ejjab maroñ kōnono ak etetal jimwe. Ñan iien ar mej.

Ke ej nañinmej ej leddik. Ak ejjañin m̧are. Im ke ar mej ar jiljinoñoul. Ejjab maroñ jerbal; m̧ōñā wōt.

Ej jokwe Ujae. Etan liin Jorbit. Ar mej ilo iien Jepaan, m̧okta jān pata.

Ri-uno in M̧ajeļ raar unok e, ak em̧m̧anļo̧k jidik ak ejjab kanooj. Eban kemour.

Iaar roñ kōn liin wōt ar kar bōk nañinmej in m̧ōjoliñōr.

Ri-M̧ajeļ rej tōmak ñan rainin. Ñe kwōj kiki ium̧win allōñ m̧ōļo emaroñ deļo̧ñe eok. Ijaje tim̧oŋ ke ta.)

[Ri-bwebwenato eo, Jelibōr Jaaṃ, ar jeje pija in kōmmeḷeḷeik jekjek in allōñ eo. Im ba, "Adik im wetaklap im āinwōt jab nana. Komaroñ kiki iuṃwin lañ im i meḷaaj eo. Ak ñe ekilep allōñ ak ñe allōñ epād tu rear, koban."]

73: THE BIG TYPHOON THAT DEVASTATED THE MARSHALL ISLANDS

As told by Jelibōr Jam, Kuwajleen 1975

Long ago, long before the white men came to the Marshalls, there was a much larger population: thousands and thousands of people. They were short of food. The only place where there was plenty of food was at Wōjjā Atoll. And so many canoes and many people sailed from Roñļap and other atolls to Kuwajleen and joined canoes from Kuwajleen and sailed to Aelōñļapļap where other canoes joined them.

And they sailed to Wōjjā. When the first canoes reached Wōjjā, they lay off shore, on the ocean side of Wōjjā Island.

A woman was sleeping there and she heard them call from the fleet of canoes, as in a dream. She awoke and heard them call out, "There are three hundred or four hundred or five hundred canoes on the way to Wōjjā to get food. Is there any food?"

The woman replied, "Yes." So, the men in the canoe passed the word to the canoe behind, and one to the next, all the way back to Aelōñļapļap where the first canoe was: "There is food on Wōjjā."

Then they came ashore and got food.

There is a large freshwater pond on Wōjjā. It was created long ago when a star fell from the sky and landed there.[1]

The islands of Wōjjā and Wōdmeej and others had many coconut trees.

So the people of the rest of the Marshalls, including those from Mājro, were able to live from the food from Wōjjā.

This went on for some time. Then a very big typhoon came up and wiped out most of the population of the Marshalls. For example, there were only about twenty or thirty people left on Kuwajleen, and perhaps two or three on Lae.

Then those who survived made more people and the population built up. But it has never reached the size of the old days before the typhoon.

The big typhoon killed all of the *rimmenanuwe,* all of the *ņooniep,* all of the *rijek,* and most of the people in the Marshall Islands. However, it did not kill the demons.

I learned this from the old people. There are some older people who know this story today.

Before the white men came to the Marshall Islands, there was no sickness. People were healthy and lived to an old age. There were many people in the old days.

Then the first disease came, *baito (*smallpox). It caused sores on the people and killed them.

It is ended.

1. Perhaps this was a small meteorite.

74: EPOON HISTORY: THE VOYAGE TO BANEP (OCEAN ISLAND)

As told by Dwight Heine, Naṃdik 1951

A group of Marshallese sailed from Epoon to Ocean Island over 150 years ago. They landed on Banep (Ocean Island) and made war and conquered there. The Marshallese *lerooj* (chiefess) in the group married a local chief and remained there.

During the German times, the Rālik *irooj* (chief) Litōkwa visited Banep. His relatives there gave him a *jebwe* (paddle) that had been on the canoe from the Marshalls. However, they would not part with the *dekeinnin* (pandanus leaf pounder) that had belonged to the chiefess.

All of the Banep people were moved by the British government to Rambi (Rabi) Island in Fiji. Kautongatonga, a descendant of the Marshallese invaders, sent a letter from Rambi to Mājro after World War II requesting information about his relative, Irooj Kabua Kabua.

Comments

Ocean Island is only about 1,500 acres in extent, and six miles in circumference (Robson 1946:174). It is called Paanopa or Banaba by its natives. The tiny island lies about 300 nautical miles south of Epoon Atoll.

The people of Ocean Island were moved to Rambi Island (which they had purchased with part of their meager phosphate mining royalties) after World War II. Their whole island had been exploited and ravaged by the intensive mining operations, as was Nauru (Pleasant Island).

Riesenberg (1965:165) reports: "Marshalls to Nauru: Sitting 1896:524. Marshallese were carried 'to the Carolines, to Pleasant Island, and still westward for distances of 2,700 kilometers.'"

Nauru is 146 nautical miles to the west of Ocean Island, with only a small difference in latitude. It is also south of the Marshall Islands. Hence a canoe voyage from the Marshall Islands to Ocean Island would appear to be feasible.

Wind, wave, and current conditions would permit a return voyage, adrift or purposeful, to the Marshalls from Ocean Island as well. For example: Riesenberg (166) lists a voyage from Ocean Island to the Southeastern Marshalls: "(Finsch 1893:71) '1880s: Three canoes fled Aranuka [in the Gilbert Islands, south of the Marshalls] for fear of wrath of king, heading for Ocean Island, arrived safely; because of lack of food at Ocean, crew of only one canoe were accepted ashore, the others started back but, went astray; one canoe with seven people (seen by Finsch) landed at [Mile] after drifting three months the other at Mājro, where they were murdered.'"

Marshallese were able to travel by ship to Banaba and Nauru during the German period. Some of them went to Nauru to work.

75: THE WAR BETWEEN THE RI-M̧WEJOOR AND THE ĻAJJIDIK AND RAARŅO

As told by Jǫwej and interpreted by Dwight Heine, Mājro 1951

Originally the Ļajjidik *jowi* (matriclan) people were fathers of the Raarņo clan people.

They fought the Ri-M̧wejoor on northern Ratak (who were *irooj:* chiefs), then elevated their children rather than their *mañden* (maternal nephews). That is how the Ļajjidik became chiefs.

This happened during the German times. About fifty men were involved in this action.

In Ratak [the eastern chain of the Marshalls], only the Ri-M̧wejoor, Raarņo, and Ļajjidik (chiefly) clans intermarried.

Bouliej, a Raarņo chief, married a Lijjidik[1] (of the Ļajjidik clan). His children, male and female, were Ļajjidik.

His children then married back into their father's clan (Raarņo).

Their children were Raarņo, the children of the males.

Bouliej's daughters married Raarņo men, but their children remained Ļajjidik.

Bouliej married Lipelik about one hundred years ago.

In the generation of their grandchildren, war was declared between the Ri-M̧wejoor who were chiefs from Arņo to Utrōk.

(I am a great-grandson of Bouliej through my mother.)

Bouliej also had a Ri-M̧wejoor spouse and had children with her. (The Raarņo were then lesser chiefs.)

The Ri-M̧wejoor children wanted to kill their Ļajjidik half-siblings. They were jealous of them. So the Ļajjidik children sided with their Raarņo cousins and fought a war. (The Ri-M̧wejoor did not want to share *ekkan* [tribute of food, mats, and the like] with their Ļajjidik kinsmen.)

The Ri-M̧wejoor were located at Utrōk, Wōjjā, Likiep, and Aelok [atolls].

They came down to Aur [Atoll] with all of their people.

(All of the Ļajjidik and Raarņo people were at Aur and M̧aļo-eļap [Atoll].)

Their spies reported to them in advance, so they were prepared for the attack. They pretended that nothing was wrong.

The invaders came to Kapen [Island] at M̧aļoeļap, and my father, Jopi, a Raarņo *irooj eļap* (paramount chief), left Jāān̄ [Island] with a large fleet of canoes.

The Ri-M̧wejoor did not suspect anything. They thought the Raarņo were just coming to welcome them.

Jopi asked them what the purpose of the trip was.

The chiefs Naņwilur, Ļoiur, Ļajikot, Ļotimno, and many *kajoor* (commoners) of the advance invasion fleet replied, "We are escaping famine *(ñita). Kōmij ko in ekkan.*"

Jopi said, "All right. Let us go to Aur." So all of the invaders went to Tōbaaļ [Island] and remained overnight.

They then went to Aur and remained at Aur for twenty-four hours.

Later, when the first cock crowed, the war started. By this time, the Ri-M̧wejoor knew that the Raarņo and "children" were aware of their plans. So they were ready.

The Ri-M̧wejoor dragged their canoes up awaiting attack (with spears in hand).

---

1. *Li* is a prefix used here to denote a female member of the clan. It is also added to names of many females.

The Raarņo launched the attack at dawn, and they fought until all of the commoners were killed. The chiefs of the Ri-Ņwejoor escaped in one canoe. (They had remained in the rear during the battle.) They were pursued by two canoes, which overtook them between Aur and Mājro and killed all of them.

When they arrived back at Aur, Jetñōl [a chief] was there with the second invasion fleet. The battle continued and Jetñōl was defeated. The war was fought on the island and on the sea. Jetñōl escaped in a canoe to Wōjjā and Utrōk. Ļajjidik wiped his force out (against Wōjjā, Kajan, and Jetñōl).

Ļaņade, chief of Ri-Ņwejoor from Mājro, had gone up to Wōjjā to aid his clan members, and came back unsuccessful.

He was killed later when Raarņo on Mājro rose up against the Ri-Ņwejoor and took over from them, shortly afterwards.

The last battle between the two clans was at Arņo. The Ri-Ņwejoor were successful because of the giant paramount chief [Irooj Eļap Rilōñ], who speared people like fish.

The Ri-Ņwejoor never attempted to retake the whole of Ratak. They remained at Arņo and held it alone.

The Ri-Ņwejoor had lands taken away on northern Ratak [*jipǫkwe* 'land and title taken away by the victor from the defeated']. They became commoners. Some of their descendants regained their lands through marriage, however.

Comments

In their outline of the history of the Marshall Islands, Krämer and Nevermann report that: "1824. . . . On the 8th of April, Kotzebue saw the Ratak Islands again, which he had promised to visit again. . . . [Ļaņade] with 40 boats (400 men) had overpowered [Mājro] and killed 5 men in 1823. The battle lasted for six days, and Kadu had distinguished himself. 100 hatchets which Kotzebue had given in 1816 had fallen into the hands of [Ļaņade].

"Now [Ļaņade] planned an attack on Otdia in the Ralik area . . . whose chieftain Lewadok had overcome Kawen [Kapen] with his people, in order to rob its iron treasure acquired at the time of the Rurik's visit. Two people from Otdia [Wōjjā] were killed in the engagement, while on Kawen no one fell. Lagediak considered this undertaking promising.

"On the second day on land, where pendulum observations were made, Kotzebue was shown the mode of warfare. By blast horns the signal was given to attack. Those approaching were dancing wildly, while the women sang and screamed. After a time the noise stopped and a few warriors came forward on both sides, seeking to exasperate each other through invectives and motions. Stimulating songs resounded. Gradually the leaders sank back into their lines and the fight became general. Spears, stones, pandanus-beans flew here and there. The leaders now blew their horns behind their troops. When one fell, the fight stopped" (1938:7–8).

Detailed information on weapons and warfare is given in the same study (198–206). See Mason (1947:90–95) for "History of land administration in Radak." He describes the maneuvering for political power by the various chiefs, and the political situation in the area.

76: *BWEBWENATO IN ARṈO:* ARṈO HISTORY

As told by Jetñil Felix, Mājro 1951

The giant Rilōñ was about eight feet tall. I was told this story by my uncles Jetñōl and Litōkwa.

There was a marker on his grave on Kōjbwe Island [Arṇo Atoll].

The Raarṇo clan had killed all of the *irooj* [chiefs] on Arṇo except Rilōñ, who was hidden away in the brush on Arṇo Island [the main island of Arṇo Atoll] by his *kajoor* [commoner subjects].

He sailed with them from Arṇo [Island] to the north, [on the] ocean side, and was taken to Pikaar-ej [Island].

One of the *aļap*[s] [lineage heads], Lujim's old *aļap,* turned the canoe into Pikaar-ej. All of the people in the canoe had said, "We are going to die in the sea."

Lujim's *aļap* said, "No. We do not belong to the sea. We must return to the land!"

He said, "We will go to Pikaar-ej." Which they did. Word was sent to all of the atoll that all of the *irooj* of Ri-Ṃwejoor were dead except for one boy and a few women. So everyone came from all over the atoll to Pikaar-ej. They remained there for a long time, until Rilōñ was twenty years old. And they guarded him. It was their headquarters.

They built many big canoes, houses, [and made] war materials: spears, clubs, and so forth.

The old men told the boy about his parents' defeat and his relatives' deaths. He remembered, but they kept telling him.

The old women made him strong with magic medicine: *anjin peran* (fearless in war): The man sits down and all of the women walk around him singing, every day for three weeks, during the day. On the fourth week, they take him to the ocean reef and make him stand on the reef. They sing one more song to make a strong wave come to him. If the big wave comes in and does not knock him down, he is ready for war. If it knocks him down, they have to start all over again.

Rilōñ was strong and was not knocked down, and everyone made *ekkan* [formal presentation of food to a chief] to him: *"dān bwijrak."*

After this, all of the Ri-Ṃwejoor led Rilōñ west to Arṇo Island. (The Raarṇo people had been there all this time.)

They went by canoe and on foot. At daybreak, there was a surprise attack. The Raarṇo saw this and moved to the north.

(Some were Mājro people.)

About eight in the morning, the war started. They fought until about three in the afternoon. And rested, and then started in after dark. At about four in the morning, all of the Mājro people left Arṇo for Mājro.

[Mājro Atoll is only a few miles from Arṇo. It is within sight of Arṇo Island.]

Rilōñ remained at Arṇo about ten years. All of the Arṇo people stayed with him.

Ten years later, the Mājro people came down again. There were many canoes and people. (Rilōñ was about forty years old. (He had married a Raarṇo.)[1]

They landed men and started fighting on the reef, to the beach. The Mājro people forced a lesser number of Arṇo people back.

1. Members of the chiefly *(irooj)* lineages of the Ri-Ṃwejoor and Raarṇo clans often intermarried. The status of the offspring of such unions was enhanced, as rank was inherited from both parents. The chiefs of Arṇo and Mājro became related through such marriages.

The Aṃo people could not handle this large number.

One of the Aṃo *aḷap*[s] sent word to Rilōñ: "The Mājro people were too strong for us. What will you do?" He was in his canoe off the island. (Rilōñ went to the canoe whenever he made war.) It was to remember the massacre of his relatives, to make him angry.

He started fighting from the canoe. (He was close behind the line fighting.) He stood in the canoe.

He replied from the canoe, "It is all right. Keep going." The Mājro people were very close, and he called his son Ḷemoden to him. "The last words I ask of you now." (He had been in the large canoe. Rilōñ was in the little cabin. The canoe was over one hundred feet long.)

His son was over on the other side of the canoe. "Who do you want to stay with? Your uncle *(wūllepaṃ)* or your father?"

The son thought it over for a while and answered "Father, I want to stay with you."[2]

Ḷañilojab, his uncle, came up then to look for Rilōñ (with four or five men).

The son told his father, "Here comes my uncle now. Ḷañilojab is about your size. And he is the strongest Mājro man. You had better kill him."

The father asked him again who he would stand by. The son did not answer him, but took his spear and ran up to his uncle, throwing the spear at his uncle. He missed him.

The uncle told his nephew "Get away from here. You are a little child." (He was eighteen years old.)

The boy remained in front of his uncle, unharmed. He called to Rilōñ, "Where are you?" The old man told Rilōñ, "Your son is here."

Rilōñ took his gear and his spear *(ṃade)* and jumped out of the canoe house ["cabin"]. He ran to where his brother-in-law and son were (by himself).

The battle was still raging on the beach. The brother-in-law ran up, also alone. Everyone stopped fighting. Rilōñ said, "I am the last Ri-Ṃwejoor, and you want to fight again with Ri-Ṃwejoor. Today is your last day to live." His brother-in-law replied the same.

Rilōñ retreated to a pandanus tree. One was a good, heavy shelter. The fruit was hanging down. He stood under the tree. Ḷañilojab started thrusting with his spear.

Rilōñ brought his spear back, point to the ground, under the shelter of the pandanus tree. When Ḷañilojab thrust his spear in under the pandanus branches, Rilōñ parried the thrust and caused the spear to go up into the tree, and to stick in the tree. Ḷañilojab held onto the spear.

Rilōñ shook the tree with his hands, and leaves came down, blinding his opponent.[3] Rilōñ then cut Ḷañilojab open across his abdomen with a shark's tooth weapon *(ñiin pako)*, which killed him.

All of the Mājro people then ran away. The Ri-Ṃwejoor killed some of them.

Some of the Mājro people swam back from Aṃo. (They had missed the evacuating canoes.) They were not eaten by sharks. Chief Aisea [*irooj ḷapḷap* of half of Mājro Atoll in 1951] knows about this—the informant replied to my question about sharks eating survivors who swam home.

The battle had been fought on canoes on the water, as well as on land.

---

2. The important decision had to be made by Rilōñ's son whether to side with his father or with his mother's brother, his fellow clansman and lineage head *(aḷap)*. This is obviously a dramatic episode in the narrative.

3. Pandanus leaves are long, heavy, and hard, with sharp edges in their natural state before processing.

Rilōñ remained on Arṃo. He had launched the attack and had won.

Later he went to Epoon [Atoll][4] and made a *bōl in iaraj* [taro pit]. He killed so many people that he made a graveyard in the taro pit. He put them in it: three hundred or four hundred people. (He had coconut leaves cut and covered the bodies with them.)

He then went to Jālooj,[5] and met the *irooj* from Rālik, Ļañinni. He met him in a canoe between Jālooj and Epoon, and asked him, "When you get to Epoon, will you check the *to in bweọ?"* (coconut husk/ coir rope). That is, he told him subtly that he had killed people.

Ļañinni reached Epoon with his entourage. He smelled a rotten odor from the land. Ļañinni told his *aḷap*[s] to check.

Some of the survivors (a few) told what had happened.

"Strangers came and killed and left the island."

Rilōñ wanted to show people who was the strongest—to build up his prestige.

The northern Ratak people (Raarṃo) brought *pej* [pandanus segment husks], to the great uncle of Rilōñ as *ekkan* [tribute], for "toilet paper." He was the strongest chief of Ratak [the eastern chain of the Marshall Islands].

Comments

See Rynkiewich (1972) for a brief history of the wars on Arṃo. He discusses "Rilung" (86–88), but without the details of Jetñil Felix's account, and with some variation in names and actions.

Rynkiewich fixes Rilōñ's reign over Arṃo Atoll as "about 1855–1865."

His account tells of the assassination. But the names of the principals in the story differ from my informant's account. However, the specific details of the act are the same.

The Rynkiewich account states "the youngest sister's eldest son, Lajinlor persuaded as assassin, a Rimejar [Ri-Ṃwejoor] clansman from Mile, to assassinate LaBeliwa [Ļapeliwa]. He did the job quietly one night by drawing a sharks tooth sword across LaBeliwa's stomach. LaBeliwa's son, Taktu, a Raarṃo clan member, watched and fled" (86).

He also describes Ļakaṃo as having allegedly "reasserted the [Ri-Ṃwejoor] lineage's dominance in the Ratak chain and terrorized the Rālik chain" (as Rilōñ is said to have done on Epoon in the story told to me).

Krämer and Nevermann state that "According to the legend, [Epoon] was once independent and had a king. A great famine came, so that many starved. Then they were conquered, killed or carried off by the people of Djalut [Jālooj]; part of the enemy stayed behind, however. So [Epoon] was subjected to the king of Djalut, but was again conquered from the north.

"In 1870 Kabuke [Kaibōke] was the head chief" (1938:41).

---

4. Epoon Atoll is 230 miles southwest of Arṃo Atoll.

5. Jālooj Atoll is roughly ninety-five miles northeast of Epoon Atoll. The informant is a descendant of the Arṃo chiefs, and of the Rālik chiefs as well. The grave *(lōb)* of Irooj Ļapļap Rilōñ is located on Arṃo Island, Arṃo Atoll. It is marked by a large earthen mound,and it has been designated as a historical site. The grave of Irooj Ļakaṃo, maternal uncle of Rilōñ, is located on Kōjbwe Island, Arṃo Atoll. It is a large grave site.

Buckingham (1949) was told a version of the invasion of Epoon by "Ļañinni under the leadership of Irooj [Jemāluut]."

His informant was Ļokrap, who was a famous *ri-bwebwenato* from Epoon. This version is detailed and contains war chants *(roro in tariņae)* and genealogical data of the chiefs. The accuracy of Buckingham's presentation of the Epoon stories, which are only in English, has been challenged by at least one knowledgeable Marshallese, a former resident of Epoon, as reported by Davenport (1952).

Erdland (1914:18) describes a catastrophe on Epoon in which the population suffered from tidal wave, famine, and death at the hands of invaders, "The old Benjamin (+1904) told me that as a little boy he had heard of a terrible tidal wave that had flooded [Epoon] and had destroyed all the palm trees. On this occasion, a certain Labunbung had killed hundreds of starving adults. He threw their corpses in water wells. When after a certain time he came back from [Jālooj] with some of his friends, an insufferabable stench met them."

77: RĀLIK HISTORY: ABOUT THE CHIEFS

As told by Ļokrap and Lobar, and interpreted by Konto Sandbergen, Epoon 1951

In the course of discussing the Marshallese land tenure system and the social system, the elderly informants, respected storytellers, gave me the following information of a historical nature.

In Rālik [the western chain of the Marshalls], the *irooj* [chiefs] never selected an inhabited piece of land as *mǫ* [personal and taboo land of the chief.][1] They always picked an uninhabited island. The *irooj* in Rālik are kind-hearted.

The more *kajoor* [commoners] the *irooj* have, the more power they have. [The word *kajoor* also means 'power' or 'strength'.] So the *irooj* tried to treat their *kajoor* well.

Nelu was the most beloved *irooj* because he was so kind to the people. He did not ask for his share [of the proceeds from copra sales]. They just gave it to him.

He was the best of the Rālik *irooj.* In Jālooj, people just handed him $200.00 on one occasion, while he was walking down the road.

Irooj Kaibōke was fair. He would pay a worker for making copra and using his own canoe to make it [to transport it].

He was a very strict man. He punished people who did wrong.

When Marshallese people stole, he would punish them by making them work, or by making them sit on a roof all day.

When European ships went through the pass into the Epoon lagoon, they had to pay him for permission to do so. They had to pay him for permission to anchor in the lagoon as well.

The foreigners said his rule was perfect. He sold Rupe *wāto* [a land parcel on Epoon] to the mission. We do not know about payment for the *wāto.*

There were only a few coconut trees on it when he gave it away. It was part of Ṃankōn *wāto,* where Kaibōke lived and ruled.[2]

---

1. *Mǫ* land. See Tobin (1958:56–61) for details.

2. See Krämer and Nevermann (1938:193–196) for discussion of the Rālik chiefs, and passim for Marshallese history, with emphasis on warfare and attacks on foreign ships. Epoon is mentioned specifically in the list of foreign contacts in the Marshalls: "1845. . . . Andrew Cheyne visited on February 23 J. Covel's group (Epoon) 4' 30" latitude 168' 42" longitude and were met by three large boats with 50 men each, who first began to trade and as the 'Najade' was swung to anchor in the wind and rain, came on board and stole everything that they could seize, and then with concealed knives and clubs began to attack. They were driven from the deck with difficulty by means of musket shots, after they had already tried to lay hands on the rudder, in order to cause the ship to become stranded. The Epoon people were known . . . as fearsome sea robbers. 1852. . . . A ship was captured at Epoon Island, the crew of which felt the wrath of the natives, because years before a great chief had been killed there by whites (Prager). Epoon was, about this time, one of the places most feared by seamen in the South Seas. Here a few years later [in] 1857 . . . the mission established itself . . ." (11–12). Ļokrap was informant for Buckingham (1949), from whom some of Grey's stories were derived (1951). He also told Marshallese folktales and other lore to James (Ļaṃooj) Milne when the latter was a youth. And Mr. Milne was Davenport's informant while a student at the University of Hawai'i (Davenport 1952 and 1953). Dwight Heine and other Epoon people also told me the story of their chief levying a tax on ships wishing to enter the Epoon lagoon. The feeling I gathered from them was one of pride that their leader could more than hold his own with outsiders despite their apparently superior power.

78: RĀLIK HISTORY: THE WAR ON EPOON

As told by Ļokrap and interpreted by Konto Sandbergen, Epoon 1952

There was a war on the ocean side of Rupe [*wāto,* land parcel] caused by a land dispute. This was the last war in Rālik. It was between Jemāluut, *irooj* [chief] of Rālik, and Ļañinni, *irooj* of Rālik also.

The war started at Kuwajleen, and they fought southward and ended at the ocean side of Rupe. Jemāluut fled to Naṃo Atoll, to Naṃo Island. They fought and Jemāluut was killed. And Ļañinni became *irooj* of all of Rālik.

The war was to see who would be *irooj* of Rālik. Their mothers were sisters. The mother of Jemāluut was senior.

They were *irooj* of all of Rālik before. The mothers were *lerooj* [chiefesses] together. Jemāluut's mother was Lijileijet. And the mother of Ļañinni was Liwātuonmour (from Ruk).[1]

These two women founded the *irooj bwij* [lineage/clan] of Rālik. Lijileijet's descendants are alive today, but they are *jipọkwe,* they have lost their lands. (They are like *kajoor* [commoners], because the war was lost by their ancestors.) Lijileijet is a large jellyfish *(jañij kiliplip)* and is found at the tip of the reef *(wōd)* off Ṃajkōn Island at Naṃo Atoll. She has been seen there.

She was not a real person. She was an *ekjab* [spirit], and she could produce children or anything by magic.

Combat Song of Ļañinni:
***Al in Ṃur* of the Last War**

Kelu kāān ilikin Barļap | bar jet ṃōṃṃaan.
Rej illu in kotak jarin erōļọk ṃadeān Epoon.
Dāpiji ūb ekkuk eļōñjak | āwilik ettepeep.
Kōmijwōj to āne me kōṃṃalijar
eloñjak āwilik ettepeep.
Keidi nejin Litōkļap rōjarōk ṃadeān Jālooj.
Dāpij ūb ekkuk, eļōñjak āwilik ettepeep.
Kōmijwōj to āne me kōṃṃalijar
eperan ļe e Ļajulobad in pilepile ṃane.
Reikuiaki bar ko, rojarōk ṃadeān
Epoon. Dāpij ūb ekkuk eļōñjak āwilik ettepeep.
Kāare lọ ob iñin Tōkā em Didi.
Raan ṃade em, jibuki im rājet erōļọk
ṃadeen Epoon, dāpij ūb ekkuk, eļōñjak
āwilik ettepeep.

***Roro* of the Song**

The *roro* (chants) of this *al in ṃur* are:

One: *Ju ilikin Epoon bwin ettiak āne em ke, āneo, rōkijbad ke.*

Two: *Rupe likin Epoon ejāmin rup, ṇo waam ar kakōṃkōṃ le āne. Ālibōke in.*

These *roro* were used during wartime only. They were made long ago. Only the Epoon people used them. (A few know them today.)

A *roro* is a song to cheer people, to aid them. It is like a yell. This song of Ļañinni was made after the battle at Rupe.

Hands were shaken in the air during the dance to describe the action of the war, the spear thrusts.

The dance has not been done within the memory of living men because it was against the wishes of the missionaries.

---

1. Ruk is the Marshallese name for Truk or Chuuk, in the Eastern Caroline Islands, far to the west of the Marshalls. See the legends concerning Liwātuonmour from Ep on pages 53 and 54.

Combat Song of Ļañinni: *Al in Ṃur* (Chant) of the Last War

(Ready for battle on the ocean side of Barļap are other men. | They are angry and this group rises and escapes the spears of Epoon.
Hold fast, for they bite. They are many. He moves. He retreats. He pulls out.
All of us land on the island which joins the battle. | The child of Litokļap makes to fight. They lift the spears of Jālooj. Hold fast, for they bite. They are many. He moves. He retreats. He pulls out.
All of us land on the island that joins battle. Ļajulobad is very brave in parrying the spears. | They look over on the reefs. They lift the spears of Epoon. Hold fast, for they bite. They are many. He moves. He retreats. He pulls out.
He makes to fight on the islands of Tōkā and Didi. | Branches of spears and one hundred allies escape the spears of Epoon. Hold fast, for they bite. They are many. He moves. He retreats. He pulls out.)

Chants *(roro)* of the Song

(Stand on the ocean side of Epoon to meet in battle. | The island and what? The island. They go after what?)

(Rupe on the ocean side of Epoon. The wave never breaks our canoe into pieces. It is risky, sir. The island on Āliboke.)

Ļokrap continued his explanation of the war on Epoon: When an *irooj* conquered another, he sometimes killed him and his followers, and sometimes simply dispossessed them.

Defeated *irooj* and *aļap*[s] would be allowed to remain on the land, but would be *kajoor*. At times, they would be ejected completely (for example, the descendants of Jemāluut), but this was not the normal practice. Usually losers were allowed to remain as workers. Some of Jemāluut's descendants are at Naṃo and Naṃdik, and they are considered to be *kajoor*.

After the land is lost, the *irooj* rank is lost. That is, rank depends upon the possession of rights in land.

For example, if the United States took away all of the land of Irooj Lañṃooj, he would still have *irooj* blood, but he would not be respected as *irooj*. He would be just like *kajoor*. Blood does not count; the land is the criterion.

Long ago, the *irooj* were respected as gods. Not like ordinary people. But once they lose a war *(jipọkwe)*, they are like ordinary people. They have lost their *ao* or dignity.[2] For example, if an *aļap* treated workers fairly, died, and had a son, the son would be respected as having *ao* from his father. (It may be lost by bad acts, however.)

Ao comes from within the heart. If you treat the people right or do something to make people respect you or be a hero (in war), it is correlated with goodness and kindness.

Anyone can have it. Also women. This term is not used today.

The last person who had *ao* that I know of was Nelu, my adoptive father who raised me. He had *ao* from *kajoor*. I think I have it. People know me and treat me with respect.[3] Kabua Kabua[4] also has *ao* from his father. All of the workers and the *aļap*[s] brought Nelu food and money without being asked.

---

2. This seems to be analogous to the Polynesian concept of *mana*.
3. Nelu was a chief of Rālik.
4. A contemporary *irooj* of the Rālik Chain, son of the late *irooj* Ļaelañ.

Comments

See Buckingham (1949:2-4) for another version of the invasion of Epoon Atoll. It differs somewhat in detail from the story collected by me, and it is longer. The two Marshallese versions of the combat song are somewhat similar, however. But Buckingham did not record the *roro*.

Ļokrap had told the invasion story and others to Buckingham a few years before I learned Marshallese lore from the aged storyteller *(ri-bwebwenato)* on Epoon.

Buckingham (3) explained; "This battle song, like the one to follow, is in ancient, obsolete Marshallese and is very difficult to translate, since the meaning of many of the words is forgotten. These translations were made by Edward Milne after careful study and in consultation with the storyteller, Ļokrap."

I did not obtain translation of the *al in ṃur* and the *roro* of the war on Epoon at the time I met with Ļokrap.

I learned that they contain elements of the archaic language *(kajin etto).*

I recently translated them as best I could without the help of one more versed in *kajin etto* than I—one who would know the *ṃwilaļ* (deep) or hidden or double meanings or metaphor, if any, in the chants. Therefore, my translation may not be the definitive one.

See Mason (1947:96–98) for "History of land administration in Rālik." He describes the maneuvering for political power by the various chiefs, and the political situation in the area.

The values and attitudes of a people are reflected in their proverbs—with which Marshallese culture is very rich—and in their folktales as well. And they are sometimes to be found in a single word, such as the word *jojoļāār.*

Ṃak Juda explained the word *jojoļāār* to me on Mājro in 1968, as a chick without its mother. It cannot scratch for its food without its mother, and suffers as a result.

It is an analogy used for landless people who have been evicted from their land, he said—the people of Pikinni Atoll and of Ānewetak Atoll, and of most of the islands of Kuwajleen Atoll in modern times, for example, he concluded.

A young Ānewetak Atoll man explained to me on Wūjlañ Atoll in 1955 that, "To be moved away from one's home atoll to another atoll is a little like dying."

79: THE CONQUEST OF PIKINNI ATOLL BY ĻAARKELAÑ

As told by Jojeb, Jokru, Juda, Birbirin, and Jojeia, Kōle 1953

According to tradition, Ļaarkelañ, a member of the Ijjidik *jowi* (clan), was living on Wōdmeej Island on Wōjjā Atoll. (This was six generations ago, according to Pikinni genealogies.)

The son of Ļaarkelañ's *aļap* (lineage head) and *irooj eļap* (paramount chief) committed adultery with Ļaarkelañ's wife, Laujik. Ļaarkelañ became angry, but he could not retaliate against the *bwidak*[1] son of his *irooj* and maternal uncle, as this would entail going to war with the latter. So he decided to go away.

The *roro* (chant) that recalls this incident is as follows: *"Elejlej Ļaarkelañ ilikin Ekǫ-eņ im kaṃōkūti."* (Ļaarkelañ is a very fierce and commanding man, on the ocean side of Ekǫ-eņ.[2] And he starts to fight him.)

He cast off Laujik and held a meeting with his *kajoor* (commoners) to decide which of them should go with him and which should remain on Wōjjā.

About fifty people of the Ṃōkauleej clan and the Ijjidik clan sailed away with Ļaarkelañ in a large war canoe *(waaļļap).*

They first went to Roñļap Atoll [220 miles northwest of Wōjjā] and remained there peacefully with the Roñļap people for many years. The former Wōjjā people intermarried with the Roñļap people and many offspring were produced from these unions. Many of their descendants live on Roñļap today and are known to the present-day Pikinni people.

Ļaarkelañ and his group, whose ranks were increased by the marriages with people of the Ri-Naṃo clan on Roñļap, next gathered his people together and set sail for Pikinni Atoll [about seventy miles to the west of Roñļap].

The expedition landed on Naṃ Island in Pikinni Atoll, where Ļañinpit, the paramount chief of Pikinni, was staying.

Ļaarkelañ chanted:

"Tōkewa tipñōl kūbijūbeja | Epo wōjļā eo | Ikar jab lierer ijōkaņo | Bwe ña i ri-jemmatol." (The canoe arrives and is poled ashore to the beach | The sail is lowered | I was not washed up with the tide | Even though I am a stranger [that is, I will not be pushed around].)

Ļañinpit did not want to fight, so he sailed to Āne-dik Island in the Pikinni lagoon, and putting to sea with all of his people, fled from the atoll, never to be heard from again.

This incident is commemorated in the following *roro:*

"Ioon i buoj ņe dien ṃwij rak in | Dien Kemelet Ļañinpit ro jeļā i aelōñ in out O | Le kañ e je ioon i buoj ke | dien ṃwijṃwij rak in." (On this main village in this atoll is the only one who can cut in the breadfruit season[3] | Ļañinpit is the only one who can com-

---

1. *Bwidak* is a title and rank in the traditional Marshallese hierarchy. The *bwidak* are next in rank to *irooj.* They are the offspring of *irooj* (chiefly) fathers and *kajoor* (commoner) mothers.

2. *Ekǫ-eņ* is the name of a land parcel *(wāto)* on Kuwajleen Atoll.

3. Open the breadfruit season by cutting (harvesting) the first breadfruit of the season. This important ceremony was the prerogative of the chiefs. See Webster (1942:342–343) and Leach (1949[1]:391) for first-fruit ceremonies. Mason (1954:21–22) had earlier recorded the oral history of the Pikinni people, including the conquest and settlement of Pikinni. This was basically the same as that recorded by me in this account, with some differences in details.

mand | Everyone in this main village in this atoll knows this—O | The only one in this main village who can cut in the breadfruit season.)

Ļaarkelañ and his group then settled down in their new home, Pikinni.

In the time of Ļairuj, the *mañden* (maternal nephew) of Ļaarkelañ—son of his sister Libaidik—a canoe from Wōtto Atoll landed on Pikinni with a war party led by Ļapelu. Battle was joined with Ļairuj and his Pikinni warriors, and the Wōtto group lost, suffering heavy casualties, including Ļapelu, who was speared to death by Ļairuj. The survivors then fled Pikinni.

Later, in the time of Ļakejibuki, the *mañden* of Ļairuj, relative conflict ensued when Loemi, the grandson of Lijimjim, sister of Ļaarkelañ and older sister to Libaidik, landed on Pikinni after drifting from Roñļap. He and his four companions tried to wage guerilla warfare against the Pikinnians, but all were killed. (Lijimjim had married into the Roñļap group and remained there with her husband and children when her brother and sister emigrated to Pikinni.)

Comments

A slightly different version of the invasion and conquest of Pikinni was told to Leonard DeBrum and me by Pikinni *aļap* Kilon on Kōle in 1952. That account is given here in what follows.

Ļatipiej, a chief of Ratak *(irooj in Ratak),* conquered Pikinni Atoll. Some of his group were of the Ṃōkauleej clan *(jowi),* some were of the Jidikdik clan, chiefs. [Pikinni / Kōle people belong to these clans today.]

Some of the people who were on Pikinni when the settlers came fled by outrigger canoes, after their defeat in battle.

Half of them remained on Pikinni and were told by Ļatipiej to remain and he would take care of them.

Ļatipiej told the people, "I am going to take care of everyone on the island. I am *irooj.*"

Ļatipiej had *ekkan* (tribute) made by *aļap* Ļañinpit—he was the number one *irooj* on the island before the Pikinni settlers arrived.

Different details of the conquest of Pikinni were given to Raymond DeBrum and me by Jǫwej, a high-ranking man of Northern Ratak, on Mājro in 1952. He stated that the ancestor of Juda [Magistrate of Kōle at the time] and other *aļap*s drifted away from Ādkup Atoll in a canoe. Two commoner *(kajoor)* brothers on Wōjjā had started to fight. The older brother wanted to kill the younger brother.

The younger man and some people went out in some canoes.

They left the island (atoll) to find new land to live on.

(The brothers were members of the Jidikdik clan of Wōjjā.)

They reached Pikinni after their first landfall at Roñļap. And then Wōtto. They were chased away by the people of these two atolls, and had to fight or perish at Pikinni. They gained the upper hand.

I do not know for sure what happened to the original Pikinni people. They either left the island or accepted the chief who had conquered them.

Jo̧wej also told me the story of the Pikinni people and the first canoe.

Long ago on Pikinni they built a large canoe. They were the first Marshallese to know how to do this.

People from Ānewetak supported them with food while they were building it.

Ļowa and Ļōm̧tal taught them how to do this. I do not know who these two were. I do not know whether these two were real men or just talk, because there is a school of sharks between the two atolls. These are the ones who brought the food. Today people may say [that] there are the people that brought the food to Pikinni when they were people—[they] later became sharks—I do not know why they changed.

These people walked on the water (like Peter).[4]

Then the Pikinni people taught all the other Marshallese how to build canoes. The Pikinni canoes were faster than the others in the Japanese times.

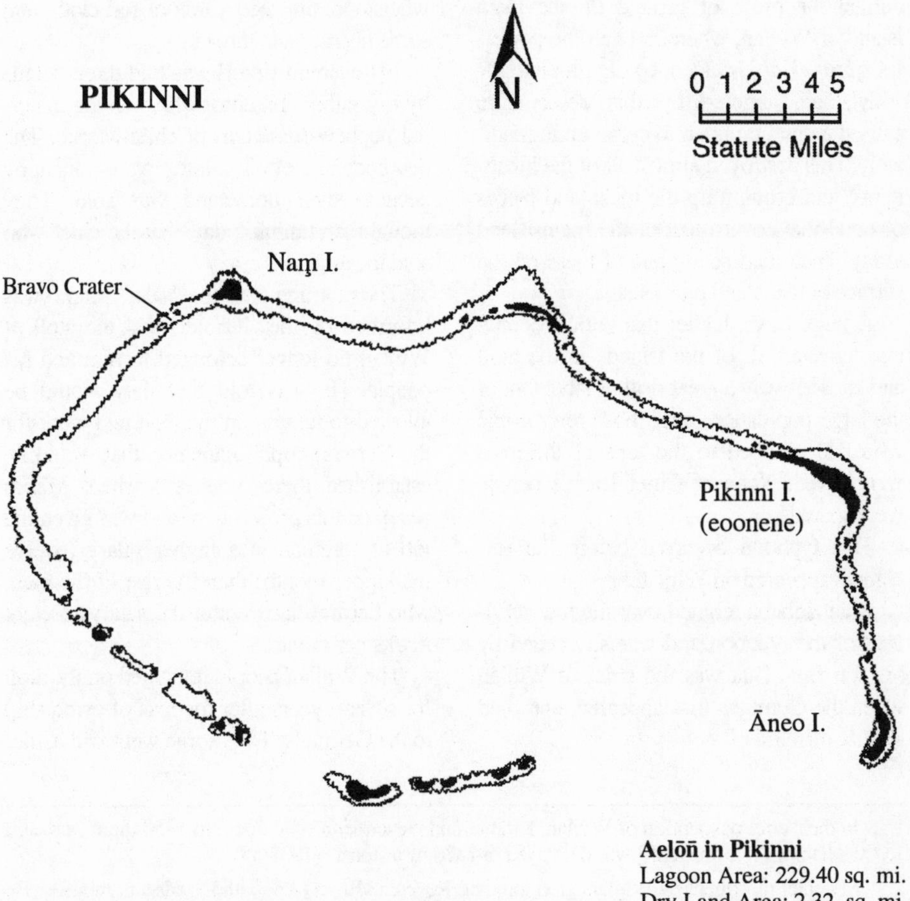

4. Holy Bible: Matthew 14:22–33.

80: EARLY HISTORY OF THE PEOPLE OF WŪJLAÑ ATOLL

As told by Reverend Ernej, Livai, and Jojeb, Wūjlañ 1955

Long ago, there were two groups on Wūjlañ, each of which was headed by a chief: Jobabu, who ruled the western part of the atoll (Rālik), and Raan, who ruled the eastern part (Rear).

The two groups fought for supremacy, and Raan won, but died in battle. Jobabu and his group, angered because of their defeat, defiled the piece of ground on the main island of Wūjlañ, wherein dwelt the powerful spirit *(ekjab)* M̧aļoeņ, by digging into it.

M̧aļoeņ, angered by this desecration, caused a great typhoon to come up immediately. This destroyed almost all of the inhabitants, and brought up the rocks and pieces of coral that cover most of the main island today. There had been none of these on the surface of the island previously.

A huge wave, higher than a tall coconut tree, covered all of the islands in the atoll and carried away a great deal of land. Out of the large population, only those few people who had climbed to the tops of the trees were saved. None of Chief Raan's people were spared.

This typhoon occurred before the foreigners appeared on Wūjlañ.[1]

Chief Jobabu reigned over the few survivors of the typhoon and was succeeded by his son Bua. Bua was the chief of Wūjlañ when the Germans first appeared, and died shortly thereafter.[2]

It is told that Marko, son and successor of chief Bua,[3] was made drunk by the German traders. After he had reached the point of intoxication, he was asked if he wanted to sell the atoll. When he replied in the affirmative: "Go ahead and take it," the Germans gave him the following articles in exchange for the atoll: a picture book, a gun, an axe, two dogs, a big knife, a box of tobacco, a whetstone, nineteen yards of red cloth, and some needles and thread.

I [Reverend Ernej] was told these details by my father, Takunto, who was the maternal nephew *(mañden)* of chief Marko. The descendants of Takunto were unhappy because their homeland was sold. They thought, and think today, that the chief who sold the atoll was crazy.

The morning after the "sale," Marko was informed by the Germans that the atoll of Wūjlañ no longer belonged to him and his people. He was told that they would be allowed to remain on the atoll and work for the German copra plantation that would be established there, if they wished. Marko accepted this proposition, and was given the job of foreman at a higher salary (twelve marks per month) than the rest of the men, who became laborers at the salary of eight marks per month.

The Wūjlañ people remained on the atoll for several years after the loss of ownership to the Germans. Then some went with Chief

---

1. In their brief description of Wūjlañ, Krämer and Nevermann state that: "In 1850 there were still 1,000 inhabitants. It [the atoll] was destroyed in 1870 by a storm" (1938:55).

2. My chief informant on Wūjlañ Atoll lore was Reverend Ernej (Anej), the Protestant minister. He was a descendant of Chief Jojabu.

3. Inheritance of the chieftainship was patrilineal on Wūjlañ and on Ānewetak, as it is today. It was and is normally matrilineal in the rest of the Marshall Islands.

Marko on a German schooner to Jālooj Atoll [over 500 miles to the southeast].

Those who had married into the Ānewetak Atoll group, and their children, did not go to Jālooj—they later moved to Ānewetak.

Kabua [the powerful paramount chief *(irooj ļapļap)* of that area] took pity on Marko and his people and gave them the island of Pin̄ļap in Jālooj Atoll.[4]

Many of their descendants live on Jālooj Atoll today, and in other parts of the Marshall Islands, and there are descendants of two women who were taken to Ponape by sailors in German times still living on Ponape today.

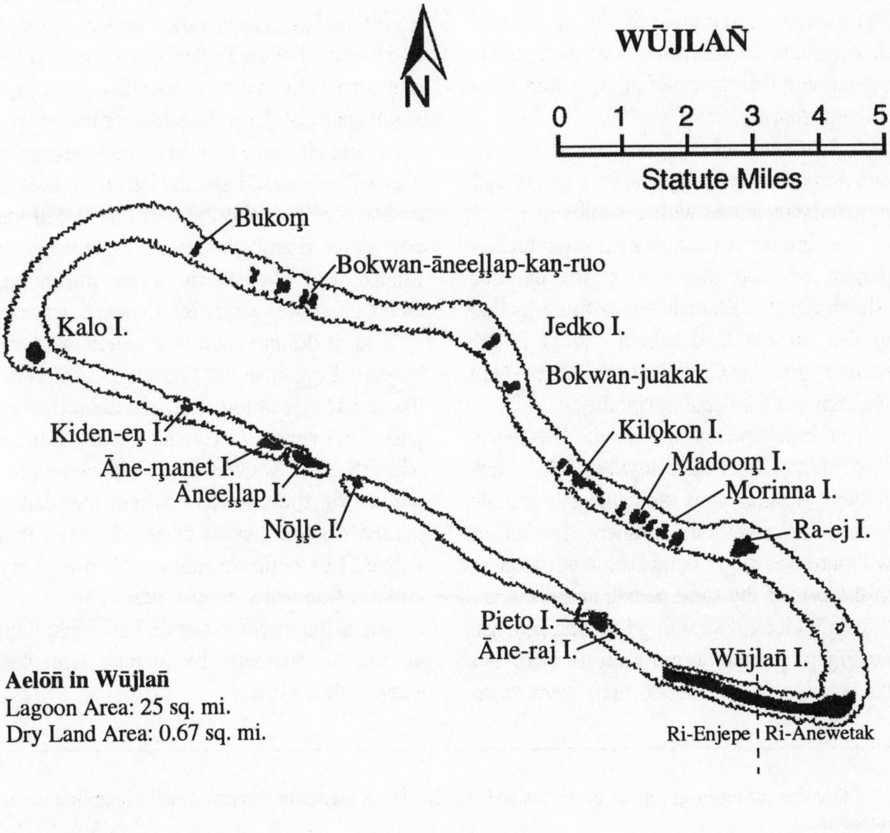

4. Krämer and Nevermann report that "in 1880 the last 20 inhabitants [of Wūjlan̄] were brought to Jaluit [Jālooj] by Chief Leuak [Ļoeak] . . ." (1938:56).

81: ĀNEWETAK ATOLL HISTORY: WARFARE WITH INVADERS

As told by Irooj Ebream, Irooj Joanej, Reverend Ernej, Livai, Jorim, and Jojeb, Wūjlañ 1955

The first arrival of outsiders was when Ļarelañ, a chief from the western Marshalls, drifted ashore in a large canoe, with many followers.

At that time, there were many more Ānewetak people than there are now, a thousand or more.

Ļarelañ first landed on Enjepe Island. The Enjepe people were living on one half of the island at that time, and the invaders moved onto the other half of the island without opposition.

A Marshallese[1] woman went to the village of the Enjepe people and started pounding pandanus leaves with a pounder.

The Enjepe woman cleaned some freshly caught fish and threw away the entrails, whereupon the Marshallese woman picked up the entrails, and asked: "What is the name of this fish?" (This is an indirect way of asking for food and hospitality.)

The Enjepe people answered, "This fish is *ban*,"[2] but did not offer any food. The Marshallese woman then took the fish entrails back to the camp of the invaders. Ļarelañ, an evil man, was angry at this show of rudeness on the part of the local people and declared, "At ten o'clock,[3] we will go to war, because the Enjepe people do not send us food." At the appointed time, all of them went to do battle with the Enjepe group at their village. All of the men and women went forward, while all of the women chanted: *"Jokwoļọk, ekwōjok ban eo, | Ikōt eo, | Du eo perak eo du."* (The net has been cast, the *ban* is caught. | What kind of fish is this? | Beat the drums, you drummers! It is *perak*.)[4]

After the challenge was given, battle was joined, and the Marshallese invaders defeated and killed all of the Enjepe people, except for one man who fled to Ānewetak Island in a small canoe. A large Marshallese canoe pursued him. He came to a very small passage in the reef between Jādool and Māddeen islands and was able to slip through first to tell the Ānewetak Island people of the disaster at Enjepe, and warn them of the impending attack of sixty or eighty invaders in the canoe.

The invading canoe was unable to enter the small passage and had to go around on the ocean side of the atoll, and enter the big pass between Ānewetak and Ikuden islands. The Ānewetak people were prepared for the invaders when the canoe landed on the lagoon beach at Ānewetak Island. The battle commenced immediately and the Ānewetak people won.

All of the invaders were killed, including, among the women, the woman who had caused the trouble.

---

1. Note the strong in-group attitude revealed by the use of the term "Marshallese" as applied to the outsiders.

2. *Lutjanus vaigiensis,* snapper (Strasburg 1964:3).

3. Note the incorporation of the Western concept of marking the hourly passage of time into the oral tradition of the islanders.

4. *Lethrinus kallopterus,* scavenger (U.S. Public Health Service 1958:1).

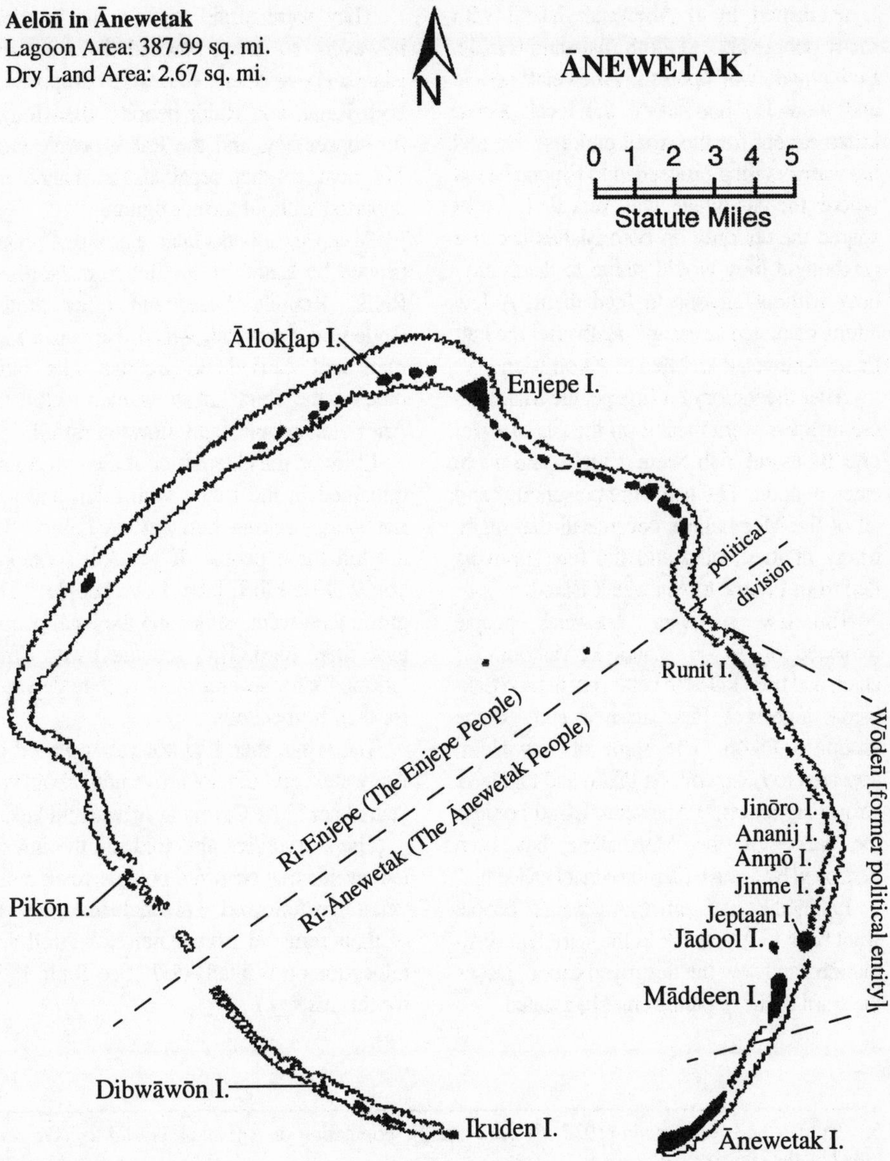

About two years later, a few, perhaps six, Marshallese drifted ashore on Ānewetak Island. Their chief was Ļakatak.

One of the Ānewetak men lied and said that the castaway chief had stolen a canoe rope from the island. The Ānewetak people became angry at this alleged abuse of their hospitality and invited the castaways to the reef to fish with them. When they got them all out on the reef and away from their canoe, they speared them all to death; even the women were killed.

About three years after this incident, the large canoe of Ļowa, chief of Wōtto and

Ujae, drifted in to Ānewetak Island with many people aboard, both male and female. Ļowa made war upon the Ānewetak people and won. He had all of the local people killed except for the small children. He and his warriors then proceeded to Enjepe Island where the slaughter was repeated. Ļowa spared the children on both islands because he thought they would starve to death anyhow without anyone to feed them. A few adults managed to escape death after the battle on Ānewetak and fled to Pikōn Island.[5]

After the victory on Enjepe, the Marshallese invaders went fishing off the island. Over one thousand fish were caught and were eaten at noon. The fish were poisonous,[6] and all of the Marshallese became ill that night. Many of them died and the few survivors fled from Enjepe to Ānewetak Island.

The few surviving Ānewetak people remained on Pikōn Island. Lewinkōm, the chief, had been killed in battle, but his son Ļakinedik, father of Pita, survived and led the group to Pikōn. The spirit of Ļewinkōm appeared to Ļakinedik on Pikōn and told him: "You may return to Ānewetak Island because the canoe of the Marshallese has been destroyed by a wave (demon)[7] that I called up."

Ļakinedik and other Ānewetak people went back to Ānewetak as the spirit had commanded and saw the destroyed canoe, just as the spirit of the departed chief had stated.

They were afraid to fight the invaders, however, so they proceeded to another island. The invaders, who were composed of both Ratak and Rālik people,[8] then fought for supremacy, and the Ratak people won. The invaders then repaired their canoe and departed without further fighting.

About six months later, a group of people headed by Ļatowan, a chief from Northern Rālik (Rońdik, Ujae, and other atolls), landed on Ānewetak Island. He was a kind man and caused no trouble. His older brother, the chief Labio, wanted to kill the Ānewetak people, but Ļatowan refused.

Lijuwor, the elder sister of the two chiefs, remained in the canoe with them and told Ļatowan, backing him against Labio, "Do not kill these people. If you kill someone, you will be killed later. Love people!" The group then went ashore and the local people gave them food. They remained with Chief Ļakinedik for several months, then departed for their home atolls.

The white men had not yet appeared on Ānewetak, and did not arrive until about two years later.[9] The Germans arrived still later.[10]

The storytellers also told me the important events that occurred on Ānewetak in the years that followed. This included the story of their removal from Ānewetak Atoll and relocation on Wūjlañ Atoll. (See Tobin 1967 for this history.)

---

5. Krämer and Nevermann (1938:56) state that the population of Ānewetak is said to have been killed by the Ujae people.

6. Toxic fish are found throughout the Marshall Islands.

7. Marshallese use the word *tiṃoṇ* (demon), introduced by the Christian missionaries and their Bible, to describe a malevolent supernatural entity. This loanword has been thoroughly incorporated into the Marshallese language. However, it has not replaced the traditional terms for various spirits.

8. Ratak is the eastern chain of the Marshallese archipelago, and Rālik is the western chain.

9. This may refer to the visit of Captain Fearn, who charted the atoll in 1798 (Morison 1944:97).

10. Note the distinction made by the informants between the arrival of the white men *(ri-pālle),* and the arrival of the Germans *(ri-Jāmne),* the former generic, and the latter specific.

82: STORY ABOUT *KIDU IN LǪJET* (DOG OF THE SEA)

As told by Reverend Ernej, Wūjlan̄ 1955

In the time before the white man came, a *kidu in lǫjet* (dog of the sea) came out of the water at Ānewetak Atoll on Pikōn Island.

When anyone came to Pikōn, the *kidu* barked, and the people were afraid and fled.

Finally, two men came, and this *kidu* again barked. And these men threw rocks at it and it died.

These men took it and cooked it in an earth oven, and ate it.

After they had finished, they again sailed to the main island and told that all of them should eat. No one would be harmed from it.

This story is alive to these days. People tell the story laid down [passed down] from those times to these days [today]. They say the thing is really true.

Comments

This particular "dog of the sea" might have been a Hawaiian monk seal *(Monachus schauinslandi)* that had drifted down from the Northwestern (Leeward) Hawaiian Islands where these animals are found today.

These rather isolated islands are located north-northeast of the Marshall Islands, and the prevailing currents and winds come from that general direction.

Certainly seals do resemble dogs in that they have dog-like heads, and they do bark similarly to canines. The German word for seal, *seehund,* literally "sea dog," indicates this.

The *kidu in lǫjet* could have been any species of the *Pinnipedia* aquatic carnivorous animals (seals, sea lions, and walruses). All of these animals make barking noises, and all of them are edible.

They make lengthy migrations for feeding, breeding, and bearing their young. Accidental or drift voyages to the Marshall Islands are certainly within the realm of possibility. They have occurred elsewhere.

For example, one such voyage of one of these animals, in the Atlantic Ocean, was described recently as follows: "In Coanna [Corunna?], Spain, residents were fascinated as a 9-foot, 3,300 pound walrus snoozed in the sun. It apparently had traveled thousands of miles from its home in frigid northern waters" (*Honolulu Advertiser,* October 28, 1986, Milt Guss).

Another such arrival was more recently reported from Southern California, "A seal of a breed that makes its home only on the coasts of Greenland and northern Canada beached herself here this week, and her appearance 8,000 to 12,000 miles from her normal habitat has marine scientists perplexed. . . . The 275-pound six-foot-long hooded seal arrived at the Silver Strand beach in Coronado, San Diego County.

"Hooded seals do have a history of wandering. Some have been sighted as far south as Florida and as far east as Portugal. Still, such trips are only 2,000 to 3,000 miles out of the animals' natural habitat. The senior curator of Sea World of San Diego, where the seal was placed stated that: 'To reach Pacific waters . . . this seal had to have swum across the Arctic Ocean and through the Bering Strait. I cannot believe that it swam through the Panama Canal'" (*San Francisco Chronicle,* July 27, 1990).

Also in the *San Francisco Chronicle* (May 12, 1992), "Brigantine, New Jersey: A baby harp seal was discovered Sunday on a beach in Southern New Jersey, the third Arctic seal found 2,000 miles from its natural habitat in a week, a wildlife expert said."

A pinniped from the Bering Sea or the North Pacific Ocean might very well have been described as a *kidu in lọjet* by the Ānewetak people, or indeed by any Marshallese group, had it beached itself on their island or appeared in their lagoon. Such incidents may have been the origin of the stories of the legendary sea dogs.

82: BWEBWENATO IN KIDU IN LỌJET

Ri-bwebwenato: Rōplen Ernej, Wūjlañ 1955

Ilo iien ko ṃokta jān an itok ripālle eaar ato juon kidu [in] lọjet ilo Ānewetak ilo āne eo Pikōn.

Ilo iien otemjej armej rej itok ñan Pikōn kidu [eo] ej kōŋaan rorror im eḷap an armej ijo mijake im ko.

Āliktata ej itok ruo eṃṃaan im kidu in ej bar rorror. Im ḷōṃa rein rej kade im emej. Ḷōṃa rein rej bōke im uṃwini im kañe.

Ṃwijin aerro kōmatte rej bar jerak ñan eoonene im peḷọk bwe erwōj en ṃōñā. Ejjeḷọk en ar jorrāān jāne.

Bwebwenato in ej mour wōt ñan raan kein. Armej raar bwebwenato liktak jān iien ko ñan raan kein. Rej ba men eo ej lukkuun ṃool.

83: THE WAR BETWEEN ĻAUNA AND THE WOLEAI PEOPLE

As told by Kabua Kabua, Mājro 1970

The Woleai people, a large number, had drifted to the Marshall Islands and landed on Kōle Island. They had their large canoes. They were very long.[1]

Ļauna and Irooj (Chief) Kabua [informant's grandfather], whose advisor Ļauna was, and Irooj Litōkwa came up from Epoon with a fleet of three sailing canoes. They had not heard of the arrival of the Woleai fleet, but had just sailed up to the Jālooj area. They had not expected to go to war.

When they found out about the Woleai people on Kōle, they went over to investigate. They met with the Woleai people and did not fight at the time.

Ļauna, who was an expert in *bubu* (divination), made the *bubu, bubu in maan̄* (folding and reading the folds of strips of pandanus leaves).

He saw that it was bad. That is, the situation was threatening. He told Kabua and Litōkwa, but they said that it was all right, and that they wanted to make friends with the Woleai men. So Ļauna said all right. That was all he could do. Then the Marshallese sailed away from Kōle toward Jālooj. Kabua and Litōkwa's canoes were ahead and Ļauna was behind. A few miles off Mājrwirōk [an island in the southern part of Jālooj Atoll], Ļauna saw the sail of Kabua's canoe raised (hoisted) and moving from side to side *(jupej)*.[2] This was the traditional signal for war.

So all of the canoes turned around and fought the canoes of the Woleai people, which had been following them. It was a naval battle. The battle was fought off Jālooj Island.

All of the Woleai men were killed. There were no survivors. (There had only been men in the Woleai group.) The canoes were allowed to drift off.

Spears and daggers *(ņade im jāje)* were used. Ļauna was an expert at hurling a spear at a target. [Kabua illustrated this by pointing to Robert Riemers' store, several hundred yards way from the Post Office where we were standing. He said that Ļauna could hit a target from the Post Office to the store if he were there.]

Then following the victory, the fleet made for Mājrwirōk. Kabua told me that the Marshallese felt that the Woleai people wanted to kill all of them, as they were the first Marshallese encountered. Then the Woleai men would be able to conquer the Marshalls, or so they probably thought. Therefore, the danger had to be eliminated.

I told Kabua that I had heard the story, but with a slightly different element. That is one of the young Marshallese men opened one of the Woleai men's magic basket,[3] which was highly taboo, although the Marshallese man did not know this.

This action made the Woleai men angry, and the war started.

---

1. Woleai (0leai) Atoll is in the Western Carolines.

2. *Jupej* is an ancient word *(naan in etto),* Kabua explained, and is a signal for war *(kakōļļe in tariņae).*

3. People of the Yap area were, and still are, reputed to be powerful magicians, and practitioners of malevolent as well as benevolent magic.

Kabua said that he had heard this part, too, and it was another reason for fighting.

In the story that I had heard about eighteen years prior to my conversation with Kabua, the battle took place just off Kōle. And Marshallese were also killed, as well as Woleai men.

One of the chiefly lineages *(bwij in irooj)* was almost exterminated, as I remember the story.

84: STORY ABOUT THE WAR BETWEEN THE MARSHALLESE PEOPLE AND THE WOLEAI PEOPLE

As told by Jelibōr Jam, Kuwajleen 1975

At the time when the canoes of the chiefs of the Marshalls saw a canoe of the Woleai people, they took the people and abandoned their canoe (the canoe of the Woleai people) because it was leaking badly—because it had drifted for a long time.[1]

And the people there (the Woleai people) were very hungry.

And Chief Ļoeak[2] took them and appointed [treated] them like his children, and gave them their food to eat and water to drink. Chief Ļoeak treated them very well.

And Ļoeak made his will [promise] known to the chiefs, all of the Marshallese chiefs, that they should not lay their hands on them (harm them), because Ļoeak said "children" [meaning that the castaways were as his children].

From that message of Ļoeak, everyone, chiefs to commoners and lineage heads, treated the Woleai people very well.

(Ļoeak took them to land and they stayed with him. I do not now where it was.)

One day the chiefs sailed to Jālooj. And Chief Ļoeak put the Woleai people, his children, aboard his canoe. The name of the canoe was *Kaiuiu.*[3]

On the day that they sailed, their food [supply] together was very good, but the evening of the next day, when their food was finished, two Woleai men went to windward on the passenger platform of the canoe, and sat there for four days.

On the fourth day, they saw Kōle and continued going when it was sunset. The men of Ļoeak's group heard the Woleai people muttering (in low voices), which the Marshallese could not understand, there where the two of them sat, with the bundle of spears that was there. (There were many Woleai people on Ļoeak's canoe. The canoe was big, more than one hundred people could be put aboard it.)[4]

---

1. Woleai Atoll is approximately 1800 statute miles to the west of Kōle, and is in the Western Carolines, part of Yap State, to the west of Truk State. Kōle Island is about thirty-three miles from Jālooj Atoll. In his detailed listing of voyages of Micronesians to distant places in Oceania, Riesenberg (1965:161) states, "Woleai to Kōle: (a) Erdland, 1914:11, 1884?: 'About 30 years ago, three canoes landed with chieftain Leon and natives from Oleai islands aboard at Kili.' (b) Krämer and Nevermann, 1938:204. 'In the '80s, a sea battle was fought near Kili [Kōle] by Woleai castaways.'" Other landings of people from Woleai and Yap have been recorded and are listed by Riesenberg. These include "Yap to Kili: ABCFM letters, Capt. Miller to Capt. Tengstrom, Jan. 1869, and Rev. Kapali, Oct. 21,1869. 1869: 'Two Yap canoes, 14 men and one woman adrift five months, reached Kili; all killed by Marshallese'" (162).

2. Ļoeak was an important chief of Rālik (the western chain of the Marshalls). He lived into the German period.

3. *Kaiuiu* is salt water and fresh water found spurting up into the air on reefs on Ellep, Piñlep, Jālooj, and elsewhere, and salt water on reefs on other islands such as Kuwajleen. These are known as "blowholes" in Hawai'i.

The usual custom in the Marshalls, and elsewhere in the Pacific, was to kill any strangers who appeared on the island. Castaway males were usually all killed and the women and children were spared and incorporated into the island community. However, exceptions to killing adult males were made, and later everyone was spared. Ļoeak's act was obviously one of compassion, and was so evaluated in this story by the Marshallese participants—and by the narrator.

At midnight, their muttering was gone. But they [the Woleai people] did not sleep. And the men, the men in Ļoeak's canoe, well recognized the custom of the Woleai people and thought it ill of them being with the spears.

When it was sunrise, the Woleai people again muttered.

And one of the men [the Woleai men] shouted out to the Woleai men who were seated on the canoe [hull] and those on the canoe platform.[5] And said "E-au!" (Woleai language. I do not now the meaning of it.) None of the Marshallese knew what the men were talking about.

When they had said "E-au!" three times, the Woleai people who were sitting on the canoe platform began to do as they had declared. (What they had said: "E-au!" And they chopped off the head of Lipepe. Lipepe was the spouse[6] of Chief Ļoeak. After they chopped Lipepe, they seized the child, the child of Lipepe, and again chopped and threw him into the sea (as they had done with Lipepe).

At the time when the Marshallese and the chief were alarmed and they went to spear the Woleai people, there was no way for them to go [gain access] to the spears, because the Woleai people were sitting on the spears. And the Woleai people quickly seized the spears and speared all of the Marshallese people on the canoe.

At the time when the Woleai people moved around fast on the canoe and chopped the Marshallese people and speared them, many Marshallese had jumped from the canoe, and some of them fended off the attack and were not hit by the spears.

(The Marshallese did not have spears and they fended off the spears with only their arms.)

---

4. Informant sketched the canoe and the location of the Woleai people and the spears, and the Marshallese crew and passengers. He explained that the Marshallese canoes in the olden days were very big—much longer than those of modern times. *"Wa eo waan irooj Ṃuto (Irooj in Rālik) ṃōttan Ļaelañ im Jeiṃata im er. Elukkuun aetok; im kiju ko rōkillep jān armej kilep. Iaar lo jebwe ko. Raar likūti ioon lōb ko an irooj Ṃuto im ledik eo nājin. Rej jutak ioon bōran ioon juon āne in Ujae iturin to, āne in edik, Bōkārōk. Rej bōk kiju an wa ñan Eañjen-Rakjen, wa eo waan Kabua. Ej pād ṃae iien an Jepaan."* "The canoe of Chief Ṃuto (chief in Rālik) part of Ļaelañ and Jeiṃata [chiefs of Rālik and sons of Chief Kabua—halfbrothers—Ļaelañ was the father of the contemporary Chief Kabua Kabua, and Jeimata (whom I knew) was the father of the late Chief Ļōjjeiļañ Kabua] and [his people]. It was really long; and the masts were bigger than very big people. I saw the steering paddles. They put them on the graves of Chief Ṃuto and his young daughters. They stood at the head on an island of Ujae beside the pass, a small island, Bōkā-rōk. They took the masts of the canoe to the *Eañjen-Rakjen* ("From North to South"), the ship of Kabua. It remained until the Japanese times." [This has been described to me as a *jikuna* (schooner).] As the informant explained further, "the *Eañjen-Rakjen* [was] a big ship with two masts. It had sails only. It was bigger than *M/V Yap Islander* [a Trust Territory fieldtrip ship of the 1960s and 1970s]. I sailed on it. Kabua took food to his people on all of his islands and was given Marshallese food and other Marshallese articles such as mats, coconut sennit, and so forth." [Canoe paddles were used to mark the graves in the old days. They were placed at the head of the grave, as informant stated. They reportedly marked only the graves of chiefs and some navigators. See Krämer and Nevermann 1938:211–212 for this and other Marshallese burial customs.]

5. Located on the side of the canoe opposite the side of the outrigger.

6. The wife of the chief was called the *lejļā,* and the corresponding name of the spouse of a chiefess was *irooj eṃṃaan.* They were respected as spouses of the high ranking persons in the society, hence the importance given the killing of Lipepe, wife of Chief Ļoeak, and their son, and commemorated in this story.

And they were tired of looking for a way to jump off [escape], for they recognized that in jumping off, the Woleai people would spear them in the water. And it would be better for them to stay on the canoe and fend off the spears so that they would not be hit.

And one man, his name was Ļejkwōnidik, was the steersman,[7] and he hurried and seized Ļoeak and put him behind himself and fended off [the spears] with the paddle that he used in steering.[8]

The Woleai people speared at the chief and tried. But they did not hit him because Ļejkwōnidik fended them off from him. When the paddle was broken up (from fending off the spears), Ļejkwōnidik thought to jump off with the chief, but because the Woleai people were throwing spears at them at the back of the canoe, there was no time to jump.

And when the paddle was finished and broken up because of the Woleai people spearing and chopping [at] those two, Ļejkwōnidik had nothing to fend off with, but he fended off with his arms.

When Ļejkwōnidik saw the group pause in their spearing at the two of them, he seized the chief and threw him into the sea. When the Woleai people speared at the chief in the water, Ļejkwōnidik seized the spears, the spears of the chief, and jumped behind the chief and swam away from beside the canoe. The Woleai people continued spearing at the two. Ļejkwōnidik made a determined effort for the chief, so that he would not be hit. And the two of them were far from the canoe. And the Woleai people stopped spearing them then.

At the time, the people in Ļauna's canoe looked around and saw Ļoeak jumping from his canoe.[9] Only the Woleai people remained on Ļoeak's canoe—all of the Marshallese who had been on Ļoeak's canoe having jumped from it. Ļoeak's canoe was very large and fast because the Woleai people had not used the line that controls the side-to-side movement of the sail.[10] And it went to leeward. But it still remained in position, and the canoe did not run very much. (In canoe language *eiair* means 'remains, does not move'.)

When the people on Ļauna's canoe saw Ļoeak and the people in his canoe jump, the people in Ļauna's canoe hurried and paddled under sail. (They helped the sail—double.)

For they saw the Marshallese jumping and they said, "It is clear that they make war on Ļoeak's canoe, for the people are jumping, but that canoe is going to leeward."

After a few minutes,[11] Ļauna's canoe proceeded ahead and touched on the outrigger, the outrigger of the canoe of the Woleai people. And Ļauna tied the outrigger, the outrigger of the canoe of the Woleai people, onto the platform of his canoe.[12]

At the time when the Woleai people were spearing Ļauna on the outrigger, he seized it and tied it up, so that the canoes would be

7. The steersman *(ri-jebwebwe)* handled the huge steering paddles on the large canoes. He was highly skilled at his work, which was important in avoiding the many reefs, negotiating the narrow and sometimes shallow passages, and keeping the canoe on course through waves and currents.

8. The informant sketched the positions of the men in the canoe and later in the water in the ensuing action.

9. Ļauna was an important chief of Rālik.

10. *liep eo.*

11. Note the use of English loanword *minit* and the accompanying concept.

12. Informant sketched the result of this action in my notebook—the canoes tied together. The *rọñ* is the canoe platform opposite the outrigger.

firmly [secured] together. The Woleai people did not stop their spearing away at Ļauna where he was tying up the canoes so that they would not separate—so that their war would be good [so that they would prevail].

When Ļauna was entirely finished tying up, he spoke to all of the men on his canoe, and said, "Well, it is already time for all of us to make this war!"

And Ļauna jumped from the platform of his canoe and went west on the outrigger to the west.[13]

The Woleai people leaped up and cut, and some of the Woleai people speared, but did not hit with the spears nor wound with the knives of the Woleai people; but when Ļauna speared a Woleai man, the Woleai men were tired of fending off the spears but that spear (Ļauna's) continued to go and speared (killed) that man.

The Woleai men saw that Ļauna was very skilled in warfare. Finally, the Woleai men stood on the canoe and each one had a spear and speared at Ļauna. When he went to the west and came close to the Woleai men, they threw about fifty spears at Ļauna. But he was not hit. He was not hit, but many Woleai men were hit by Ļauna and jumped from the canoe and swam away from the canoe.

And Ļauna again returned Ļoeak and his people to his [Ļoeak's] canoe. All of the Woleai people who were still alive were swimming upon the sea.

At the time, Ļauna was really sorry about the women (Woleaian) and cried, but because the Woleai people had started the war and had killed the spouse of the chief, Lipepe, and the boy her son, Ļauna meditated upon these things. And only went ahead of some of the canoes, but he said to himself, "If those canoes will take the Woleai people aboard, good." For he was very sorry, and because he wanted to make peace thus, he proceeded westward on the place to sit on the outrigger to the west, and came near the canoe of the Woleai people.[14]

And at the time when he speared the men, they speared first.[15] But when he came near the group, they did not throw away their mistake [apologize], but they jumped from the canoe. And Ļauna did not speak to the them, but he did not spear them in the sea. And he ended the war.

And Ļauna's canoes went away, and went away to Jālooj. The Woleai people were gone. They [the Marshallese] took perhaps one Woleai woman. Her name was Leon. But all of the Woleai people remained in the sea and swam. But they were not able to reach land, and perhaps they died.[16]

(The thought of Ļoeak, when he took the Woleai people to be his children, was that he would take them to Mejatto [an island in Jālooj Atoll].)

It is ended.

Ļauna was Iroojin Eañ im Rōk: Chief of the North and the South [in Rālik, the western chain of the Marshalls]. He was the father of Neimat, spouse of [Irooj] Ļaelañ and mother of Kabua Kabua [a contemporary chief].

---

13. Informant sketched this scene for me—the relative positions of the chief and the enemy on the canoes.

14. Informant sketched this scene for me. In all of his sketches of the action and his description of the battle, it was as if he was explaining very recent events. There was no hesitation whatsoever. It was like an eyewitness account. Indeed, this was typical of his method of narration.

15. Informant recapitulated the action to explain Ļauna's attitude and justification of his final action toward the enemy.

16. Note the discrepancy between the identification of Leon in the story as a woman, and as a chieftain by Erdland.

Perhaps there were no white men on Jebwad [Island, Jālooj Atoll] at the time of this story.

Ḷauna gave the atoll of Rōn̄dik to Ḷejkwōnidik so that he would be *aḷap* [hereditary head of the atoll], because he had saved him. It was *ṃadejinkōt.*[17]

Ṃakwilōn̄, father of Aronean̄, was *aḷap* later.[18]

I learned the story of the war from Ḷojōr, the old man who adopted me on Jālooj when I was twelve years old.

I stayed with him until I was twenty-one years old.

He was in the war when he was a boy. When he revealed [told] the story to me, he was a real old man.

Ḷauna was very brave, and he was not afraid of any person. He was not afraid of the German official, as the story tells.[19]

Comments

A certain amount of upward mobility was possible in traditional Marshallese culture. Special rank and status could be achieved, albeit limited, in this highly structured society.

As informants have explained, the title of *ḷeatōktōk,* or leader, was awarded to deserving individuals along with land tenure rights that became hereditary.

Other individuals were able to achieve positions of leadership and authority in relation to their chiefs, who were at the apex of the feudalistic society, for specific service rendered to their chiefs.

These specialists include war leaders *(ḷakkūk),* stewards *(ri-kōṃōn̄ā),* executioners *(ri-ire),* the navigators *(ri-meto),* the weather forecasters *(ri-lale lan̄, ri-katu),* and others. But their titles were not hereditary except insofar as their maternal nephews or sons might be trained by the specialist to succeed them in their positions if qualified. And this was often the case, apparently.

The specialists were also often rewarded with gifts of land for their services.

The fine gradations in hereditary rank and title are no longer as important nor as sharply delineated as they once were. And there is obviously no longer a need for certain specialists.

17. *Ṃọrjinkot*: "take from the spear" (Rālik), *bōkṃaanṃade* or *ṃade* (Ratak). This is land given by a chief for bravery in war. See Tobin (1958:34–37) for details.

18. Ṃakwilōn̄ (who was also a well-recognized navigator) and Aronean̄ were both living when I was in the Marshalls. I knew and respected both of these intelligent, prominent, and likeable men. They are now (as of 1984) dead.

19. Informant was referring to an incident that he had related to me previously. He told it to me to illustrate the character of the famous chief Ḷauna. Ḷauna had had an angry confrontation with a German official. The German was in the wrong, but he challenged and threatened Ḷauna. But Ḷauna refused to back down. He challenged the German, and concluded his remarks by saying, "Go ahead and kill me if you want to!" standing in front of the official and waiting for his reaction. The result was that the German backed down. So Ḷauna won the argument (and obviously enhanced his prestige with the Marshallese, as the remembrance of the incident over so many generations attests). The story has a sort of David and Goliath flavor to it—an "underdog" victory over the bully theme.

The details and dynamics of the traditional system are probably known to very few Marshallese today. And with the elimination of warfare and the introduction of foreign institutions, the role of the chiefs has changed considerably, as could be expected.

84: BWEBWENATO IN TARIŅAE EO IKŌTAAN RI-ṂAJEĻ IM RI-WOLEAI

Ri-bwebwenato: Jelibōr Jam, Kuwajleen 1975

Ilo iien eo ke wa ko waan irooj ro i Ṃajeļ raar lo wa eo waan ri-Woleai raar bōk armej ro im joļǫk wa eo waer (wa eo waan ri-Woleai) bwe enana ettal. Kōn an to an peļǫk.

Im armej ro ie (ri-Woleai) rekanooj in kwōle.

Im Irooj Ļoeak eaar bōktok er im likūt er āinwōt nājin. Im leļǫk kijeer ṃōñā im limeer dān. Ekanooj eṃṃan an irooj Ļoeak kōṃṃan ñan er.

Im Ļoeak eaar kalliṃur ñan irooj ro, irooj in Ṃajeļ otemjej bwe ren jab leļǫk peier ñan er (kǫkkure er). Bwe Ļoeak ej ba, "Nājin ro." Jen wōt ennaan in an Ļoeak, aolep, irooj ñan kajoor im aļap ro ekanooj eṃṃan aer kōṃṃan ñan ri-Woleai ro.

(Ļoeak eaar bōkļǫk er āneļǫk im raar pād ippān ie. Ijaje ia.)

Juōn raan eaar jerak tok irooj ro ñan Jālooj. Im Irooj Ļoeak eaar ektake ri-Woleai ro nājin ñan Jālooj. Im Irooj Ļoeak eaar ektake ri-Woleai ro nājin ņa ilo wa eo waan. Etan wa eo Kaiuiu. Ilo raan eo rej jerak ekanooj eṃṃan aer ṃōñā ippān doon kab boñōn eo raan wōt juon ṃōjin wōt aer ṃōñā ej etaļǫk ruo eṃṃaan ñan likiej in keepep in wa eo. Im jijet ie iuṃwin emān raan.

Raan eo kein kemān rej lo Kōle im etal wōt ke etulǫk aļ. Eṃṃaan ro doon Ļoeak rej roñjake an ri-Woleai ro alliñurñur ijo rejro jijet ie, ippān tūr in ṃade ko rej pād ie. (Elōñ ri-Woleai i wa eo waan Ļoeak. Eļap wa eo, jibuki jiṃa armej emaroñ ektake.)

Lukon boñōn eo ejako aerro alliññurñur. Ak rejro (ri-Woleai ro) jab kiki. Im eļap an eṃṃaan ro, eṃṃaan in wa eo waan Ļoeak ekkōl kōn ṃanit eo an ri-Woleai ro im rej ļōmņak nana kōn aerro pād ippān ṃade ko.

Ke ej tak aļ, ri-Woleai ro rej bar alliñurñur. Im ļeo juon (ri-Woleai eo) ej laṃōj ļǫk ñan ri-Woleai ro rej jijet ioon wa eo kab ro i rǫñ. Im ba, "E-au!" (Kajin Woleai. Ijaje meļeļe eo.) Aolep ri-Ṃajeļ ro rejaje ta eo ļōṃaro rej kōnono kake.

Ke ej jilu alen aer ba, "E-au!" Ri-Woleai ro rej jijet i roñ rej jino aer kōṃṃan āinwōt aer kōņaan. (Ta eo raar ba:, "E-au!") Im raar jek bōran Lipepe. Lipepe ej lio ippān irooj eo Ļoeak. Ṃōjin an jek Lipepe rej jibwetok ajiri eo, nājin Lipepe im bar jeke im joļǫk ņa i lǫjet. (Āinwōt raar kōṃṃane ippān Lipepe.)

Ilo iien eo, eļak iruj ri-Ṃajeļ ro kab irooj eo im ļak iten wekar ri-Woleai ro, ejjeļǫk iiaļ in aer etal ñan ṃade ko bwe ri-Woleai ro rej jijet wōt ippān ṃade ko. Im eṃōkaj an ri-Woleai ro jibwitok ṃade ko im wekar aolep armej in Ṃajeļ ro ioon wa eo.

Ilo iien eo, ke ej ellewetak ri-Woleai ro ioon wa eo im jek ri-Ṃajeļ ro, im wekar er, elōñ wōt eo ri-Ṃajeļ raar kāļǫk jān wa eo ak jet iaer rej kattōrak im rejjab lel kōn ṃade ko. (Ejjeļǫk ṃade ippān ri-Ṃajeļ im raar kattōrak ṃade ko kōn peier wōt.) Ak rōṃōk in pukot iiaļ in aer kāļǫk bwe rekkōl in kāļǫk bwe ri-Woleai ro renaaj wekar er ņa i lǫjet. Ak eṃṃan wōt aer pād ioon wa eo im tōōri ṃade ko bwe ren jab lel.

Ak juon eṃṃaan, etan Ḷejkwōnidik ej jebwebwe im ej kaiuri im jibwetok irooj Ḷoeak im likūt ṇa ilikin im ej kattōrak kōn jebwe eo ej jebwebwe kake.

Ri-Woleai ro raar wekar irooj eo im ṃōk. Ak ejjab lel, kōnke Ḷejkwōnidik ej kattōrak jāne. Ke ej pedakilkil jebwe eo Ḷejkwōnidik ej ḷōmṇak in kāḷọk kake irooj eo ak kōn an ri-Woleai ro jellelikḷọk erro ṇa iḷọkan wa eo ejjeḷọk iien an kāḷọk. Ak ke ej maat jebwe eo im pedakilkil kōn an ri-Woleai ro wekare im jek erro, Ḷejkwōnidik ejjeḷọk an kein kattōrak ak ej kattōrak kōn pein.

Ke Ḷejkwōnidik ej lo an jaad emmeḷo aer wekar ḷọk erro, Ḷejkwōnidik ej jibwe irooj eo im joḷọk ṇa i lọjet. Ilo iien eo ri-Woleai ro rej wekar ḷọk irooj eo ṇa i lọjet, Ḷejkwōnidik ej jibwe ṃade ko ṃade in irooj eo, im kāḷọk iḷọkan ḷọk irooj eo im aō ḷọk jān turin wa eo.

Ri-Woleai ro reḷak wekar ḷọk erro. Kōn an ḷap an Ḷejkwōnidik kate kōn irooj eo bwe en jab lel. Innām rejro ettoḷọk jān wa eo. Im ejeṃḷọk an ri-Woleai ro wekar er.

Ilo iien eo ke armej ro ilo wa eo waan Ḷauna rej erreilọk im lo an Ḷoeak kāḷọk jān wa eo [wa]an. Innām ri-Woleai wōt rej pād ilo wa eo kar waan Ḷoeak im aolep ri-Ṃajeḷ ro kar ioon wa eo waan Ḷoeak raar kāḷọk jāne. Wa eo waan Ḷoeak eḷap an ṃōkaj ak kōnke ri-Woleai ro rejjab doorḷọk iiep eo im kabbwe. Ak eaer im wa eo ejjab kanooj ettōr. (Ilo kajin wa eaer ej pādwōt. Ejjab eṃṃakūt.)

Ke armej ro i wa eo waan Ḷauna rej lo an kāḷọk Ḷoeak im armej ro i wa eo waan, armej ro i wa eo waan Ḷauna rej kaiur im aōṇōōṇ iuṃwin wōjḷā. Bwe rej lo an ri-Ṃajeḷ ro kāḷọk im rej ba, "Alikkar ke rōtariṇae i wa en waan Ḷoeak, bwe armej ro raar kāḷọk ak wa eo eṇ ej kabbwe."

Ḷọkun jet minit etakeakḷọk wa eo waan Ḷauna im atartar ilo kubaak eo, kubaak in wa eo waan ri-Woleai ro. Im Ḷauna ej lukwōj kubaak eo, kubaak in wa eo waan ri-Woleai ro ṇa i roñ in wa eo waan.

Ilo iien eo ke ri-Woleai ro rej wekar Ḷauna ṇa i ilo kubaak eo ke Ḷauna ej eọeo bwe in pen wa ko ippān doon, ri-Woleai ro rejjab bōjrak aer wekar ḷọk Ḷauna ṇa ijo ej eọuti wa ko bwe ren jab jepel jān doon. Bwe en eṃṃan aer wōj tariṇae.

Ke ej dedeḷọk an Ḷauna eọeo, ej ba ñan aolep ḷōṃaro ioon wa eo waan, im ba, "Ekwe ej kab iien ñan adeañ tariṇae in!"

Innām Ḷauna eaar kāḷọk jān roñ in wa eo waan im itoḷọk ioon kubaak eo toḷọk.

Ri-Woleai ro raar kātem jike ak jet ri-Woleai rej wekare ak ejjab lel kōn ṃade ko ak ejjab kinejnej kōn jāje ko an ri-Woleai ro, ak eḷañne Ḷauna ej wekar juon eṃṃaan in Woleai ri-Woleai ro reṃōk in tōri ṃade ko ak ej ja etal in ṇe ṃade wōt, ak elel ṇe eṃṃaan.

Ke ri-Woleai ro rej lo an Ḷauna kanooj in jeḷā kilen tariṇae. Āliktata ri-Woleai ro rej ekkar ioon wa eo im kajjo ṃade im wekar ḷọk Ḷauna. Ke ej itoḷọk im kepaak ḷọk ri-Woleai ro ṇa ioon wa eo ri-Woleai ro rej jellelikḷọk Ḷauna tarrin lemñoul ṃade. Ak eaar jab lel. Ke ejjab lel ak eloñ wōt eo ri-Woleai relel ippān Ḷauna rej kāḷọk jān wa eo im aō ḷọk jān wa eo.

Innām Ḷauna ej bar kejepḷaak ḷọk Ḷoeak ṇa ilo wa eo waan im armej ro doon. Aolep ri-Woleai rej mour wōt im aō ioon lọjet.

Ilo iien eo eḷap an Ḷauna būroṃōj kake kōrā ro (ri-Woleai ro) im jañ, ak kōnke ri-Woleai ro raar jino kōṃṃan tariṇae im ṃan lejḷā eo, Lipepe, kab ledik eo nājin eḷap an Ḷauna kōḷmānḷọkjeṇ kōn men kein. Im eaar etal wōt iṃaanḷọk wa ko jet ak ej ba ilo būruon make, "Eḷañne wa kaṇe iḷọkan renaaj ektak tok ri-Woleai eṃṃan." Bwe eḷap an būroṃōj ak kōnke eaar kōṇaan kōṃṃan aenōṃṃan iñeo ej itoḷọk wōt ioon petak in wa eo toḷọk im kepaakḷọk ri-Woleai ro.

Im ilo iien eo eaar wekar wōt ḷōṃaro raar wekar ḷọk ṃokta. Ak ke ej kepaak ḷọk jar eo rejjab joḷọk bwōd ak re kāḷọk jān wa eo. Im Ḷauna eaar jab ekkonono ḷọk ñan er. Ak eaar jab wekar er ṇa ilọjet. Ak eaar kejeṃḷọk an tariṇae.

Im wa ko waan Ļauna raar etal wōt im ilo̧k ñan Jālooj.

Ri-Woleai rejako. Juōn kōrā in Woleai bōlen raar bōke. Etan Leon. Ak aolep ri-Woleai rej pād i lo̧jet im raar aō. Ak rejjab maroñ wōnāneļo̧k im bōlen raar mej.

(Ļemn̦ak eo an Ļoeak ke ar bōk ri-Woleai ro bwe en nājin, enaaj kar bōkļo̧k er ñan Mejatto.)

Ejem̧ļo̧k.

(Ļauna eaar Irooj in Eañ im Rōk, jemān Neimat, lejļā eo an Irooj Ļaelañ im jinen Irooj Kabua Kabua.

Bōlen ejjeļo̧k ri-Pālle i Jebwad ilo iien bwebwenato in.

Ļauna eaar leļo̧k aelōñ in Roñdik ñan Ļejkwōnidik bwe en aļap, kōn an lomor eo. Ej m̧orjinkwot.

M̧akwilōñ, jemān Aroneañ ekar aļap tokālik.

Iaar katak bwebwenato in tarin̦ae eo ippān Lojōr, ļōļļap eo ar bōk eō [im] kōkaajjiriri[k eō ke ej] joñoul ruo aō iiō. Iaar pād ippān [ñan ke ej] roñoul juon aō iiō.

Ļeo ar pād ilo tarin̦ae eo ke eaar ļaddik. Ke eaar kwaļo̧k bwebwenato ñan eō eaar lukkuun ļōļļap.

Ļauna eļap an peran. Im ejjab mijak kōn jabdewōt men ak armej. Eaar jab mijak kōn komja in Jāmne, āinwōt bwebwenato eo ej ba.)

85: STORY ABOUT KABUA WHEN HE DRIFTED TO M̧AKIL

As told by Jelibōr Jam, Kuwajleen 1975

Irooj [Chief] Kabua[1] in a canoe with fifty people, men and women, made a round [voyage] in the Marshalls.[2]

They sailed from perhaps Nam̧o to Kuwajleen, Lae, Ujae, and Wōtto, and were blown astray in a big wind and drifted ashore on Piñlep and Koro[3] (an island).

When they drifted ashore, the people of the island took very good care of Kabua and his group.

After a while, it was the right time for the day of celebration for the people of the island. And they made a lot of food and all of the people prepared to go to the celebration. As is the custom of the atoll, it would be bad if one person were absent.

And they dug an earth oven [pit] nine meters square[4] in size, the size of this area.

At the time when the earth oven was finished, there was a very big bed of hot coals/fire; at this time they pushed over any person inside the earth oven so that [if] he could not jump to the side of the earth oven, to the other side; well he would burn up and die.

But those able to jump at the time they pushed them inside the earth oven, [if] they jumped and landed on the other side, they would not die. This was the custom when it was the right day to do it.

And when Kabua's canoe drifted to Piñlep and Koro, after three days it was the right time for the celebration. And they invited Kabua and all of the people in his canoe to participate in the celebration.

And when the Marshallese went, they were surprised with the custom that they [the island people] performed.

When it was the right [time], they called Kabua that he should go, so that they could push him into the fire. Kabua did not stay put; instead, he went.

When they pushed Kabua at the time, a man named Ļaibwijtok hurried and jumped behind Kabua and took hold of Kabua and jumped with him across the earth oven to the edge on the other side.

And Kabua was not burned, for Ļaibwijtok jumped with him.

When Kabua and Ļaibwijtok reached [the other side of the fire], they assumed the responsibility, the responsibility to put the people [of the island] into the earth oven (all the people who were near the fire trying to destroy Kabua, but they only destroyed those [particular ones] of [all] the people of the island). [They did not destroy those who had not tried to destroy them.]

And when the people who came to the celebration were finished, they ended the

---

1. Kabua was an important paramount chief *(irooj ļapļap)* of Rālik (the western chain of the Marshall Islands). He lived and reigned into the German period.

2. See footnote 4 on page 259.

3. Piñlep (Pingelap) is a small atoll about 400 statute miles, roughly southwest of Ujae Atoll, and M̧akil (Mokil) is about fifty-miles northwest of Piñlep. Note that the informant introduced the story with reference to M̧akil, than changed the locale to Piñlep. The two were obviously associated in his mind, and in the story, perhaps because they are in the same culture area, the Ponape (Pohnpei) area. M̧akil is about one-hundred miles east and slightly south of that large high-island.

4. Note that the English words *meter* and *square* have been borrowed and incorporated into the Marshallese language as *mitō* and *jukweea.*

time of celebration with Kabua; because he was so tough, as was Ļaibwijtok. (They did not continue the ritual. It was worship, *kabuñ.*)[5]

And they gave Piñlep and Koro to be Kabua's (gave the islands to him as the chief), because Kabua threw very many people into the fire.

It was a game, but it was like war, and Kabua won,[6] because he did not burn up. He was like a flying bird.

After some days, the people on Piñlep came and brought a great deal of food and bowed down to Kabua in order to acknowledge that he was to be their chief.

From the time that they saw his toughness in flying and that of Ļaibwijtok—from this time on, they said Piñlep and Koro belong to Kabua.[7]

After a week or two, Kabua said farewell to the people living on Piñlep and Koro and again returned to the atolls of the Marshalls. (In the ancient language, *wurin* means tough, and *matan mej ro* means 'the living people'.)

They arrived there at the atoll of Pikinni. When the canoe neared Pikinni, Ļaibwijtok showed his toughness and leaped up to the top of the mast and dove down headfirst.

And the people thought that he would pierce the deck of the canoe and break his head into pieces, but he tumbled to his feet.

When the island was a little distance away, Ļaibwijtok did this again [leaped up to the top of the mast, dove down headfirst, and tumbled to his feet] until the time the people of the island saw his leaping away and falling headfirst.

And the Pikinni people said that he would pierce the deck of the canoe and break his head into pieces. But Ļaibwijtok tumbled to his feet. Ļaibwijtok showed that he would never be killed in time of war. If there were a bigger customary celebration, he would meet it [just as he had done] in Piñlep and Koro. (That is, he would show his bravery again and he would not lose.)[8]

When the canoe arrived at Pikinni, the people were happy, because the chief was alive. But in the days before, the message was that Kabua and Ļaibwijtok had died at sea. And the people in the Marshalls did not know that Kabua had reached Pikinni.

After a few days, he again sailed from Pikinni and came to Kuwajleen. From Kuwajleen to Naṃo, the assembly place of the chiefs. And [he] remained there.

It is ended.

(Naṃo was the place of the chiefs from long ago. From Naṃo they moved to Buoj, Aelōñļapļap, in the time of Ļauna,[9] because of the good pass [in the reef]. And the graveyard of the chiefs is there.[10] Never mind typhoons. [That is, it is a safe location in regard to the often destructive typhoons.]

They [had] made *bubu*, divination,[11] and saw that Naṃo was good. And they made *bubu* later and saw that Buoj was good.

---

5. This was apparently an ordeal by fire, perhaps part of the religious practices of the people of Piñlep (unless it was fictive). There was no corresponding ritual in the Marshall Islands that is known either in the oral tradition or in reports of European or American observers.

6. Note use of the English loanword *wiin.* The traditional Marshallese word is *anjo* 'victory, to be victorious'.

7. See Krämer and Nevermann (1938:300–301) regarding this claim.

8. This appears to be a show of strength, perhaps a challenge of sorts by the chief's "champion," although this story does not indicate a need to challenge the Pikinni people.

9. Ļauna was an important Rālik chief who lived into the early German period (latter part of the nineteenth century).

At the time of the story, when he was at Piñlep and Koro, Kabua was a very young man, perhaps eighteen years of age, and he was of the blood of the chiefs—he had not yet taken the chair of the chief [succeeded to the chieftainship].)[12]

Comments

Another version of the experiences of Irooj Ļapļap Kabua and his party on Piñlep is recorded in Krämer and Nevermann (1938:300–301). "One day the head chief Kabua wanted to sail from Ebon [Epoon] to Jaluit [Jālooj] with a fleet *ínet* [*inej*] of about 100 boats. They only wanted to sail a little for pleasure, *djerakerik badjik* [*jerakrōk bajjōk*]; but the weather was unfavorable, and they did not reach their destination. In Kabua's boat was also his father Djibë [Jipe], his uncle Labídjĕtak

---

10. Chief's graveyard (*wūliej ļap,* 'big/important grave'). This is the plot of land in which *irooj* are buried. The area is forbidden to anyone not of *irooj* ancestry, with the exception of the guardian lineage. It is believed that supernatural sanctions will automatically operate against those who violate the taboo (see Tobin 1958:61). Irooj Ļapļap Ļōjjeiļañ Kabua was buried with his ancestors at Buoj, Aelōñļapļap in 1981. His body was brought there from Kuwajleen. There is another *wuliej ļap* of Rālik chiefs on Jālooj Atoll.

11. *Bubu* 'divination by means of folding pandanus leaves *(bubu in maañ)* or by knotting coconut leaves *(bubu in kimej in ni)*'. See Krämer and Nevermann (1938:250–251) for the latter technique. The technique by means of coconut leaves is also practiced in the Carolines. See Lessa (1968:188–210) for a detailed discussion of this method of foretelling the future. The Marshallese also practiced a technique called *boļā.* Beach pebbles were counted out in series to find the answer to a question or problem. See Tobin (1958:38–39) for the role of the diviner *(ri-bubu).*

12. The expression *bōk jea an irooj* 'take the chair of the chief', means to succeed to chieftainship. The loanword *chair (jea)* and the concept of succession symbolized by enthronement (using an article of furniture) are associated in this expression. There were no chairs or enthronement ceremonies in traditional Marshallese culture. The concept may have come from the Bible, for example, Matthew 5:34 ". . . God's throne." (Matu 5:34 ". . . *an Anij tūroon.*") However, the word *tūroon* is not used in a secular context in the Marshalls. On the other hand, the concept of succession to chieftainship symbolized by installation on a throne (special chair) may have come from German traders or officials. However, the German word *thron* would also have been borrowed as *tūroon*, and thus is also found lacking in secular contexts. Whatever the etymology, the expression and concept are now integrated into Marshallese culture. It is also used for succession to the position of *aļap* (lineage head in charge of land holdings). I heard the expression when I first arrived in the Marshalls, on Arņo Atoll, and many times since then. A Marshallese voyage from Epoon to Kosrae, to the west, is said to have occurred many years ago. As Dwight Heine told me in 1951, "The old people say that Marshallese sailed from Epoon long ago. They landed on Kosrae and fought the Kosrae people and defeated them. Some of them married Kosrae people and remained there. The section of land on which the Marshallese lived on Kosrae is named Epoon. Later on, the Marshallese went to Pohnpei and fought the Pohnpeians—and defeated them." An old Pohnpeian tale ("A story of Rālik and Ratak island chains") tells of Marshallese settling and marrying on Kosrae, and how many of their descendants accompanied the Kosraen chief Ijokelekel when he took Pohnpei. The story tells of the founding of the Rulujannamou clan on Pohnpei by two women who arrived on the island at that time with their husbands (Bernart 1977:104–105). The clan is called Ri-Luujien-Naņo in the Marshalls, where it has many members. It probably originated on Naņo Atoll. See Riesenberg (1965:162) for drift voyages, Marshalls to Kosrae.

[Ļaibwijtok], his younger brother Geidju [Keju], Kabua's mother Liboreang, her daughter Litelínedj, and her younger sister Lima͡iang, and finally Kabua's brother Lagadjímui [Ļakajiṃwe], and a few kadjur [*kajoor*]. The boat reached Pingelap, where Djoumanger was king. For three months they remained on Pingelap in peace with the inhabitants. But then Djoumanger wanted to get rid of them. Thus it came to a quarrel. Djoumanger threw a stone at the forehead of Labídjĕtak, and cried '*ĕ̄am,* that is yours.' Soon the one who was hit and Kabua seized a spear and knocked him down, so that he died. Then all the Pingelapese ran away and gave up the battle. Then Kabua had a still larger boat carved (*djekd-jekō̄a* [*jekjek wa*]) than the one he already possessed, and when it was finished, he sailed home to Jālooj with his people, which was his seat from old times. Kabua now claimed the domination of Pingelap; but the German government did not acknowledge his claims and took the island from him. There is a proverb about Kusae and Pingelap from old times: *'Idjolo geii berang gei i djike góro:* I will eat bananas, I will go (to) Pingelap'. That means, I go to Kusae, then to Pingelap.

"Pingelap was visited by Edao, when he returned from Ep. He cut palm wine there. It flowed so abundantly that the bowls attached to [the trees] always ran over, and dripped down, so that a big water-hole with good water originated. It was near the house of Maiep. When he did not need the waterhole anymore, he covered it up with stones, so that nobody knows where it is any more. Because he made it only for himself.

"He made a large oven, upon which a big fire was able to burn called um in djerodui. While the fire burned, he played 'pulling' with the people, who pulled the other person into the fire. Thus he caused many to be burnt, and many also died in the fire.

"When the Peiho landed again at Pingelap on March 19, 1910, on its return trip (Bd. 1, p. 331) with chief Ladap from Lae aboard, who told the story above, I sailed ashore with him, in order to look at the spot of the water-hole, and the oven. Obviously, there was little to be seen, and the Pingelaps seemed rather ignorant. . . ."

This is an excellent example of how folk-tales change over the years. In this case, the exploits of the trickster Etao told to the German ethnographer in 1910 have been incorporated into the story that was related to me in 1975 of the voyage of Irooj Ļapļap Kabua, the powerful Marshallese leader.

It should be noted that my informant, Jelibōr Jam, is a native of Ujae Atoll, which is very close to Lae Atoll, the home of Ladap, Krämer's informant, and it is part of the Kapinmeto (Western Rālik) area.

This would seem to rule out variation in the story due to geographical isolation or communication factors. The other elements in the story, collected by me, and not found in the earlier version, might have been added later. Or perhaps they were not told to, or recorded by the German ethnographer, due to communication problems with his informant.

It should also be noted that the names of Kabua's relatives were absent in the version recorded by me.

Riesenberg answered my query about the purported drift voyage of Chief Kabua to Piñlap as follows,[13] "In the James L. Young papers, which are Pacific Manuscript No. 21 and which I copied when I was at the Australian National University, is the following, under date July 29, 1876, written while Young was at [Epoon]: 'Kabua, who is a

13. Personal communication (1976).

man of some 50 years of age, has been a famous warrior and sailor, having been once drifted away to Pingelap 500 miles to Westward and having with his crews fought and defeated the Natives there who endeavored to kill him. He also took a ship to Jālooj lagoon in 1852 and killed the Captain (Mackenzie) with his own hands.'

"As for Pingelap and Kabua, Young's date of writing, 1876, and his remark that Kabua was 'once' drifted to Pingelap, suggest that this happened earlier than the 1870s, which is implied in Krämer and Nevermann on page 286."

Those interested in voyages of Marshallese and other Micronesians outside of their home areas should consult Riesenberg (1965:155–170), which includes an extensive bibliography. It is a supplement to his larger South Pacific voyages study (1962).

85: BWEBWENATO IN KABUA KE EAAR PEĻǪK N̄AN ṂAKIL

Ri-bwebwenato: Jelibōr Jam, Kuwajleen 1975

Irooj Kabua ilo juon wa kōn lemn̄oul armej, ṃōṃaan im kōrā, rej rawūn ilo Ṃajeļ. Rej jerak jān bōlen Naṃo n̄an Kuwajleen, Lae, Ujae, Wōtto, im jatōp ilo juon kōto. Im eǫtōk ļǫk ilo Pin̄lep im Koro (juon āne).

Ke rej eotōkļǫk ekanooj in [ri-āne eṃṃan aer] [eṃṃan ri-āne] lale er, Kabua im [doon eo an] [ro doon].

Pād im ļak juon iien ejejjet raan in ṃōņōņō an ri-āne eo. Innām raar kōṃṃan elōn̄ ṃōn̄ā im aolep armej rej kōppojak in etal n̄an ṃōņōņō eo. Āinwōt ilo ṃanit in aelōn̄ eo. Enana n̄e ejako juon armej.

Innām rej kūbwij juon uṃ dettan ruatimjuon mita jikwea dettan peļaakin.

Ilo iien eo n̄e [ke] ej mejļǫk uṃ eo ekanooj ļap an emmelle ilo iien in rej jipeļļǫkwe jabdewōt armej ņa ilowaan uṃ eo, bwe eo eban kāļǫk n̄an tōrerein uṃ eo tu-jimettan rājet in uṃ, ekwe, enaaj bwil in mej. Ak ro reppin̄ ilo iien eņ rej jipeļļǫkwe ņa ilowaan uṃ eo. Renaaj kāļǫk im jok itujab eo jimettan im rejāmin mej. Āindein ṃanit eo n̄e ej jejjet raan in kōṃṃane.

Innām ke wa eo waan Kabua eaar peļǫk n̄an Pin̄lep im Koro ļǫkun jilu raan ejejjet iien keemem eo. Innām raar ān̄inļǫk Kabua im aolep armej ro i wa eo waan bwe ren pād ilo iien ṃōņōņō eo.

Im ke ri-Ṃajeļ rej ilǫk rej bwilōn̄ kōn ṃanit eo rej kōṃṃane. Ke ej jejjet aer kūr Kabua bwe en ilǫk bwe ren jiperļǫkwe ņa ilowaan kijeek eo. Kabua eaar jab pād ak eaar etal.

Ke rej jiperļǫkwe Kabua ilo iien eo, juon eṃṃaan etan Ļaibwijitok ej kaiuri in kāļǫk iļǫkan ļǫk Kabua im jibwe im kāļǫk kake n̄an tōrerein uṃ eo tu jimettan.

Innām eaar jab bwil Kabua bwe Ļaibwijitok eaar kāļǫk kake.

Ke etōprak Kabua im Ļaibwijitok rejro bōk eddo eo, eddo in ettaak armej (ri-āne ro) ņa ilo uṃ eo. (Aolep [ro] repād iturin kijeek eo im rej kajjeon̄ kǫkkure Kabua. Ak er wōt rej kǫkkure [an] ri-ān ro.)

Innām ke eiten maat armej ro raar itok n̄an keemem eo raar kabwijrake iien eo im ṃōņōņō ippān Kabua kōn an kijon̄ kab Ļaibwijitok. Im raar leļǫk Pin̄lep im Koro bwe en an Kabua, kōnke eļap an lōn̄ armej eo Kabua ar joļǫk ņa ilowaan kijeek eo. Ikkure ak ej āinwōt tariņae. Ak Kabua ej wiin bwe eaar jab bwil. Ej āinwōt bao in kāļǫk.

Ālikin jet raan armej ro ioon Piñlep rej itok im bōktok elōñ ṃōñā im badikdik ñan Kabua bwe rej likūt[e] bwe en aer irooj. Jān iien eo raar lo wōden an maroñ in kāļǫk, kab Ļaibwijtok. Jān iien eo rej ba an Kabua aelōñ in Piñlep im Koro.

Ļǫkun juon wiik ak ruo Kabua eaar iǫkiǫkwe matan mej ro ioon Piñlep im Koro im bar jepļaak ñan aelōñ in Ṃajeļ.

(Ilo kajin etto "wurin" ej 'an kijoñ'. Im "matan mej ro" ej 'armej remour'.)

Ijo eaar tōkeak tok ie ilo aelōñ in Pikinni. Ke wa eo ej epaakļǫk Pikinni Ļaibwijitok ej kwaļǫk wōden an kijoñ. Im kālōñļǫk ñan ṃaan kiju eo im lōrak tu bōran. Im armej ro rej ļōmņak enaaj wekar eoon wa eo im rup bōran. Ak ej kaiuri [im] jutak.

Ke ej ettoļǫk jidik āne, ej kōṃṃan rot eo ṃae iien eo ri-āne rej loe an kālōñļǫk im wōtlǫk kōn bōran.

Im ri-Pikinni rej ba enaaj wekar eon wa eo im rup bōran. Ak Ļaibwijtok ej kaiuri im jutak. Ļaibwijtok ej kwaļǫk ke ejāmin kar mej ilo iien tariņae. Ñe eaar ļapļǫk wōt ṃōņōņō, ṃanit eo (keemem) eaar iioon ņa ilo Piñlep im Koro.

Ke wa eo ej poļǫk Pikinni eļap an armej ro ṃōņōņō bwe ej mour wōt irooj eo. Ak ilo raan ko ļǫk ṃokta ennaan eo in ke emej Kabua kab Ļaibwijtok i lǫmeto. Ak armej in Ṃajeļ rejaje ke eṃōj an Kabua tōprak Pikinni.

Ļǫkun jet raan ej bar jerak jān Pikinni. Im itok ñan Kuwajleen. Jen Kuwajleen ñan Naṃo, jikin kweļǫk eo an irooj. Im pād ie.

Ejeṃļǫk.

(Naṃo ar kar jikin irooj jān etto. Im raar eṃṃakūt ñan Buoj, Aelōñļapļap ilo iien Ļauna. Kōnke eṃṃan *pass.* Im wūliej in irooj epād ie. Jekdǫņ taibuun. Raar bubu im raar lo eṃṃan Naṃo. Im raar bubu tokālik im lo eṃṃan Buoj.

Ilo iien bwebwenato ke ar pād Piñlep im Koro, Kabua ej likao jidikrik. Bōlen joñoulrualitōk an iiō. Ilo iien eo ej bōtōktōk in irooj. Ejjañin bōk jea in irooj.)

86: STORY ABOUT AN AMERICAN SHIP

As told by Jelibōr Jam, Kuwajleen 1975

Perhaps one hundred and seventeen years ago, a ship sailed from America. It was going to Japan to purchase tea.

The ship was loaded with kerosene, and it did not reach Japan, but it came and they saw the main island of Ujae. When they saw it ahead, they tacked to windward, northward. And the captain thought that they had passed the island, and he said, "Tack to leeward now." Now the ship tacked again to leeward. He looked out and was surprised; there were many waves ahead. Then the ship suddenly tacked to windward. Now the captain said, "Throw out the anchor."

When they threw out the anchor, the anchor stopped the ship, and the ship turned around. Then the waves surged over the stern of the ship.

Now the people of Ujae woke up in the morning. They looked out and saw the ship outside of the reef, and they launched their canoes and sailed to the ship.

When the white men saw the big canoes, great was their fear and panic. Then the canoes of Ujae went out and anchored opposite the ship, and the men jumped out and ascended to the ship. And the white men poured kerosene on the water, and the surging waves did not destroy the ship—did not swamp it because the kerosene smoothed the waves.

And there were two men (men of Ujae). They said, "Never mind if we die, but we are going to the ship in the name of all of the people of Ujae." The names of these men: Mr. Ļakien and Mr. Ļañibuñ. They went seaward and the white men threw a line to them. And they seized the line and the white men pulled them up to the ship. When they reached the ship, they took hold of their hands (the white men grasped the hands of the men from Ujae) and lifted them onto the ship and gave them hats, gave them cigarettes, gave them shoes, gave them clothing, and took them away and fed them things to eat—beef, biscuits, potatoes—and gave them many different kinds (of food).

And they lowered the boats (the ship's boats) and loaded them with people (white people). And they just put them next to the ship. But they brought the men (the Ujae men) to where the captain was, and he asked them, "What atoll is this? What is the name of the chief?" And Ļañibuñ, [who] understood a little of the white men's language, answered and said, "Ujae Atoll, and the name of the chief, King John." (The English or the Germans, I do not know which, gave the name to King Kabua.)

Now the white men understood and were very happy.

And Ļañibuñ said, "Do not be afraid, for Ļakaien and I will take care of you as best we can." Now the white men were happy and went to the island with their boats. When the boats arrived on the beach, they moved the young white girl named Emma, and a cat and gave them to Ļakaien (so that he would take them away from the boat).

And Ļakaien took them to where he saw was the best place on the reef—no water, and smooth—and put the cat and the girl there, and stood there with them.

And all of the white men disembarked from the boats and went to where the girl and the cat were. And waited for the sailors who were working on their ship. (They were bringing goods to the reef from the ship.)

Ļañibuñ was also working with them. And people from the Ujae canoes came to Ļakaien and the young girl. And Ļakaien said, "See that you do not kill them. Just be kind to them." Now he took the girl and gave her to some men so that they would take her and the cat to the Ujae canoes.

Now these men, the captain and the mate, went with the girl to the canoe that was there (the canoe of Ujae). And Ļakaien called Ļañibuñ to him, "You keep on working and help these men. For I will take that girl and those officers. But I will hurry back." Now he sailed off and took them to the main island of Ujae. (The ship had struck on the island named Lo̧ñba.)

Now he took them and put them on Ujae. And Ļakaien decreed to them, the Ujae people, and said, "Take very good care of them and bring their food here." And Ļakaien returned again and unloaded from the ship goods, food, kerosene, [and] people, and returned again to Ujae. And stayed there for it was night. This was the first day.

The second day, he sailed again to the ship and worked again until noon. All of the food and kerosene was gone and off-loaded from the ship.

Now the white men gave kerosene to the Ujae people. They filled their lamps with this great amount of kerosene and they burned from day to day. The white men taught them how to make lamps with wicks and tins. And they did not extinguish them. But they kept them in tins. The people of Ujae were very happy, and they took very good care of the white people.

And the white men made two ships, and when the ships were completed, the mate sailed to Hong Kong, and the boatswain sailed to Jebwad, Jālooj.

A woman (the chief had brought her from Likiep previously) named Nerija, spoke to the white men in English, because the demon was speaking (the demon Lōm̧kein). But the woman did not know English previously. Now Nerija, or we should say the demon, said, "Do not worry, for a ship will come here and take you (the Americans) away."

A week later, the ship appeared and came to the ocean side of Ujae (the main island). The Ujae people looked out and saw the ship. The covers were thrown off of the big guns.

(The Americans were at Jebwad and at Epoon at this time, but they had not been to Ujae. Ļañibuñ was chief, the son of a chief, as was Ļakaien, son of Ļañibuñ. And Ļañibuñ had been on Jebwad with white men previously, and knew a little of the white men's language.)

And the white men from Ujae ran and went seaward, out on the reef. And the white men on the warship saw them and covered up the guns again.

And the Ujae people loaded boats with goods and coconuts and taro and breadfruit. And they said farewell. And the white men brought the old lady who had said that the ship would take them away at this time, and they thanked her and went seaward to the ship.

Many years later, during World War II, Allen, an officer in the navy on an LCI[1] came to Ujae. And he sought that ship, the ship of his family that was wrecked there. He brought a book—it was very old and small. And he said, "Are there one or two old men who were here at the time that Will Jackson's ship was wrecked?"—the name of the owner of the ship. He said, "The captain's name was Morrison."

Two old men answered and said, "We two saw this at that time. We were small boys."

Now the man said, "I came here to verify the place where the ship of my family was

1. LCI is the U.S. Navy designation for "Landing Craft Infantry."

wrecked. And I give my word of gratitude to you all, because of your ancestors taking care of the people. With this, I give you an ending [repayment] from my elders to those who are living on Ujae Atoll, for a day of celebration, commemorating the time that you were kind to us.

"Tomorrow we will meet together for a party that I will put on. Thank you very much."

They slept and woke up on the following day. Now food was prepared on the LCI and brought onto the island—the LCI was beached. And the food and all of the servicemen on the ship came off the ship, and joined the Ujae people and had a party. At that time, there was plenty of food from Ujae, [and] there was a very small amount from the ship—not a lot.

They met and ate food together and played baseball. There were two teams. One from the ship and the girls of Ujae. And the team from Ujae lost.

When everything was finished, Allen said, "This is a day you will remember every year on the ninth of June. The name of this day is 'Will Jackson's Day of Ujae'."

It was ended, and we clapped and parted.

And from that day to this, they do so [celebrate that day].

Comments

In his perceptive comments concerning firsthand reports by islanders, as opposed to European accounts of specific events, Lewis (1977:127) states, "It is nothing less than a tragedy that only one-sided accounts of the first contacts between Europeans and South Sea islanders have come down to us. . . ." He concludes, "We can only guess, therefore, at the reactions of the Tongans and Futunans to the things from another world . . . creatures whose incomprehensible equipment and patent ignorance of proper behavior effectively removed them from any kinship category and put them outside Maoritangi (the right and correct way) altogether. For their part, the Western captains were responsible for the safety of their clumsy vessels on dangerous uncharted coasts; the requirements of safety from attack, fresh food, and fresh water were for them imperative."

While Lewis was referring to the initial contacts with representatives of Western culture, his thesis is applicable to later contacts or events as well. Although at least some of the Ujae people apparently had had some contact with Europeans and Americans, the wreck of the "American ship" was of considerable importance to the little community.

The fact that the story has been transmitted orally for generations, and that songs have been written about it, attest to this, as does the annual celebration of the event.

It is interesting to compare the reactions of the people of Ujae with those of the passengers and crew of the American ship, and the preconceptions and attitudes of the people from two quite different cultures toward one another. This can be done to a certain extent by reading the account of the wreck written by one of the survivors. It was published under the title "Wreck of the Rainier in 1887." The author was O. J. Humphrey.

I have excerpted pertinent material from this interesting book for this purpose on the following page.

Excerpts from "Wreck of the Rainier: A Sailor's Narrative"

By O. J. Humphrey, 1887

"The ship was headed from Philadelphia to Kobe, August 12, 1883.

"January, 3d . . . At three P.M. the island of Lae, one of the Marshall group, was made on the port bow.

"At 4:30 P.M., the island bore abeam about eight miles distant. . . . The captain went below and returned in a few moments and spoke to the mate saying, 'The course is northwest, and we are now clear of all the islands at last, with nothing to trouble us until the shores of Japan heave in sight' (pp. 24–25).

"At two bells breakers sighted. Captain gave the order 'hard a-starboard', but too late. The ship struck on the reef.

"Heavy seas crashed against the stern and the ship was in danger (p. 27).

"Holes were made and cargo drifted away (p. 28).

"White sails appeared in the far distance, which on approach proved to be canoes swarmed with dusky natives, coming down inside the lagoon. . . .

"Canoes were made fast to the coral, and the natives then approached up to the inside surf line and commenced to shout and gesticulate which sent a chill of terror to the unfortunate mariners who clung to the wreck which soon must go to pieces (p. 29).

"Natives beckoned on board and came aboard. (By line from the ship.) They knew a few English words (pp. 31–32).

"They were given shirts and dungaree pants. They then wandered about, stealing anything they might see that they could hide from sight (p. 32).

"A boat was hoisted overboard, the captain's daughter was sent ashore. She was wrapped up in the American flag and hoisted to a chair. And lowered over to the boat.

"All of the boats went over the reef and into the lagoon with provisions . . . we could only wait the will of the savages (p. 35).

"During all this time, the savages had been examining everything, and their wild, demoniac looks and yells accompanied all their movements, either swimming or on the canoes. They were clad only with a small mat, fastened about the waist, with holes in the ears large enough to put one's hand in. In other words, a hole was made in the ear, and then the skin of the face was cut down to the jaw-bone. Small rolls of coconut leaves, about two or three inches in diameter were put in these holes to keep them open until properly healed, and these then filled with wild flowers. All this sent a thrill of terror through the stoutest heart, as all hands only expected to be a Thanksgiving feast for the savages. The firearms were loaded and kept in readiness; each boat's crew was armed, and at the present time outnumbered the savages. But with no land to be seen, to be left on a coral reef in mid-ocean was rather a dismal situation (pp. 35–36). Canoes towed the ship's boats to Ujea Island.

"The captain was taken to the king's house and coconuts were given to the crew and passengers" (p. 37).

[The fears of the Americans were overcome by this friendly reception, and by the treatment accorded them by the people of Ujae during the months spent on the atoll before the Americans were rescued.

The seance with the spirit (demon) Libogen is described in some detail by Humphrey, and can be compared with the version of the incident related in the Marshallese story from Ujae.]

86: BWEBWENATO IN JUŌN WAAN AMEDKA

Ri-bwebwenato: Jelibōr Jam, Kuwajleen 1975

Bōlen jibuki-joñoul-jiljilimjuon iiō remootļǫk juon wa eaar jerak jān Amedka. Ej iten etal ñan Jepaan in wia ti.

Wa eo ebooļ kōn karjin. Innām eaar jab tōprak Jepaan ak eitok im lo eonene in Ujae. Ke ej lo ŋa iṃaan, ej bwābwe niñaļǫk. Innām kapen eo ej ļōmņak emootļǫk āne eo im ej ba, "Kabbwe kiiō." Kiiō wa eo bar kabbwe. Reļak ilbōk elōñ ŋo iṃaan. Reļak iten bwābwe ejidimkij. Kiiō kapen eba, "Joļǫk añkō!"

Ke rej joļǫk añkō ebōjrak añkō im jitļǫk. Eļak ibweeb ej rup ŋo ŋa iļǫkwan wa eo.

Kiiō ilo jibboñōn eo eruj armej in Ujae. Rej reilem lo wa eo ŋae ilikin baal. Innām rej bwilǫki [wa ko] im jerak ñan ippān wa eo.

Ke ripālle rej lo wa ko eļap [aer] mijak kab lōļñǫñ. Innām wa ko an Ujae rej etal im po ikijjien wa eo im kālǫk im wōnlōñļǫk ñan wa eo. Innām ripālle ro raar lutōk karjin ŋa ioon lǫjet. Innām eļak ibweeb ŋo ejjab rup. (Ejjab kōṃṃan ṃōrṃōr kōnke karjin ekōmatōltōle.)

Innām eor ruo eṃṃaan (eṃṃaan in Ujae) rej ba, "Jekdǫǫn ñe kemro mej ak kemij ro [kemro ej] etal ñan wa eŋ ilo etadwōj." (Ilo etan aolep armej in Ujae.) Etan ļōṃaro: Mr. Ļakaien kab Mr. Ļañibuñ. Rowōnmetoļǫk innām ripālle ro rej joļǫk juon to ñan erro. Im rejro jibwe to eo im ripālle ro rej tōbwe ñan wa eo. Ke retōprak wa eo rej kabjōr peier (ripālle ro rej jibwe pein ļōṃaro jān Ujae). Im kotak er ŋa ioon wa eo im leļǫk aer at. Leļǫk kijeer jikka. Leļǫk aer juuj. Leļǫk aer nuknuk. Im rej bōkļǫk er im naajdik er; ṃōñā kau, petkōj, piteto im bar lōñ jabdewōt kain raar leļǫk.

Im rej door[e] booj ko (booj in wa eo) im kanne kōn armej (ripālle) im doore wōt ŋae iturin wa. Ak rebōk ļōṃaro (ri-Ujae) ñan ijo jikin kapen eo, im ekajjitōk, "Aelōñ in ia? Etan irooj eo?" Innām Ļañibuñ emōlele kōn jidik kajin pālle, ej uwaak em ba, "Aelōñ in Ujae im etan irooj eo, King John." (Ri-Iñlen ke ri-Jemane, ijaje. Raar door etan in ñan King Kabua.)

Kiiō ripālle ro remōļeļe im kanooj eļap aer ṃōŋōŋō.

Innām Ļañibuñ ej ba, "Koṃin jab mijak bwe kemro Ļakaien naaj kōjparok koṃ joñon wōt amro maroñ." Kiiō ripālle reṃōŋōŋō em wōnāneļǫk kōn bǫǫk ko. Ke booj ko rej tōprakļǫk ioon pedped ripālle ro rej kōṃakūt ledik [eo] in pālle, etan Emma, kab juon kuuj im leļǫk erro ñan Ļakaien (bwe en bōkļǫk er jān booj eo).

Innām Ļakaien ej bōk er im etal ñan ijo ej loe ioon pedped im eṃṃantata (ejjeļǫk dān im metaltōl). Im door kuuj eo im ledik eo [ilo] ŋa eo. Im jutak ippāer ļǫk.

Innām aolep ripālle rej to jān booj ko im etal ñan ijo ledik eo ej pād ie im kuuj eo. Im kōttar [an] jeeļa ro jerbal ioon wa eo waer. (Bōktok ṃweiuk jān wa eo ñan pedped eo.)

Ļañibuñ ej bar jerbal ippāer. Innām rej itok armej ro jān waan Ujae ko ñan ippān Ļakaien im ledik eo. Innām Ļakaien ej ba, "Lale koṃ ar jab ṃan[e] er. Koṃin jouj wōt ñaner." Kiiō ej bōk ledik eo im leļǫk ñan jet eṃṃaan bwe ren bōkļǫk ñan wa ko waan Ujae ko kab kuuj eo.

Kiiō ļōṃaro, kapen eo kab meej eo, retal ippān ledik eo ļǫk ñan wa eo ej pād ie (waan Ujae eo). Im Ļakaien ej kūrtok Ļañibuñ, "Koṃin jerbal wōt im jipañ ļōṃaraņ ŋe. Bwe ña ij ṃōkaj kōn ledik eo kab kapen rā. Ak inaaj bar ṃōkajtok." Kiiō ej jerak im bōkļǫk er ñan eonene in Ujae. (Wa eo ar itaak ioon āne etan Lǫñba.)

Kiiō bōkļǫk er, door er ŋa Ujae. Innām Ļakaien ej kalliṃur er ri-Ujae ro em ba, "Koṃin kanooj lale er em kōṃṃan tok kijeer." Ak Ļakaien ebar rǫǫl em aljōktok ṃweiuk, ṃōñā, karjin, armej im bar rǫǫltok ñan Ujae. Kab Ļañibuñ im aolep jeeļa ro ioon wa eo rej etal ñan Ujae. Em pād ie bwe eboñ. Raan eo kein ka juon.

Ran eo kein ka ruo ebar jerak ñan wa eo im bar jerbal ñan raelep. Emaat aolep ṃōñā, kab karjin im to jān wa.

Kiiō ripālle rej leļǫk karjin ñan armej in Ujae. Joñan an lōñ karjin rej ittil ļaaṃ im urur jān raan ñan raan. Ripālle raar katakin er wāween kōṃṃan wiik ippān tiin: ļaaṃ. Im jab kuni. Ak rej bar kōṃṃane ŋa ilo tiin. Innām kanooj in ṃōŋōŋō armej in Ujae. Im kanooj eṃṃan aer lale ripālle ro.

Innām ripālle ro rej kōṃṃane ruo wa im ke tōprak wa ko meej eo ej jerak ñan Hong Kong im bojin eo ej jerak ñan Jebwad, Jālooj.

Juōn kōrā (irooj eo ar bōktok jān Likiep ṃokta) etan Nerija, ej ba ñan ripālle ro ilo kajin Iñlij, kōnke tiṃoŋ ej ba (tiṃoŋ eo Lōṃkein) ak kōrā eo ejaje kajin Iñlij ṃokta. Kiiō Nerija, ak jen ba tiṃoŋ eo, ej ba, "Koṃin jab inepata bwe enaaj itok juon wa im bōk koṃ." (Ri-Amedka ro.)

Ļǫkun juon wiik ewaļǫk wa eo im itok ñan lik in Ujae (eonene). Ri-Ujae [ro] reilǫk [er reilǫk] ñan wa eo. Ej joļǫk kōba ko jān pakke ko.

(Ri-Amedka ro rej pād i Jebwad im i Epoon ilo iien eo ak rejjañin pād i Ujae. Ļañibuñ ej irooj, nājin irooj āinwōt Ļakaien, nājin Ļañibuñ. Innām Ļañibuñ eaar pād i Jebwad ippān ripālle ṃokta, im ejeļā jidik kajin pālle.)

Innām ripālle ro jān Ujae rej ettōr im wōnmetoļǫk ioon pedped. Im ripālle ioon ṃōnwa eo rej lo er im bar kūtmi pakke ko.

Innām ri-Ujae rej kanne booj ko in ṃweiuk kab ni kab iaraj kab mā. Im rej iǫkiǫkwe doon. Im ripālle ro rej bōktok leļļap eo eaar ba enaaj waļǫk wa eo im bōke er wōt kiiō. Im rej koṃṃoolole im wōnmetoļǫk ñan wa eo.

Ālikin elōñ iiō remootļǫk, iuṃwin tariŋae kein karuo, ej itok ñan Ujae, Allen, juon opija an Navy ioon juon LCI. Im pukot ijo wa eo waan baaṃle eo an eaar rup ŋa ie. Ebōktok juon bok, kanooj ṃor ak edik. Im ej ba, "Eor ke juon ak ruo iaan ļōļļap ro raar pād ilo iien eo ej rup wa eo waan Will Jackson?" (Etan ļeo wa eo kar an.) E ba, "Kapen eo etan Morrison."

Ļōļļab ro ruo rej uwaak im ba, "Kem ro lo ruo iien in. Kemij ro ļaddik."

Kiiō ļeo eaar ba, "Ña iaar itok bwe in kaṃool jikin eo eaar rup wa eo waan baaṃle eo aō ŋa ie. Innām ij lewōj aō naan in koṃoolol koṃ kōn an kar rūtto ro ami kōjparok armej ro. Kōn menin ij lewōj juon jeṃļǫkan jān rūtto ro aō ñan ro rej mour ioon aelōñ in Ujae kōn juon raan in keemem.

"Kememej iien eo koṃar jouj ñan kem. Ilju jenaaj ioon doon kōn juon bade inaaj kōṃṃane. Kanooj in eṃṃool."

Kiki im ļak ruj raan eo juon kiiō eaar kōṃṃane ṃōñā ilo LCI eo em to ānetak (LCI eo epād i perijet eo). Em ākto ṃōñā kab aolep ri-tariŋae ro an wa eo. Im koba ippān ri-Ujae em kōṃṃane iien bade eo. Iien in elōñ ṃōñā jān Ujae, eor jijiddikrik jān wa eo (ejjab eļap).

Raar kweļǫk [im] ṃōñā ippān doon im iakiu. Eor ruo kumi. Juōn an wa ak juon an Ujae. Innām eluuj kumi eo an Ujae.

Ke ej ṃōj jabdewōt Allen ej ba, "Eñin raan eo koṃ naaj kememej ilo iiō ko otemjej ej Juun ruatimjuon raan. Etan raan eo 'Will Jackson Day An Ujae'."

Ejeṃļǫk im kemwōj kabbokbok im jepel jān doon.

Innām jān raan eo ñan rainin rej kōṃṃan [āindein].

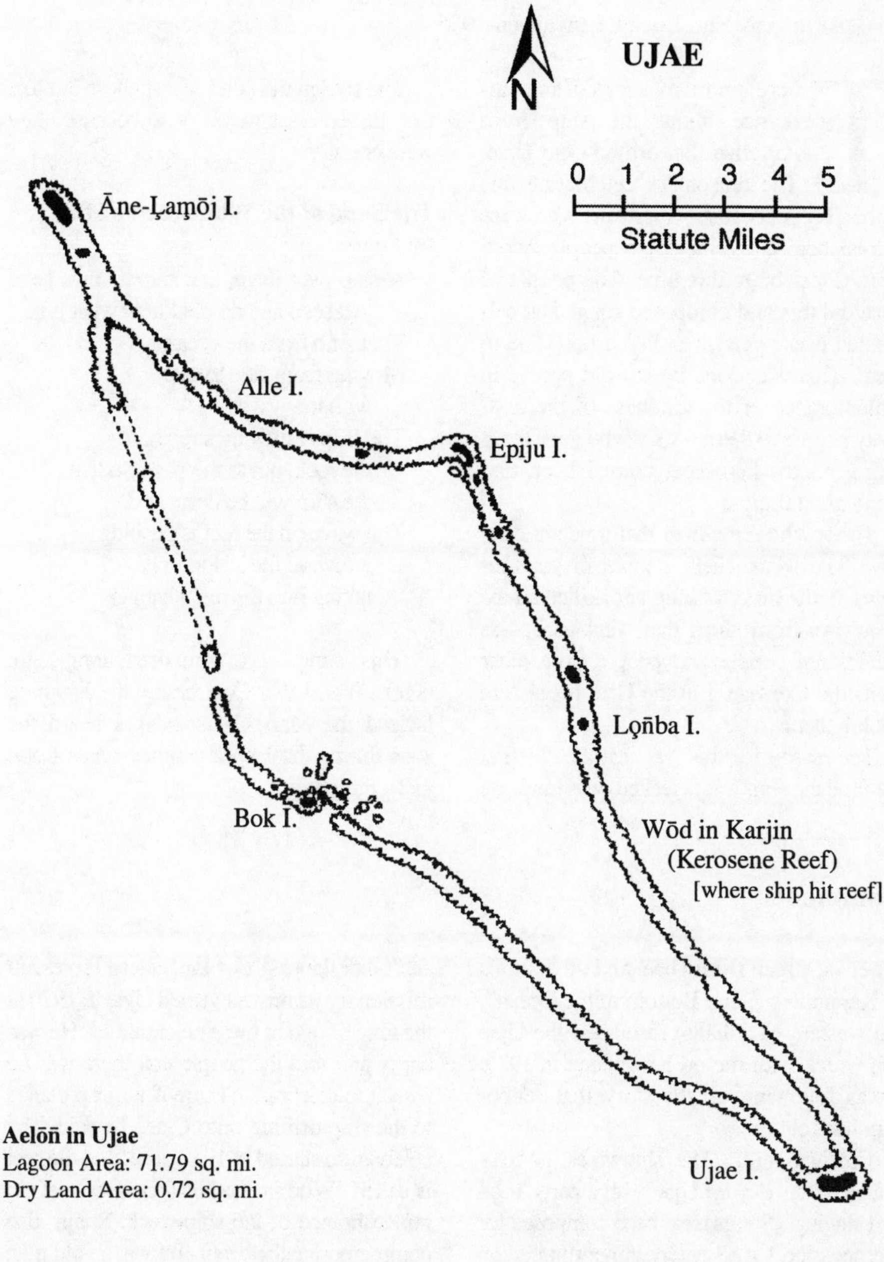
UJAE
N
0 1 2 3 4 5
Statute Miles
Āne-Ļaṃōj I.
Alle I.
Epiju I.
Lo̧ñba I.
Bok I.
Wōd in Karjin
(Kerosene Reef)
[where ship hit reef]
Ujae I.
Aelōñ in Ujae
Lagoon Area: 71.79 sq. mi.
Dry Land Area: 0.72 sq. mi.

87: STORY ABOUT AN AMERICAN SHIP: FURTHER EXPLANATION

As told by Enti Lucky, Kuwajleen 1975

There are many songs of remembrance about the ship from America that drifted onto Ujae. The reason for celebrating this to this day is because Americans who were helped before by the Ujae people asked them to celebrate this time. The people of Ujae did this and composed songs and celebrated every year. It is like a fairy tale to them. This was done by the old people in remembrance of the kindness of the castaway people to them—they who gave them cargo, goods, kerosene, corned beef, and many good things.

Those who remember that time are dead now. The Marshallese people in previous times, in the times of long ago, killed all the castaways from ships that went adrift—as the Pikinni people and people from other atolls did likewise. But the Ujae people did not kill them.

The reason for this was that the chief, at the time the ship was wrecked, was kind.

The reason the other Marshallese did like this [killed castaways] was because they were crazy.

The Song of the White Men's Ship on Ujae

A ship over there, that ship that we have
just seen and do not know what it is.
That ship from the ocean.
Moving from side to side
with the waves.
The ship is moving straight to
the rock, not to the pass. So that
the ship will be destroyed.
The wave on the reef is pushing
it toward the island. It is
taking it to the reef channel.

This song was composed long ago, before World War One, before the Japanese [seized the Marshall Islands]. I heard the song during the Japanese times, when I was just a little boy.

Comments

Emejwa, a man from Ujae, and other atolls of Kapinmeto ("The Bottom of the Ocean", the western Marshalls) discussed the Ujae shipwreck with me on Kuwajleen in 1975. I was following up the story that Jelibōr Jam had told me.

Emejwa said, "The shipwreck is celebrated to this day on Ujae with a party, food and singing. (Songs have been composed for the occasion.) And entertainment including Marshallese dancing (*jebwa*, stick dancing, and other dances). A Marshallese Protestant missionary (minister) visited Ujae in 1970 at the time of one of these celebrations. He was angry and told the people that there was no reason to celebrate. 'There is no importance to the ship drifting onto Ujae,' he said. The celebration started in 1917 or so, and the reef is called 'Wōd in Karjin' (kerosene reef) in remembrance of the shipwreck. Songs also commemorate the event. Tokwa, an old man of Ujae, knows the songs."

87: BWEBWENATO IN JUŌN WAAN AMEDKA: KŌMMEĻEĻE KO JET

Ri-bwebwenato: Enti Lucky, Kuwajleen 1975

Kōn wa eo jān Amedka ar kar peļo̧k ñan Ujae elōñ al in kememej kake. Wūnin kaṃōļo kake ñan rainin kōnke ri-Amedka ro ri-Ujae ṃokta raar jipañ er eṃōj an kajjitōk ippān ri-Ujae bwe ren kaṃōlo kake iien in. Ri-Ujae ro raar kōṃṃane āindein im kōṃṃan al ko im raar kaṃōlo aolep iiō ko.

Ej āinwōt juon ino̧ñ ñan er. Rūtto ro eṃōj an kōṃṃane āinwōt ilo ememej an jouj eo an ri-peļo̧k ñan er. Ro raar leļo̧k *cargo,* ṃweiuk, karjin, ko̧o̧n piip, im elōñ men in eṃṃan.

Ro raar ememej iien eo remej kiiō. Ri-Ṃajeļ ilo iien ṃokta, iien etto, raar ṃane aolep ri-peļo̧k jān wa. Āinwōt ri-Pikinni im ri-aelōñ ko, raar kōṃṃan āinwōt. Ak ri-Ujae rejjab ṃane er.

Wūnin irooj, ilo iien eo an wa ejorrāān ejjab melim, ej jouj.

Wūnin ri-Ṃajeļ rej kōṃṃan āinwōt kōnke rej bwebwe.

Al in Wa in Pālle ilo Ujae

Waan meja waan meja
ne waan lo̧meto keien ko i
kejepele ki im kōṃleñi
in ale i iñe bwe waan
rup ŋo in ad e kakkūṃkūṃ
le āne le wa in ŋa
ioon bōke in.

Al in ar kōṃṃane ettoo'm etto; ṃokta jān Tariŋae Kein Kajuon. Ṃokta jān ri-Jepaan. Eṃōj aō roñ al eo ilo iien Jepaan ke iaar ļaddik bajjek.

88: THE PEOPLE OF MĀJEEJ AND THE GERMAN TRADER

As told by a Mājeej *aļap,* Kuwajleen 1975

Mājeej was never conquered by outsiders, including the Germans. Big waves always arose at the critical time and prevented this.

There was an incident of a German trader setting the price for copra lower on the beach at Mājeej Island and higher on the outer edge of the reef *(baal).*

The people objected and said, "We won't work. We won't load our copra into the boat."

The German said, "All right. I will shoot you and kill you!"

The people said, "Go ahead. It is all the same with us."

The German then attempted to land on the island and shoot the people.

A big wave, bigger (taller) than the island, the tops of the coconut trees, arose and prevented the German from landing.

The Mājeej men who were on the German's ship were taken to Jebwad [the German administrative headquarters on Jālooj Atoll].

There was a court case there. The judge ruled that two prices would prevail (as the German had said).

The reason: it is easier to load on the beach and much harder on the edge of the reef.

So it was done, from then on.

Comments

Mājeej is a raised coral island without a lagoon and with a wide fringing reef. It has a dry land area of only 0.72 square miles. The island is located in the northern part of the Ratak chain. The fringing reef is covered with water at high tide and canoes and small boats are able to gain access to the open ocean. This enables the Mājeej people to go deep sea fishing and to go alongside the larger ships that come to the island for trading purposes and government business.

The larger ships cannot enter the reef area but must anchor off the reef edge of the island. Loading copra and offloading cargo can be difficult if the tide and weather conditions are not right. And the ease of small boat transit from ship to beach on Mājeej varies with the tide conditions.

Mājeej is not part of the Ratak chiefdoms and, it is said, has always been independent politically. It is divided into two political entities: the northern sector of the island, and the southern sector. Each had its own *irooj* (chief).

Perhaps the geographical and political factors have contributed to the independent attitude of the Mājeej people, as seen in the story of the confrontation with the German.

The story seems to imply that the Mājeej people received supernatural aid (from benevolent spirits) when the big waves always arose when the people needed help, and prevented would-be invaders from getting ashore and conquering the Mājeej people.

The use of a large wave or waves to intervene in human affairs was related to me by Reverend Ernej on Wūjlañ Atoll in 1955. In that story, a typhoon and large waves were brought up by the powerful spirit *(ekjab)* on Wūjlañ to punish islanders who had desecrated his dwelling place (see story 80, "Early History of the People of Wūjlañ Atoll," page 336).

As one might expect, other factors also thwarted invading enemy fleets at Mājeej Island. Informants M̧aikel, Jurenki, and L̦aruñ explained the independence of their island to me on Mājeej in 1952, "This island was never conquered. Attempts were made, but they all failed. Irooj Jetñōl tried, later Irooj Jortōkā[1] tried. They came up on the beach but saw that there were too many people on the island. So they left.

"This happened before the white men came to our island.

"The people of Mājeej were armed with their spears and were ready for the invaders.

"We Mājeej people never paid tribute *(ekkan)* to anyone.

"And we have always lived on Mājeej."

1. Jortōkā was *irooj l̦apl̦ap* (paramount chief) of northern Ratak toward the later part of the nineteenth century. One can see how this small island with a fringing reef that drops off sharply into the depths, could be easily defended by a determined population, which the Mājeej people obviously were.

89: STORY ABOUT THE MĀJEEJ *IROOJ*

As told by Jurenki, Mājeej 1951

The *irooj* (chiefs) of Mājeej came from two women, sisters: Litokbuñ and Limenwa. They were born on Mājeej and were human beings. This was long ago.

They married *kajoor* (commoners). The two women had parents, [who] were *kajoor.*

Litokbuñ, the older sister, started a fight on the island because there were many headmen then. She defeated all of them. She killed them all. (She fought her sons.)

After she won, she fought her sister. The younger sister won. The older one lost. All of the *irooj* on Mājeej come from this. This was before the white men came to the Marshall Islands.

Mājeej was divided into two parts during the Japanese times, North and South. Many people have *ruo aer* (two shoulders)[1] here on Mājeej. The *irooj* get along together, though.

Long ago there were no *irooj* on Mājeej (only headmen). This was way back. They were just *kajoor.* Then later the two sisters who were Raur (clan) said, "Our *jowi* (clan) is *irooj."* So they started the war to become *irooj.*

Note: Storyteller had never heard of the legendary Liwātuonmour.

---

1. This term comes from the old Marshallese custom of the *kajoor* honoring the infant *irooj* by carrying them on their shoulders. The term *ruo aer* (two shoulders) implies carrying two *irooj,* that is, owing allegiance to two *irooj* (see Tobin 1953a:10).

90: THE HISTORY OF THE CHURCH ON ĀNEWETAK ATOLL AND ON WŪJLAÑ ATOLL

As told by Reverend Ernej, Wūjlañ 1955

Jaṃuel came to Ānewetak in 1927. Ṃakwilōñ came in 1928. They were the first ministers to come to Ānewetak.

The Ānewetak people did not know about Christianity. I and Jonni had heard a little about it at Jālooj before. Jaṃuel came from Ṃakil and spread the gospel. He remained for one year. Then Ṃakwilōñ arrived. He was a Kusaiean preacher. He and Jaṃuel had been trained by Miss Hoppin. She sent them both. Jaṃuel was not so good. Ṃakwilōñ was better.

Jaṃuel taught reading and songs. But he did not baptize or marry people. He did not have this authority.

He had brought his wife Klara, a Ṃakil woman with him. She helped him teach.

The Japanese knew about this and allowed them to preach almost all the time. But they stopped it some days, perhaps three or four times a month. They did this whenever they thought it interfered with work.

The people built a small church out of local materials.

There were no Christians before Jaṃuel came. The religion *(kabuñ eo)* before was of spirits, *ekjab*. The *ekjab* names and locations:

1. Deñle: A rock on Ānewetak Island.
2. Luroñroñ: A rock on Jādool Island.
3. Jālooj: A coral head near the shore of the small island of Jādool.
4. Jari: A rock on land on Māddeen Island.
5. Debjen: A rock on Ānewetak Island.
6. Ļakaowōd: A rock on Enjepe Island.
7. Lepenak: A rock, a tall one, on Ikuden Island.
8. Ļabwilbwil: A coral head on Dibwāwōn Island.
9. Joonbar: A big rock on Pikōn Island.
10. Wūnbar. A rock on Pikōn Island (close to Joonbar).

Jālooj moved at high tide, not at low tide. People spoke to Jālooj—only people who wanted to get good sailing. They brought mats and food, and so forth, and said, here is your food or your mat, and so forth. Then they sailed away.

There are two *ekjab* in the lagoon of Ānewetak Atoll. They are Lijeieōn, a large wave, and Lijeilōr, [another] large wave. These destroy canoes that do not see them in time to escape. I do not know whether they are male or female, or if they can talk. Waves may only hurt people.

There is a *roro* (chant) to the *ak* (frigate bird) *ekjab*. It is a black *ak*. *"Ak eo | lik eo | Jakeo. | Lik eo jān—Jinme | ak eo."* (The frigate bird | the sea | Jakeo. | The sea from—Jinme | the frigate bird.) It flew above Jaļo Island. This is a *roro in kautiej* (a chant of respect, honor).

People worshipped these *ekjab* before Jaṃuel came. Some even continued to believe in them (old and young). Today all believe in Christ. Requests are made to *ekjab* for luck in fishing only.

Ṃakwilōñ had a second wife, Jepe, a Kosraean. She was a great help to him. He baptized and married and gave new names to people. They built a big church on Ānewetak.

He held school every day: writing, spelling, Bible, arithmetic, and singing (in Marshallese). Both he and Jaṃuel, only a little.

M̧akwilōn̄ taught for two years. The Japanese allowed him to teach every day.

The old people did not learn. The people who had to work also did not learn.

I had learned the Bible from Jālooj people who had worked on Wūjlan̄ Atoll, and then I went to Kosrae to be confirmed. I was there for two months; then I returned to Ānewetak and worked with M̧akwilōn̄ for eleven months.

The Japanese told M̧akwilōn̄ to leave Ānewetak.

A small English schooner, the *Penora,* came to Ānewetak.

There were two Japanese traders who were permanently stationed on Ānewetak. They did not know English.

Pita [one of the two chiefs, *irooj*], M̧akwilōn̄, and Joanej went to the schooner with the Japanese. M̧akwilōn̄ only knew, so he thought, what was going on.

The Japanese asked what the conversation was about and M̧akwilōn̄ said, "Nothing." One of the Japanese understood a little. Later the Japanese wrote to the Office at Pohnpei.

A big man-of-war came to Ānewetak, and Japanese officials on it beat M̧akwilōn̄. They said that it was bad that M̧akwilōn̄ spoke to the white men.

A trading schooner came almost immediately afterward and took M̧akwilōn̄ away, and the Japanese told him never to return to Ānewetak.

The Japanese were very angry. They had found out that M̧akwilōn̄ had given information on a chart of Ānewetak to the Englishmen. Joanej [presently one of the chiefs] denied knowledge when he was questioned by the Japanese. And M̧akwilōn̄ did not admit it either.

I was the only minister after M̧akwilōn̄ left. I received money and books for our church from Kosrae. There were no church meetings or contact with the Marshallese church organization.

I went to my first meeting of the Marshallese church in the Marshalls in June 1951. It had been called by Miss Wilson [Rev. Eleanor Wilson].

I have not seen the *Morning Star* [the Protestant Mission schooner that was based at Jālooj Atoll].

All the church funds have come from the Ānewetak people.

I do not know who will [succeed] me as minister.

Almost everyone knows how to read the Bible [in Marshallese]. Only ten of the older people do not know how.

The rocks of the spirits *(dekā in ekjab)* were not destroyed.

The Word of Christ came to Wūjlan̄ when I was a young man. L̦aman̄in̄i, a preacher from M̧aļo-eļap, came and taught the Gospel to the people.

A small church was built for the Marshallese. He converted me and Jonni. My wife did not want to learn, and she died later.

Jonni's wife also did not wish to learn. But she became converted later, on Ānewetak.

My present wife studied with M̧akwilōn̄, and she preaches to the women at the Thursday afternoon meetings.

APPENDIX A: BIOGRAPHIES OF STORYTELLERS

Jelibōr Jam. He was born on July 4, 1914, on Ujae Atoll, Kapinmeto, Rālik. He is of the Ri-Kuwajleen *jowi* (matriclan). His father's name was Jam, and his clan was Ejowa. The name of Jelibōr Jam's mother was Likno. Jelibōr is *nukwin irooj* (relative of the chiefs), as his mother and father were part of the chiefs before—maybe just *ļajjibjib* (lesser nobility), he said.

He was educated at the Protestant Mission School on Jebwad, Jālooj with Mother Hoppin, and at the Japanese school for five years.

He worked with the Japanese government at Jebwad as an interpreter and field trip officer's assistant for many years, one year of which was spent on Kuwajleen. He was Magistrate [Mayor] of Ujae Atoll for five years, into the American times, then continued in office for the one year period 1944–1945. He then went to Ruot [Roi-Naṃur] on Kuwajleen to work with the Americans as a carpenter, laborer, and cook for six months. Then he returned to Ujae and remained here until 1957, when he returned to Kuwajleen and took a job with the U.S. Navy at the Snack Bar, where he has continued to work.

He was married in 1937 to Taila. They have nine children, three boys and six girls, all of whom are living. One boy is a student in the school for ministers at Tarawa, Gilbert Islands. One boy is a student in the Philippines, one is at Emaus Protestant High School in Palau, and the rest are at school on Epjā.

Jelibōr Jam is an *aļap* (lineage head) of Irooj Ļapļap Jeimata (his son is Ļōjjeiļañ Kabua) in Kapinmeto (both are now deceased) and of Irooj Ļapļap Kabua Kabua in Rakinmeto and Eañinmeto (Kuwajleen). He further explained that his grandfather was Ļatōb, a *ri-meto* (navigator) and *ri-bwebwenato* (storyteller).

The Germans took Ļatōb and put him on a ship, inside the ship. They released him on deck, near but out of sight of Ānewetak. This was to test his knowledge of Marshallese navigation—the location of the atolls (his ability to find them). Ļatōb correctly told them, because of the presence of arrowroot detritus in the water. (This is called *liṃliṃ*.) It is in the water west of Ānewetak, and it is the *kōkļaļ* of Ānewetak Atoll, as Ļainjin said in "The *Ikid* of Ļainjin" [page 131], Jelibōr Jam concluded.

Mr. Jelibōr Jam speaks Japanese in addition to his Marshallese mother tongue, but only a little English, he said. He, and all of the other Marshallese who shared part of their traditional knowledge with me, were very conscientious in imparting this valuable information. Indeed, they were meticulous in narrating this lore, and they wanted to be sure that I understood what they were telling me.

Jobel Emos. He was born on September 9, 1918, on Wōjjā Atoll in Northern Ratak, and was reared mainly on Epoon Atoll in Southern Rālik. He was of the Ijjidik clan. He was an *aļap* on Wōjjā Atoll and on Ādkub Atoll as well.

Mr. Emos had three years of Japanese school on Epoon, and spoke Japanese and fluent English, as well as Marshallese.

He became an employee of the United States Navy shortly after the American victory over the Japanese forces in the Marshall Islands. He worked on Kuwajleen as work-crew supervisor and recruiter for workers from other atolls. Mr. Emos worked for civilian contractors on the Kuwajleen military base from about 1947 until his death in 1983.

Mark (Ṃak)[1] Juda. He was born on Jālooj on September 13, 1903. And is of the Ri-Ṃae clan. He is *kajoor* (commoner), but is an *aļap* (lineage head in charge of land) on Jālooj. He worked most of his life as a carpenter and as a boat builder. Mr. Juda graduated from the second school class established in the Japanese period of administration of the Marshalls. He is fluent in Japanese and understands some English, he stated. He first worked as Marshallese interpreter for the Japanese administration. He then worked as carpenter during the United States naval (civil)

1. Names of informants given in parentheses are their original names.

administration, and later for the Trust Territory Community Development Office at Mājro.

Mr. Juda married and had two daughters, one of whom is now deceased, and a number of grandchildren. He has retired from government service and now lives on Mājro Atoll.

Jǫwej. He was born in Ratak Eañ (Northern Ratak) during the German period, and was an elderly man when I first met him in 1950. He was the great-grandson of Irooj Eḷap (Paramount Chief) Bouliej, and was of the Ļajjidik clan.

Jǫwej was a famous *ri-meto* (navigator) and was advisor to Irooj Eḷap Ļaañm̧ooj Ran̦n̦o (who was also his kinsman). He explained that he was with Irooj Eḷap M̧urjel when he died, also Irooj Eḷap Ļabadeo, and he also stayed with Irooj Eḷap Jajua. M̧urjel made Ļabadeo promise to keep Jǫwej with him as *ri-bwebwenato* (storyteller/ advisor/historian), and Ļabadeo made Jajua promise. He then became *ri-bwebwenato* and *ri-meto* for Irooj Eḷap Lañm̧oj, who succeeded to the domain of northern Ratak after the death of his brother Tōmeiñ.

Jǫwej explained that he acted as a sort of advisor to these chiefs when they became paramount chief. He said that Ļabadeo always consulted him before he made an important move. He advised all of the *irooj eḷap* how to treat the *kajoor* (commoners)—how to act toward them. Jǫwej advised the new chiefs, he said.

Jǫwej possessed a wealth of knowledge of Marshallese history and traditional customs and lore. He was truly a living repository of Marshallese culture, and I can personally attest to his navigation skill, using the traditional techniques.

Ļaañm̧ooj Ran̦n̦o. He was the *irooj eḷap* of northern Ratak. The son of Ļaibne and Lerooj (Chiefess) Luliej of the Raarm̧o clan. Ļaañm̧ooj married Almira, daughter of Joran, an *irooj* of Mājeej Island, and later married Libarju. He had three children, one of whom, Emmi, a son, he made *irooj edik* (subchief) of Ādkub Atoll.

Ļaañm̧ooj succeeded his brother Tōmeiñ as paramount chief. His domain was the largest political entity in the Marshalls (as it remains). It stretched from Aur Atoll north of Mājro, to Bokak (Taongi) Atoll in the far north, excluding parts of M̧aḷo-eḷap Atoll (which were under a junior line) and all of independent Mājeej Island. Likiep Atoll, formerly part of the realm, was sold to the ancestors of the DeBrum and Capelle families by Irooj Eḷap Jortōkā in 1877.

Ļaañm̧ooj was a very kind person and was reportedly highly respected and liked by his people, and by other Marshallese as well, as indeed he was by me. He was very knowledgeable about traditional Marshallese culture and the history of the Marshalls. Ļaañm̧ooj died on Mājro in 1952 and was succeeded by his sister, the late Lerooj Lim̧ōjwa.

Kabua Kabua. He is an *irooj ḷapḷap* (paramount chief) of many islands and land parcels *(wāto)* in the Rālik Chain. Kabua (as he is commonly addressed) is the son of Irooj Ļapḷap Ļaelañ and Neimat, the daughter of Ļauna, a famous and powerful chief of Rālik. Kabua Kabua was named after his grandfather Irooj Ļapḷap Kabua, and he is of the Ri-Kuwajleen clan. He was born in 1910, and attended Japanese schools on Jebwad. He has been an appointive official under both Japanese and American administrations, and has been a member of the judiciary for many years. He speaks fluent Japanese and some English.

Dwight Heine. He was born on Epoon Atoll in 1919. His paternal grandfather, Reverend Carl Heine, was an Australian of English and German descent. Mr. Heine was of the Look clan. His Marshallese ancestors were from both Rālik and Ratak. He was educated in Protestant Mission schools on Epoon and on Kosrae (Kusaie) and was the first Micronesian to receive a college degree (Bachelor of Arts from the University of Hawai‘i).

Mr. Heine held many important positions, including that of Director of Education for the Marshalls, District Administrator for the Marshalls (the first Marshallese to hold these positions), and Special Consultant to the High Commissioner of the Trust Territory of the Pacific Islands at Saipan, a position that he held for a number of years until his retirement. He died in November of 1984. He was married to Morgiana, also from Epoon, and had a large family. He was very knowledgeable about the history and traditions of the Marshalls, and was a skilled raconteur and public speaker.

James Milne. He was born on Tarawa, Gilbert Islands, in 1921. He was of the Ri-Pit clan, and his paternal grandfather was an Englishman. Mr. Milne had Marshallese connections through his father, who was born on Epoon of a Gilbertese mother.

Mr. Milne was educated at the government school on Tarawa, then moved to Epoon at the age of eleven. He attended the Protestant Mission school there for five years. He worked for the Japanese government, then became a scout, and then a scout-interpreter for the United States Navy. He worked as interpreter for the U.S. Navy Civil Administration of the Marshall Islands. He later attended Mid-Pacific Institute and the University of Hawai'i. He knew a great deal about Marshallese culture, as well as that of his native Gilbert Islands, and spoke Japanese and English fluently (in addition to Marshallese and Gilbertese). Mr. Milne later engaged in a number of business ventures and had worked on government projects as well, including the Kōle Project, an attempt to help the displaced Pikinni people develop a viable economy on Kōle Island. Mr. Milne was married to Atina, an Epoon Atoll woman, and had a large family. He died in 1980.

(Litarjikūt) Dorothy Kabua. She was a *lerooj* (chiefess) of Mājro Atoll and was closely related to *irooj* (chiefs) of Arņo Atoll. Her brother Aisea Devij (David) was *irooj ļapļap* (paramount chief) of half of Mājro Atoll, and was succeeded by her son Joba Kabua. Her younger son, Amata Kabua was the first President of the Republic of the Marshall Islands.

Litarjikūt was married to the late Irooj Ļapļap Ļōjjeiļañ Kabua of the Rālik Chain. She was of the Raarņo clan and also related to the Ri-Ṃwejoor clan through her *irooj* kin on Arņo Atoll. She was educated at Protestant Mission schools and spoke Japanese and some English. She was very articulate and intelligent, and quite knowledgeable about the traditional culture of the Marshalls and of the events of her lifetime as well.

Reverend Ernej (Anej). He was born during the German period *(iien an Ri-Jāmne)* on Wūjlañ Atoll and was of the Jowa clan. Rev. Ernej was a descendant of the original chiefs of Wūjlañ. He probably knew more about the history and customs of that remote atoll than anyone else, and a great deal about Ānewetak Atoll as well. He was an *aļap* (lineage head) and a *bwidak.* (His father was *irooj* and his mother was *kajoor* (commoner). Rev. Ernej studied on Ānewetak with Rev. Ṃakwilōñ, a missionary from Kōsrae (Kusaie), in his missionary school on Ānewetak. Rev. Ernej spoke a little Ponapean and a little Trukese (in addition to his native Marshallese), he said. He was quite old when I took a census of the Wūjlañ population in 1952. He thought he was eighty years old. He was very alert mentally and active physically when I knew him.

Livai (Kar). He was born on Ānewetak during the German period and was of the Ijjidik clan. And was a *bwidak kia* (son of an *irooj*) and was an *aļap.* He said that he had no formal education. Livai said that he spoke a little Ponapean. He knew a great deal about the history and culture of Ānewetak. He died several years ago.

Ebream (Ļañiñi). He was born on Enjepe Island, Ānewetak Atoll. He said that he was 40-plus years old in 1952. He was *irooj ļapļap* of the Enjepe half of Ānewetak (and later Wūjlañ) and was of the Ijjidik clan. He stated that he had no formal education. He was also one of the two magistrates (mayors) of Wūjlañ Atoll.

Ebream said that he spoke a little Ponapean. He was married and had a large family. Ebream died several years ago.

Joanej (Lajukwe). He was born on Ānewetak Island, Ānewetak Atoll. He said he was 40 years old in 1952. He was *irooj ļapļap* of the Ānewetak half of Ānewetak Atoll (and later Wūjlañ) and was of the Ri-Pako (shark clan). He stated that he had had three years of school with Rev. Ṃakwilōñ on Ānewetak. He was also one of the two magistrates (mayors) of the Wūjlañ community for many years. Joanej said that he spoke a little Ponapean, and he was married and had a large family. He died recently.

Tiṃa Ṃarin. He was born on Roñļap Island, Roñļap Atoll, during the Japanese period *(iien an Ri-Jepaan).* He is an *aļap* on Roñļap Island. Mr. Martin had gone to Japanese school in the Marshalls and had worked as a seaman on a Japanese ship. He had visited Japan in that capacity, one of very few Marshallese to have done so.

Juda. He was born on Pikinni Atoll during the late German or early Japanese period. He belonged to the Ijjidik clan, and was the magistrate (mayor) on Pikinni and on Kōle Island after the Pikinni people were relocated there when the United States took Pikinni for an atomic test site.
He had a large family and died a number of years ago. Juda was spokesman for the Pikinni exiles during the very difficult and trying times of their uprooting, relocation, and attempts to adjust to their new environment.

Birbirin. He was born on Roñlap Atoll and had kin on Pikinni, and he married Tarpit, a Pikinni woman. He shared the exile of the Pikinni people on Kōle. He stated that he was 60 years of age in 1953, when I took a census of the Kōle Island population. Birbirin is a skilled navigator and very knowledgeable about traditional Marshallese culture.

Jorim. He was born during the German period, on Ānewetak Island, Ānewetak Atoll. He is of the Jowa clan. Jorim had a little Bible study with the Rev. Ṃakwilōñ—all of the older people were taught, he said. He is an *aļap* on the Ānewetak part of the atoll.

Jojeb. He said he was 39 years old when I took a census of the people on Wūjlañ in 1952. He was the son of Rev. Ernej, and was of the Ijjidik clan. He was descended from the original Wūjlañ people, as well as Enewetak Atoll people. He had three years of education with Rev. Ṃakwilōñ in his mission school on Ānewetak and three months with the United States Navy.

Jojeb said that he spoke a little English, a little Japanese, and a little Ponapean. He was conversant with the history and traditions of both Wūjlañ and Ānewetak.

Rev. Ļamān, Ļajekkein, and **Titōj** were elderly Roñlap Atoll men. They were born during the German period. None of them spoke English, but they all knew some Japanese.

I became well acquainted with them after they had been relocated to Ājej Island on Mājro Atoll. The entire Roñļap Atoll community had been moved there following the contamination of their home atoll by radioactive fallout in 1954. These informants, who died some years ago, left many descendants.

Raymond DeBrum. He was born on Likiep Atoll during the latter part of the German period. He was the grandson of José DeBrum, a Portuguese trader and planter, and part-owner, with German trader Adolph Capelle, of Likiep Atoll.

José's first wife was a woman from Ṃaļo-eļap Atoll, and their son Joachim was Raymond's father. Joachim, also a shipmaster, trader, and planter, was very knowledgeable in traditional Marshallese culture, including navigation, which he taught his sons. One of them, Leonard DeBrum, became a licensed shipmaster during the American administration of the Marshalls.

Raymond DeBrum was an expert in Marshallese navigation and many other aspects of Marshallese culture. He possessed land rights on Likiep Atoll and on Jāmo̧ Island, Majuro Atoll, and elsewhere. He worked for the Japanese administration and later for the American administration. He held a number of responsible positions, including that of Clerk-of-Courts of the Marshall Islands District. He served in this capacity for many years. He spoke some German, fluent Japanese, and good English.

Jetñil Felix (Bilik). He is from Arņo Atoll, and was born there during the Japanese administration of the islands. He belongs to the chiefly lineages of Arņo and Rālik.

Mr. Felix served as interpreter and field assistant in the early days of the American administration of the Marshalls, and became an employee of the Trust Territory Government, and later of the government of the Marshall Islands. He worked in the Supply Department at Majuro in supervisory capacities for many years. Mr. Felix speaks Japanese and English.

Ijikiel Laukōn. He was born on Arn̄o Atoll during the period of the Japanese administration of the Marshalls, and was educated in Japanese and in American schools. He spoke English well.

Mr. Laukōn was a trained and knowledgeable agriculturist, and worked as an extension agent in the outer islands. This included agricultural rehabilitation and education on Wūjlan̄ and Kōle on behalf of the relocated Ānewetak and Pikinni people.

He was later promoted to the newly created position of Community Development Officer for the Marshall Islands. He died in 1968 while still holding this office.

APPENDIX B: MOTIFS OF THE STORIES

"A motif is the smallest element in a tale having a power to persist in tradition. In order to have this power it must have something unusual and striking about it. Most motifs fall into three classes. First are the actors in a tale—gods, or unusual animals, or marvelous creatures like witches, ogres, or fairies, or even conventionalized human characters like the favorite, youngest child, or the cruel stepmother. Second come certain customs, strange beliefs, and the like. In the third place there are single incidents—and these comprise the great majority of motifs. It is this last class that can have an independent existence and that may therefore serve as true tale-types. By far the largest number of traditional types consist of single motifs" (Thompson 1951:415–416).

Motifs of the Stories (in order of appearance in each story)[1]

1. The Beginning of This World

A2. Multiple creators.
A21.3. God falls from heaven to earth.
A120. Nature and appearance of gods.
A513.1. Demigods descend from heaven.
A515. Pair of culture heros.
A139.9. Extraordinary physical appearance of gods.
A417. Gods of the quarters. A god or spirit for each of the world-quarters, north, south, east, and west.
A500. Demigods and culture heros.
A465.5.1. God of tattooing.
A1465.1. Origin of tattooing.
A515. Pair of culture heros.
A520.1. Gods as culture heros.
A630. Series of creations.
A665.2.1. Four sky columns. Four columns support the sky.
A665.2.1.1. Four gods at world-quarters support the sky.
A830. Creation of earth by creator.
A920. Origin of the seas.
A955.0.1. Islands created by order of deity.
A958. Origin of reefs.
A970. Origin of rocks and stones.
A2100. Creation of fish.
A2110. Creation of particular fishes.
A1900. Creation of birds.
A1970. Creation of miscellaneous birds.
A200. Creation of insects.
A2170. Creation of miscellaneous animal forms.
A2411. Origin of color of animal.
A2411.2. Origin of color of bird.
A2217.1. Birds painted their present color.
A2411.4. Origin of color of fish.
A1319. Origin of other bodily attributes.
A1423.3. Origin of coconut.
T555. Woman giving birth to a plant (coconut).
A2681.5.1. Origin of coconut tree.
A1400. Acquisition of human culture.
A1420. Acquisition of food supply for human race.
A1439. Acquisition of other necessities.
A1440. Acquisition of crafts.
A1446.5.5. Origin of baskets.
A2820.2. Origin of particular kinds of baskets.
A1170. Origin of night and day.
A541.3. Culture hero ordains how houses are to be built.
A1445.1. Origin of boat building.
A1438. Origin of medicine (healing).
A1570. Origin of regulations within the family.
A1640. Origin of tribal subdivision.
A1590. Origin of other customs.
A541. Culture hero teaches arts and crafts.
J140. Wisdom (knowledge) acquired through education.
A665.2.0.1. Pillars supporting sky.
A1171.5. Day begins when sky lifted.
A1435. Acquisition of habitations.
A1490. Acquisition of culture—miscellaneous.
A722.7.2. Place from which the sun rises.
A760. Creation and condition of the stars.
A720.2. Formerly great heat of sun caused distress to mankind.
A2600. Origin of plants.
A2681.11. Origin of breadfruit tree.
A2684. Origin of cultivated plants.

---

1. I have not tabulated motifs in the *Ikid* (Song-story) of Ļainjin, story 30, beginning on page 131. It is basically a recitation of topographical features, natural phenomena, and animals that I have identified and annotated.

A913. Origin of tides.
A1150. Determination of the seasons.
A750. Nature and condition of the moon.
A1120. Establishment of present order: winds.
A1127. Winds of the four quarters established.
A2650. Origin of flowers.
A1131. Origin of rain.
A530. Culture hero establishes law and order.
A1540. Origin of religious ceremonials.
VO. Religious services.
A1546. Origin of worship.
A176. God ordains ceremonies and regulations.
D231. Transformation: man to stone.
D150. Transformation: man to bird.
D170. Transformation: man to fish.
A901. Topographical features caused by experiences of primitive hero (demigod, deity). Footprints of the gods.
A972.1. Indentation on rocks from imprint of gods and saints.
A520.1. Gods as culture heros.
W100. Unfavorable traits of character—personal.
W154. Ingratitude.
Q380. Disrespect punished.
Q325. Disobedience punished.
Q550. Miraculous punishments.
Q580. Punishment fitted to crime.
A1013. Flood as punishment.
D2151.3.1. Magic tidal wave.
D215.1.3. Magic control of waves.
F200. Fairies (elves).
F235.2.3. Fairies become visible or invisible at will.
F239.4. Size of fairies.
F216. Fairies live in forest.
F219. Other dwelling places of fairies.
F441. Wood-spirit.
F423. Sea spirits.
A1330. Beginning of trouble for man.
A1335. Origin of death.
A1337. Origin of disease.
V100. Human sacrifice.
C564. Taboos of chiefs.
C755. Taboo: Doing thing during certain times.
V67. Mourning rites.
E722. Soul leaves body at death.
E722.3.1.1. Soul remains about dead body.
A955.11. Islands originally from continent (larger island), then separated.
A955.8.0.1. Islands fished up from underworld.
A955.8.1. Bait used by hero to fish up island.
A955.3.1. Origin of island's position.
QO. Rewards and punishments.
Q2. Kind and unkind (obedient and disobedient).
W31. Obedience.
F420. Water-spirits.
F420.1. Water-spirits as man.
F403. Good spirits.
F403.2.3. Deeds of familiar spirits.
F402.6.1. Marriage or liaison of mortals and water spirits.
F402.6.5. Spirits who live underground.

2. Story about Bōrraan
P231. Mother and son.
P200. The family.
W100. Unfavorable traits of character—personal.
Q325. Disobedience punished.
Q557. Miraculous punishment through animals.
A2100. Creation of fish.
A2110. Creation of particular fishes.
A2122. Origin of bonito.
A2138. Creation of porpoise.
A2139. Creation of fish—miscellaneous.
A1013. Flood as punishment.
Q431. Punishment, banishment (exile).
A1335. Origin of death.
E481.1. Land of dead in lower world.
A2213. Animal characteristics from squeezing or stretching ancient animal.
A901. Topographical feature caused by experiences of primitive hero (demigod, deity).

3. Story of the Heaven Post Men
A417. Gods of the quarters. A god or spirit for each of the world-quarters, north, south, east, and west.
A665.2.1. Four sky columns. Four columns support the sky.
A665.0.2. Gods who hold up heavens.
A260. God of light.
A432. God of agriculture.
P.O. Royalty and nobility.
A1653.1. Origin of kings (chiefs) from gods.
499.8. God of harvest.
A487. God of death.
A1335. Origin of death.
A1330. Beginning of trouble for man.

4. Origin of Tattooing
A513.1. Demigods descend from heaven.
A465.5.1. God of tattooing.
A1465.1. Origin of tattooing.
A515. Pair of culture heros.
A520.1. Gods as culture heros.

A72. Original creator followed by transformers. These demigods change the original creation into the present forms.
P.O. Royalty and nobility.
1653.1. Origin of kings (chiefs) from gods.
A2411.4. Origin of color of fish.
A2411. Origin of color of animals.
A2411.2. Origin of color of birds.
A2212.1. Birds painted their present color.
D680. Miscellaneous circumstances of transformation.
A192. Death or departure of the gods.
A901. Topographical features caused by experiences of primitive hero (demigod, deity).
D2090. Other destructive magic powers.

5. The Origin of the *Irooj* (Chiefs) of the Marshall Islands
A515. Pair of culture heros.
A520.1. Gods as culture heros.
A520. Nature of culture heros (demigods).
A592. Culture heros and descendants.
A1653.1. Origins of kings (chiefs) from gods.
A192. Death or departure of the gods.
V1.5. Sacred stones.
A419. Local gods—miscellaneous.
V10. Religious sacrifices.
V12. Nature of sacrifice.
PO. Royalty and nobility.

6. Liwātuonmour
PO. Royalty and nobility.
A520.1. Gods as culture heros.
V1.5. Sacred stones.
A592. Culture heros and descendants.
A192. Death or departure of gods.
A419. Local gods—miscellaneous.
A454. God of healing.
A520. Nature of culture heros (demigods).

7. Story of Liwātuonmour and Lidepdepju
A515. Pair of culture heros.
A520.1. Gods as culture heros.
V1.5. Sacred stones.
A419. Local gods.
V10. Religious sacrifices.
A192. Death or departure of gods.
A592. Culture heros and descendants.

8. About a Woman Named Lōktañir
9. The Story of Lōktañir
L10. Victorious youngest son.
P231. Mother and son.
QO. Rewards and punishments.
Q2. Kind and unkind (obedient and disobedient). Churlish person disregards request of old person (animal) and is punished. Courteous person (often youngest brother or sister) complies and is rewarded.
Q65. Filial duty, rewarded.
A1459.2. Acquisition of seamanship (sailing, etc.)
D21977. Magic dominance over animals.
D2150. Miscellaneous magic manifestations.
P.O. Royalty and nobility.
A770. Origin of particular stars.
A761. Ascent to stars. People or animals ascend to sky and become stars.
A773. Origin of the Pleiades.
A779.4. Origin of the star Antares.
D293. Transformation: man to star.
D2141. Storm produced by magic.
D2151.3. Magic control of waves.
D2142. Winds controlled by magic.
D2142.1. Wind produced by magic.
D214.2. Wind stilled by magic.
A1150. Determination of the seasons.
A760. Origin and condition of the stars.
W1O. Kindness.
W154. Ingratitude.

10. Story about Jebwa
F401. Appearance of spirits.
F420. Water spirits.
F420.1.1. Water spirit as man.
F402.6.7. Spirits dwell on island.
F403. Good spirits.
F200. Fairies (elves).
F239.4. Size of fairies.
F402. Evil spirits. Demons.
A1542.2. Origin of particular dance.

11. About a Young Man of Jālooj: Story about Anidep
PO. Royalty and nobility.
F402.1.4. Demons assume human forms in order to deceive.
0400. Person falls into ogre's power.
A1495.1. Origin of ball game.
D1710. Possession of magic powers.
D1781. Magic results from singing.
RO. Captivity.
0420. Capture by ogre.
R10. Abduction.
0440. Ogre abducts victim.
0422. Ogre imprisons victim.
R11O. Rescue of captive.
P231. Mother and son.
R169. Other rescues.
R210. Escapes.
R220. Obstacle flight—Atalanta type.
R260. Pursuits.

G11.10. Cannibalistic spirits.
G500. Ogre defeated.
G530.2. Help from ogre's mother.
G550. Rescue from ogre.

12. A Young Man Who Saw Jebrọ
A762. Star descends as human being.
A773. Origin of Pleiades.
P230. Parents and children.
P231. Mother and son.
A2687.5. Origin of banana.
E765.4. Life bound up with external event. Death to come when certain thing happens.
E571. Extremely old person.
D56. Magic change in person's age.
Q235. Disobedience punished.

13. Origin of the Banana Plant on Arņo Atoll
P200. The family.
P230. Parents and children.
RO. Captivity.
G10. Cannibalism.
G80. Other motifs dealing with cannibalism.
A2687.5. Origin of banana.
Q65. Filial duty rewarded.
Q11O. Material rewards.

14. Coconut Drifting onto the Sandbar: The Beginning of Coconut Trees
P231. Mother and son.
A2681.5.1. Origin of coconut tree.
A995. Origin of islands.
A999. Other land features—additional motifs.
Q65. Filial duty rewarded.
Q11O. Material rewards.

15. Story about the Beginning of Pandanus in the Atolls of the Marshalls
A200. Origin of plants.
A2681.11. Origin of breadfruit tree.
A435.4. God of pandanus.
A520.1. Gods as culture heros.

16. The Story of *Bōb* (Pandanus)
A200. Origin of plants
A435.4. God of pandanus.

17. A Fairy Tale *(Inọñ)*
A1599. Origin of additional customs.
T554.0.5. Woman gives birth to an insect.
F402. Evil spirits. Demons.
0500. Ogre defeated.

18. Stories of Roñļap and Roñdik
A955.3. Origin of island's shape and position.
A980. Origin of particular places.
W150. Unfavorable traits of character—social.
W151. Greed.
F402.6.7. Spirits dwell on an island.
F403. Good spirits.
Q272.1. Greed (gluttony) punished.
Q590. Miscellaneous punishments.
Z71.1. Formalistic number: three.

19. Story about Ellep in the Days of Long Ago (and Stories 20 and 21)
W31. Obedience.
W150. Unfavorable traits of character—social.
Q325. Disobedience punished.
A955.3. Origin of island's shape and position.
A980. Origin of particular place.
C610. The one forbidden place.
A920.1.0.1. Origin of particular lake.
D150. Transformation: man to bird.
G312. Cannibal ogre.
P231. Mother and son.
F402. Evil spirits. Demons.
D52. Magic change to different appearance.
D10.1.1. Ogre can become either a man or a woman.
D42.2. Spirit takes shape of man.
0500. Ogre defeated.
F405.12. Demons flee from fire.
0512.3. Ogre burned to death.

22. Story about the Atoll of Wōtto in the Olden Days
F401.6. Spirit in human form.
QO. Rewards and punishments.
F402. Evil spirits. Demons.
G312. Cannibal ogre.
G512. Ogre killed.
A901. Topographical features caused by the experiences of primitive hero (demigod, deity).
G346. Devastating monster. Lays waste to land.
D150. Transformation: man to bird.
G36. Ogre monstrous as to mouth.
F911. Person (animal) swallowed without killing.
F912.2. Victim kills swallower from within by cutting.

23. The Story of Ļabōkjānwut
B211.2.9. Speaking rat.
B437.1.1. Helpful rat.
E631. Human offspring from marriage to animal.
A901. Topographical features caused by experience of primitive hero (demigod, deity).

24. Ļaio, the Demon Who Stole from the Atoll of Mājro
G11.10. Cannibalistic spirits.
F401.6. Spirit in human form.

F402.1. Deeds of evil spirits.
G420. Capture by ogre.
G402.1.11.2. Evil spirit kills and eats person.
Q325. Disobedience punished.
Z71.1. Formalistic number: three.
PO. Royalty and nobility.
F420. Water spirits.
F420.5.2.1. Malevolent water spirits.
A955. Origin of islands.
B463.1.1. Helpful seabird.

25. How the Large Inlet on Wōtto Island Was Formed
R260. Pursuits.
R210. Escapes.
G131.2. Cannibal ogre.
D55.1.1.4. Woman stretches neck over horizon.
G346. Devastating monster. Lays waste to land.
G36. Ogre monstrous as to mouth.

26. The Beginning of the Appearance of Navigation in These Atolls
P231. Mother and son.
J140. Wisdom (knowledge) acquired through education.
PO. Royalty and nobility.

27. The Reason the Kapinmeto People Know Navigation: Story of the Beginning of the Knowledge of Navigation
PO. Royalty and nobility.
J140. Wisdom (knowledge) acquired through education.
P231. Mother and son.

28. Story about Weather: The Way the Old People in the Marshall Islands Used (Forecast)Weather
A740. Creation of the moon.
A750. Nature and condition of the moon.

29. About the *Ikid* (Song-story) of the Lōrro And Likakōj
PO. Royalty and nobility.
P230. Parents and children.
C830. Unclassified tabus.
J140. Wisdom (knowledge) acquired through education.
W31. Obedience.

30. The *Ikid* (Song-story) of Ļainjin
See footnote 1 on page 378.

31. Our Mother Forever, Our Father and the Father of Others

32. Story About Inedel
P210. Husband and wife.
P230. Parents and children.
P231. Mother and son.
T610. Nature and growth of children.
T145. Polygamous marriage.
S10. Cruel father.
S31. Cruel stepmother.
W150. Unfavorable traits of character—social.
Z271.1. Formalistic number: three.
A901. Topographical features caused by experience of primitive hero (demigod, deity).

33. Story about Living Things (Animals) in the Marshall Islands
B210. Speaking animals.
B211. Animal uses human speech.
B773. Animals with human emotions.
E211.3. Speaking bird.
B211.3. Speaking cock.
B211.5. Speaking fish.
B211.5.3. Speaking octopus.
L100. Unpromising hero.
B211.2.9. Speaking rat.
B295.2.1. Animals make voyage in canoe (usually have shipwreck).
B296.2.2. Animal (who is land dweller) crosses water on back of another animal.
A2412. Origin of animal markings.
A2494.16.7. Enmity between octopus and rat.
A2455. Animal's occupation: stealing.

34. The Tattler and the Triton: A Parable about the Coming of the Missionaries to Epoon
B140. Prophetic animals.
E143. Prophetic bird.
B211.9. Speaking shellfish.
B211.3. Speaking bird.
B211. Animal uses human speech.
V311. Conversion to Christianity.

35. The Story of Lijebake
P230. Parents and children.
Q325. Disobedience punished.
Z122. Rain personified.
B2116.3. Speaking turtle.
B211. Animal uses human speech.
B211.3. Speaking bird.

36. Story about a *Kakwōj*
F420.5.2.1.0.1. Water spirit pulls people into water, drowns them.

37. Leppeipāāt (Low Tide)
B211.5.3. Speaking octopus.
B175.6. Magic octopus.
B773. Animals with human emotions.
B211. Animal uses human speech.

Z71.1. Formulistic number: three.
B874.9. Giant octopus.
G308.9. Demon octopus.
A901. Topographical features caused by experiences of primitive hero (demigod, deity).

38. Two Women
B211.5.3. Speaking octopus.
B175.6. Magic octopus.
G308.9. Demon octopus.
B211. Animal uses human speech.
B874.9. Giant octopus.
B773. Animals with human emotions.
A901. Topographical features caused by experiences of primitive hero (demigod, deity).

39. Story about a Woman on Kōle Island
P231. Mother and son.
F402. Evil spirits, demons.
G30. Person becomes cannibal.
G11.6. Man-eating woman.
G312. Cannibal ogre.
F401.6. Spirit in human form.
K520. Death escaped through disguise, shamming, or substitution.
K525. Escape by use of substituted object.
M231. Obstacle flight—Atalanta type.
G36. Ogre monstrous as to mouth.
G500. Ogre defeated.
G650. Unclassified ogre motifs.

40. Story about a Mejenkwaad
V61. Various ways of disposing of dead.
G402. Evil spirits, demons.
G312. Cannibal ogre.
K1880. Illusions.
Z71.1. Formulistic number: three.

41–46. Other Mejenkwaad / Lōmkein Stories
No additional motifs.

47. Story of Two Brothers on Jālooj
D231. Transformation: man to stone.
G111.5. Cannibal demon.
F402. Evil spirits. Demons.

48. About a Woman Who Had Ten Boys
P231. Mother and son.
F516.2. People with one arm.
F517.0.1. Person with one leg.
K512.1. Person with one eye.
G131.2. Cannibal ogre.
L10. Victorious youngest son.
L101. Unpromising hero (male Cinderella). Usually, but not always, the unpromising hero is also the youngest son.
K520. Death escaped through disguise, shamming, or substitution.
G500. Ogre defeated.
K512.31. Ogre killed by throwing hot stones (metal) into his throat.

49. Story about Eleven Boys
F516.2. People with one arm.
F517.0.1. Person with one leg.
F512.1. Person with one eye.
E101.1. Unpromising hero (male Cinderella). Usually, but not always, the unpromising hero is also the youngest son.
G308. Sea monster.
Z71.1. Formalistic number: three.
K2388. Man stows away on canoe to make journey upon which he is not wanted.
G512.3.1. Ogre killed by throwing hot stones (metal) into his throat.
L10. Victorious younger son.
Q280. Unkindness punished.

50. Story about Two Epatōn Women
P.231. Mother and son.
G131.2. Cannibal ogre.
G510. Ogre killed, maimed, or captured.
0550. Rescue from ogre.
R153. Parent rescues child.
E125.5. Resuscitation by mother.

51. About a Woman Who Had a Boy Child
P.231. Mother and son.
G111.5. Cannibal demon.
G84. Fee-fi-fo-fum. Cannibal returning home smells human flesh and makes exclamation.
R210. Escapes.
R260. Pursuits.
G36. Ogre monstrous as to mouth.
G100. Giant ogre.
D631.4. Supernatural creature change size at will.
K1600. Deceiver falls into own trap.
G512.3. Ogre burned to death.

52. About a Man Named Jemerkinene
P200. The family.
C610. The one forbidden place.
C615. Forbidden body of water.
P210. Husband and wife.
P230. Parents and children.
F200.5.2.1. Malevolent water spirits.
G111.5. Cannibal demon.
F401.6. Spirit in human form.
Q325. Disobedience punished.
D42.3. Spirit assumes appearance of man's wife.

F402.1.4. Demons assume human forms in order to deceive.
G512.3. Ogre burned to death.

53. A Story of Two Men in Ratak, on Wōjjā Atoll, Island of Mejjen
C640. Unique prohibitions—miscellaneous.
Z271.5.2. Formulistic number: three.
Q325. Disobedience punished.
G111.5. Cannibal demon.
F401.6. Spirit in human form.
RO. Captivity.
R210. Escape.

54. Story about a Young Mājeej Girl
F200.5.2.1. Malevolent water spirit.
Z271.5.2. Formulistic number: three.
PO. Royalty and nobility.
G111.5.1. Cannibal demon.
R310. Refuges.
J140. Wisdom (knowledge) through education.

55. The Girls from Ep
PO. Royalty and nobility.
C515. Taboo: touching (plucking) flowers.
Q325. Disobedience punished.
Q590. Miscellaneous punishments.
P600. Customs.
Z71.1. Formalistic number: three.
F401.6. Spirit in human form.
RO. Captivity.
G111.5. Cannibal demon.
R260. Pursuits.
B478. Helpful crab.
B211. Animal uses human speech.
B211.8.1. Speaking crab.
B295.2. Animals build canoe.
R210. Escapes.
R220. Flights.
G500. Ogre defeated.
G512. Ogre killed.

56. Lijibokra
F402. Evil spirits.
F403. Good spirits.
F401.6. Spirit in human form.
T415. Brother-sister incest.

57. Story about Lōrro
P210. Husband and wife.
E700. The soul.
E720. Soul leaves or enters the body.
E721.10. Soul takes a voyage.

58–60. Other Lōrro Stories
No additional motifs.

61. About a Woman on Ujae Named Libwiner
W100. Unfavorable traits of character—personal.
J200. Choices.

62. The Story of Ļañinlur
PO. Royalty and nobility.
P200. The family.
T50. Wooing.
P130. Marriage customs.
T10. Falling in love.

63. About a Chief on Epatōn, Kuwajleen
PO. Royalty and nobility.
C564. Taboos of chiefs.
C41. Taboo: singing.
F1083. Object rises into the air.
D390. Magic object rescues person.
C310. Taboo: looking at certain person or thing.
W150. Unfavorable traits of character: social.
Q380. Disrespect punished.
Q450. Cruel punishment.
K910. Murder by strategy.

64. Story about Two Young Men at Wōja, Aelōñļapļap
Z271.5.2. Formulistic number: three.
D1812.3. Means of learning future.
W150. Unfavorable traits of character: social.
W151. Greed.
F1083. Object rises into the air.
F1083.0.1. Object floats in air.
D2135.O.2. Object magically raised in air.
D2135.5. Objects sent through air.
K40. Labor contest won by deception.
K300. Thefts and cheats—general.

65. Story about a Boy Named Deelelpo Jāpo
P200. The family.
P210. Husband and wife.
P231. Mother and son.
P600. Customs.
G11O. Cannibalism.
E35. Resuscitation from fragments of body.
F402. Evil spirits.
A999. Other land features. Additional motifs.

66. Story about Ņooniep
67. Stories from Ānewetak Atoll
F230. Appearance of fairies.
F235.2.3. Fairies become visible or invisible at will.
PO. Royalty and nobility.
F271.2.3. Fairies build canoe.
H1594.3. Canoe race.
F403.1. Spirits give money (fish) to mortal.

68. Stories about Etao
P200. The family.
A2770. Other plant characteristics.
K2370. Miscellaneous deceptions.

69. Maui on Mājeej, and Woneņak Stories
D1710. Possession of magic powers.
PO. Royalty and nobility.
D719.1. Contest in magic.
D2149.1. Thunderbolt magically produced.
A9O1. Topographical features caused by experience of primitive hero (demigod, deity).
F441. Wood spirit.
F441.4. Form of wood spirit.
V60. Funeral rites.

70. Maui on Mājeej
D1710. Possession of magic power.
D719.1. Contest in magic.
PO. Royalty and nobility.
A901.1. Topographical features caused by experience of primitive hero (demigod, deity).

71. The Chant of Mile: Fishing Up from the Bottom of the Sea
F899.4. Marvelous fish hook.
A4955.8.0.1. Islands fished up from the underworld.

72. About a Woman Who Was on Rōn̄dik
A750. Nature and condition of the moon.

APPENDIX C: WEATHER FORECASTING AND NAVIGATION

The Marshallese, who have been sailing their large canoes throughout their scattered islands and atolls for untold centuries without benefit of navigational instruments, such as the compass and the sextant, have developed a reliable system of navigation with only a knowledge of wave patterns, currents, the position of heavenly bodies, and other natural phenomena.

The knowledge of navigation and the associated weather forecasting were the property of the chiefs *(irooj),* who jealously guarded it and passed it down to their close male relatives, usually their maternal nephews and their own sons, to favored nonrelatives, and occasionally to their own daughters.

Knowledge of navigation, a necessity in making expeditions of conquest to distant atolls, and for ordinary communication, was restricted to a few individuals in order to maintain and enhance chiefly power and prestige. Among the few men who thoroughly know Marshallese navigation today, only two are said to be of commoner ancestry.

A commoner *(kajoor)* who wished to learn navigation (or obtain land or any other favor from the chief) followed a stylized pattern in asking for the favor. It was a serious breach of etiquette to ask directly. He silently presented food and fine mats to the chief and waited for the chief to speak.

An elderly informant, Jo̧wej, a famous navigator *(ri-meto)* and a subchief *(irooj edik)* of Wōjjā Atoll, described such a petition made to his father, Jibūinem̧m̧an, who was an important subchief under M̧urjel, ruler of most of northern Ratak.

The commoner brought food to the chief, who, knowing full well that a request was going to be made, asked, "What is this for?" The reply came, "To seek for light." The chief then asked, "For what?" And the commoner replied: "I want to learn navigation, give me life." He meant "Teach me navigation so I will not miss the landfalls while sailing, and die."

The chief then agreed to his request and taught him *ialeplep* 'the main road', a lesser type of navigation. Commoners were very rarely allowed to learn *meto,* the complete knowledge of navigation.

The associated and necessary knowledge of weather, based on empirical knowledge, on trial and error—gained like the other aspects of navigation over centuries of observation and experience—is known as *lañ.* The weather expert is called *ri-lale-lañ* ('weather watcher' or 'observer'). His services are valuable not only for navigation but for fishing and other economic activities.

My informants all agreed that, in the old days, the chief hid the secrets of navigation and could kill people or throw them off of the land if they revealed the secret knowledge.

Even today, one must obtain permission from one's chief before revealing this knowledge to anyone. However, the consensus of informants, navigators and nonnavigators alike, was that most navigators want to hide their secrets.

Chants *(roro)* are learned and used as mnemonic devices by the weather forecaster (and the navigator). Although some of them are obviously descriptive of specific conditions or phenomena, most of the chants are meaningless in the literal translation because of the extensive use of metaphor and allusion. The deep meaning *(m̧wilaļ)* must be learned. Archaic or esoteric words or terms further tend to obscure the meaning of the chant to the uninitiated. See *Land Tenure in the Marshall Islands* (Tobin 1952:25–26) for details.

Navigation signs or sea marks—certain fish, marine mammals, birds, floating logs, and the like, and large rocks on reefs and other natural phenomena called *kōkļaļ* or *kakōļļe*—are learned as indicated, and form part of the navigation chants (*roro* or *al*) and help the navigator / voyager to his destination.

Sailing canoes have almost disappeared from the Marshalls, supplanted by motor-driven vessels (and recently aircraft). With the large seagoing canoes have gone the old navigators and their highly specialized knowledge and skills, through natural attrition. There are probably very few Marshallese who possess this once highly prized knowledge, and it will undoubtedly die with these old men. The modern Marshallese navigators learn their skills at maritime academies or from those who have graduated from these institutions; not from a *ri-meto,* and without seeking their chief's permission.

I was able to observe the techniques of Marshallese navigation while on long trips with the famous *ri-meto* (navigators), Jọwej and Raymond DeBrum, on schooners (converted United States Navy fifty-foot motor launches) in the early 1950s. We did not miss a landfall on trips with either of these men in charge. (The bright lights of Kuwajleen naval base at night provided a navigation sign unknown to the old Marshallese navigators, but were used by these navigators of the post–World War II era as navigational aids *(kōkļaļ).* The terms used in the folktales of the beginning of the knowledge of navigation in the Marshalls were used by the *ri-meto,* and are still known to the few survivors and some of the older Marshallese.

A fleet of canoes was known as an *inij.* As Ṃak Juda explained to me on Mājro in 1973, "The Marshallese used to sail in fleets of 60 to 80 sailing canoes that were 50 to 60 feet long. They were used for warfare and to visit other atolls, by the *irooj* (chiefs).

"An exchange of goods was made between Eāninmeto and Rakinmeto (north and south Rālik). *Pinniep* (coconut oil), *eokkwaļ* (coconut sennit), *ṃakṃōk* (arrowroot 'flour') from the north were exchanged for *jāānkun* and *bwiro* (preserved breadfruit), and pandanus and other foods from the south.

"This was done until the 1920s, when the large canoes were replaced by schooners. However, Kabua's ship, the *Eañjen-Rakjen,* a 120-ton, two-masted schooner built in San Francisco began operating in the German times. It continued operating in the waters of the Marshall Islands into the Japanese period of administration."

Krämer and Nevermann (1938:222),[1] in a rather lengthy discussion of traditional Marshallese navigation, state, "When a [*kajoor*] comes to a [*ri-meto*] and asks for instruction, he says: [*letok jidik*] *mour,* i.e., 'teach me something', upon which the [*ri-meto*] answers, if you give (give some life) me little, I shall give you little, if you give me much, I shall give you much." The correct translation of *letok jidik mour* is 'give (me) a little life'.

As noted previously, the formal presentation of food and other valued items to the chiefs *(irooj ro)* was an important part of traditional Marshallese custom, the traditional culture (*ṃantin Ṃajeļ* or *ṃantin aelōñ kein*). Indeed, it still is. The act of formal or even informal presentation of food is one of recognition of the rank and authority of the one who is so honored. The *irooj* functioned as redistributive chiefs.

1. For other descriptions of the Marshallese system of navigation, see Winkler (1898:1418–1419, English translation 1899:487–508). This contains sketches and photographs of the various "stick charts," and photographs of canoes and canoe models. Also see Krämer and Nevermann (1938:215–232, English translation no. 10003:221–242). Erdland (1910:16–26) discusses specific courses plotted and stellar navigation, and Davenport (1960:19–26) provides an extensive bibliography of the subject in his succinct discussion of Marshallese navigation.

APPENDIX D: A NOTE ON CANOE BUILDING IN THE OLDEN DAYS[1]

Informant: Jǫwej, Mājro 1951

Erentōp means something (in other words, a gift) to put your shavings from the canoe in (a reward for canoe building). In the old days canoes were very important in the economy and in the frequent wars. In the absence of metal tools, canoe building was a difficult and time-consuming task.

When the chief *(irooj)* wanted a new canoe, he sent hundreds of his people out to cut a huge breadfruit tree for the hull. And other trees for the supports of the outrigger, the platform, and so forth. Clamshell-bladed adzes *(māāl)* were used.

Only a few men in a few lineages *(bwij)* knew how to construct a canoe. Special knowledge of measurements was and still is handed down within the lineage.

Folded pandanus leaves were used to "blueprint" the canoe. Two of these skilled men were usually in charge of the building of a huge canoe for the *irooj.* These men were rewarded by the *irooj* with gifts of mats, rope, food, and so forth—never land. The other workers received nothing from the *irooj* but food while they were working on his canoe. I saw Irooj Ṃurjel's[2] canoe built, and land was not given. I have never heard of land called *erentōp.* [Other informants have told me the same thing.]

A man in charge of the canoe building was forbidden to have sexual intercourse while the canoe was being built. A *ri-bubu* specialist in magic made magic to aid in building a good canoe. *Boḷā* [divination by counting out beach pebbles *(ḷā)* in series] was used before the canoe was built to find an auspicious time. A canoe should be made when there is no danger of a surprise attack that would prevent completion or allow capture of the canoe by the enemy.

1. The methods, customs, and rituals involved in the construction of canoes in old Hawai'i are described in some detail by Malo (1976:126–135), and the special rituals involved in the major undertaking of felling a tree, shaping the canoe hull, and bringing it down from the forest in old Hawai'i and Tahiti are described by Beckwith (1970:273–274). These customs and rituals indicate the importance of canoes to the islanders in the past. The seeking of supernatural protection and assistance in the construction and operation of canoes has been observed in many other cultures in Oceania.

2. A paramount chief *(irooj eḷap)* of northern Ratak.

APPENDIX E: THE OLD MARSHALLESE METHOD OF COUNTING

Informant: M̧ak Juda, Mājro 1973

Fish *(ek)* are counted by twos: *juon, ruo, jilu, emān, ļalem.* In the present-day method of counting, this means: one, two, three, four, five. In the old method, counting fish, they mean: two, four, six, eight, ten: *jabjet.*

Then it continues from *jabjet* as follows:

Jabjet em juon: twelve.

Jabjet em ruo: fourteen.

Jabjet em jilu: sixteen.

Jabjet em emān: eighteen.

Jabjet em ļalem: ruokor: twenty.

Ruo̧kwōd em juon: twenty-one.

Continue as above.

Jilkwōd: thirty.

Continue as above.

Limakwōd: fifty.

Continue as above.

Juonibuki: one hundred (fifty times two). *N̄oul* is ten. That is, *juon noul (joñoul)* is one ten. *Jiṃa* is 'plus'. That is, *joñoul jiṃa* [is 'ten plus', 'ten some', 'ten and more'].

Jilñuul is three tens.

Eñoul is four tens.

Count to double fifty or one hundred and then repeat.

This method was used by fishermen to divide their catch when a large number of fish were caught. This was usually by the surround method *(alele),* or catching fish with scoop-nets *(bo̧bo).* For shellfish, the one–ten regular count was used.

The double-count method was also used by the chiefs *(irooj)* to distribute catches of fish (and was also used for porpoise). The double-count method is not used today. It was used as late as the Japanese times to divide fish, and by the *irooj.* It was used for group net fishing: the surround method and the like.

It may have been used for copra and other things long ago, but I have never heard of it being done in the days of Irooj Kabua (the German period and later).

Today people use *juon, ruo, jilu* (one, two, three). This was used before, in the old days, for counting people and for dividing food at a feast, or for other distribution. (*Wōtbar* is the term used for this activity.)

For counting, *jikut* (two hundred) and *rukut* (four hundred) were used in stories *(bwebwenato).* This was for big counting, in the language of stories *(kajin bwebwenato).* [See notes 114 and 115 on page 137 in story 30.]

The largest count was *jikut* and *rukut.* The larger counting: one thousand *(juon taujin)* count and upward—and the concept—came to the Marshall Islands and the Marshallese language with the Europeans. *Jikut* and *rukut* were used for the counting of spears *(ṃade),* and came from stars in the skies (constellations). There was no point in counting coconuts prior to the start of the copra industry in the Marshalls.

In the old days when the chief *(irooj)* prepared a feast, he would not specify how much to provide. He would say *"Jej eo̧jek"* (bring a bundle, a big one, for the place where people live, one island). But for people who visit from elsewhere, he would say *"Ni badbad"* (bring food).

REFERENCES

Abo, Takaji, Byron W. Bender, Alfred Capelle, and Tony DeBrum. 1976. *Marshallese-English dictionary.* PALI Language Texts: Micronesia. Social Science Research Institute. University of Hawai'i. Honolulu: The University Press of Hawai'i.

Abrahams, Roger D. 1983. *African folktales: Traditional stories of the Black World.* New York: Pantheon Press.

Alkire, William H. 1977. *An introduction to the peoples and cultures of Micronesia.* 2d ed. Menlo Park, Calif.: Cummings Publishing Company.

Alpers, Antony. 1970. *Legends of the South Seas.* New York: Thomas Y. Crowell Company.

Anderson, Donald. 1951. *The Plants of Arno Atoll, Marshall Islands.* Atoll Research Bulletin No. 7. Washington, D.C.: The Pacific Science Board, National Research Council.

Baker, Rollin H. 1951. *The avifauna of Micronesia: Its origin, evolution, and distribution.* Museum of Natural History, vol. 3, no. l. Lawrence, Kans.: University of Kansas.

Barrau, Jacques. 1961. *Subsistence agriculture in Polynesia and Micronesia.* Bernice P. Bishop Museum Bulletin 223. Honolulu: Bishop Museum Press.

Beamer, Winona. 1984. *Talking story with Nona Beamer: Stories of a Hawaiian Family.* Honolulu: Bess Press.

Beckwith, Martha Warren. 1970. *Hawaiian mythology.* Honolulu: The University of Hawai'i Press.

———. 1972. *The Kumulipo: A Hawaiian creation chant.* Honolulu: The University of Hawai'i Press.

Bender, Byron W. 1969. *Spoken Marshallese: An intensive language course with grammatical notes and glossary.* Honolulu: The University of Hawai'i Press.

Bernart, Luelen. 1977. *The Book of Luelen.* Trans. and ed. by John L. Fischer, Saul H. Riesenberg, and Marjorie G. Whiting. Honolulu: The University Press of Hawai'i.

Brost, F. B., and R. D. Coale. *A guide to shell collecting in the Kwajalein Atoll.* Rutland, Vt.: Charles E. Tuttle Co.

Bryan, Edwin H., Jr. 1946. *Maps of the Islands of Micronesia.* Honolulu: United States Commercial Company.

Buck, Peter H. (Te Rangi Hiroa). 1966. *The coming of the Maori.* Wellington: Maori Purposes Fund, Whitcombe and Tombs, Ltd.

Buckingham, H. W. 1949. Collection of Marshallese Legends: Told by Ļokrap, Ebon. Typescript. Kwajalein, Marshall Islands.

Bulfinch, Thomas. 1978. *Bulfinch's Mythology.* Avenel Books. New York: Crown Publishers.

Carr, Denzel, and Samuel Elbert. 1945. *Marshallese-English and English-Marshallese Dictionary.* Honolulu: 14th Naval District, District Intelligence Office, Marshalls-Gilberts Area.

Catholic Mission. n.d. *Marshallese-English Dictionary.* Likiep: Marshall Islands. [Post–World War II.]

Cernohorsky, Walter O. 1967. *Marine shells in the Pacific.* Sydney: Pacific Publications.

Chambers, Keith. 1969. A preliminary collection and study of Marshallese folklore. Unpublished MS. Honolulu: University of Hawai'i.

———. 1972. Tale traditions of Eastern Micronesia: A comparative study of Marshallese, Gilbertese, and Nauruan folk narrative. M.A. thesis, University of California, Berkeley.

Davenport, William H. 1952. Popular sayings and tales of the Marshallese. Typescript. Honolulu: University of Hawai'i.

———. 1953. Marshallese folklore types. *Journal of American Folklore* 66:219–237.

———. 1960. Marshall Islands navigational charts. Imago Mundi, vol. 15. Indianapolis: Bobbs-Merrill Reprint Series in the Social Sciences. A-48:19–26.

Dixon, Roland B. 1964. *Mythology of Oceania: The Mythology of All Races,* vol. 9. New York: Cooper Square Publishers.

Elbert, Samuel H., and Torben Monberg. 1965. *From the two canoes: Oral traditions of Rennel and Bellona Islands.* Honolulu: University of Hawai'i Press.

Erdland, P. August. 1910. *Die Sternkunde bei den Seefahren der Marshall-Inseln.* Anthropos: Internationale Sammlung Ethnologischer Monographie. Ed. 5:16–26. Munster: I. W. Aschendorff.

———. 1914. *Die Marshall-insulaner: Leben und sitte, sinn und religion eines Südsee-Volkes.* Anthropos: Internationale Sammlung Ethnologischer Monographie, Bd. 2, Hft. 1. Munster: I. W. Aschendorff.

Finsch, O. 1893. *Ethnologische Erfahrungen und Belegstücke aus der Südsee.* Annalen des K. K. Naturhistorischen Hofmuseums, ed. von Hauer, 8. Wien: Alfred Holder.

Fischer, John L., and Ann M. Fischer. 1957. *The Eastern Carolines.* New Haven: Human Relations Area Files Press.

Fosberg, F. R. 1953. *Vegetation of Central Pacific atolls.* Atoll Research Bulletin No. 23. Washington, D.C.: The Pacific Science Board, National Academy of Sciences, National Research Council.

Gifford, Edward W. 1924. *Tongan myths and tales.* B. P. Bishop Museum Bulletin 8. Honolulu: Bishop Museum Press.

Gittings, Anne. 1977. *Tales from the South Pacific.* Owens Mills, Md.: Stemer House Publishers.

Gladwin, Thomas. 1970. *East is a big bird: Navigation and logic on Puluwat Atoll.* Cambridge, Mass.: Harvard University Press.

Goo, Fannie C. C., and Albert H. Banner. 1963. A preliminary compilation of Marshallese animal and plant names. Mimeo. Hawai'i Marine Laboratory, University of Hawai'i, Honolulu.

Grey, Eve. 1951. *Legends of Micronesia,* books 1 and 2. Micronesian Reader Series. Honolulu: Department of Education, Trust Territory of the Pacific Islands.

Grimble, A. 1972. *Migration, myth and magic from the Gilbert Islands: Early writings of Sir Arthur Grimble.* London: Routledge and K. Paul.

Hager, Carl. 1886. *Die Marshall-Inseln in Erd und Völkerkunde, Handel, und Mission. Mit einen Anhang: die Gilbert-Inseln.* Leipzig: G. Lingke.

Halstead, Bruce. 1959. *Dangerous marine animals.* Cambridge, Md.: Cornell Maritime Press.

Hamilton, Edith. 1942. *Mythology.* Boston: Little, Brown and Company.

Hathaway, William. 1953. *The land vegetation of Arno Atoll, Marshall Islands.* Atoll Research Bulletin No. 16. Washington, D.C.: The Pacific Science Board, National Academy of Sciences, National Research Council.

Henry, Teuira. 1928. *Ancient Tahiti.* B. P. Bishop Museum Bulletin 28. Honolulu: Bishop Museum Press.

Hiatt, Robert W., and Donald Strasburg. 1951. *Marine zoology study of Arno Atoll, Marshall Islands.* Atoll Research Bulletin No. 4. Washington, D.C.: The Pacific Science Board, National Academy of Sciences, National Research Council.

Hines, Neal. 1962. *Proving ground: An account of the radiological studies in the Pacific.* Seattle: University of Washington Press.

Holy Bible. 1962. Saint Joseph New Catholic Edition. The Old Testament confraternity —Douay version, and the New Testament, confraternity edition. New York: Catholic Book Publishing Company.

Humphrey, O[mar] J. 1887. *Wreck of the Rainier: A sailor's narrative.* With Preface By Robert Rexdale. Portland, Maine: W. H. Stevens and Company, Publishers. Printed By B. Thurston and Company, Portland.

Johnson, Rubellite Kawena. 1981. *Kumulipo: The Hawaiian Hymn of Creation.* vol. 1. Honolulu: Topgallant Publishing Company, Ltd.

Kalimur Ekāl an ar Iroij im dri lomor Jisōs Kraist (The New Testament). 1948. New York: American Bible Society.

Kamakau, Samuel Manaiakalani. 1964. *Ka po'e kahiko (The people of old).* Trans. by Mary Kawena Pukui, arr. and ed. by Dorothy B. Barrere. Bishop Museum Special Publication 51. Honolulu: Bishop Museum Press.

Kato, Susumu, Stewart Springer, and Mary H. Wagner. 1967. *Field guide to Eastern Pacific and Hawaiian sharks.* Circular 271. Washington, D.C.: United States Department of the Interior, Fish and Wildlife Service, Bureau of Commercial Fisheries.

Keightley, Thomas. 1978. *The world guide to gnomes, fairies, elves, and other little people.* New York: Avenel Books.

Kirtley, Bacil F. 1955. A motif-index of Polynesian, Melanesian, and Micronesian narratives. Ph.D. dissertation, Indiana University.

Kirtley, Bacil F., and Edith T. Mookini, eds. and trans. 1979. *Essays upon ancient Hawaiian religion and sorcery by nineteenth century seminarists.* Honolulu: *The Hawaiian Journal of History,* vol. 13.

Knappe, Konsul, Dr. 1888. *Religiöse Anschauungen der Marschall-Insulaner.* Mitteilungen aus den deutschen Schutzgebieten. Berlin.

Knight, Gerald. 1982. *Man this reef.* Majuro, Marshall Islands: Micronitor News and Printing Company.

Kotzebue, Otto von. 1821. *A voyage of discovery into the South Seas and Beering's Straits . . . Undertaken in the Years 1815–1818.* Trans. by H. E. Lloyd, 3 vols. London: Longman, Hurst, Rees, Orme, and Brown. (Vol. 3 written by Adelbert von Chamisso.)

Krämer, Augustin Friedrich. 1906. *Hawaii, Ostmikronesien und Samoa, Meine Zweite Südseereise (1897–1899) zum Studium der Atolle und ihrer Bewohner.* Stuttgart: Verlag von Strecker und Schröder. Trans. no.1033, 59 pp. ms.

Krämer, Augustin Friedrich, and Hans Nevermann. 1938. *Ralik-Ratak: Ergebnisse der Südsee Expedition 1908–1910.* 2 B, Band 2. Hamburg: Friedrichsen, De Gruyter Co. Trans. no.1003, 234 ms. pp.

Leach, Maria, ed., and Jerome Fried, assoc. ed. 1949. *Standard dictionary of folklore, mythology, and legend,* vol. 1, and vol 2:1950. New York: Funk and Wagnalls Company.

Lessa, William A. 1959. Divining from knots in the Carolines. *Journal of the Polynesian Society* 68:188–210.

———. 1961. *Tales from Ulithi Atoll: A comparative study in Oceanic folklore.* Folklore Studies 13. Berkeley and Los Angeles, University of California Press.

Lewis, David H. 1972. *We, the navigators: The ancient art of landfinding in the Pacific.* Honolulu: The University Press of Hawai'i.

———. 1977. *From Maui to Cook: The discovery and settlement of the Pacific.* Sydney: Doubleday.

Lons, Veronica. 1975. *Egyptian mythology.* New York: The Hamyln Publishing Group, Ltd.

Luomala, Katharine. 1949. *Maui-of-a-thousand tricks: His Oceanic and European biographers.* B. P. Bishop Museum Bulletin 198. Honolulu: Bishop Museum Press.

———. 1950a. *South Sea superman.* Reprint from *International House Quarterly,* Autumn 1950. New York: International House Association.

———. 1950b. Micronesian mythology. And Polynesian Mythology. In *Standard Dictionary of Folklore, Mythology, and Legend,* vol. 2, ed. by Maria Leach. New York: Funk and Wagnalls Company.

———. 1955. *Voices on the wind: Polynesian myths and chants.* Honolulu: Bishop Museum Press.

———. 1975. *Cultural association of land mammals in the Gilbert Islands.* Occasional Papers of Bernice P. Bishop Museum, vol. 24, March 1975, no. 12. Honolulu: Bishop Museum Press.

Malo, David. 1976. *Hawaiian antiquities (Moolelo Hawai'i).* Honolulu: Bishop Museum Press.

Marshall Joe T., Jr. 1951. *Vertebrate ecology of Arno Atoll, Marshall Islands.* Atoll Research Bulletin No. 3. Washington, D.C: The Pacific Science Board, National Research Council.

Mason, Leonard. 1947. The economic organization of the Marshall Islanders. Economic Survey of Micronesia vol. 8. MS. Washington, D.C.: United States Commercial Company.

———. 1954. Relocation of the Bikini Marshallese: A study in group migration. Doctoral dissertation, Yale University.

Minton, Sherman A., and Madge Rutherford Minton. 1973. *Giant reptiles.* New York: Scribner.

Morison, Samuel Eliot. 1944. Historical notes on the Gilbert and Marshall Islands. *The American Neptune* 4(2):87–118.

Mōton Kalimur eo Mokta: Kab Kalimur Ekāl: Jeje ko re Kwojarjar. 1966. New York: American Bible Society.

Piggott, Juliet. 1975. *Japanese mythology.* London: Hamlyn Publishing Group, Ltd.

Pukui, Mary Kawena, and Samuel H. Elbert. 1971. *Hawaiian Dictionary: Hawaiian–English, English–Hawaiian.* Honolulu: University Press of Hawai'i.

Pukui, Mary Kawena, E. W. Haertig, and Catherine A. Lee. 1972. *Nāna i ke kumu (Look to the source),* vols. 1 and 2. Honolulu: Hui Hānai, Queen Liliuokalani Trust.

Reed, A. W. 1963. *Treasury of Maori folklore.* Wellington: A. H. and A. W. Reed.

Riesenberg, S. H. 1962. *Tables of accidental and deliberate voyages in the South Pacific.* Memoir No. 34. Wellington: The Polynesian Society.

———. 1965. Table of voyages affecting Micronesian islands. Sydney: Australasian Medical Publishing Company Ltd. (Reprinted from *Oceania,* December 1965, vol. 36, no. 2.)

———. 1972. The organization of navigational knowledge on Puluwat. *Journal of The Polynesian Society* 81:19–56.

Robson, R. W. 1946. *The Pacific Islands handbook, 1944*. New York: The Macmillan Company.

Rynkiewich, Michael A. 1972. Land tenure among Arno Marshallese. Ph.D. dissertation, University of Minnesota.

Sherlock, Philip. 1966. *West Indian folk tales*. London: Oxford University Press.

Spoehr, Alexander. 1949. *Majuro, A village in the Marshall Islands*. Fieldiana: Anthropology, Vol. 38. Chicago: Chicago Natural History Museum.

Stone, Benjamin. 1960. The wild and cultivated pandanus of the Marshall Islands. Doctoral dissertation, University of Hawai'i.

Stone, Earl L., Jr. 1951. *The soils of Arno Atoll, Marshall Islands*. Atoll Research Bulletin Number 5, Washington, D.C., The Pacific Science Board, National Research Council.

Strasburg, Donald W. 1964. List of marine fauna of the Marshall Islands. Honolulu: University of Hawai'i. Mimeographed.

Thompson, Stith. 1932–1936. *Motif index of folk-literature*, 6 vols. FF Communications Nos. 106–109, 117. Helsinki.

———. 1951. *The folktale*. New York: The Dryden Press.

———. 1966. *Tales of the North American Indians*. Bloomington: Indiana University Press.

Titcomb, Margaret, and Mary Kawena Pukui. 1952. *Native use of fish in Hawai'i*. Wellington: The Polynesian Society.

Tobin, Jack A. 1953a. An investigation of the socio-political schism on Majuro Atoll, Marshall Islands. Majuro. Mimeographed.

———. 1953b. The Bikini people, past and present. Majuro. Mimeographed.

———. 1954. Ebeye village: An atypical Marshallese community. Majuro. Mimeographed.

———. 1955. Special field study of Ujilañ Atoll. Majuro. Mimeographed.

———. 1958. Land tenure in the Marshall Islands. Revised. In *Land tenure patterns, Trust Territory of the Pacific Islands*, vol. 1, ed. by John E. de Young. Guam, Mariana Islands: Office of the High Commissioner, Trust Territory of the Pacific Islands.

———. 1967. The resettlement of the Enewetak people: A study of a displaced community in the Marshall Islands. Doctoral dissertation, University of California, Berkeley.

———. 1970. Jabwor, former capital of the Marshall Islands. *Micronesian Reporter* 18:4. Saipan, Mariana Islands: Public Information Office, Trust Territory of the Pacific Islands.

Toor, Frances. 1950. *A treasury of Mexican folkways*. New York: Crown Publishers.

United States Navy. 1943. *Military government handbook*. OPNAV P22-1 (formerly OPNAV 50-1) Marshall Islands. Washington, D.C.: Office of the Chief of Naval Operations, U.S. Government Printing Office.

———. 1945. *Sailing directions for the Pacific Islands*, vol. I. Hydrographic Office Publication 165. Washington, D.C.: United States Navy Hydrographic Office, U.S. Government Printing Office.

United States Public Health Service. 1958. List of marine fauna of the Marshall Islands. U.S. Public Health Survey. Majuro, Marshall Islands. Mimeographed.

Webster, Hutton. 1942. *Taboo: A sociological study*. Stanford, Calif.: Stanford University Press.

———. 1948. *Magic: A sociological study*. Stanford, Calif.: Stanford University Press.

Winkler, Captain. 1898. *On sea charts formerly used in the Marshall Islands, with notices on the navigation of these islanders in general*. Trans. from Marine-Rundschau, Berlin 1898, pt. 10, pp. 1418–1439. Smithsonian Report, United States National Museum, Washington, 1899.

Wright, Glen. 1981. *The pigeon with nine heads and other fascinating legendary tales of Samoa*. Provo, Utah: Aro Publishing Company.

INDEX